B.W. GOODWIN
DROGEN
GOTTDRAK'S RISE
BOOK 2
DRAKREGUS SERIES

Drogen: Gottdrak's Rise

By: B.W. Goodwin

First Edition

www.drogenbookseries.com

drogenbookseries@gmail.com

I dedicate this book to my mother and father. Who, no matter the circumstance, always stand beside me.

Part 1

Lord of War

Part 1

He comes with mountain son,
Namesake nipping at his heels,
Connection, Protection, opposing direction,
Understanding,
The pounding drumbeats have wrought.
He meets them halfway,
Tips of blade drawing iron lines in the sand,
The bodies a pile,
Sinew and Bile
No strike can abate a body filleted,
Wading the bloody shore,
None can save the Lord of War.
Bludgeons of might,
Ring through the night,
There he lie upon stone of floor,
Pronounce him dead,
He'll rise no more,
Nevermore the Lord of War.

Prophecy of the Dwarven King

Prologue

Death's scythe surged with power as he lay his hands upon its cylindrical haft, feeling their connection renewed after two decades of separation brought a jubilant grin to his tired face. Holding Lisana's soul in his hand garnering a renewed sense of hope. A hope he long thought lost in torturous isolation. Thoughts of his cherished love his only solace.

Though he'd been racked for two long arduous decades, Deaths body lacked any signs of atrophy. *I could be here a thousand years and never lose my edge,* thought Death as he swung his prized scythe through the air. Where all things withered and died their bodies succumbing to harsh conditions, the elements, or the effects of time itself, he remained steadfast, strong, and wholly alive, no matter what might befall him.

The walls of his cell were decorated with the instruments of his torture and Death recalled when, and where, each of the implements had been used. Knives to fillet the flesh and blunt instruments to fracture bone. The sections ran from his hips to the ceiling, and all had been used multiple times. His demonic torturer taking great pleasure in cutting his ribs one by one while another of its kind pulled him ever tighter upon the rack. *A love of the rack that he surely received from Lucian. If only Daelon retained the power to keep them in line,* thought Death.

The damned rack lay only feet away from where he'd been suspended upon the wall. A constant reminder of the pulling torture to come. Lucian, although a fan of the stretching functions of the rack, never used it for its intended purpose, instead using it to hold Death steadfast and unable to move an inch or resist what was to come. A rat would be placed upon his exposed stomach and covered with a cauldron. Then came the embers, embers that would heat the pot and fall upon his body as more were added. However, the embers paled in comparison to the feeling of the rat, scratching and gnawing at his skin under the pot. He lost track of how many times rats had scratched and gnawed their way through his intestines and out the other side their terrified bodies eliciting a wet smacking sound as they fell and skittered across the floor.

I have lived through many tortures, some mild, others gruesome, and others worse than the rat, but not by much. Still, I did not, and would not allow myself to break. Far too much is at stake. No, the demons, goblinkin, and Lucian could never hope to break me nor could they hope to understand my true torture. Being without her touch and soul knowing that the method to reach her once again lay just beyond reach all these years, thought Death caressing the shaft of the mighty scythe; Reaper of Souls.

The torture had been constant for the first decade but the second came with more infrequent visits, leaving Death to look upon the scythe day in and day out unable to free himself from the abyssal bindings that held him indefinitely. The infrequent visits were punctuated by the arrival of beings from the demonic race, though paling comparatively in form and power to their former selves. *If she knew how her people were being used by Lucian, would she choose another path,* contemplated Death.

Pushing the thought aside Death moved to the door of his cell. *Thank you Drogen for allowing me the freedom I so desired, but to think help would come from such an unlikely source. I will make great use of this opportunity. If only there was music to accompany my escape. Oh well. I'll just have to make music of my own,* smirked Death maniacally, *out of their screaming flailing corpses.* The thought of killing those who had imprisoned him enticing a smile of righteous anger to spread across his visage. *I hope some of those demonic bastards are among them. I have to repay them for their hospitality above all.*

Death knocked with a heavy hand on the door moving swiftly to the hinged side. His knock drawing a scrambling sound from out in the corridor. The feel and size of their souls told him they were nothing more than cannon fodder, and not one or more of the Gods. *Mere Peons.* Knowing the ogres to be more brutish than intelligent he sank into a crouch. *the door will come next.* The door flung open swiftly the brunt of the weight from its swing dissipated through his arms and down his legs into the ground cracking the stones under foot.

Two sets of large beady eyes scanned the room from the corridor before entering. The ogres stood ten feet tall and had to walk through the door hunched over and single file. Each held a large cudgel, weapons most often used to bludgeon the rats that scurried through the cells feeding on the flesh of prisoners while they slept, or once he had claimed their mortal souls. The lumbering brutes would eat the vermin whole upon crushing the life from their bodies.

Almost a shame I have to kill them. The world could do with a few less rats, thought Death with a sneer.

With both ogres inside his cell Death pushed hard against the door forcing it out of his way and in the same instant swinging Reaper of Souls out with a quick forward step and slip. The sharpened Dragon scale blade careened around the neck of the furthest ogre and with a single pull Death severed both of their heads clean through, faster than the blood could spill from the wounds at both creatures' necks.

The ogre's bodies knelled upon the grimy dungeon floor their severed heads rolling from their shoulders into the waiting maws of dozens of rats. Ogre blood began to flow across the cell floor as Death walked through the portal away from his twenty years of torturous imprisonment. Stepping through he did something he hadn't done in all that time, he allowed himself to breathe.

The souls of the ogres finally realizing their deaths, came to him as all souls do, however he would not grant them a peaceful afterlife allowing their souls to be reborn, through life, instead he eat them. The act of eating their souls further bolstering his power, although the taste left much to be desired.

There really is no substitute for the souls of the longest-lived races. Gods and dragon's chief among them. Nor can it compare to the surge of power brought forth by their consumption, thought Death licking his lips. With thoughts of the dragon kin came more thoughts of Lisana, the woman he wished to see above everything else. *Worry not Lisana. We'll be together once again; you have my word. Then, we will search out our son.*

With those thoughts as motivation Death moved through the underground catacombs with abandon. Running through the underground passageways to find a way up into the castle proper killing orcs, trolls, and other goblinkin along the way.

Rounding a bend, he noted a change in the craftsmanship of the masonry indicating the work of a far more refined hand then those that constructed his underground prison. *This is where my accent begins,* thought Death.

It took only a minute to find a large spiral staircase through an unguarded archway. He ascended the steps three at a time in a constant run going until the staircase stopped and a steel reinforced door once more stood before him, its design exactly that of his cell door. Death heft Reaper of Souls down through the door from top to bottom kicking half of the door into the arms of an orc who had been fast asleep on the other side.

The doors impact crushed the breath out of the orc as its head cracked against the wall as its fellow orc came around blade drawn and spoiling for a fight, but Death was behind the outclassed warrior before it ever registered the movement and with a single touch the orc lay dead upon the ground. As the lifeless orc fell at Deaths feet the partial door shifted and fell to the side. Death could tell from the creature's shallow breathing that it wouldn't live much longer.

"Unlike others that claim to be gods I am not cruel. I will not allow you to suffer this life much longer," said Death in goblin tongue as he looked upon the orc piteously. "How far am I from the surface," asked Death. Bringing the orcs eyes up to meet his own.

"Not far," breathed the orc. His final inhalation, as Death snuffed out the light in his eyes with a single thought.

"Thank you, young orc. For this I will grant you another chance at life. The others of your ilk will not be so lucky." Death harvested the orcs soul and allowing him to pass into the well of souls that fed the entirety of existence. If only I could gorge upon the lives of those from the other realms as I once could," sighed Death "Why am I unable to do so, are my reapers not gathering their souls, or are they being used in some other way. Yet another problem that I must solve to regain the strength I once had."

A squadron of goblinkin, a mixture of trolls and orcs, came around a blind corner as Death made his way through yet another door. *If I cannot find a way out, then I'll just have to make one.* Seeing Deaths fleeing form they tore across the flagstones each drawing weapons and charging forward with abandon, hoping to be the one to take down the escapee. A feat that would surely garner them higher standing with both Grock; their deity, and their tribes as a whole.

The troupe sounded like a stampede of elephants as their footfalls echoed off the walls. Death didn't bother to stop or take the time to regard the fast-growing band behind him. He was far too focused on what lay ahead as he continued his search for an exit. He was about to give up hope when he felt a dampness in the air. The dampness grew in its intensity the higher he rose inside what he surmised to be a spiral tower. Through a ventilation slit, Death felt cool clean air flow towards him, a welcome sensation in contrast of the stale air he'd inhaled for two decades.

Death cut through the stone wall with Reaper of Souls and sent the freshly cut stones flying out with a powerful forward kick. He'd unknowingly ascended many stories above ground, which garnered him a surprisingly great vantage point. He walked through his self-made doorway, dropping three stories to touch down lightly on the ground. A chorus of guttural cries of alarm sounded throughout the settlement, bringing hundreds of goblinkin out of their slumber and into the damp morning light. The sun's rays casting a massive shadow as it came through the towering spires present upon the castle that stood at his back.

A ring of orcs and ogres formed ranks around him. He could hear their many prayers to Grock, beseeching him for power, while archers placed bolts into their crossbows training the bolts upon him. He'd been flanked on all side by an army of goblinkin within mere moments of his escape, but Death held no fear of capture at their hands. He waited for his enemy's ranks to number in the thousands before choosing to speak above the throng. "Do you know who stands before you," bellowed Death in goblin tongue. Sending a chill through the thousands that stood around him. "If you part from me now, you'll live to see another day. However, should but one of you attack me... Then all your lives are forfeit. Your rotten souls will be mine for all eternity."

With their invocations done the shamans let loose divine magic's upon Death and those closest to him. A shockwave of electrical energy pouring through their ranks, touching even the furthest orcs with its radiating magical power. At the epicenter of the blast stood Death as though he felt nothing but a tickle from their Gods given power. Death smiled a cruel and sadistic smile into the crowd of goblinkin. "Your God is weak," laughed Death. "And you're all fools. I'll show you the power of a true god. How about a display of magic yet unknown to this world," said Death with a snap of his fingers.

A hundred goblinkin suddenly exploded outward showering everything in blood, bone, and pieces of shrapnel. The volley of shrapnel lay a further fifty upon the ground dead or dying from the gashes and severe wounds they produced. *Dranier and all other plains of existence will feel my return as the rivers flow with the life's blood of over a thousand exsanguinated souls. I wouldn't have it any other way,* thought Death as he manifested his true form sending a chill through the air and down each spine as the breadth of his power pulsed from his body and into the sky above him. Cascading like a wave covering everything for miles in an impenetrable darkness, not even the sun could hope to permeate.

Lisana felt each touch and gentile caress upon Reaper of Souls through her soul chain, sending a shiver down her spine. Death himself had taught her how to use the ability shortly before his departure from Lundwurm Tul twenty years prior. He'd told her it was a lost art of the Gods. Something only he, and his counterpart Gaia, retained knowledge of, though they'd never had cause to use the power themselves. Death had taught her how to reach the chamber and what to do inside, although much of what she'd done within the chamber came from instinct and feeling alone.

Through the link she was able to feel Death's touch, and glimpses of what he saw upon closing her own eyes. So long as he held the weapon in his hand. Her connection had diminished over the two decades to the point of being nearly untraceable. Something that in the first few years of separation would have been entirely possible. Though she was rendered unable to track it precisely Lisana could still interpret the pull within her mind, a constant call for her to come find it and him.

Her love had left Lundwurm Tul to throw Lucian off his tyrannical warpath to the dragon's front door. Luckily for them both it had taken Lucian a few months to consolidate his power through his subjugation of the gods who dared oppose him, and his iron fisted rule. In the time before Lucian's power had been solidified, Death set up false trails leading the gods far away from Lisana and the rest of the dragonkin. It hadn't taken long for Lucian to figure out who'd been pulling his strings however, and once he'd realized the errant paths put forth by Death, he executed his plan to capture one of the only Gods aware of Lundwurm Tul's location and the knowledge with which to find it.

Lisana had felt Death's desperation to get away through the connection and knew the moment his thoughts and actions turned from anger to despair. The last emotion she'd felt from him in twenty years and a feeling she felt constantly over the years of separation. Taking care of, and raising Drogen during that time had given her some solace but once Drogen could mostly take care of himself her placation of the emotion faded and she found herself longing to feel his touch and the connection they shared again. Her inability to run to his aid, was a point of absolute inconsolable despair. She tried to hide her feelings from Drogen forcing them down whenever he was in her presence, but buried emotion inevitably boil to the surface. In one night she'd felt both overjoyed at Drogen's birth and powerless at her inability to help Death culminating complete physical and mental exhaustion.

She tried and had been successful, in her eyes, of hiding her underlying feelings of despair from Drogen. Lisana found out the opposite was true, which Drogen made clear years before she'd left Lundwurm Tul. *He could tell how much I missed his father even though I never told him the entire story, or who his father is. Well aside from inside the letter I suppose. I only prey he doesn't think ill of me for leaving him as I did.*

The cave Lisana had called home for over a year doubled as her base of operations. She'd chosen the location as it was central to the goblinkin's most defensible stronghold and the connection, though faint, had led her to the massive prison complex the goblinkin controlled. Her cave home though close was easily defensible and out of reach to any without wings or a great deal of climbing ability. Her only wish was that the view and smell could be more pleasant for the goblinkin homeland known as Grock; the namesake city of their deity, was beyond grotesque. The smell of putrid flesh, rancid fat, and fermenting hides filled her cave most nights and, at first, had turned even her iron stomach, but she'd grown used to the stench over her year of occupancy. *I'll never know how so much grease and grime could collect from the highest spires to the ground on which they walk.*

Before coming to reside in her cave, Lisana had traveled across Dranier to find any information she could about Death and his location. Most of the beings she'd talked to either didn't know, or didn't want to suffer the wrath of the gods for letting slip information about his whereabouts. Whether they would die by her hand or not. Lisana understood. It had been many years since his capture and few, if any, had witnessed his detainment. She also knew Lucian had planted false trails in order to throw anyone who was looking for him off the trail.

At least that's what she thought before she'd entertained Gaia's company. Lisana had nearly decapitated her out of sheer rage at seeing a god for the first time in so long. Their battle had been fierce and fervent, though in the end she'd defeated Gaia, it was a hollow victory. Realizing that the rage she felt was the pain of her own inability to save Death all those years prior. After the battle, they were both exhausted and passed out from the sheer exertion. Unlike the other times she'd faced one of the Gods, Gaia awoke from her slumber, something that had only happened once before. They sat and talked about their counterpart and his son for quite some time. Gaia had been overjoyed hearing about Drogen and all he'd been able to accomplish in such a short time.

It was at this time Lisana struck a barging with Gaia, though she was initially apprehensive to the idea, Gaia agreed to teach him soul binding. When Gaia asked for a description of Drogen she had simply said "You will know him when you stand within his presence." Lisana could tell from the way Gaia nodded that she really didn't believe it. Over the years away she often wondered if she should have given more of a description, but in her heart, she knew that such a thing was unnecessary. Wherever he walked his presence was known, no small feat among a race as long in life as theirs.

Gaia had been the one to suggest going to Grock, the orc capital and giant underground prison system, to look for Death. It had been her one and only lead in the years since her departure from Lundwurm Tul and as she gained ground her hope turned to knowing for she could feel her blade Reaper of Souls, grew stronger the closer she came to the settlement. Lisana had rejoiced in the first few days, knowing her love was so close but that exuberant joy diminished as realization struck her, though he felt so close that she could almost reach out with her soul and touch him, Death was still so far away.

Two months after her arrival the number of campaigns by the Goblinkin had increased leaving much of the inner city deserted though far from defenseless. She also noticed much of the living quarters, used by the generals and Grock himself, had been completely deserted as if they'd taken up new residence elsewhere. Knowledge, she figured might be helpful to one of the other races populating Dranier. *Not to mention profitable,* smiled Lisana.

She watched over the many giants, trolls, orcs, ogres, hobgoblins and a slew of other goblinkin from her perch each day waiting for any sign that Death was amongst them. Any sign or signal that he was okay and coming to her side. Lisana knew him to be there, just below the surface. She wanted nothing more than to leave the smell and grotesque displays put on by the creatures, but she had nowhere else to go. *I will not return to Lundwurm Tul until I have Death by my side, though returning is only a snap away.*

Lisana above all else wished she could have taken Drogen with her on the journey to find his father. She wanted to express upon him all that she'd kept locked away over the years. She wished that their reunion, when it happened, could have been complete. Still she knew Drogen had at least a year's worth of training left before he left Lundwurm Tul and a couple of months more once he found Gaia and journeyed into his soul chamber to perform the soul binding. It had taken her just over three months to complete the binding and resonance with her soul, thus she thought she'd give Drogen the same amount of time to complete the task.

All of a sudden Lisana heard a resounding crash as bricks from three stories up came crashing down to the ground, and a dark figure dropped from the new exit. In the back of her mind she could feel a greater sensation, that of joy. Running from the cave with sword in hand she leapt into the night sky silently gliding down to the castle's walls to see what the commotion was about. As she drew closer, she heard and felt the call of Reaper of Souls pounding into her mind. Joy welled up inside her knowing that Death would be able to feel her elation through the sentient blade.

Death had begun to talk in goblin tongue, which she still couldn't understand, sending chills through her body and all those below her before a magical bolt of lightning struck Death killing those unfortunate enough to be close when the spell was completed. Over a thousand Goblinkin had him surrounded and she grew fearful that his capture was all to imminent, facing off against so many after years of captivity. Such thoughts where quickly dispelled as with a click of Death's fingers at least 100 bodies exploded into shrapnel killing at least half that number and injure many others. Then she witnessed Deaths true manifestation the true Reaper of Souls as he swung the scythe of the same name once and fell five giants from the concussive force of his swing alone.

Death mowed through the goblinkin forces with all-out abandon taking limbs, heads, and torsos of thirty to fifty with each swing of Reaper of Souls. Within a minute the castle square was flowing with a river of blood and not a single being was left standing in his wake. A thousand souls came to his call. He thought to let them all pass to the afterlife, but chose instead to fill his stomach to the brim, further bolstering his already overwhelming power. Not far away he could make out the distinctive cadence of large wings, but didn't bother to look and see who it might be for one enemy wouldn't be enough to capture him, not with the power of so many souls coursing through his undying veins.

With a single circuit swing with Reaper of Souls Death cut through the brick castle that stood at his back in its entirety. The castle stood strong for a fraction before it collapsed in upon itself crushing the life out of any who still remained cowering within its walls as he walked away, regaining his diminished form as he did so. As Death looked up into the sky, he saw a set of draconic eyes staring back at him, eyes he'd pictured in the throes of a restless sleep and the waking dreams solitude had brought. He thought himself dreaming once more, and wondered if Lucian had finally found a method to break him entirely after all. But then he felt Reaper of Souls reaching out to her and knew that his vision wasn't fooling him that the woman he loved had found him.

Death moved across the ground as if he where gliding upon the rivers of blood he'd created as Lisana set down and closed the door in her mind starting out in a run as she touched down. Blinking once her eyes turned sapphire blue and tears began to form upon her eyelid. So too did they form within Death's as they both rushed for the others embrace jumping over corpses and skating across the blood-soaked ground fervently.

They embraced each other at a run wishing to envelop each other for eternity and never let go, fearing that breaking their contact would ultimately wake them from their mutual dream. It took them many heartbeats to realize once more that this was no dream, but reality. *Only a nightmare would smell so rank of blood, well someone else's nightmare,* thought Death with a slight grin as he held her out to arm's length in order to look into her sapphire blue eyes. With a gentile caress to Lisana's cheek he gingerly lifted her mouth to his kissing her with abandon that she reciprocated with a fervor all her own.

"I cannot believe that you stand before me my love. I thought I might die before once again reuniting with you," purred Lisana lovingly.

"I wouldn't wish to live in a world without you in it my dearest Lisana. Should you have died, I would not have let your soul leave my side. I would bring you back to this world even if a true death awaited myself for doing so. You were the only solace, the only beacon of light in my bleak years of torturous captivity."

"Soon there will be another, for which your affections will surely grow," said Lisana. Smiling with pure joy. "We can go see him now if you want." Making a snapping gesture with her hand.

"If you speak of our son those affections began the moment he came to me, in the form of a Reaper."

"WHAT," shouted Lisana in surprise. "A year's worth of training remains for him to accomplish before he is able to walk free of the barrier surrounding Lundwurm Tul. Tis no way he could already be in Dranier. No way."

"But he is my love," said Death. Pulling her face up to look into his eyes. "And he's both resonated with his soul and killed the Gods Ether and Uther," drawing a look of complete astonishment to Lisana's visage as she contemplated the possibility. "Just wait until you hear his full name Lisana, it will give even you chills."

"Wh-What is it," questioned Lisana.

"I think it best you heard it from his mouth instead of mine, for my words cannot convey the strength and weight of his name. I cannot do it justice or convey its implications in the way that he can."

"Please just tell me," said Lisana pleading.

"No, you will understand once you see him my beloved dragon, just know that Drakregus is far more fitting then even the elders of your race realize."

Looking dejected at being told to wait she conceded, though Death knew she was conspiring in her own mind to gather the information from others. "Fine I'll wait to hear it spoken from his own mouth, though I do so begrudgingly," said Lisana with a sneer. "Have you any inkling to his location. I've longed to see him again since the moment I left Lundwurm Tul in order to find and bring you home."

"Most of my power has yet to return to me so I cannot place his soul from this distance, but he did have the soul of a zephyrian in tow upon leaving my presence, one with ties to an elder bloodline among their kin," said Death.

"Then that is where we'll start. There is an outpost city just outside the goblinkin lands. Should we begin there?"

"The city of Zephyr has fallen to the goblinkin hordes. At least that's what the zephyrian's soul, which Drogen came to collect, said. I surmised the same a month prior when a large number of goblinkin, and a few zephyrian's came to pass through me. No...I believe him to be in Zephyria."

"Is their capital where I believe it to be," asked Lisana. A sense of foreboding coming over her at the prospect of seeing once more the city of a people who had once been under the protection of the Dragonkin. A people who had been completely wiped from the face of Dranier.

"Yes it is. They took the land and made it their own erasing those who came before them and their connection with the Dragonkin," said Death. Wrapping her in a sympathetic hug.

The news drew a long-held sadness to Lisana's face. "Then I suppose we have a heading now. What do you say we go find our son," she said. Somberly trying to smile through the deep-seated emotion. *An entire race decimated, how could they have been so cruel? To wipe them out for siding with the dragonkin, I suppose our seclusion from the world gave them ample time to poison the other races against us as well.*

"I thought you would never ask. Though I dare say the both of us could use a bath before we meet up with him." To which Lisana raised an eyebrow questioningly. "Me far more than you," said Death with raised hands. "It seems I've gone a little overboard and drenched myself in blood not to mention the smell of the dungeon that has undoubtedly permeated to my very soul. We can do so along the way, but I believe it best we make haste. I don't want him slipping through our fingers, not when we're so close to reuniting."

"Very well milady let us make haste we don't want to keep Drogen son of Lisana; Reap... waiting," said Death with a wry smile. Leaning down to kiss Lisana again love coursing through him. As if the imprisonment had never happened.

Lisana with a mischievous grin and a purr that sent shivers down Deaths spine, "You're going to pay for that."

Chapter One

Drogen awoke with a start feeling a surge of power coursing through the air, though he didn't understand what could have caused the cascading surge of pressure. What concerned him was the distance the power had to have traveled without dissipation. What surprised him most however was the ominous nature the presence put forth which had silenced even the sound of birds through Natalia's casement window.

Seraphine and Natalia rested peacefully beside him their beautiful features blissfully unaware of the strange atmosphere that had spread throughout the land. It felt like something primordial had returned to Dranier and that primal power was something not to be trifled with. *Could that be Death... my father? Has he been released from his confinement with the help of the twin god's souls, or is it something else? Either way tis best not to worry those around me unnecessarily. Maybe I can distinguish the source by losing myself from corporeal bonds,* thought Drogen as he took another look at the two beautiful women lain out on either side of him.

Drogen escaped his corporal form with a few inhaled breaths his body remaining on alert Godslayer; Envoy of Death assuring him of their presence with subtle feelings at the back of his mind, although something about the interaction felt off. The radiating magic's deployed far into the distance was both dark and beautiful as the sunlight began to ascend across the early morning sky and filter through the trees and onto the plateau that Zephyria set upon. As quickly as the power had come so too was it leaving as though it had sealed itself away, just as he did when hiding his Draconic form. *I swear I can smell blood upon the wind. An ominous omen indeed, It look to be receding back toward Moongrove or beyond,* thought Drogen.

With a thought he returned to his body. Natalia and Seraphine where just beginning to stir as he regained himself. Drogen knew that slipping out of the bed without waking them wasn't an option again, especially with the maids whose presence he'd witnessed fluttering about the room. *I tried escaping their clutches once before, doing so again would be a start down the path of insanity.*

Natalia was the first to wake relieved to see Drogen hadn't tried to escape again. As she heard the footsteps of the maids she understood why. With a cheeky grin she smiled "Good morning Drogen. Did you sleep well?"

"Yes, it was restful," said Drogen thinking about the aura that had cascaded across miles to wake him from his slumber. He'd thought to mention the sensation and information, but he didn't want either of them to worry about what may or may not be coming. *Even I, at my current strength, have no chance against something that can throw out such monstrous power.*

"Yay, it seems you learn quickly. You didn't try escaping again," came Seraphine's voice.

"What are you still doing here? This is my bedchamber. I told you to leave him to me," said Natalia.

"Sorry, *buuuuuuut* that's not going to happen," said Seraphine in a teasing voice accentuated with a quick wink at Drogen.

"Might we be away from this bed for a while? I do believe we were requested by Lord Vladimir," said Drogen.

"Yes, we were summoned. Fread hasn't come back since then, but I suspect we must make an appearance before too long. Else my father will come for us himself," said Natalia as she rose from the bed and out into her room drawing back the curtains on her four-poster bed as she did so. The maids rushed to her side and began dressing her. Drogen surmised from the sound of her heartbeat that it was a practice she both disliked and was embarrassed by.

Seraphine was the next to rise from beneath the coverings, which she made a show of by putting her completely naked body on display.

"Will you stop that and put some clothes on already we have to go meet my father and nudity is not acceptable attire," bit Natalia as the maids spun her around.

"Fine what do I have to wear if I can't go as the forests intended," questioned Seraphine cheekily.

"The maids already have something prepared. Now get out here and suffer with me like a true friend," said Natalia haughtily.

Seraphine moved the curtain aside stepping out into the room, "Well if I must then let's be done with it."

As the two women changed Drogen continued to ponder his first few months outside of Lundwurm Tul and wondered what the next two would have in store for him and those who had begun to gather at his side. Then his thought drifted back to Ether and Uther, as he wondered what ramifications their deaths might have upon Zephyria and its people. *I wonder why tis that I have not been thrown back into a prison cell after killing their divinity. Furthermore, how am I sharing this room with two princesses and not being detained? Tis as if everyone is treating such action as ordinary activity... when tis anything but,* thought Drogen.

"Why are you not out here as well? The maids are waiting for you to get out of bed. It was you who wanted to get up in the first place," scolded Natalia through the curtain.

"Right. Right. I was simply waiting for you to garner your robes before proceeding. I did not wish to further perturb you whilst present in the process," said Drogen as he pushed himself up and off of the bed in one smooth movement. The moment his feet touched ground the maids were on him stripping him to nothing before adorning his body with, what he viewed as, gaudy attire. The clothes proving much the same as those the aristocrats of Zephyria wore during the ball he'd attended inside the castle.

Each garment was designed to be overly ornate for special occasions. Where there was a seam there was a layer of gold or silver running through it denoting the rank of the aristocracy. Platinum belonged to those of Royal rank. Natalia and Seraphine's dresses with their layered plumes had platinum running through every seam. Even the fringes of each beautifully decorated gown, though done in frills and lace, had been hand weaved with the precious metal.

Drogen's clothes where weaved with metal as well, but he could tell it differed from the two royals. Though both his and theirs looked the same to the eye the density of the metal expertly woven through his clothing was significant. Drogen knew the difference in material had to hold some significance, but decidedly pushed it aside as he looked down at the color scheme of his apparel with a heavy frown.

The final denotation of rank came from the color of the garments, which perturbed Drogen as they made him stand out far beyond his liking. Where Natalia's dress was as blue as the sky, and Seraphine's shone the green of the forest, symbolizing their being near, or at, the pinnacle of their respective hierarchies, Drogen was adorned in the pure white robes of a god. The realization of which only adding to the annoyance growing within him.

The radiance of the garments only grew as sunlight drifted into the room through Natalia's casement window. The maids, finished fussing over his two companions, moved aside finally affording him a full view. The full-length corset with flowing plum dresses only further bolstered what Drogen knew to be all too true of the two women "Beautiful," said Drogen out loud drawing a blush from both as they turned away shielding their eyes from the glare of his white attire. *How does one breathe in such attire I suspect if the tops of their dresses became any tighter, they might fall to death from lack of air. Such things must be exceedingly uncomfortable.*

"Why does my attire differ so greatly from your own? Tis also curious that I am not a prisoner here having killed your divinity." The two women made to protest but Drogen silenced them with an outstretched hand, "There's no denying what I've done. Numerous zephyrian's witnessed the fated battle, may-hap not the entirety of it, but most certainly the end result."

"I can shed some light on your questions," came a voice as the door to the room opened. Fread's heartbeat was unmistakable to Drogen as was Willows, who followed him closely. "You see the gods have long tortured and destroyed many of the zephyrians with their overwhelming power. Even Lord Vladimir was powerless to stop their bloodshed. By Ether and Uther dying at your hands, the zephyrian people, aside from a few zealots, feel free from the burden of their rule. Most are taking their deaths as reason to celebrate for those they had lost at divinities hand."

"Will the other gods not search for the one responsible and lay waste to our kingdom? We cannot know the path other gods may take having two of their own killed in battle," questioned Natalia.

"Natalia is right on this Fread. There is no telling what the gods are conspiring to bring down upon your people. Furthermore, your kin are predisposed to worship at the altar of the gods. What I've done is take their divinity away. The repercussions of which is likely to cause strife among not only the zealots, but the people as a whole. Will they be able to move past their current system, find another god to worship, or continue in their worship of the dead gods Ether and Uther. Some of your people might seek to worship no gods after being subject to their calamity," said Drogen.

"Well, aren't those some existential questions," remarked Seraphine with a rueful frown.

"The truth is no one knows how to proceed forward. Everyone is still in a state of shock after losing Ether and Uther. I've seen many people praying to them for guidance only to remember that their prayers will go unanswered for death has claimed their souls. Even Lord Vladimir is at a loss as to what path to follow moving forward," said Fread.

"How can anyone of them know what to do moving forward. The future is unclear and uncertain to them all without guidance from the Gods, which just proves how wrong the methods Ether and Uther used were," remarked Willow in a quiet solemn voice.

"None of this explains the new attire or the colors for which I wear. Not to mention the difference in metal between those woven through Seraphine, Natalia, and... even Willows clothing." *Have they left unrealized the truth of her divinity,* thought Drogen.

"The rarity of metal denotes the rank of those who wear it," to which Drogen nodded. "Most people recognize the rarity of copper, silver, gold, and platinum but there is one much rarer and denotes the ranks of the higher beings. The metal looks the same as polished platinum to the untrained eye, but is less cumbersome and denser than platinum. What's weaved into the fabric of your clothes is palladium. A metal that's far more scares than the other metals that are used as currency. It also fetches a much higher price when sold," confirmed Fread.

"So they have seen fit to adorn me with the attire befitting those that I've slain," said Drogen not bothering to stifle the disdain in his voice.

"Yes... and no, it is the attire of the Gods, but everyone knows you're of a different race. This is to show respect to you, it's not meant to be an insult. They know you're of the dragonkin but were unsure what attire to give that would be to your liking. So in lieu of knowing, Lord Vladimir had these garments fitted for you, hoping they would do until such time as you suggested something more... to your liking," said Fread.

"I think I'd much rather wear the attire I used during the zephyrian ball." Much like the garments that had adorned his body during the gala, to him, they were both ostentatious and impractical. The contrast between his hair and the garments looking unnatural to him as well. But everyone else looked at him as though they were looking into the sun, something they couldn't, and shouldn't touch for fear of the repercussions. Even with the impracticality of the design being overlooked he still couldn't see it as anything more than adorning himself in the armor of his enemies. The worst shock to his sensibilities still remained the kindred design to the two Gods he'd killed just one day prior.

With a touch on the shoulder Fread shook Drogen from his inner musings. "If everything is set then we best be off for the audience chamber. We mustn't keep Lord Vladimir waiting."

Drogen only nodded to his friend absentmindedly as he mused over the connotation of being presented the strange garments a rage slowly building as he realized what Vladimir was after by doing so. *Don't think that my beating the gods for your people is acceptance of rule over their dominion. I believe tis time you think for the good of your people, and not the good of the gods,* thought Drogen as a group of armed and armored guards escorted the small band from Natalia's bedchamber door and down the tower staircase before filtering into a hallway familiar to him but only in memories from a waking dream he had when he was but a hatchling.

The memory was through the eyes of a young girl moving through her castle home running into the library they passed on their way to the audience chamber. She read obsessively studying everything from language to history, against the librarian's wishes from what Drogen remembered of the dreams. He knew that girl now to be Natalia.

In his waking dreams she went to the library to learn as much as possible moving like a ghost around the room so as not to disturb the others and to use the library even when she was supposed to be in bed asleep. The first days of her nightly wanderings brought her face to face with the librarian, but she adapted quickly viewing it as a game of hide and seek up until the day of her mother's death at the hands of Ether and Uther. Skills she also used to ride one of the few horses stabled in Zephyria for the King and Queen. After her mother's murder at their hands, and her father's sudden marriage to Nefar, Natalia trained herself further in order to spy on and steal from her greedy stepmother and sister in order to help those within the kingdom most affected by their avarice.

Thinking about Natalia's skills brought back the memory of her flight from the palace guards where she'd had to flea capture after stealing a great number of jewels and coins from the Queens vault, using a key that she's fashioned out of wood. Although he thought it a dream at the time Drogen knew beyond a doubt that the woman whose black wings shined in the morning light was the one who had perpetrated the caper, and who had so excited his dream.

How I wish I could escape into those dreams once again to feel the world through another person's eyes once more. If seeing through the eyes of Natalia, Seraphine, and Willow all came to be true then the others, whose eyes I saw through, must be out there as well. I wonder what it is that connects us together. I wonder if I'll ever meet those whose worlds, I've only caught glimpses of, in the future. The builder, the hunter, and the one whose hair dances around their head like the ebb and flow of the sea.

As he shook himself from his inner musings Drogen found himself taking in the beautiful decorative tapestries denoting former Kings and Queens alongside battles and representations of zephyrian history that hung from the castle's massive walls. But what really caught Drogen's eye was the stained-glass window, which allowed light to filter more freely into the castle. Each window had been formed into the shape of a crest, one that Drogen recognized from a story Lisana had told him once, long before her flight from Lundwurm Tul.

As the group neared their destination the artworks above them grew in both number and majesty drawing his attention and providing distraction from the worry creeping through every fiber of his being finally a duo of guards pulled open the last set of doors allowing them to enter the audience chamber without impediment.

Although the room was crowded it didn't entertain nearly as many as was present when the Gods had arrived for him. Amongst the congregation where aristocrats, soldiers, clergymen, a few citizens; there for other business, and the royal family. As they spotted Drogen the room grew so silent the rustle of the soldier's armor reverberated throughout the room adding a somber tone to the already intense atmosphere.

Drogen looked around the room watching and waiting for the conflict to begin anew, but he couldn't hear the telltale rise in the heartrates around him that occur when battle looms on the horizon. *They might not seek battle now, but I shall be prepared should conflict arise.* His eyes settled on Vladimir only after taking in the two deep gouges left in the Queen and Bernadine's thrones by Godslayer; Envoy of Death.

I've received no respect from them though I've given my fair share. I will not bow unless they do so first. Although he'd only been in front of the royal family a couple of times, they noticed the change immediately. Their heartbeats skipping dangerously inside their chests. Natalia, Seraphine, Willow, and Fread moved to bow, but stopped as Drogen bade them hold with an upraised hand.

Vladimir stood up, beckoning both Nefar and Bernadine to do the same. Though Drogen could sense she wished to protest, Nefar followed Vladimir's lead pulling Bernadine up by her hand as she did so. Vladimir stood on shaky legs for a few seconds before bowing his head in Drogen's direction. The act drew gasps from everyone in the room, the biggest of which came from Nefar, followed closely by Bernadine. Both looked as though such action was beneath them choosing to curtsy towards him begrudgingly, as they were unable to bend at the waist.

Drogen abstained from any action for four heartbeats before bowing in kind; with those who accompanied him. "My name is Drogen; Son of Lisana Reaper of Souls, Godslayer; Envoy of Death, Drakregus of Lundwurm Tul." With his full name spoken allowed many in the room paled feeling the astronomical weight of each spoken syllable even though they couldn't understand the latter portion of his name. *Many underestimate the weight of a name and its connotations with regard to both lineage and future until the name is spoken with the feeling and weight of the one who bares it,* thought Drogen.

"Ye..." said Godslayer; Envoy of Death at the declaration. Giving Drogen another bad feeling, as if something within was wrong.

"To bow is to show respect to another. It shows that none are above humility nor those they represent, even if those beings set upon an ornate throne," said Drogen. His eyes changing and adding a degree of menace to his every word. "Only yesterday I stood before you a heretic and criminal in your eyes and in the eyes of the Gods you worshiped. What has changed?"

"Y-you killed our Gods, but in so doing saved my daughter a-and my people," spoke Vladimir.

"You took no issue with Natalia's condition yesterday as she lay before your raised dais, wings scolded and plucked clean upon her back, whilst clothed in soiled rags, her body a-fever from the pain and agony suffered at the hands of your guard, and family. I ask once more what has changed?" Drogen's eyes penetrating Vladimir's own. Making the hardened warrior shrink as though he where a child scolded by his parents.

"I-I lis-listened to what everyone had to say about you," stuttered Vladimir.

"You and yours were disinterested in what any of my companions, or I, had to say in way of defending ourselves both yesterday and during our other, less than pleasant councils leading up to this point. No Lord Vladimir the Crimson King, that is not what has changed. You did not only wake this morn and decide to take what was stated before as truth. You've lived in fear of the Gods and their wrath for the entirety of your lives. In that time, you grew accustomed to placating those of divine birth so the destruction of your cities and people alike could be kept to a minimum. Tis not you, your people, or your methods that have changed tis your placement of fear."

"Why shouldn't we fear one who can kill two of divine birth without dying himself? Whose skin is impervious to attack or damage of any kind."

"Simply put... a Dragon cannot lie. If you wish to know whether or not I speak the truth, ask Seraphine her blade possesses powerful magic's that can understand the deceit in others. Those cut by the blade, if ever a lie is told, are punished. Though it never had an effect on me, it can still monitor those whose blood it has spilled," said Drogen.

"Drogen is telling the truth my sword does affect any who have felt its sting and while under its spell they are incapable of lying even if the lie is minuscule. Only Drogen has ever been able to hold and touch my blade freely and not feel the weight of all the lies he's ever told. Not once since I've met him has he ever lied, and my sword tells me he speaks the truth even now," stated Seraphine without hesitation.

"Tis not my wish for harm to befall you or your ilk. However, should I be attacked, those who have come against me will be defeated through submission or death," stated Drogen.

"V-very well, but what do we do now that Ether and Uther are no more," inquired Vladimir. Accusatory in his intonation. As if finally remembering his role as ruler of Zephyria.

"That is for you and yours to decide. I will not stop their worship of Ether and Uther, nor any of the other Gods in the pantheon of Dranier. Whether you worship the old, the fallen, or the new is of no consequence. Tis your people's decision as to what course of action should be taken. I only ask one thing of you and that is to disavow those who have done your people so much harm. Those who sit beside your throne of hewn wood and feign friendship while holding a dagger to your back, and the purses of your people," said Drogen.

"We've done no harm to the people of Zephyria. How dare you speak out against us. You have no proof of any wrongdoing," shouted Nefar as she leapt from her throne.

"Careful Nefar those closest to you may very well hear the pounding of your lying heart as it beats in your chest... as I can. You need not go any farther for the truth of these words than the outskirts of this city where the lower-class serfs of your country take shelter. Their greed," said Drogen. Gesturing toward Bernadine and Nefar. "Has stripped them of all possessions, shelter, and food. All to support the lust for gold displayed by the adopted heiresses to the royal family of Zephyria."

"I've listened to the pleas of those who've come before my court, but how can I trust that any of them speak the truth. When they accuse those who sit beside me of such acts while they." Vladimir pointing to Bernadine and Nefar. "So ardently deny raising such burden upon our people."

"Those low in station have far less to lose then those whose only thought resides upon the fullness of their coffers. Did you ever send one of your own guard to check on the legitimacy of their claims, or did you take the word of those beside you as more meaningful than the voice of the people you tenuously rule," questioned Drogen witheringly.

"I... We," stumbled Vladimir. Struggling to find the words as Drogen began talking again.

"Although these crimes pale in comparison to the conspiracy perpetrated in conjunction with the now deceased Necromancer Kethick. I would think that knowledge more than sufficient," stated Drogen. Staring at Nefar and Bernadine who flushed at the mention of Kethick's name. Both nearly fainting as their hearts pounded uncontrollably in their chests.

Vladimir set upon his throne looking at the two beside him down to those below his mouth dry and un-moving.

"I will take your lack of acknowledgment as a no," said Drogen flatly. Returning his eyes to Vladimir. "The decision of what to do with them is for *you* to decide. In my opinion, for their crimes against Zephyria, they should be stripped of rank and forced to live in the conditions wrought of their avarice."

The two women at Vladimir's side moved to object but fell back to their seats as Drogen's eyes shifted to them. As they returned to their thrones Drogen once more shifted his attention back to Vladimir.

"Do not take this suggestion as an order. Tis simply a suggestion for your consideration. As I stated the decision is yours and yours alone," said Drogen.

Vladimir looked at the ground in contemplation unsure of the actions to take. The Gods had governed over and given down their words to him and his kin for so long he found himself looking to them for guidance even though he knew they could no longer heed nor hear his calls. "I must attain more information on what is transpiring within my kingdom, then I will take appropriate action," concluded Vladimir.

Drogen could hear Natalia's heartbeat rising in her chest to a thunderous torrent before she ever started speaking. He rushed to her holding her close to him hoping to sate the torrential beat of her heart, but he knew that the release of everything she held in would be better than simply pushing it down. *She fought off the trauma for the entirety of the night. Tis as if someone is holding off what she's feeling,* thought Drogen as he sunk to the floor beside her.

"Father," she started. Balling her fist to fight off the rage threatening to boil to the surface. "They've done horrid things too our people, you, and I. What other information could you possibly need," said Natalia. Tears in her eyes.

Drogen taking his place behind her, a rock to lean on as the experiences came flooding back into her mind like crashing waves.

"They stood by while their personal guard scolded and plucked my wings. I-I can still feel the pain of the boiling water as it flowed down my feathers blistering the skin beneath. The unending agony as they mercilessly pulled each individual feather. I can still see their faces turned up in cruel smiles of pleasure in my mind as plainly as they sit beside you," her recounting of the events raked with sobs of anguish and tears she could not stop.

"Do you know how long they took to pull my feathers father, because I don't. I lost track of the number of times I passed out and awoke screaming out in agony for someone to save me before every feather was pulled from my wings," sobbed and convulsed Natalia. "Even though Drogen healed me with his magic," she sobbed. " I-I can still feel the pain, it's something that will remain to haunt my dreams for the rest of my life, and no amount of magic can ever take that pain away. Does that not give you enough knowledge to make a decision," she questioned in incredulous frustration.

Tears streamed from Fread's eyes as he looked on in silence standing behind them while tightening his grip on Willow's arm in apprehension and heartache hearing Natalia sob inconsolably as she forced herself to recount the ordeal, she'd suffered at the hands of those who were supposed to be the pillars and aspiration for all of Zephyria and its people. It made him feel completely powerless, exactly how he'd felt seeing her broken and chained before them on the floor.

Drogen comforted Natalia enveloping her in his arms as he wrapped them around her body wings and all. "I am here for you Natalia." Even with his words of solace Drogen could hear Natalia's heart beating furiously inside her chest. Within her mind she relived the torture over and over quickly loosing herself in the abyss as it encroached upon her from all sides.

Lifting Natalia's forehead to his own Drogen pressed himself into her. Feeling the conflict within her mind, as if it were warring within himself. Slowly her heartbeat began to decrease, and her tears dried. The last tear fell from her cheek, Drogen wiping it away with a finger as he brushed her messy long black hair away from her swollen face.

"I will not tell you how or force you to act Vladimir. However, this inquiry is concluded. I bid thee farewell, unless of course, you have news or charges for those gathered to hear," said Drogen threateningly almost daring Vladimir to act recklessly.

Vladimir shook from his contemplation with tears brimming his eyes. Looking around at his trusted guard, the aristocracy, and the serfs who had come asking for aid he noted the tears of his people and the emotion that even his trained soldiers were trying desperately to hide. Anyone else might have looked upon the swaying and hunching of his trusted guard as simple movement to forego fatigue, but he knew the look of men weighed down by torturous emotion. "No you may come and go as you please from this point on. None will stop you. Should you need, or want anything, it will be provided."

"There is always an expense or consequence for the actions that we take Vladimir. Who bears the weight is the only matter left to be determined. I will not lay weight upon another unnecessarily. If I need anything I will retrieve it myself, or through my comrades, either way it will come at my expense. Thus, I'll be returning these distasteful garments."

"Do you dislike them," questioned Vladimir fearfully.

"No, I don't like them in the slightest, and for future reference, I would prefer not to be draped in the colors worn by those I have slain," said Drogen as he looked down upon the brilliant white robes interlaced with precious metal. I will gather garments more to my liking shortly and these will be returned to you. On a side note, what, if anything, lies four to five days northeast of Moongrove," posited Drogen.

Vladimir thought about the question for a moment before his eyes lit up. "That is believed to be the location of the goblinkin homeland of Grock. At least, that's what rumors say of the area. Grock is believed to house an underground prison complex that boasts many prison cells and rooms of torture. It's said that even Death himself would be unable to escape. We modeled much of the under-city prison in Zephyr after the stories."

"Thank you for the information," Drogen bowed to Vladimir. Who bowed back. As Drogen returned to full height he glared at Nefar and Bernadine with his draconic eyes. A cobra waiting for the right opportunity to strike. With a wave of his hands, he called his friends in close feeling them all connect together he snapped his fingers. They vanished into thin air drawing gasps of surprise from the entire congregation. The shock within the room was palatable, but nothing compared to the horror plastered upon the faces of Nefar and Bernadine as they came to realize how swiftly death could overtake them. A click of the fingers and they would be no more than corpses upon the thrones they fought to protect for their own selfish gains.

Chapter Two

Drogen listened to the air and heartbeats around him as he and his friends stood in the house he'd built, in the wilderness outside Zephyria. He couldn't hear any other heartbeats within earshot at first, but smiled as he heard two familiar rhythms coming through the tamarack trees along the dirt path he'd formed through the wood.

"Well, you certainly gave Lord Vladimir something to think about. Why did you do it as a suggestion, instead of a demand? You're far more powerful than anyone else who would stand against you, especially in the court. You could have called for Nefar and Bernadine to do exactly as you suggested without question," posited Willow.

"And that Willow is your answer. Those who do not question their existence or the orders of those they see as all powerful beyond taking them at their word are sheep who will fall flat when chaos, either minimal or catastrophic, comes knocking upon their door. Tis the same reason tyrants become overthrown. What I've done is give Vladimir a chance to rule for the good of his people, instead of the gods. I have simply forgone destroying him in lieu of him either ruling or destroying himself by other means. I will not dictate demands to any people whether I know them intimately as a people, or not. I will not pretend to speak for the people, nor will I work as an executioner."

"So, you've given Lord Vladimir the power to change the fate of our people and their future, or destroy himself with the power he wields," said Fread.

"Those who cannot govern themselves cannot hope to govern a people," said Drogen.

"The creativity of his solution to the problem Drogen has given him will show you, and the other Zepyrian people, what kind of leader he will be moving forward," said Seraphine as her gaze shifted to Drogen. "Should he choose to follow your advice to the letter then he may very well fall short of what he must become to effectively serve Zephyria, and its people."

"Should his reasoning and inquiries show the actions to be justified, then it may be the correct course of action. This is a test for him, to hear the will of the people he governs. He is their ruler, but without them he is nothing but a man setting upon empty lands on a carved chair. Tis my hope that he can see the truth through the clouds masking his vision. The fall of a ruler occurs when they can no longer hear the voice of the people they serve over their own ambitions."

"Am I the only one here whose wondering what that last question was about? Why did you ask about the lands outside of Moongrove? You could have just asked me. Grock is closer to Moongrove then it is to Zephyr, or Zephyria after all." said Seraphine in a dejected huff.

"I knew that it was close to Moongrove, but I wished to see if they had any current information aside from speculation. I cannot say for certain, but I believe that their impenetrable dungeon, the one in which Death himself would be incapable of escaping, has been destroyed by one they thought to be forever sealed within its confines," said Drogen cryptically.

"Shouldn't we find out what's happened before we go jumping to conclusions? It could be an after effect from the battle you had with Ether and Uther. It could be that their magical power lingered and you're sensing its rapid dissipation," said Willow whose arm hadn't left its interlocked hold with Fread's.

"All I can say for certain is that a massive power was unleashed, and it came from that direction. The weight of that power awoke me from my slumber this morning and silenced even the insects as it cascaded across the sky. Whether to take the phenomenon as foreboding, or fortuitous has yet to reveal itself. None the less, I doubt the goblinkin, or their God Grock, will be at all pleased with its destruction. And where there is destruction there's knowledge to be garnered," said Drogen

Drogen bade everyone to set down at the fired wood table at the center of the house making a mental note to do the same to the chairs whenever the chance to do so presented itself.

"Fread... Are you ready to move to the table," questioned Willow as she tugged upon Fread's arm. Looking around the room he looked at the table and then at Willow, before standing up and moving over to the table to sit.

"I can still feel the connection to the home runic sigil I placed at Seraphine's, so we can get there quickly. However, there's no telling what we might be getting into. Arriving in a large group could further complicate matters as well. Furthermore, I don't wish to drag any of you into a fight unnecessarily. Especially since the last one concluded only yesterday. I believe it best if I go through with this part alone," said Drogen.

"Don't think you can get rid of us that easy." said Seraphine. You would undoubtedly get lost without a guide, or do I need to remind you of our first meeting," she said with a coy smile. "I know the area like the back of my hand, so I'm going with you whether you like it or not."

"Well, if she's going then so am I. I won't be left out of this adventure like I was the last one. Plus, I need to keep an eye on her, and make sure she doesn't do anything inappropriate," said Natalia pointing at Seraphine while sticking out her tongue.

"Well, that's not very proper of you princess. You just don't want me to get any further ahead of you than I already am," teased Seraphine back.

Fread cleared his throat to stop the two women's back and forth waiting for them to stop sticking their tongues out at each other long enough for him to speak. "Unfortunately, I'll be unable to participate in this adventure with you. I left my duties here for far too long and have a mountain of paperwork regarding the kingdom and its allies to go through. A stack I swear grows every time I look away from it," said Fread with a hearty laugh.

"I too will be staying," stated Willow. "To help Fread and the other guardian knight's that were injured during the battle yesterday. Not to mention the collateral caused by Ether and Uther's use of magic."

"There is also an effort being made to retrieve the dead from below in order to give each of them a proper burial," said Fread.

"I'll also be helping Fread get through his workload of course. From what I've seen, it's going to take quite a bit of time. Even with both of us working to get it done."

"Still, I cannot, in good conscience let princess Natalia go without guard. Not when there is certain danger where you plan to go. I will send you two well suited warriors who'd be happy to accompany you wherever you go. I'll only need a little time to find them, and a small window for them to prepare. I'm sure I can get them to you within an hour's time."

"Tis no need Fread. Two loyal guards are already coming this way, and they are more than up to the task. Assuming they, and Seraphine can get along without fighting… too much," smiled Drogen mischievously. "From the sound of the armor they wear they're ready to go as soon as we are."

Seraphine thought about what Drogen said contemplating what he could mean until her heart sank. "You could pick anyone, does it have to be the Dwarves," she said with despair. Before looking to Fread. "You know I think finding some other guards sounds like a good idea. You couldn't possibly let your princess out into the world without proper protection. You know, guards that can defend her above her waistline. Why don't you run along and get them for us," Seraphine smiled sweetly batting her eyelashes at both Drogen and Fread.

"What are you afraid of Seraphine. That they will give me an unfair advantage," prodded Natalia.

"On second thought bring the stinking dwarves. After a week of smelling them Drogen will be begging to bring the three of you back here. Leaving him with me, and me alone." Both women continued their back and forth while Willow laughed, and Fread stared off as if recalling a memory.

A loud knock brought everyone back from their bickering, laughter, and musings as it echoed through Drogen's house. "Come in Rumble and Tumble we've been expecting you," he said shaking his head at the two warring women stopping briefly on Fread's far away expression.

"Oud you know it be us," came Rumble's startled reply as the door flew open. The two dwarves were covered in chain mail armor from head to foot with partial plate covering their vital areas. They carried with them two weapons each, a war axe; tied to their belts, and a long sword, which had been strapped at their back in a scabbard cut down the side allowing it to be quickly drawn.

"It seems you're both ready. I believe you'll both enjoy what's to come. You do enjoy killing goblinkin, do you not," said Drogen as he rose to his feet and bowed to the dwarves.

"Ay," came Rumble's reply while his brother nodded vigorously bowing in kind.

"Are you sure there isn't anyone else we can ask," questioned Seraphine desperately.

"What elf, ye afraid me brother and me'll be superior to ya in battle," grinned Rumble.

Seraphine's expression was one of sheer disbelief. As if the statement was simply too ridiculous for any consideration. "No, I'll show you just how effective I can be. I'll kill more than both of you combined. You'll see just how far below elves' dwarves truly are, and I don't just mean in stature."

Drogen gestured to Natalia coaxing her closer to him while the others held their own discussions. "Is this normal," posited Drogen in a whisper. His forked tongue tickling Natalia's ear and forcing blood to her cheeks.

"For them yes. I have no idea why they constantly try to one up each other, and I'm unaware of what relations are like between the two races in general. I know they've fought territorial disputes in the past, but that information is from books made long ago. Nobody I've been able to ask on the subject seems to know when, or why the conflicts actually started. What I do known is that each race has their own special name for the other. For example, Elves will refer to dwarves as uncultured mole people while the dwarves will call elves dandy tree lice," said Natalia. "Often I think it's simply a battle to see which side can come up with the more cleaver insult," chuckled Natalia under her breath.

"So, working with them is going to be more than a little entertaining," sighed Drogen as he moved away from Natalia and in between the two warring parties. "Maybe I'll get in on the action. Should we come up with some kind of prize for the victor in this little foray of yours?"

Rumble and Seraphine paled at the prospect, dispelling their arguments as their boasting turned to stuttering and finally to silence.

The deflated look from both sides threw all but Fread into hysterical laughter. Fread smiled at the laughter as he saw Rumble and Seraphine's deflated looks, and the elation on everyone's face.

"Now you two quite your boasting and show what you can do on the field of battle. Tis the only true test, would you not agree," Drogen questioned drawing a strained *"yes"* from each of them.

"Well as entertaining as this is to watch, you have your guards now, and I know they are capable enough for the journey ahead. So, with that, I believe it's best that Willow and I take our leave. There's a lot for me to do as captain of the guard, and many bodies that still need to be collected from the battleground below," he said as Willow grabbed him by the arm once more pulling him towards the door."

"Very well," said Drogen with a bow. "I wish the both of you well and hope to see you again soon. As I'm sure everyone else does. However, before you disembark, might you return these garments for me, and give the seamstress my thanks for their hard work on the attire. Drogen stripped out of the garments handing them over to Fread before drawing out a fresh set of clothing from his extra-dimensional bag.

"I'll be sure to do just that," said Fread.

"What about the dresses worn by the two princesses, they too will prove to be a hindrance... especially where you're going," stated Willow. I cannot imagine trying to fly through the air, or move through the trees in a corset, not to mention fending off enemies."

"I suppose tis time for you two to change into more appropriate attire as well," said Drogen with a nod.

"I know where we can go. There's a shop not far from here just inside the shopping district. They don't have anything that's pre-made but the seamstress works fast. We can go to Seraphine's home in the Moongrove from anywhere can we not," questioned Natalia.

"Of course we may," confirmed Drogen.

"Well let's get going then. The dwarves are getting smellier with every passing second and they're just standing here," said Seraphine with an outstretched tongue toward Rumble.

"At least me brother an me don't smell of uh mildewed forest like yerself. Anyway, it only been three weeks gots one more tago till it be time," said Rumble as though a bath at any other time would be a waste.

"Come now everyone let us start this adventure. I wish to see the Moongrove as soon as we're able to get there, and your constant back and forth is hindering our progress," said Drogen as he pushed the entire party out the door. They only made it a few steps before their bickering started up again. *Well at least we're moving,* thought Drogen. *This could be a very long trip.*

They walked through the cut in path to get back into town, and to the tailor shop Natalia had spoken of her dwarven guard taking up positions in front and behind the group as they moved through Zephyria. As they entered the city everyone greeted Natalia and Seraphine excitedly before moving away so as not to interrupt their progress. Natalia made sure to greet everyone she passed smiling at them warmly.

As they walked through the throng of people hearing the rustle and bustle of the street vendors and those people walking between shops a small band of zephyrian children accidentally bumped into their group unknowingly. The children turned around tentatively to see what they'd inadvertently struck and shrunk back in fear as they realized the mistake they'd made. A couple of them tried to run away in fear but were stopped by Rumble and Tumble before they could take even half a step away.

"You need not fear little ones. It's good that you can have fun with your friends, but you might want to play in a more open area. Somewhere where others won't be inconvenienced by your play. Now if I remember right there's a big open field just over there that would be perfect for your games," said Natalia a bright smile gracing her features and melting the fear from the children's faces. "Now run along and play to your heart's content, but remember not to get in anyone's way, or you might get yourselves into trouble. We would not want that now would we," asked Natalia as she patted each of the children on the head reassuringly.

"We promise we be more care-ful princess," came the children's reply. With toothy smiles, and excitedly flapping wings.

"I'm glad to hear it, now run along and play well," said Natalia pushing them on their way and waving them off before they continued on to the tailor shops front stoop. At the entrance everyone waited for Natalia and Seraphine to finish gathering their new clothes. All except Drogen who both women pulled inside behind them. Fread and Willow stopped Rumble and Tumble who had made to follow before they could enter holding them back by the shoulder as Drogen disappeared behind the rapidly shut door.

Seeing the smile of love shared between Fread and Willow as the door closed behind him Drogen couldn't help but smile. *It seems that their relationship has developed further, and that Fread has not forgotten anything of himself, nor holds a grudge against me for bringing him back before his soul could pass. I'm delighted to see them experience happiness. I know Willow has had none for quite some time.*

"Hello and welcome to the Wild Seamstress I'll be with you shortly," came a voice from behind the counter. After a minute of waiting patiently the seamstress rose with a smile. Hello, my name is Jesha how can I help y..." As she looked at the people gracing her shop, she found her voice had stopped working entirely. Until her mouth stood agape.

"Hello Jesha," said Natalia warmly, "Is my order ready?"

"P-p-p-p-princess y-you ordered something from my shop. I-I don't remember seeing such an order I would assuredly remember getting an order from the palace," stuttered the seamstress uncontrollably.

"Well, the thing is," started Natalia sheepishly. "It wasn't done under my name, but it was commissioned by one of my guards, one of the dwarves, either Rumble or Tumble. Oh, and We'll also be needing something for my friend Seraphine over there. It needs to be something easy to move and fight in."

"Yes. Yes. Of course, we can make something perfect for her." Looking around the room Jesha nodded looking her up and down before settling back on Natalia. She looked at Natalia for a second more before realization struck, "That armor's for you," shouted Jesha. Covering her mouth to stop the outburst but being wholly too late in doing so.

"Yes. Is it finished," questioned Natalia patiently.

"Ye- yes princess j-just give me a moment to grab it from the back."

"Shiesa, come out here and help this beautiful elven lady find some materials." Hearing Jesha's call a little winged girl came running out from behind the counter her tiny white wings flapping excitedly just enough to push her slightly off the ground.

"On second thought it might be better for you to come back with me. Just to make sure the fit is to your liking," said Jesha sheepishly as she ushered Natalia behind the counter, "I'll take you to my private fitting room, as it may take some time to get the armor on and the other items you requested situated properly."

"Thank you, Jesha," said Natalia. "I cannot wait to see how it fits and feels."

As Natalia disappeared the little winged girl stopped in front of Seraphine. "Hello pretty lady how can help you," questioned Shiesa

"What would you recommend Shiesa," questioned Seraphine.

Shiesa looked overjoyed to be asked what she thought and went about the room looking and feeling the different fabrics while looking back at Seraphine each time.

The room boasted bolts of fabric from the floor to the ceiling ranging from the brightest whites to the blackest nights in color.

As Shiesa found fabrics she liked, all of which were green, Seraphine would take them off the rack and place them on the front counter for Jesha to use when she returned. After bringing out a fourth bolt, Shiesa came back skipping happily along the ground. Wings beating about her back joyously.

Drogen felt a sense of peace as if he too were experiencing the same joy the little winged girl displayed as she sat down in a chair behind the counter awaiting Jesha's return. *The simple joy of children is something to behold. I wonder what became of those children that were playing in the streets before Zephyr was attacked by the goblinkin. Do the little ones we saw this morning play with them as well.*

Jesha reappeared a moment later shaking her head. Shiesa be a good girl and see if you can help the princess. Maybe your smaller hands can untangle the mess of that knotted corset.

Shiesa jumped down from her chair fluttering off into the back of the shop a look of clear determination on her face.

"Ah these fabrics will do quite nicely," said Jesha while she inspected the bolts for any damage.

"I'll leave the design up to you; all I ask is that it's functional and easy to move in through the woods. I cannot have it getting stuck in trees and branches should I need to move through them," said Seraphine.

"Right then I just need to take down your sizes and I'll get straight to work."

Jesha took down all the measurements she needed and quickly began cutting and forming the fabric her hands working expertly as she cut and threaded the fabrics together into a beautiful one-piece dress which she handed to Seraphine, the moment it was done, to put on and test the fit. "Walk around a bit and see where we may need to improve upon the design," she said.

Taking the opportunity Jesha went to the back again to check on Natalia and Shiesa's progress. "I hope they've been able to remove that blasted dress by now. I would loath having to cut the corset off, even if the string is replaceable. Oh, you can change in the room just to the right over there," pointed Jesha before once again disappearing.

Seraphine was the first to come out her green dress forming tightly to her body, resembling much the same design as her mother's dress in Moongrove. The dress was slightly shorter, however it allowed her more flexibility. With the accompaniment of her sword belt, which she had worn atop the previous dress, while the sword Truth at her side was held upon her hips by a small belt.

"Tis fitting, your movements look as though they will not be hindered, either should we find ourselves in trouble," stated Drogen

A clearly irritated Natalia came out from behind the counter clad from head to foot in form fitting black studded leather armor. Her Raven black hair had been braided falling down her back to nestle between her abyssal black wings. The deep black of the doeskin leather held her tightly within its embrace only punctuated by strategically placed metal studs that would help deflect blows around her vital organs. Natalia no longer looked like the princess they knew, and even Seraphine couldn't help but marvel at the transformation her friend had undergone.

Drogen turned away from her realizing he was staring. His own heartbeat pounding through his head as he turned toward the door of the shop. *I wonder what everyone else's expressions will be at seeing such a drastic change in the princess of Zephyria.*

"I never imagined that I would be wearing this on my first journey into the larger world. Thank you for this and my friends new attire Jesha. And thank you too Shiesa," smiled Natalia eliciting a big grin and hearty flap of Shiesa's tiny wings. "Now let us settle up so that we may be on our way."

Jesha tried to decline payment, but Natalia wouldn't take no for an answer and even left a silver for Shiesa as thanks for all her help, receiving a wide eyed thank you, before the three of them ventured out of the shop.

"For a princess ye be terrifyin," said Rumble as Tumble bobbing his head in agreement.

Natalia felt blood pooling in her face. "Well, I cannot be going out into the world unarmed or armored now can I," said Natalia hotly.

"I must say I doubt that Lord Vladimir would approve of the world seeing you in such things but, since he's not here to protest... I hope your travels go well, and you remain safe out there. Natalia this will be your first time leaving the city though you are quite skilled in many aspects of battle, I know that most of your knowledge stems from books. Your practices with me, though great, will not make up for a lack of experience. Don't hesitate to rely on the others for the things you don't yet know. You must all work together in order to come back alive remember that," said Fread. Clear signs of worry furrowing his brow as he looked upon Natalia. "I will tell Lord Vladimir of your departure, but I believe it best not to give him any details regarding what you're doing. Unless you feel an explanation to be wise."

Natalia thought about what Fread said and looked to those around her for guidance, ultimately knowing the decision to be hers alone to make. "T-Tell fath... tell my... tell Lord Vladimir nothing of what we are doing. Drogen gave him much to think about and knowing the dangers I face will likely cause greater hardship.

"What if he ask's us where you have gone. What would you have him told," questioned Willow.

"If he does ask, tell him I have gone out to see the world with my trusted friends, and guard by my side, but nothing more," stated Natalia. "I only hope he can see the truth that's before his eyes before it's too late," she said under her breath.

"Very well princess your words will be passed along. I..." Drogen could tell that Fread wished to convey something else, but Rumble's antics pushed those thoughts aside.

"HEY, will ye quit the lollygagging there be orcs needin cuttin right above the shoulder," grumbled Rumble as he made a few practice swings with his axe scarring away a few onlookers.

"And how are you going to accomplish that feat. I didn't think the dwarves liked anything to do with magic, aside from what they use to forge. What did you find? Some magical way of gaining stature or something," scoffed Seraphine.

"Ya it be a closely held dwarven magic, only problem be it make us irresistible ta elves," said Tumble as he stuck his tongue out at and danced around her. Drawing a fit of laughter from everyone but a rather perturbed Seraphine.

"Before we go there is one other item that I need help with," said Drogen as he pulled his dragon-scale bowl with a thought from his soul chamber. "There is still much of the writing on my bowl that needs to be translated," he said passing the bowl to Willow. "I leave it in the care of you and Fread, for when we return."

"I believe tis time for us all to part ways. Now everyone who's going with me simply place your hands anywhere upon my body and we'll be in Seraphine's house in the blink of an eye." The first to move in where Seraphine and Natalia both of their hearts fluttering in excitement and apprehension for what was about to come. The dwarves hesitated for a few seconds before stretching out their hands and grabbing hold of Drogen's tunic. "We'll see both of you soon, but for now take care of yourselves... and each other," winked Drogen as he clicked his fingers together and disappeared with the others.

"I'm really glad they left after that. I feel quite embraced," said Fread as blood pooled in his face.

"What it's not like he didn't know after that morning in his house. And even if he didn't, he can hear our heartbeats. There's no doubt he would have figured it out even if we tried to keep it secret from him, or the others," said Willow.

"I still can't believe he can distinguish between heartbeats, especially in large, crowded areas like the market. But there again, it explains why no matter how hard either Princess Natalia or I tried we could never sneak up on, or catch him off-guard," said Fread.

"I only hope he can keep them all safe, and they don't find too much trouble along the way. Still, the fact of the matter is, trouble is exactly what they're leaving to find," said Willow with a shrug.

"Although I am worried for the safety of both the princesses, they have the dwarves and Drogen to protect them, should anything happen," said Fread. Well, I suppose we should get to work. The first order of business telling Lord Vladimir of her departure," stated Fread with uncertainty. "Or maybe a letter?"

"*No Fread* you promised Natalia and you need to keep your promise."

"I know. I know. What about the bowl he gave you. Can you understand anything that it says. Gaia said it was the language of the Gods, and she said only a God would be able to translate it."

Willow brought the bowl up to her eyes and dismay swept across her face. "I have no clue what any of this writing is. If this is the writing of the gods, then it's an old and forgotten system of writing that came before my birth into divinity."

"What could that mean for Drogen and the others," posited Fread.

"I don't know. Our only hope is finding someone who might be able to decipher what it says before Drogen gets back to Zephyria."

The connotation of what that statement meant wasn't lost on Fread, but he didn't want Willow to see the worry that it brought. "Until we find someone, we can have the scholars inside the castle take a look. See if there's any reference to it in the castle records, whether it be a lost tome, or sacred text they might be able to give us some idea of what it says."

"I don't think having this out where just anyone can take a look at it is a good idea," said Willow.

"True, I'll have Krail and Our head Librarian figure out a good method," said Fread as they began their journey back to the castle.

Chapter Three

As they opened their eyes Rumble, Tumble, and Natalia where awe struck, jaws slack in amazement. The look in their eyes and the skipping of their heartbeats telling Drogen that they could hardly comprehend the different environment before their eyes.

"It's nice to know that there's at least one thing that can silence a dwarf," smirked Seraphine.

"I be sorry to disappoint ye Seraphine. Tumble an me just tryin to figure what be best to get it down. Fire or axe," came Rumbles retort.

"Don't you dare," said Natalia menacingly.

"Sorry princess," said the dwarf shrinking away a bit, "It only be a joke."

Nothing within the room looked as if it had been disturbed to Drogen and a nod from Seraphine all but confirmed his thoughts. *Now lets see if any surprises await us through the door,* thought Drogen as he set his ears to work seeking out anything else within the estate. At he outer limits of his hearing the distinct sound of heavy armor and footsteps traversing wood floors came to him.

"It seems there are some people taking refuge inside your house Seraphine, although through the walls, tis unclear whether they be friend or foe. Either way I feel it best to be cautious. There's no telling what might await us outside. For now we should see who resides within this house and if they're enemies, dispatch them quickly and quietly, before they have chance to call for reinforcements," said Drogen

"Well that leaves you and the dwarves out of the question. You and the dwarves are not much for subtlety," said Seraphine. "I think it best if Natalia and I go out and take care of things," garnering a look of uncertainty and concern from Natalia before she gave Seraphine an approving nod. You three can just sit back and relax for a bit. I'm sure that using your rune, as you called it, took a lot out of you with so many people tagging along.

"Bagh. Ye just wanna get a head start on the kill count. Though I suppose it wouldn't be right, not to start ye off with a handicap," said Rumble with a malicious grin.

Seraphine made to retort but stopped short scanning the room as if finally noticing something out of place.

"If you three are quite finished. Had you been paying attention you would have noticed that Natalia has already gone through the door," said Drogen.

"She what," cried Seraphine sprinting to the door and pulling it open. Quickly darting out into the main foyer as the door swung back closed behind her.

I'll show them I can do this. That they can trust me now and in the future even if this is the first time I've traveled outside of Zephyria. I've trained myself for this. I can do this, thought Natalia. Working her way along the limbs, branches, and vines formed along the walls to give the structure stability, was easy for Natalia. Each part of the structure lending itself as a hand or foothold of varying sizes throughout the entirety of the mansion making traversing up the inside the structure silently easy. *It's like this entire house was made to climb,* thought Natalia giddily. Natalia worked her way up the side of the mansion like a spider crawling across its web. Just beneath the second story banister Natalia let herself hang and listen for any sign that an enemy was near.

Natalia worked her way across the banister silently until the guttural utterings of the orcs came to her ears from behind a door that had been left slightly ajar. To her ultimate surprise she found that she somehow understood what they were saying, as though they spoke in the common tongue.

The sound of near silent feet coming up the stairs shook Natalia from her thoughts as a sense of guilt overwhelmed her at seeing Seraphine's angry face pointed directly at her. Unsure if the gesture would make her angrier or not Natalia bid her to be silent and pointed towards the door where she knew the goblinkin to be. The anger disappeared from her friends face instantly as she backed herself to the door-frame.

Natalia proceeded over the banister with a small silent push of her wings resting herself against the door-frame on the other side. Looking at Seraphine apologetically she mouthed "I'm sorry." Seraphine dismissed the apology with a wave of the hand and Natalia knew that her friend would more than likely tell her exactly what she thought about her initiative when they could talk without the threat of enemies to hold back conversation. *I'm not looking forward to that conversation,* thought Natalia as she listened in on the conversation the goblinkin were having just beyond the door.

"We must go to new Grock. You see what done to old one. New one bigger anyways."

"Yes, I see what done. None left but rubble. How we get there. You know where it is, my tribe never told."

"Me hoped you knew. Been told its north in conquered lands."

As the two orcs continued to converse in their broken language Seraphine and Natalia slipped through the door unnoticed. They covered the distance to the two orcs in a few swift footsteps in which Seraphine had pulled her sword Truth from its scabbard. From thigh pocket in her leather armor, Natalia pulled forth a short sword a forearms length moving against the other orc.

Recognizing the threat the orcs moved to draw their swords but Seraphine had struck before the first orc had time to pull out even half of its blade. The other orc retreated quickly as his companion fell to the floor giving him ample time to block Natalia's strike. A strike without weight behind it. Seeing the light blow as it fell upon the orc told Seraphine how right she had been to chase after her friend.

The orc recognizing its opponent for the novice made a counterattack that would have severed Natalia's hand had she not retreated in time negating the effectiveness of the counterattack. With a feral snarl the orc pressed forward forcing Natalia back on her heels and off balance. As the orc's strikes slapped against her defending blade she felt her arms growing numb. With her arms all but useless the sword fell from her hands to clatter on the ground at her side.

As the orc drew back Seraphine plunged Truth through its back and heart. The sound of the orc's sword hitting the ground brought the breath she'd been holding back into her lungs, but it was swept away again upon seeing the look of horror Natalia had set upon her face.

"They would have slaughtered me if you weren't here," said Natalia tears starting to form in her eyes. "How could I have been so reckless thinking that I could do this without help, or proper training?"

"Taking another life isn't easy, especially not the first one," said Seraphine sinking down beside her friend. "Even if the life taken is done so to save your own, or in the defense of your people. There's no real way to combat the weight that burden puts upon a person's heart and soul. Seeing another being to death's door can be traumatic, but taking the life of another creature away is even more so."

"Then how can you take the life of another so easily," bit Natalia.

"It's not easy Natalia, even now I will have to live with the knowledge that I've added another to the list of beings that I've killed. But...the simple truth is they've taken much from the both of us. For me they have taken away many of my people and my home within the Moongrove. They've taken the same from many of your people as well. Imagine what the people of Zephyr feel knowing they may never get their lives back to what they once were. They no longer hold residence among the other races and have been sequestered once again to your main city, just as you've been your entire life. The only difference is that they tasted freedom as you do now. That knowledge is what makes it easier for me to take the lives of those who would destroy mine and other people's homes for their own purposes. It makes it easier to do. but will never decrease the weight."

"What if I can't do it."

"There will come a time that you may be forced to do it. It may not be today or tomorrow, but it will come to pass. I hope you choose to keep living instead of fearing the feeling it will undoubtedly give you. Every one of us want to see you continue to live, and that includes everyone in Zephyria. For now push it from your mind and dry your eyes or Drogen might see me as the better choice," said Seraphine teasingly. "You wouldn't want that would you?"

"No. I am clearly the better choice after all," said Natalia with a smile. Taking a long steadying breath through her nose to calm herself.

"We better make sure there aren't any more orcs in here before we tell them they can come out from the room," said Seraphine as she helped Natalia back to her feet, "But first." she said, sweeping over to a large framed picture, set into the wood through a tangle of living vines. Feeling along the large frame the vines receding as Seraphine pulled upon its edge revealing a set of branded armor. "Though it seems a shame to cover up this figure from Drogen's eyes, but it's probably for the best where we're going."

As Seraphine and Natalia came back into the room Drogen saw the swollen flesh about Natalia's eyes, as well as Seraphine's banded armor, that told him she'd been crying. He thought to ask her what was wrong, but dismissed it a moment later knowing she'd confide in him, if and when, she was ready to do so. "Are all the enemies taken care of," questioned Drogen.

"Ya only two orcs were inside the house and they're both dead," said Seraphine with a reassuring look at Natalia who shrunk back at the comment.

"Well then, let's be gone from this congested room and discuss where we're to travel next," stated Drogen.

Drogen opened the door for everyone to walk through and shutting it behind him before joining the others. He only took a couple steps before stopping in his tracks, hearing shifting feet and heartbeats coming from the forest just beyond the French doors that opened out into the Moongrove. One of which he recognized, but it somehow felt off, a shift that he recognized in himself whenever he changed form. "Someone else has come to say hello it would seem," sighed Drogen as he motioned toward the French doors. "I believe it best for the rest of you to wait here while I go see what awaits us."

Everyone agreed with a nod though Rumble made to protest wishing to go along too, thinking he might be able to claim a few heads should battle ensue, but Tumble stopped him with the side of his axe in order to bar his way. "Let him go Rumble there be no need to kill anything but what be aimin ta kill us. He be knowing the difference sooner then we."

"Fine," said Rumble silently. Cursing under his breath.

Drogen walked through the door cautiously his draconic eyes peering into the shadows descending from the canopied forest casting the small clearing into near complete darkness, even with the sun hanging at its highest in the sky. In the distance, he could make out seven heartbeats one of which was finally close enough for him to recognize. *Alya,* thought Drogen. *No wonder the rhythm sounded familiar?*

Drogen maneuvered himself between the door and the wilderness outside so that his friends would have enough warning to ready themselves for a fight, should it come. I can hear your heartbeats out there, don't think you can hide yourselves from me. Out of the shadows appeared six White tigers. *This reminds me of the elders,* thought Drogen offhandedly. At the center stood a woman whose body housed the familiar heartbeat. To that woman Drogen bowed, to which she did the same, fumbling with the movement, as if unsure in her own skin.

"It seems there's more than one species upon Dranier that has the ability to take on a different form. My kin never mentioned yours, though they did lock themselves away for many years, in Lundwurm Tul. I find I must ask, which is your true form Alya. This, or the tiger who comforted me whilst I was nestled in the crook of a tree," asked Drogen.

"I didn't think you out of everyone would recognize me, not in this form. Although, I'm sure the ears would have given anyone else suspicion," smiled Alya. "I would never have thought my heartbeat would be what gave away my secret. The tiger is my true form, this is but another I can take. I think you and your kin would be surprised to know but, from what I understand, there are other people, those who live across the forbidden plains that have the same ability. However, very few, if any, have the knowledge or fortitude to travel across the harsh environment without serious repercussions."

"So there are others who can take on other forms besides the ones they're born into. How very interesting." *I wonder if the magic of the dragons influenced those races more than the Gods did as it is here. I would very much like to witness and know these other races not present in this part of the world. How many more races could there be,* thought Drogen.

"Yes many other races it would seem and most if not all have the ability to shift as we do."

"Is that what these other races refer to the release of constrained power as," asked Drogen.

"Yes."

"Well I suppose in a way tis an apt representation."

"Within my race, the Warren, many choose to go the entirety of their lives shifting only once. The practice has all but gone from my people in the last century because of the relationship we formed with Gaia and the elves. Out of the last generation born to the Warren only one that I know of took on this form more regularly. That was my mother Avren, who fought alongside your father."

"Was she there when my father was taken prisoner?"

"Yes. She killed one of the Gods who tried to ambush him. However, by the time she had returned Lucian; the supreme God, had subdued him in abyssal black chains. Bindings even he couldn't break. She followed their trail and wound up deep in the territory controlled by Grock and the bloodthirsty goblinkin. Death told my mother to run so she did and I've not seen her since that day over twenty years ago. She told me a great deal about Lisana and asked for me to keep an eye out for her to tell her what happened, but Gaia ended up telling her what I knew in my stead. Why is it that my mother never mentioned you?" said Alya.

"Quite simply my father didn't know. My mother kept her pregnancy from everyone, and that included him. She feared he would refrain from his vital task of stalling the Gods and their conquest of Lundwurm Tul if he'd known the truth so she hid it."

"Why is it that you and others of your kin are here? I thought you would have escaped with the elves as they made their way back to the main city," asked Drogen listening intently to their heartbeats in order to discern whether or not an attack might be forthcoming. *The rhythm of a heart and the changes it makes when faced with death will reveal whether you face an ally or an enemy. Just be careful that allies do not become enemy's once you've turned your back to them,* remembered Drogen as the words Thane once said range clearly in his mind from one of the many aerial battle's the two had engaged in.

"My kin have long held a contract with your father. It is a familial contract and is passed down through our line from one generation to the next. You might call it a familial bond between two people. I have come to fulfill the contract that my mother took upon herself, as is my duty."

"You do this out of need to fulfill a contract? A contract passed down to me because I am the son of Death," asked Drogen as Alya nodded. "If that tis the only reason for which you would follow me into what comes next, then no. I will not risk another person's life on a mission that could result in everyone I know being captured, tortured, and or killed for something as fickle as that. Those who have followed me here trust in me, not because of obligation, but because they believe in both the mission and I. Life is far too precious to waste on a task that you may not believe, nor have stake, in."

"But... the co-contract."

"Is following a contract adopted by our parents what you really want Alya?"

"If we don't follow the path our parents have lain out for us are we not disgracing their memory," replied Alya.

"Our parents should want for us what brings us joy. Will coming with me result in joy or sorrow and is it worth it for you to do so. What do *you* want Alya."

Alya thought on it long and hard before she spoke. "I want to find my mother."

"Then we have something in common. I seek my parents as well, but do you view this as reason enough to risk your life, throwing yourself into the throng of battle that is sure to come?"

"Yes it is. To me my family is more important than the contract formed between our parents, though that contract might be what leads me to her. I won't use the contract as an excuse."

"If you believe coming along will bring you closer to your goal then I will gladly bring you along. But should our paths begin to divert at any time, we will go our separate ways without guilt or malice derived from some parental agreement. I will leave you to think about what you wish to do, as it stands there are others inside with which I must confer regarding your addition to our party." Drogen bowed low to Alya before turning around and disappearing back into the house. Leaving her with the twelve other warren to think.

As Drogen entered, the questioning faces of Natalia and Seraphine assailed him, while Rumble and Tumble held their axes out ready for a fight. "No need for weapons. That part of our journey may very well be upon us soon, but tis not now." Everyone relaxed knowing more enemies weren't waiting for them on the other side of the door. The dwarves however, looked disappointed as they tucked the axes back into their belts, so they rested comfortably upon their sides. "Alya of the Warren may, or may not, be joining us. I'm sure she'll be in before long with a decision. Is it alright with everyone here to have another comrade come along," questioned Drogen.

"Alya of the Warren," asked Seraphine skepticism written all over her angular face. "Alya, the white tiger who's always getting me in trouble with my mother? That Alya?"

"Yes. Actually, it would seem that her clan, the Warren are much like the dragon's. They too can manipulate their form. I met her as a white tiger, but she can also take on a form similar to ours with three major differences. She retains her predatory cat eyes, her feline ears, and the color of her hair retains the white and black striped pattern of her fur. I can see from the shock on your face that this is all news to you," chuckled Drogen seeing Seraphine try to wrap her head around the idea.

"Ye be tellin me there be not only dragon people, but cat people as well. Ye be attracting weird friends Drogen," said Rumble.

"Ay and the hair be getting weirder," said Tumble drawing a short laugh from everyone.

"Seraphine, you know her best. Has she been in combat before? I'm sure she accompanied you on at least a couple of your scouting missions. You told me as much during your visits to Zephyria, though I don't remember the details. Although I've trained with the best my kingdom has to offer, I know I sorely lack experience. Having two rookie fighters, instead of just one. Truthfully, I feel that my lack of experience might hinder our progress," said Natalia.

"You cannot hope to learn the ways of battle for yourself if you stay locked away forever. We all lack something such is the way of life. Tis what we do to turn our greatest weakness into our greatest strength that we all need to see to get past our own shortcomings," said Drogen reassuring Natalia that she would prove just as valuable in what was ahead as anyone else.

"She's actually quite skilled. I've only seen her in her feline form though I don't know if she will be more or less powerful in this other form. She and I once encountered a fist of orcs. They encircled us and where wading in to deliver strikes. Using Truth I killed one orc, but Alya killed the other four. She's a force of nature. Her speed, maneuverability, and strength are superior to my own. She has kind of a primal ferocity. All of this while using no other weapons aside from her own claws," said Seraphine.

"So ye sayin a kitty cat be stronger than ye and yur's," poked Rumble drawing a scowl from Seraphine.

"Then she be stronger than ye, and me-too Rumble," said Tumble.

"Bah, I be believin it when I be seein it." With Rumble's denial, there came a knock on the door. Drogen turned around and opened the double doors wide affording everyone a view of Alya as she came walking through the doors.

Alya bowed to the group just as Drogen would have done and they bowed back. "Sera-Seraphine I-I'm Alya, your f-fr..." Seraphine came up to Alya cutting her off and wrapped her in a tight embrace drawing a deep purr from her throat.

"Why didn't you tell me about this? We could have had even more fun together wreaking havoc and pulling pranks nobody would have ever known since you can change," said Seraphine with a wicked smile.

"You would've been the one getting into trouble. I didn't want to burden you with keeping my secret from the other elves. Your sword Truth would have forbidden such a thing from happening anyways."

"Wow her hair. It be white with black streaks. I thought ye be kiddin us all," said Rumble before Tumble could prevent his brother from speaking.

"It seems you wish to join us on our journey, *until* such time as our courses divert," questioned Drogen. To which Alya bobbed her head in agreement. "Well then it seems that introductions are in order. You of course know Seraphine and I. Might I present Natalia Princess of Zephyria." Natalia came forward, bowing to Alya before stepping back. "And the dwarves Rumble and Tumble are her trusted guard," he continued pointing each of them out in turn.

"It be a pleasure ta meet ya Alya," said Rumble. "I ear from the tree lice ye be good in battle. I hope ta see just how good."

"Alya thanked them all for the warm welcome although Drogen could still feel the apprehension harbored in her heartbeat as she wondered what the others thought of her being of a different race, and one they didn't know actually existed. Her heartbeat settled down once she realized the menagerie of races that surrounded her in Seraphine's house. "Never thought I'd see Dwarves in here," said Alya.

"Ya neither did me brother an me," said Rumble

"Never thought we be seein a two-legged cat," said Tumble.

"Since the pleasantries have been taken care of. I believe tis time to get going, or else the daylight will wane before we can make any progress toward Grock."

"You know you didn't say anything about what this mission is about. I gather it has something to do with the energy you felt this morning. Are we really going to the goblinkin homeland? There's going to be a lot of resistance before we can get close enough to see Grock," said Natalia.

"That may be true, but we need to know what happened, and if luck be with us, we might be able to glean what the goblinkin have planned for the future. Tis also an opportunity to see if Grock is willing to forgo the path he's set the goblinkin upon. Although I don't know if this is his doing or Lucian's behest, as it was with Ether and Uther when they pulled me from Lundwurm Tul."

"Bah enough uh the talkin there be orcs needin killin me axe is hungry fur a fight."

"Dwarves cleave orcs about the neck, an loose thar heads with a kick, the snaggletooth's they fall ta ground an with a chop another's down," sang Tumble gleefully.

"How does a dwarf reach the neck of an orc in order to cleave it," questioned Alya.

"Ye need be asken the tree dandy that one," said Rumble with a toothy grin drawing an audible harrumph from Seraphine.

Before leaving Seraphine's estate, the group scoured the structure for the necessities that everyone needed in order for their journey to begin. Alya thinking ahead had already packed for a long journey including some road rations dried, fresh fruits and vegetables, hard dry bread, as well as freshly plucked pheasant clearly killed with exceedingly sharp teeth.

Finding everything they needed for the journey to Grock inside the mansion they exited the house. Looking up through the trees Drogen tried to discern what time it was but found no clues through the density of the forest canopy. *It seems that without elves being present more of the sky is obscured by the canopy of trees. I wonder why I didn't notice it before,* thought Drogen. *What distance do we have to cover in order to reach Grock?*

"Grock's going to be in that direction," said Seraphine as she pointed past the Moongrove mansion and into the dense woods beyond. "With all of us going we won't reach the boarder of the goblinkin territory for at least three days."

"Then we best be heading out. As it stands, avoiding battle would be the preferable option. However, should anything attack us, don't hesitate to cut it down," said Drogen as they began moving through the brambles and deeper into the surrounding wood. Never looking back at what had once been a thriving elven city only a day and a half prior.

Chapter Four

They worked their way through the woods single file as the forest grew thicker around them making traversal especially hard for the dwarves whose chainmail was constantly falling victim to the intrusion of branches and thorns present in the forest around them. Far worse for them was the presence of stinging nettle which seemed to creep underneath even the tunics and breaches they wore beneath the half-plate chain-mail armor. Putting Rumble into a prickly mood while two days passed without incident and very little discussion.

As they broke to make camp the second night Natalia came to Drogen meekly. "Might I talk to you Drogen I would like your help with something... *privately*."

Intrigued Drogen agreed telling Alya where they were going just in case something happened before following her out of camp while the others went about making preparations for the nights sleeping arrangements.

"What is it that you wish to discuss princess," Drogen asked with a bow.

"First off don't call me princess just use my first name," said Natalia bowing in kind, to which Drogen nodded. I want you to train me to fight beyond what Fread has taught me."

"Fighting is going to be necessary and self-preservation a must, but why ask me and not Seraphine or your own guard? I'm sure even Alya would help aid in your training should you ask her," stated Drogen.

"It's simple really. You cannot be hurt by my attacks, and you won't hold back just because I'm royalty like the others would. Fread was the only one who didn't treat me with squab gloves when I tried to find someone to train with. The others inside the castle would often allow me to win without putting up a real fight. Although, I believe they did so out of fear more than anything. With how often Bernadine and Nefar sent people to the dungeons, I cannot blame them for being fearful," said Natalia.

"Training with me isn't going to be easy Natalia. You are going to need to listen to everything I say following my instruction. From that instruction you will also need to find the ways that work best for you. Everyone is different and with different limitations knowing those limitations will allow you to better understand your strengths, and what you can do to cover those weaknesses."

"I-I understand. I will do my best and show you that I am worthy of your guidance," stated the clearly determined Natalia.

"All are worthy of tutelage Natalia. You need only know in your heart that you're worth being taught. Now let us see where you're at in your training."

"What I-I didn't think that you'd want to start so soon," said Natalia clear worry in her eyes.

"You never know when an enemy is going attack. The sooner you're able to defend yourself, and the others in our party, the better for everyone. So don't hesitate Natalia. When you see an enemy, attack without mercy, for they will do no less to you and those you care for. Now do you want to improve or not, is the question you have to ask yourself. If you wish to be trained then come on Natalia, *attack now,"* exclaimed Drogen.

From hidden folds in her studded leather armor Natalia produced throwing knives, which she threw expertly at Drogen who didn't even bat an eye as they hit him right above the heart, before falling to the ground at his feet. "Very good Natalia it seems your marksmanship is excellent but, lets see how precise you really are. Instead of aiming for the heart aim for the other softer vital areas. Spots that can disable and kill your opponents that isn't as protected by bone, and often times, has far less armor for protection."

"Where should I aim then," questioned Natalia.

"You must look for chinks in the armor your enemy wears. The leather armor you wear is good for moving around quietly and offers better protection than your skin will but far less than the armor worn by your dwarven guard so you will be fighting at a disadvantage. Come in close now and I'll show you what I mean."

Natalia came in closer to Drogen holding a dagger out to him as she did so.

"Very good never let your guard down when in battle, you never know from where or when an attack might come." Pointing to each spot on his body Drogen began to work through the list. "The best places to land a blade are going to be the neck, the wrist or forearm, the thigh, or the tendon at the back of an enemy's ankle."

"I understand why I would aim for each of the vital areas, but why the back of the ankle."

"Cutting there will ensure victory, for once tis cut, your enemy can no longer do anything but crawl. All that being said, in close with a dagger you have more options. Up close you'll be able to discern more prominent gaps in your enemy's armor, gaps for which you can exploit. Take plated armor for example. To save on weight most often the sides of the armor are made with far less substantial material, giving a point of failure. Stabbing upwards through that chink in the armor will give you access to their vital organs and possibly even their hearts. The same goes for the arm pit. Some armors are far better constructed leaving only subtle deficiencies, making finding an exploit more difficult. If you cannot find a weakness to exploit go for the eyes. Most will be unable to fight without sight making for an easier kill. Lastly, if the opportunity presents itself, go for the groin."

Natalia took in all the information that Drogen gave her quickly devising within her mind means of attack and methods of garnering blows that could incapacitate or fell an opponent, but she also knew that knowledge, although powerful, was useless without experience to back it up.

"We have a few minutes before the others come looking for us so attack me where I've stated. We'll see how good you really are with those knives of yours. Your first test, can you hit a moving target," said Drogen as he sprinted behind a tree coming out the other side. A dagger came flying by, clearly aimed at his neck. "Very good Natalia, if I'd been moving as slowly as I was getting away, your dagger would have definitely made contact with my throat."

The duo kept up the routine for nearly half an hour Drogen darting between and climbing trees to test Natalia's ability to adapt to whatever environment he chose to be in at any given time and each time there was a throwing knife or dagger their mere inches from hitting him each time. But never making contact.

"I believe we've trained enough for now Natalia, you look exhausted and putting your body through too much too fast will only make your training inefficient. So, for now, I'll call our first session to a close. There is one other piece of advice that I would give you. None who hold back in training will succeed in battle. You are precise with each placement of your throwing knives but if you refuse to hit your target now, you're most likely to do the same in battle," said Drogen.

"I-I'm sorry Drogen," said Natalia.

"You asked me not to treat you as the others you've tried to learn from have. I expect the same courtesy," said Drogen with a bow which Natalia reciprocated.

"I will do better when next we train," said Natalia.

"Excellent. I have a little homework for you as well. I want you to look at the armor that the others in our party wear. Find the strengths and weaknesses of each, including your own, before our next session."

As they entered the camp site everything had been set up each of the companions having their own personal tent to themselves aside from the brother dwarves whose large tent was made to house themselves and Natalia so they could better guard her against a night raid. The three tents during the first night had been relatively close together but had separated greatly upon the discovery of Rumbles frightfully loud snoring.

Tumble was just beginning to stack wood to start a fire while Rumble began skinning and gutting a fist of rabbits for them to eat. "Here you can add this to the meat to cook," said Drogen producing a pork loin from his bag. Which he cut into chops to cook above the fire, Tumble was struggling to light.

"Here Rumble you can add this to what you're cooking it will give you all enough to eat. Tomorrow we'll reach Grock so having enough to eat will help us be at our best for what tomorrow might bring," said Drogen.

"Thank ye the tree lice be sulkin in er tent cus we take from the forest so ye might wanna stear way awhile. Ey Dragon ye can light the fire faster then me brudder, so help em out will ya," said Rumble.

Without a second thought Drogen placed a hand on Tumbles shoulder drawing him back out of the way before he sent a jet of flame to the wood igniting it instantly.

"Ye be a good fire lizard," said Tumble with an appreciative whistle.

I need to ask Seraphine about what Grock looks like and what we might expect going forward, but tis probably best not to disturb her at this point in time if what Rumble stated is accurate. Tis information that concerns everyone so them hearing what we discuss would be most prudent anyways, thought Drogen as he sat down beside the fire keeping a close eye on Natalia as she stealthily surveyed the two dwarves. *Alya and Seraphine seem to be in discussion. Maybe Alya's trying to get her out here to join the rest of us. Well tis none of my business, unless they make it so.*

Rumble tied the rabbits and pork around sticks driving them into the ground around the fire to start them cooking, after the first rotation of the meat Alya and Seraphine emerged from the tent and sat down around the fire, Seraphine staying away from the roasting meat, but not running from it.

"Although they might not tell you, I thought you'd like to know. Everything they took from the rabbits they returned to the forest. Nothing they took is going to waste Seraphine. Not even the blood," whispered Drogen.

Seraphine mouthed "thank you," but said nothing more as she stared into the fire.

Alya took up position on the opposite side tying her pheasant to a tree limb and holding it over the fire instead of beside it.

"Do you not have something for which you can eat," asked Drogen.

"I've already eaten," said Seraphine.

"Oh will ye come off it already. They be rabbits thar be thousands of the blasted things in this forest don't ye be doubtin. An thar be thousand more afore long," bellowed Rumble. "Ye be the only one ear not be eaten meat."

"I know, but it doesn't mean I have to like it," retorted Seraphine.

"How about we discuss more pressing matters instead of those that have come and gone. Do you have any idea when we'll be within the goblinkin territory tomorrow, or what we could be walking into?"

"Truthfully I have no idea. Reports over the past month have shown a massive decrease in activity coming from Grock. They could've abandoned it for someplace else," posited Seraphine.

"Let me see if I can find anything out while everyone else eats." Within his mind Godslayer; Envoy of Death gave off a feeling of safety bringing ease to his body as he slipped his corporal form. Drogen moved his astral form up through the trees to look into the sky above them hoping to find any trace of the disturbed currents that could tell him where to look, but found no traces left to follow. *With no baring to follow and only a general direction I could be searching the woods for hours and find nothing. Let's see if I can find anything of interest at least.*

Drogen searched the surrounding area until he heard a call from the others for him to return. At first he thought the call to be that of Godslayer; Envoy of Death, but they remained silent within him. With a thought he returned to his body sucking in a deep breath as he did so. "I found no evidence of the phenomenon left upon the air, not surprising given how quickly it receded but I'd hoped it could at least guide us in as we gained ground. Either way, We should know what happened around mid-day tomorrow, if I've properly judged the distance. The first thing we will come across is a well-traveled road through the forest."

"It should be easy to find because the goblinkin burn paths through the trees instead of cutting through most times," said Seraphine who had visibly relaxed.

"We should probably get some rest while we can there's no telling what tomorrow will bring," said Alya with a wide mouthed yawn which exposed her sharp pointed teeth.

"I'll cover the watch for tonight," said Drogen. "The rest of you should get some sleep."

"You've taken the watch for the last two nights are you not tired," questioned Natalia clearly worried that he would be exhausted.

"I've no need for sleep for at least another day. Once I'm tired I'll be sure to let the rest of you know, but for now, you all need rest far more than I do," said Drogen.

Everyone agreed as the infectious yawn began to travel between them all. Only Natalia didn't gravitate towards her tent. The twins looked to her expectantly but seeing her unmoving near the fire by Drogen they decided to forgo sleep as well standing guard by the tents entrance.

"I still have a lot of energy maybe we can do a little more training in the meantime," asked Natalia.

"As you wish, but it will not be the same training we did. Come sit in front of me and fold your legs upon each other as I do," said Drogen. "Good. Breathe in through your nose and out through your mouth letting your mind wander till you're empty of all thought and feeling besides the rhythm of the breath you take in and out. In and out," he finished in a whisper.

It was hard for Natalia to get into the rhythm and Drogen could tell from her breath that she didn't understand what the exercise was trying to do, but soon the tension left her body completely, as if the weight upon her shoulders had lessened and melted away.

These will be the first steps in dealing with what was done to you Natalia. None could go through so much and not feel the effects of it. There's only so much I can do to help you work through the trauma the rest will depend on you. If you deal with it and fight through you'll be much stronger. I hope you can fight against the darkness, before it builds to something you can no longer control, thought Drogen.

Drogen noticed immediately when she'd finally drifted off to sleep and knew her sleep would be more peaceful than it had been the night previous, having awoke from a cold sweat screaming at the top of her lungs reliving the trauma she'd undergone at the hands of her own people. With barely a whisper he picked up her lithe form whisking her into her tent followed closely by Rumble and Tumble. The twins grunted in thanks before they took up positions a few paces away their axes and swords ever within reach.

Drogen set himself up beside the campfire to catch its glow listening to the heartbeats of his companions and the wildlife that surrounded them listening intently for any sign of an emanate attack as the hours slipped away and the sun began its accent through the sky denoting the start of another day.

When everyone had awoke from their slumber they quickly broke camp looking forward to reaching their destination as quickly as possible. For the first morning since they'd left Zephyria Natalia looked well rested and joyfully helped her guard break down there tent, all the while looking upon their armor and its exploits.

As they worked through the forest traveling became easier for everyone as the number of bushes and brambles that dotted the forest floor lessened making cutting through the brush unnecessary. Much to everyone's relief a road became apparent as Seraphine said it would. Halfway through their early morning jaunt, a burnt out path had been cauterized into the trees scorching them too their roots on one side causing half to wither away from where the fires had ravaged.

"The poor trees they'll never grow as they once did. I hope the animals made it out before it was too late," said Seraphine sadly as she sidled up beside Drogen. "I might need your help to take care of this sadness a little later," she said with a mischievous wink.

"Are you sure you wouldn't want Alya to comfort you. She seems quite good at it," said Drogen.

"Well maybe I can ask her to help too," said Seraphine snaking her arms through Drogen's as they walked. "Oh... but what would Natalia think. I'll have to invite her too," she said breaking contact and walking off adding an extra sway to her hips.

Something tells me she's going to get me into a lot of trouble. Tis surprising however that more trouble has not already presented itself to us. Why would the orcs, with the furiosity they attacked Moongrove, abandon lands they've conquered? Furthermore, why have we seen no other goblinkin since leaving Moongrove, thought Drogen.

The forest around them began to thin out little by little allowing more of the mid-afternoon light to filter past the natural canopy that remained overhead. With still no sign of enemies and no heartbeats for Drogen to focus on they continued forward cautiously, watching and waiting for any signs of an ambush or impending attack, but none came. Clouds began forming in the sky overhead and a chill filled the air as the smell of ozone wafted to their nostrils foreshadowing rain.

The burnt-out path through the forest suddenly stopped overlooking a massive clearing housing what had once been a massive castle, though the burn marks still remained the tree line had receded away, not front burning or any other natural cause leaving them as grotesque malformed amalgamations of branches and trunks. *They look like the trees around Kethick's cave where he'd preformed his necromantic experiments. Tis as if there very lives have been stolen from them.* The taking of life extended into the forest all around them only stopping at what seemed to be the third tree in line in all directions forming a ring of death around the fallen castle.

Somberly they moved through the lifeless tree's weapons in hand, as they walked into the abandoned black lands of Grock. As they drew closer the sky opened letting out a downpour. "I've visited this part of the forest a couple of times. This is different than the last time I was here, and not in a good way. I don't remember the ground being black either it was, if I'm remembering correctly, made of stone," stated Seraphine. "Wh-what could have caused so much destruction to rain down upon this land? I doubt even Grock could have done something of this magnitude?"

As the rain pounded the ground with abandon, they happened upon the first of a sea of corpses the blood washing away to reveal the green skin beneath. "This land was not painted black in any natural way. Twas raining blood painted the ground such an ominous color," said Drogen.

"There has to be at least a thousand corpses here, and not all of them orcs and goblins. I see trolls, giants, hobgoblins, and many other races of goblinkin among the dead," said Natalia.

"I doubt Grock would have done such a thing to his own with the amount of time he's spent conquering lands," said Alya.

"Aye they life a good fight, as any good warrior do, an fightin themselves be no exception. But I be Agreeing with ye this be someone else. This not be their doin, but they could have left a few of um for me at least. Whoever they be they be inconsiderate."

"Well, that's a big word for a dwarf. Maybe there be a one to cut for ye around ear somewhere, said Seraphine mockingly."

"I be careful elf ye start talkin right an ye might be getting attracted to us dwarves yet," said Tumble with a laugh drawing a blush to Seraphine's cheeks and a scowl to her mouth.

"From what Ether and Uther said before their deaths Grock is just above them in terms of power, although he could be far more powerful than they let on... I don't believe this to be his doing either. Someone else did this. There's still much to see I suspe..." said Drogen stopping mid-sentence as he heard heartbeats heading directly for them. "We need to get over to the ruins and hide ourselves quickly. We have company."

"Bah that be leavin us open ta attack if we be spotted," roared Rumble.

"I didn't think a dwarf would be afraid of a few goblinkin," poked Seraphine.

"It not be goblinkin that gots me worryen," bit back Rumble.

"Well, I say we follow Drogen's lead. He wouldn't do anything to put us in harm's way without thinking through the situation first," said Natalia.

"And how would you know that Natalia, it's not like you've spent a lot of time with him," said Alya.

"Ye be right most ah it be in da bedroom," spoke Tumble with a stifled laugh.

"Really," smiled Alya. "I would have never guessed the Princess of Zephyria would allow a man to sleep in her bedchambers before marriage. Although Seraphine did do it first," she said sending an exaggerated wink Tumble's way.

Their conversations naturally died out as they ran through the corpses and rain in order to get to cover. Drawing closer to the epicenter of death and destruction, the scope of the slaughter became more evident, trees nearby had been cut clean through along the same line as the goblinkin had been, clearing more of the land. Trudging onward through the devastated landscape Drogen listened intently to the many enemies that converged upon them, hoping they could hide themselves well enough not to draw attention, until they could mount an attack.

From the looks of this once looming castle's bricks, it was done with a single weapon in a single strike. The enemy's this god faced outnumbered them, thousands to one still they reigned supreme. The power of a God is the only explanation. Which God could do something like this? Could this be the work of Lucian, no this is nothing like the power that destroyed Lundwurm Tul. Maybe this is my father's doing. Whomever it may be, the goblinkin fled this area for good reason.

Everyone scattered, hiding themselves in the castle's rubble, luckily the rain hid the sound of their heavy armor greatly masking their movements in the downpour from everyone but Drogen. As the troupe of goblinkin came through the trees an overwhelming sense of malice and bloodlust poured over the area stealing the breath from everyone and arresting the heartbeats of what little wildlife still remained in the area as they skittered away in absolute terror.

A half-orc and a white robed being, scarred beyond anything Drogen had ever seen, walked through the rubble of the collapsed castle, talking as though no one else was around to overhear them. The other goblinkin in his company had disassembled and moved to inspect the corpses of their fallen brethren, or so Drogen thought, but found them taking arms and armor instead of tending to the dead as the other races he'd fought beside had tried to do.

Drogen, knowing that the two were relaxed and unlikely to perceive a threat from amongst the debris, took a chance by moving in closer to the pair hoping to glean some information from their conversation. *I only hope they speak in the common tongue and not the guttural goblin tongue.*

As he drew in closer, Drogen was dismayed, for they spoke goblin tongue and nothing more, as they walked through the wreckage. Although Drogen couldn't understand the strange language, full of grunts and growls, he understood the anger prevalent upon the white robed figures scarred visage and the body language he displayed with his subordinate.

Godslayer; Envoy of Death came into his mind, but their voices were muted to the point of indistinguishable whispers in his mind. *From the robes that adorn his body, tis safe to assume this to be Grock; God of the goblinkin, who stands before me,* thought Drogen. Shrinking back into the rubble Drogen backed away slowly so as not to draw any unwanted attention.

Ether and Uther overestimated themselves with their self-comparison to Grock. Please everyone remain undiscovered. If battle ensues, we'll all meet our end at Grocks hands. It seems that threatening Grock with war was reckless of me having never met him or felt the weight of his presence. He far exceeds the power of both Ether and Uther combined. Still if he doesn't forgo this crusade of his then I will need to act, for a dragon never goes back on its word, thought Drogen.

As Grock and the half-orc walked along, another, small but familiar faced orc came racing up to the duo breaking free from the back of a riding Worg which scurried back into the woods fearfully away from Grock. The legs of the small orc pounded the stone as fast as they could carry him until he stood breathlessly before Grock. Its heartbeat was like a drum to Drogen's ears, and he knew then that his threat was moments away from delivery. *What terrible timing,* thought Drogen with a wince.

The little orc finished recounting the events that brought him taking small but noticeable steps back, as the creature frantically spoke. Grock didn't give the small orc a chance to run any further. Gripped its neck within his powerful hand, Grock suspended the orc off the ground. The orc struggling futilely to break Grock's grip around its throat. The wretch's struggle ended as Grock crushed its throat breaking its neck in one motion before tossing the broken orc over his shoulder. The lifeless creature landed in a heap its body breaking further as it struck against, what had once been, one of the castles desolated walls.

The heartbeats of his companions told Drogen that the display had been witnessed by them all as fear gripped each of them tightly. *If they give away their position, I'll have no choice but to fight Grock, until I can gather my companions and retreat. I only hope I can hold him off long enough to do so. No wonder Ether and Uther laughed when I told them of my threat,* thought Drogen. *No wonder Death was enthused by the prospect,* he scoffed under his breath.

Fortunately, Grock's rage filled voice covered up any other sound as he growled out orders in their guttural tongue. The orcs saluted Grock with a fist over their heart before running off at full speed to gather those still salvaging before retreating back into the forest. After they disappeared Grock pounded a pile of bricks into dust letting out a long sigh, before following his underling into the forest, an evil snarl contorting his scarred face.

Nobody dared to move or risk coming out from their hiding places until the sun had started to descend behind the trees until they knew, for sure, the danger had passed. Even Drogen, with his enhanced hearing, stayed still, making doubly sure they were all safe from the Gods menacing presence, before attempting to relax the white-knuckle grip he retained on Godslayer; Envoy of Death.

Rumble was the first to move and he did so tentatively. "I believe it be safe... for now," he said, his voice cracking though his bone-dry throat.

"Ay," Agreed Tumble as they walked out in the open.

With the declaration, the others slowly came out from hiding, meeting where Grock had just stood. Everyone was shaken to the core, unsure of what to do, or how to react having seen the imposing figure of Grock. Fear holding them all tightly, so much so that none dare speak.

Shaking where she stood Seraphine shuddered. "Grock said an enemy escaped from their hold, and that if left unchecked could jeopardize their campaign. Though he didn't show it, I could tell that he is fearful of whoever escaped."

"He said something about someone named Lucian being less than pleased with the news," said Alya.

"Wha happen with little snaggletooth," questioned Rumble.

"It seems that someone threatened to bring war down on the orcs if their warning went unheeded. Before he died, he told Grock about what happened in Moongrove," said Seraphine to the group in a hushed tone. Fear continuing to grip her tightly.

"Then my assumption would be accurate, that the one who received the news was none other than their God Grock, whom the goblinkin worship so fervently," stated Drogen. "Is there any chance that the threat will be taken seriously his crusade ended without more blood being spilled?"

"Do we know where they plan to attack next, or their numbers," questioned Natalia a feeling of dread sweeping over her.

"NO," exclaimed Seraphine. Leaving no room for doubt. They only discussed what happened to the underground prison and castle that is now nothing but rubble, fallen trees, and corpses. They didn't even mention who broke out of their hold and caused all of this devastation," finished Seraphine.

"For now, we have far more questions than answers and I see no clear path forward since we have no idea where the military force of goblinkin is congregating, nor where they plan to attack next. The factor this destructive force brings to the forefront cannot be disregarded either," said Drogen.

"We need more information, but how are we going to get it," questioned Alya.

"One solution is ta infiltrate the orcs, we be needen information, somthin we be severely lackin," said Rumble.

"That's tantamount to suicide," quipped Seraphine who quickly covered her mouth looking around to make sure her outburst hadn't alerted any nearby enemies.

"Seraphine's right, if anyone were to be caught and imprisoned by the orcs, tis likely you would die before enough information was gathered to point us in the right direction. Tis also probable that many unknowable tortures await those whom they've captured," said Drogen.

"What do you mean by any of us Drogen," questioned Seraphine drawing glances from everyone before they turned their gazes back to Drogen.

"Tis far too dangerous for any one of you to be captured by the orcs... but for me."

"NO," shouted Seraphine and Natalia in unison.

"If you have a better idea then I'm willing to hear it, but as of right now this is the only path forward that I can see. I'll also be able to leave their clutches whenever I've gathered the information that we need with a simple click of my fingers," said Drogen. "The truth is I'm the only viable candidate for this mission."

"Aye maybe ye be da best option but there be another problem with ye doin it. Ye don't understan orc," barked Rumble caring no longer to stifle his voice.

"There's no better method of learning then necessity," said Drogen.

"An what might we be doin while ye be playin house wit the smelly ones," said Tumble holding his nose to accentuate his point.

"Making sure nobody else gets caught and imprisoned by the orcs while keeping a close eye on their movements. We need to understand their movements, it might just give us an idea as to where they plan to advance. The more information we can ascertain the better off we'll be when the time comes to bring the fight to them," said Drogen.

"I don't care how strong you are, there's no way we're letting you go in there alone. You have to take someone with you, preferably someone who knows the orcs language," said Natalia.

"Ay I be agreein wit the princess on this," said Rumble stomping his foot.

"It'd be easier for me to get myself out then it will be with others. I don't know what possible tortures could await us, or what might happen should we become separated by the orcs and interred in different areas. I cannot guarantee the safety of anyone that comes with me, such is the dilemma we all face in this dilemma," said Drogen.

"Nothing is ever guaranteed Drogen. We all could die at any point going forward. We could be killed by the orcs on the spot instead of imprisoned by them. Either way it has to be done in order to gather the information we need, and although learning out of necessity is possible, you'll lose valuable time and information in the time it takes you to understand them. Time we could using to stratagize," said Seraphine.

"Shouldn't we go to Moonclave," questioned Alya. You know gathering the council is going to be a challenge to say the least. They don't do anything in a timely manner, and they'll need to hear any information that is brought to them. It may be too late to get them all together if we don't get there as soon as possible." said Alya.

"You do have a point," said Seraphine. "But it's an emergency surely they will convene quickly given the possibility of war."

"We don't know that they're planning for war," said Natalia. All we know is they're planning something; we don't know anything about what they're planning."

"Orc want war, all dem blasted snaggletooths ever want," barked Rumble.

"We should get back to Moongrove before we decide anything," said Drogen. "We can come up with a plan from there."

"Me brother an me prefer ya take the elf. We be likin fuzzy ears," said tumble with a wide smile as he looked toward Alya.

"Down boy, you're not my type," said Alya with a slight grin and chuckle.

"Give it some time, we be changin yur mind," rhymed Tumble with a small dance and massive grin.

"OK, OK can we get back to the problem at hand," said Natalia impatiently. "We still have a long journey back to Moongrove from here."

"You're right," said Seraphine with a sigh looking at Natalia. "I think we need to get you some different armor. What you have on is seriously going to your head," said Seraphine sticking her tongue out at Natalia. "But I suppose we all have to grow up sometime."

Chapter Five

Over the next three days their group ran across a few war-bands moving through the wood. Rumble and Tumble wished to attack and take out the war bands, but Drogen and the rest stopped them before they could go through with the action.

"We don't need to draw attention to ourselves we're alone out here and even though we have Drogen with us the chances of one of us getting seriously injured or killed are far too great to risk it. Even if we're not killed by them what are you going to do if they bring you in front of Grock. I don't know if any of us could hope to face him and survive," scolded Seraphine.

"It is for the best," said Natalia.

"Damned pigs need slaughtered. We could be thinin their ranks at least," said Rumble with an enthusiastic single nod of his helmed head.

"Where there's one there's ten," said Alya. "We all know how bad it gets when it comes to orc war bands. This place was under there rule before whatever came and went decimated them completely. It's a wonder we didn't run into one on our way out here."

"Yes, it is. I think these war bands came with Grock whoever turned that place to rubble didn't leave a single one alive to tell the tale. Grock must have been on his way there following the same release of power that woke me from my slumber," said Drogen.

"We need to keep a low profile, or we risk running into Grock himself," said Seraphine.

"Ye kill two of his kin and ya be fearin a one," grumbled Rumble.

"I feel the difference in the both of us, and I do not fear death, but I do fear a meaningless death. Facing him, as I am now, would prove to be my ultimate downfall. Ether and Uther had the power of the zephyrian people's worship. Grock hath the support of far more. And the power of the Gods is directly related to the number of their worshipers. Grock... he would be like facing six Ether and Uther's all rolled into one. I may be immortal, longevity wise, but I can still be killed through different means. Most of those means are harder to manage due to my scales. However, being crushed is still a possibility or the force of a significant blow, which he could more than manage. I have internal organs and they can be hurt or burst as anyone else's could," cautioned Drogen.

"Could you use the spell you used to bring us to Moongrove again," questioned Seraphine.

"I could, but there's only one more use that can be managed from the rune I placed both here and in Zephyria. Three uses are all I get," said Drogen with a frown. "I can make another, but it takes time to do so. Time we might not have, if we arrive surrounded by a warband. I would rather save its use for an emergency, or in the case of Zephyria, to send information that needs to be given. We don't know enough about what might be coming and Zephyria is not likely since they're protected atop the plateau."

"I didn't realize that there were limits." said Natalia.

"Everything and everyone have their limits. Magic is no different. The effectiveness also decreases with each use. The first use; I can take six and myself, The second use; four and myself, and the third use; two and myself. I remember my mother telling me that it wasn't always the case. I know not what could have happened to cause such a change," said Drogen.

"I heard something to the same effect from my own mother," said Seraphine. "That there was a time when many different creatures roamed Dranier, and magic was as easy and natural as breathing."

They moved through the overgrowth that surrounded them being warry of any open area's that might house orcs. They passed unseen by three different war bands the first day only stopping when Drogen told them it would be safe to bed down for the night. They didn't bother to set up camp in case they needed to get away quickly.

Drogen kept watch as his companions slept through the night trying many times in vain to hear the voices of his soul, but Godslayer; Envoy of Death remained silent as though their voices were never there to begin with. He tried many times to meditate but even that didn't alleviate his worry. *Does this have anything to do with my killing of Ether and Uther. They would talk to me just fine up until their demise. What could this mean, and why do I feel so alone within my own mind,"* thought Drogen.

The first night went by without any trouble but getting around the orc contingents the next day became a long arduous task. Each group they encountered was larger than the last and slow moving through the overgrowth. Although they wished to use the overgrowth to their advantage even Seraphine had a hard time navigating through the sheer amount without alerting a passing warband. Leading to them giving an even wider birth to any heartbeats Drogen could make out in the distance.

By the end of the second night everyone was exhausted from the constant stress of not getting caught and detained by the many warbands that always appeared to surround them on all sides, as though they were tightening a noose around their necks.

Rumble and Tumble were getting tired of dodging the many patrols and being quiet when they wanted nothing more than to jump out of the underbrush and get rid of the "mangy beasts," as they said any time, they came across yet another group in their travels.

As they bedded down for the night Natalia moved in close to Drogen. "I'm glad to see that you were able to sleep these past nights," said Drogen.

"Yes, thanks to you, and the meditation technique that you showed me. The nightmares seem to be at bay, at least for now," said Natalia with a shiver.

"We cannot avoid our trauma's forever Natalia. There are many ways of dealing with them, you must find the method that suits you. Often acknowledgment is the first step in dealing with such things, of course that could be different for you," said Drogen.

"I know that I am a victim of what they did to me," said Natalia.

"NO, Natalia. Not a victim. *Never a victim.* Be a survivor, an avenger. Or anything else but never a victim. The moment you choose to see yourself as a victim you surrender the control that you have over your trauma to those who inflicted the wounds upon you. The wounds that we receive in life leave us scared and bruised while others might go unseen except by those who've experienced similar events or simply seek to understand." Drogen told Natalia emphatically.

"How did you deal with it," questioned Natalia. "We've only mentioned it a couple of times, but I was connected to you when we were children, and I know from what you've said that the same goes for you. When you went before the people in robes."

"For which time are you referring. I stood before the elders many different times during my childhood," posited Drogen.

"The time they forced you to change. I remember feeling it through the connection it forced me to scream out. The pain was so very intense. That night was the precursor of many difficult events to follow. The start of Kethick's influence over me and Ether and Uther killing my own mother in front of my father and I," whispered Natalia as the visions of what she had witnessed came flooding through her mind once more. "I have relived those memories over and over again since that time. They have only been supplanted recently with what Nefar and Bernadine perpetrated against me."

"I take it that you never experienced that pain again through the connection," questioned Drogen.

"No after Kethick began giving me his medicine I no longer saw through your eyes, and even when I stopped the connection never returned," confirmed Natalia.

"I'm glad you didn't have to experience the pain that the change brings again, although the first time was the most painful for sure. I only wish you didn't have to experience that pain at all,"

Drogen thought for a minute trying to put into words how he was forced to get through the trauma of that time. Deciding quickly that he should tell her the whole story since it could help her conceive a method of overcoming her own trauma.

"For many years after that I refused to change at all. Which proved to be my own detriment. I was so afraid of the pain that I didn't realize that fighting through the pain was my best course of action. My failing as a young hatchling was not embracing my true self. Of course, being young and naive, I thought to short term. I didn't look to the future more than a couple of days at a time. I got through my trauma by being forced to relive it repeatedly. Till I could not think or speak and was exhausted. I got through it by exposing myself to it until I could no longer feel the pain. Each time the transformation became less and less painful and became nothing short of natural for me. I would call this method acceptance through exposure. I only hope that the method you use is not so painful as my own had to be," said Drogen.

Natalia had visible tears in her eyes at the end of Drogen's story. Having felt the transformation through there connection the first time she knew how hard it had to have been for him to go through so many transformations, but she knew that the transformation no longer pained him, in fact he transformed as though the pain was no longer there, whenever she had the pleasure of experiencing the beauty of his transformation firsthand.

"Until you're able to deal with the conflict within yourself you may lean upon me, and I will help as much as I can to take the weight off your shoulders, but ultimately it is within you to deal and get past the trauma of past events. Even if at times It feels as though the pain will never fade or dissipate. So come Natalia, lay down beside me and rest your body knowing that I will be watching over you till you awake."

With the sound of the dwarven brothers snoring into the night sky Natalia moved in close to Drogen laying her head down on one of the pillows that Drogen had made for them to improve their rest on their journey through the woods. It didn't take long for Natalia to fall into a deep slumber beside him adding her own small breaths to the symphony of sleeping sounds that surrounded him.

I know that even if what they did to you has broken something deep within yourself that you will be able to bear it. You're stronger than you know Natalia, I hope that you come to see it yourself. You are already trying to fix yourself, tis an admirable quality. One that I wish I had developed myself long ago.

Drogen surveyed his friends looking for any disturbance to their slumber. Alya, lay in her feline form curled up next to Seraphine who was cuddling her as though she were much smaller than her form would suggest. Rumble and Tumble, the loudest sleepers of them all, had dug small ruts into the earth for themselves to sleep in. A ritual which they performed each night without fail, since leaving Zephyria.

Noticing nothing out of the ordinary and tuning out the sounds of his companions Drogen listened to the wood around him blocking out the natural sounds of the forest as he came by them to focus on what would be unnatural and disruptive. With his ears attuned to the area, he looked around once more before falling into himself.

There in his meditative state Drogen thought himself into his soul chamber to look upon the blades locked in their respective pedestals speaking to them but receiving no reply at all from those pieces of his soul. He looked for any reason at all for their silence but the more he looked the further he felt from the answer.

He walked out of his soul chamber from between the two doors that housed the twin sides of his soul. The left side housed the Dragon's soul, but to the right was the door that he chose to look upon. The white chains that blocked the door had diminished for reasons unknown to himself. After Ether and Uther's deaths only one lock remained for him to remove but nothing seemed to budge the lock from its eternally closed state.

"Does the fall of the other locks have an unknown effect on my soul. I suppose that I may just need to look for the answer in my bowl, if only I had brought it with me instead of leaving it with Fread. Not that I could decipher the language of the Gods myself," thought Drogen. *"I can only hope the lack of communication will not hinder my ability to protect my friends."*

With a last pull on the remaining chain Drogen pulled himself from his mind meditating the rest of the night.

Each of them awoke from there slumber fully rested having slept peacefully through the night. Drogen cooked up some pork that had been preserved in his extradimensional bag for them to eat before they broke camp.

"Do you think we can make it back to Moongrove by tonight," questioned Alya.

"It all depends on the number of orc warbands we come across on our way," said Seraphine drawing a disapproving grunt from Rumble and Tumble.

"I know you don't like doing nothing with so many enemies around us, but we still need to be careful," admonished Natalia.

"Jus need a few leg seperatins from torsos, they not be needin all their legs," said Rumble.

"Yeah, seem kinda greedy keepin all them legs attached," chimed in Tumble.

The absurdity of Tumble's statement drew a hearty deep guttural laugh from Drogen as he pictured a group of orcs hopping on one leg because of the brother dwarves. "If something happens that we need some orc legs you'll be the first I call upon to harvest," laughed Drogen.

The levity of Drogen's laugh brought a smile to each of their faces as they moved to continue their journey deeper into the woods. "It seems that the warbands are getting fewer the closer we get to Moongrove. It seems that we can move forward at a greater pace from here," said Drogen.

"Good we be growin tired of this dodging and runnin from them stinkin pigs," grumbled Rumble.

"Well then let's get going I hope we can finish this jaunt off and make a plan as to how we can get you two in with the orcs without dying."

"Natalia and I will figure that part out, you four need to begin your journey to Moonclave said Drogen. I will be able to find my way there once we get all the information that we need.

Grock is moving a massive army. We need to figure out where they plan on attacking and warn them so that everyone is fully prepared for what is coming their way. It would probably do to have them expect my arrival as well. I know the elves don't care for outsiders within their home. I just hope that your word will allow me passage without undue hostility," said Drogen.

"Ya dem tree folk not be likin any but themselves. Right pain in the ass ye ask me," said Rumble. "Be needin a huimblin dem ones."

"Well then it's a good thing nobody asked your opinion then isn't it," chided Seraphine as she stuck her tongue out at him.

"Enough you two we still have a long way to go and the both of you being at each other's throats isn't going to make our journey any faster you know," said Alya with a sigh of consternation at the all too likely prospect. "Is this how it's going to be the whole way to Moonclave," she questioned.

"Nah they be cuddlin afor long," chimed Tumble drawing a look of anger and disbelief from Rumble and Seraphine respectively. Natalia tried furtively to suppress her giggle, but it didn't escape Drogen's notice, drawing a genuine smile to his own visage.

With fewer orc patrols they made good time but could not go any further as the rays of the sun were hardly able to penetrate the canopy above them. It was a good sign that they were getting closer to their destination, but it also meant that visibility for Natalia was close to non-existent once the sun receded to a certain degree. Rumble and Tumble offered for her to ride upon their backs but she refused saying that resting for one more night couldn't possibly hurt.

"Relenting, everyone went about making camp for the night the canopy of the trees making perfect cover for the night."

"When is the last time you rested Drogen," questioned Natalia. It has to have been nearly a week that you have went without sleep are you sure you are, okay?"

"Tis only one more night Natalia. I will rest when we get back to Moongrove where we might be able to relax before starting the next part of our journey. We still need to figure out how to gather information," said Drogen.

"Yes, getting rest in a safe place and having a clear rested head will allow us to better strategize," said Natalia.

"We will reach our destination tomorrow. We're not that far away I can feel the pulse of my rune the closer we get," said Drogen *I only wish the same could be said of Godslayer; Envoy of Death,* he thought.

"May I lay next to you again tonight. Your presence seems to make the nightmares a little more bearable."

"Tis fine with me," said Drogen beckoning her over to his side.

"I do not know what I will do to get over what has happened to me but knowing you believe it possible for me to do so I too think it possible. Thank you for believing in me," yawned Natalia as she fell asleep.

I wish it was that easy princess. Yes, my belief may help but your belief in yourself is what truly matters, but you will come to find out the truth of your strength in due time.

Drogen thought back to the conversation that Natalia had brought up referencing his trauma of transformation. *There were many people within my dreams that had made me wish to go out into the world beyond Lundwurm Tul. So far, I've met two of them, Natalia and Seraphine But, there were others as well.*

Thinking back to those long ago dreams he remembered peering through the eyes of no less than five others. Thinking back upon them the memories were hazy at best. *I hope that I will meet them and know that they're the ones from long ago memories. Oh, what fun it was to experience things outside of Lundwurm Tul. Even if I couldn't interact with them in any way back then it was so wonderful... most of the time,* thought Drogen, as the distinct memory of many tragedies born across many people propelled themselves through his mind.

"It seems there are still trauma's that I need to work through myself," confessed Drogen in a whisper.

Instead of going within himself once again Drogen spent his time outside himself waiting for the sun to rise. Scanning the area through the trees and making sure their route forward would be clear of any obstacles.

As the sun started its rise into the morning sky Drogen returned to his body to check on his companions before they awoke. Like they'd thought the night previous it would only take them half a day to reach Moongrove even if they slowed their pace down to what it had been at the start of there journey back.

They broke camp quickly taking some preserved meat from Drogen before they began moving with renewed vigor. They made the Moongrove long before mid-day drawing a sigh of relief from each of them that they had finally made it back in one piece. Drogen listened intently to the sounds coming from inside the forest manor that had once been Seraphine's residence for any indication that there was anyone or anything inside. Hearing nothing, he opened the door wide ushering them in.

Moved into the house cautiously, the dwarves secretly admired the wonderment of elven architecture. And how they could achieve such complexity within living trees, though neither brother cared to admit so.

"You need to get some rest Drogen. We can take care of the preparations. You protected us without sleep for an entire week. I know dragons differ in many ways, but I know lack of sleep is bad for anyone. We can all see you're tired. Why don't you go into your room and get some sleep for a while?"

Drogen made to argue that he was fine, but they all looked at him and pointed. Getting the hint and knowing that it would be useless to argue any further he went to the room that he'd previously stayed in lay upon the bed and passed out the exhaustion he refused to acknowledge overtaking him completely.

With Drogen securely in his room and asleep for the first time in over a week they decided as a group to allow him to sleep as long as possible while they gathered everything they could.

"When we got here, we went through many of the shops to find things that we needed and a couple of the houses to get supplies, but we didn't go through all of the houses in Moongrove it would have taken too long," stated Seraphine.

"I say we go through the houses this time," said Alya. "We have plenty of time to gather supplies now. We will need as much as we can get with the four of us going to Moonclave."

"Me brother an me not be liking leaving the Dragon as only one goin wit de princess," said Rumble.

"I understand your feeling Rumble and Tumble, but that doesn't change the fact that it will be better for you to go with Seraphine and Alya instead of with Drogen, and I," stated Natalia.

"We all have a long journey ahead of us, and getting out of hard situations such as an army of goblinkin should be left to one who can deal with it, but the more people that go with them could lead to many more casualties on our side," said Alya.

"It's better to divide ourselves into groups in order to be the most effective at what has to be done," said Seraphine although the look on her face showed in no uncertain terms that she was not looking forward to the trip.

"It could be worse, we could be traveling with orcs," said Alya. "And at least he's funny," she said pointing to Tumble who gave a deep bow which dropped his helmet into his outstretched hand and his lengthy beard to scrape the floor. "See funny."

"How long will it take for the four of you to get to Moonclave," questioned Natalia.

"That will depend on two factors, resistance and overgrowth along the route," said Alya.

"We don't know if the orcs who attacked here followed after their retreat back to Moonclave," said Alya.

"It has only been a week since the attack," said Seraphine.

"I be more surprised tha there be so little resistance," said Rumble.

"I suspect that Grock had something to do with that," said Natalia. "Whosever decimated that place must have been important for Grock to go himself. Ether and Uther didn't do anything unless it was important in some way, or for their own sick enjoyment."

"To answer your question Natalia, all things go smoothly, and we encounter little to no resistance, we can be there in a little over a month," said Alya.

"How will we find you, when we're done with our part," questioned Natalia.

"Drogen said he'll be able to find us. I don't know what method he'll use but I suspect we'll know when the time comes," said Seraphine with a confident smile.

"This be enough talkin we be needin supplies an standin round ain't gatherin um up," Rumble grumbled angrily.

"Fine. Fine. Let's get this done quickly so that we can get this journey done and over with already," snapped Seraphine.

Tumble ran over to the door and ushered everyone outside hearing Alya whisper, "This is going to be a long journey," under her breath as she walked past. With everyone out Tumble closed the door.

"We will go to the south and gather supplies from the residences outside of the city center," said Seraphine as she motioned for Natalia to join her. "Once we get everything useful, we'll bring it back here. The rest of you should take the residences just north of the training grounds," said Seraphine.

"There are more places up where we're heading, so once you're done, you'll come help with the remaining residences right," questioned Alya.

"Ah come-on you didn't have to tell them that," chided Seraphine playfully.

"Done you be worryn about us. We be back wit all the supplies afore you even get bak ear," said Rumble.

"Does everything have to turn into a competition or argument with you two," said Alya with an eyeroll and a sigh of exasperation.

Natalia and Seraphine worked their way through many residences but found getting into many of them to be less than ideal. Each house had been ransacked and burned on their path leaving nothing but ash or fallen trees that would never grow again.

"Destroyed all destroyed," said Seraphine.

"This is simply heartbreaking. I only hope the others are having more luck than we are, said Natalia."

"At least we found a machete," said Seraphine. "This will at least save our blades from unnecessary wear. I only wish we could have found food or water to take with us. I kind of hate leaving it up to those ground hogs but maybe just maybe they are having better luck than we are," she said shaking her head in disgust. Natalia knew that the disgust wasn't for her dwarven guard but for the scene of her destroyed home. "Your people can and will rebuild Seraphine. It's the people that are important."

"I know they can and will, but it doesn't make it any easier seeing the devastation," said Seraphine. "There are only a couple more houses, then we can go and help the others."

They walked forlornly down the road that connected all the residences together and to what had been the market of Moongrove. Seraphine's sadness growing with each passing footstep.

They were heading through the last copes of trees that would bring them to the final residences along the path when Natalia suddenly put out her hand stopping her dead in her tracks.

It was only then that Seraphine heard them the distinctive grunts and guttural language of the orc's the same creatures that had destroyed her home and the peace that had once been present within it.

"I know that you want to kill them, and you would be justified in doing so for what they've done to this place, but sometimes we have to temper our anger in order to gather information," said Natalia.

"Oh, how would you know," raged Seraphine as she stepped forward. Starting to draw Truth from its sheath at her hip.

Natalia held her hand in place upon the hilt of her sword not allowing her to draw it from its scabbard. "You think I don't understand, when my mother was killed Nefar and Bernadine came into the castle. Nefar married my father after Ether and Uther killed my mother in front of me. You think I didn't plan ways in which to get my revenge on them, for taking the place of my mother. If you think that then you are sorely mistaken and think far too highly of me. I'm not above plotting the end of those who've wronged me, but we must be smart about how we do things."

Seraphine looked hard at Natalia gazing into her eyes with a sorrowful look. "I... I didn't know that's what happened to your mother. I'm sorry Natalia. I'll try to control my rage, but I cannot promise that I won't snap."

"I understand Seraphine. Let me at least see if I can understand what they're saying maybe we will at least make this trip through this area worth it by garnering much needed information."

Natalia listened carefully to the back and forth of the orcs for a while before speaking. "Most of what they're speaking is nothing but shameless boasts. I don't know if maybe these two were simply left behind by all the others when Grock came through."

"Does that mean I can kill them and not worry about it," said Seraphine.

"Wait. This might be something," said Natalia. "We need one more for the quota. Where are we supposed to find someone when this place has been completely abandoned."

"How should I know. If we don't find someone then it will be one of us added into the cages when we get back to... Grammora," Translated Natalia. Is Grammora a place that you've been told about," she questioned.

"No, I can't say I've ever heard the name of any goblinkin settlement spoken aloud. That I'm aware of at least. What do you think they mean by a quota, were they tasked with capturing people," questioned Seraphine angrily?

"Yes. That's what it seems to be. Wait... this could be the perfect opportunity," said Natalia clearly formulating a plan in her head.

Seraphine looked through the trees at the orcs in the distance talking in front of a cage that had been filled with some of the local wildlife. "Wait, you cannot be thinking what I think you are. You cannot be seriously thinking about becoming their prisoner."

"They're fearful that they haven't found anything worth bringing back, which means that they'll have to treat me well or risk getting taken for whatever purpose they're afraid of being taken for," said Natalia clearly deciding it to be the best course of action.

"And what do you expect me to tell everyone else when they ask where you are. We're supposed to meet up with the others and there's no way that they're going to allow you to do something so foolish, and neither will I. We're leaving there's clearly something not right with your line of thinking," said Seraphine clearly concerned for the wellbeing of her friend. "You were a prisoner in your own kingdom just a few days ago Natalia I'm not going to allow my friend to go through that again if I can do something to prevent it."

"Yeah... you're right I'm thinking carelessly I promise I won't do anything that puts me in unnecessary danger," said Natalia.

"I think we should leave these last couple of houses and go find the others. At least we now know the name of one of their encampments, or cities, or whatever it might be. My mother might recognize the name... Look I know that the plan is for you and Drogen to find a way to get information from the orcs, but there must be a better way than sacrificing yourself to them as a prisoner," said Seraphine trying to comfort her friend and help her to see that there are other options.

"Alright I get it I'll try and think of some other way of getting information. Let's get back to the others. There may be other goblinkin around so we should at least warn them of that possibility," said Natalia. "It would probably be best to do so before Rumble and Tumble start taking legs off," she joked.

"Quite right, we don't need any unnecessary attention we don't know if Grock might be coming back through here on his way to... Grammora," said Seraphine.

They backed away from the tree they were spying from slowly careful not to disrupt any of the foliage that might alert the orcs to their presence. They both breathed easier the further they moved away from the orcs and their prisoner cages. Working their way quickly back to Seraphine's former home.

They reached the house without incident and waited a couple of minutes to make sure that the orcs had not picked up their trail following them back to the house. Seeing no sign, they each let out a breath they were unknowingly holding in.

"What should we do now," questioned Natalia.

"Well, I think we should go and find the others. They may be on their way back here with whatever they were able to find, and they may need some help depending on if they encountered any orcs themselves," said Seraphine.

"I agree," said Natalia. "However, I think it will be better if you get to them as fast as possible. I don't know my way through the forest so I will only hinder you, whereas you grew up here and probably know a more direct and faster route to get to wherever they might be," reasoned Natalia.

"You're planning on going in and laying down next to him aren't you," said Seraphine with a raised eyebrow. "Well, I can't say I blame you. I did the same thing the first night he was here, only I was naked laying beside him," she teased.

"Well, I cannot have you getting ahead of me now can I," said Natalia with a mischievous grin.

"I swear that new outfit of yours has got you acting all sorts of non-princess like," said Seraphine. "I like it."

"Go, they may be in danger, I'll hold things down here with Drogen," said Natalia.

"Oh, I'm sure you will," said Seraphine with a suggestive gesture.

"Will you just go already," said Natalia with a wide yet bashful smile.

"Fine. Fine. I'll be right back with the others, so let him rest at least a little while longer he's guarded us all for a week, and you'll be monopolizing his time in the future without me as it is," said Seraphine as she walked through the door, closing it behind her.

Seraphine found the others as they were clearing the last house. The dwarves had their hands full with many preserved foods they found while Alya seemed to be holding a number of water skins.

"Before you ask, Natalia is safe and sound with Drogen at the house. Drogen will protect her if anything happens. She need only call to wake him from his sleep. Now hand me some of what you've found so we can get out of here. Natalia and I found a couple of orcs on the outskirts of Moongrove. We don't need to bring any unwanted attention to ourselves. We don't know if Grock will be coming back through here."

"What were you able to find on your end," questioned Alya.

"There wasn't much left down there being that its where the orcs attacked from. Most of the houses had been burned or felled in some way that made them inaccessible to anyone. The only thing we were able to find that was of any use was a machete which will be helpful for cutting through the underbrush and foliage on our way to Moonclave," said Seraphine with a frowning shrug.

"Wha bout dem orc's ya get nothin from dem," questioned Rumble.

"No we didn't interact with them at all. Natalia translated some of the things they were saying for me but most of it will prove to be less than useful, I fear. It seems the orcs are looking for things to take prisoner for some place called Grommora. They seemed quite concerned about reaching a certain quota, from what Natalia said. But that had nothing to do with us, so we left them and returned to the house."

"An whose idea would it be to leave Natalia with Drogen," questioned Rumble the sound of fear rising in his voice.

"Well, it was Natalia's sug...," started Seraphine.

"Bah, Ye stupid elf. And it not seem be da slightest bit suspicious to ye that she wished to be left," yelled Rumble.

"Oh no," said Seraphine. "She said it was a way in for them. I didn't think. I thought I dissuaded her from being rash. No. No. No. Noooo. We need to hurry before it's too late. It took me some time to find you we should go directly to where I saw the orcs," said Seraphine in a panic.

"Lead the way," said Tumble who had lost his usually joking demeanor for one of fierce determination.

They ran through the forest not caring if anything or anyone were to hear them thundering through, they were up against a clock and Natalia already had a head start on them. There breakneck pace brought them through the market in a flash and past into where the tree homes had once stood as part of the charming landscape of Moongrove.

Seraphine led them around the final outcropping of tree's just before where the two orcs had stood but when they came through there was not a single soul in sight. The two orcs the cages that they had filled with wildlife nothing. It was all gone, and Seraphine's stomach sank further still as she realized that, if they were gone, then so too was Natalia she did exactly what Seraphine feared her friend had done. "Why. Why, would she do something so dangerous?"

"Stupid, stupid, stupid pigeon headed girl. Why she gotta be doin somethin so stupid," raged Rumble.

"There's nothing we can do about it ourselves," said Alya. "She made her choice, of course it was a stupid and irresponsible choice, but it was hers to make all the same. We need to get back to Drogen and tell him what's happened. He'll be able to come up with a plan to get her back from wherever they're taking prisoners."

"An what bout her life. She be dying afor long," cried out Rumble.

"Me brudder an me charged wit her care. We be goin after er," spoke Tumble.

"No. We have no clue where they're going. We need to think about this logically."

"We done be needin logic we be needin action," cursed Rumble.

"How do you expect to find and rescue her. If you can't find her in time, and she's taken into their prisoner hold, what then Rumble. How're you going to retrieve her surrounded on all sides by goblinkin? Without getting yourself and her killed," raged Seraphine. "I don't like this any more than you do. You're her guards and I'm her friend. I should never have left her alone after she talked about being captured by the orcs to get information."

"Why wasn't Drogen able to stop her," questioned Alya.

"He be sleepin. He protect us fur a week. There be no doubt he not be knowin, or he be ear," said Rumble.

"I be thinkin it bad wakin a sleepin dragon," said Tumble going pale.

"You might be right, especially with the news we have to deliver, but Drogen is our best bet for a conclusion that will bring both Natalia, and him back alive," said Seraphine.

They ran full speed back to the forest manor hoping, against hope, that they'd simply overthought the absence of the orcs. *Maybe they simply left with what they had, and she didn't go with them. She's just going to be in bed laying with Drogen asleep and safe,* thought them all, but each in their own way knew that their hope was moot. Natalia would not be there to greet them. Still, they could hope.

Rumble was the first to reach the door throwing it wide with enough force to have its force reverberate through the entire house.

"Well, if he wasn't awake yet, he will be now," sighed Alya. "I suppose it does get across the desperation that we're feeling thought."

"Drogen, we have trouble," exclaimed Seraphine desperation and worry afflicting her voice.

Drogen heard the slam of the door feeling it reverberate through the bed and he jumped up out of bed as though stabbed with a sharp blade. By the time he heard Seraphine's voice through the closed door he had summoned his blade cut the door and kicked it down within a second's time.

Seeing the display of power, the rest of them were left speechless.

"Where's Natalia. I don't hear her heartbeat and each of yours are racing far faster than if you had only just run here. Your hearts beat with worry. What has happened to her," questioned Drogen.

"That pigeon head dolt went an god herself taken on purpose," roared Rumble.

"Why would she do something so reckless," posited Alya.

"Tell me what happened," said Drogen. "All of what happened."

Seraphine recounted their walking up on the orcs, and what Natalia had said about the orcs looking for a prisoner, so that neither of them became imprisoned themselves.

"Good that means that the ones who captured her are going to do everything they can to get her to where they're going in one piece. There is nothing like fear as a motivating factor to ensure the safety of another."

"You be sayin she safe in the hand ah them pigs," raged Rumble. His voice raising louder with each syllable.

"No, I don't think anyone is safe in their hands, but they are going to get her there alive. If they don't, they're the ones who will be imprisoned. Did she know where she was being taken," questioned Drogen as he stared into Seraphine's eyes.

"Some place named Grammora is all I know," said Seraphine. "I've never known the name of any orc encampments, and if Natalia hadn't been translating, I wouldn't know even that much."

"Grammora well a name is better than nothing at least," said Drogen. "Here take this with you, you'll have far more use for its contents than I will in the coming days." Drogen threw Seraphine his extra-dimensional bag as he made for the door.

"Wait, how will you find us in Moonclave... How will we know that you're coming," questioned Alya.

"You'll understand both at once," said Drogen touching his shoulder blade as he fled the forest manor. Running into the woods beyond with abandon.

"Well, what we be doin now," questioned Rumble as he watched Drogen disappear into the woods.

"We should head to Moonclave. There we can come up with a strategy, and it will take some time to get the council together to tell them about Drogen's emanate arrival. especially since we don't know when they might be back from this Grommora place," said Seraphine.

"It would be a good idea to send word to Fread in Zephyria as well, to tell him what we've found out, as well as what has happened since we left," said Alya. "Maybe your mother will have heard something about Grocks plans, or what broke out of that prison."

"Yes. She may have some information that will be good to give to Fread in correspondence. We can send a hawk from Moonclave and it will fly directly to Fread. A letter will take at least a fortnight round trip."

"Thar be another thin we be needin to discuss, what bout me brudder an me. We be less than welcome in the land of tree fairies. We probly be killed on the spot bein that Moonclave a secret location," said Rumble.

"We could play two dwarves in an overcoat," posited Tumble.

"You'd still be too short and far too round to pass as anything close to an elf," said Seraphine shaking her head at the ludicrous notion.

"It's a funny thing to imagine though. Thank you Tumble. At least we have someone who can make us laugh during the journey," smiled Alya.

"To answer your question Rumble... I don't know. I'm an elven princess so I'll just have to use my authority to get you in. It might take me a while to get approval though. So, I think it's best if you two camp out near Moonclave. Until I can get you into the city proper."

"Me brudder an me herd much the same a time afore," said Rumble biting back bitterly on his words. Before replacing them with a wide smile.

They began putting everything they'd found in their search into Drogen's extra-dimensional bag which would allow them to continue traveling quickly. Unencumbered by unnecessary burdens.

"Will the two of them be alright," inquired Alya looking back to where Drogen had disappeared.

"They be more-en alright when the sky lizard get to ur, by me accountin," said Tumble with an exaggerated wink directed specifically at Seraphine. Inciting a glare, which made Tumble chuckle gleefully.

"I wone be relaxin bout er till I be known she safe, but how ye suspect they be findin us when Moonclave be secret an all," Rumble questioned.

"We'll know when we know," said Seraphine.

"I hope you're right about that," stated Alya somberly.

"I'm more concerned about how I'm going to explain Drogen to the council," said Seraphine with a sigh.

"What ye fairies be scared of ah little lizard," asked Tumble with a chuckle.

"No, they keep little lizards as pets and ride them through the woods on patrols," said Alya, not catching onto the joke.

"Ye migh wanna keep the breathen fire part to yeself to start. Migh turnum against us afore we begin," said Rumble.

"You don't have to tell me what I already know but it's not like I can lie about him if they ask specific questions. Lies are not permitted within Moonclave. There's a barrier around its entirety that works much the same as my sword Truths magics. However, it's far more powerful and can, if a big enough lie is spun, be fatal to those who initiated the deceit without correcting their mistakes. From what I've heard. It's one of the many reasons smaller prefectures and places in the woods are settled by my race. We all grow weary of the burden, for it is a harsh reality to live with, even amongst my kin."

"Can truth not counter the effect the barrier has and fend it off to some degree," asked Alya who was growing ever more concerned. For their mission and the probability of its success.

"If I be guessin right ye sword be made from the barrier," said Rumble. "Do ye know who formed the magic barrier?"

"No. Truth goes dormant whenever I cross the barrier. I don't know who made the barrier it, was in place before we ever called the Moonclave our home. My ancestors thought the Gods built it as a place of knowledge and understanding. It's where we learned much of what we know about the world, but even the Eldest of my race has no idea who made the barrier, or the purpose for which it was erected. This sword "Truth" is our refinement of the powerful magic garnered through our study of the ancient barrier."

"Doesn't Gaia understand it," questioned Alya.

"She plays ignorant of the barrier's origin. Many of my kin have asked but she speaks around the information always hiding it from us. It seems that only she is immune to the barrier's effects."

"Me only hope be they listen ta reason, whether it come from tree, cat, or stone," said Rumble.

"Not cat warren... war-ren that's my kins name *not cat*," said Alya wagging her finger before turning her attention back to Seraphine. "Maybe Gaia can help us convince them."

"Maybe, but we won't know anything until we get there. With any luck they'll see reason enough to offer aid to Drogen against the goblinkin and the threat they pose to the rest of Dranier. Our ties with the Warren, and the word of two dwarves and myself I hope will be enough to convince them that there is a legitimate threat and to take what information Drogen brings with him as actionable," said Seraphine.

"I know Drogen will be able to find Natalia and bring her alongside himself to Moonclave," said Seraphine.

"Alongside or in is arms," said Tumble with a wide toothy grin.

"Okay that's enough of that its time that we get moving we have a long journey ahead of us," said Seraphine.

"Well, this trip should be more than a little interesting," said Alya. "Especially with two dwarves in tow."

"That's exactly what I'm afraid of," said Seraphine wish a shake of her head and an exaggerated exhale.

Chapter Six

Drogen inhaled the air brought to him upon the wind for any sign of goblinkin. *Did she take this action because of me? This is not the method I would have chosen for her to deal with the trauma that she's been through. But it wasn't my decision to make for her. Was this simply the opportunity that she thought we needed to get information? Still, why, why didn't she wake me from my slumber. We could have tried to infiltrate together. Or did she fear that I would say no to such a request,* contemplated Drogen with a heavy sigh. *Either way I suppose it was not my decision to make.*

Moving swiftly to the last place Natalia had been seen, Drogen found the footprints of the orcs leading off into the woods excrement from the many animals that had been caged by their hands leaving another form of trail for him to follow.

The cart that the orcs transported their prisoners on had two large wheels which helped them pull the cart swiftly even through the heavy and plentiful underbrush that plaguing the forest floor. It also made their trail through the woods that much easier to traverse and track.

A few miles into the woods following there laden wagon's trail brought Drogen to an outcropping that had hosted an orc warband their heavy footfalls and multiple carts moving away from most of which circumvented Moongrove all together.

The tracks of the large warband seem to be going to meet up with there God for unknown reason. If they stayed on the track they cut through the woods it seems as though the ones who took Natalia are heading in the opposite direction to the warband, contemplated Drogen.

It took till the sun was about to set in the sky casting darkness through the forest but Drogen was rewarded for his efforts as he spotted there wagon track once more. There wagon having pushed down the underbrush between two trees in order to form a path for themselves through the forest.

As I suspected. Now we can get moving, Thought Drogen hoping for a word a feeling anything from his swords, but nothing came locking his face in a forlorn frown. *I don't know how far ahead they are now. My only hope is to catch up with them as quickly as possible. "Please be safe Natalia."* thought Drogen aloud.

Drogen moved through the woods as quickly as possible, however the closeness of the trees and the overgrowth present throughout made the use of his wings, and there speed impossible. Leaving him with one option, to run.

Without want of sleep he traveled through the night an into the light of the next day. *How can they be so far ahead of me still. They couldn't have gotten that far ahead. Unless I followed the wrong trail. Maybe they did turn and follow the warband,* thought Drogen, doubt and anxiety of neither seeing, hearing, or smelling Natalia within the eerily quiet forest causing his heart to race.

As the anxiety of not knowing was about to overtake his usually calm heart a gust of wind came hurtling through the trees around him bringing with it the smell of rancid fat, iron, and feces.

Found you, thought Drogen with a grin. *I still have a long way to go but at least now I know I'm heading in the right direction. But how could they have traveled so much faster than I did.*

With renewed purpose Drogen bounded through the woods the stench of the orcs upon the wind egging him on into a fervor to reach his destination. As he drew closer the sound of thunderous footsteps gave pause to his forward momentum. The footfalls were still some distance off. However, with each step taken reverberations cascaded through the forest floor and into the soles of his feet.

The footfalls were accompanied by the crashing of trees falling to the ground the limbs cracking and breaking as they collided with the earth.

With the sound as a non so subtle guide for his pursuit, Drogen moved with purpose to cross the distance hoping that he would be able to pick out Natalia's heartbeat through what was sure to be a chaotic environment.

With each step he took forward the sound of thunderous footsteps got closer coming across a massive clearing in the trees. The massive trunks of uprooted trees littering the ground all around. Small fire pits had been snuffed out just before dawn. Drogen could tell from the heat which continued to radiate from the coals that he was not far behind those he pursued. Though there numbers had grown significantly from when he started.

Hearing no heartbeats around him he broke straight through the clearing deciding it best to use the trees for cover as he drew closer so as not to alert those he pursued. Although, he doubted that anything could be heard over the racket he followed.

The sound of massive footsteps soon became near deafening as the shock wave of each footfall became much more emphatic. As he came through yet another cleared area he finally caught a glimpse of the ones he pursued.

The heads of giants loomed over the tops of the massive trees. Three giants in total moved forward grabbing any tree that blocked there way forward and chucking them aside. They shared a singular focus pulling each up roots and all before discarding it like a piece of scrap and moving on to the next making a wide path through the woods.

Drogen moved away from the giants making a new path through the woods instead turning to the path they'd already created. Hearing heartbeats from behind the Giants his heart sank. For behind the giants came the heartbeats of not only one warband, which the camp he'd gone through had suggested, but far more than he could reasonably count.

Taking to the tree tops Drogen brought himself alongside the army of goblinkin. An army that stretched from the backs of the giants they followed all the way to the horizon line. Among them were species that Drogen had heard tale of before from his time in Lundwurm Tul and the stories his kin had shared.

Ogres, trolls, orcs, goblins, and giants, So many of them together. Grock has been rather busy bringing so many together under his banner, thought Drogen.

Within the thousands of goblinkin gathered were many cages filled to what some might consider there breaking point with prisoners. Within there confines were zephyrian's, elves, and gnomes, yet another race he'd as of yet come in contact with. Hundreds were imprisoned within the cages no rhyme or reason prevalent in there captivity aside from taking up the space within there prison.

Just within earshot between the footsteps of the giants Drogen heard the voices and heartbeats of still more coming up behind him. His heart fluttered in hope, that was quickly dashed as Natalia's heartbeat was not among those that he could hear within the coming warbands confines.

The orcs and goblins who joined the others moved there cages, which had far fewer in them alongside the others before falling back to the marching ranks that followed closely behind. Falling in file just behind the prisoners they had added to the train.

Drogen watched the procedure carefully as the new prison wagons were added one by one to the rest and the anguished faces of those that had been captured as realization of there plight began fully setting in. He wanted to do anything he could to set the prisoners free but he could fight the horde around him for weeks and still get nowhere close to freeing any of them.

Anything I do would likely result in not only my death but the death's of all those who have had the misfortune of being captured, thought Drogen.

Seeing no way into the camp without raising the alarm, and no way of knowing where they were going Drogen instead chose to follow alongside them. Hoping that a chance would come that he might slip in with the other prisoners.

I can only hope that the ones who took Natalia are truly going in this direction, thought Drogen. *Only time will tell. Barring that then my only hope is that this caravan through the woods is heading in the same direction that Natalia has gone. To Grammora.*

The train lead by the giants went on until just before nightfall when the note of a loud horn rang out behind the giants. As soon as the bellow of the horn died down the giants sat where they had just cleared pushing yet more trees aside as they did so.

Those following behind the behemoths stopped as well setting up fires and collecting materials to burn. Even with the thousands of orcs setting up there camp for the night there were still eyes trained upon the prisoners and sentries keeping a watchful eye over each cage in turn.

Drogen watched and waited for any opportunity to get into one of the cages unnoticed, but no such opportunity presented itself. The sentries were ever watchful not sparing even a second without there eyes upon there captives all while the other's were preoccupied with there own tasks before nightfall cast them in darkness.

As nightfall came over the camp security around the prisoners began to dwindle to fifteen minute patrols around the cages. *Tis time to descend and see what havoc must be rot in order to garner the information I seek.*

Drogen dropped from the tree he'd used to spy on the goblinkin without a sound. He moved in between the makeshift structures listening to those sleeping inside and hoping that he might come across the information he needed to see, or hear. Knowing that the smaller structures were likely those of subordinates where as the larger were made for the ones leading the army around them. The larger structures were at the center of everything, and the most heavily guarded. Ogres and orcs alike surrounded the tents which housed the collective of the army commanders.

Drogen sat out among the tents moving with the guards and keeping to the shadows watching and waiting for them to say the word, the one word that he needed to hear to know that he was going in the right direction.

I don't need to see what they're doing I only need to hear one thing Grammora. As long as they're going to Grammora then my next steps are set. I will do as she did and become there captive, though it will be on my terms not there's.

Unfortunately the commanders were fast asleep in there beds and not a word escaped there lips through the night, still Drogen did not move away from them. Even as the sun began to ascend through the sky Drogen remained among the tents keeping his ears out for both

Grammora and the ever watchful security that moved around the tents. As a ray of sunlight came through the trees an orc who was on patrol began rousing those inside before moving on to the next.

The orcs each gathered themselves within there respective tents before moving out to the central tent between each of the commanders sleeping quarters. It was then that there meeting started.

Drogen didn't understand a word of what they were saying, but he didn't need to understand he only needed the one word to be said aloud and he could put his plan into action. *Grammora. I only need to know that you're going to Grammora tis all I need to hear,* thought Drogen. The stress of not being caught as well as keeping his ears trained on the grunts and sequels that comprised the goblinkin's language adding to the anxiety he felt not knowing if he would be able to catch up to Natalia.

With the rays of light growing brighter behind the camp more and more of the goblinkin were roused from there slumber and starting to tear down the camp for another long day of moving forward toward there destination.

The commanders were still talking back and forth with each other and Drogen had to move further away so as not to rouse suspicion of his presence among them, with the distance between them. Drogen could barely hear them speaking at all, as if they whispered incoherently in his ear. Still none said the name Grammora.

Have I made a great mistake in following these goblinkin. What if they're not going to Grammora. I have allowed too much time to pass between Natalia and I. How am I supposed to rescue someone when I cannot even find where they are, Drogen chided himself. *If only Godslayer; Envoy of Death could have warned me, as they could have in the past. Or guide me to the right path as they guided me to the elves of Moongrove.*

With nothing to show for his efforts Drogen moved back into the woods watching the caravan move forward through the day and resting during the night. With each day and night that passed his heart sank deeper and deeper. He even thought about capturing one of the soldiers, but knew that without understanding there language he would garner little to no useful information as it seemed most did not speak what would have been considered the common tongue.

He continued with the same methods watching and listening to any who spoke listening for Grammora, the last vestiges of his own positivity at rescuing Natalia waning with each passing minute he remained among the goblinkin as the giants who led there caravan tore the forest asunder.

Still he hoped listened and waited till he heard it. The name that he'd been hoping to hear. It came from a group who brought a great number of cages full of animals and a multitude of prisoners. It was not said by an orc or goblin but by a man who looked no taller than a boy. Drogen thought him to be a dwarf at first but he was neither stout of shoulder nor bearded as dwarves were known to be.

He must be one of the gnome race thought Drogen. *I wonder how he wound up here among the prisoners?*

Noticing the curious actions of the gnome Drogen decided it may behoove himself to keep a watchful eye. The gnome constantly took in his surroundings and clocked all who moved through the encampment as they passed by. As though he were awaiting the right opportunity to enact a plan he was only just forming.

A few minutes before nightfall Drogen saw the gnome reach into a deep pocket set within his cloak and pulling out a thin wire which he set to work with on the lock in which he was captive. It only took the gnome a second to have the pins pushed up and the lock open wide.

Even though the lock was open and his escape ensured the little gnome did nothing to escape from his captivity he simply watched and waited for something to happen, something that Drogen could only contemplate as he kept his eyes and ears out for anything else the Gnome had to say.

It seems that this gnome knows about Grammora I wonder if I might be able to get the information I need once he escapes his imprisonment. All I know is that Natalia went to Grammora, thought Drogen.

As his thoughts raced hoping that the Gnome would be the answer to his plight a thunderous sound came blaring through the forest. As though a tree had burst apart pelting the nearby foliage with the last vestiges of its life. And from the sound of the explosion came a deep thunderous wail from the giants who led the warband's way through the woods.

A breeze blew a short while after wafting the smell of burnt flesh and hair back through the lines of orcs and into the trees that surrounded them. Then came another. An explosion followed by a wail. The orcs and goblins knew for certain that they were under attack breaking all attention away from those they had imprisoned as they formed rank and file lines in front of the prisoner wagons.

All those who stayed behind the prisoners looked out into the forest around them waiting for any signs of an ambush from the side or the rear of there massive train.

Drogen, seeing the commotion caused by the explosion and the havoc being rout did not waiver in his concentration for the gnome was the only one who might know where to find Natalia. *You might have found a way to distract the goblinkin around you, but you will not get past me. Not without telling me of Grammora,* thought Drogen.

As the last vestiges of Drogen's inner vow ran through his head more explosions sounded all around him bringing the army that had traveled unimpeded for nearly a week to a complete stand still. The rank and file of the military power before stood in unexpected terror at the sheer number of explosions sounding around them and many of the goblins ran in fear back down the trail from whence they came.

With the terrified goblins running in all directions the orcs themselves started to succumb to the chaos and terror as the explosions seemingly drew nearer and nearer from each side. The sound made one think thousands of giants had come to destroy them.

This was the chaos that the gnome seemed to have been waiting for as he flung the door to his prison open running out and over to the many cages that had been occupied by many other races other than his own. The gnome unlocked each cell in seconds bidding those inside to follow him quietly so as not to catch the attention of the orcs who were otherwise engaged by the running goblins and the multitude of explosions occurring around them. The last cages door was open and the occupants within released from there captivity when one of the orcs finally noticed the attempted escape taking place.

The orc warrior yelled out to those around him. His voice drowned out by the many explosions still occurring, but many orcs still heard the call bringing their attention to the escapees. The orcs now had other things to focus on and charged toward their captives to once again secure them. Those who turned soon found themselves being attacked from the forest behind them. Arrows flew through the air striking down those closest to those escaping with deadly precision. Still more arrows and projectiles flew through the ranks of orcs and goblins as they fled further distracting from there already escaping prisoners until not a one was left within.

The many prisoners disappeared into the woods before any others became aware of their great escape. With the thunderous noise happening all around them and the ambush they expected but were unprepared for drawing them in it would be some time before they realized the truth of what they had lost.

Drogen ran through the camp like a panther making no noise and drawing no notice from any of the distracted goblinkin. *This may be the last chance I have to get the information I need. If only these blasted explosions were not so loud. I could track them from farther off, but if I lose the gnome now, I will be right back where I started.*

It didn't take long for Drogen to catch up to the group of escapees choosing to mix in with them seemed like the best idea, so he did so, and did so just in time since more seemed to be showing up as well.

Elves, gnomes, zephyrians, and many other races came rushing out of the forest around them leading them deeper into the woods and their salvation from the fate that would have inevitably befallen them at the goblinkin's hands.

Drogen worked his way up to those he'd seen imprisoned with the roguish gnome listening for the gnome's heartbeat among them. The gnome kept a comfortable pace behind those he had rescued. Knowing that chatting with the gnome would have to wait until they were out of danger Drogen he simply ran alongside biding his time till he could finally ask the question burning within his soul to be answered.

Everyone ran without rest until some of the weakest among them began falling due to their exhaustion catching up with them. Even then the group did not stop they simply took those who could no longer run under their arms and ran on. They traveled for more than an hour before finally coming to a stop so they could rest and recoup their strength before continuing on.

The gnome Drogen followed took refuge against a tree resting his back against the mighty trunk to catch his haggard breath. Taking the opportunity Drogen sat down on the next quarter of the massive trunk so as to give the gnome his space.

"Thank you for rescuing all of those the orcs had imprisoned. Your ambush had to take much preparation and perfect execution in order to save so many," stated Drogen when the gnome had finally caught his breath.

"Funny how you know it is I who saved many of the people here when I know I did not have a hand in saving you." stated the gnome.

"Because you my friend did not save me, but I witnessed you save many more than I could have possibly done on my own," said Drogen.

"Surround," cried the gnome. The cry barely had time to escape his lips before ten bows arrows knocked and strings tight were pointed at Drogen's head.

"I did not come here to fight you I need only information and I will be on my way," said Drogen.

"How do we know that you're not a spy? Placed among us by the orcs or Grock himself," said one of the elves who drew his bowstring even tighter.

"I give you, my word. I am neither of those things. Although, I suppose if that is not enough... What might I have to do to garner the information I seek, and leave without an unnecessary battle," posited Drogen with a sigh.

"And what makes you think we will let you leave after you receive the information you seek," said the gnome.

"I suppose we will have to see how things transpire, although I hope you choose to let me go peacefully. I will be leaving regardless," stated Drogen.

"What information do you seek," questioned the gnome after a few moments of contemplative silence.

"Are the orcs you escaped from going to Grammora," questioned Drogen

"Yes, they're going to Grammora," said the gnome his curiosity peaking at the question.

"That is all I needed to know," said Drogen. "It seems my journey has not been in vain after all."

The gnome waved for those he summoned to put their weapons down.

"Do you not still suspect me of being one of Grock's minions, or a spy," questioned Drogen.

"No, because I recognize that emotion in your voice. However, I must warn you that none who have gone into Grammora have ever come back alive," said the gnome.

"Then I will need to do something to change that." said Drogen.

"What makes you think that you can succeed where all the others have failed," questioned the gnome.

"Because I am different from all who've tried before," said Drogen.

"Might I know the name of one who thinks so highly of themselves," stated the gnome annoyed by the perceived arrogance.

Drogen rose to his feet before bowing to the gnome in his usual manner. "I am Drogen, and tis not arrogance with which I proclaim such. Simply a statement of the truth." Looking into the gnome's eyes Drogen's eyes shifted to those of his birthright and with a blink they returned to normal.

Taken aback by the display and then unsure if his eyes were simply deceiving him the gnome rose to his feet. "I am Deus," stated the gnome extending his hand which Drogen took in kind responding back to Deus with a firm grip and shake.

"Tis a pleasure Deus, now I must be leaving," said Drogen.

"It seems that my warning will be going unheeded. Well, if you do manage to make it out alive then I would ask that you look for someone for me. Her name is Carme. I don't expect much but if there's any chance," trailed off Deus.

"I will see what I can do," said Drogen understanding the feeling of heartbreak and sadness of his gnome friend all too well.

The bowmen looked to the gnome as Drogen began walking away but he waved them off again, so they continued on with getting the people around ready to strike out once again.

Drogen ran through the woods a breath of fresh air rushing into his lungs as his conviction that he was on the right path was fully restored. By the time Drogen had returned along the trail the escapees had run through the orcs had already begun marching again leaving the bodies of the dead, as though they were a part of the underbrush, where they had fallen.

With the help of his wings Drogen made up the distance the orcs had traveled in under half an hour. Hearing the heartbeats of those at the back of the still massive army that lay ahead he slowed down furling. His wings and taking to the trees so as to make his way back to the cages.

It was nearing nightfall when the cages finally came into view before him. Many of the cages looked to have been discarded or destroyed all together only those caging animals remained.

Drogen followed along the route the orcs traversed through the woods trailing alongside the cages until night fall came and the orcs, still on guard for possible ambush, were ready to bed down for the night. Having no prisoners to look over the orcs paid no attention to the cages they carried simply going about setting up camp and keeping an ever-watchful eye to the woods that surrounded them.

Guards took shifts to look over the cargo they still carried but they lacked the motivation they once did with regards to there captives growing extremely lax around the cages that housed there left over spoils. Taking the opportunity for what it was, Drogen made his way to the cages a silent shadow in the night. The lock holding the door shut easily broke in twine within his powerful grasp. Depositing himself within the cage alongside a wyvern, who held no wish to share its already confined space with the likes of him, until it witnessed the change in Drogen's eyes.

The wyvern made no contest of its space instead curling its tail around itself to take up as little room in the cage as possible as far away from Drogen as it could manage within the far too confined space.

My only hope is that I make it to where Natalia is before she suffers a fate from which none may return. Although, I do not doubt that she likely could escape on her own, depending on the environment she is retained in. At least with me by her side her chances will be greater than alone, thought Drogen. *Please just remain alive so that we may return to our friends unscathed and with the knowledge we need.*

Chapter Seven

With Drogen's departure accompanied by their previous entourage, Fread went to work on the pile of paperwork. Paperwork which had been left undone since before his hunt in Moongrove for Drogen. When he wasn't working on matters of state, he kept a close eye on Vladimir and the decision the monarch had yet to come to concerning his wife and step-daughter's punishment. Fread understood that Vladimir had to work through his thoughts and feelings, but after a weeks time, Fread hoped his decision would be made soon. Whether the decision was the right one was ultimately up to Vladimir.

The one thing that helped Fread through the countless meetings and ever-present emergencies that plagued the entirety of his waking hours and days was Willow's unyielding presence. They'd only been together for a few passion filled days, but their connection was unmistakable to them both. Every time she swept into the room his worries and apprehensions vanished as though they'd never been. He often found his mind wandering through their nights together, locked in the thralls of uninhibited passion.

I suppose there's nothing like a near death experience to bring two people together, thought Fread.

Yet even her presence couldn't lay aside the worry gripping his heart concerning the whereabouts and probable trouble that his friends were undoubtedly finding themselves in. "I only hope they can find some way to deliver messages to us if they need any help," said Fread to the ever-growing stack of papers littering his desk and floor.

With their relationship being so new Fread tried to put Willow at ease, not showing the worry that gripped him, but he knew she could see through the façade. He found keeping his innermost feelings secret from her near impossible though he couldn't understand exactly why. Her presence both put him at ease and disconcerted him. He knew for sure that he had feelings for Willow even though their romance was only days old she felt like a part of him that he's been missing and hadn't realized its absence until she came into his life.

Pushing his musings aside he went back to work reading over a missive requesting guard for a caravan's journey through goblinkin territory in order to facilitate trade with a couple of outlying elven communities. An order that worked alongside Vladimir's request for more armor sets to be procured from elven smiths.

I'll have to see if the merchants can gather the armor since they're going to the elves already, thought Fread stretching back in his chair to release the building tension in his limbs. They will also need to be compensated for their time and the armor itself. As he signed orders to fulfill both contracts, he placed a wax signet beside his signature ensuring that the authenticity of the orders wouldn't be questioned.

Willow came sweeping in through the closed door. She wanted to do something to alleviate at least a portion of the stress that plagued Fread's days since the departure of their friends, but nothing she could think of seemed a plausible solution. So, she decided to take it upon herself to watch over the royals in order to report any news or rumors she might overhear whilst he remained walled in by stacks of never-ending requests.

"You've been locked in this office for nearly three days Fread. You're just going to waste away at this point."

"You're probably right... has it really been that long," posited Fread seeing the pile of used dishes set at his feet from the meals both Willow and Krail had brought him during his days of solitude. "I suppose I have been here for at least that many days. I apologize for getting so lost in the paperwork."

"With the amount of paperwork that's still left to go through, I don't blame you for getting lost. The parchment around you is enough to form a small forest," said Willow with a wry smile.

"Heard any interesting rumors in your wanderings these past days," questioned Fread.

"No. It seems that things are quieting down, although, many people are having a hard time coming to terms with their deity no longer hearing their prayers. I've actually heard quite a few of your kin sending prayers to Drogen. Thanking him for taking care of Ether and Uther," said Willow.

"I think it best to keep that information from Drogen. I don't believe he will take very well to people worshiping him as they once did Ether and Uther. I can't tell you how many requests I've found, among the thousands of others, requesting a monument be placed in the castle's courtyard where Ether and Uthers effigies once stood," said Fread whilst reading through yet another document.

"I almost wish you'd approve it just to see Drogen's reaction," said Willow with a mischievous grin.

"Believe me I thought about it, not for Drogen's reaction however, but for the religious zealots that have come in protest of Drogen not being ostracized for his killing of Ether and Uther," said Fread clear annoyance radiating through his voice. "I swear over half the requests here are from them asking for everything from death to banishment."

"Yes, they've gotten quite bold going as far as to show up at the audience chamber every day holding up other's, who are wishing for their requests to be heard," said Willow.

"I suspect the real discussion on everyone's mind is when Lord Vladimir will render his verdict upon Nefar and Bernadine," said Fread.

"Some have started a betting pool as to what the outcome will ultimately be," said Willow. "But that's something we can talk about later. I think it's time for you to get out of this stuffy office. "You can't expect to get through all of this in one setting."

"You're right," said Fread with a long drawn-out yawn. I told Krail to go home hours ago to spend time with his wife. I suppose I should take my own advice at some point. I've been here far too long all the words are starting to run together. I need to return all these dishes to the kitchen as well," said Fread picking up the large stack of plates and utensils before heading out the door leaving his stuffy office behind.

"By the time we're done in the kitchens it should be time for the hearing of requests within the audience chamber to start. Maybe Lord Vladimir will have come to a decision," Willow shrugged taking hold of half the plates Fread carried as they walked.

"I fear that the decision he makes will likely result in some unforeseen consequences, but we cannot know for sure what they might be until such time as they strike," said Fread.

"Living in the past and fearing the future is no way to live. Believe me Fread I was stuck in that place for longer than I care to admit, even to myself. We have to look on the bright side.

Not at some consequences that may or may not arise. We cannot hope to know what fate has in store for any of us," said Willow.

Willow's words gave Fread much to think about and they arrived to the kitchen in contemplative silence. Fread deposited the dishes in the wash basins without so much as a thought to his actions as Willow's words worked their way to combat the uneasy feeling, he was having in regards to Nefar and Bernadine.

One of the scullery maids, seeing Fread lost in thought upon depositing the dishes, came over and dropped a loaf of freshly baked bread into his hand. He made to protest but she waved him off disappearing without a single word into the larder.

"Thank you," he called but received no reply.

He split the bread with Willow who happily ate the hot yeasty loaf alongside him as they made their way to the audience chamber where they hoped the long-awaited decision would finally be made. They finished eating just steps before entering the audience chamber.

Many were gathered within its confines, but most of those present were guards. The view remained the same, Vladimir sitting upon his central throne on the raised dais Nefar to his left, and Bernadine to hers. The heir of superiority the two step-monarchs had ruled with had returned with vengeance since Drogen and Natalia's departure, while Vladimir looked old and frail, far beyond anything Fread had ever witnessed.

"It would seem the weight of this decision is causing restless nights, whispered Willow into Fread's ear drawing a slight, but decisive nod of acknowledgment.

The dilemma placed before him by Drogen, weighting heavily on Vladimir both mentally and physically. All who stood before the once mighty unshakable ruler of Zephyria could tell at a glance that the decision, which had been set upon his shoulders by Drogen, was weighing him down.

Acting as though nothing was amiss however, were Nefar and Bernadine. Their usual antics of talking down to the people, and disregarding those they did not see as worthy of their attention growing with Vladimir's decline.

"I would like to request that the one who killed our deity be punished for his crimes against the zephyrian people," came the voice above the crowd that Fread had grown all to familiar with since Ether and Uther's demise.

"When will they quit with this line of requests? I have enough to deal with without having yet another of their demands to go through," thought Fread with a heavy sigh. *As though they themselves have not suffered loss by their cruelty."*

"Yes, I think that such things must be taken into account for the sake of the zephyrian people. We cannot possibly have the killer of our Deity running around our people acting as our savior when we were perfectly happy before he took it upon himself to interfere in affairs that were not his own," came Nefar's voice.

"I agree, and the fact he's taken Princess Natalia with him shows he has no regard for Zephyria at all," stated Bernadine with a scandalized countenance.

Fread grew increasingly enraged at the arrogance and malign speech coming from both Nefar and Bernadine. He tried in vain to hold his tongue, but it all spewed forth as though there was nothing there to prevent the outburst. "How dare any of you speak with such venom about the person who saved us from our oppressors. Not one person here has not had a loved one lost by the hands of Ether and Uther. Not a single one of us has gone unscathed throughout all there years of cruelty. Yet you dare speak foul of the one who has saved us from the fear and oppression rout by there hands," raged Fread taking a sideways glace at Willow who held an apologetic look upon her face.

"You have no right to speak to a royal in that manner, I will have you taken to the dungeon for such behavior," Nefar raged back.

"Banishment," yelled Vladimir.

"Yes, that is a far more fitting fate for your transgression against royalty," said Nefar.

"Not him," said Vladimir venom coming into his voice. "You two are hereby banished from Zephyria and any place upon which a zephyrian calls home. You are never to set foot upon zehpyrian soil, or death shall be served upon you both." Vladimir pointed to Krail who stood at the head of the guards stationed right next to the throne. "This order is absolute make sure it is carried out and that none who would harbor them among our people will do so, or they too will suffer the same fate."

"*Noooooo,*" cried Nefar finally comprehending the reality of there situation. "We. We can work something out. There's got to be something we can do. P-P-Please, don't banish us. Are you really going to do this to us after what he just spouted. We are royalty appointed by Ether and Uther."

"You are royalty no more, and you're lucky to be getting off this easily. I thought many times of simply having you killed for what you have done to me, Natalia, and the people of Zephyria," stated Vladimir. "Krail take them from my sight at once."

Nefar and Bernadine broke down in tears flailing and denying the banishment as guards, led by Krail, grabbed their flailing sobbing forms.

"Stop," said Vladmir getting up from his throne drawing a look of relief from both Nefar and Bernadine, "Give them as much food and water as they can carry at the bottom of the cliff. Now take them away."

"Yes, Lord Vladimir," came Krail's reply. As Nefar, and Bernadine renewed their useless struggle.

"You all will regret this I will make sure of it," screamed Nefar as the newly hung double doors that had been destroyed by the bodies of Ether and Uther closed with a resounding thud behind the swiftly moving guards.

"Fread and Willow come forward," came Vladimir's call.

"Yes Lord Vladimir," acknowledged Fread. Willow grabbing Fread's arm to interlock her own with his as they came to stand before the throne of Zephyria.

"I think it is time Fread. I no longer have it in me to rule over the people of Zephyria for I am no longer fit for the role. My inability to act upon what is right and inability to listen to the hardships of my people and family further prove that I am no longer fit to lead our people."

"I think I understand where this is going, would it not behoove us to clear the audience," questioned Fread.

Vladimir raised his hand cutting him off before he could continue with his inquiry."No Fread it is time for the truth to come out and everyone in Zephyria will know soon enough," said Vladimir.

"Very well," said Fread.

"You must reclaim your title, Fread. I know you wanted to work alongside the others and garner respect through your own deeds. A feat you've more than accomplished by becoming a respected member and leader of the Royal guard. However, the zephyrian people need a leader in my stead, until the rightful ruler of Zephyria succeeds us," said Vladimir.

"Since you've stated as much with so many present... I have no room to negotiate for more time in my duties," rhetorized Fread.

"So it is, and unfortunately has to be Fread. As your father, I am sorry, but as the reining Lord, I felt it... necessary," said Vladimir sorry creeping into his voice as he spoke.

"What is he talking about," questioned Willow. "Does that make you Natalia's brother," she questioned in a whisper.

"We will need to discuss these complicated matters later, but the short answer is no," whispered Fread.

"Very well my love, I'll save these questions for later," said Willow. Both turning their attention back to the patiently waiting Lord Vladimir.

"You didn't believe me when Natalia and I came back with Drogen from Kethick's hideout. You clearly didn't trust in either of us enough to acknowledge what we said was factual. You never questioned the legitimacy of the one who sat at your side even though the proof of their evil was plain as day to everyone else. So yes, I acknowledge that you, as you are now, are unfit for the role of Lord over the people of Zephyria. Do you acknowledge and agree," questioned Fread.

"I agree my actions and ineffective rule has lessened the existence of Zephyria as a whole thus I abdicate this throne to a living heir as is prescribed in the laws set forth by the first King of Zephyria, My Son Prince Freadrick Zephyr," Vladimir took the crown off his head as he rose from Zephyria's throne. "I former king Vladmir of Zephyria do hereby acknowledge thee, King Freadrick of Zephyria," said Vladimir placing the crown upon Fread's head before kneeling in front of him, lord no longer.

Vladimir's declaration garnered more than a few gasps, they looked upon the show taking place before them as though they were all dreaming. The royal family had all been cast out and the King was now abdicating his position to a son that none of them knew existed, However, upon seeing the former King kneeling before Fread all within the audience chamber followed suit kneeling to Fread in acknowledgment of his rise.

"With this declaration, and with the former Lords blessing, I King Freadrick take my place upon the throne of Zephyria," said Fread walking past the still kneeling Vladimir to set upon the throne. "All rise and be seen by your new Lord Freadrick Zephyr," said Lord Fread and all rose.

"Now I ask that you all go and tell the people of Zephyria that I have been appointed as their knew Lord," said Fread to the entirety of the audience chamber. "Now go we will resume hearing requests on the marrow."

All present within the audience chamber ran as though their lives depended on it to tell everyone that there was a new Lord set upon the throne of Zephyria leaving only a couple of guards Vladimir, who stood before the throne, and Willow who still had so many questions and not nearly enough answers as to what was going on.

Fread sat upon the throne exhausted both mentally and physically from the spectacle that had just taken place. *I thought I had enough work before, but now, there will be so much more,* thought Fread.

"You mentioned that I would set upon the throne until the real ruler of Zephyria came. Am I to assume that those documents recount the truth of Zephyria," questioned Fread.

"If you have already seen the truth then you are correct," said Vladimir.

"Then the concern becomes how are we going to tell Natalia," questioned Fread.

Chapter Eight

They had traveled through the woods for a fortnight moving rather slow as they had to cut a path through the forest. They had hoped to move along the same path as those who had fled when Moongrove was overrun.

Seraphine, Alya, Rumble, and Tumble had grown closer, in their own way during their travel although the brother dwarves were constantly looking behind them, to where they had just been, for their charge Princess Natalia. Although Seraphine, and Alya tried to give them encouraging words as to Natalia's survival, they could not, or simply would not, hear any of it.

The brothers were responsible for Natalia, and they took that job seriously. Thus, in Natalia's stead they would guard Seraphine and Alya with their very lives on the line.

During their travels there had been no threat to their lives, and they had mysteriously not seen any goblinkin traveling through the forest. Something that seemed strange to them all with how they had chosen to overrun Moongrove.

"Maybe they just don't want to send people off on a wild chase when they have no idea where Moonclave is located," suggested Alya.

"Or they be buyin time fur the moment to strike out against ye tree faeries," said Rumble.

"Although I don't much care for the tree faeries comment, I can't see any other explanation. One of my people could have told them where Moonclave is and with the number of our people that have been captured over the years I would view it as a truth rather than just a possibility," confessed Seraphine.

"How much longer till we reach the barrier," questioned Alya.

"We should be getting to the barrier today. We may need to split up once we reach it," said Seraphine.

"What ye be meanin tree sprite, why we be needin ta do somethin like that," said Rumble.

"I thought we would be able to bring them into Moonclave with us," said Alya as Tumble put on a sad puppy dog like face to look up at Seraphine.

"That won't work on me, and it definitely won't work on any of the other elves," said Seraphine with a slight smile.

"Ye be tellin me brudder an me what we be expectin going into yer Moonclave then once we be at this barrier ye be talkin bout," questioned Rumble.

"Yes, but we don't need to make a decision on what to do until then," said Seraphine. "Although, it is something we need to think about, and that's why I brought it up."

"Ay, I think we be better off not goin into Moonclave. Then at least ye can move freely," said Rumble.

"I agree," said Seraphine. "But it should be put to a vote so that we can all agree or disagree after hearing all the information."

"As ye wish," said Rumble moving away and speaking to his brother in a hushed tone.

The dwarves conversed back and forth until Rumble let out an exasperated sigh, waving his hands in the air fed up with how their conversation was going.

"They continued to walk in silence only speaking in short bursts until seemingly out of nowhere," Seraphine said, "We're here."

"We be where ye daft tree bug. It be the same ear as it been a fortnight," grumbled Rumble in a tirade.

"This is the barrier's edge, beyond this point none can speak anything but truth, and the closer you get to the center of the barrier the harder it is to fight against the barriers influence. I have lived here all my life and have never seen anyone defeat the barriers influence."

"Come here Rumble and you will understand," said Alya with an outstretched hand.

Rumble waved away her outstretched hand moving up to where they stood stretching out his own hand to what was invisible to his own perceptions. It was only slight, but he felt a pressure against his hand, pressure against something that he could not physically see himself, but pressure all the same.

"How can something like this exist," questioned Rumble clearly at a loss.

"We, the elves as a whole don't know either. Strangely though within the barrier we feel a higher affinity for the nature around us and its influence. It's as though the world comes back to life the moment we go beyond its' boarders," a sense of melancholy overtaking her sing song voice. *If only the repression from the barrier were not there,* she thought.

"It be strange ye know nothin," said Rumble.

"Not for a lack of trying. We simply can't decipher the language surrounding this place is written in. Although we have developed our own systems of writing based upon it. We are nowhere close to actually understanding the meanings behind the words that have been written," said Seraphine.

"We have other more important matters to discuss don't we," questioned Alya.

"Yes, we have a choice to make. Rumble and Tumble could come with us into Moonclave, but that could further complicate what we need to do within. They would be the first and only dwarves to walk into Moonclave. Even though I'm of noble heritage my people will need more than a little explanation. Likely, it would lead to the two of you being imprisoned, if not all of us," said Seraphine.

"Ye not really welcomin folk are ye. I be thinkin forest a sight better than a cell," said Tumble.

"I be thinkin it better we go witum. Not be out ear in the forest awaitin them returnin. What happen if we be taken by patrolin tree sprites. We be in same position if not be worse," countered Rumble.

"I agree with Rumble, I think we should take them with us. If a patrol comes through and they're captured we have far less room to talk things through than if they come with us to Moonclave," voiced Alya.

"Ay, we be needin as much as we can get when comes to the likes of faeries. They not be listening to anythin they not wantin to ear," said Rumble.

"An what if ye plan not work. An talkin not enough. Ye be expectin us ta wait for the flyin lizard," questioned Tumble.

"It seems like their roles have reversed, does that mean Rumble is gonna be the funny one now," questioned Alya trying to cut through some of the tension with some levity.

"Not on yur life, fuzz foot," scoffed Rumble.

"I understand your thinking Tumble, but it will be for the best if we all go in together. I feel like the weight of our words will have more weight than if Seraphine and I go in alone, said Alya.

"Maybe ye be right fuzz foot, an at least if ye be attacked we be there ta defend ye. As best we can," said Tumble. I be sure to gnaw a few ankles off afore I get captured at least," said Tumble.

"I wouldn't, elf probably taste terrible," said Alya.

"May be ye just not cookin it right," said Tumble.

"Okay, that's more than enough of that," said Seraphine clearly over their back and forth drawing a deep and hardy belly laugh from both Alya and Tumble, the former trying to imitate the latter.

"So, it be decided then. We be goin in together," said Rumble.

"It seems that way. Yes." said Seraphine looking at each of them in turn and getting a nod in return."

"Very well let us be off ta the land of the faeries then," said Rumble. At least we be able ta get off our ackin feet," Rumble grumbled.

Seraphine, Rumble, and Tumble moved through the barrier waiting on the other side for Alya to join them.

"Ya not be gettin cold feet are ya fuzz foot," questioned Rumble.

"Is that really my new nickname," said Alya with an exasperated sigh before walking through the barrier.

It took half an hour for the outskirts of Moonclave to come into view. The walls of the great elven city drawing them ever closer to their destination. Along the outskirts stood two massive trees shaped into watchtowers that overlooked the woods around them. Hawks and the like coming and going from the highest point of the tower flittering off in all directions paper scrolls strapped to their legs.

From the guard towers blocking the entrance to Moonclave came three fists of guards. Each guard wore a sword at their side and brandished bows with nocked arrows pointed directly upon them.

"Phaylor, don't you recognize me. It hasn't been that long has it," announced Seraphine.

"Seraphine, I thought that might have been you, but what, pray tell, are you doing bringing the likes of ground hogs into Moonclave, are they prisoners or something. And who might the one next to you be. I don't recognize any of your entourage," said Phaylor as they all came forward still wary and brandishing their weapons.

"They are friend's," said Seraphine. "I really can't believe I can say and mean something so ridiculous, but they're friends."

"Even the dwarves," questioned Phaylor.

"Yes, even the dwarves," said Seraphine exasperated.

"As for me. We do know each other, but you might not recognize me as I am now. Maybe this will help," said Alya as she bent forward. Her hands shifting into paws, and fur springing forth from everywhere. Till she was looking up at him with her large feline eyes, and a big toothy smile.

"How is it that I didn't know Alya could change forms to match our own," Phaylor questioned.

Tumble looked at Alya and couldn't help but laugh at the absurdity unfolding before his eyes. "I never be thinkin a seein a tiger wearin clothes," he said choking out the words between fits of utter glee.

"Oh, hardy har har, it was a lot faster doing that then having to undue all these clothes," said Alya with a harrumph that made even the battle-ready guards let out a slight chuckle.

Phaylor raised his hand up and motioned the guards away with a swipe of his hand. "Go back to your tasks." As soon as the guards disappeared back into the tower Phaylor began shaking his head. "What made you think bringing dwarves to Moonclave was a good idea Princess," questioned Phaylor.

"Well, it wasn't really my idea. I was asked to do so by another friend. A friend that will be coming later. Although, I don't know how he plans to find us. He's trying to find out more information regarding the goblinkin's movements against all the people of Dranier. And save Princess Natalia from her own harebrained scheme," said Seraphine.

"Then I take it these two are actually Princess Natalia's guard from Zephyria then. I heard that there were dwarven brothers who guard the princess, but this is the first I've ever met them," said Phaylor.

"The grumpy one is Rumble, and the funny one is Tumble," piped in Alya.

"We be capable ah introducin ourselves fuzz foot," grumbled Rumble.

"See told you," said Alya with a smile. Sticking her tongue out at Rumble, and drawing a laugh from Tumble.

"I see," said Phaylor nearly getting swept up in the boisterous momentum of Alya, and Tumble. Almost.

"What are the chances of convening the council, is there a convening scheduled for any time soon," questioned Seraphine paying no attention to the antics going on beside her.

"No. The next scheduled council meeting is still a couple of years away. I doubt you'll get any of them to come together before then," said Phaylor.

"Then I must ask my mother for help convening the council. If we work quickly, we may just be able to get them together by the time Drogen gets here. From wherever they wound up. Do you have any idea where my mother might be. Or those who that had to flee from Moongrove," questioned Seraphine.

"I would suggest you look for them in the residential district, I suspect that they would be there since the roots of the Moongrove were unaffected by what happened," said Phaylor

"Thank you Phaylor, that will cut down on the time we need to find the queen," said Alya finally tuning into the conversation.

"I would suggest the dwarves stay here with me. It seems getting to the queen is top priority and they will ultimately slow you down especially when it comes to the residential district," said Phaylor.

The dwarves made to protest, but Phaylor raised both hands bidding them calm. "Nothing bad will happen to you while you're under my watch. The reason that I am suggesting this is because once they get to the residential district, they have to move along the treetops, and although there are bridges between the trees for swifter travel ultimately there are sections that have no such bridges."

"It seem as though, we be partin ways ear then," said Rumble. "Ye be makin sure ya get back ear in one piece. Or I be cutten ya down to me size fur the trouble."

"Is that concern I'm hearing," questioned Alya.

Rumble didn't say anything other than letting out a bagh and waving his hand dismissively.

"Well, we better get going then. We have a lot of work ahead of us to convene the council," said Seraphine.

"Oh, before we leave here, I wish to send a hawk to Zephyria to tell them of the current situation taking place, in case Drogen or Natalia get there first. I know that Fread would like to know what has transpired since our leaving as well."

"Very well do you have anything written out to send," questioned Phaylor.

"Yes. We had quite a bit of travel time, so I've written something in advance. Make sure that this goes to Fread, He's the commander of the royal guard of Zephyria," said Seraphine.

"It shall be done," said Phaylor. Taking a rolled piece of parchment from Seraphine. "Follow me Rumble and Tumble you can stay in the guard barracks awaiting Seraphine, and Alya's return."

"Ay, lead the way tree sprite," said Rumble.

"Yes, right this way mountain troll," said Phaylor.

"Oooh this may be a diffren kinda fun," said Tumble.

With Rumble and Tumble off trading insults with Phaylor, Seraphine, and Alya felt slightly better going off on their own into the city proper.

Upon entering the large tower gate, the city itself came into view and the expansive elven city of Moonclave lay before them, in all its splendor. Divided into seven distinct districts, At the heart lay the tower of the counsel and the focal point of the barrier that encapsulated the whole of Moonclave.

"Moonclave is kind of strange looking compared to the way Moongrove was laid out. It seems as though everything is divided up into sections," said Alya as she carefully scanned the new environment around them.

"That's because it is." said Seraphine. "We don't know what the builders of this place did, but each section of the city has its own kind of draw depending on where you stand within it," said Seraphine.

"To the left of us is the aviary, where all the winged creatures within these woods, and some found elsewhere, are trained and raised as either mounts or as messengers."

"Further up past the aviary is the district of Knowledge. This is where research is done with regard to the barrier and all that was written by our predecessors is studied and hopefully at some point will be translated. There's a complete library with many hundreds of books with knowledge that we are simply unable to grasp at this time. At least that's what my mother has told me," shrugged Seraphine. "Last I heard they found some kind of lost magic."

"To the right of us is where we raise animals that provide us with essentials of living without any harm coming to the animals themselves. Chicken's, among other birds, give eggs; of which we only eat the infertile. Goats and cows provide milk. Bees: honey, and there are many others which provide material for clothing.

"To the right of where we raise livestock are the farm and wetlands. That is where grains, fruits, and vegetables are grown. The wetlands also house aqueducts that provide clean water to the city as a whole.

"And up past that," questioned Alya.

"Up from the wetlands and aqueducts, adjacent to the aviary, is the crafter's district. It's the place where passions are explored and marketed to others. Forging, weapon crafting, armor making, or giving enchantments to items. It is here that all things produced within Moonclave are bartered and traded for," said Seraphine.

Alya thought through all the information that Seraphine spoke processing everything she could as they walked toward the massive tower which blocked their view of the other districts which Seraphine had spoken of. "I thought you said there were seven districts in Moonclave by my count that's only five," said Alya.

"Oh, you're right," said Seraphine. "The military district is the one we traveled through to get into Moonclave proper. It's the first line of defense against any and all invasions. It houses the guard barracks, as well as the main messenger outpost," said Seraphine.

"I'm guessing that the last district is where we're currently headed then. You've mentioned nothing about where your people actually live after all," said Alya.

"You're quite right it's the living district that we are heading to. Unfortunately for us it's the furthest away from where we currently are. If I had to guess the ones who made this place did that intentionally," said Seraphine.

"Are the towers, like those the guards were in built for defense or something else," questioned Alya.

"I think they were for defense, but nobody knows for certain. There are actually thirteen in total twelve all around and at the center is this tower," said Seraphine stretching out her hand to touch the tower as they began to move around its exterior.

"These towers are also the reason behind what the council chose to name this place, not knowing or surmising the name given by our predecessors. From the sky Moonclave looks like the phases of the Moon," finished Seraphine.

"You're a lot chattier than you were with the dwarves. You're reminding me of Drogen and his long way of speaking," said Alya.

"It's the barrier. It's pulling it all out of me. Hence why my people talk so little to each other. Speaking can do more harm than silence, so a majority choose silence in opposition to possible offense," said Seraphine.

The layout of the city made travel within easy. Each section had its own paths through it and each of them was a main artery that led to the counsel tower. One simply needed to move along the right path, and they would reach a point along the outskirts where the outer perimeter of Moonclave would lead you to any and all of the districts. Although this method also took significantly more time to traverse.

Still many elves chose to traverse the circle of Moonclave. The concept of time to the elves being far laxer than many other races of Dranier. Thus, arriving when they felt like it, and not when others might wish for them to be there. Something that made it nearly impossible to get anything of importance done quickly. The elven counsel never convening willingly for anything short of disaster. Everything else was viewed as insignificant and thus unimportant. The only one who could get around the lackadaisical nature of the elders was another member of the council, or High Queen of the elves.

"Do you think the dwarves will be alright," questioned Alya concerned for their safety.

"I'm sure they'll be fine. They are in good hands." said Seraphine.

"We know so little about what the goblinkin are planning. Do you think we can convince the counsel to convene with such little information," questioned Alya.

"It is likely the council will not see fit to convene until Drogen is here. Still, they need to be made aware of what we do know through a member of the council in order to get them to convene when the time comes.

"I miss Moongrove already," whined Alya. "At least there we could get everyone together at a moment's notice to take care of problems whether it be to help someone or to fend off an attack. No wonder the others looked so dejected at the prospect of having to come back here."

They walked toward the council tower ignored by everyone they passed because that was the way of the elves within Moonclave and the barrier as a whole. Their lack of communication with each other made it increasingly hard to collaborate with anyone on anything within the city's walls. Even harder was finding out any information one might need out of necessity. Especially if the elf in question didn't know you personally.

"How long do you expect it will take to get to the Living district," questioned Alya.

"We won't be getting there until tomorrow. We're both tired from traveling this far. We will need to make it to the crafters district and find an inn for the night. We can get up early and head into the living district from there.

"Should we get a message to the dwarves then," posited Alya.

"No. Phaylor will hopefully have told them that it will take a while for us to get there and back," said Seraphine.

"You put a lot of trust in Phaylor," said Alya.

"We grew up together and he's my oldest friend. So, of course I trust him," said Seraphine.

They continued to walk around the circumference of the tower until they had reached the opposite side. Seraphine moved to lead them on, but Alya stopped to look into the tower itself. Curiosity getting the best of her.

Within the room set two massive half-moon tables the halved sides facing the walls of the chamber. Between the two half-moons lay a massive black circle with golden runes engraved around and through it forming an encircled star.

"Alya, we need to get going its already mid-day and we still have a long walk before we can sleep for the night," said Seraphine.

Alya looked at her giving a single nod before prying her eyes away from what she saw within. They continued walking down the path that would lead them directly to the crafter's district thinking about what might be upon the horizon for them all.

"I wonder how long it will take Drogen to come back with Natalia... I do hope that she's alright," said Alya.

"As do I Alya. We can only place our trust in Drogen that he will bring her back safe and sound. For now, we will do as he asked and prepare for his arrival and for conflict. The goblinkin have attacked Zephyr and the Moongrove. Who knows what other people's they've displaced or killed in their conquest. It's only a matter of time before they find Moonclave and come knocking. I'd rather be prepared to defend our homeland from the eventuality of war then be caught unaware of an emanate attack, like what happened in Moongrove," said Seraphine.

Hundreds of elves walked by Seraphine and Alya, but none came close they garnered only simple nods at most and even then, they made no sound.

"From the looks of your people the barriers effect is bringing them down," said Alya.

"Yes, once we learned of the barriers effect many of our kind wanted to leave this place and start anew. Two towns were made. My mother made Moongrove and another Queen, I believe her name was Lyra, formed a settlement in the forest somewhere south of Zephyria," said Seraphine.

It took until the sun was nearly set for Seraphine and Alya to make it into the crafters district and until the moon started its accent into the night sky for them to find an inn. As they walked in, they heard many merrily singing songs clearly having partaken of alcohol at one of the bars within the crafters district.

"This is more like it. I thought I wouldn't be hearing any music in Moonclave," said Alya.

"It is the only time they're really able to relax within the barrier. It has caused many to lose themselves in drink so that they can sing dance and be joyous without thinking about the barrier and its influence over us all," said Seraphine.

A rather rambunctious elf who had partaken of more than his fair share of libations came dancing by them singing happily to the room accidentally bumping into them in his drunken state.

"Thorry," said the elf as he backed away.

"No worries, would you be able to point us to the inn keeper," asked Seraphine.

The elf looked at them confused in his drunken stooper for a few seconds before turning haphazardly and pointing to a rather severe looking elf sitting by himself in the corner staring out the window toward the council's tower.

"Excuse me. I apologize for interrupting your musings, but we wish to inquire on a room for the night," said Seraphine apologetically.

The elf turned around to look at Seraphine but paused on Alya. "I bet dwarves just love you, don't they?" He didn't linger upon either of them for long before going back to what he was doing. "We have one room available it will be five coppers or a large copper coin for the night. Two large coppers if you want food tonight and before you leave."

"Sounds fare enough, thanks for the hospitality," said Seraphine clearly perturbed by his comments toward Alya, though she tried to hide it from her expression. Alya noticed the look in her eyes grabbing her by the arm. Dragging her away from the innkeeper.

"Hey let me go. I can walk on my own," spouted Seraphine.

"We cannot have you berating the innkeeper for what he said especially since he already agreed to house us for the night," said Alya. "I doubt we would have been allowed if you let your lips run loose, as I suspect might have happened."

"I was going to tell him to keep his opinions to himself is all," said Seraphine.

"Right," said Alya, "And it would have undoubtedly escalated from there. Then we may have had to look for another inn."

"Fine. Fine. I see your point," said Seraphine.

"It's not like he's wrong," said Alya with a wide toothy grin.

Looking around the small inn they noticed a woman moving through the drunkard's taking money and handing out food that they clearly needed to sober up.

"I suppose that would be Phatropa," said Alya.

Seraphine nodded before looking around for an empty table. "Let's get some food and rest for a while. Our journey and day will be easier tomorrow once we're fully rested."

"Do you know how much longer it will take to reach where your mother is from here," asked Alya as they sat down.

"It shouldn't take us very long from here. Our home within the living district is quite far in though so it will take some time for us to get there," confirmed Seraphine.

Seeing the two new additions Phatropa set down a couple plates of food and made her way over to Seraphine and Alya's table. One of the elves stopped her along the way and asked for something, but she came straight to them.

"What can I get the two of you," said Phatropa.

"Yes, the owner said that you had a room available with meals for two large coppers," said Seraphine.

"Yes, we do. I'll make sure the room is ready and come back with tonight's meal. It might be a little while before I can get the room ready but once its done I'll show you the way," said Phatropa.

Seraphine fished out a small coin purse from a pocket in her dress pulling out two large copper coins and handed them over to Phatropa.

"Very good. I will be back with you shortly," said Phatropa leaving from their table and into the kitchen.

Phatropa worked herself around diligently at her tasks dropping plates of food and pitchers of water as she went. She ran back into the kitchen a second time carrying out five plates of food on one arm and two with the other which she dropped off along the way leaving the remaining two for Seraphine and Alya.

"Oooh the food looks good. It will be nice to eat something fresh instead of, stale bread, dried fruits, and vegetables," said Seraphine.

"There would have been a lot fresher food for you if you eat meat," said Alya.

"Yeah, I know, Drogen's bag was full of fresh meat, which I still don't understand the possibility of. I'll have to ask him to store more fresh fruits and vegetables as well when he gets here," said Seraphine.

"Speaking of Drogen," said Alya taking a big bite of a juicy apple. "How are things going with you and him."

Seraphine looked at Alya embarrassed, as she grabbed peach slices, some apple wedges, grapes, and berries to a bowl of yogurt. Over the top she sprinkled some honey granola and started eating. "How did you know I liked him," questioned Seraphine.

"We've known each other for a long time Seraphine and gotten into plenty of trouble together during that time. It was clear from the look on your face whenever you look at him, said Alya.

"I suppose I'm just not good at keeping my face in check when it comes to feelings. I might have to work on that," said Seraphine with a sour expression. "Things seem to be progressing smoothly, Natalia will be an obstacle for sure, or she might not be, depending on her pliability to the way we elves think," she said with a wide grin.

"Hmm, if anyone can convert her to the way elves think I dare say it would be you," said Alya. "Do you think Drogen would go for it?"

"I don't think he'll have any complaints," said Seraphine.

Phatropa came dancing up to them once more as they were nearly done eating. "Your room has been prepared just let me know when you're finished eating and I'll show you the way,", said Phatropa. Filling glasses of water from a pitcher for each of them.

They finished up quickly ready to get some rest signaling that they were ready to Phatropa who was taking care of another customer as they rose from their seats.

"This way," said Phatropa as she passed them taking them to a room set off to the back corner of the inn.

They moved into the room taking it in. The room had no decoration just a large bed and a couple of stands to either side. In the corner set a single wooden chair with a small corner table.

"Thank you Phatropa its exactly what we need," said Seraphine.

"Good if you need anything else you know where to find me," said Phatropa before she shut the door.

"I call the right side," said Alya taking her clothes off as the door closed. And transforming into her feline form and stretching out over the bed like a cat. "uhhhh this is so much better than sleeping in that other form."

"Then why don't you just stay in this form," questioned Seraphine.

"I like being able to walk and talk with everyone as they are, and being in that form just made it easier," said Alya.

Seraphine looked at the bed for only a second before just deciding to lay down. The exhaustion of traveling from Moongrove and through Moonclave overtook them both.

Chapter Nine

Natalia awoke to the sound of her orc captures discussing once again joining a caravan through the woods in order to make travel easier. Which was once again shot down by the other who reiterated that they were only a short distance away from their destination. Grom the most experienced of the two looked at things with more of a level head then his compatriot who wanted nothing more than to lessen their burden by dumping Natalia in with the multitude of others.

"No Bogger, we take to Grammora. They see we better than other who bring nothin. We get out from under foot, we move forward, join arena guard," reiterated Grom.

"I like travel with others Grom, what wrong wit that," questioned Bogger.

"Nothing wrong, but her special. Wings not same. She get us to arena. No more attack and imprison," said Grom. "We aster alone, cut time in half, or more."

Bogger could not argue with the fact that they were getting through the woods at a much faster rate than the army cutting a path through the woods would take.

"We reach Grammora tomorrow," said Grom. "You see."

Bogger, tired of arguing, decided it was time to gather wood for a fire.

Natalia had gotten used to the orcs and their guttural language quickly taking her time to fully understand what they were saying and translating it with little effort on her part. *I wonder why other languages are easy for me to understand, and comprehend. I only read about their speech structure. I didn't think doing so would allow me to understand and even speak the language,* thought Natalia.

Grom came over to Natalia a hint of sadness in his eyes as he looked upon Natalia.

"You have nightmare again. Is because of us," questioned Grom.

It was the first time Grom had asked her anything, although she doubted Grom or Bogger knew she could understand them.

"Nightmare not Grom, not Bogger," said Natalia shaking her head. She unfurled her glossy black wings and pointed to them making a plucking motion. My people give me nightmares, not you."

"I understand well. My people give me nightmares too, they hurt Grom, and Bogger because we different than others, I try protect Bogger, but he do not understand," said Grom a look of sadness upon his face. Only bugbear understand,"

Natalia nodded her head wishing she understood what the forlorn orc meant by bugbear, but she'd never heard or seen the word written anywhere in her studies. She only hoped that the information would prove beneficial at some point in the future.

"Wish could let you free, but need black wing so no more this," said Grom pointing to the wheeled cart on which she was imprisoned.

"Why do you have to take prisoner," questioned Natalia.

"If we fail to find prisoner, we become prisoner. Forced to fight in arena. Forced to die in arena," said Grom.

"So, others suffer so you don't," said Natalia "I understand this too."

"I have Bogger bring food you eat. We make to Grammora tomorrow. Know who take black wing to she taken care of. Grom and Bogger be given new place. No longer imprison," said Grom moving away from Natalia in order to set up there night camp and get food rations out and ready to use.

"Thank you Grom," said Natalia.

Bogger came back a few minutes later arms full of dry firewood. Grom moved some of the dried underbrush into a large pile while Bogger set about stacking the wood atop it. With all the firewood placed Bogger retrieved a flint stone from his pocket using and used the dagger at his side to shoot sparks. The underbrush ignited the moment the sparks touched the dried leaves.

The two orcs did not utter more than a few grunts until their stew was complete. "Take some to the black wing," said Grom.

Bogger looked more than a little perturbed by his compatriot but did as he was told giving Natalia a bowl of stew through the prison bars.

"We need make sure. She go to arena tomorrow," said Grom.

"Sneak her in with others?" questioned Bogger.

"Yes, with others," confirmed Grom.

Both of them nodded looking up at Natalia at the same time. "She our ticket to better," said Grom.

Bogger looked less than convinced but knew that Grom would not be persuaded otherwise.

With dinner complete Bogger snuffed out the campfire with a few buckets of dirt the three of them bedded down for the night.

Natalia awoke screaming in a cold sweat phantom pain radiating from her wings which she curled around her to feel that the feathers were indeed still there. Her cry of pain had alerted Grom and Bogger who jumped out of bed fearing that they were surrounded.

Grom looked over to Natalia clearly saddened by her outburst of fright. Bogger however looked quite angry having been woken up yet again by her screams in the night and wanting nothing more than to get rid of her and the problem she was to his rest.

"It still early but getting an early start will bring us to Grammora faster," said Grom.

"Yes, and her far away while we sleep," grumbled Bogger.

"I'm sorry," said Natalia, drawing a raised eyebrow from Bogger.

"Now understand why she go to arena," confirmed Bogger nodding his head. "She be happy with this one. As long as she useful."

The two orcs packed up everything they had set up taking out rations of hard bread and dried meat to eat before continuing on with their journey.

The forest around them was steadily beginning to thin out which made traversal a lot easier on everyone and allowing the cart to move much more freely without having to crush and move over overgrowth and underbrush that had plagued most of their journey.

Halfway through the morning as the sun rose behind them the edge of the forest came into view causing Grom and Bogger to draw renewed breaths and move forward more quickly, there destination finally within reach after traveling for so long.

Natalia looked around as more and more orcs began to come out of the woods accompanied by ogres, trolls, and worgs, many of whom were pulling heavily laden carts forward towards the crumbled walls of a seaside city. There were sentries around each entrance through the fallen walls allowing everyone into the city proper.

Natalia looked upon the crumbled walls but didn't think much of them as they were all covered in refuse and other unmentionable liquids that had a pungent smell all their own. Instead, she looked forward hoping that she'd be able to get the information that her friends would need in order to prepare everyone involved for what Grock had planned.

I will have to figure out a way out after I get the information that I need. I can only hope that they will forgive me for taking this upon myself, thought Natalia.

A guard looked over her two orc captors and Natalia herself without a word simply waving them forward and into the city proper. Grom and Bogger moved along with a group moving towards the arena keeping their heads down in order to blend in with the rest of them. They gradually relaxed as the arena came into view before them.

It took nearly three hours before Grom and Bogger were at the head of the line going into the arena.

"UH... Not you two again came an agitated voice, what have you got for me this time a ferocious rodent that will be slain in seconds or how about a mythical snail whose slime can melt iron," came the condescending voice.

"No No Golga we have something you need this time. We swear. We earn our spot in arena you see," said Grom drawing a slight but none too enthusiastic nod from Bogger.

Golga looked at the two orcs less than convinced by their lip smacking but allowing them entrance anyways with a sigh. "At least with you two here I know it won't be boring."

Natalia looked up at this new person with great interest. Golga as they had called her spoke the guttural goblin tongue, but in a much more sophisticated manner than Grom or Bogger had. It drew Natalia in, and she wondered whether it was a difference in dialect or something to do with a difference in education.

Golga wore no armor nor weapons though she moved much like she had seen seasoned warriors move. Without a single step wasted.

They Golga, Grom, and Bogger continued to talk amongst themselves while they released Natalia from the confines of her prison cell. More prisoners were being filtered in so the group as a whole moved into a larger hall just beyond waiting for the rest of the prisoners to be filtered in.

Most of those present looked to be on their last legs, many of whom were to the point of starvation or dehydration from the amount of time they spent as prisoners and the lack of care shown by their captors when it came to keeping their charges alive on the long and arduous journey of getting to Grammora.

Many orcs waited by those they brought in while others simply chained those they brought to others and left without a word. Natalia watched as Golga moved through the crowd pushing her way to the front of them all. Her larger and more robust stature aiding in moving any and all who stood in her way to part before being trampled underfoot.

Golga stood nearly two heads taller than the other orcs and towered like a giant over the goblins that Natalia noticed running around. Golga's voice rang out over the crowd of sick and fearful prisoners that filled the room drawing what little conversation had started to complete stark silence. The only sound that could be heard throughout the area was the nervous shuffling of feet as all looked upon her fearfully.

So many differences between this one and the others that I have seen so far. Is she of a different race among the goblinkin or is she simply the size that the females of the orc race grow too. Come to think of it I've only ever seen male orcs this is the first female I have ever come across, not that I've seen or met many orcs in my short time outside of Zephyria, thought Natalia.

Then Golga looked upon the selection of prisoners with great displeasure, whether the displeasure stemmed from the selection of sick and dying prisoners, or simply that the prisoners were standing there, Natalia didn't know. The orc started out speaking in the deep guttural language of the goblinkin drawing confused looks from everyone. Everyone except Natalia who looked to the Golga attentively. A difference Golga did not miss.

Golga pointed at Natalia and bid her come forward with a curled finger. Grom and Bogger moved with her through the crowd pushing through the others to get to the front where Golga waited.

"You understand," questioned Golga.

"Yes, she understands," spouted Grom excitedly.

"I did not ask you or Bogger., I asked *her*," exclaimed Golga pointing her finger at Natalia.

"Yes, I understand your language," said Natalia changing the intonation and pattern to better replicate the nuances present in Golga's form of speech.

"And a quick study as well. It seems that you two have actually brought back something useful for once," said Golga. "Very well I will give you both entrance to the arena guard. You," pointed Golga to a large orc with a crossbow in hand. "Take and train them in how the arena works and their new duties within."

"Thank you. Thank you. Thank you Golga," spouted Grom and Bogger in unison.

Golga let the three of them walk out of the hall before turning to once again address Natalia who waited patiently beside her.

"You translate and make sure the others understand," said Golga

Natalia nodded her head in acquiesce translating every word Golga said as she said it. "You are the cleaners. That is what you will be doing for the entirety of your time here. However, unlike those outside the arena, you will remain here. The lot of you will oversee removing the bodies of the dead within these halls, and within the arena itself. All the dead will be hauled to designated dumping grounds. And you should understand that no matter where you might go, *you will be,*" emphasized Golga "surrounded by guards Any attempt to flee will be met with death."

"There is a way to a better job within the arena however that is a matter that is handled by the arena champions. They may choose to raise any one of you from a cleaner in the arena to their, personal cleaner and should your champion fall, so too will you go back to clearing bodies. Now I will show you to your job areas and finally to where you will sleep. Once the larger group of prisoners arrives the fights within the arena will begin. Those fortunate enough to be chosen will live with your champions, as concubines," said Golga.

The prisoners did nothing to combat the orcs they simply followed along. The sheer number of crossbows trained upon them quickly killed any thought of disobeying or flight that any might have otherwise entertained.

Natalia didn't know how to feel as they moved through the different areas. She felt as though she was doing the bidding of the orcs by translating for Golga, but wanted to make sure she could save as many as she could by laying down the rules that Golga herself had set out for them. She felt as though she were being pulled in multiple directions at once. Her heart wished to help everyone, her stomach said that helping the goblinkin was wrong, and her inquisitive mind wondered why she felt something different from Golga, as she had with Grom and Bogger. Whatever turmoil Natalia felt within herself she did as she had been requested to do. She translated.

Golga kept Natalia by her side in front of everyone her own personal translator. Drawing looks of ire and fear from those within the group some thinking her in great danger while others looked to her as a traitor. Someone who deserved to die alongside those who captured them.

The coliseum was split into four sections. The prisoner hold, the cleaner's quarters, beast hold, and the arena itself. Each faction within the coliseum were to remain in their designated areas unless otherwise authorized, or having been given special privilege through there overseers.

The prisoners hold, was split between the imprisoned, which included many goblinkin who had disregarded or failed in their duties. And the champions of the coliseum. The prisoners worked to regain the honor, or station they once held by surviving and proving their worth in the arena. Whereas the champions had garnered the favor of the crowd and risen above the rabble. Few outsiders garnered this achievement and those who had were subsequently done in by beast or numbers. None had survived their fame for long.

As with the prisoners hold, the cleaners hold, was further broken into two sections. Living quarters and the mess hall where most of the cleaners would spend their days slaving to produce large quantities of food for those within the coliseum and many captured beasts.

The last section housed all the dangerous animals and beasts captured throughout Dranier. Beasts that would be released at irregular intervals as special hazards. Those who manage to kill the beasts are automatically promoted to champions within the arena. The lucky ones fight against smaller beasts such as young worgs or a pack of wolves. Most would find their luck far from enough to save them from a quick death should anything else within the beast hold be released.

"It's here that all the beasts of note are held as special battles within the arena. Their cages will be cleaned out by end of each day. Should it fail to be done. One of you will be killed. There is always someone out there to take your place," translated Natalia, who made sure to capture the serious and threatening tone Golga clearly wished to impart to the others.

The last stop for the group was their sleeping chamber. Which is all it was, a single chamber hardly large enough for them to move, let alone sleep comfortably. No beds no padding simply a room with no windows, aside from the one upon the only door. The lot of them were pushed into the room, except for Natalia, who waited beside Golga.

Golga motioned for the guards to watch over the prisoners, and for them to be shown to the bathing pool. Once they had settled in. Golga and Natalia leaving brought worried mutterings from those inside, but their mutterings soon became not but whispers, as they moved further away from the others. Natalia was worried for those they left behind but put on a neutral face as she continued to follow behind Golga.

Natalia traveled a couple of steps behind Golga timidly. Not understanding if her job was over or if there was still something the imposing figure needed her for. The orc led her to a section of the arena she had yet to see. She deduced from the surroundings, as well as the abundance of guards, that it was the section of the arena for the champions.

Natalia looked around with interest. Wishing she could be seeing her friends looking back at her. *I wish that I could tell them that I am alright, that they don't need to worry about me and that I'll be sure to get as much information as possible and return to them no matter what. This is something only I could do,* thought Natalia. *I will see you all again soon.*

Natalia was lost in thought when Golga stopped causing her to bump into Golga's thigh. She backed away timidly hoping that her lack of attention had not become reason enough for Golga to lash out and punish her.

Golga looked down at Natalia but paid her transgression no heed simply moving away slightly to allow Natalia opportunity to see what lie beyond.

Looking around Natalia understood where they were. At the center of the large, cavernous hall, sit a pit of sand. Within the pit came the sound of wooden sticks slapping against each other. It took Natalia only a couple of seconds for her eyes to adjust. There in the pit were two people striking and sparring against each other. One of them a large orc where the other was an elf. They came together striking, blocking, and dodging each trying their hardest to best the other. The elf was using his speed and agility to his advantage while the orc he faced used his weight and more rigid movements to withstand and bring down heavy strikes.

The quick and precise movements of the elf proved too much however as the orc found the wooden blade placed at his throat in what would have been a fatal strike. Both combatants broke apart placing their wooden blades in a second's hands before facing each other once more placing an open palm over one fist to signal duels end.

Natalia could tell that there was not even an inkling of animosity between the two combatants, which she thought would be present in everyone. However, the match, from what she could garner was more to make themselves feel excitement. They were sparing because it helped them feel alive despite what might have happened in the past or would happen in the future. They were living in the moment and making the most of it they could.

Golga moved them both in beside the pit as two more went down into the pit taking up the wooden swords the seconds held out to them before starting their spar. Golga pushed through the crowd making her way to another who was twice her size and covered in scars and wore a set of armor just slightly too small for his massive frame. *This orc clearly grabbed the armor from a downed opponent,* thought Natalia. *Or maybe his armor that has grown too tight against his muscles?*

The two of them talked for a short time before Natalia was beckoned forward. The gesture and excitement present in Golga's face made Natalia feel like she was being shown off as a shiny new bobble. She moved from foot to foot awkwardly unsure what was going to come next.

"Roccan I've found an interesting one it has obediently followed since getting here as well. I've used her as a translator to the others. I don't think it knows that I've been speaking different languages, and she's translated all of them without effort," stated the orc she'd been following.

"How interesting. Do you understand this language," beckoned the largest, and hairiest goblinoid Natalia had ever seen.

At first Natalia was confused by the differing inflections and certain words which the change in the guttural language put infuses on but quickly grasped the linguistic differences before shakily replying to his words.

"Yes... I understand, although it differs from the other language's I've heard before it has many similarities."

"You've found an interesting one this time Golga, did she come in with the newest acquisitions," asked the massive hulking figure.

"Yes, of all it was Grom and Bogger who brought her in. I gave them what they've been wanting positions in the arena. This one will be useful for our purposes. This one will make communication easier."

"You always find something new and exciting to do, but mind that she doesn't get herself or you killed. She might have been able to tell the difference in language but, she must also be able to differentiate based on species too. You know what happened to the last one when it misspoke," said Roccan.

"Yes, I'll make sure that she learns properly. The gnome didn't work out, but something tells me this one will be different," said Golga. "I'll be sure to teach her properly the differences. It seems all who are not of our kind think all taller than hob to be orc."

"Good now I must get back to the champions, the first battles will begin once the main forces arrive. I believe that to be in about a week. The giants will help cut a path, but their journey will still be slow with so many."

"They must be prepared for what is coming and be entertaining. Or it will be our heads on the block," said Golga

"The troops demand a show, and we must give them one. For the glory of Grock," said Roccan grinding his teeth and almost snarling as the words left his lips.

Natalia thought the behavior odd but didn't say anything for fear there would be consequences by doing so. However, upon looking at the almost proud expression on Golga's face she thought that the gesture held more significance than she knew.

Maybe I'll uncover the significance of what I just witnessed the more I observe, thought Natalia.

Roccan went back to his tasks not bothering to see them out as Golga started walking away Natalia upon her heels they moved along at a quick enthusiastic clip. Moving back along the same route they'd used to reach the training pit.

"You will be given a special place reserved for our most distinguished captures. You'll be by my side translating to the others. Using your skills in order to convey what I wish conveyed in your silly common tongue for the captured and the respective dialects of those you would refer to as orc's or goblinkin," said Golga opening an iron door and ushering her into it.

Within the small room were a couple of beds. One of the beds was clear and tidy, while the other was covered completely in a smattering of paper and books, strewn out to cover the entire surface.

"You will sleep here. This place was used by the previous person to hold this position. It was a rather pleasant gnome who had a gift for language and was able to translate well, unfortunately she angered a rather ill-tempered ogre, and was dispatched for her transgression. You don't want to make the same mistake," said Golga shaking her head. "Those books were hers. She studied them in order to understand our ways and our languages it helped her to live among us longer than most. Study well or you'll succumb to the same fate."

Golga took Natalia's hand almost tenderly in her own. Reaching into her pocket she produced a special band and placed it around Natalia's wrist. "With this you'll be able to go out of this room whenever you like within the arena. However, going outside of these walls will be impossible for you unless accompanied by me."

"I will make sure to learn my role well," said Natalia using the same dialect. She had heard Roccan and Golga use only a few minutes prior.

"Since you're mine now, I will tell you something important. The beast pens must be cleaned without fail each day," with a nod of her head Golga left Natalia closing the door behind her.

As the door closed all the tension that had been holding her body up suddenly let loose dropping her to the floor where she lay for many minutes trying to recover the strength that she had suddenly lost. Once she had recovered, she pulled herself up using the bed that had books piled upon it for balance and strength.

Unsure of what else to do Natalia started by tidying up the room. The books and manuscripts were not in any real order so to make them easier to look at she group them together by size placing them against the wall on the bed giving her a place to start reading. She was about to grab and start when what Golga said as she was leaving came to mind "The beast pits must be cleaned, every day, without fail."

Natalia moved into the hallway closing the door behind her. "I hope that there are others who've started cleaning. If not, then I have a very long night ahead of me," thought Natalia.

The goblinkin that passed her by paid her no mind, as if she couldn't be any sort of threat in the slightest to them as she walked quickly to the beast quarter. As she rounded the corner to the areas her worst fear was realized as the area had not been disturbed since they'd been there a few hours prior. *Maybe someone will come along and help me with the cleaning process,* thought Natalia but she doubted it even as the thought crossed her mind.

Within the beast pins stood only one other to help her, a goblinoid whose stature and facial features was much the same as those of Golga, and Roccan. "Hello sir bugbear may I know your name," posited Natalia, cautiously in the bugbear dialect.

Ah you were the one translating for Golga earlier. I see she's given you the job. Good it seems that you have gained some knowledge this day in how to differentiate between at least us and the orcs. Such knowledge will be of great import to you here. Oh, right my name, I am Cauron," said the hulking bugbear.

Natalia noted the many scars and cuts that adorned his skin where he'd been either cut or bitten many times. The most egregious of which being a scar that went from his hairline through his right eye and down his check and disappeared into his armored torso. *That wound must have been grievous, I wonder how he received it,* thought Natalia. *I hope it wasn't caused by one of the beasts trapped within this place.*

"I see that you're the only one who has understood that the pens need cleaning or else there will be major consequences. Well shall we get started," asked Cauron.

"Yes, let's get started," said Natalia determined to be done with the dirty work quickly.

Cauron moved to the first set of pens within the large section pulling a leaver attached to a pully netting the beast within. The first set of rooms were wild beast on the smaller side. A couple of larger than average wolves and feral worg. Natalia cleaned up the piles of excrement from each of the pens with a crude shovel and a piece of bent iron.

Once collected the waste was disposed in a dung heap quarantined from the rest of the pens. Each bucket full was added to the pile which grew steadily as each pen was cleaned. Steadily the beasts contained within the pens grew to more ferocious heights and included a set of rather angry bears who gnawed and reached out in vain from the confines of a raised net that held them above the ground while Natalia cleaned. Nearing the end of the network of pens she knew something strange was going on as Cauron simply ushered her inside of the second to last pen without raising the rooms net.

Inside was more like a room similar to those she'd seen the others of her group ushered into. Within the room stood two humanoid species that she'd never seen before. Both covered in fur but clearly of different lineage. The largest of them looked to have the ears and eyes of a bull, whereas the other was more akin to the wolves she had just cleaned up after. *Why have I never heard of such people before, where could they have come from.* Thought Natalia as she retrieved the pail of waste from inside the room.

She tried to talk with them, but they seemed unwilling, or simply could not understand what she was saying to them. "Can you understand me," posited Natalia to each as she diligently worked cleaning up plates of finished food.

"I'll figure out a way to communicate with them, it might just take a little bit of time to do so," said Natalia under her breath as she finished and closed the door behind her.

Cauron looked quite impressed that he heard so little out of her as she came through the door. "Most who've seen those two recoil in fear. Yet you do not hold such ideas. Golga has certainly found someone interesting," finished Cauron.

Cauron quickly ushered her forward to the very last and largest room and door that were present inside the beast quarter. He looked at her apprehensively before ushering her inside the room and closing the door tightly behind her silently and without a word but a simple gesture warning her to proceed silently within. *It seems the stealth skills I learned stealing from the treasure vault are going to come in handy yet again,* thought Natalia wish a silent sigh.

She moved into the room quietly looking around the dark room as she searched for the waste that needed to be disposed of. Natalia stopped suddenly as a gust came pushing through her hair. As her eyes adjusted to the dimly lit room she saw where the breath came from. "Drogen," she spouted without thinking and was greeted by a set of large green eyes, the pupils of the creature's eyes deep black slits. "I-I-I am sorry to disturb your rest, but you looked like someone I know."

The creature looked almost startled at Natalia's comment and raised its head following her as she moved through the room. "I'm here to clean up, is there anything you would like for me to get rid of," posited Natalia to the creature. *Why am I trying to talk there's no guarantee that it can communicate with me, or even wishes to do so,* thought Natalia trying to diffuse the anxiety building up in her stomach.

Natalia looked at the creature with sympathy knowing that it was far more trapped than she was. "I wish I could do something to help you and everyone, maybe if Drogen was here he could do something more," she said depositing its waste into a bucket before heading for the door. "Maybe the next time we meet you will feel comfortable enough to talk to me, if you can." said Natalia. As she moved to the door a breeze blew through her hair whipping it around her face. "I'll take that as a maybe."

Pulling the door closed Natalia let out a breath she didn't know she'd been holding in. Cauron watched her with interest as she moved the waste into the waste closet before returning to Cauron. "Is the one in here the last," posited Natalia.

"Yes, the work is done you may leave to your quarters," said Cauron. As he said that she could leave he looked at her as though he were impressed. At least it looked to her to be so, but only for a split second, before the more reserved and demure expression returned to his face.

"Is there a place where I can clean up after getting rid of the waste," questioned Natalia.

"Ah yes, it seems you came here before being taken to the baths. Near to the kitchens there's a place where you might clean yourself up, just look for guards standing in front of a door. Be careful how long you spend. Its nearly time for the champions to be done sparing." Again showing a slight hint of concern before wiping the expression from his visage as though it never was.

"Thank you," said Natalia nodding to him in acquiescence as she moved through the dungeon door closing it lightly behind her.

Let us see what I can do in these dark corners, Natalia hugged her wings around her torso blocking out the light around her and becoming one with the shadows. Everyone she saw walked by her as if she wasn't there at all. Even their infra-vision eyes unable to see her in the darkness. Keeping herself hidden the entire way to where she could wash the stink from her hands and body.

Looking around she found a side door that the earlier tour of the grounds had only alluded to two orcs standing guard outside. She walked out of the shadows furling her wings behind her and into view of the orcs who were more than a little surprised by her sudden appearance before them.

"Is this bath," questioned Natalia using the same dialect that Grom used.

"Yes bath," said the guard.

Natalia walked past the guards and through the archway. *It seems I can get around rather well with my skills, even with people around. With more people it could be harder for me to hide, or it could prove to be a great asset.*

The room itself had been formed into a large bath that many people were already soaking in. The freshest water being closer to the front of the room while the dirt and grime filled part lay closest to the entrance. Water flowed in and out in the same fashion. The filthy water disappeared under the floor, where it would wind up Natalia could only guess.

Looking through all the people present she noticed that there were no divisions between the men and women within the room and everyone simply co-mingled as they pleased. A group of orcs had grabbed a couple of female elves and were touching them in ways the elves clearly didn't like. But were too scared to speak any objection. The fear of being killed for doing so clearly present in the looks they shot back to the others within the pool.

Natalia stripped herself realizing quickly that privacy was something she was lucky to have any of within the arena. She was nervous being naked in front of so many but none of them paid any attention to her, any more than they did to each other. Still, she kept her wings closed around her until she dropped into the murky water. Not wanting to stay any longer than necessary she scrubbed herself, as clean as she could in the dirty water.

As she was about to get out of the bath one of the orcs noticed her and motioned for her to come over to him. Natalia's heart sank to her toes at the gesture hoping that the orc had meant someone, anyone else, but her hopes were dashed quickly as she pointed to herself and received a deep nod. Knowing that disobeying the orc might prove detrimental to her health she waded through the water timidly hoping that something anything would happen to divert his attention from her.

As she neared the orc the sound of many footsteps whoops and hollers came flooding into the room the first of the group who came in cannon balling, fully clothed, into the pool covering everyone and everything in greasy dirty water.

Taking advantage of the distraction caused by the new entrants Natalia quickly left the baths collecting her clothes and escaping out the door her wings covering her naked body as she melted into the shadows on the other side the two guards fully distracted by the champions and their rambunctious behavior not even noticing her leave and melt into the shadows.

Chapter Ten

Drogen had been within the cages of the goblinkin army for nearly a week, ever moving forward to a destination that seemed never to come. During that time, He had taken only short respites choosing instead to maintain his conscious state in order to figure out exactly where they were in correlation to where they'd started. It had been only an hour since the caravan had started moving once again but his nose picked up the scent of an ocean breeze wafting through the trees and to the cage in which he continued to feign sleep alongside his wyvern companion.

Along the journey as had happened before, more prisoners and cages were added in along the way and none of the goblinkin paid him any heed after the first day of his self-imprisonment.

Drogen felt many of the prisoners beginning to stir around him and knew it wouldn't be long before the rest would be waking wondering if their journey would continue for yet another day, or if their destination would finally be revealed. He could tell from there heartbeats they were both anxious and curious as to the army's final destination.

Those around him looked worse for wear having been given only what the goblinkin did not eat or drink, which was little to nothing to be shared between all the overflowing cages. Furthermore, many chose to feed the hungry predators instead of themselves. Some had been successful while others had become food for the many predators to eat upon. A fact that often garnered more than a few laughs from the goblinkin who seemingly enjoyed the spectacle whenever it took place.

I wish I could help everyone here to escape, or at least to give them water that is not tainted to the point of being nearly undrinkable except by those desperate enough to need the water to live. There are far too many of them around and they have taken guarding those imprisoned much more rigidly than before Deus and his party raided the caravan. I cannot do anything to garner attention to myself. Unwanted attention could make finding Natalia even harder, and it would ultimately put everyone here, even more mortal danger than they are right now. Though it pains me to do so I must bide my time Natalia and I can figure out how to help as many people as we can once we're together, thought Drogen although it weighed heavily on his mind that some, if not all the people that surrounded him would likely die, by disease or by their captors themselves.

Each time a new legion of goblinkin joined ranks with the others Drogen listened intently for Natalia's heartbeat with each new addition to the caravan. Her heartbeat, voice, a whisper anything that could impart to him that she was still alive and well. That he had not come so far in vain. Any sign that he wasn't too late to help his friend.

The trees ahead of them began to thin out and the giants, without anything else to do were tasked with carrying the wheeled cages of prisoners upon their backs making their travel, although still slow, significantly faster.

The ocean breeze became much more noticeable as the giants drew closer to their destination, although not even Drogen could see through the hulking behemoths that carried them forward. Not until they reached the start of a downed wall did Drogen fully understand where they were.

I recognize these walls. Only a few months' time has passed since I defended them as the zephyrians escaped from the army who knocked upon their door. These are the walls of Zephyr," thought Drogen.

The Giants sat the prison wagons down on the ground throwing the ropes they had used to hoist them off as soon as the wagons touched ground. Their jobs complete they wandered into the city itself not paying heed to any of the structures in their way.

It appears that the city has suffered more than its share of collapse since last I was here, thought Drogen as one of the giant's hips toppled a structure to the ground as it was forging its own path. *It appears that the Orcs treat their conquests without the respect it truly deserves. I only wonder, is this simply the nature of the goblinkin or is this a byproduct of their own deity's ambition. I suppose time could provide a truth that my eyes, at this juncture, do not see.*

It wasn't long before the many cages that housed the captured were opened and the people within were prodded out forcibly at spear and crossbow point. Any who resisted were simply killed in the cages and left to bleed out within. Such was the fate of those too injured to stand, and the sick who didn't move fast enough for their captors liking. Another couple prisoners broke away looking to make a daring escape into a downed structure, but they too were felled. Crossbow bolts rained down upon those swiftly fleeing forms dropping them to the ground where they writhed in agony. The orcs cheered at their anguished cries letting them succumb to their wounds as an example to all the others around them.

After witnessing the cruelty of the orcs yet again and the way they just left the ones who tried and failed to flee to die, nobody else resisted the poking and prodding as they were forced forward to the center of the city where one towering presence stood out among the rubble that surrounded it. The coliseum.

The coliseum had to have been formed by the hands of the very giants that had brought them to Zephyria for they too could walk into the massive structure. It had been formed from the ground itself with some of the existing buildings added in for structure and dwellings within.

Outside of the coliseum stood many thousands of structures ranging from makeshift tents to rain covers formed out of collapsed or collapsing buildings. The structures made up what Drogen could only conclude to be over a million goblinkin their ranks soon to grow far more with the addition of the caravan's forces.

Each prisoner was chained to another in line and separated into two separate groups before they reached the massive portcullis of the coliseum. Those with good muscle mass, or fit in some way, were separated further from those that looked near death, and taken in opposite directions once within the coliseum proper.

As Drogen walked with those he was tied to a group of chained goblinkin came up beside them following the same path. Some of them looked to be confident, as though they knew what was coming and that they could overcome it, whereas others looked to know what was coming and wishing they were anywhere else. They dragged some of their own kin behind them who were either dead or bleeding out from fresh wounds waiting for death to release them from their suffering.

There groups moved to a makeshift barracks area where captured and imprisoned would ultimately sleep and live while not fighting in the arena where the largest orc he'd ever seen took tally of them all before speaking in the common tongue.

"I am Roccan and this," he said pointing to the room around them. "Is your new home. You will all be living here until such time as you die or distinguish yourselves from the rest within the arena. Those who find themselves at the top will ultimately be allowed to go to the champions quarter there you will be assisted by another of the prisoners within these halls. The only way to survive here is through strength and determination. Ultimately you all will die. The question is will you die on your feet or on your knees. That choice is yours to make.

"Until the first round within the arena you will all be living in tight quarters within a select set of rooms. You will have some freedom of movement but should any of you try to escape you'll find a weapon dispatching you before you ever have a chance. All of those within these walls are viewed more favorably with each battle fought and won, running will reward you nothing but death."

Drogen moved through the area listening intently to the heartbeats around him hoping to hear Natalia's specific rhythm, but only in vain. *If only I could find her and we could get out of here and to Moonclave,* thought Drogen looking around the crowded room.

"Now we will test your combat skills to see who will stand out among each of you. I suggest going all out because holding back in any way within the arena will also mean death. The question is do you wish to die uselessly, or will you channel your rage in order to live one more day," said Roccan as he began handing out extremely dull swords to each of them.

This one seems different than those I've met before in more than just his larger stature. I don't think him to be an orc at all. Maybe he is of another species. I doubt he would even have need to fear the likes of an ogre, troll, or any of the other species, aside from the likes of a giant. I wonder if he will differ in other ways, thought Drogen

"Tomorrow will be the first day for each of you in the arena. I just hope that your luck is good, and you needn't face off against impossible odds. Unfortunately, not all will have luck on their side."

Drogen found that the giant orc was looking at those imprisoned with almost kindness as if he wished to help them all in some way, if that was at all possible. *Strange, truly strange, is it possible that there is dissension within their ranks?* Drogen could only ponder the possibility and wonder if there was something that could be done to both garner information that could be useful and help to break up the massive force that could prove detrimental to the other races of Dranier.

"Now it is time to grab a weapon may you find a good one because it will be your only companion within the arena. Grom," said Roccan pointing to one of the many orcs around them.

The orc moved to the corner of the room pulling on an ore cart full of weapons each of which had seen far better days in the past. He pulled the cart up in front of Roccan with a single hand Roccan pushed the ore cart over spilling the contents out on the floor at their feet.

A show of strength to dishearten anyone who even thought about fighting back against him and the rules he sets forth. Interesting, thought Drogen.

Each person grabbed a bladed weapon hesitantly before backing away from the overturned cart. Drogen being the last to do so garnered him a bent useless dagger that couldn't have been used to pick his teeth clean let alone cause a fatal wound. However, to Drogen having such a weapon was of no consequence.

Even though Godslayer; Envoy of Death are unresponsive to my calls to hear their voices they will still come to my hands upon my call. They have not abandoned me completely so there must be something that I'm missing, some reason that they no longer speak to me, but those are questions for a different time, thought Drogen.

Drogen went to the back of the room to observe everyone else within the group, but keeping an attentive eye most upon Roccan who truly intrigued him. In a way Roccan reminded Drogen of his time with the elders, and the methods in which they guided him.

"Form groups of two and get ready to spar those who spar well will find their conditions far better tomorrow than those who are found lacking," said Roccan.

Groups of two fought in the sandy pit until Roccan bid them stop guided them in striking and movement then sending them off to rest before calling up the next group. He worked diligently with each of them, and each would ultimately be better for his teachings. Still, nearly all of them dismissed his teachings, thinking themselves above the likes of him and his teachings from their ultimate dismissal of any and all critique he gave. Although most rejected his teaching's he remained steadfast in doing so.

Drogen found himself moving closer to Roccan, wishing to posit a question but was stopped by his pointed finger. Taking the cue, he moved into the sand pit awaiting his opponent. An orc that had been following Drogen around stepped into the ring a dull short sword in hand.

Roccan raised his hand in the air signaling them both to stand at the ready. And with a drop of his large hand the match began.

Drogen and the orc circled each other, the orc looking for any method or opening in his defense. An opening that Drogen was more than happy to provide acting distracted by all the other things going on in the area and leaving his side wide open to attack, or so thought the over eager orc. The orc sprang forward thrusting his blade out with a triumphant yell.

As the orc closed the distance Drogen did not move he simply brought the folded dagger up catching the orcs blade within the fold and pushed it harmlessly aside. The untrained orc expecting the piercing of flesh with his weapon over sold the thrust drawing himself past Drogen entirely. An advantage Drogen didn't waste as he grabbed the orc by the collar with his left hand throwing him, effortlessly to the floor like a stone.

Roccan came forward stopping the match and checking the fallen orc, "Do you understand your mistake young one," he said picking the orc up from the ground. Still dazed the orc shook its head clearly finding it hard to understand what had gone awry. "You underestimated your opponent and went for an obviously staged opening. You should all take this as a lesson. Whether it be beast or otherwise never underestimate the ability of who you're facing. Doing so is guaranteed to get you killed... quickly."

Drogen moved closer to Roccan dropping his dagger to the ground as he did so to stand in front of him. Roccan looked at Drogen with respect, a respect he knew to be of a martial nature.

"Your features the way you're with everyone here, is interesting. I have fought many orcs and goblins alike but you, you are different, honorable. I must know, from what clan do you hail Roccan," posited Drogen inquisitively.

"You are quite astute, just like a few of the others that have come before. Of course, you are correct I am not an orc, nor a goblin, or hob, no I am what is known as a bugbear. The real question is what you are," questioned Roccan. "You lack the ears of an elf, and your face is far too pure even among that race. No, you yourself are different to the others I have seen as well."

Drogen nodded slowly acknowledging Roccan's comment. "I must warn that you do not want to know the truth as an enemy," whispered Drogen so only Roccan could hear.

"I will keep that in mind," said Roccan as Drogen walked back into the crowd his back to Roccan the entire time his blade remaining in the sand exactly where he dropped it. Roccan motioned for the same orc who had pulled up the cart to pick up the discarded dagger before continuing with the last few sets of matches.

The last few matches continued as the others had, with Roccan giving advise that often fell on deaf ears. Upon the completion of the matches Roccan again spoke to the group. "Tomorrow will test you all. Think about the advice I've given you and try to improve upon yourselves before your battles within the arena begin. The only other help I can provide is to play to the crowd. We see strength as truth above anything else. The crowd can prove to be your saviors or your death sentence, playing to them will allow you to live, even if you will only live one day longer." finished Roccan.

"What are we to do until tomorrow," asked an elven captive.

"You may eat, drink, and sleep until tomorrow comes, because it is coming. So, what you do with your time is up to you. If you wish to practice and improve then do so. If you wish to bathe, there is a bath located by the kitchens, where there is food for you all to eat as well. I will explain more about this place and take you around to the other sections tomorrow, those who survive at least. For all those that will inevitably fall tomorrow, may your deaths be swift yet glorious upon meeting your end."

Only a couple stayed within the dueling pit, but most began wandering off in their own chosen directions there dull and mostly useless weapons with them as well as an escort of heavily armed and armored orcs who followed the groups as they split off in each direction.

Drogen took it upon himself to explore more of the area around hoping that he might be able to hear Natalia's heartbeat if he listened close enough to the world around him. He moved through each area listening intently for her heartbeat sifting through the multitude of beating hearts around him. Many of those within the area were clearly close to death, in one way or another whether it be from injury or sickness.

Luckily, she's not among those within these cesspools of disease. I wonder if there's something I may be able to do for them. If they die of disease or die in the arena, they will all more than likely meet their end.

Does my interference amount for anything in the larger picture if they're simply going to die regardless? If I save them here, they still have a chance at life. 'Tis better to live on your feet than to die on your knees,' thought Drogen remembering Graven's words during one of the many days of training he participated in with the elder Dragons.

Knowing what he must do Drogen worked his way down the hall opening each door to find a massive numbers of dying people. And in each instance, he blew his flame into the murky pools of water within each room turning the once disgustingly dirty water into one of golden radiance that would be sure to cure any and all within the disheveled rooms. *I only hope that I am not too late in healing those within the rooms, and that they help themselves as well as each other. The effect the water will diminish greatly once they dilute it with more of the dirty water and eventually it will fade all together, but I know that I've helped at least a few survive,* thought Drogen. *I only hope tis enough.*

As he left the final room Drogen felt he had accomplished much with his abilities and wished to rid himself of the foul stench that now wafted from his skin, a favor seemingly granted to any who dared to enter the rooms of the dead and dying.

Drogen continued walking through the halls listening and hoping that he would pick up on Natalia's heartbeat if only to know that she was alright. In the distance he made out the sounds of those he'd been brought in with, and the splashing of water. *I suppose the baths are this way then,* thought Drogen. Many guards surrounded the portal to the baths their numbers less than the heartbeats within but still significant enough to kill any and all inside should the need arise.

A split second before stepping into the doorway he heard it, it was distant almost beyond the ability of even his enhanced hearing, but he could hear Natalia's heartbeat, and just as quickly as it came it left. *At least I know she's safe and that coming here was the right thing to do. Tis likely that we will cross paths and when that time comes, we will be able to come up with a plan. For now, tis best to bide time and see what information might come our way that may help us in aiding those who have been put on the wrong side of Grock's machinations.*

Drogen moved quickly through the door to the open baths where he observed for a short time to denote all customs that were being observed within. Seeing that each person was naked, uninhibited in their conversing, and splashing around he did as the others had obviously done stripping and wading into the cold pool of dirty water moving swiftly to the cleaner area of the pool where the fresh water came rushing in. As he drew closer two elves stopping him in his tracks.

"I wouldn't get much closer they are the champions of the arena. Unless you want a fight, you should move to the lower part of the pool," said one elven man. Drogen noted their lithe forms and the almost wispy way they walked even in the pool of water. The characteristics of their races grace on full display even through the murky waters.

"They're the only ones who are allowed to bath in the fresh flowing waters, aside from those with whom they consort themselves," said the other elf. Drogen looked past them and to two massive figures in the distance one with the head and fur of a wolf. The other stood out even more with their blue fur and large horned head and large round eyes.

Drogen looked at them both giving them a slight bow stopping just before his nose touched the water of the pool. "My name is Drogen, thank you for stopping me."

"Just be sure you don't make that mistake in the future," said the first elf as they moved away from him.

Drogen didn't raise from his bow but looked up at the wolf and bull men waiting for them to speak.

The wolf man looked up at the bull and back to Drogen inquisitively seeing his actions as extraordinary. The wolf looked to his companion as if looking for permission to share the information receiving a decisive nod in return. "I am Mai-Coh and this is my companion Chian" The massive Chian with her blue fur stood nearly two heads taller than her companion. Making everyone else in the room seem tiny in comparison.

Mai-Coh looked skeptically at Chian but followed suit. "You should move back to the shallows unless you want to attract more unwanted attention," said Mai-Coh

"Thank you friends, for the chance to converse," said Drogen as he waded back to the shallower end of the massive pool where the scummy filthy water awaited him. "I feel as though I've met you two before, said Drogen as he moved away, "or... maybe it was only a dream."

As Drogen waded back to the filthy waters he noticed others moving away from him quickly fear moving through them as the heartbeats of Mai-Coh and Chian came up behind him their own hearts sinking at the fear present around them as they moved.

"Tis a shame that people often fear that which they do not understand," comforted Drogen with a shake of his head. "I would have you know that you are most welcome to speak with me any time, and I would ask you to pay the others no mind. However, I can tell from your heartbeats that such a thing is unlikely to occur."

"Did you just say our heartbeats," said Mai-Coh skeptically.

"Yes, I did, we all have our secrets to bear until the moment is right, and those things that we must not say with so many prying ears and piercing gazes around," said Drogen drawing a knowing nod from Chian.

"Chian and I though we have enjoyed your company these few minutes need to get back to our cage before the grumpy old caretaker comes looking for us. He seems to be one of the only decent beings in this place," complained Mai-Coh catching himself on the last syllable and pushing his hand in front of his mouth as if he could catch the words before they left.

Drogen pretended not to notice but realized that there were likely others like Roccan. *I wonder how many bugbears there are within the goblinkin ranks, and if all of them are of the same mind as Roccan,* pondered Drogen.

"I too feel as though I've bathed enough in these filthy waters," said Drogen each of them emerging from the pool drying themselves with less than clean rags before dawning there attire once more Chian was the last to emerge turning away from them while drying.

Out in the hallway Drogen began to move off in the direction of the arena fighter's barracks but stopped when he noticed Mai-Coh and Chian heading in the opposite direction. "Do you not participate in the arena as the other's do?"

"Yes, we participate in the arena much the same as those within the baths will. However, we are different from the others our appearance being seen as more beast like has caused many a problem, so we are kept in the beast pits with the captured animals. Luckily our jailor isn't so bad," said Mai-Coh.

"Then tis likely we will meet once again in the arena tomorrow," said Drogen "So I'll bid you good night and hope tis not on opposing sides that we meet." Drogen bowed low to them both before moving off to find a place in which to meditate."

"What is it about him that causes me to talk so freely," said Mai-Coh in disbelief of his own lack of ability to hold his tongue. "It's as if I've known him the entirety of my life yet I've never seen him before. How is that even possible? Do you feel the same way, Chian?"

Chian contemplated for only a few seconds before nodding.

"Maybe this is fate finally catching up to us and giving us our way out of this situation and back on track. To think we made it through that desert only to be captured and imprisoned," grumbled Mai-Coh. "I thought we were destined to die here fighting in the arena, but maybe fate has some other plan for us. We'll know more tomorrow and can draw conclusions from that. For now, let's get back to Cauron, don't need him coming to look for us."

Chapter Eleven

Although they wanted to wake early the next morning the soft bed of the inn didn't wish to release them from there slumber and held them fast for far longer than either of them wished to openly admit. By the time they rose from their beds the sun had nearly reached the pinnacle of its accent.

Seeing Seraphine and Alya come out of their room Phatropa went into the kitchen and grabbed them bowls of oatmeal, honey, fresh fruit, and a pitcher of milk to eat and drink. She set it down on a table in front of them as they rubbed the sleep from their eyes.

"We need to eat fast and get going," said Seraphine with a yawn.

They mixed everything Phatropa had brought them into there oatmeal allowing the sweetness of the fruit to mix with the freshly cooked oats honey and milk. They ate their breakfast quickly but savored every bite they took.

"Lets get going. We still have a distance to travel and we've already overslept," said Seraphine getting up from the table.

"Yeah Rumble is probably going to be extra grumpy when we get back if we take too long," said Alya.

"Yeah it's best we get this done as fast as possible and return to them before they cause trouble," confirmed Seraphine her full belly giving her a renewed sense of purpose.

"I hope we'll be seeing you again soon," came Phatropa's call as they walked back out into the crafter's District.

"At least there's one of your kin that the barrier doesn't seem to be putting down. More of the elves should follow her example," said Alya.

"I couldn't agree more," said Seraphine.

Getting back on track they made for the main road through the crafter's district and further on to the living district. A journey that took them very little time to complete. They reached the edge of Moonclave and everything around them seemed to change. Where the very heart of Moonclave had felt oppressive and nearly lifeless the living district sang in harmony with the world, creatures and the forest alike.

Tree houses and rope bridges connected and formed in the canopies of the trees while the root systems of some of the trees boasted accommodations from small one bedroom houses up to sprawling mansions, which were lain out in, to the untrained eye, a random order.

"Now comes the hard part," said Seraphine.

"Do all of the elves live in the living district? How far back does this part of the forest go," asked Alya in shock at what she was seeing for the first time.

"This is the home of and birthplace of all elven kind. There is a place for every elf within the living district, but not all elves choose to live here. Some choose to live in the city itself where they do what makes them happy despite the barriers influence like Phatropa," said Seraphine.

"I see the barrier still has its effects out here," chuckled Alya. "So why is this the hard part?"

"The elders all have residences on the forest floor, their importance being the most among the elves. And my mother is among the first so she's near the back of the living district. I just hope that she's at home when we get there, and that I remember how to get home after being gone for so long," said Seraphine.

Seraphine started tentatively through the trees taking her time to get her barring's while Alya stuck close to her side. She took them up into the trees through one of the thirteen towers that lead to the many natural rope bridges that flowed through the treetops.

Seraphine led them to the main bridge which was tied into other smaller bridges which led further into the living district. She looked at the vines that made up the natural bridges looking for something, for what Alya could only guess.

"This is the right path," said Seraphine. Heading down the right most bridge.

Alya was skeptical but said nothing choosing to trust her instincts.

They moved through many different interchanges of bridges each time taking time to look at the different options and Seraphine choosing the correct path to follow. Having to stop and look each time slowed their progress considerably.

"We're making good time all things considered," said Seraphine.

"Yeah, if we're actually going the right way that is," said Alya.

"It may have been a while ago, but I can still feel my way home," said Seraphine.

"How many different paths are there through these woods," questioned Alya.

"The number of council members is equal to the number of districts within Moonclave. Each council member takes care of both a district and those under their purview inside the living district. They rule on disputes between couples, divorces, or disputes over problems. Anything viewed as heinous or against the wellbeing of the elves as a whole gets brought before the entire council for ruling," said Seraphine.

"So, anyone who wanted to find where the leaders of the elves are would have a very difficult time finding one let alone a specific one through this mess of natural bridges and swing ways," said Alya. "Wait I thought you said the elders don't convene very often, so what happens to those who are awaiting there judgment?"

"Those who are unfortunate could be jailed for years waiting for the elders to convene. The last time the elders convened, as far as I know, was nearly a decade ago now. It was for the discovery of what the barrier does to us and our wishing to sojourn from Moonclave," said Seraphine.

"I know that the elves take their time in doing things with such long life, but once every decade seems like a long time to go between meetings," said Alya.

"Yet another reason we wished to leave. We had more control over ourselves, and when we could come together to get things accomplished as a community. The council is far too slow moving in far too many ways, and not to mention unreasonable," said Seraphine with a snicker.

Seraphine looked around at yet another intersection when something caught her eye. A large slice in the bark of the massive trees around them distinguishing that tree from all the others around them.

"Now our journey will be swifter," said Seraphine.

"I didn't think you elves liked to cut trees," said Alya.

"We don't but I was far younger, and in a rage when I did this. My mother was not happy with my assault on this tree. I don't even remember what I was mad about. It had something to do with a bad dream, if I remember right. Anyways, I got into a lot of trouble for cutting into its bark, she lectured me for what felt like days. At the end I remember her letting out a deep sigh and looking up at the cuts I had made. She said 'at least some good can come out of your anger Seraphine. With this mark you've made, you will always be able to find your way home.' She did warn me that it would be a far less lenient punishment if I ever did such a thing to a willow," reminisced Seraphine a look of nostalgia gracing her refined features.

They continued their journey at a much faster pace having to traverse using the larger branches of trees far more as the number of bridges decreased greatly the closer, they came to Seraphine's childhood home.

The ground below began to open as the canopy above started showing more of the midafternoon sky. A tree that stood twice as high as those around it came into view shortly after. The massive mansion had been built into the roots of the colossal tree. The top half of the mansion stood out to Alya for it was the same structure as the one they had been forced to abandon within Moongrove.

Seraphine dropped to the forest floor using a hanging vine to slow her decent to the ground bidding Alya to do the same.

Alya seeing no need to slow her fall simply dropped to the forest floor hitting the ground without a sound and walking up beside Seraphine with a smile.

Seraphine winced at Alya's landing knowing that falling from such a distance herself could have broken at least one or both of her ankles if not her legs, though she could make the lowest branches of the trees at a standing jump, falling from that distance would have hurt severely.

"I suppose being feline has its privileges," said Seraphine.

Alya simply purred in response taking Seraphine under the arm before they started walking toward the mansion.

As they approached guards lined up at the front doors pole arms resting at their sides.

"This is quite the fanfare. Especially since we didn't send word ahead," said Alya.

"This isn't for us Alya," said Seraphine in a whisper as they approached the double hung doors.

The first two guards raised and crossed their pole arms in front of themselves barring their way forward. "You are not welcome at this time. The counsel has convened and are not to be disturbed," said the first guard as the second looked on menacingly.

"I am Seraphine her daughter and this is my house." growled Seraphine at the guard giving him a shrinking stare down that made even Alya recoil.

"S-sorry milady w-w-we were told not to let anyone in until the proceedings have concluded," said the first guard as he shrank away.

"What proceedings," said Seraphine not removing the menace from her voice in the slightest.

"The trial concerning Silf's inability to retain control of Moongrove," said the second guard.

"Why do you reference an Elven Queen within her own district by her first name instead of the proper designation," questioned Seraphine a sinking feeling dropping to the pit of her stomach. "She's one of the council."

"The guard visibly swallowed before answering the question. "B-because Silf has lost her status on the counsel and thus her seat. These proceedings are to determine further punishment for her failings within the Moongrove.

Rage filled Seraphine's eyes causing her pupils to dilate. "Let me in or I'll force myself through you all! You won't like the bite of my blade," she said as she unsheathed Truth from the scabbard at her side. The elvish runes upon Truths flat showing them all that she ranked far above them all. If you think the barriers influence is bad just wait till you feel the effect this blade has on you all.

The threat of being cut by the terrifying blade was enough for them to drop their pole arms once more to the ground at their side. "P-Please proceed, Princess Seraphine," said the guard nervously watching them both as they passed by. Seeing her threat didn't fall on deaf ears, she sheathed Truth at her side.

The other side of the door hosted a cacophony of raised and aggravated voices. "They're in the dining room," said Seraphine. "At least we don't have to find the members of the council since they're already here," she said shaking her head. Leading Alya into the kitchen, drawing everyone's gaze, quieted their voices to dead silence.

"Seraphine and Alya greet councilors Silf, Elise, Boramil, Llewellyn, Elmar, and Terill."

"Seraphine, Alya wh-what are you doing here," posited her Queen Mother with concern. "Drogen wouldn't happen to be with you would he," she questioned a clearly hopeful look on her face that fell as Seraphine shook her head. "I suppose it was wishful thinking."

"Drogen, and Natalia of Zephyria are trying to figure out the goblinkin's next move. He sent us here to prepare for his arrival within Moonclave so the Elders will be ready to convene and hear what he has found. Either way, we need to do something to stop Grock before more fall into the goblinkins hands," said Seraphine.

"We can discuss the smelly goblinkin when next the council convenes, for now there are far more pressing matters to attend to," said Terill who sat opposite Silf at the head of the table.

"Then you clearly don't understand what is happening beyond the barrier, or you simply don't want to," said Seraphine.

"Who are you to Speak so flippantly to counselor Terill," said Elise with a frown as she shifted in her seat to the right of Terill.

"It's okay Elise she clearly doesn't look upon the counsel favorably. Yet another demerit for it must be her mother's influence," said Boramil a rather severe elf who chose to take a seat at the center of the table between Terill and Silf.

"It is not my mother's influence, but that which I see happening in front of me that shows the true demerit and overreach of the council," said Seraphine with a withering stare.

"I was told that all matters involving the council were to be conducted within the council tower in Moonclave proper," said Seraphine.

"That may be true, but" came the voice of Llewellyn who sat at Silf's right side.

"There are no buts, councilor Llewellyn. this is the truth known to all the people of Moonclave. How can anyone trust the council when they are unable to follow the rules, they themselves have set," said Seraphine menacingly.

"We are the council, and we make the rules," said Boramil. "We do not answer to you or anyone else. We are trying to determine whether or not to strip Silf of the remainder of her property for her failure to save Moongrove."

"From the sound of it you've stripped my mother of her seat and status, which means that this house will no longer belong to her or I, as her descendant," raged Seraphine.

"Surely losing one province without a massive loss of elven life cannot warrant further punishment than this," said Llewellyn "I don't see why we're coming down so hard on another of the council."

"Silf is no longer of the council," said Terill raging back at the room.

"We need to set an example for those who think leaving Moonclave to be an option. She is of our blood but lost a city to the hands of such lowly beasts as goblinkin. The only thing worse would be defeat at the hands of those grubby little dirt mites," said Boramil.

"And what if their God Grock is the one leading them to our city?"

"You cannot control or know the will of the Gods," said Elmar with a sneer.

"Are we to be subject to their petty squabbles like Zephyria wa...," said Seraphine.

"We follow the word of Gaia if we were in trouble Gaia herself would come to protect us and she is nowhere to be found," said Terill

"The one that I'm coming ahead of has been seen and approved of by Gaia herself. You can ask any of the elves from the Moongrove," said Seraphine anger prevalent in her voice. The weight of truth pushing its power out so the elders could grasp the gravity of her words growing stronger with the help of the barrier.

"We are not in any danger. If the dwarven dust mites can't find us here, then the goblinkin are even less of a threat. We can discuss such matters if the need arises when next the council meets." said Boramil.

"You stubborn fools. You won't do anything until we have an army knocking upon our door," yelled Seraphine.

"That is enough, know your place little elf, Councilor Boramil has spoken," seethed Terill.

Seraphine moved to object, but Alya stopped her with a hand over her mouth knowing full well what her friend's tongue would do to their chances of gathering forces should she continue. "Drogen is counting on us," whispered Alya just loud enough for Seraphine to hear. "Calm yourself," said Alya.

She still made to protest but decided to calm herself instead because Alya was right if she continued forward, especially after Terills dismissal *Things look like they're going to be far more problematic than I thought. It would have been hard even with my mother on the council but now...I knew it was going to be an uphill battle before Drogen arrived, I just hope nothing else makes it harder.*

"Now as for the Moongrove, it too will be returned to the council. Everything remaining within the province is now a part of the council's treasury as well," said Terill. "You have failed in your duties to protect your people and will be stripped of everything. A fitting punishment for your failings. Do you have any objections?.

"I have ruled on the council for over a hundred years why must I be stripped of everything for one failure. I dare say that anyone here, if put in the same position, would have fled the province and escaped back to Moonclave," said Silf tears brimming her eyes.

"I agree," said Llewellyn. If Lyra were here, she would agree as well. We should not be taking Silf off of the council for a single mistake," said Llewellyn.

Seeing an opportunity to help her mother, with Llewellyn's help Seraphine moved toi speak but was interrupted before a single word could escape her lips when a heavy knock came upon the door to the kitchen and a guard, who held a messenger hawk entered. The guard held a scrolled letter in his hand as he approached the council.

Terill popped the wax seal and read the letter silently accompanied by a slight but wicked smile spread across his face, before it was covered over with a look of feigned anger. "You dare to bring dwarves to your own homeland," said Terill looking down at Seraphine as he rose from his chair. "To betray your own people by bringing them here. It should be considered treason. This is a far more pressing matter than some supposed attack by the goblinkin."

"They're the dwarves given charge over Princess Natalia of Zephyria, and I brought them here at Drogen's behest. He had to go and save Natalia from the goblinkin. You think two dwarves are a bigger threat than a thousand goblinkin," questioned Seraphine.

"You've brought our oldest enemy to our doorstep and thus committed treason against the Moonclave. Guards detain Seraphine and Alya for questioning and trial," yelled Boramil.

As the guard came on Seraphine meet his charge blocking his path forward and standing between him and Alya. Knowing her own escape would be impossible she yelled at Alya who she knew could escape capture. "RUN ALYA! Wait for Drogen and tell him what's transpired here."

Alya made to protest but saw no room for debate in Seraphine's voice or the look of fierce defiance that spread across her normally demure countenance. Seeing no way to save Seraphine from capture as more guards came flooding into the house Alya ran for the double hung doors forcing herself through.

The first set of guards that had let them through jumped back in surprise as she came crashing through dropping them back onto their backsides. Causing the row of guards giving Alya all the time she needed transforming into her feline form as she jumped over the sitting guards.

"Capture her quickly," screamed a voice from the other side of the door. But Alya was far faster than the elves could ever manage to be. The elven guards and the entirety of the council came running out as fast as they could manage seeing only a speck of white fur disappearing into the woods.

Alya ran for her life looking for any means of hiding within the woods to where the elves would be unable to find and capture her. Some place that would allow her to watch and wait for Drogen's arrival. She blew through the living district with abandon unsure of her course but needing to get away from any and all pursuers.

Her heartbeat thundered in her head as she slowed down trying to discern her next course of action when the branches of the trees around her began to writhe like snakes gripping her around all four of her legs and torso arresting her completely before she could cry out.

Chapter Twelve

"Its time to rise and face the day,"came Roccan's call. The arena is full and awaiting the arrival of the champions. If you're lucky you too will become a champion, but if you're not then you will know death for those are your only two options moving forward."

Drogen rose from his place of meditation as Roccan's call came billowing through. With Roccan's call came the sinking of all the hearts that surrounded Drogen within the confines of their small stone room. Each of the prisoners got up slowly, clear looks of dread present on all of their faces as they made their way to the door and what many knew would be there last living day.

Roccan came into the room and ushered everyone up and out to the sand pit they had used the night previous for training. Drogen waited for all the others to leave before he rose to his feet and over to the waiting bugbear.

Drogen bowed to Roccan slightly before moving past his hulking figure and into the training room. Roccan looked at Drogen curiously but let him pass unimpeded closing the door behind him once Drogen had moved past.

The room was a mixture of fear, body odor, and uncertainty as Roccan once more stood before them all.

"This next part gives me no pleasure, but it is part of my duties within the arena. You will all be tested today by creature and sword alike. Should you survive and be accepted by the crowd then you will move on to the next. Most if not all of you will die this day, whether it be from bad luck, or the superiority of your opponent. Those who survive this day will be given the rank of champion and may choose from among the cleaners quarter for a companion or concubine. If two champions pick the same concubine then they will fight to the death for their claim," said Roccan looking over the faces of everyone that stand before him and letting out a small but noticeable sigh. I will guide you to the arena door and from there your survival is entirely up to your own abilities.

Roccan turned away from them starting down the long stretch of stone walkway that would lead them to the fight for their lives. They all moved forward guards bringing up the rear of their group making any thought of escape completely disappear.

Roccan continued forward without another word and Drogen could hear many around him preying to deity that he knew would. Or could do nothing to save them from the fate they had been unfortunate enough to receive. They walked as slowly as they could to prolong their lives but were greeted by the tips of blades and spears from behind keeping them moving ever forward to their demise.

Drogen stayed at the back of the group wishing for those in front to receive a better weapon should one be available to them in the hopes that more of them would be able to survive the coming life or death struggle.

I don't need weapons, they are in need of them far more than I am, thought Drogen. *I can only hope that more than I am able to survive past this first day. Although it seems we all may be on borrowed time, especially if there are giants involved in the fighting within the arena.*

Cheers could be heard through the stone walls as they approached the door that signaled the end of their journey. The ravenous cheers for blood brought a chill through each of the prisoners in quick succession.

Drogen looked to the guards that pushed them along and noticed that they all had a feverish, almost frenzied look on their faces as they were undoubtedly looking forward to the spectacle that was about to take place. Then he looked upon the face of Roccan and saw something he truly did not expect a look of sadness as he looked over all of those who stood before him. Clearly and undoubtedly pained by what was about to transpire.

Roccan looked up at Drogen and wiped the look from his face as he moved almost uncomfortably to the portcullis signaling for a couple of orcs to raise the gate that barred them from the arena.

The orcs worked a rope and pulley on both side of the door lifting it up just high enough for them to pass through. The guards behind them pushed them on with the tips of their blades forcing them all through and into what lay beyond.

Cheers sounded all around them as they were pushed through into the wide sandy arena floor. The number of goblinkin and their cheers becoming defining as the last of the prisoners were pushed through.

Drogen paid no attention to the crowd around him only to Roccan who he bowed to once more before the massive door came crashing to the ground and sent sand flying.

Natalia had been among the goblinkin for a week and noticed many things about their ways that differed greatly from what she had previously known to be true. Most of those peculiarities had stemmed from the bugbears she had met within Grammora. They did the jobs they wanted to do. In the case of Roccan, teaching the way of the sword and of the warrior. Cauron wanted nothing more than to tend to the animals in his care, and then there was Golga. The one who wished to maintain things and have everything clean and tidy. They were unlike the orcs who thirsted for war or conquest beyond anything else.

Natalia had grown closest to Golga, followed quickly by Cauron who she helped most nights with the cleaning of the beast hall. Even more surprisingly she had also gotten closer to Bogger and Grom two others who seemingly stood out as different that the others.

Bugbears, orc, hobgoblin, raush, goblin, vaudune, and so many other races that would be considered goblinkin yet they're all completely and totally different from one another," thought Natalia. *And so many differences in dialect.*

Laying on her bed she grabbed another of the books that had been left in the room, well aware that Golga would soon be coming round to rouse her. She had read only a quarter of the books within the room greatly fascinated by the information within pertaining to all their different characteristics and species.

Opening a new book simply titled 'Titan's First or Other,' Natalia noticed something written in a beautiful script on the first page. There were three sets of numbers columned next to each other. Raising Natalia's curiosity and intrigue. She was all set to investigate but heard the distinctive rapping of Golga's fist upon the chambers door.

"Coming," yelled Natalia sliding the book back onto the second bed and covering it with a couple of others before opening the door.

Golga came rushing in excitedly as if she were coming in to see and talk to an old friend. "The arena battles are starting today. We are only an hour away from there start. Its such an exciting time for everyone. Although I don't like that they are using prisoners in such a way at least they get to have some kind of choice in how they will go out," said Golga.

"Does that mean all in the cleaning quarter are to report to the arena," questioned Natalia.

"Yes, once everything starts that is where everyone will be, watching the matches as they unfold and choosing our arena champions from among the prisoners. If you're lucky one of the champions will choose you as there own," said Golga. "It will give you much more livability if that happens although I will still be using your abilities so make sure you keep studying these books as much as possible.

Golga picked up a few of the books on the bed and riffled through them. "The one that will help you out the most moving forward will be this one," said Golga holding up the book 'Titan's First or Other.' "Many fascinating things written about our massive... cousin. Although it is a *short* book, it has valuable information.

"It will be my next book to read then," said Natalia.

"Good. Good. Well then let's get going. I need you to translate for the others in the cleaner's quarters. There will be many tasks that need to be accomplished within the arena and those tasks will need to be done with urgency lest they be taken as a part of the battle," said Golga.

Golga held the door open for Natalia to walk through and closed the door behind them both before they traversed the short distance to the room in which the rest of the cleaners quarter prisoners lay resting.

They passed many a door on their way, which were open and vacant. "I thought they were full of the sick and dying," questioned Natalia.

"They were," said Golga. "Now they're empty."

Natalia's heart sank knowing that the room that had been rather full were now empty meant that they had all finally succumbed to there disease or otherwise. "At least they're no longer suffering," said Natalia visibly saddened.

"No time to worry about that now," said Golga as they moved past the last of the rooms.

As they moved to the end of the cleaners quarters Golga pointed to the two guards that held position outside the room that housed the prisoners. "It is time," said Golga pointing to the door which the guards swiftly opened. On the other side the others who were sleeping soundly jumped as the door slammed against the brick behind its hinged side.

"Time to rise everyone. The arena is open and there is much to do," translated Natalia to the room. Once the battles begin we will be in charge of clearing the bodies from the arena itself. We have only a small amount of time to get the deceased out of the arena. Those left within are guaranteed to die so work diligently and don't dawdle," translated Natalia. "We will make our way to designated areas and await the announcement of the first rounds conclusion. Follow me."

The whole of the group followed quickly behind Golga she would point to an area just large enough to fit a body through as they went and assigned two per area having Natalia reiterate when they needed to move out and get the bodies with each pair.

They kept going until all but Natalia had been assigned an area. "Come with me, we will cover the final area. I must worn you however, that it will most likely be the area with the most bodies to recover," said Golga.

"I will do my best," said Natalia.

"It think that Bogger and Grom were also assigned to that area so they will help with body retrieval as well," said Golga.

"Are they liking their new position within the arena," questioned Natalia.

"Yes they're fitting in quite nicely and I see much potential in them. They seem to be of the same mind as well, although Bogger would probably argue otherwise, his words often do little to match his actions," said Golga with an amused smile which she quickly wiped away. "You need not mind any of that. We need to listen and be ready to do what must be done."

"Right," said Natalia steeling her expression and heart for what she would undoubtedly see upon the commencement of their job. *I'm ready,* thought Natalia. Trying to convince herself although her heart beat, if any could hear it, betrayed the apprehension she dare not show.

The group of them walked out tentatively from beyond the portcullis that slammed to the ground behind them barring any chance of fleeing the mortal peril sure to befall them within the confines of the arena. Seeing a large stack of weapons strewn upon the ground some ran with abandon. The weapons on the ground seemingly far better than those they'd received only a day prior.

Drogen looked around at the number of prisoner's that accompanied him and realized quickly that there were far more among them than he had been roomed with. Nearly thrice as many as he thought had been imprisoned with him previously. Where he thought there only to be 30 at most now stood nearly 100 people of varying shapes and sizes. *And not a single dwarf among them. I wonder how such a possibility can be,* thought Drogen.

As the first in line came into contact with the weapons strewn upon the arena floor the portcullises around them opened up once more and with it a flood of goblins and gnolls. Numbering nearly three to one. The arena erupted in cheers as the first of the goblins was taken down by the deft swing of a surprised elf with a dull short sword.

The sound of the dull blade ripping through the goblins flesh made two others close by loose what little food they had eaten before the battle. Seeing that the battle was upon them others began brandishing the new weapons they had run for and those with previously procured weapons got into defensive stances awaiting the coming onslaught.

Drogen could see that there were many versed in swordsmanship to vastly varying degrees, most however, were holding their weapons in shaky and unsure hands that had clearly never held one before.

It would seem that those taken in by Roccan are far more prepared for the arena than the others. His advice will save many from death this day, thought Drogen.

Drogen moved through the crowd observing those locked in battle and taking in their struggles to hold off the goblinkin surrounding them on all sides. Drogen listened to every heartbeat around him focusing on two that seemed, from his knowledge, out of the ordinary. There were two among the goblins who fought together taking down a couple of gnomes who had failed to mesh their skills well enough together to be an effective team.

Looking at them both with another as reference he saw their eyes turn yellow and housed an intelligence that the others did not posses. The two of them were vicious in their fighting one dropping an enemy low while the other waded in, blade ready to pierce the heart or cut the artery of those that were falling.

These two are the real enemy. The others are cannon fodder comparatively, thought Drogen. *Everyone sees them as nothing but goblins and thus are attacking in error against the goblins and gnolls. I'll take it upon myself to take care of the real threat while everyone else is distracted by the numbers.*

Blood was quickly turning the sand at their feet to a red mush clumping to the bottom of everyone's boots and causing them to become sluggish. An elf, unaware of her surroundings jumped back from a thrust for her foot to slip upon the blood soaked ground dropping her and two others to the ground fully at the mercy of a pack of gnolls that showed they had none with a downward thrust that pierced each in turn through the heart, head, and lungs. The elf who felled the other two being the worst off choking on her own blood as it filled her lungs.

Drogen stood before the two goblins that were not goblins at all his hands bare of any weapon and locked eyes with them each in turn. It was clear from their reaction to jump back and run that their instincts were telling them to run away, though they fought the urge.

With a look at each other and a nod they roared to the sky shredding the clothes that had adorned their small frames as hair sprang forth from every corner of their rapidly changing bodies. They had the fur of a hyena and a body similar to the worgs Drogen had seen the orcs riding. One of the gnolls who witnessed the transformation only had a single word come across his lips before being felled for his lack of awareness. "*Barghest.*"

They stood at double the size of there goblin counterparts and there yellow eyes scanned the scene around them diligently.

Drogen awaited their first move against him as a gnoll, metal spear in hand, came running up from behind in an attempt to skewer him. The gnoll was feld by another combatant before it ever got close throwing its spear as it fell. Hearing the whistle of the weapon as it moved through the air Drogen shifted his balance the spear narrowly missing the small of his neck.

Snatching it out of the air with his left hand Drogen held its tip down toward the ground stepping forward and into a balanced and refined spear stance his hands gripping the haft of the spear as though he had always done so. The audience erupted in cheers all around them but neither Drogen nor the barghest acknowledged their cheers.

The initial shock of their unceremonious start was quickly starting to be overcome. Those who had been taken by surprise were finally starting to turn the tables and the odds that had been stacked against them back around. The defenders started forming groups and protecting each other from the onslaught dropping many more goblins, and gnolls low than they had previously been able to achieve. Still even though the number of goblinkin were dwindling so too were the number of defenders.

The pair of barghest's circled Drogen taking in every inch of him as he stood in the middle of their circle calmly waiting for them to initiate their attack. The other goblinkin, not wanting to be anywhere near them, gave a wide birth forcing everyone out and away from Drogen and the barghest's.

Drogen looked away, pretending to be distracted by the sound of cheers that once more erupted around them. Seeing the opening the barghest at his back charged its jaw wide open as it launched itself high aiming for Drogen's exposed neck. It was met with the butt of Drogen's spear down its throat as he drew back toward his attacker. Feeling the weight of the barghest upon its end and hearing the creature gag upon its haft he turned the spear point down driving it into the sand. Not wanting the barghest to suffer unnecessarily he threw a single punch breaking the spear in half and destroying the head of his attacker in one strike.

Seeing the death of its partner the second barghest came in with haste. Snapping its jaw trying to gain any kind of purchase it could manage from Drogen to no avail. Grabbing the barghest around its head with his hands he grappled the enraged beast to the ground its body followed its head to the ground and Drogen with a single stomp stopped its struggle forever crushing the ribs around its heart.

With the barghest's dealt with, Drogen looked around to see how many remained. They had broken off into smaller groups allowing them to attack and defend far more effectively. Still their numbers had dwindled greatly. Where there had been nearly a hundred to start only 40 remained. Blood, sinew, steel, bones, and broken bodies littered the sand and with each death came more cheers for those who remained.

As the last gnoll fell to the floor the cheers around them became deafening. Having won victory over the day, those remaining, raised their hands and weapons in triumph garnering even more robust cheers from their adoring audience.

Drogen looked around at the meaningless loss of life and could do nothing but frown. All the body's commingled together as a cesspool of blood turning the ground to a black ichor causing his stomach to turn sadly as he took in all the destruction.

So many dead in order to provide entertainment, thought Drogen as he shook his head. *Is this the entirety of the existence Grock wishes for. I cannot see it as anything more than a waste.*

The portcullises opened up once more around them bringing with it Roccan and two others. Roccan locked eyes with Drogen as if he was searching for him in the crowd. Roccan dropped his head in an almost imperceptible movement as though he was acknowledging Drogen.

Drogen walked past Roccan's large bugbear form and into the area beyond the portcullis as the cleaners hold began filtering out onto the battlefield to start their duties. He stopped only for a second as Natalia's heartbeat came into focus. He wanted nothing more than to go to her side but thought better of it. *If what I suspect is true, we will be seeing each other soon enough. If they know we are acquainted too soon it could pose more danger to her wellbeing.*

Natalia knew from the sound of Golga's exhale that things were going to be far more arduous on them all than previously thought.

"Grom and Bogger gather the rest of the guards and carts there are far more bodies than we were told there would be," barked Golga clear anger in her voice at the sight that lay before her.

Natalia didn't know what she was about to witness but knew it would undoubtedly change her, as she saw the change that came over Golga at the sight that lay before her.

"Such senselessness against those that should be treated as kin," said Golga under her breath as she shook her fur covered head. "Be strong young one for this is a sight that I would not wish upon any," she said clear sadness present in her massive brown eyes.

Grom and Bogger came back with a large group of orc guards following laden with heavy wheeled carts to transport the dead. "All of you spread out and assist the people of the cleaning quarters lest we take too long and become a part of the festivities ourselves. We only have until the sun reaches its peak to clear the arena. Move swiftly," barked Golga allowing all but Grom and Bogger to pass.

"Look like we with you again," said Grom with a nod to Natalia.

"Yes, it would seem so," said Natalia speaking in Grom's natural dialect.

"Enough talking let's get to work," said Bogger pushing past them and through the smaller portcullis from which the cleaners garnered access to the field beyond.

Natalia nearly threw up the moment she lay eyes upon the scene. Everything she saw was covered in a soupy mix of blood, urine, and feces of those who had died. She looked over the bodies of them all seeing elves, gnomes, goblins, hobgoblins, and zephyrians collapsed upon each other in a slaughter she had not thought possible. The smell of the battlefield brought her another bought of near sickness, but she resisted the urge to puke that welled up from the depths of her soul.

I made a terrible mistake in coming here. I thought, maybe just maybe I could stop my sleepless nights and the nightmares that haunt me from my own torture at the hands of Nefar and Bernadine, but this...this does not bode well. How could I think that there was a way out of here. How could I be so naive to think that I was safe. What have I done, thought Natalia.

Natalia began loading the cart pushed up beside her by Bogger, who took hold of the corpse's feet helping to lift the body of a hacked goblin into the cart. The look of those around her was dour and nobody dared speak the feelings of fear and hopelessness that move over them all as they worked to clear the corpses.

Not even Golga was immune to the weight that burdened their hearts as they cleared corpse after corpse without rest until they had retrieved the last corpse. Having worked diligently to remove the bodies the cleanup was done just before the sun had reached its highest point over the arena.

"It looks like the next round of battle will begin shortly," said Golga as they returned through the portcullis from whence they came. Both mentally and physically exhausted by the sheer number of corpses, and the truth of their own mortality.

"How many rounds will there be today," questioned Natalia.

"Today there will be two, the ones who are left will be viewed as champions and be gathered with the previous champions, they will choose from among the cleaners hold to be their personal property or concubines, for as long as they live," said Golga no emotion no change to her demeanor simply stating a point. The strain of the job they had just, and would have to continue, performing taking its toll on her as well.

Chapter Thirteen

With Death, set upon Lisana's back, they set down on the summit of Zephyria and took in their surroundings. Death was quick to dismount as Lisana shifted to her smaller form. From a fold in his cloak Death produced Lisana's extra-dimensional bag.

Lisana kissed Death on the cheek pulling out and donning red leather armor and breaches, the same color as her scales. After getting dressed she pulled a water skin from her bag pouring water over her exposed scales which growing the skin back.

"Tis good that some magics still work in this world," said Death.

"Yes, tis good, but maybe if we had not sealed the majority of it when we did. Seraphal would still be here and the zephyrians would have been repelled instead," said Lisana with a deep melancholy in her voice. "Coming back here after such tragedy feels like a nightmare. I know that none of them survived but still I hope, beyond hope that I will see her black wings and beautiful face looking back at me as we enter the castle. Stacks of books around her with her nose stuffed into a book, as it had always been."

"We cannot make up for tragedies of the past that is what makes them the past. All there is to do is to look to the future and make sure that such a tragedy does not manifest itself again. Drogen has befriended one of the zephyrian people so I believe them to have changed from how they once were, and they will have changed further with the demise of Ether and Uther."

"Yet another thing that has me nervous," said Lisana in a rare show of vulnerability. "Will he be able to forgive me for leaving him in Lundwurm Tul as I did those many years ago?"

"Even if he doesn't at the start, he will in time Lisana. He had the Lundwurm Tul itself to raise him in our absence, he's the result of all those experiences. Furthermore, he knows you didn't abandon him, you went out in search of me," said Death.

"I fear I'm the one who should be most worried for I neither knew I had a son, nor that I had missed the entirety of his life. If he has any issues of abandonment, they'll likely be pushed upon me. I wasn't there at all," said Death dropping a few more of the mental barriers. He had placed in order to guard himself during his years of torture and isolation from both Lisana and the outside world.

Of the countless tortures I've experienced across the boundless eternities of life, this was by far the hardest. Love awaited me outside of my cell. That knowledge hurt far more than any torture Lucian or any of those under his command could ever suffer upon me. It was truly torturous, but that love that I knew to be waiting for me also provided something I never had before, hope, thought Death as he stared into Lisana's beautiful calculating eyes.

Lisana was still troubled not knowing how their reunion would turn out springing to the forefront a feeling she'd only ever experienced in such quantity when she was a young hatchling. Fear and anxiety.

This is more nerve wrecking then staring down an army on the battlefield. Although your words do comfort me my love, I still feel guilty having left Drogen in Lundwurm Tul. He has every right to hate me for what I did. Even if it was to find you his father. We've been apart for years without contact. I don't see how he can be fine with how things are, or how I left him. A note and a few trinkets, thought Lisana. *I should have done more, something more to prepare him.* Lisana continued to pondered the many avenues, twists, and turns that might occur upon reuniting with Drogen, most of which became worst case scenarios within her mind.

"Stop my love, your worry does nothing but temper your radiance," said Death as he held Lisana by the back of the neck to bend down and kiss her on the lips. With their embrace, Death felt the tension wash from Lisana. Lisana broke off from him a few seconds later though she wanted nothing more than to lose herself in the passion of the moment and have it wash her worry and stress away, Lisana knew they had wasted enough time journeying and she wanted, more than anything, to see her son again, even if it could only be done from a distance.

Death smiled down upon her and bid her forward so he could gaze upon her fine figure as they walked. "In these many years that we've been separated your beauty has only grown more magnificent."

"Careful honey because my beauty isn't the only improvement," said Lisana with a wink. Sashaying her hips.

"Oh, I've no doubt about that. You were fierce before we met and only proved yourself more so as we grew closer those decades ago. You think Drogen would be interested to learn exactly how we met," questioned Death with a mischievous smile.

Lisana tried to hide her embarrassment remembering the circumstances of their meeting by not giving Death any response but he knew her well, even after being separated for so long. He knew that every time the story was brought up, she would become embarrassed even if she tried to hide it. Knowing that it continued to have the same effect warmed Death's heart as he continued to walk behind her and into Zephyria.

"Quite odd that we've seen no guards," said Lisana.

"It seems they truly have changed. When they destroyed the Angelos they must have also destroyed the battle towers that used to be here," said Death.

"Or they think it useless to guard against a threat when only those with wings might pose any kind of threat," said Lisana.

"I suppose tis lucky for them that magic is sealed, and the daelons cannot excerpt their true existence," said Death

"Don't they know there are other flying races out there. They would foam at the mouth if they knew such a place existed especially so unguarded," said Lisana with a sneer at their utter lack of preparedness.

"You are right but the dragons and zephyrian's are the only ones living in this part of Dranier at the moment, aside from the locked daelons. I doubt they've seen another flying species aside from Drogen, their deity, and themselves," said Death.

"If Drogen even revealed himself to them," said Lisana. "I'm sure that Lundwurm Tul itself told him none knew of our abilities."

Engrossed in their conversation Lisana stepped into the market street of Zephyria where many an eye stopped to stare at them in concern. Their many visages showing them to be fearful, clearly hurt by recent wounds. Lisana knew instantly why they looked so pained and Deaths previous statement came to mind.

They used to be the subjects of the twin Gods Ether and Uther. Tis clear that though the Gods were cruel they too where loved by them. Even if that love wasn't ever repaid in kind, thought Lisana.

"We seek an audience with your ruler, is there someone who can take us to him," questioned Lisana.

One of the zephyrian's, although fearful, pointed out a fist of knights making their way through the markets streets reciting news that boosted the moral of those around them. With her sensitive hearing, she discerned that someone named Fread was being placed upon the throne. All of a sudden the feeling in Zephyria changed and became one of elation as if a massive weight had been lifted by the news.

It would seem that this Fread is much loved by the people of Zephyria. At least we know who we will be meeting. What kind of man so hold the love of his people. Maybe I should test his mettle, thought Lisana with a mischievous smile.

Death looked at the smile that sprung to her lips and tensed up in ways he hadn't done in decades. *I recognize that smile and that look never bodes well for me. Ah but it's always a thrill with her, not knowing what she might do or say when she dons that expression. Oh how I've missed her,* thought Death reverie prevalent in his eyes.

"We seek an audience with this new ruler named Fread," said Lisana to a guard looking quite amused by the two who stood before him. Krail unfurled his wings for a second before turning to the others in his contingent, "Continue to spread the word around so the whole of Zephyria knows, once you're done with the markets go around to each door you find on your way back to the castle. You'll receive further orders once you've returned, so don't dally all day. Many other jobs need accomplishing."

The quartet shouted a resounding, "yes sir commander Krail." Holding a fist to their heart in salute before scrambling through the streets excitingly to inform the other zephyrians of the glorious news of their new Lord Fread.

Satisfied that those under him were going to follow his orders without protest or delay Krail bade Death and Lisana forward. "I'm Krail commander of the zephyrian forces. I work directly under Lord Fread. Why, if you don't mind my asking, do you seek an audience with our new lord. Word could not have traveled outside of Zephyria at this point. My other question is, more pressing; however did you reach this high plateau without wings?"

"We have our ways," said Death with a sidelong glance and mischievous grin directed towards Lisana.

Lisana didn't notice the subtle nod by Death as she tried to gauge the man who walked beside her. With a thought, her eyes changed to slits giving herself more of an imposing and predatory look. She hoped that the change would startle the zephyrian as soon as he glanced over, but it had an entirely different effect than either she or Death anticipated.

As Krail glanced over he noticed the change to Lisana's irises causing him to draw in an excited breath before he could stop himself. "Now I understand why you're here. Fread will want to meet with you as soon as possible," danced Krail excitedly.

Death and Lisana looked at Krail and back to each other in bewilderment not quite sure how to take the giddy nature of the zephyrian commander. "Do you understand what the woman who walks beside us is," posited Death in bewilderment.

"Yes. Yes. I'm quite aware of her heritage as I've met one of her kinsmen. I owe him much for all he's done to protect the people of Zephyria. More accurately, I owe him my life. He did something none of the clerics and clergymen thought possible even with the magic of the Gods flowing through them. He reattached and made useful my wing again," said Krail extending his once disembodied wing out to its fullest in order to show the scar. "If not for Drogen I would no longer know what it means to be one with the sky. Being one with the sky is what it means to be zephyrian."

"That should not be possible, not even with our healing water," whispered Lisana.

Death nodded but said nothing as they walked behind Krail.

"Are you not afraid for the safety of Fread and your King allowing two complete strangers to meet with them," questioned Lisana.

"If you meant to do harm to anyone you would have already acted by now. Also, the last thing someone who wishes to attack the hierarchy through nefarious means does is seek out a group of guards on patrol," stated Krail in a matter of fact tone. "One thing I would like to tell you however, is that our leader does not like the term king he would much rather be seen as a lord of his people instead of a king."

"Tis Lord Fread then, does he wear the same shiny gold armor that you do on the fields of battle," asked Lisana curtly. Seeing the practicality of the design, but not for the shine and radiance produced by the armor, especially in the sun.

"I would hope none of your guards stand behind you with the sun at your back," said Lisana. "I fear they might go blind."

"No, his armor though similar is of a different color entirely compared to the two you've seen. Fread's will be the color of arterial blood, the same as all our previous rulers. Our previous Lord Vladimir had been given the moniker the Crimson King by some dignitaries, which is probably why he preferred Lord over King," said Krail.

There back and forth discussion ended as Krail ushered them up the steps, leading into the audience chamber. The doors were in complete disrepair, half hanging, and the other half, simply gone as if an explosion had claimed the gargantuan door. Noticing their looks of intrigue, Krail just smiled giddily as though joy was the answer to each question they felt needing answered.

Maybe we can infer more from that giddy look than I previously thought, pondered Lisana This was likely caused by *Drogen, and if that is the case then I wonder what he did to cause so much damage. This door was no doubt solid hardwood, not only that, someone reinforced it with tempered mythral bracing.*

Krail only let them gawk for a few moments before he pushed them both through the opening and into the audience chamber where a small band of gnome traders were asking for an escort back to their homes a great distance south of the Moongrove forest and through what they described as goblinkin infested lands.

Fread set upon the Throne of Zephyria with a large man in crimson robes sat beside him listening to the gnomes request intently.

"Many have been taken by orcs and imprisoned. They are all being taken to a place known as Grammora. Although none of us know where this Grammora is located. The orcs seem to be imprisoning any they come across gnomes, elves, and your kin none are safe from imprisonment," said the gnome.

"It seems that more guards are going to be needed, for all merchant caravans moving forward. We will send two fists with you on your journey to make sure you get back to your homes safely. It will take a couple of days to gather the necessary supplies. You will stay in Zephyria as a guest of the nobility, while you wait," said Fread.

Krail moved through the swaths of people working his way up to the thrones disappearing into the throng of guards and guests. He methodically wormed his way up beside Fread on the dais exchanging only a brief few words before Fread bent Vladimir's ear.

Fread dropped down from the dais as Death felt the hairs on the back of his neck stand up telling him that someone was staring at him. Looking around a pair of golden eyes caught his attention. The eyes remained trained on them growing steadily closer and matching Fread's pace.

To have won a God to his side, thought Death with a low whistle, *This one might be even more interesting than previously thought. This soul I recognize them both a goddess of destruction with a zephyrian who has experienced death. Quite interesting indeed.*

"Before we exchange formalities might I interest you in a change of scenery this place is far too crowded and loud," said Fread.

Lisana nodded in agreement bidding Fread and Krail to lead the way.

"Will your other friend be joining us," questioned Death as he pointed out a set of sunflower eyes. Staring daggers in their direction.

"Willow," called Fread in a voice just audible enough to penetrate the last few rows of people.

Willow pushed her way through the crowd carefully so as not to hurt anyone grabbing Fread's hand and taking her place at his side.

All five of them walked with purpose out of the audience hall. Taking a side path alongside the castle walls they came to a large grassy area only broken up by outbuildings set at equal distances for storage.

"This part of the castle is mainly used by servants though there are regular patrols at night, we can talk here without disruption, or unnecessary distraction," Fread bowed gracefully to both Death and Lisana, My name is Fread I am comman... Lord of Zephyria."

"It would seem your new title continues to trip you up Lord Fread," said Krail with a smile. Bringing a wide smile to Willows lips in kind.

Lisana bowed first with a smile directed toward Krail. Lisana Reaper, tis a pleasure to make your acquaintance Lord Fread.

Both straightened up and waited for the others to perform introductions.

"I am Willow." she bowed, "Fread's Beloved." Drawing a sidelong glance, and deep heartfelt smile from Fread.

Death bowed only slightly so as to gauge the reactions of everyone around him. "I'm known and feared by all living things and command the ability to choose for you a life in luxury or anguish based upon your actions in..." Lisana smacked him lightly on the back of the head with her open hand. "Okay, fine I'll cut my fun short. I am Death."

Everyone except Willow and Lisana backed a pace away quickly, drawing a wicked grin from Death.

"Oh, come on why is it you get such a great reaction from people while I get nothing but a giggle and smile," growled Lisana. Her voice far deeper than the others thought her capable of producing. The eyes usually do it. I even scared your sister Gaia. Maybe I'm just losing my touch," pouted Lisana in displeasure.

"You lose your touch. Not in a million years my dearest Lisana," said Death.

"Will you quit it. I'm trying to be threatening over here. You're making it far harder than it should be," chastised Lisana.

"D-d-d-d-Death," stammered Krail at the realization of his previous actions being far too casual came to mind.

"Yes, I am Death. Tis a pleasure to meet you all. Now where might we find our son."

Chapter Fourteen

"It is time for the next round. The sun is at its height in the sky and the corpses from earlier have been cleared by the cleaners," said Roccan.

"How many rounds must we suffer this day," questioned an elf that had a rather severe gash running down his hip that refused to stop bleeding.

"Two, you must survive two rounds this day only then will you be given the title of champion and a member of the cleaners hold as your own," said Roccan.

"We started out with so many, yet... nearly all have been killed this day," came the reply of a gnome who looked to have gotten through the battle relatively unscathed.

"Better to fight an die. Then die without fight," said an orc who had been among the captives.

"Then it seems I will be greeting Death this day," said the voice of an elven female who was loosing far too much blood far too quickly.

Drogen looked at all those within the room and knew that he could do nothing to help them survive their predicament. There was no source of water from which he could craft his draconic elixir. Nor would it prolong their lives in any meaningful way.

The sound of a horn rang through the passageway they stood in announcing that it was time for their return to the arena. They moved as a group, the well off helping the wounded, who found it hard to move back to the arena. Where they all knew they would inevitably breath there last, holding tightly to their weapons as they did so.

Drogen helped two elves who had broken legs by lifting them up so that they could walk even without the use of their opposing broken legs.

"Do you think the council will do anything to save us," questioned one of the elves Drogen carried to the other.

"No the council will do nothing because they cannot see past Moonclave," said the other.

"If I could live I would give them a piece of my mind," said the other elf. Garnering a single nod from the other as they moved once more through the portcullis to what they knew would be there final resting place.

"Thank you for helping us we'll burden you no longer," said the first elf.

"We will die, but I promise we will take more than our fair share before we meet our end," said the second.

Drogen let them down slowly to the ground before turning to face them giving a deep bow of respect to each. "May Death embrace you as family ushering you both to a peaceful afterlife," said Drogen rising from his final bow to the elves.

The portcullis they exited fell to the ground as the last of them moved into the arena. The crowd around them erupted in excitement at their return and the prospect of more bloodshed upon the already soaked ground on which the combatants tread before them.

As the sun reached its most prominent point in the sky above them a second horn blew, and three other portcullises opened around them. Releasing to the arena hobgoblins and worgs, which some of their enemies rode.

Drogen paid close attention to all of the goblinkin and worgs as they gained ground in the arena noticing the difference in size compared to the worgs he had seen ridden by the orcs who attacked Moongrove. Those worgs being ridden differed further from those he had seen previously as well for they were smaller than their brethren but larger than the other worgs that came into the arena.

If these are what worgs are supposed to be... what was the species I saw the orcs ride into Moongrove. These worgs would fit not more than a goblin upon their backs. The larger ones however, remind me of the barghest that I took down earlier. Could they be a crossbreed, thought Drogen.

Drogen wasted no time going into battle against the hobgoblins and worgs aiming for the riders hopes that he could take down the more agile and deadly enemies.

Listening out for those around him he heard as the first of the worgs came into contact with the elves he had personally brought to the arena and couldn't help but smile as they dispatched one after the other piling the bodies of the worgs around them. His smile disappeared as he heard each of them cry out in rage and agony as they became overwhelmed and overrun dying with their weapons in their hands.

Still more of the injured and dying fell to the pack of veracious worgs their sacrifices allowing for those left behind to attack and kill more of the worgs as they were distracted by the easy meal that lay before them.

Some found piercing the hairy hide of the worgs difficult with their dull blades, but they eventually were able to land killing blows that felled the beasts as they continued to chew on the corpses of the deceased.

The hobgoblins, upon their worghest mounts, ran around the arena itself looking for and dispatching all the wounded they could find whether it be worg or prisoner it mattered not to the tips of their long spears. Once the wounded were taken by their weapons they began targeting the weakest of those remaining. Taking down any who showed sign of succumbing to the inevitability of exhaustion.

Matching the trajectory of the nearest rider Drogen moved to intercept them on their path. The hobgoblin rider thrust its rusty blood soaked spear out aiming at Drogen's neck. Drogen paid the spear no head instead going for the mount using a fist to crush the skull of the worghest and sending the hobgoblin flying past to skid its face across the blood soaked ground. The spear landed point first at Drogen's side. Picking up the spear he threw it like a javelin.

The spear flew through the air piercing three worgs through their sides who had teamed up against an elf. Drogen had noticed the elf's struggle against the three beasts having no chance at victory if they had been able to surround her, but unable to escape the murderous hunt she was an unwilling participant in. Seeing her opportunity the elf struck out against the injured worgs crushing their skulls with the small hammer she had procured as a weapon.

Seeing the felling of its brother the worghest fought against the reigns of its hobgoblin rider nearly throwing off the rider as it tried to puncture a clearly tired and unsuspecting gnome through the back. The twist of the worghest threw off the trajectory of the hobgoblins spear driving it wide and causing the hobgoblin to loose its spear in the process as it tried to regain control of its enraged mount.

The elven female Drogen saved took the opportunity the worghest afforded her tackling the hobgoblin to the ground off the back of its mount. The elf brought down its hammer on the hobgoblins back as she worked her way up to its head delivering crushing blows as fast and hard as she could.

The worghest ran full tilt at Drogen shifting its form into something that more resembled an orc, but of a slightly smaller stature. It grabbed up a two handed long sword that had been dropped by a fallen orc defender. The worghest brought its long sword down in an angled swing striking for Drogen's exposed left clavicle.

Drogen squatted down pushing out with his left leg dodging the sword strike completely. But drawing the eyes of the transformed worghest. Using his right foot like a spring Drogen launched up with a solid fist landing a solid hit to the worghests chin rocking its head back over its shoulders producing a loud resounding crack as the creatures spine snapped from the weight of the blow. As the worghest fell the crowd around them cheered in a defining show of support for the defenders.

Only a couple of worgs remained to be dispatched. Drogen took down two more while the others fought and took down the remaining enemies. Where there had been twenty defenders to start the round now stood five able bodied defenders and three heavily injured who had taken a lot of damage from the vicious worg attacks. Blood continued to drain from their injuries as the remainder of those alive came together at the center of the arena.

The remaining defenders brought their weapons and fists up in a show of victory drawing out the exuberant cheers of the crowd around them. Their cheers further propelling out as the portcullises began to open up once more around them. Unsure if what was coming would be friend or enemy the defenders dropped their blades to a ready stance waiting for an attack.

The first to come out was Roccan accompanied by four others. Each had weapons adorning their armored forms and they cast their shadows of superiority over the arena. After the champions came those from the cleaners quarter. Leading the cleaners quarter were Golga and Natalia. Golga ushering Natalia forward quickly so that she could translate to the defenders as Roccan spoke silencing the zealous crowd.

"These are your arena Champions," boomed out Roccan's voice. These new champions will join the champions that you have become most familiar with during these past months. Tomorrow they will fight against harder more vicious foes as your champions. May they show us battles worth remembering for years to come," said Roccan bringing his fist up in the air to garner applause before silencing them once more as his hand dropped. "Grock the God of all our kin will walk among us tomorrow bringing his divinity to this arena and to the champions that have been selected."

The goblinkin around them began to chant at the mention of Grock. "Destroy all weakness, slaughter to prevail," translated Natalia.

With a wave of his massive hand Roccan silenced the crowd once more a look of ire on his face, which he quickly covered up with a smile. "For now we have one thing to give our champions starting with the most distinguished of them all. Their pick from the cleaners quarter," said Roccan pumping his fist in the air to draw the cheers and attention of the crowd.

"Let the selections begin," bellowed Roccan over the crowd.

"First will be Goral our greatest champion and winner of fifteen arena bouts who do you choose," roared Roccan to the crowd more than Goral.

"I choose the elf," came Goral's call as he pointed to an elf that had clearly been trying to shy away and hide during the selection process. Golga moved over to the elf, ushering her forward, and out to stand beside Goral.

"With no challenge we move to the second champion. Gulvon with twelve victories. Who do you choose," came Roccan's guttural call.

"I choose garden sprite," said Gulvon who in turn pointed at a small but lively gnome. The gnome didn't wait for Golga simply accepting her fate and going to Gulvon's side.

"No challenges," called out Roccan. "Alright then on to the next with ten victories Hargo the raske, who do you choose."

"I take Orna as my own," proclaimed Hargo.

"So she shall be," said Roccan in kind.

From among the cleaners came a hobgoblin that looked much the same as Hargo with her hard stone like skin contrasting with the yellow hue of her eyes.

I wonder if raske is a race among the goblinkin, thought Drogen. *So many questions I do not have answers to. Could they also be different than the orcs and goblins that make up the vast majority of Grocks army?*

"It seems that this too will go unchallenged," said Roccan curiously. "Very well then on to the last of our past champions. Champion of eight bouts Girhok."

Natalia froze in place fear clearly gripping her heart as it beat within her chest as she spoke the name during her translations.

"The black wing will be mine," came Girhok's call.

Natalia needn't even turn around to know for whom the orc was referring. She had been dodging him for over a week since being spotted in the baths by him on her first night. And since then he tried many times to entrap her. She had turned into his latest obsession. Her only out and only solace from the orc advances upon her being Golga's influence within the arena and near constant presence.

It seems my luck has finally run out, thought Natalia as a slight tear began to trickle down her eye.

"I challenge," called Drogen. His voice drowned out by thunderous applause as he stepped forward.

"Get back everyone we have a challenge for the black wing," roared Roccan.

Golga hurriedly pulled Natalia and the others in her care away from the arena's center. "It seems that you're quite popular this day," said Golga trying to cheer her up.

"Do you know anything about Girhok's challenger," questioned Natalia. "Or their chances?"

"I'm afraid not they came in with the last group of prisoners. I don't have any idea about them. They're not of my kin nor yours. Not look like elf either. As for chances of victory, I would say low, Girhok may be forth but he better than Goral in fight," said Golga. "Doubt anyone dumb enough to challenge Girhok, that know better."

"I suppose all that's left is to wait and see what fate has in store for me this day," said Natalia.

"If you don't want to watch your fate be decided I can understand. Girhok is not who I would choose to send you with, if I had a choice. Hopefully this challenger can save you from such a fate," said Golga.

"No, I will watch my fate as it unfolds. It does no good to go into the future, blind of your own free will, when knowing the truth can guide you to something brighter," said Natalia.

"As you wish," said Golga as they turned their focus back to the battleground still stained with blood and covered with bodies.

"Destroy all weakness, slaughter to prevail," chanted the crowd fully re-energized by Drogen's declaration of challenge.

Those not within the contest of strength went running from the battle area not wanting to become casualties in the battle about to ensue. Girhok wasted no time taking the weapon from his side to point it out toward Drogen in a low defensive guard. The orc cautiously watching Drogen as they circled each other.

Girhok looked at Drogen for a second before stopping and yelling for Roccan. Roccan came forward throwing a sword down at Drogen's feet for him to pick up.

"It would seem that you are more honorable than most I have come across. Very well I'll use the sword you have provided," *though it is entirely unnecessary,* thought Drogen with a slight bow to his opponent in thanks for the weapon.

The orc came in feigning a strike to Drogen's side before pulling the sword short and stepping back clearly trying to gauge Drogen's competence and ability to read his movements.

Drogen took not a step, nor did he move from the spot on which he stood at Girhok's strike. Standing as still and unmoving as a statue. Drawing a smile to Girhok's lips, in understanding and anticipation.

Girhok moved in snaking his weapon around in strange thrust and jabs trying to throw Drogen off, each strike being met by a parry as Drogen moved back and away from the Orc's tightly controlled and vicious onslaught.

Tis clear that this orc has trained himself diligently in swordsmanship where most of his kin would strike with abandon and improvised movements from unskilled hands. This one has taken the time to master his movements. To master his sword and fight in the most efficient way in order to down his opponent. An accomplishment that truly deserves praise, thought Drogen.

Not wishing to prolong the match any longer than truly necessary Drogen began his attack dropping into a crouch using the tip of his sword to strike at the weak points on the leather armor Girhok wore as protection. With a couple strategic twisting strikes Girhok's armor plating became entirely too lose forcing discard or interference with Girhok's decreasing movement speed.

Drogen allowed Girhok to strike and attack as much as he wanted in order to have Girhok tire himself out. As Girhok came in for a thrust Drogen side stepped it putting his hand on the back of Girhok's sword gripping hands fastening them tightly to his blade rendering him unable to release himself from his hold. With the sword in his other hand Drogen brought the blade up to Girhok's neck a single thrust enough to end the orcs life.

Girhok closed his eyes waiting for Drogen's strike, but it never came. "Roccan," called Drogen.

Hearing his name Roccan walked out once more into the arena appraising the scene.

"I will allow him to live if he concedes to my victory," said Drogen.

Roccan spoke to the orc in their language turning back to Drogen after listening to a series of grunts from Girhok.

"I have lost. It is my time to die. Destroy all weakness, slaughter to prevail. For honor of Grock," recanted Roccan. Clear sadness in his eyes having to translate the words.

"It seems that even a warrior of such caliber cannot see past deity to anything more. Such a pity that indoctrination so takes root in the soul," said Drogen piercing through Girhok's throat pushing the dull blade through his spinal column before releasing his grip from the swords hilt.

Drogen lay Girhok down upon the ground the sword his grave-marker. And the arena erupted in roars of glee and elation as Drogen lay him gently to the blood-soaked dirt.

"Such a senseless death, and for what. Some crusade by a deity that clearly cares not for his own people," spoke Drogen to himself, but Roccan took in each and every word as he spoke. "Peace is a far-off notion for those that cannot think for themselves and have no mind for anything but to foolishly follow based on faith alone. Only death awaits those unable, or unwilling to see a world outside of themselves. They worship without thought of the consequence their actions bring. Not only to those around them but to those whose lives they touch with their own. And the crowd cheers the death of one of their own as though a life lost is nothing more than sport or inconvenience. May you become more than you were in this life should you garner another chance at living through Death," said Drogen rising once more to his feet.

The remaining champions, and those from within the cleaners quarter, who remained to be selected moved forward drawing the eyes of the crowd away from Drogen and Girhok for only a split second, but it was all the time Drogen needed as he sent out a burst of white flame from his mouth turning Girhok's body, bones and all, to ash.

Only one person's eyes never left Drogen witnessing the bright flash of light firsthand, but even Roccan could not fathom what had just transpired. "How... What..."

Drogen paid Roccan no mind nor service of answer for his inquiry simply choosing to take his place once more among the champions.

Roccan looked around for a few seconds before recognition of his surroundings once more graced his visage. "We have a winner in the bout of champions. Those under champions Girhok's care will once more belong solely to the cleaners quarters while the right of challenge gives our newest champion right to the black wing. Come forward black wing and take your place at the victor's side."

Natalia moved in sheepishly. Still unsure if her new patron would be any better than Girhok would have been.

Please be someone I can trust, thought Natalia. Only when she was close to the victor did she look up from the ground. She stopped suddenly not truly believing her eyes blinking in order to combat what clearly had to be a trick of the eyes.

"Drogen," whispered Natalia still not believing the truth of who stood before her.

Drogen look upon his friend, hearing her voice for the first time in weeks, bringing a smile to his face despite how he felt inside.

This is for a purpose. Finding out about Grock's plans for the rest of Dranier will in turn save many more, should they heed my call and take the information in bring them to heart. Although, that does not parlay the feeling of loss that I feel from having to take their lives, and the lives of so very many. At least Natalia is safe, thought Drogen.

Natalia ran to Drogen tears in her eyes seeing his friendly face once more.

“Now if there are no more challengers then we will move onto the next Champion,” yelled Roccan.

Natalia stopped dead in her tracks not realizing that her plight might not actually be over. She looked around at the rest of the Champions a sigh of relief escaping her mouth as none of the others came forward. Seeing no opposition to her advancement Natalia continued quickly to Drogen’s side.

With the death of Girhok, the number of champions decreased to nine. Two within his group of new champions would likely not survive the night with their severe wounds leaving at most seven to fight the trials ahead.

“Asche come forward and choose,” came Roccan’s voice. Pointing to the elf Drogen had helped with a well-placed spear. She chose quickly and without contest.

“Champion Goya come forward and choose.”

Drogen and Natalia waited through the final choices but were far past hearing anything as the crowd cheered with each and new announcement of champion and choice until the last among the cleaners quarters were chosen, and the others followed behind Golga.

“I will go with them and find you after my work is done,” said Natalia seeing Golga and the others going about cleaning the arena of the dead bodies.

Drogen simply nodded his head in acknowledgment as she moved away from his side helping her fellows clear away the arena floor. The crowd continuing their defining cheer as the Champions moved back through the open and waiting portcullises.

Chapter Fifteen

"If you want me to tell you, you need only prove who you are," said Fread feigning confidence.

"And how do you suggest we go about proving ourselves to be who we say," said Lisana in amusement. Relieved to know Drogen made a friend who wouldn't simply trust others at their word. Or give any information over without verifying his safety.

Not that his safety is of any real concern, thought Lisana.

"Drogen told me much about his life in Lundwurm Tul. Up to, and past the point of your... flight," said Fread.

"Good, there is much I wish to know, you will prove to be an invaluable fount of information. I assume the sword you carry upon your hip for more than decoration," poked Lisana licking her lips in anticipation. "Lets see if you know how to use it."

"Krail, you'll be the referee for our bout," said Fread pulling his sword to mid-guard.

Lisana pulled a short sword free from a fold in her leather armor, a fold which housed her extra dimensional bag.

I cannot help but see the similarities between the first time I faced Drogen and now, We even stand upon the same ground, thought Fread as they touched weapons and began to circle in an imaginary ring.

Lisana looked at Fread menacingly trying to throw him off by allowing her eyes to change to those of her inherited power, but no such response came from Fread his heartbeat didn't even fluctuate at the sight of the change.

I continue to glimpse reasons for Drogen's friendship with this one. To have no reaction of fear when facing against an enemy you have no chance of beating is beyond admiration. The zephyrian people have found in him a fine ruler, thought Lisana with a wicked grin. *Let's test to see how long his reign might last.*

She came on in a torrent, her blade seeming to disappear and reappear instantly giving Fread only seconds to react or be hit with her vicious strikes and thrusts. Lisana retreated a few steps before circling again giving Fread a moment of reprieve. Lisana's movements as they circled each other akin to a viper ready to strike and devour its prey.

Fread was astounded by his ability to remain calm given the predicament in which he found himself. He faced off against the terrifyingly fast and deadly woman keeping pace around their imaginary battlefield, he felt not a touch of fear or anxiety. *What could have caused my fears to disappear. My body moved as though adrenaline coursed through my veins but my heart beats slower than when I rest. I've never known this amount of focus before it's as if the world has drifted away leaving only my opponent and I.*

"Will you not ask your questions or are too scared to talk and fight at the same time. I promise I won't leave you incapable of running your country. Even if it has to be from a chair," breathed Lisana tauntingly under hear breath. Trying to illicit a rise from Fread to no avail.

Fread brought the fight to Lisana feigning a thrust which he turned into an upward slash at the last possible moment putting Lisana, for the first time in many years, on the defensive against him. "Lets start out simple what is your sons full name," bellowed Fread as he chopped down from on high barely missing Lisana's neck as she parried the blow harmlessly to the side.

"I cannot answer a question I don't know the answer to," said Lisana as she parried Fread's sidelong cut with the flat of her sword pushing it out and stepping into Fread's territory with a curled fist which he sidestepped following along the path of his parried blade.

"You don't even know Drogen's full name that is a... pitty," taunted Fread

"I left before Drogen had reached that stage of his training, but I gave him two swords and other equipment the day I sojourned from Lundwurm Tul to procure his missing father."

"Exactly the answer I was looking for, what else did you leave for Drogen," questioned Fread as they came together in a sticking parry. Both striking from opposing direction at the same interval. They circled closely for a short time before back-stepping to begin circling once more.

"I left Drogen a letter explaining why I had to leave, hoping that he would understand. In an extra-dimensional bag I left him a back scabbard with two swords forged by my own hands," said Lisana.

Fread nodded his head in acknowledgment to Lisana and how well her story matched up to Drogen's own. Fread went in for a slash at Lisana's side but suddenly went still and unmoving as if he had lost consciousness dropping his sword tip digging into the dirt as his hand lost tension.

Lisana moved in for a strike at Fread's neck but pulled short before making any contact. "I told him of the cowardice I felt leaving him to find the one I loved without saying goodbye," said Lisana her mischievous side falling away as tears welled in her eyes reliving what she'd done all those years prior, and the guilt she'd buried.

Willow moved to Fread quickly as the rest of the tension that had been present within his body loosed itself and he began to fall.

Krail came running to Willow and Fread's side unsure about how to proceed.

Wiping her tearful eyes she looked down upon the concerned Krail and fussing Willow weary of her own outburst of emotion and the scene rapidly unfolding before them. "I didn't touch him with my blade. What caused him to faint," questioned Lisana.

"I fear I know more about whats going on here than anyone else at the moment," said Death.

"What is happening to him," questioned Willow suppressing all emotion within and around herself.

"He will be fine Willow, but his journey will be rather difficult going forward until he truly accepts what he has been through."

"What do you mean," posited the emotionless Willow.

"He has known me, not in this form, but as a soul that could have passed back into the Ether. His soul, although his, fights to embrace me as it has seen beyond itself and its shell," said Death.

"What... What do you mean he died," said Krail.

"Yes Sir Krail Fread died in the Moongrove Drogen brought his soul back to a fully healed body, from what I can see. However, even if the body is healed that does not mean the soul is. Fread has been touched by me and thus his soul has known Death. There are many changes that can come with that. Loss of time, fearlessness, and a wish to be embraced once more are only a few that may present themselves. Tis something that might be tempered, but the likelihood of such things disappearing entirely are... minimal. Although, I have seen the bouts of lifelessness go away entirely in the past," said Death looking down at Fread.

"I take it that Drogen did not know the possible consequences of bringing Fread's soul back," questioned Lisana before releasing a forlorn sigh. "None can know the true depth of consequence without first taking the action. I learned much the same myself here in the past."

"There are consequences in all actions. The question is do such consequences outweigh the benefits. Tis lucky his soul was returned hastily so his mind was not compromised as well," said Death.

"Does he realize that any of this is happening to him," asked Krail.

"No, he doesn't. I noticed it a while ago. That he was losing track of large swaths of time. He confirmed it for me as well. When he said that every time he looks away, the stack of papers that surround him seem to grow," said Willow.

"It will be easier for him to understand and take the steps he needs to take for his new state of being," said Death. "His soul is realigning with his body it will only take a moment more for him to regain consciousness."

"I will tell him about what has happened to him and why. Can you guide him in the ways he might overcome this new state," questioned Willow.

"Yes, I can guide him through what I know of his plight but most if not all of the revelations and discoveries that he will need to go through will be on him to find and figure out. I can do not more than guide him," said Death.

Life returned to Fread's eyes and body as quickly as it had left. He jumped back to his feet and into position holding his hand out as though he still retained his weapon. Fread looked around noticing the lack of weight in his hand before grabbing the hilt of his sword from the ground and pointing it at Lisana once more.

"Fread there are some things that we must discuss," said Willow hollowly. Continuing to restrict all emotion within and around her.

"What could there be to discuss? I 'm in the middle of a bout," said the emotionless Fread.

"You need to stop your manipulations Willow. They do neither of you any good at this juncture," said Death.

Willow let loose her hold and they all breathed in relief having the entirety of their faculties back within their grasp. The sudden onset of emotions brought tears to Lisana's eyes having left her prematurely.

Fread slid his sword away but didn't approach thinking the action unwise with Lisana's outburst of emotion.

"I believe you are who you say," said Fread

Death, floated across the ground as if it were covered in ice, pulled the sword from Lisana's hand and into a deep embrace against his chest. She lay in his embrace for only a moment before clearing her eyes and pushing her love out to arms length.

"I must apologize for being rude, especially to my dear friend's family, but I couldn't have just anyone looking for him know his whereabouts. Drogen has made many enemies after defeating our former Gods Ether and Uther. Even among my people, who he has saved from their hardships, there are dissenters who would wish ill upon him," said Fread

"One can never be too careful when it comes to protecting those closest to them my Lord," said Krail coming up beside his dearest friend.

Fread looked lovingly towards Willow as he reflected upon Krail's words. He smiled upon her with a deep admiration and love that he had never felt previously in his life. It took Krail's touch for him to pull his eyes away from Willow's enchanting golden eyes. Taking the cue Fread moved his gaze to Lisana.

"I hope my questions didn't garner ill will between us. I thought it fitting seeing as I witnessed Drogen use the same method too defeat a God by the name of Gaia in the Moongrove."

"Drogen defeated my sister without being fully awake," questioned Death in surprise.

"Yes. He did, and he did so by speaking truths she refused to see herself. Truths, she said, that even you did not see," said Fread looking up into the eyes of Death.

"Interesting. It seems there are still things, even after living so many life times, that even I can be surprised by," said Death with a chuckle.

"Oh enough of your pondering I'm sure our son will tell you all about it when we find him," said Lisana turning her attention to Fread. "Now where is my son? He's long due an apology, and to meet his father."

"Truthfully we don't know," said Fread shaking his head. "However, I do believe we can find out where he will be. If I can receive Death's help with a rather frustrating translation," said Fread.

"You have my interest, But the goddess by your side should be able to translate any and all languages present upon Dranier, as easily as I can," said Death. "All the Gods, and Goddesses are born with such ability after all."

Willow shrank back at Death's declaration of her being a Goddess not wishing to start a conflict.

"Well speak up little goddess, can you not translate the text," questioned Lisana in a motherly tone.

"N-no I cannot. The text is written differently from anything I've ever seen. It's completely indecipherable to me."

"Where did this text come from," questioned Death his intrigue peaked by Willows inability to translate.

"That's actually the interesting part it came from the bowl formed from Drogen's third scale. The one that prophesies his future. Gaia translated it once saying it was the language of the Gods but it must have changed from then," said Fread

"We had Willow try to translate the text as Gaia did," said Krail.

"But I was incapable of figuring out anything," said Willow a look of defeat written on her face.

"Well then let us see about this translation," said Death. "However, there are other matters that Willow wishes to discuss with you, after which you will likely seek more of my help. So I would ask you leave me to translate while you speak with Willow."

"And what am I supposed to do in the meantime," questioned Lisana sourly. "I need... time."

"I would love to take you into town. From what I understand it has been along time since you have seen Drogen. We can look for a present to commemorate your reunion," said Krail as he hooked his arm into Lisana's. "And I can tell you all about how your son saved us in the battle for Zephyr."

"Don't tell her his full name," said Death a chill flowing out from him as if the world would be cast in never ending darkness. "Lisana must hear it from Drogen and non else."

Lisana scoffed under her breath, "How does he always know?" Lisana moved off with Krail leaving Death with Fread and Willow.

"You have tested Lisana. However, you have yet to test me," said Death

"I knew the moment that I saw you somehow. Although I cannot, for the life of me, figure out why." said Fread. "Plus you came here with a dragon and proclaimed yourself Death. I know one thing about the dragons, and that is, they do not lie."

"Point taken," said Death with an amused grin "now let's say we take a look at this untranslatable text."

Chapter Sixteen

"It seems that luck shines upon you this day champions for Grock has yet to arrive within Grammora. His guard has signaled ahead and they will be here this evening. So you have garnered an extra day of life," said Roccan an almost sarcastic undertone to his speech as he spoke Grock's name.

"What will we be doing until tomorrow then," questioned Asche.

"That is entirely up to you," said Roccan. "However, I would suggest that you train, or at the very least, garner what information you can about the enemies you might be facing in the arena. Cauron may let slip some information if you go in looking to learn more about the creatures that fall under his care."

"What about those we won in the arena," questioned Hargo.

"Yes, those who wish may lay with their concubines or any such activities," said Roccan with a sigh. "You are the arena champions after all. However, I would suggest using the baths first. You reek of death."

"Bad luck ridding smell of victory," said Goral.

"The only one with bad luck is the one who wound up with you," said Gulvon.

"Enough of this. You are free to roam and do what you want till tomorrow," said Roccan. "Be sure you sleep early this night for your first bout will likely be early tomorrow morning."

Drogen left the champions hold quickly in search of Natalia within the cleaners quarters. Some of the cleaners came up to him as he passed but most moved away fearing what could happen if he became impeded in his forward progress.

With his ear attuned to her heartbeat Drogen moved along the halls listening for her distinct tambour. He moved past dozens of guards and prisoners alike as he walked but payed none he passed any more head than a scurrying mouse.

Where are you Natalia, thought Drogen. As the thought left his mind, he heard the first vestiges of her heartbeat coming from the other side of a solid wood door that had been cut and formed to match the opening to the room perfectly.

Found you, thought Drogen as he knocked upon the door.

"Come in," came Natalia's call from the other side of the door. Clear distraction in her voice as she called out.

Drogen opened the door pushing down upon the doors handle and giving a small nudge. The door swung wide freely allowing him his first sight of the room beyond.

Natalia set upon a bed of books riffling through the pages without looking up dark circles present underneath her eyes as she worked through a problem which clearly distracted her,

"It seems you're in the middle of something. It may be best if I come back later," said Drogen.

Natalia looked up from her book and into Drogen's face. Simultaneously, Natalia threw the book she was reading back onto the bed and got up rushing to him.

"I cannot believe it is really you," said Natalia tears growing in her eyes as Drogen embraced her. "I was careless and stupid for what I did to get here. Although, I was right about Grom and Bogger I didn't think that things would become so... Bloody," she confessed the tears streaming in pools down her face.

Drogen wiped her tears away with his fingers bringing her eyes up to look into his own. "I fear that my suggestion of immersion therapy caused you to think in such a way. I am sorry for giving you such a suggestion. I wished above all else that you could have found a better way," said Drogen sadness gripping him fully as he looked into Natalia's eyes.

"I chose this path Drogen. Your words were not what drove me to do this. I wanted to help in any way I possibly could. Coming here was the logical thing to do. But, in doing so I left you all to worry," said Natalia. "I am certain Seraphine is angry with me, for what I did as well. Especially since she told me not to."

"She was far angrier with herself for not bringing you along with her when she went to find the dwarves and Alya," said Drogen

"I will have to apologize to her in some meaningful way once we get out of here with all the information we can," said Natalia drying her eyes once more.

"I think that would be for the best. I can see from the dark circles in and around your eyes that you are not sleeping well," said Drogen.

"You're right. I haven't slept much since leaving with Bogger and Grom from Moongrove. Although I haven't had the dream of Berandine and Nefar's men pulling out my feathers in a while, I fear I've replaced that trauma with what happened yesterday," said Natalia with a shiver.

"I apologize Natalia, for some of that trauma indubitably came from those who fell before me in the arena," said Drogen with a low bow. "Tis a shame that such bloodshed is deemed necessary here."

"Surprisingly, I don't think we are the only ones here who think so," said Natalia with a gleeful expression as she walked back to the book laden bed and picked up the book she had discarded upon seeing Drogen.

"What makes you say that," inquired Drogen walking over and sitting on the empty bed opposite Natalia.

"I was just rechecking my work, but I found something written within this book by my predecessor," said Natalia holding open 'Titan's First or Other' to the first page. Where three scribbled columns of numbers had been written.

"And what do those numbers mean," questioned Drogen.

"They lead to books, or I should say letters within this book," said Natalia positively beaming with excitement. "I thought at first that it pointed to specific words but it actually pointed to the first letter of each word."

"And what does it say," questioned Drogen.

"There are only three words that it makes although I haven't been able to figure out the last word I suspect it is a name. It says bugbear, friend, Carme," said Natalia with a wide grin. "Although the last word is only speculation."

"Did you say Carme," questioned Drogen.

"Yes, I did. Why what do you know," said Natalia.

"It would seem that the gnome I met along the way here knew more about this place than he let on," said Drogen before relaying the events of the gnome and his compatriots daring rescue and escape.

"I'm sorry they made it so hard for you to come after me," pouted Natalia.

"Tis not your fault that your captors bore you here faster than I could come myself. Tis all in the past. Where might we find this Carme," questioned Drogen.

"I'm afraid that is gonna be difficult. I didn't get this position by taking over for her. I got it because there was a vacancy," said Natalia with a grimace.

"Then I suppose we will need to go to those she claimed to be friends. The bugbears," said Drogen

"I think Golga wanted me to find this message and wished for me to come to her once I had been able to decipher its meaning," said Natalia.

"Do you think she will talk to the both of us," asked Drogen.

"No. I think it best I go to her alone. I might be able to get some information out of Cauron as well in the beast hold," said Natalia. "If I can ask the right questions that is. I think wolf and bull, who are being held there might know more than they're letting on as well. If only I could get them to talk to me."

"Mai-Coh, and Chian are their names," said Drogen.

"What... how... I have been trying wince I got here to get them to talk to me," said Natalia.

"Sometimes a bath is all you need in order to relax defenses. That and a lost look doesn't hurt either," smiled Drogen. "You might find them more talkative now you know their names, and saying mine may not hurt either. Mai-Coh seems to talk for the both of them although I do not understand why."

"I will go to Golga first. If nothing comes of it then I will go to Cauron, Mai-Coh, and Chian," said Natalia.

"Then I will go to Roccan and see what information I can derive from him as well," said Drogen.

"Where should we meet when we are done then," questioned Natalia.

"How about we meet in my room in the champions hold. You have been won by my actions in the arena after all," said Drogen drawing blood up to Natalia's face.

"So I was," said Natalia looking away in her embarrassment.

They walked out of the room together Natalia locking it behind them before they moved off in opposite directions knowing that they would be back together soon made Natalia's heart flutter in anticipation and excitement. A fact that didn't go unnoticed to Drogen's attuned ears.

Natalia moved through the cleaners quarters looking out for Golga, or the ever reclusive Cauron.

I did not expect Drogen to be the first one greeting me this morning. It was a pleasant surprise to be sure, but now I wonder what could have happened to Golga this morning. Maybe I should look for Bogger and Grom. They might know where Golga has gone, thought Natalia.

The cleaners quarters were mysteriously silent up until the kitchens came into view. She had only ever gone into the kitchens once with Golga and that had been to prove her translation abilities with the many dialects present with the kitchen staff.

The kitchens were abuzz with work, far more abuzz then Natalia had ever seen it before drawing upon her curiosity. She looked through the doors of the kitchen but stopped in her tracks before ever entering. There on the ground just beyond the entrance lay a massive pile of filthy bloody fabrics the sight of which sent her stomach into knots.

They're using the dead to feed the living, that's why they're having so many fight and die in the arena. To feed their army, thought Natalia tears brimming her eyes as she turned away from the atrocious scene. *We need to get out of here as soon as possible, and save as many as we can.*

I don't see Bogger or Grom anywhere where could they have gone off too. Maybe they're with Golga as well, thought Natalia.

Finding none who she really wanted to see or talk to Natalia decided it was time to see Cauron, Mai-Coh, and Chian hoping they could provide the information she wished to learn.

Entering the beast hold Natalia was again surprised, for Cauron too was missing.

There has to be something to all these disappearances. Can I really trust the bugbears as friends or are they doing something more sinister behind the scenes, thought Natalia. *Do I trust what was written in that book? Have I some how miss translated the note?*

Still pondering upon her own thoughts Natalia opened the door to Mai-Coh and Chian's room hoping for at least one person she wished to talk with would be present.

Mai-Coh was sitting in a chair resting his back against his chair while manipulating something Natalia could not see, in his hands. He looked up, quickly putting the item away as she walked inside. Chian still lay on her bed facing the door with a clenched fist.

"Hello, sorry to disturb you so early in the morning, but I have some things I would like to talk to you about. If you can spare a moment that is," said Natalia.

They looked at her, but still said nothing.

"So that is how it is going to be," smiled Natalia. "Mai-Coh and Chian; Drogen said you might be a little more talkative if I knew your names. And that you had spoken to my closest friend," said Natalia.

Mai-Coh looked at Natalia his eyes squinting as he spoke only one word. "Dreams."

Dream... what could he mean Dream. Is it some kind of code... no... it has to have something to do with Drogen. Drogen; Dream. How are the two... Oh.

"You both dreamed through his eyes as he did through ours. Then we are far more alike then previously thought. I too dreamed through his eyes, until an herbalist stopped those dreams from coming through. I know of only one other that had those dreams and we too are friends her name is Seraphine. Although, in coming here, I feel that friendship may have become strained. It is my hope that I might become friends with you both as well," said Natalia.

Mai-Coh looked over to Chian who nodded in acceptance. "Friends sound good to us. Can not have too many friends. Not here," said Mai-Coh.

"I have also found reason to call the bugbear's friends as well, although I don't know if I trust the source of the information. Can one trust that a dead person is telling the truth," questioned Natalia.

"My people would say, death brings truth to light," said Mai Coh.

Chian sat up on the bed in order to better hear the conversation between the two but did not speak, as Drogen mentioned would happen.

"It would seem that you both believe Carme's words to be true then I will have to trust in her words as you have confirmed them for me. I suppose I should be on my way then as it seems you are both just getting up," said Natalia.

Chian motioned to Mai-Coh with a hand bidding him to go further.

"Some stories are told to shift focus," said Mai-Coh.

"I will keep that in mind. Do you know where our friendly captures might be this morning," questioned Natalia as she opened the door.

"Cauron is not outside," questioned Mai-Coh before shaking his head. "No Cauron is always here. I know not where he may be."

Natalia nodded her head before walking back out through the door and into the beast hold proper. *It seems that their absence was supposed to go unnoticed by everyone for some unknown reason. What could they be doing that has them acting so secretively,* thought Natalia as she began her walk to the champions quarter hoping that Drogen might have been able to find Roccan where she had been unsuccessful.

Going over all the information Mai-Coh and Chian had provided she thought over the many things Golga had said since their initial meeting taking into account Mai-Coh's statement about stories being used to shift focus.

Could my predecessor still be alive and well. And what about all those rooms that had been cleared out. Is there something else going on here that we're not yet seeing, thought Natalia. *I suppose talking to Drogen might help stem some of these uneasy feelings that continue to come over me with the number of questions that continue to grow.*

Working through her musings Natalia walked into the champions quarter to search for Drogen.

He never told me which chamber his room is in, thought Natalia. *Oh well I'm sure I can find someone who will be willing to show me along the way.*

The first sounds that came to her through the hall on the way to the champions hold were those of swords clashing. The sound coming closer with each step she took. As the sand pit came into view, she took note of the two fighters the first was the champion Hargo, who Natalia understood to be raske a race of hobgoblins that had exceptional defensive skin that could take a sharp blade and have little to no damage. Hargo's opponent was Goya a gnome that used his wits more than weapons to remain alive in the arena, and while facing his clearly more skilled opponent in the sand ring.

Off to the side watching the show unfold stood Asche, the elf champion. Natalia recognized for having stood beside Drogen the previous day.

"Can you tell me where Drogen's room is," questioned Natalia as she came up beside Asche. Having heard nothing of Natalia's movements Asche jumped away in fright.

"Oh, sorry I didn't mean to scare you," said Natalia.

"It-its okay." said Asche catching her breath. "You asked about Drogen right? Oh you're the one he fought for against that orc."

"Yes, I am. Where might I find his room," questioned Natalia.

"Go back along the hall to the first door on the left. On the other side of the door, you will find six others. He's the second door on the right," said Asche.

"Thank you," said Natalia.

"You may want to be careful, there's something about him that feels far more dangerous than anyone else here," said Asche.

"Only to those who would view him as an enemy," said Natalia as she walked back down the hallway to find Drogen's room.

Asche looked at Natalia curiously but didn't dwell on it as the sound of steel striking steel stole her focus once more.

Natalia followed Asche's directions coming quickly to his door but couldn't bring herself to knock remembering how she had felt earlier in the morning at Drogen's declaration of winning her from Girhok.

You won me long before the arena Drogen. I will simply have to show you once we are far away from this place, thought Natalia.

With a balled fist she knocked upon the door, which swung wide without her doing anything else.

Whoever made these doors knew what they were doing, thought Natalia.

Drogen sat in the room un-moving his legs crossed and his hands folded in front of him. Thinking something wrong Natalia closed the door swiftly before moving to Drogen's side. She listened to his steady breath taking a steadying one of her own as she sat down beside him waiting for him to stir.

Drogen had looked for Roccan everywhere he could think of within the arena listening intently to all of the heartbeats he could looking for Roccan's but to no avail. Finding the search to be fruitless Drogen returned to his room to await Natalia's arrival.

With everyone else who might disturb him doing whatever they wanted for the day Drogen took the opportunity to meditate falling within himself in hope that he might glean the truth of what had, thus far, eluded him.

As he closed the door behind him, he called in his mind. *Godslayer; Envoy of Death.* As they had every time before, they came to his hands filling them as an extension of himself, but they would not, or could not speak to his mind. Not since his killing of Ether and Uther could he hear their voices within his thoughts. Voices he wished beyond all else would speak to him once more.

He lay his swords upon his leg's hands upon their hilts and the chains that connected them to his soul visible as he fell within himself, they too fell from tangibility.

"*Something has changed, but what could it be. What am I missing. Could the deaths of Ether and Uther have affected me in some other unknown way that I could not foresee. I have far too many questions and no answers to dissuade the feelings of uncertainty that continue to creep into my mind. Tis best I forgo these thoughts for now and focus on what I can figure out and control,* thought Drogen within his mind.

Drogen called forth the white door once more looking at the final lock that stood between him and the rest of himself and pushed its image away fleeing his mind and projecting himself out into his astral body to see what information he might garner from outside himself.

Maybe there are souls that I might be able to commune with in order to garner useful information. Since Roccan is nowhere to be found, thought Drogen.

Drogen moved around the living of the champions quarter looking for the dead in his astral form. Although those around him spoke within his astral form he could not understand a word of what they were saying. As if their voices could not reach his ears and his voice could not reach theirs.

I suppose the first place to look for souls to converse with would be the arena itself. Maybe I will find someone there, thought Drogen.

It took him only a second to cover the distance from his room and into the arena proper he needn't bother with walls or any other mortal constructs within his astral form, so he simply passed right through them.

Within the arena stood hundreds of souls. Souls that refused to move on even though a reaper appeared before them to drag them away from their suffering. Reapers were moving through swaths of souls trying to drag them away, but they could do nothing against the stubbornness of the souls that stood before them. They would not go to Death and pass through him. They could not and would not.

Drogen moved to one of the reapers who looked to hold beauty not unlike the angular featured elves. *Maybe they take pleasing forms to the dead in order to help them come to terms with passing on while their souls are taken to my father,* thought Drogen.

The reaper stood before Drogen ushering him forward with an outstretched hand. One which he would not take either. I have come seeking information regarding Grock and his plans for the army he has amassed here in what used to be Zephyria.

"You are dead what happens from this point on concerns you no longer," said the reaper.

"That is where you're wrong, I'm afraid. I am not dead simply projecting outside my own body," said Drogen. "Now who among the dead here would know what Grock is planning."

"The dead need not concern themselves with the plight of the living," said the reaper. Clearly tired of the back and forth as she reached out grabbing hold of Drogen's hand.

The reaper tried futilely to carry Drogen away, instead she found herself being pulled back to the ground by the un-moving and unwavering astral form of Drogen.

"You will not be taking me, but maybe I can help you take the souls who remain trapped here," said Drogen.

"How is this possible," questioned the Reaper.

"For that answer, you would have to ask my father," said Drogen as he moved past the slack jawed reaper.

Realizing that Drogen was even more unwilling to acknowledge his own demise the reaper simply chose to follow him. For when realization of his predicament set in.

"From whom might I garner the information I am looking for reaper. I'm sure you have someone in mind, that knows something useful," said Drogen.

Looking around the reaper seemingly communicated with the others of her kin through some kind of unseen connection Drogen didn't have access to. "Yes, there is someone that might know the information you seek. Come this way," said the Reaper.

Drogen followed behind the reaper garnering quizzical looks from the others of her kind as he matched her movements and speed.

"This is the one I would suspect you seek. Standing before him was Girhok. The same orc that had refused to concede to him in life. *Maybe death has offered him perspective that he would not afford himself in life.*

"Death does not suite a warrior such as yourself. Although I understand wanting to go out as you did," said Drogen.

"I see you've joined me in this purgatory as well," said Girhok

"No. I'm afraid that I am only visiting," said Drogen with a smile. "Tis nice that in death all is equal and we can converse unimpeded by the confines of language. Although, this is not the way we speak as warriors. We speak through battle. I saw the depth of practice that you bore through and the precision of your strikes as they came in. I only wish your devotion to your God had not outweighed your proclivity for knowledge and combat," said Drogen clear signs of grief weighing upon him.

"I thought Grock would be here to greet me, but all I see are the dead, and those who wish to take them away from this place. I thought I was doing what had to be done, but it turns out all Grock told us we were fighting for was a lie. He was never on our side, and the number of souls that haunt this place prove to further that point. We're nothing but pawns in some larger scheme," said Girhok.

"I would like nothing more than to help end the tormenting reign of Grock for good. Would you be able to help me free your people from his influence," questioned Drogen.

"I know very little about what Grock has planned for the rest of Dranier. All in know is there's to be a meeting of the generals the day Grock arrives. To go over the next stage of his plans," said Girhok.

"Would the bugbears who guided our lives in the arena be attending such a meeting," questioned Drogen.

"Yes, they are the leaders here and the Generals in Grock's army. They would need to be at any and all meetings," said Girhok.

"Thank you Girhok. You have been most helpful. I promise Grock will find his path forward blocked at every turn, until he reaches his end at my hands. Starting tomorrow, when we'll undoubtedly be fighting to death for his pleasure," said Drogen.

"I suppose I have nothing left but to wait and see the start of his demise," said Girhok.

"My only hope is that it is enough to allow all those within this arena to move on knowing that they need not worry for those they have left behind. For now, rest your spirit and know that tomorrow the fun begins," chuckled Drogen.

"What is your name reaper so that I may tell my father of your help," questioned Drogen.

The reaper looked Drogen in the eyes as he spoke. "If it will help you to move on, I'll tell you my name. I am Asmora. Lucky for you I have a name, most of us do not remember, or never had one."

"Tis nice to meet you Asmora. I'll be sure to speak well of you and those under you to my father when next we meet," said Drogen.

"You're dead and it is time for you to recognize it," said an exasperated Asmora. The truth of which was not lost on Drogen, as he knew reapers drew no breath.

With a thought Drogen pulled himself back to his corporeal form regaining all his senses he was drawn wholly to the sensation of Natalia's heartbeat and sleeping form lying next to him. "I apologize for my late return Natalia, but I will allow you to sleep. We can do nothing until Roccan, Cauron, and Golga come back so tis best you get your rest," said Drogen stroking Natalia's abyssal black wings as she slept soundly.

Chapter Seventeen

It was a few hours later that Natalia finally stirred from her slumber in Drogen's chambers. Natalia awoke embarrassed by her own perceived indiscretions. But looking up into Drogen's eyes, as he caressed her wings, calmed Natalia's embarrassment and served to quicken her heartbeat.

"Tis good you've gotten some much deserved rest Natalia," said Drogen. "When you're ready we can go over what we have been able to find out on our respective searches."

"Okay. I want to rest my eyes for a little while longer it's been so long since I have felt safe," said Natalia as she nuzzled herself down into Drogen's lap. Pressing her free wing out into his caressing fingers.

She rested for only a few minutes more, but they were the most peaceful she had experienced since sharing her bed with Seraphine and Drogen after Ether and Uther's demise. *I wish we could stay like this forever,* thought Natalia as she begrudgingly sat up and started clearing the sleep from her eyes.

I could not find Golga or Cauron in either the cleaners quarter or the beast hold. So I could not ask them any questions," said Natalia.

"Twas the same here I'm afraid. Roccan was nowhere to be found since his speech to the champions this morning," said Drogen patting his shoulder which Natalia lay her head against.

"I did have luck with Mai-Coh and Chian however. As you thought Mai-Coh was much more talkative after I learned their names and mentioned yours. Although he started our conversation with a single word it turns out the three, or I should say four, of us have dreams in common," said Natalia.

"And what information did they impart," questioned Drogen.

"They told me that some stories are there to divert attention. Most importantly they confirmed what Carme wrote in the book of titans. That the bugbears are friends. There may be more like the bugbears as well among the goblinkin like Grom and Bogger. The two who brought me here," said Natalia.

"I believe I know where our bugbear friends have disappeared to this day. If Girhok's information is accurate," said Drogen.

"When could you have talked to Girhok, he died in the arena. I doubt you had time to speak with him in depth about anything during your bout," questioned Natalia.

"No, he is quite dead but his soul is stuck within the arena. Reapers are trying to clear the souls of the fallen from the battlefield but have, thus far, been unsuccessful. They are stuck in this place. I hope that disrupting and, if necessary, killing Grock will allow the souls of the dead to move on. So many have died unnecessarily. At least I was able to save some of the sick and dying the day I came here," said Drogen.

"What do you mean you saved the sick and dying," questioned Natalia.

"On the day I came to the arena with, what I assume to be, the bulk of Grocks army there were many rooms filled with the sick and dying on the way to the baths. Within each was a reservoir of water which I blew flame into in order to help those inside," said Drogen.

"I remember those rooms being empty and asking Golga about it. She said that all the sick and dying were there no longer. I thought she meant that they had all succumbed to their wounds or afflictions," said Natalia. *But if that's not the case then where could they have gone,* she thought.

"I believe there are many things going on within the shadows that not but a few are privy to know," said Drogen. "We will have to wait for our bugbear friends to return from their meeting with Grock and the other generals."

"How do you know that they're meeting with Grock," questioned Natalia.

"Girhok told me that the bugbears are within the higher ranks of Grock's army, and that they would have to attend any council that is convened," said Drogen.

"Do you think they will tell us anything about Grock's plans," asked Natalia.

"I believe that we can convince them, although it might take some persuasion on our part, and convincing of course. I believe them to be just as tired of this senseless bloodshed as we are," said Drogen.

Natalia recalled the look that had come over Golga's face as they entered the arena to clean up the bodies. "I think you're right about that as well... and, I suggest you not eat any of the food they serve tonight, or tomorrow," said Natalia as a shiver ran down her spine.

"It has been a few hours since we looked for Golga, Roccan, and Cauron so maybe they've returned to their duties," said Drogen.

"Only one way to find out," said Natalia as she hoped up off the floor and began dusting herself off.

Drogen rose to his feet behind Natalia hugging her from behind. "I hope we can get out of this place as soon as possible, and back to our friends in Moonclave and Zephyria. Maybe we can save a few along the way as well. So that coming here, even if we garner no usable information, will have still been worth it," said Drogen.

Natalia turned around in Drogen's arms kissing him softly on the lips before shrinking away embarrassed by what she thought to be brazen behavior. *Oh how jealous Seraphine will be,* thought Natalia.

Drogen brushed the hair away from Natalia's face bringing her into his embrace kissing her on the lips in kind. "There are many things that need to be taken care of at this juncture, but know that I feel deep affection for you," said Drogen.

Natalia nodded as blood rose to her face, but could not form any words so she simply turned to the door flinging it wide before walking through it.

She need not say a word to Drogen for her heartbeat spoke louder than words ever could.

"There is little time left before the arena tomorrow. It will be best if we find out what we can together," said Natalia.

"I believe that to be the best course of action as well. With any luck tomorrow will be our last day among the goblinkin for a time," said Drogen.

"I wish I could share your optimism," said Natalia.

Drogen followed Natalia to her room where Natalia knew Golga would come for her. He heard Golga's heartbeat coming from the other side of the door and the heartbeats of two other goblinkin coming from further down the corridor, as if they were waiting to descend on the room.

Natalia opened the door to a frantic Golga who she had to force herself past while Drogen came in behind.

"We have to get you out of here. There's no time left tomorrow is the end of everything here and I don't want you to suffer and die here as so many others have before," said Golga clear worry and brimming tears coming to her eyes.

Seeing Drogen for the first time Golga stood up straight hiding her face as she tried desperately to conceal the bubbling emotions.

"You need not worry, Drogen is a friend and possibly the only one who might be able to stand up to Grock," said Natalia.

Golga looked Drogen up and down looking for the reason that the one before her could give the usually timid Natalia so much confidence. "I see not a thing about this one that differs from any that have died here before," said Golga.

"You've never seen one like him before Golga. I can guarantee that. However, there are things we need to know before we can leave. We need to know what Grock is planning and where this massive army is headed," pleaded Natalia. "I know that you're a friend that we can trust Carme made sure to tell me so in the books she left behind."

"It's too dangerous, if I don't get you out of here, you'll be forced into the arena. I don't wish to see you die," cried Golga.

"I will not allow her to die," said Drogen as Natalia finished translating.

"Can we get everyone out, including those within the champion hold without raising suspicion upon you or your kin," questioned Drogen.

"No there were many of Grock's generals that laid eyes upon the champions. If any of them disappear, aside from those who were seen to be beyond saving, then we will be sacrificed to the arena ourselves for lacking in our duties," said Golga.

"It seems logical then that all the champions must be present and accounted for, as well as those that serve them from the cleaners quarter," said Drogen.

"No, only one of each of them will be forced to take part in the arena tomorrow," said Golga.

"So, one champion and one cleaner. I have taken care to remove any who do not need to be here through the underground. I was hoping to have Natalia escape with Carme as well," said Golga.

"I will stay with Drogen," said Natalia.

"It is good to hear that Carme is still alive. Could you tell her that Deus sends his regards for me," said Drogen.

"You can tell her yourself. I don't care if I get sent to the front for doing it, but I am getting you out of here Natalia," said Golga.

Drogen moved up in front of Golga as she lunged for Natalia. His eyes shifting to his birthright in front of her making her recoil back. "You... You are... impossible."

"I assure you I am not, and if you give me a chance I will save as many as I can from Grock and his plans," said Drogen.

"V... Very well," said a shaking Golga. "I will confer with Roccan and Cauron to see if there is anything we can do to help tomorrow in the arena." said Golga.

"Thank you Golga," said Drogen with a bow. "I am glad that Natalia was able to find someone that she can truly call friend."

"Don't let anything happen to her Drogen," said Golga in the common tongue as she opened and walked out the door. "Grom, Bogger we have matters to attend to with Roccan and Cauron lets get a move on," translated Natalia for Drogen.

The two heartbeats Drogen heard from down the hall came running up to Golga. "We be seein ya again," said Grom.

"Yeah, be seein her dead in the arena tomorrow be more accurate. Be a waste it would," said Bogger.

"Thank you for your concern you two but we will be fine. I hope that one day we can meet under better circumstances, but I'm thankful that it was you two who brought me here regardless," said Natalia.

"Ah, ye were a terrible prisoner, wakin Grom an I all hours of the night," said Bogger with a slight smile.

"Why can ya not say what ya actually mean," said Grom.

"Come on you two that's enough. Let's get moving. They need their rest for tomorrow," said Golga.

Grom and Bogger ran after Golga but turned to look back at Natalia and Drogen clearly worried about what was to come for them.

"It seems there are more like the bugbears than we may have previously thought," said Drogen.

"I hope you are right about that," said Natalia.

Chapter Eighteen

Death, Fread, and Willow walked through the castle of Zephyria going deeper into its depth to the library. As they walked in their eyes were forced to adjust to the brightly lit room from the darkness of the passageways leading through the castle.

Inside the room was abuzz with activity many zephyrians silently flapping their wings and running around sporadically with books in their hands delivering them to tables where others of their race sat reading and writing. Even in their haste barely a sound resonated over the rustling of pages.

"I didn't want anyone else to have access to Drogen's bowl, so I had Krail take etchings of the inscriptions. This also allowed more priests and scholars to have access," said Fread. "Gaia, while we were in Moongrove, told Drogen that the inscriptions were in the language of the Gods."

"If that were true then I would have been able to translate it," said Willow

"Let me see one of these etchings," said Death.

"Brena," called Fread as those sitting in the room turned around to look in their direction.

One of the zephyrians, working on a set of etchings, came over to them looking around at each of them with a slight look of disappointment crossing her face as she did so.

"Brena here is Zephyria's librarian and the one overseeing the translation teams," said Fread. "Can you please gather a set of etchings for us. We may have found someone who is able to translate the text," said Fread.

"You're the Lord of this land Fread. You need to start acting like it," said a grumbling Brena. "You need not say please, for you are the one who presides over all of Zephyria."

"I know Brena. However, you have been many things to me over the years, including a teacher and friend. I will not forgo the manners you instilled in me when I was not but a squab even if you're only a few years older than myself. You may see yourself and others as lower than myself through status, but I wouldn't have been able to be as I am now without your help and influence," said Fread.

"Very well Lord Fread," said Brena. "I have an extra etching made from the first half of the bowl that I can give you. For the second half however...I will need Krail's help."

"As you wish Brena. Once Krail gets back from the markets I'll be sure to send him here to help you right away," said Fread with a smile.

Brena backed away while looking each of them up and down once more and smiling. She fluttered her wings propelling herself toward the table she had previously been working at and began moving papers and books around looking through the mess of literature and notes that covered its entire surface.

"It looks as if this may take a while," said Fread with a smile that quickly faded to dower. "I wish to discuss what is happening to me."

"There are many who have gone through what you have in the past the most important part is to have something or someone here with whom to anchor yourself to the here and now," said Death.

"What about all the times when my soul tries to escape my body and I...die," questioned Fread.

"That is less up to you and more up to your soul. From looking at your soul as it sits within you now, it will likely try and escape once more through other means, such as recklessness. Your soul has touched the other side and thus wishes to join the others and escape this mortal coil. Because of this, you will find emotion harder to feel, and that could make you a danger to more than just yourself," said Death.

"Is there a way to know when it is coming on, or a way to prevent it from becoming a larger issue," questioned Willow clearly feeling deep anxiety hearing what Fread is likely to experience.

"There are any number of clues that I have seen over many lifetimes. The biggest issue is that the one experiencing them often has no idea until it is far too late. It has to be someone close who recognizes what is going to happen. As Willow did earlier when you fainted," said Death looking at Fread.

"So, I'm stuck like this till my soul gets its way and returns to you," questioned Fread.

"I didn't say that all hope was lost. No there are a few things that we might do in order to eliminate your souls wish to leave your body. The problem is that all the methods I know are nothing short of cruel. It would be wise to go over your options and make sure that is the right path forward for you," said Death.

"Are there no other options," questioned Fread.

"There are others, but they're unavailable for anyone upon Dranier. If true magic were to be released then your soul could be rebound to your body in a way that would allow you to live without the lifeless times, but nothing can change the other aspects that you and everyone around you will need to get used to," said Death.

"We will have to wait and see what the future hold at this time, it would seem. Something always happens that decides the path that must be taken. It always does," said Fread.

"How can someone release true magic," questioned Willow.

"For the answer to that you would have to ask one who saw it sealed," said Death cryptically. "It would seem that Brena is coming back."

Gripped in her hand was a small roll of parchment which she gave to Fread. "I will have the other etching to you as soon as Krail returns to help me make them," said Brena before walking back to her book and paper littered desk.

"Can no others within this hall help her to procure the rest of the etchings," questioned Death.

"Oh, I'm sure that anyone else here could help her make them, but she has ulterior motives on why she requested Krail," said Willow with a giggle.

Catching on Death chortled slightly. "Well, I suppose a partial translation will have to do then."

Fread walked with the rolled piece of parchment over to one of the only empty spots within the entire library. A small desk with only a few books strewn out upon its surface. Using some of the books set upon the table Fread weighed down the parchment flattening it against the desk's surface.

Death walked over to the parchment and surprise crossed his typically somber visage. "Yes, this is the language of the Gods. Not your Gods, nor those from thousands of worlds before. This is the language of the primordial gods of Dranier," said Death.

"You mean that the gods we know today are not the ones that were here in the beginning," questioned Fread.

"No, they are not. The primordial's were made by Gaia and I, as the gods of Dranier. With our vastness of age and knowledge we thought all worlds needed Gods to bring order to chaos. In our ignorance we brought primordial forces to this world and they in turn bore children. Those and later generations, are those you call gods," said Death a look of sorrow forming a dower cloud around him.

Willow feeling the emotion radiating off of Death moved to internalize it before it got out of hand and affected all around him but death shook off the feeling seconds later becoming enthralled by the text before him.

"Does it say where Drogen is, or what he has planned," questioned Willow.

"It has been many centuries since I have seen let alone read this language. I know it is within me to translate these etchings, but even for me it will take time to do so. I do recognize some of these words for they are similar to many others that came before most languages are after so many lifetimes, the question then becomes meaning for often that is the thing that changes over time. Every word can have its own interpretation and meaning behind it so looking through the words to the context beyond will prove...difficult," said Death.

"We have many here that can help with such things. I will have Krail talk with Brena and the others that are struggling to translate the etchings. They will help in finding any and all meanings," said Fread.

"Good that will be most helpful. There is one word that I am all too familiar with and that stands out among all those I see it is Daelon. Without any other context, there might just be hope for binding your soul yet," grinned Death, staring down at the parchment he furrowed his brow "This is not in the right order. It seems this is actually the middle and not the start or the finish and the writing of the primordial also differs from many in that it is read from right to left and bottom to top." From a fold in deaths cloak he pulled out Reaper of Souls slicing the parchment in twine with the sharp blade before returning it from whence it came. The parchment curled back on itself, but as Death rearranged and stacked the cut etchings above and below each other Willow dropped another set of weights on the table to hold it all down flat. "There now it's in the right order," said Death.

"I still cannot read it, even though it's in the right order. I thought that I could read all the languages of this world," questioned Willow.

"You can read and understand all the languages of this world, with the exception of those that came before your existence. The progenitors are such beings. There are of course exceptions and I believe, being that his bowl is covered in this writing, that Drogen will be an exception to the usual rule. It's possible that the side of his that came from me has been born imperfectly through countless lives and he'll garner the knowledge of those past existences when he finally awakens. Tis possible that he has existed in such a state for as long as Gaia and I have been alive."

"What do you mean born imperfectly," questioned Fread.

"He is what would be considered a universal truth there is life; Gaia, Death; me, and now we know there is a third; Drogen. Although, we don't truly know what universal truth he encompasses with his existence." *I do have a good idea what it is,* thought Death to himself. "It took two powerful bloodlines coming together as one for him to be born into this world with power that will rival Gaia's, and my own. He could have lived countless lives before and been struck down without knowing the truth before now. Being born from the mix of a powerful being such as a primordial, a god, or any number of other deity, and one of a lesser power of soul. It would be like mixing a human and elf together. You get a half elf, which has a longer life span than a human, but less than that of the elf who helped spawn them."

"What is a... human," questioned Fread, unsure of the word.

"Ah, that's right they've not been discovered yet, or simply do not exist upon Dranier." Death seemed to lose himself for a short time before shaking his head and focusing on the task that lay before him.

"Gaia read the etchings on the bowl and was right about the deaths of Ether and Uther at his hands as well as the requirements necessary for their successful defeat. He was none to pleased to know that his destiny was mapped out for him in such a way, and he admitted as much to Seraphine," said Fread.

"Do you know exactly where Gaia stopped reading," posited Death.

"Unfortunately, I was not there it was Seraphine who told me. I needed hope that Drogen could and would succeed in his fight against Ether and Uther, for the sake of Zephyria. She told me of the writing on the dragon scale bowl and what Gaia translated. It was the hope I needed and allowed me to confidently get behind the actions he took," said Fread.

"From what I am told, he came looking for me in the ravine between Moongrove and Aragorth, because of Gaia's translations." said Willow.

"I suspect that this will have everything to do with the goblinkin and Grock. There has been a massive uptick in threats to merchant caravans especially in the last couple of months. This morning there was a caravan that requested a larger escort because of the threat of goblinkin attacks through the woods and roads," said Willow.

"The goblinkin have been wreaking havoc across Dranier. Two settlements, that we know of, have been either razed to the ground or taken over by orcs these past months. The first to fall was Zephyria, the second Moongrove, and who knows where the band might strike next," said Fread. "I hope that Drogen can get information to us so that we might aid him in the fight, the kingdom owes him that much, and far more, for ridding us of the travesty the Gods brought to our doorstep."

"For now, it looks like all we can do is watch and wait, while I work on these translations. When the time comes, we will know where to go, for the birth of a God is something that the entirety of Dranier will feel and have to acknowledge." *Oh, how nice it will be to once again have brand new experiences, I thought my time with new, exciting, and unknown had ended long ago,* thought Death.

"I wish to find something for my son Krail, do you know what he likes. To see him in all his glory is my sincerest wish, but I have no idea how he's changed over the years. Nor what I can do to make up for my lack of being there. It was the hardest thing for me to do, leaving him how I did. I knew he'd be safe in Lundwurm Tul, while I ventured to find his father. I'd hoped to be there when he awoke fully from the meditative sleep, but it seems the gods broke through first, and without my knowledge," said Lisana with a deep rumbling growl from the core of her being.

Krail was half expecting her to breath fire with how deep her growl seemed to be and was glad to see that the results were little more than smoke puffing out her nose. "I think Willow and Fread would have been better at this than I," said Krail. "I'm afraid I really don't know Drogen all that well. Other than him healing my wing so that I retained my ability to fly. I really don't know much."

"On the contrary Krail you know far more about my son than even you realize, and far more than I do having gone without seeing him for so long. You have informed me that he saved your ability to fly, but I'm sure that you're not the only one he saved with the golden dragon water," said Lisana.

"You're right he healed many of the injured and saved many lives in Zephyr that would have no doubt perished if he had not risked recapture and informed us of the goblinkin army that knocked upon our front door," said Krail as he motioned Lisana into a small shop of small mechanical trinkets and curiosities.

"From that alone I know him to be kind and steadfast in his principals. He was willing to turn back to those who had him imprisoned when danger was present for them, at his own risk. I raised him well," said Lisana with a smile that denoted her still stinging sadness that lay just beneath the surface.

Lisana looked through the trinkets the store had to offer admiring the tiny mechanisms and meticulous craftsmanship with which each had been made. Mechanical birds that flapped their wings, figures of creatures which ran across the tables they sat upon, and many other curiosities. Yet none of them could draw her eye until she came upon a waterfall surrounded by willow trees which cascaded into a pond at its base. "This is it," said Lisana.

"It's quite beautiful," said Krail.

"Yes, it will remind him of home in Lundwurm Tul," said Lisana a look of nostalgia washing over her as she took the waterfall to the front counter paying for it with two large silver coins.

"This is to be sent to the castle," said Krail to the young shop attendant before they left.

"You didn't need to have it sent to the castle. I could have carried it myself in my extra-dimensional bag," said Lisana.

"Many of the younger generation of Zephyria are used to deliver packages. It is a great opportunity for many of them to come to the castle and see other aspects of life within Zephyria. It could give one of the younger generation inspiration for the future, and for the future of Zephyria," said Krail.

"My son truly has surrounded himself with many thoughtful friends. What else can you tell me about him," questioned Lisana

"Although many among the clergy of Zephyria would heartily disagree, he has changed Zephyria for the better. We, as a whole have a new sense of hope for the future which we did not have under the oppressive rule of Ether and Uther," said Krail.

Krail, walking with Lisana into the heart of the zephyrian marketplace received many hellos and waves from those they passed. Krail led Lisana to a couple of outdoor stalls where many rambunctious squabs were running around giddily flapping their young wings. Not paying attention a young zephyrian girl ran into her legs falling backwards before she could catch herself.

"Lisana bent down and assisted the girl in righting herself helping her pat some of the dirt from her expertly crafted clothes. "Make sure you watch where you're going, you don't want to hurt yourself, little one," said Lisana.

"How are you doing Shiesa. I haven't seen you around in a while," said Krail.

"I'm good Mr. Krail. Mama let me come out and play since the shop is not too busy," said Shiesa.

"What kind of shop do you help your mother with," questioned Lisana.

"Mom and I turn fabric into clothes," said Shiesa shyly.

"So, you're a seamstress," questioned Lisana.

"Yes," said Shiesa. "Mama's teachen me how to be simtress."

"I'm sure that you will make a fine seamstress, being taught by your mother," said Krail.

"I even helped fit two princesses," said Shiesa proudly as she puffed out her chest.

"Truly great indeed," said Lisana.

"When next I come to the market, I will have to come see you about some garments then," said Lisana.

"I can take to mama now," said Shiesa.

"I'm afraid my time for today is coming to its end," said Lisana.

"Okay pretty lady. I go play now. Sorry for bumping you. I'll see better," said Shiesa running off after her friends.

"We could have gone," said Krail.

"No, it seems the goddess named Willow has come to gather us. Which means, the other two are probably not far behind," said Lisana. *This seems like a good opportunity to figure out whether or not this Goddess means any harm,* thought Lisana.

"What brought a goddess down here to live, with those other gods feel are inferior to their own," questioned Lisana as Willow finally came into view.

"The short answer... Drogen and love," said Willow in reply. Not shrinking back from Lisana as she stared her down.

The look in Lisana's eyes softened a little seeing that Willow would not back down from her declaration, but they remained trained on her trying to see any lies or deceit within Willow as she had so often seen in her many years of battle with the Gods.

Lisana learned to be especially critical regarding their motives since the talks between the two races broke down. "And where, pray tell, did Drogen stumble upon you," she questioned.

"He saved me from myself in the ravine between Moongrove and Aragoth. I locked myself away, and my own kin would come and try to kill me. The stress caused me to purge myself of emotion. So I couldn't feel anything. I lost myself in my own blood lust. Your son. He put me back together again," said Willow tears forming in her eyes. "I tried to kill him when we first met, but he wouldn't go down, and refused to fight back. Drogen brought back the emotions I had purged until I was whole again." Willow's words were becoming harder to understand as she openly let the tears fall from her eyes. Although she tried to hide her emotions, the side effects from becoming whole again had yet to fully subside.

Hearing the tale Lisana visibly relaxed. Seeing the genuine emotion, and greenery which accompanied her falling tears she lost all prejudice. Wrapping Willow in a deep hug. "I can see that you have seen and endured much, as have most of us in the eldest races. We all have pasts we wish could be different and regrets. The important thing is we move forward, and make sure we do not commit once more the mistakes of the past," said Lisana.

"Now, do you know what my son might need," posited Lisana with a smile, as if the previous conversation hadn't happened. Krail and Willow looked at each other for a second before laughing at the speed in which Lisana moved on.

"He's always going through clothing, especially if he has to change in haste," said Willow.

"Clothing simply isn't personal enough. It has to be something more personal than clothes. How does the harness I built fair with his forged blades," questioned Lisana.

"If it's the same one he wore in Zephyr... It was destroyed beyond repair, while he fought off the goblinkin," said Krail.

"That wouldn't be a necessity, not now. He can summon them with a thought. He has no need for scabbards," said Willow drawing a curious look from Lisana.

That's not something I've heard any Dragonkin being capable of, could it be a manifestation of Death's blood flowing through his veins, thought Lisana. *I cannot wait to hear his full name. Although I still don't understand what all the fuss is about.*

"Anyways, I was sent here to get everyone you and Krail. I came just ahead of the other two since they had some things to discuss," said Willow. "I will help with whatever I can, but I spent most of my time with Fread in Moongrove. I know even less than Krail does I fear."

Lisana stopped and looked at a few more shops but found nothing stood out. "If only I had an idea of his name, maybe I could find something worthy of him," pouted Lisana as she held up a pair of expertly stitched and carved wrist cuffs.

"Don't say it," said a voice above the crowd. Lead by Fread, Death came floating through the rapidly dissipating crowd.

"You always show up when I'm finally about to get the answers I'm looking for," said Lisana coming towards Death threateningly.

"And I told you it had to be heard through his lips, not another's. So... stop trying," said Death with a crooked smile.

Lisana's feigned anger with Death's interference in the matter completely fell away as she returned to her interrupted musings over the many cuffs before her. "What can I possibly get to make up for so much lost time."

"If I may interject," said Fread. "You act as though your presence and that of Deaths would not be enough."

"He's right my love. Nothing we buy will make up for time that's been lost. But the three of us can be together in the future."

"If you really want to make it up to Drogen I remember something that he said about his time within Lundwurm Tul," said Fread. "He told us a few stories that the dragonkin told while sitting around their tables in, what he referred to, as the *feeding hall*. You never told him about his father or how either of you found each other. It may be that the stories you've held close to the chest are the gift you need to give," said Fread wrapping his arm around Willow's shoulders. Pulling her in close and placing a kiss upon her forehead. Drawing a big smile to Willow's face.

"Tis good Drogen found such grand friendship since leaving Lundwurm Tul. You might be onto something with telling our story," said Lisana. Wrapping her arm around Death's waist drawing him close to kiss him on the lips. "And oh, what a story it is," she quipped with a devilish smile as Death visibly cringed.

Chapter Nineteen

"It's nearing time for the first bout to begin. All are expected in the arena before Grocks arrival. Should any come late they will be fed to the beasts within the beast quarter, bellowed out an unfamiliar voice," Natalia heard within her dreams. Unwilling to acknowledge what she heard as anything else as she lay comfortably upon Drogen's lap.

Drogen had not slept the entirety of the night but had fallen deeply within himself. Coaxing his blades to his call through their connection within the soul chamber. Even over the hours of inner solitude, they made not a sound, their resonance waning with each probe within his mind. Yet they continue to appear at his mental call. They would not leave him completely. Godslayer; Envoy of Death returning to that of simple blades which he could summon with a thought, but having no sentience left with which to communicate. The loss of his weapons minds bringing about a persistent fragmentary feeling.

The door of his champion hold room opened a short while after the guttural announcements, which Drogen could not understand, rang their last vestige. Trailing off as the voice moved along the passageways leading to the next hold.

Golga, accompanied by Grom and Bogger, pushed through and into the room. Drogen awaiting them, while Natalia rested wearily, having worried herself to sleep in the night.

"Natalia, tis time to get up and face what is to come," said Drogen stroking her abyssal black wings.

Natalia stirred from her slumber rising up from Drogen's lap with a start as her eyes gazed upon Golga, Grom, and Bogger's presence within the small room.

Golga looked into Natalia's eyes with a look of pervasive sadness that betrayed itself through the smile that shone upon her face.

She is worried for Drogen and I, thought Natalia. "I have only been around you for a short time, but I cannot help count you as anything short of friends," said Natalia in the bugbear's dialect followed by a long yawn.

"I only wish we could have met under better circumstances," said Golga. "Maybe we could have gone on adventures together as friends. I suppose that would go for these two as well," she said with a chuckle.

"I supposing so," said Grom. "Although Bogger might think differently."

"Should have sent away long time ago, too much trouble," grumbled Bogger.

"I'll miss you too Bogger," said Natalia drawing a loud harrumph as Bogger crossed his arms over his chest.

"We should get going to the arena," said Drogen. "I can hear many heading in that direction as we sit here."

"Right you are," said Golga. "A-are you sure you don't want to get out the other way. There is still time," she said hoping that Natalia, at least, would take her up on the offer.

"I'm sorry Golga, but I cannot accept running from this while Drogen fights to save the others within the arena," said Natalia.

"I hope you and all the others find some way to make it out alive, but I cannot see a method through which you might escape death this day," said Golga. "Not within the arena, and not with Grock here."

"There is a way, if what Natalia has told me about one of the creatures curated by Cauron is, what I believe it to be," said Drogen with a smile. "Many will survive this day, far more than Grock will like."

"Wish could be sure ourselves," said Grom.

"Dead and they know it," said Bogger. "I wont morn one with death wish."

Ignoring Bogger's dower attitude, they moved through the champions hold as a group making their way to one of the three large portcullises allowing access to the arena floor. Mai-Coh and Chian stood at the arena's center with the other champions ready for the fight that would soon arrive.

Golga, Grom and Bogger stuck close to Natalia as they walked into the arena. Grom and Bogger surveyed their surroundings and the multitude of goblinkin filtering into the stands all around them. Golga however did not look away from Natalia's lithe form fearing her dead the moment she was out of sight.

Natalia stayed with Golga wishing to remain by their side, to parlay their fears as well as her own. *Others might think me insane but even though I am and was always a prisoner of theirs I felt safe with them around. Especially Golga who has treated me most kindly since my arrival in Grammora,* thought Natalia.

Drogen, outpacing them all, moved swiftly to the side of the champions.

"It would seem that today is our day to die," said Asche as he walked up beside her.

"Roccan came and retrieved us early this morning, and brought us here for encouragement it would seem," said Hàrgo.

"There is only one way this ends, and it is for the glory of Grock," said Goral.

"Destroy all weakness, slaughter to prevail," said Gulvon. A cheer taken up by many in the stands as they filtered in. Gulvon raised his tattered long sword into the air garnering more than a few cheers from the crowd as the chants died down.

"Why must we fight for the glory of Grock. We're not even his subjects, said Goya. The only beings we will ever worship are, the Anu."

"It would seem we fight together this day," said Drogen moving close to Mai-Coh and Chian.

"It only day we fight together dream walker. Death surrounds this place, and we are next," said Mai-Coh.

"Oh, I think not Mai-Coh. There is still much for you and the other champions here to live for," said Drogen. "The question is when the time comes will you come with me, or will you embrace death unnecessarily."

"You are confident dream walker, but confidence doesn't mean right," said Mai-Coh

"True. Very true," said Drogen. "Hmmm it would seem Grock has arrived."

The crowd around them burst into cheers as a massive being walked out to sit upon an intricately carved throne that had been centrally placed between the two sides of the stands. The seating that had once filled the area demolished in order to accommodate Grock's stature. Grock stood out in stark contrast with the worshipers around him as a giant. A difference accentuated further as his booming voice filled the breadth of the arena.

"Today starts our day of glory," said Grock to the goblinkin around them while Natalia translated for those who could not understand on the arena floor. "For on the morrow we begin taking our plight to the other races of Dranier."

"Destroy all weakness; slaughter to prevail." Came the call of his worshipers. Which Drogen noted, filled Grock with more power, further amplifying the gravity around him and his words.

"We will take our place as the dominate race of Dranier taking all who stand in our way down along the way. Starting with these insignificant beings that have shown themselves capable within this arena. NO MORE will I allow them to live within my presence. However, killing them myself would be far too easy. Thus, your generals have brought forth challenges that are sure to delight, destroy, and crush all who stand against us," barked Grock to the enthusiastic crowd's cheers the deep scars on his face contorting as he smiled.

"There are those among the arena who are of my blood as well. True champions of our people. Those of my blood among the arena are to take their place alongside their kin, forgiven for their insolence and failings. For all have use among the legions moving forward. Bring them forth my generals and raise them from the tarnish of the arena to the battlefield where they will no doubt be of great inspiration to their kin. So that all may bare witness as the captured fall before our might," exclaimed Grock with a raised fist.

"Destroy all weakness; slaughter to prevail," chanted the crowd. As those who thought themselves to be cannon fodder were redeemed in Grock's eyes.

"For the glory of Grock," shouted Goral and Gulvon. Raising their swords triumphantly in the air.

Hargo however displayed not a hint of happiness regarding the new development. "Idiots, we are destined to be the first to attack and the first to die," said Hargo under his breath. "Grock does not forgive failure. Simply taking us all for cannon fodder or to die pressed up against an impassable wall."

Drogen, although incapable of understanding Hargo's language could tell from his scrunched face and saddened expression at Goral and Gulvon's display that Hargo felt much the same as the bugbears. Armed with that knowledge he moved back to Golga, Grom, and Bogger who had surrounded Natalia subconsciously.

"We will stay and fight with you," said Grom. Enthusiastically grabbing for the blade at his hip.

"Suppose I have death wish too," said Bogger.

"It would seem there are more like you among the goblinkin," said Drogen as he came within earshot of the trio surrounding Natalia. "Make sure that wherever you end up, you take Hargo with you as well. It seems, from the lack of enthusiasm, he feels much the same as you three."

"I wish I could stay and fight, but should I not follow orders I will be killed by Grock himself," said Golga.

"All three of you have to go," said Natalia. "I do not wish to see any of you die."

"I don't know if it is possible for you to escape this fate, but if you do, then I want you to open this," said Golga as she threw a small notebook down at Natalia's feet.

"Once this is over, I will do just that," said Natalia picking up the small notebook. Stuffing it in one of the many hidden pockets within her studded leather armor.

"Your end and end of everyone," said Bogger.

"Roccan and Cauron feel the same way and wish there was more we could have done to prevent your, and so many other deaths."

"All wish the same," said Grom.

"You will know when the time comes that your assistance is needed, but this is not that time," said Drogen.

"Go you three before anyone grows suspicious that you are not moving," said Natalia anxiously.

Golga bid Bogger and Grom on, although they looked back at the both of them a few times to make sure they had not succumbed to the trials already.

The champions, generals, and guards all vacated the field of battle being followed closely by those they had won during their time in the arena from the cleaners quarter. They were just about through the three portcullises, when two giants and an ettin walked out into the arena. All those who were not fast enough to move out of the way were unceremoniously splattered underfoot. The sound of bones cracking under the immense pressure of their colossal feet sending fevered cheers throughout the arena.

As the last of the goblinkin, and those retained through their arena battles walked free of the arena grounds, the only avenue of escape fell to the ground with a loud crash and spray of sand.

"Let the battle begin," roared Grock.

"Destroy all weakness; slaughter to prevail," rang out from the crowd as two caged creatures fell from the audience wall to the sand breaking open as they hit the ground spilling their contents which burrowed deep into the sand obscuring all movement from view as the giants and ettin dropped to the ground sitting against the wall adjacent to their portcullis.

"What are those things," yelled Asche.

"I think it's more important to ask where they went," remarked Goya.

"Silence," exclaimed the normally silent Mai-Coh motioning for everyone to remain silent with finger placed against his lips.

The rumble of the giants sitting brought the creatures to the surface launching themselves through the air at the giants who had created the noise. Each of the creatures went for a different giant having swam through the sand in opposite directions. The first bit into the flesh of the two headed ettin's foot and was summarily kicked away by the massive foot sending the shark like creature flying to the opposite side of the arena.

As the sand shark hit the ground it burrowed once more into the sand disappearing from sight once more. The second land shark was far luckier in its attack biting into the unsuspecting giants forearm sinking its teeth in and ripping flesh free with ease.

The giant jumped up from its seated position letting out a howl as it stomped around madly. Drawing the attention of the other sand shark as it sent vibrations through the ground.

"Move now," called out Mai-Coh.

Goya and Asche hesitated for only a second before running with the rest of the champions whereas many that had no battle experience, from the cleaners quarter, were stuck where they stood. Fear gripping them too tightly to move.

The second sand shark hurled itself out of the sand attacking the giant from behind snapping its teeth shut around the giant's achilles tendon. As the tendon gave way under the weight of the sand sharks teeth the giant fell into the arena flailing about trying to get rid of the creatures by any means possible.

The flailing giant hit many of the stunned people splattering their corpses against the arena walls. However, the sand sharks would not relent sinking their teeth into the giant's fleshy body.

Those that remained at the arena's center finally fought through their fear and began running some choosing to run to the champions, where others decided it best to run for the many small doors around the arena. Taking to banging on the doors, which they had used to remove corpses previously.

All around the arena laughter and glee came pouring forth as they witnessed the struggle of those desperately fighting to stay alive.

The giants wound quickly became far more severe, the sharks taking large chunks from anywhere they could gain purchase along the giants' body. The giant's fight came to an end as one of the sand shark tore through the giant's neck and down through its throat ripping and tearing through the corpse to the sand beneath where it disappeared once more.

The cleaners closest to the fallen giant were the first to realize their mistake, far too late as the still bloody sand shark that had gnawed through the giant launched into their back the mouth of the sand shark ripping them in half as it pulled them down into the sand.

The second sand shark remained upon the giant's corpse until it fell still trying to pull the giant down into the sand as it would any of its other prey. It pulled and tugged the giants arm for a short time before all went still where the sand shark had disappeared.

Seeing yet another die who had been pounding on the door to be let out those who remained stopped moving completely watching and waiting for someone to mess up and give them an opportunity to run.

Removed a small dagger from one of the many folds in her studded armor, Natalia threw the sharp blade as far as she could the dagger flipping end over end until it hit the ground thirty yards away creating a small metallic clanging noise. Still even the small amount of noise proved enough for the sand sharks which moved through sand like water.

The dagger fell between the teeth of one sand shark as the other had jumped far too high. As the powerful jaws of the sand shark bit down it broke the steel blade in twine.

"Does it have any weakness," whispered a clearly shaken Asche. While the sand sharks were flying through the air homing in on the ringing dagger.

Mai-Coh, hearing even the most silent of whispers covered his eyes with his hand, pointed down his mouth with his finger and then to the base of his spine.

"Well at least there's a weakness," said Asche under her breath. As the crowd around them erupted in cheers seeing another of the cleaners fall. Who had chosen to run the exact moment the sand sharks began burrowing once more.

It would seem that there will need to be a distraction if who remain are to survive this, thought Drogen. Looking to his side at Natalia he motioned for her to move away silently. As he himself moved back away from the rest of the group. The boots he had received coming in handy yet again as they made his footsteps silent.

Natalia moved like a ghost upon the wind her own natural ability coming into full use as she backed away from Drogen and to the rest who had wisely come close to the champions while they safely could. The other champions looked at Drogen fearfully as he silently moved away from the others and into the far more open arena center.

Seeing Drogen moving away from the others brought a cheer through the crowd as they awaited what would inevitably come. The sand sharks. However, the crowds' voices caused the sand sharks to spring from the ground near the walls allowing Drogen to move quickly while they were in the air to further the distance between himself and the others. The champions took the opportunity to draw in closer around Mai-Coh and Chian who clearly knew more about the situation they found themselves in than the others.

Once Drogen reached the arena's center he caught Mai-Coh's attention. The crowd cheered once more as the sand sharks came closer to the surface looking for any prey that might be disturbed by their movements drawing them to the arena walls. As the sand sharks broke ground launching themselves toward the crowd Drogen touched his fingertips together his thumbs wide before touching them together to form a circle.

Mai-Coh looked at Drogen confused by his split from the group and further perplexed by the hand motions clearly meant for him to understand. Drogen made the motion a few more times while he looked to Chian, who appeared as clueless as he, and then to Natalia.

Natalia threw two more daggers hitting the walls twenty yards away on either side of the large group drawing the two sand sharks in opposite directions giving herself time to whisper so that Mai-Coh could hear. The sand sharks flew through the air attracted by the clanging and clattering blades. "Horseshoe to Drogen encircle and strike," she whispered while performing the same hand gestures but thumb to finger instead pointing always at Drogen.

Hearing the explanation, Mai-Coh understood why Drogen had chosen to move away from the group. And what needed to be done in order to successfully deal with both sand sharks. Mai-Coh nodded his head to Natalia and Drogen in kind. Pulling out a small, but clearly dull blade from a sheath at his side.

Natalia produced many more daggers from the many folds and pockets within her studded leather armor handing them out to anyone who remained unarmed many within the group were shaking holding the daggers, and other blades but grew less so as they looked to the champions and their determined demeanor.

Once everyone was armed and ready Mai-Coh nodded to Drogen signaling their readiness.

Drogen stomped on the sand at his feet compacting it into rock and alerting both sand sharks to his location as his thunderous stomps sent tremors through the ground. Mai-Coh's ears moved as he followed the sound of the sand shark's movements under their feet. Making sure the sand sharks would come for him and only him Drogen continued stomping compacting the ground to accentuate the sound.

The sand sharks broke ground jumping into the air at the same time going for his upper and lower body at the same time. For anyone else it would have been a death sentence but for Drogen it simply made what came next easier. Because he could hear their heartbeats through the sand Drogen knew exactly where they would be, stepping out of the way as soon as their heads left the sand in attack.

Mai-Coh seeing Drogen move yelled "horseshoe toward Drogen blades ready." They all moved at his call forming a semi-circle toward Drogen watching and waiting for their opportunity to strike.

The sand sharks began burrowing into the ground, but Drogen wouldn't allow them both to go. Stepping up and behind the sand shark Drogen grabbed it by the back plate that shielded its weak spot beneath. Hefting the struggling sand shark over his head he began to sink into the sand, helping to secure his footing adding strength to his throw as he sent the sand shark flying through the air and into the waiting champions and cleaners.

Drogen made sure to make throwing the sand shark as loud as possible drawing the other to his struggle as he sent the hulking beast flying through the air.

The second sand shark launched itself at Drogen as its brother landed upside down its armored head scraping along the ground to a halt at the center of them all. They wasted no time striking out against the sand shark driving their blades between the armored plates on its stomach along its tail and anywhere else they could wound and kill the beast that had killed many of their friends.

The sand shark struggled against the onslaught eventually regaining its feet, but that only allowed for a faster death as Asche, and Mai-Coh struck out with their longer blades piercing the sand shark into its ocular cavity and into its brain. As it fell to the ground dead many continued to stab that creature most until the blades in their hands broke.

Mai-Coh, Chian, Asche, Goya, and Natalia stopped their assault the moment life left the creature turning their attention once more to the one who came up with the plan to start with and the one who continued to face off against the creature, which had taken an entire group to take down, alone.

Drogen dodged the sand shark trying to determine the best method moving forward. *Should I summon Godslayer; Envoy of Death then the possibility of Grock coming down before the others have a chance to escape is likely. So, I must wait. I am nowhere near Grock's power, and he would likely crush me before they can escape this place. Saving them needs to be the priority. Maybe displaying my strength to early was a bad idea, but I cannot think of that right now,* thought Drogen admonishing himself. *Well then how about another feat of overwhelming strength.*

Stomping the ground once more Drogen grabbed the sand shark at the base of its armored head pulling it up straight and exposing its weakest area the sand shark bucking and shaking its head and body desperate to break Drogen's grasp. Partially transforming his hand, he sunk his fingers between the plates along its spine severing it with a flick of his finger. Dropping the creature to the ground at his feet.

The audience and everyone were in shock at the overwhelming display of strength not believing that the creature had fallen so efficiently and fast. However, as the sand shark's muscles stopped twitching all together and it grew still the crowd went wild cheering the champions success, much to the ire of Grock

"Bring out the wyvren, the ogre's, and the trolls. We will crush them all under the might of Grock," yelled Goral seemingly sensing Grock's irritation.

The crowd began chanting Goral's name, but Grock was focused entirely on the one who'd single handedly bested a sand shark. A sand shark that had taken forty orcs and two giants to capture and contain for the arena. At least that was the number that survived. Finally noticing the chants of those around him, Grock curled a fist and thrust it into the air. "Let the next round begin," he exclaimed.

Chapter Twenty

The portcullis, guarded by the etten, opened and out poured a fist of trolls, a fist of ogres, and two wyvern who were chained to the hands of a troll and ogre respectively. Leather collars affixed around the necks of the wyvern would pinch tightly, restricting their ability to breath. So as to render them unconscious, should they try to go against those who held their chain leash.

The crowd around them went wild seeing the ogres, trolls, and wyverns. "Destroy all weakness; slaughter to prevail," cheered the audience followed by loud pounding of their feet through the stands, which reverberated into the arena through the walls that protected them.

As the trolls, ogres, and wyverns entered the arena many, who thought victory feasible, dropped to their knees in surrender. Feeling the last vestiges of hope fade with their decreasing odds of survival. Some, who survived the first round, chose instead to take their own lives. Rather than give themselves false hope of survival. Bleeding out where they kneeled in the sand. Death on their own terms.

Those around, including the champions, tried to stop the daggers from their deadly plunge, but were too slow in reacting to stop them all. Natalia looked upon them with both sadness and understanding, wishing she had not given them all daggers. The loss of so many weighting heavily upon her heart.

Looking around Natalia counted those who remained, The six champions; including Mai-Coh, and Chian, herself, and five others remained. A paltry sum compared to the amount that had once called the cleaners quarter their home. *I hope that most have not died here and were taken away from this place instead,"* thought Natalia.

Twenty have died so far this day, and more to follow, for nothing. A senseless crusade against beings that simply want to live and be left alone. What is the point in all of this bloodshed. I could take them all down with a breath, but Grock would then overwhelm and kill us all. My life being forfeit is a distinct possibility. But I'll not see them all die due to inborn arrogance on my behalf. I am not Grocks match. Not this day, thought Drogen.

"Those willing to face the threat ahead follow me, everyone else get as far back as possible," said Drogen

Those unwilling or unable to fight ran to the body of the fallen giant in hopes that the corpse of the larger beast could provide some form of protection. Only the arena champions, Natalia, and one other from the cleaners quarter remained to stand before the overwhelming numbers.

"What is your name," questioned, Natalia. To the only one willing to stand and fight with the rest of them. "My apologies that I didn't have a chance to ask before."

"This is Keltus... my sister," said Asche who walked up beside Keltus wrapping her in a hug.

"A pleasure to meet you Keltus. However, there is still the issue of seven. How are seven supposed to survive against the twelve of them," questioned Goya as he stomped the ground.

"I count nine," said Drogen. "Although our two compatriots seem to be detained at the moment."

"Wait you're not talking about. How are we supposed to control those things," said Asche.

"If we free them, they'll attack everything and everyone. They've likely never been trained at all," objected Keltus. "I've seen what an untrained wyvern can do, and it is not pretty. They're indiscriminate in a rage."

"Likely not trained, but from the looks of the scales around their neck they have been tortured for some time," said Natalia. "Cauron would have never allowed that. These wyverns are likely those that came with Grock's army."

"Enemy of enemy is friend," said Mai-Coh.

"And a little persuasion couldn't hurt," said Drogen with a shrug.

"Who can deal with choker," questioned Mai-Coh.

"I can probably get one of them off. If I can concentrate on a single target. Although, help would be greatly appreciated," said Natalia.

"I can help," said Goya. "Especially if you have more of those daggers and other components hidden in that armor of yours."

"My sister and I will deal with the other," said Asche.

"What task lie before us dream walker," questioned Mai-Coh.

"We will sow chaos and distraction while the others free the wyverns, if you two are up for the task," said Drogen.

Receiving a decisive nod from Chian's furry blue head. "We are dream walker," said Mai-Coh.

"Drogen, just call me Drogen Mai-Coh."

"Okay Drogen we are ready when you are."

"Then let us begin," said Drogen taking off toward the two fists of enemies that lay ahead. Picking up a discarded dagger Natalia had thrown Drogen began attacking indiscriminately. Poking into each piece of ogre flesh that stood before him, a wasp in their midst.

Mai-Coh and Chian, following Drogen's lead began poking and prodding any bare flesh they could find on the trolls, who healed quickly, but still felt the pain they caused. Ultimately separating the two fists into four smaller groups as they tried to fight against the stinging threat attacking their legs and ankles. The wyvern handlers had their hands full with their charges and were forced to split from the group as well working their way out along the circular walls of the arena further dividing them.

One of the ogres facing Drogen's stinging flight around its legs, bent down trying to swat Drogen away, but found itself bleeding out for its trouble. Envoy of Death slicing through the ogres neck with a single strike before disappearing once more as though it never was.

The ogre fell clutching its throat, blood gurgling out from its severed artery. Stepping out from the dying ogres forward lurch, Drogen move past, not a single drop of blood falling upon him. As the creatures life force began to pool beneath it the audience's fevered cheers rang out once more.

"What do you have other than daggers," questioned Goya.

"Not much. I have some leather string, for emergency fixes to the armor, a few extra studs, and that's it," said Natalia. "And I only have... ten daggers left," she said Feeling around her armor.

"That's more than enough with this," said Goya, pulling a small vile from his pocket.

"What is that," questioned Natalia.

"A little something I cooked up in the kitchen last night," said Goya. "I almost didn't have time to complete it, but fortune seemed to shine upon me as I was left undisturbed and unattended," he said with mischievous smile.

"They did tell us to prepare," said Natalia with a smile.

"That they did," said Goya.

"What does it do," she questioned.

"All we need to do is get this liquid onto the chain the ogre is holding. We'll have to choose the right spot, but this will weaken the chain to the point that it will break. Be mindful however, this is all I could prepare," said Goya.

"We need to aim for as close to the collar as possible, don't want them to be restrained again. How do you suggest we get it up there," pointed Natalia.

"I suppose we'll just have to figure that out as we go," said Goya.

The ogre and wyvern duo worked their way along the right side of the arena wall coming closer to those hiding behind the giants corpse with each step forward.

Scoping out the contraption placed around the wyvern's neck she could see that it was made of a thick leather. Something that would not be easily cut through, not in a short amount of time. Similarly the chain which the ogre grasped in its massive fist would prove far harder to make yield with force as its links of metal chain showed little signs of ware.

I hope that Goya's bottle of liquid does what he says it does, or else we will have to go back to the drawing board, thought Natalia.

Goya hid himself in front of the giants corpse while Natalia worked her way up to the ogres hand with her wings drawing out a couple of daggers to throw once its hand came into range. The ogre tried and failed to swat her out of the sky with the chin wielding hand pulling back on the wyvern's collar and causing it to fall to the ground in its overbalance.

Goya taking the opportunity ran out from his hiding spot but the wyvern was already righting itself leaving him out in the open and an easy target for the angry wyvern who lurched forward against the collar and chain.

The ogres arm was pulled down and away by the wyvern's forward momentum giving Natalia the perfect opportunity to strike. She sent out three daggers along the arm and wrist of the ogre aiming for precise points along its outstretched arm. The first dagger missed its mark stabbing the ogre between the ribs instead of the deltoid of its right arm where she had intended. The second dagger struck true however piercing into the fold of the ogres arm releasing black blood from its opened artery.

With the third dagger Natalia was able to strike the ogres right wrist joint. The small dagger piercing through the back of its hand cutting multiple tendons. Rendering the ogre's hand completely inoperable. However, the chain didn't fall from the ogres grasp as its hand and fingers went limp. The ogre pulled hard upon the leash the wyvern wore causing the creature to pass out from lack of air.

Flapping her wigs quickly Natalia fled from the backhand the ogre made against her dropping swiftly to the ground as the wind from the ogre's swipe caused turbulence within the air currents.

Righting herself just in time she saw Goya pouring the contents of his vial onto the chain. Which lay upon the ground dangling from the knocked-out wyvern's neck.

Natalia landed in a run making her way to the giants corpse where she knew the others to be hiding and watching Goya's own run to cover as the ogre gained ground upon the wyvern kicking it back to waking life.

The wyvern, none too pleased with the rude awakening made to go after the ogre. Seeing the intent in the wyvern's eyes the ogre pulled mightily upon the collars chain to stop the wyvern. Its heart sinking to the dirt as the chain pulled away leaving the wyvern unshackled and enraged.

Natalia, and Goya hurriedly ushered the non-combatants in close to the corpse of the giant knowing the dead body would likely be there only way of fooling the wyvern into thinking there to be no more pray in the vicinity.

The wyvern without the chain to bind its service battered the ogre with its wings raking and clawing its foe to the ground before ripping the ogres throat out, all throughout the ogres left hand trying desperately to rip the wyvern off as its right hand slapped at its attacker feebly till its dying breath.

Asche and Keltus split off to the left following the movements of the troll struggling to keep the wyvern in check even with the collar around its neck. Keltus stopped before the wyvern trying to garner its attention and tell it their plans but the wyvern, would hear nothing in its rage striking out with its clawed feet at Keltus forcing her away and back to Asche's side.

"I don't see the wyvern listening to anyone or anything in the state its in. Far too much rage at those imprisoning it," said Keltus shaking her head.

"Well if anything that means it will attack those that imprisoned it first before it comes for us," said Asche with a sigh as they ran around the struggling troll.

They followed the troll's path until it was a comfortable distance away from the others of its kind who were being successfully annoyed by Mai-Coh and Chian.

"How do we deal with the troll," questioned Keltus. "They can regenerate quite easily unless something stops the process."

"I'm assuming that's where the wyvern's come in," said Asche. "That collar is meant to prevent their use of fire breath, and assume control in general."

"Is there any way we can cut through the leather around its neck," questioned Keltus.

"That would be the best method, but these swords are far too dull, to cut through such thick hide," replied Asche.

"Too dull for the collar, and we can't simply break the chain its far too strong. That leaves the troll as our only weak point then," said Keltus.

"Some weak point," commented her sister incredulously.

"We can do it sister. We just need to work together."

With a nod the sisters ran for the trolls back. Asche stabbed her dull sword into the trolls back as high as she could jump holding her hand out to Keltus who grabbed it flinging her further up the trolls back where she gained purchase in the same manner.

The troll roared out in pain and began moving erratically but would not, or could not, let loose of the chain holding the wyvern. The wyvern fell to the ground toppling over backwards as the chain holding it by the neck pulled back hard. The troll in its search for what was causing pain pulling back far harder than he should have.

The troll danced around wrapping itself in the chain and drawing the wyvern in closer with every jerk and turn until its large mouth was in striking distance. However, it didn't strike out with its powerful jaws first, but with its tail. The wyvern's tail broke through the trolls stomach. Then with its razor sharp teeth claws and stinger it clamored through the troll with abandon.

Asche and Keltus dropped to the ground at a run to get away from the very angry wyvern as it attacked indiscriminately at any bit of flesh it could find its tail delivering a powerful toxin that even the trolls regenerative ability could not fight against.

"I guess I forgot," said Asche with an audible gulp as they ran.

"Forgot what," questioned Keltus.

"They don't breath fire," said Asche.

"I thought it was strange that it didn't try to breath fire at me when I was in front of it.," said Keltus. "I almost wish it were fire instead. That poison is nasty."

Mai-Coh and Chian kept up their assault upon the trolls but were growing exhausted from the exertion. the constant movement and strikes putting straining their bodies. An exhaustion further perpetuated by the constant regeneration of the trolls they faced. The desperation becoming nearly overwhelming to them both as a massive primal roar filled the arena, followed quickly by the cheering crowd around them.

Asche and Keltus came running through the trolls with abandon trying desperately to get away from the wyvern chasing them. Taking the cue for what it was Mai-Coh and Chian ran after them stabbing each troll foot they found on their way out.

The four ran desperately, not daring to look back should the wyvern have decided to continue pursing them instead of killing those in front of them. They only slowed down when they heard the cheers of the crowd erupting once more.

They dared not stop, but looked around to see who or what had been downed. They all took a breath of relief as they saw the wyvern Natalia and Goya set out to free, attack its captor making mincemeat of the flailing troll until it could raise its hands in defense no more.

Mai-Coh looked where they had come from, breathing a sigh of relief, seeing the trolls desperately trying to apprehend the wyvern dragging the severed hand of its captor behind it. On a blood-soaked chain they could not garner grip upon, without facing the deadly claws, teeth, and stinger of the enraged wyvern.

Drogen threw the dagger he had been using to stab the final ogre as the wyvern's finished taking down their prey garnering more cheers as the many battles found their conclusion's. The dagger slammed into the ogres throat the hilt pushing through and widening the opening in the ogres throat before stopping. The ogre fell to its knees grabbing desperately for the small dagger that was restricting its airway but couldn't pinch the hilt with its massive fingertips.

With the ogre distracted by the dagger Drogen walked up to him looking up into the creature's eyes with sadness. "So much death in the name of your deity. Yet he would not sacrifice himself for you, if the roles were somehow reversed. He treats life as fodder and his own life as more than those he needs to maintain his power. Such backward thinking," mourned Drogen.

The ogre continued its desperate grabbing until it could no longer lift its arms and with a kick Drogen sent the dagger the rest of the way through the ogre's neck, severing its spine on the way out. The ogre fell back from the weight of Drogen's blow its last breath a gurgle of blood.

Drogen walked away from the corpses that lay around him, paying no head, as he focused on the battlefield around him. Most of the trolls were dead or dying from the wyvern's poison destroying their regenerative abilities. However, one still remained trying desperately to free itself from the wyvern's constant enraged attacks.

Asche, Keltus, Mai-Coh, and Chian ran up to Drogen fully exhausted by their efforts against the wyverns and troll. The wyvern Natalia and Goya had released had yet to turn away from its captor striking repeatedly against the troll's corpse, dismantling it piece by bloody piece. Drogen roared in a deep reverberating guttural language that none of them had ever heard before the sound of which turned the heads of both wyverns toward Drogen.

"I ask that you move away, but once the time comes you will need to get on the wyvern's backs taking one other with you upon the wyvern's backs. For that is all they will be able to carry and fly to Moongrove. Once it starts, we must act quickly in order to leave this place."

The wyverns ran for Drogen seeing him as the next big threat against them paying no more attention to the corpses left in their wake, nor those left living behind the giant's corpse.

"You cannot hope to survive against two wyverns' alone," protested Asche

"There is much that I can withstand that others could not," said Drogen. Watching and listening to the wyverns' progress, as they started running for him, drawing a fevered cheer from the crowd as the wyverns gain ground.

"Cannot leave you here to die alone Dream... Drogen," said Mai-Coh.

With a blink Drogen's eyes changed to those of his heritage so that he could look at each of them in kind. The gravitas of his words punctuated by the truth. "Gather the others quickly and bring them as close as is safe, while I take care of the wyverns. GO," roared Drogen. As he met the charge of the wyvern Asche and Keltus had freed.

The crowd went wild as Drogen leapt into the wyvern's midst his fist colliding against the wyvern's jaw sending it toppling to the side. Just as the second wyvern approached from his side. Drogen sidestepped the attack as the wyvern pounced its stinger coming down against the other wyvern who remained prone.

With a thought Godslayer came to his hand only appearing long enough to cut through the wyvern's stinging tail rendering it useless as it spurted blood. The wyvern roared in pain as its tail was cut raging at Drogen even more as it stared into Drogen's draconic eyes and fear gripped its heart. The wyvern jumped away from Drogen daring not approach even as Drogen turned his back to the wyvern presenting a perfect opportunity. The second wyvern began to stir raging as it felt the tip of its tail being severed.

Its rage brought its head up to Drogen's face and to his draconic eyes. The eyes that brought innate fear to the wyvern's heart causing them both to shutter as they set down on their haunches and waited. "Your stingers will grow back in time," Drogen told the wyvern's, who couldn't understand the language, could discern their meaning as any of draconic blood could.

The wyvern's scratched the earth at their feet anxiously as they continued looking into Drogen's eyes. "You will take two each from this place when the time comes. If any die by tooth or by claw, so too will you," threatened Drogen as those that remained alive came walking up to Drogen and the two wyverns. "Once this task is complete, you're free to return to the wilds from whence you came."

"It would seem that this battle is over with the cutting of a couple tails," roared Grock. "Then it seems it has come time for the grand finally. Be weary for the next beast will surely kill you all. For it is an ancient beast. One the likes of which the world thought lost. But we have found enslaved one. It is a beast the Gods know all too well and one that plagued this land hunted to extinction, for their crimes against divinity. The most ancient of evil's," hyped Grock.

"Destroy all weakness; slaughter to prevail." roared the crowd at Grock's declaration.

Chapter Twenty-One

"The ancient enemy of the Gods of Dranier," restated Grock raising his hand into the air to raise the Etten's portcullis once more. "A dragon," He shouted the crowd cheering in triumph with his declaration. Out of the portcullis came Grock's dragon.

"You would dare call a drake a dragon," roared Drogen as he looked upon tits chained neck. *I will be sure to burn the difference into your soul Grock and the soul of the giant who think to bind him.*

"Bow before Grock's might, and I may allow you to remain in my service," bellowed Grock. Those who remained standing throughout the trials and hardships thought about taking Grock's offer. Many starting to descend to their knees until they heard Drogen's voice through the crowd's cheers.

"And what if I alone am enough to best your dragon," projected Drogen over the crowd. "What would you do then. Let us all go free," he questioned as the crowd quieted to the point a pin drop could be heard.

"If such a lowly and insignificant creature as you can best my dragon, then all of you may leave. Free of this place," spouted Grock with a malicious smile.

So, either way death awaits those that cannot fly free. The words of gods always have double or triple meaning. He means to set us free from life, thus releasing us from this place, and existence, thought Drogen with a grin of his own.

"Very well Grock, I will take this challenge and face your dragon alone. If I succeed, we'll be free. If not, we'll be yours to do with as you please. I only ask a moment with my new friends before this fight comes to its conclusion." said Drogen walking over to his friends and those who remained alive from the cleaners quarter. Not giving time for Grock to answer, simply taking it.

Grock waved his hand in dismissal knowing, he had already won, although the slight Drogen had given him did not go unnoticed. Those around the arena cheered once more before reciting their favorite saying with a renewed vigor. "Destroy all weakness; slaughter to prevail. destroy all weakness; slaughter to prevail." A chant they would maintain until the final battle's start.

Natalia and the others came rushing up to Drogen and the wyverns, although they remained cautious, weary of a possible attack. The entirety of the group looked with concern over to the drake, that Grock called a dragon, with fear and anxiety pounding in their hearts knowing they would be no match for such a creature. Natalia, Mai-Coh, and Chian were the only exceptions their expressions sympathetic despite their fear.

"I've never seen a dragon before," said Asche. "They look more like a larger wyvern with four legs."

"That is no dragon. That is a nothing more than a young drake. Grock seems to have forgotten that truth," said Drogen.

"Wait then that means, you're..." muttered Goya. A distinct sparkle in his eye.

"This one is far younger than I would have liked. Tis likely he will be incapable of carrying more than a few upon his back. Still, it should be enough to get the majority of those left out without much difficulty. I will need one with knowledge of the Queens manner in Moongrove to provide baring for your coming flight.

"I can take us to the Queen's manner. I've been there a couple of times before. As has my sister," said Asche.

"Good, then I will have one of you go on this drake and another on one of the wyverns. I have a way to get a couple out of here myself. However, tis limited. I can take at most three with me. So, it would be best to get as many out as possible with the resources at our disposal. I leave it to you to decide, who will stay, and who will go. To those who stay, be ready for a fight far more strenuous than we've faced thus far," said Drogen.

"Chian wishes to stay and fight with you Dre... Drogen," said Mai-Coh. "As do I."

"Then we should have more than enough room for those that are left," said Drogen.

"I wish to stay as well, but I fear this next phase goes beyond my capabilities," said Natalia with a solemn crestfallen look at Drogen.

I fear that what comes next is beyond my capabilities as well, thought Drogen. "Then we have our duties," said Drogen. "I will also caution you, no matter what Grock decides to do in order to kill everyone here I will not allow it to happen. Do not worry for me, and do not help with this part. I will need everyone as rested and ready as possible. Is that *clear*," posited Drogen as he looked upon each of them.

"Yes," they all called back or nodded.

"Thank you, my friends. Now all of you run for the giant's corpse southeast of here and wait." said Drogen bowing to the group before turning to face the threat of Grock.

Drogen moved away from friends both new and old to take his place at the arena's center, as his compatriots ran for the giant's corpse at his back. Drogen stood before the goblinkin's deity, saying nothing to acknowledge Grock's presence any further.

The lack of acknowledgment coupled with the earlier disrespect bringing an irritated air to Grock's words. "I'll give you *one last chance.* Do as you just did to that running filth behind you, and *bow* to me. I may yet show you mercy."

"You are unworthy of such respect," bit Drogen dryly.

"Then you will feel for yourself a god's wrath. *Let the final round begin,*" bellowed Grock and the crowd went wild with excitement. Their fervor further amplified, as the remaining giant and ettin rose to their massive feet to accompany their new companion holding tightly to the drake's leash.

So, this is how he's going to play it, thought Drogen with a smile. *Then play I shall. And watch the crown fall.* Drogen watched and waited to see what each of the giants would do as the rest of his party continued their trek across the arena's radius.

"You two protect the others until I can free the drake," said Drogen to the two wyverns. The wyvern's, one dragging a bloody chain, jumped into the air. Each flap of their powerful wings raising them up just enough to glide across the arena toward the downed giant. They set down in front of the giant's corpse standing as sentinels.

The new giant, try as he might to stay against the wall, struggled against the power of the young drake's pull toward the center of the arena, its four powerful legs far stronger than the giants two, as it struggled to maintain any semblance of control.

The ettin surveyed the arena clearly sizing up the biggest threat, settling on the watching and waiting Drogen, before it began moving in earnest. The twin headed giant's massive footfalls shaking the arena as it gained speed coming straight for its prey at a run.

Drogen awaited the ettin's arrival at the arena's center most point without fear. For there was not a giant in the world that could stand up to the might of a dragon no matter their form or function.

Thinking Drogen no more significant than a fly the twin headed giant leapt into the air coming down with both feet in order to crush Drogen to pulp in the sand beneath. With a thought Drogen brought out Godslayer; Envoy of Death the two abyssal black blades pulling all light away, black smudges against the brightness of the sun that none could truly see.

Drogen kicked off of the sand launching himself away from the ettin's incoming stomp. Godslayer; Envoy of Death cutting into the bare flesh at the bottom of its colossal right foot.

The ettin's double stomp sent reverberations through the arena. The crowd and Grock cheering in response to the blood flowing out from beneath the ettin's foot. "Look all who think themselves more than the will of a God. Look and repent for these are what your last desperate moments will look like."

Thinking victory his, the ettin raised its fists in the air bellowing in victory. A mistake made in hubris that the ettin would come to regret. Drogen moved around the ettin's right leg while it was distracted. And with a swift strike to the back of the twin headed giant's ankle, the ettin began its decent to the ground. A scream of surprise escaping each set of lips, as its ankle gave way, toppling it to the sand below.

The audience grew quiet, astonished by the ettin's unforeseen fall. Drogen ran up the ettin's spine using Envoy of Death to cut from sacral to cervical in one long running stroke exposing the giant's spine to the air, and sand, its body sent cascading through the air. Drogen stopped his cut just below the two heads of the ettin where its spine deviated. The ettin made to rise from its prone position, but with a downward thrust into both sides of its deviated spine the ettin could rise no more.

With the ettin's fall came Grock's rage. "*Kill him now*," roared Grock. Calling on the two remaining giants and the drake riling the entirety of the audience as the shock of what happened began setting in. Shifting their focus away from his comrades completely.

Yes, Grock focus all your efforts on me, thought Drogen with a smile. Instead of waiting for the giants to arrive Drogen ran for the one holding the leashed drake. His breakneck speed creating gasps of confusion and surprise all around the arena.

The giant pulled the drake back, so it faced Drogen's incoming assault. The drake loosing fire against him, but Drogen paid the fire no more head than a summers breeze. The flame doing little more than scorch his clothes. "Your fire is weak drake," roared Drogen in Draconic. "If you don't wish to feel true fire then duck."

Drogen let out a stream of white-hot flame scorching the sand and everything else within its path the drake flattening itself to the sand just under Drogen's fire breath milliseconds before. The chain held by the giant turned to molten metal. The giants body scorched to the bone, leaving not but a charred husk behind. All the moisture in its body evaporating instantly.

Fear gripped the crowd seeing the white-hot flames turn the giant into not but a cinder and the sand around and behind it into a sheet of glass. The remaining giant stopped, in fear unsure of what to do next.

"We don't have any time now. Pleasantries will have to wait. Go to the wyverns and those on the other side of that rotting giant's corpse. Take as many as you can upon your back and fly.

One of the elves will guide you to your destination. *GO,"* belted Drogen. The guttural draconic asserting both dominance and urgency upon the drake.

"Yes, old one," said the Drake. Launching itself into the air raising high enough to glide to the giant's corpse.

As the drake ascended Drogen took in a deep breath. Breathing flames upon the portcullis the drake had come through, melding the metal into the stone structure locking it forever, before turning his breath upon the arena's wall covering the drake's flight from Grock's view.

"Does that mean he can change into something else as well," questioned Keltus.

"Is the same for many of my people," said Mai-Coh.

"Does that mean you can change into another form as well," questioned Natalia truly surprised by the revelation.

"No, I am strange in wolf tribe. I cannot change form; I came to this land in search of a way to change. Before returning to my people.

"Is it the same for Chian," questioned Keltus.

"No. Chian and taurean do not change. Not as wolf clan do. Chian come as builder," said Mai-Coh.

"The drake is coming," exclaimed Asche.

"Do you know how hot that fire must be to cause the sand to turn to glass, and all the liquid within that giant to evaporate in an instant," questioned Goya excitedly.

"I'm just glad he's on our side," said Keltus with a shiver. "We should hide the drake might be coming to eat us."

"You don't need to worry, said Natalia.

"And why should we not worry," questioned the four remaining survivors of the cleaners quarter.

"Because, dragons cannot lie," said Natalia.

The drake dropped out of the sky a short distance away from Natalia and the others. All were weary of the drake until the wyvern's began dancing around it happily. The drake breathed some fire from its mouth melting through the long chain still being drug around by the wyvern Asche and Keltus freed.

Natalia, Mai-Coh, and Chian were the first to come out from around the giant's corpse. Motioning for the drake to come closer, Natalia hoping it would recognize her from the times she helped Cauron in the beast hold.

"Black wing," said the drake in the common tongue.

"It is nice to hear your voice for the first time," said Natalia. "I knew you and Drogen would get along. If you had chance to meet."

"Old one free me. I free friends of old one," said the drake proudly. "Hurry on. Leave smelly place."

"It is time to go everyone," yelled Natalia who motioned for those who remained hidden to come out.

Still very much afraid of the drake and wyverns, but fearing being left behind more, everyone ran to their salvation. The drake lowered its head to the ground allowing Asche, Natalia, and two from the cleaners quarter to get on before rising back to full height.

On one of the wyverns Keltus drug another of the cleaners quarter into mount, with Chian's help. Goya, arguing with Mai-Coh about staying, was pushed up onto the second wyvern followed quickly by the final cleaner who locked their arms around Goya holding on for dear life.

"Go," exclaimed Mai-Coh. The drake and two wyverns started their accent as a rumble of footsteps came into focus making Mai-Coh's ears twitch.

Trying in vain to stop the drake and wyvern's from flying away orcs let fly crossbow bolts from the top of the arena. However, untrained in fighting a flying enemy, the crossbow bolts fell to the ground missing their fast-moving targets completely.

The sky bound entourage were above the flame before Grock could fully comprehend what had transpired under his nose. "Kill them all now," roared an enraged Grock.

Mai-Coh and Chian drug the giant's corpse over to the portcullis they knew would soon play host to an army of goblinkin. Rigor set in the giant's body making it impossible to move the corpse out of the way without a massive feat of strength that the orcs and ogres could not achieve as it pinned the portcullis shut under the giants' massive dead weight.

With only one entrance remaining viable for the remainder of the goblinkin forces. Mai-Coh and Chian began running as fast as they could back to Drogen.

They made only a short distance before a flood of orcs came rushing into the arena letting loose a volley of arrows which fell short. Behind those with the crossbows came orcs and ogres brandishing bludgeons and polearms of refined steel. The numbers behind them growing steadily as more and more came out from beyond the portcullis and into the arena weapons drawn and ready for martial combat running to make up the distance, they needed to travel to block Mai-Coh and Chian's path forward.

The second volley of arrows came far closer than the first barely missing their mark over the distance. Drogen motioned for Mai-Coh and Chian to drop to the ground sending fire over the battlefield taking care of the deadly crossbow bolts before they could inflict harm upon them. The fire breath scared the orcs enough that some dropped their weapons entirely running away in terror to get as far away from the all-consuming fire as possible.

As Drogen's fire breath abated, Mai-Coh and Chian jumped to their feet running for Drogen as quickly as they could manage. Those not scared off by the dragon's fire started running after them weapons drawn, and bolts quickly finding their place upon bow in order to let loose another volley.

With each passing second more of the goblinkin came flooding out of the remaining portcullis. The army moving swiftly to block Mai-Coh and Chian's path forward. The orcs coming in with thrusts, slashes, and overhead swings. Ogres with bludgeons following the steadily growing half legion of their orc cousins into the arena as swiftly as their feet would carry them.

The ground and wall in front of Drogen had turned into molten flowing glass under the heat of his white-hot fire. Cutting his fire off. The walls and ground caught under his breath turned into a single sheet of quickly cooling molten glass.

Grock looked down from his vantage heatwaves dissipating just enough for Drogen to glimpse a massive warhammer at Grock's side. A weapon Drogen had not seen there before. As the heat receded and clear glass formed Grock took hold of the warhammer's haft raising the maul up over his head before jumping from the wall and into the arena below.

A wall of orcs and ogres fully solidified behind Drogen, blocking Mai-Coh and Chian from getting to him. *If only they could have made it here before the line formed,* thought Drogen. *I will just have to get to them instead.*

Grock's massive form came running for Drogen standing four times his height and five times his width he came on with a two-handed swing narrowly missing Drogen as he sank to the ground beneath the swing. Pulling back the warhammer he raised the maul above his head bringing it crashing down to earth as Drogen flung himself backwards. Grock's warhammer hit the blood-soaked ground scattering dried sandy blood across the arena in all directions and cracking the glass formed by Drogen's fire. The cracking glass forming small fissures through the entire glass structure.

That will be another surprise for Grock, thought Drogen. With a smile. *Tis time to get out of here.* Listening for Mai-Coh and Chian's heartbeats Drogen found them fighting and running as necessary each second forcing them further away.

Grock came at Drogen with a fast swing that Drogen barely dodged with a back-step feeling the push of air from the massive maul as it careened past. With the warhammer past he stepped into Grock's space Godslayer coming in with an upward thrust to Grock's chest, while Envoy of Death moved in with a downward slash against Grock's hands.

With a back-step of his own, Grock moved out of Drogen's reach an opportunity Drogen took advantage of by disengaging and running into the fray behind him. Spitting Dragon's fire at Grock in hopes that it would slow his progress. The white-hot flames enveloped Grock completely but made no contact. A thick golden barrier encasing his body nullifying any and all harm that might have befallen him.

Drogen dared not turn his back to Grock completely, knowing that one false move would spell his end, and the end of Mai-Coh and Chian. *We will be free of this place soon,* thought Drogen.

Grock ran into his forces searching instinctively for Drogen's retreating form and with each step gained ground.

The small dagger he had procured was worn out beyond repair. The sword he had found lying on the ground in their hasty retreat proved no better, breaking in two against an orcs armored torso. However, Mai-Coh was far from defenseless against their onslaught. As they drew in close their arms raised Mai-Coh used his superior speed to run beneath their downward strikes chomping into and through any exposed skin that might stick out ripping fingers, and arms off with each bite of his powerful jaws.

Still, the battle was far from easy with arrows careening in and around them every time they thought about gaining ground. Luckily for them and their continued health most of the arrows struck orc and ogre instead of their intended targets. Killing more than a few of their own people in the process.

The deaths caused by their own comrades did nothing to stem the flow that continued to grow in front of them for as one fell dead three more took their place leaving no openings for Mai-Coh and Chain to run through. The dire situation further amplified with the additional threat posed by the larger goblinkin gaining numbers with each necessary retreat.

Chian skewered a couple of orcs upon a horn throwing them into their brethren pushing back on their line. The bodies of their comrades proving little more than a nuisance to those they struck.

"Can you see Drogen Chian," questioned Mai-Coh ducking a crossbow bolt just in time for it to penetrate the eye of an orc that had circled in behind them.

"No," bellowed Chian skewering an ogre with a devastating goring horn. Throwing the ogre back the way it came, it crashed into the line of orcs tumbling them to the ground like domino's.

"Not survive much longer," said a clearly worried Mai-Coh.

Chian, from the natural vantage of height, looked over the army for any sign of Drogen. Drawing eyes down upon the one figure likely to denote Drogen's location. Grock. Chain pointed a furry blue finger Grock's way as he raged through his own people the devastating warhammer sending tens of goblinkin to their untimely grave taking collateral along the way.

"I believe that to be the most logical place for the dream walker to be as well," said Mai-Coh. "We need to get closer, so he might find us." The goblinkin line began to encircle around them placing Mai-Coh and Chian in mortal peril. They continued to fight their way along the goblinkin line toward Grock's rampaging form flinging bodies and biting off limbs as they went, but the line of enemies continued to heed the dead in the same manner one shows an ant.

Mai-Coh listened intently for any sign of Drogen but found it difficult to hear anything between the goblinkin surrounding them, and Grock's tireless killing of his own people as the deity tried and failed to find and kill Drogen. Grock's continued rampage behind enemy lines bringing a bit of renewed strength to Mai-Coh and Chian's rapidly fatiguing stamina.

Two giants came running through the only open portcullis at the exact same time, sending block and debris out over the battlefield and killing many with the spray of materials and many more as they fell to the ground crushing any unfortunate enough to be in the path of their descent.

The giants quickly righted their blood-soaked bodies brushing the bodies away as they righted themselves running toward Grock's side stomping orcs and ogres alike with each footstep taking more to the grave as they gained on their deity's position.

Within the fray unfolding beneath Grock's feet Mai-Coh finally spotted Drogen's red tipped black hair a golden barrier forming a thin shell around him as he cut, sliced, dodged, parried, and countered orc and ogre attacks. All the while Drogen's eyes never loosing contact with the true threat, Grock. Every dodge and retreat bringing Drogen closer to where he somehow knew Mai-Coh and Chian to be.

Drogen heard their heartbeats getting closer as he moved through the ranks of orcs and ogres. Knowing Mai-Coh and Chian would be hard pressed to gain any more ground. *I could send dragon fire upon the entirety of Grock's army, but it would in turn hurt or kill Mai-Coh and Chian,* thought Drogen.

Grock's warhammer came down upon an ogre, who had errantly stepped into his path, splattering those around the crushed creature in sinew, blood, and bone fragments.

Drogen retreated further into enemy lines taking out any and all who hindered his progress. Mai-Coh and Chian coming closer with each step, until two more giants joined Grock's side. The orcs quickly dissipated from around him, forming a path of retreat, but in turn leaving him open for more precise attacks.

The giants carried with them massive wooden bludgeons which they haphazardly used to crush the sand before them turning any goblinkin that had not retreated from around Drogen to paste beneath heavy blows that sent a mixture of wet and dry sand careening through the air.

"It would seem there is more to you than meets the eye brother," said Grock noticing the golden barrier taking shape around Drogen. "Still, you are far too lacking to think yourself worthy of taking me," roared Grock as his hammer came down crushing the bloody sand, as Drogen jumped back out of harm's way.

Drogen felt a surge of power within himself. A power that felt new, yet eerily familiar. As the army continued to grow around him so too did the power, he felt swell. There in his mind he swore he heard the voices he had longed to hear since Ether and Uther's Death. *Home. Tis like I have come home,* thought Drogen. The golden barrier began to thicken and compress around his form as he pulled upon the subconscious string that had suddenly come to light within his mind.

In that single moment Drogen lost sight of Grock his concentration broken from the sudden thread of life shown by Godsalyer; Envoy of Death. Drogen realized far too late his mistake as the maul of Grock's warhammer crashed in at his side sending him hurdling uncontrollably through the air. As he hit the ground the entirety of the feeling dissipated to non-existence drawing silence to his mind once more.

Mai-Coh and Chian came running up to Drogen closing the distance quickly as Grock and the two other giants came on in a rush to deliver their finishing blow upon their downed foe.

Grock was the first to reach Drogen casting his warhammer down from on high as Mai-Coh and Chian slid in beside Drogen's hard breathing form hoping to pull Drogen free before the hammer could finish what it started.

The hammer and bludgeons fell in succession upon the ground pounding anything and everything beneath into the ground. "This is what will come to any who stand in my way, *DESTROY ALL WEAKNESS; SLAUGHTER TO* PREVAIL," roared Grock. "Now lift your weapons and witness the devastated flesh of our foolish foes." Lifting his hammer into the air Grock shouted to the arena around him.

Many took up the call, but it was short lived as all the weapons that had come down were pulled away revealing the ground beneath, and the unmistakable truth it held for Grock his command.

As he looked down upon the compacted ground where he knew his enemy to be, he found nothing. No blood, bone, or sinew graced the ground at his feet. Grock's eyes pulsed wildly, seething in unfettered rage. Behind him yet another call of surprise drew his eyes yet again, as the glass structure cracked and crumbled sending the throne, he'd been sitting on within the stands, to the blood-soaked ground below. In his enraged state, he attacked the two giants that had come to his aid, crushing each of them fully and completely from head to toe with the maul of his warhammer before his anger subsided.

Those on the battlefield dissipated quickly, running from their enraged god. To any place that might provide safety.

Looking down on the arena bellow Golga, Roccan, and Cauron frowned upon their enraged deity.

"Did you see it Roccan. The glow he emitted. It was only for an instant, but I know I saw it," said Golga.

"Your eyes are simply playing tricks on you Golga," admonished Cauron.

"Cauron right Golga. Only a god can manifest golden aura. It had to be a trick of the light, and nothing more," said Roccan.

"Well even if the two of you won't recognize what I saw, at least you acknowledge he's a dragon," said Golga. "You just refuse to see it is all. He talked to those creatures, the ones with the lizard heads and they worked with him," said Golga.

"Drogen did look quite offended by Grock's characterization of the drake," said Roccan with a smile.

"Still, I didn't expect the drake to take to that one so easily, but what does it change anyways. You saw how hard he struggled against Grock," said Cauron as if chewing on each word.

"It changes everything," said Golga

"It changes nothing. We still move against the other races of Dranier on Grock's order," said Roccan. "It is nice that so many could be saved from death here but, they will die anyways with this senseless crusade. We have simply allowed them to live a short time longer."

"He said there would be a time when he will call upon us for assistance," said Golga

"We are nothing more than cannon fodder for Grock's purposes," said Cauron. "I doubt another of the Gods or the Dragon's will be any different in that regard."

"I know that he will be different, you cannot tell me you do not feel the same way Roccan," questioned Golga hopefully.

"I do hope that what you believe comes to pass, but we cannot truly know until the time comes," said Roccan.

"What information were you able to give them," questioned Cauron.

"I gave them all the information, in a nice book" said Golga.

"Are you insane. What if they would have all died, and Grock found out," chided Roccan. "He would pound our heads down to our feet in an instant.

"Then make sure he does not find out," said Golga with a huff.

"It seems his rage has finally dissipated," sighed Cauron.

"Let's hope the two giants are the only other casualties this day," said Roccan with a nod.

"Will the two of you help him when the time comes," questioned Golga apprehensively.

"The question is Golga, are there any willing to help us, if such a thing does come to pass," questioned Roccan.

"We cannot be the only ones who disagree among our cousins," said Golga.

"I fear we might be," said Cauron.

"We cannot think in such a way Cauron. If we do then everything is lost," warned Golga. "I know that Grom and Bogger are with us, and Hargo may be as well."

"We are the leaders of our people. Where we go, they will follow," added Roccan.

"Yes, they will follow. But the orcs are a different story," said Cauron. "I fear most are unwilling to go against Grock. They follow his word absolutely."

"We need to recruit more if we have any chance of winning a battle of attrition against own kin," said Roccan.

"No better time to start than now," said Golga with a twinkle in her eye.

"Best mind that ambition doesn't cause you and everyone else to lose their heads," said Cauron.

"Well, there is an upside to such things," said Roccan with a slight forlorn smile.

"And what could be the upside to losing our heads," questioned Cauron.

"If we lose our heads, it's no longer our problem to solve," said Roccan.

Chapter Twenty-Two

Mai-Coh and Chian could not believe their eyes as they looked around the room struggling to gather their bearings with each blink of their eyes. So instead of focusing on what they could not understand they focused back on the one they knew had made it happen, Drogen.

His breathing was shallow and growing weaker as the injuries beneath the crushed surface began to take hold bringing him closer to the end with each breath.

Chian picked Drogen up off the floor placing him on the soft leafy bed of the small room so they could have a closer look at Drogen's injuries. As Chian lifted Drogen's upper body off the bed, Mai-Coh carefully pulled the blood-soaked tunic up over Drogen's head.

The small amount of light passing through the rooms window proved barely enough for Chain to see, but it was more than enough for Mai-Coh. "The light dies as it touches the dream walkers' side, where hammer struck."

"What might heal the wounds beneath," questioned Chian.

"I know not what can heal the dream walker. Wounds below the surface are hardest," said Mai-Coh as he scanned the room for anything that could help the one who had saved them. He noticed a bright red light coming from the floor of the room, for a split second. Displaying an unfamiliar symbol that dissipated as he blinked.

"Water," came Drogen's shallow almost nonexistent voice as the volume of air filling his lungs wheezing in a raspy agonized breath. "And its Drogen... not dream walker," he struggled to say, trying in vain to lighten the mood.

"Watch over the dre... Drogen, said Mai-Coh admonishing himself internally. "I know not what water might accomplish, but likely to be his last request," said Mai-Coh with concern. "Watch over him."

Chian nodded grabbing hold of Drogen's arm and hand with a delicate but firm grip listening intently to his erratic heartbeat. Taking in what he thought might be his final look upon the one who had rescued them, Mai-Coh went running out the door of the small room.

Drogen moved into unconsciousness, and back again multiple times with Chian gripping his hand and arm tighter each time. Hoping the feeling would bring comfort to Drogen's weakening form. Many minutes passed as Chain waited with Drogen. Minutes that felt like hours with each flutter of Drogen's heart.

Mai-Coh came rushing into the room carrying a flower vase filled with water in hand. "The stream is not far; however no other vessel could be found. Is Drogen conscious?"

"Yes, bring it here," said Drogen with a strained whisper barely audible to even Mai-Coh. His voice gaining some strength as he forced himself up into a seated position with Chian's help.

"Hold it out before my mouth, do not be afraid," Drogen coughed, "This flame will not touch you."

Mai-Coh gave the vase over to Chian who placed it in front of Drogen's mouth waiting for him to muster the necessary strength. With a shallow breath in Drogen let out a golden flame turning the liquid within to a golden syrupy. "Drink this for your wounds and give what remains to me," bid Drogen.

Mai-Coh and Chian looked at each other for a split second quickly deciding in their silence that it was best for Drogen to take the entirety of the golden liquid himself. Chian put the vase to Drogen's lips bidding him to drink, and drink he did, pulling the entirety of the liquid from the vessel and down his throat. The dragon water started working instantly as they heard Drogen's bones move back into place. His lungs regaining their full breadth as they regained their former capacity.

The effective elixir healed internally and externally. Bringing with it cascading waves of anguish, forcing Drogen to cry out from the suffering that raked his body and mind. He let loose a roar of pain. Blue fire foaming at his mouth, as the remaining injuries within his body mended.

Chian and Mai-Coh looked at each other with concern as Drogen's body went limp and the healing of the wound finally subsided leaving his skin a clammy mixture of blood, sweat, and tears.

"Has been ages since I have felt such all encompassing pain," shivered Drogen as he began moving towards the beds edge. "I will need to ingest more to fully heal. What about your injuries," questioned Drogen. Fighting against the unhealed bruising he moved to, and sat on, the edge of the bed.

"How long until the winged ones arrive," questioned Mai-Coh clearly diverting from Drogen's question.

"When I came here initially, I had no inclination as to where I was heading, Godslayer; Envoy of Death guided me to this place," said Drogen clear tension showing upon his face. "Asche and Keltus know how to get here. Their journey will prove shorter than mine... Still, I suspect it will take them at least a day to get here if not two," he said while contemplating. "Plenty of time to heal before we receive them. Now let us go to the place you found water, that we might heal our wounds at once. Before the others arrive."

Mai-Coh and Chian nodded in confirmation before taking hold and lifting Drogen to his feet carefully. Wary of the pervasive injuries neither of them could see, Mai-Coh let Chian be Drogen's crutch as he led them to the spring he had found. Chian looked at Drogen with concern noticing that every step forward elicited a nearly inaudible wince, A wince that Mai-Coh tried hard not to notice as their pace slowed to a crawl.

The pain wrought havoc though Drogen's body and mind distorting the world and everything around him into an extension of agonies influence. Each step calling for more focus than the last to keep his legs and feet going despite the pain. With one final step his legs buckled, nearly dropping him to the ground. With his right hand raised, he successfully steadied himself against a tree trunk.

Chian, noticing the failure of Drogen's legs grabbed upon the back of his breaches hoisting him up and taking away his need to walk as the sound of rushing water quickly intensified to a thunderous tempo around them.

The small, yet swift creek appeared only a few feet wide, but the ripple-less current upon its surface, conveyed more depth than its width would suggest.

Mai-Coh dropped to his knees in front of the spring filling the vase once more with water bringing it back to Drogen quickly. Drogen breathed fire into the vessel once more forming the thick golden dragon's water before it was put to his lips to drink by Chian. Drogen drank the syrupy liquid down in one gulp feeling the healing effects take hold immediately as the pain that had plagued his every step subsided to a dull ache, and then, to nothing at all.

"Thank you, my newest friends. Now tis time to heal your wounds," said Drogen.

Mai-Coh and Chian, even though they had seen the proof firsthand, found it hard to believe that Drogen's injuries had actually healed. Both Chian, and Mai-Coh looked at each other clearly hashing out whether to partake of the liquid themselves or not. Each of them shrugged in answer and Mai-Coh filled the vase once more.

Drogen patted Chian's hand, which still had him suspended in the air, so that she would release him to the ground once more taking the vase of water from Mai-Coh and releasing his dragon's fire upon it. With a shaky hand he handed it back to Mai-Coh. "I do have one request," he said as Mai-Coh took a drink handing it over to Chian. "I ask that you not bring up my injuries until the question arises. I do not wish to worry the others, nor impose unnecessary strife after what we all had to survive," said Drogen concern upon his face as he looked into both of their eyes.

"As you wish dream walker Drogen," said Mai-Coh drawing a nod from Chian as well as they both looked over their fully mended injuries. They both bowed to Drogen as they had seen him do before, to which he replied in kind.

"We should get back to the Queens Manor. I don't wish to be away should the others sojourn here take less time than I estimated. We also need to rest. Our injuries are healed however, only rest or meditation can recover stamina, and from strain," said Drogen.

As two days and nights came and went all three of them continued to look into the sky hoping to see the drake and wyvern's decent through the trees. As the sun reached its zenith Mai-Coh came running up to Drogen and Chian excitedly. "The winged ones come," he said.

"I was growing increasingly worried that something had befallen them as they escaped," said Drogen with a sigh of relief.

"Most have doubted my ears, yet you do not," questioned Mai-Coh inquisitively.

"Although, I may not have the ability to hear over the distances you are capable of, I can still hear far further than most others," said Drogen. "As I mentioned before, I can hear each of your heartbeats," he said with a warm smile. "I could have used your abilities when I was trailing the goblinkin on their way to Grammora. Maybe then I could have forgone some of the anxiety that plagued the first half of my journey."

The drake and both wyvern's descended through the canopy of trees above the Queen's mansion touching down lightly with a steadying beat of their wings. "I sorry old one. Try get here fast, but others go another place first. Many go away but cousin's do not," said the drake.

The drake bent down so that those upon his back could descend to the ground bowing his head to Drogen as he approached.

The two wyvern's set down beside the drake, having no passengers upon their backs, looking at Drogen fearfully.

"The important thing is that everyone is safe," said Drogen with a slight bow of his own. "I am Drogen, Godslayer; Envoy of Death; Drakregus of Lundwurm Tul."

With Drogen's declaration the drake dropped its head down even further to the ground, only raising from his position when Drogen did. "I am Strom old one," he proclaimed proudly.

The others joined him, listening to the two of them speak in draconic and not understanding a word. Except for Natalia who seemed quite interested in what each of them were saying.

"Tis good to meet you Strom. Now that your task for me is done, what will you do."

"Seek family, Separated from others. I captured put in smelly place," said Strom with distain.

"I wish there was something I could do to help you find your family, but I have only been away from Lundwurm Tul a short time. You're the only drake I have come to know," said Drogen sorrowfully.

"Tis okay old one. Know where family is. Take much time, but Strom find," said the drake enthusiastically.

"Very well then Strom when you see fit, journey to find your family. You are a prisoner no longer," said Drogen with a kindly expression and bow.

"I hope to see you and your family the next time we meet Strom," said Natalia in guttural draconic. "And thank you for teaching me these last few days."

"I glad to help black wing," said Strom.

"How is it that you learned how to speak to him in another language in only a couple of days," said Asche.

"I still don't understand how that's even possible," remarked Keltus.

"I don't understand it myself really. Languages simply make sense to me, or maybe it is all the books I have in my head," said Natalia with a shrug.

Drogen moved over to the two wyvern's who looked up at him terrified. "You need not worry cousins, you did as you were told and you are free once more," said Drogen the wyvern's looked at each other for a second before beating their wings and flying as far and fast from Drogen as they possibly could. "I wished to heal their tails, but it seems they wish to be away from this place quickly."

As the wyvern's left Natalia flapped her wings covering the distance between her and Drogen quickly, enveloping him with wings, arms, and legs. "I feared I might not see you again," said Natalia. Tears streaming down her face.

With his arms locked by Natalia's impassioned embrace Drogen caressed her leather covered leg causing her heart rate quickening at his gentile touch. With the realization that her actions garnered an audience Natalia dropped her legs from around Drogen's body but refused to let her arms go from around his neck forcing her to use her wings to maintain altitude before him.

Drogen wrapped his free arms around Natalia's waist in a tender embrace of his own. "I'm glad you have returned unharmed," said Drogen whispering into her ear his forked tongue tickling the helix sending a shiver down her spine.

"Ahem, we don't mean to interrupt, but is there some place we can clean ourselves up," questioned Keltus, Asche smacking her sister's arm for interrupting them.

Mai-Coh and Chian came walking up behind the group. Staying back, not wanting to make the others uncomfortable with their presence.

"You two don't need to worry," said Drogen. "You're among friends, nobody here will treat you differently than we would another."

Mai-Coh and Chian, at Drogen's declaration came in only slightly closer. Seeing their reluctance to fully join the others, Asche and Keltus grabbed hold of their hands dragging them into the group.

"Should we all go and wash then," questioned Drogen.

"That's fine with us, we kind of got used to it being in the arena," said Asche.

"True, it somehow feels like a natural thing to do now," said Natalia.

"It was much the same way in Lundwurm Tul. Although nudity was not uncommon in general, most of my race used a communal hot spring to cleans themselves of fatigue," said Drogen.

"I know not what hot spring is, but we shall join you, if we are permitted," said Mai-Coh.

"What about you Chian," questioned Keltus.

"I will come too," said Chian in a feminine voice that surprised all but Drogen and Mai-Coh.

"Wait, you're a woman," questioned the others with wonder in their eyes.

Chian looked at Drogen skeptically understanding all but his reaction. "Why does it seem like you knew," questioned Chian.

"Simply put women have a different heart rate than men do. The question is, why did you feel the need to hide it," said Drogen.

"While Chian explains, I will lead us," said Mai-Coh beckoning them all to follow as they listened to Chian.

"My people; the taurean, and Mai-Coh's; the pawnee view being a warrior as a man's profession. Women stay home, support their family. It is a peaceful life, but I wanted to learn how to fight and build. Like the men of my village. I passed each trial the chieftain had for me. I come to this land for my final task."

They walked through the trees following behind Mai-Coh and listening intently to Chain's every word. Mai-Coh looking back at her every now and then to make sure she was alright.

"The chieftain gave me the task of finding a method of building that improves Taurean life. I traveled to this part of the world, from which none have ever returned. To show them all that I am capable of building a house of my own. I need more proof of my ability, that I am capable of working alongside the strongest of my kith," finished Chian.

"Tis strange, the ways of this world. My race is that of warriors, everyone within takes part in war efforts. Whenever necessary," said Drogen.

"All elves are taught to fight, so they might defend our lands from invasion," said Asche.

"I was a part of the wyvern guard when we lived in Moonclave," said Keltus. "They are considered Moonclave's elite."

"What about you Mai-Coh. It sounds like you came from the same place Chian does. Are you here for the same reason," questioned Natalia.

Mai-Coh slowed his pace slightly at the question, the sound of water filling their ears as they drew closer to the water way. "I follow Chain in coming to this land, but my goal is different. My clan change shape to fight, and to run. I cannot change, so viewed as outcast among Pawnee. Come to find answer why."

With a wave forward Mai-Coh led them into a clearing along the bank of the creek where they could all clean themselves comfortably without fear of being swept away by the unforgiving currents above. As a group they wasted no time getting undressed, jumping feet first into the cold flowing water.

Natalia and Drogen stole glances at each other as they cleansed their bodies of grime and dirt. Natalia, for the first time in what felt like a lifetime, felt clean. Still images of those that had been lost during their time in the arena, and all the dead plagued her. A mark on her mind that she could not shield herself from.

All the others cleansed themselves and their clothes in the flowing water before getting out to hang the clothes on nearby branches to dry. Mai-Coh and Chian gave their own clothes to the elves to hang while they continued basking in the cool water. Asche and Keltus returning a short time later cannonballing into the creek splashing water over them all with joy filled musical laughter.

Natalia continued cleaning herself by dunking herself under the water and flapping her abyssal black wings which glistened in the sunlight as the water-droplets fell away. She moved closer to shore feeling her wings grow in weight as they retained water threatening to drag her down should she not be careful.

"I can help you, if you would like," said Drogen after seeing her struggle against the weight trying to rid herself of the last vestiges of grime.

Natalia was both embarrassed and excited by the prospect agreeing as she grew tired of struggling against her own body. "Thank you," said Natalia as Drogen's hands gently caressed the feathers loosening and pulling away everything that clung to them to have it wash down stream.

Asche and Keltus looked at the two of them with giant smiles ushering Mai-Coh and Chian out of the water to grab their clothing from the trees. They grabbed their clothes and began journeying back to the Queens Mansion unencumbered by garments as they drip dried.

Finished with her right wing Drogen moved his hand to her back massaging away the filth that remained. Eliciting a slight moan from her mouth at his gently massaging fingers. He worked the tension from her back and shoulders before starting on her left wing.

"Thank you, Natalia. If not for you tis likely we would have little more information than we started with about the goblinkin. Although it may be hard for those we had to leave here to understand, in the long run, it proved to be the right thing to do. Now we know there are allies among the goblinkin. Although those that died will haunt our memories, we will make certain their deaths do not go without meaning, said Drogen

Natalia turned round slowly fighting against her wings weight till she faced Drogen and embracing his muscular form and planting a tender kiss on his lips before moving out of the water expunging tears from her eyes.

Drogen wrapped his arms around Natalia's waste lifting her naked flesh against his stomach careening his neck down to meet her impassioned lips. Breaking the kiss only to catch her breath. "Are you sure," questioned Drogen.

"Yes, I'm sure. I've been sure since we danced together in Zephyria," said Natalia. "I don't know why it took me so long to see it, or why you didn't do anything when Seraphine and I were naked in bed beside you."

"Nudity was natural in Lundwurm Tul," said Drogen. "And... we would have been interrupted," he continued with a smile.

With bated breath she kissed him once more. Drogen walked with her lithe body laying her upon the grassy bank. Drogen scanned her smooth body taking in every inch before kissing her clavicle and down to her exposed breast caressing her with his forked tongue as he made his way down her body kneading her breast with his right hand eliciting soft moans and shivers of anticipation.

Drogen kissed around her pubic mound dropping lower to touch upon her sensitive folds with a gentile kiss and flick of his forked tongue. Her moans became pervasive and sensual as his tongue probed her every furrow. Edging Natalia closer and closer to ecstasy as his tongue found her most sensitive areas to caress. As she neared release his tongue pulled up from beneath her prize propelling Natalia into waves of rapture as he continued his gentile assault stimulating her further with his left hand between her legs while his right traced lines upon her stomach and attending to each of her sensitive peaks.

Drogen positioned himself above her his phallus touching her opening as he kissed her lips feverishly Natalia pulled him in closer wrapping his neck with her arms and wings, wishing to become one with him in body and soul. Natalia positioned herself under him feeling another release of pleasure as he slowly pushed into her. The feeling of him probing her most sensitive areas causing her to gasp and moan in excitement and anticipation.

As he pushed forward, they felt a tear and tears began streaming down her face Drogen stopped allowing her to become accustomed to the new sensations, as she continued her assault on his lips. They continued further only after she began to move herself along his length moaning with pleasure anew falling into ecstasy together the pleasure of each other's carnal desires coalescing with a final thrust of both their hips.

Drogen rolled off of Natalia carefully his energy more spent than if he'd been fighting the entire day but feeling altogether more fulfilled than he'd ever felt before. He scooped Natalia up into his arms holding her close and kissing her lips as they lay upon the bank basking in their collective glow.

They wanted nothing more than to lay there forever, embracing each other and forgetting the world around them, but they knew too well that if they chose to do so the deaths of those whose lives had been lost would be for naught. Begrudgingly, they returned to the water and washed themselves of sweat and shared fluids drying off in the grass embracing each other before returning to their waiting companions.

"Are we to ask Asche and Keltus to guide us to the Moonclave," questioned Natalia.

"I thought of that before I left to find you. If they're unable to help me find Moonclave, I simply need to activate the rune I placed on Seraphine's back. I need only activate the magic, and I can guide us to Moonclave.

As they approached their companions through the trees Drogen could hear the disturbed heartbeats of everyone from what should have been inside the Queens mansion. "We need to move quickly, something's wrong," said Drogen.

They ran through the trees and into the clearing that housed the manor finding nothing but those that had returned, clean and dressed, from the creek.

Natalia looked at the clearing with slack jawed amazement for where the mansion once stood was bare of all but grass. "What could have caused something like this to happen, and so suddenly," she questioned as both her and Drogen ran for their clearly baffled friends.

"I don't know either," said Asche. "I have never heard of one of our structures disappearing in such a way. Have you Keltus?"

"No, this is something new. I've never witnessed anything like this before either.".

"Is Strom still here," questioned Drogen.

"No, he left while we cleaned ourselves," said Chian.

"So, asking him if he has seen anything like this is also out of the question then," stated Natalia. "This doesn't look good. Could something have happened to Seraphine and her mother in Moonclave."

"There can be no other explanation," said Asche.

"Wait, you know Seraphine and her mother," questioned Keltus.

"Yes, Seraphine is a close friend," said Natalia agonizing over what the structures disappearance could mean. "I think you better get going to Moonclave and quickly," she stated looking Drogen directly in the eyes. Take this as well, she said bringing out a book she had hidden inside her armor. This is a translated copy of Grock's plans, I thought it best to translate it, and I am glad I did."

"Can you guide me to Moonclave," questioned Drogen to both Asche and Keltus.

"We can, but it may take us some time to find the right path," said Keltus.

"Are you not coming with us," questioned Asche to Natalia.

"No, I need to get back to Zephyria. With any luck we can help dismantle Grock's plans more effectively if we come at it from multiple directions, and I will be needed to efficiently translate this book again," said Natalia turning to Chian and Mai-Coh, "Do you wish to join Drogen or will you come with me to Zephyria. I cannot guarantee that we will have all the answer's you seek, but we have a beautiful city and builders that Chian might learn from at least."

Mai-Coh went off to confer with Chian about while Natalia stepped up to Drogen's side kissed him on the cheek. "I'm sorry that I cannot continue on this journey with you," stated Natalia clearly heartbroken. Although I wish to be by your side, I cannot let you fight Grock and his army without any support. The dwarves, and elves are both under threat of the goblinkin. Should Grock succeed the other races that call this world home are under threat as well. I need to return to Zephyria and convene a force that can help.

"If the information that Golga gave us is completely accurate then we seriously underestimated the number's we are dealing with. I do have one question, since you came in later than I did, and with what was supposed to be the majority of their forces. How many goblins were in Grammora," questioned Natalia.

Drogen looked down at Natalia going over his time with the goblinkin outside of Grammora. "There were many among the warband when I started moving with them, but once we came to the city, I saw not one," said Drogen comprehending the problem. *Where are all the goblin's,* he thought. "It seems we're in a far more desperate situation then we truly realized." Drogen lifted her eyes to his own, kissing her once more as Mai-Coh and Chian came back with their answer.

"We will go with you to the place of the sky people," said Mai-Coh. Chian nodding her head in agreement. Both of them looking around to determine the right bearing.

"No need to search you'll be there before you know it. Simply touch upon my shoulders." They moved behind Drogen tentatively taking hold of his shoulders. Natalia embracing him with a kiss upon the lips. As their lips touched, she closed her eyes wanting to keep hold of the sensation as long as possible as Drogen snapped the fingers on both his hands, sending a strange sensation through her body. The sensation faded, as did the feeling of his touch, and she opened her eyes to see Mai-Coh, and Chain standing with her in a dark musty room. With the others nowhere in sight.

"Can anyone see where the door is, that will be the best way to let in some fresh air and light," questioned Natalia feeling around in the darkness for a wall or anything else she could find to figure out where she stood.

Chian found the door pushing it wide letting the rays of the setting sun filter through the door and into the room. The three of them looked around at the craftsmanship used to build the house in which they stood, but Chian truly understood the beauty and detail. "You were right my kith could benefit greatly from such craftsmanship," she said.

"This house was actually built by Drogen. Just wait till you see the buildings of Zephyria," said Natalia proudly.

With a flash of fire Drogen's rune appeared, burning to ash at their feet.

Drogen felt them leave his side the moment he snapped his fingers the secondary snap a focus to stay. *I will need to place a permanent sigil, but that would take far more time than I have to waste at the moment.*

Asche and Keltus moved in beside Drogen waiting. "We need to move quickly to Moonclave," he said picturing the rune he's drawn upon Seraphine's shoulder before they parted company. With a click of his fingers power flowed through the rune providing direction to Seraphine. *I'll be there soon my friends,* thought Drogen.

"Asche; Keltus. You know that I am of the draconic race," said Drogen to which they nodded. "I ask that you stand back and not be afraid for what you are about to see. Tis my truest form, and I will not hurt you," he said as they moved back.

Drogen stripped his clothes off taking a nail to cut away the flesh upon the outside of his scales that it would not cover the other two in skin and blood. As his flesh fell away the scales beneath pulled in the last rays of light from the world around them, as if night had suddenly come to the forest. With a thought the door in his mind flew open transforming in an instant into his true form. "Climb up on my back and let us fly swiftly to Moonclave."

Part 2

Caught Upon the Breeze

"Do you feel it upon the Breeze, an old one is coming."

"Can one of you at least tell me what is going on," I appreciate you saving me and all, but I could be doing something else to help my friends," protested Alya hanging upside down upon a willow's branches.

"The old one is coming. We all know what that means."

"We must greet the old one, must we not?"

"Yes. It's an old one after all."

"You need not worry he will seek us out. If he really is an old one, he will come to us,"

"What of those born of us. Will the old one not be angered by their transgression? They had the aura of the old one upon them. Will the old one be displeased by their capture and imprisonment.

"Will the old one be angry at us. They were wrought upon Dranier from our very trunks."

"What is an old one and how does any of this help my captured friends," questioned Alya angrily.

"The old ones understand the ignorance of children, far better than any others could. No, the old one will love those born of our trunks. The old ones differ from the deceivers for whom they sought truce.

"They will be angry at the imprisonment of those who came before.

"But unlike the deceivers, they will not take it out on those who did so without reason."

"Yes, deceivers need no reason."

"It's the folly of children to be ignorant until the time they are forced to open their eyes.

"Some cannot see the truth before them. What of those who care only for their own gain. Those that seek for themselves above others."

"Those like the deceivers."

"To try and double-cross the old ones in their own council, foolish deceivers.

"They will find deceiving the old one fanciful."

"Should we go to the saplings now?"

"How will the saplings react?"

"They view us as nothing more than what they see. As it's been since the time they walked from our trunks."

"Would it not be better to go to them now."

"Can I at least have a vote in this, since I'm here, after all" questioned Alya as the Willow tree holding her turned her right-side up passing her along its rope like branches onto its trunk.

"Once they gaze upon our moving forms, the saplings will understand themselves all the more."

"They are born of us, as we were born of the old ones.

"Their origin is one of peace, and ours is one of war. We are not the same."

"The saplings view the world through peace, their only conflict with dwarves."

"When will the old one arrive?"

"Such knowledge is irrelevant."

"We serve the old ones we need only wait for the old one to arrive. And with the old one's arrival, we will move once more.

"Until then we needn't concern ourselves. Let the saplings live as they have. Ignorant of their true origins and unknowing of the old one's path."

"Let them live in bliss for a short time longer, for the arrival of an old one after all this time can mean only one thing."

"War is coming."

"Will it be as it was before their self-exile."

"Will the ground quake with their power once more as they fight the deceiver's?"

"Um excuse me, but what do you mean war is coming. Could you mean with Grock," questioned a severe looking Alya as more branches began to encircle her fur covered body.

"We cannot know if the deceivers are aware of the old one's arrival."

"Do you think they would suffer an old one to live if they knew?"

"The deceivers wish to destroy the old ones."

"Then what are we to do? Should we try to keep."

"Protect them from the deceivers."

"No. we are incapable of doing anything to stop an old one. It is for the old one to decide, ours and our saplings fate."

"May the old one be kind, and bring about a future that all life may prosper and thrive."

"For now, we sleep and awake with the old one's arrival."

"Woe to the deceivers."

"Can you at least let me go, I'm bored just hanging around here," said a rather perturbed Alya. Her eyes widening in fear as thousands of blossoms began to bloom upon the willow trees around her.

"You will be released when the old one arrives."

"Don't want another imprisoned."

"It could anger the old one more."

"Can you at least get me some meat to eat I can't stand just eating vegetable's and mushrooms any more... Oh come on," raged Alya, as one of the willow's branches brought a tray of freshly picked fruits and vegetable up for her to eat.

The willow trees the breadth of Moonclave opened into a display of fragrant molten flowers, appearing to be alight with flame along their ground sweeping branches. Each limb swaying in a wind none, but the willows, could feel. Each branch a tributary of dancing flame. Many of the Elves looking upon the blooming trees in awe and fear. For most, it was the first time the willows had ever bloomed. As if they had been waiting for something that had finally come. The question on the mind of the elves soon became whether to take the molten blooms of the willows as a sign of providence, or calamity.

Chapter Twenty-Three

No light could be seen from outside her underground chamber. The only rays of light penetrating the round room making up her cell being iridescent vines, which gave off just enough light to outline the three objects within its confines. Seraphine lay upon the uncomfortable root bed looking at the remaining two objects a small table and a wooden bucket used to collect her waste.

Why does it have to be so dark in here. The least they could do is give more light. I am, or was, a princess after all. That should count for something, should it not.

I hope Alya was able to get away in time, and able to get a message off to Drogen... Somehow. She has to tell him what's happened. Maybe he can clear up this mess somehow. I hope my mom is okay as well. If only I knew he was coming then maybe... I would have more hope. Sitting here in this dark room the smell of my own excrement filling the air... please hurry Drogen.

But how will he find us, he has no method of doing so unless another elf brings him. Although, if that is the case how will he know that something is wrong and hurry to get here. He could travel the wood for weeks and still never come upon Moonclave. I fear the same to be true if he flies here. The barrier might detour him from approaching as well.

I feel so alone here, how long has it been, has it been a few days or a few weeks, maybe it's been a month. I can no longer tell. I feel like a caged animal. What can I do. If only I could bring down the door. If I could bring down the door then I could get out of here and run away, I would run far away, and never return.

Seraphine curled up on the mildew riddled bed. Tears filling her eyes again as the room around her began to constrict a snake coiling and threatening to take her life with each passing second that felt like hours. *I failed and now the council will sentence us all to death for a treason that would never have come to pass. Maybe if I could have said something about the dwarves when I stood in front of the council this wouldn't have happened... That too seems... unlikely. The council took great pleasure in removing my mother from her position and relieving her of every possession.*

"*Damn* the council and *damn* this cell," screamed Seraphine to the empty air.

"Who be there," came a familiar voice. "That you Elf? Where be fuzzy ears? She be ear too," questioned Rumble.

"You're here Rumble? Alya escaped. I don't know where she went. Wait... how long have you been here," questioned Seraphine. "What about Tumble, Is he here as well?"

"Good at least fuzzy ears got away. They add us in anudder area down ear, when we first be tossed in a cell. We be moved ear yesterday. Tree sprite took me brudder an our ago an haven't seen em since. Drogen be ere yet," he questioned hopefully.

"No. I've received no word of his arrival. Although, getting anything out of the guard hasn't been easy. Is Phaylor the one that's been taking you and Tumble out for questioning," posited Seraphine.

"No, an he not be the one who bring me brudder an me down ear either," said Rumble. "We not seen em since arrivin ear with ye and Fuzzy Ears."

"I don't think Phaylor knows what's going on down here. If he did, he would have come looking for us," said Seraphine. "I noticed those who came down here look around a lot before and after they enter my cell. Could it be they're doing this without Phaylor's knowledge," questioned Seraphine.

"Me brudder an me be noticin the same," said Rumble. "There be somethin amiss among the tree folks."

"I hope Drogen and Natalia get here quickly. Who knows what the council has planned for us. Whatever it is, if they're keeping our imprisonment a secret then we may be in for far more than I originally thought," said Seraphine.

"He say he be findin us. No need for them to know how he get ear. I not be knowen how he'll go about it, but I got no doubt, where that one be involved. One thing be for sure. Dem tree bugs be in for a shock," Rumble said with a hearty yet dry laugh.

Seraphine wanted to be as unshakable in her faith of Drogen as Rumble was, but still found herself doubting the possibility of rescue. "Quiet I hear someone coming."

"Get in there you dirty mole. I can't wait for the counsel to convene and execute all four of you. Treasonous scum." The boots of their jailor continuing to scrape the floor, until Seraphine heard them stop just beyond her door. "But first, I think I'll have a little bit of fun with our *former* princess," came his oily voice. As the door to her cell receded into the ground.

"Would you look at this, oh how the high have fallen." said the guard as he came into the cell. Using his magic, he quickly bound Seraphine's hands and legs. "However, my fun will have to wait. Members of the council have questions for you. Maybe they'll hand down your sentence today. Wouldn't that be nice," said the elf with an audible sneer.

"What would Phaylor think if he knew we were down here rotting in a cell," questioned Seraphine with a sneer of her own.

"What Phaylor does or doesn't know has no bearing on me. I work for the council," raged the elf. Roughly pulling Seraphine to her feet.

"I'll be sure to let him know you think so little of him," said Seraphine gritting her teeth. "What is your name council stooge?"

"I am Manzine, and I will gladly be your executioner," he said with a deep sneer back.

"Whether you follow through on that threat or not, I'll make sure you pay dearly for it," seethed Seraphine spitting in Manzine's face.

"You're lucky *former* princess. They expect you in pristine shape standing before them. Else I would take your head for what you have just did," said Manzine gnashing his teeth.

"Then you better take me to the council so we can get this over with. I want to see the look of disappointment on your face when things don't go according to your plan."

"That's enough out of you," bit Manzine creating another vine to wrap her mouth. Gagging her from uttering another word. "Oh, how surprised you're going to be when things go exactly to the councils plan," he sneered contemptuously.

Manzine grabbed Seraphine under her arm pulling her roughly toward the door, and with a firm hand, he pushed her through it. Forcing her to trip, her decent only halted by her face and shoulder crashing against the opposing wall. "Oh no you almost fell. What would the council think if you had damaged your face before seeing them, it simply won't do to be so clumsy," he chortled.

The council will listen to what I have to say. *Whether they like it or not*, thought Seraphine. As she struggled to bite through the vine in her mouth.

Manzine laughed as he followed closely, poking and prodding her as direction, whenever they came upon an intersection. Until they finally came to a set of carved stairs, runic script carved upon their every rise.

The runic symbols drew Seraphine's eye as they shared similarities with symbols she had seen before. Symbols she had seen in only one other place outside of Moonclave. On Drogen's twin blades. Her realization bringing a smile to her face. A smile Manzine quickly took note of.

"You won't be smiling after the council is done with you," said Manzine. Releasing the vine around her mouth as they transcended the stairs.

"That's where you're wrong Manzine. The one unable to smile will not be me. It will be those on the council after he arrives," said Seraphine shaking her head in disbelief of her, and subsequently the dwarves' luck.

"There's nobody who can save you now," he said. Pushing Seraphine in ill-mannered demand to open the door. Even with the push, and Manzine's egotistical threat the wide smile did not, disappear from Seraphine's face. Realizing nothing he did would take away her smirk, ire flowed like blood through him.

Seraphine pushed open the sturdy hardwood door, leading to the dungeon's depths, to reveal the council chambers beyond.

"Good you've brought her," came Terill's voice as they entered the round chamber room. "We can get on with the trial quickly and attend to... other duties."

"Yes. Let us be done with this quickly. I have other matters to attend to," Elmar said impatiently.

Terill bade Elmar to slow down with the rise and fall of his hand. "Boramil will be back with Elise shortly. Once they return, we can get on with the trial."

"Speaking of," said Manzine. Looking out the clear glass doors of the council tower.

Elise and Boramil walked quickly through the door. Closing and barring it from within, that no others could disturb the proceedings.

"It looks like everything is ready at least. I hope you weren't waiting long," said Elise.

"Looks as though we've come just in time," stated Boramil with a broad wicked smile.

"Yes. Yes. Take your seats. Now we can get this trial formally under way," said Terill dismissively.

"Where are Llewellyn and my mother," questioned Seraphine. Concerned by the lack of people who would likely be on her side.

"Llewellyn is the only other member of the council, and she is otherwise... indisposed," commented Elise.

"As for your mother Silf. She's no longer a member of the council and can no longer pass judgment," said Boramil.

"We have a majority of the council here, so rendering a verdict should be simple enough," said Terill.

"Let's get this trial under way then, shall we," said Elmar. As Boramil and Elise took their seats at the large crescent moon table to the right of the central dais.

Manzine pushed Seraphine toward the central dias. The vines around her wrists and ankles growing and wrapping themselves, and her, around the circular dais. The concentrated energy of the barrier surging through her, unlike it would be for others, was a feeling she had grown accustomed to with the use of the sword Truth.

"We the Elven council call this trial to start," proclaimed Terill vehemently.

"The accused has no representative for themselves. So, one will be appointed for this proceeding," said Boramil.

Terill made a show of looking around the room before stopping, in feigned surprise, upon the only other person in the room. "Manzine will you represent the accused."

"I must protest. Manzine will not give impartial representation. Had the council asked, they would know I have someone who can act as my representative. It will simply take time for them to arrive," proclaimed Seraphine.

"That is quite enough. Do you have any proof this representative is on their way here. Or are you just trying to waste this council's precious time," questioned Elise.

"He is coming, but it will take time for him to arrive. I'm standing here, at the barriers strongest point. Lies are not permitted within the barrier of Moonclave. And they are certainly not permitted upon this dais. Is this not proof enough that I tell the truth," decried Seraphine.

"And why should it be considered proof this representative elf of yours is actually coming. They may have told you they would be, but who's to say they've not been bound to duties elsewhere," countered Boramil.

"My representative will not be an elf. I don't know who among my own kin I can trust," stated Seraphine spitefully.

"Now you further admit you have disclosed the secret location of Moonclave to another outsider. Here I thought your treason fully known, as you have seen fit to bring our greatest enemy, the dwarves through the front gate," roared Terill.

"I disclosed the location of Moonclave to no one," asserted Seraphine.

"You may have not disclosed our location. But you have led enemies to our front door. That in of itself is an act of treason," raged Elmar slamming his fist into the crescent table.

"I have not disclosed the location of, nor led any enemies into Moonclave," said Seraphine.

"Such insolence will not be tolerated within these chambers," fumed Boramil.

"If you did not disclose the location of Moonclave to this *representative*. How do you know they can find Moonclave," questioned Elise.

"Yes... You have no proof. Aside from your word, this representative is coming. You're simply trying to eat up more of this council's time. Waiting on someone who may never come," remarked Terill.

"Without proof there is no reason to delay anything. Do you have any proof," questioned Elise smugly.

"What is that," blurted out Manzine covering his mouth, but he couldn't resend what he'd already spoken aloud, as he stared wide eyed at Seraphine's left shoulder.

Remembering Drogen's finger tracing a symbol upon her back, Seraphine breathed a sigh of relief. "You wanted proof my representative is coming. Here it is," smiled Seraphine triumphantly. Shrugged away the thin rags the council had seen fit to imprison her in, she exposed her shoulder. However, try as she might to turn and show the gathered council, she couldn't break the vines. Though she struggled valiantly against them.

Manzine loosened his hold on the vines, just enough for her to show the council. The slow pulsing glow of a runic sigil gracing her shoulder.

"How might this be considered proof," questioned Elise whose triumphant smile had quickly faded.

"Because he is the one that drew the symbol on my back. You never said what the proof had to be. Your question was if I had any proof. It's not my fault that you were not specific," said Seraphine.

"So, what. We could just sentence you and be done with this farce without anyone else ever knowing," proclaimed Elmar boisterously.

"He is the one that sent me here. And it seems to me you all have all forgotten something quite important."

"And what, pray tell, could we have forgotten that would change our mind in sentencing you right here and now," questioned Boramil with a sneer.

"Has anyone upon this council detained Alya," questioned Seraphine with a wince, she quickly hid suddenly remembering Manzine's wish for the four of them to be sentenced. Hoping she had not just overplayed her hand.

The council members looked at each other and back to Seraphine realizing quickly that none of them had locate the elusive warren. Although they had all tried to do so.

"Now imagine, if you will, that my representative arrives. I have already been sentenced by this council. A fact he comes to know through Alya," proposed Seraphine.

"You act as though you have won Seraphine, but your friend will not learn of what happens within this chamber. None other than those present will ever know. You have no leverage," stated Terill imperiously. His words garnering enthusiastic nods of support.

"That is where *you're* wrong. Where *you're all* wrong. The representative, you can see for yourself *is* coming, has power enough to raze Moonclave to the ground. He killed Ether and Uther, the twin gods of Zephyria after all," said Seraphine. Drawing gasps from everyone within the audience chamber.

"You lie. There is no existence that can stand before the gods," yelled Elmar. Slamming his fists down on the table again.

"Those who stand within the barrier of Moonclave, and especially at its core, are incapable of telling *lies*," asserted Seraphine. "Now imagine what someone capable of killing the twin gods of Zephyria *by himself* would be capable of... *Should he learn...* those he sent ahead were put on trial... by *this* council."

The entirety of the council, and Manzine, turned a deathly shade as they collectively contemplated the possibility.

"W-we will allow you this... representative," said Terill trying desperately to regain his former hold upon the trial's proceedings. "However, should your representative not arrive in a timely manner. W*e will* move ahead with your trial. And Manzine, *will be* your representative. This council will reconvene in a week's time. Should your representative not arrive within this allotted time, you will have no choice but to accept, *your fate*," he affirmed.

"Very well. I would however warn you. If anything untoward should happen to me, or those I arrived with, you will not like the consequences," insinuated Seraphine.

"You dare threaten this council," raged Elmar.

"It is not a threat. Tis a *promise*."

"Manzine take her away. The council has much to discuss," seethed Terill.

"It shall be done," said Manzine. A deep frown on his face. With a wave of his hand the vines ensnaring Seraphine to the dais returning to their original form. Wrapping around her wrists and ankles. Grabbing her by her long hair he pulled her off the raised dais forcefully. Only releasing his iron grip of her hair when they had reached the door of her cell.

Chapter Twenty-Four

Natalia couldn't help the wave of sadness, which washed over her upon witnessing the bright flash of Drogen's rune, as it turned to ash. With a sigh she pushed away her thoughts of Drogen knowing the task that lay before them both to be of utmost importance. With war on the horizon, not only for allies of her people, but for all the races of Dranier, they needed to prepare quickly for the coming conflict.

Many of my people have lost their lives and livelihood to the goblinkin who overtook Zephyr. More still lost their lives when Grock's minions attacked during Drogen's battle with Ether and Uther. We can no longer set on the sidelines and watch as Dranier is taken over. Many preparations need to be overseen and prepared to help, not only ourselves and our allies, but the whole of Dranier against what is coming, considered Natalia.

"If everyone is ready, we should make haste to the castle. Speaking to my father about Grock's plans, which I will need to translate for his review, needs to take priority. Once we deliver our information, it will be up to Zephyria to decide on the right course of action," said Natalia.

"May the sky people make the right decision," said Mai-Coh.

"I do not wish to pressure either of you into coming with me. However, pleading my knowledge before Lord Vladimir may be more... convincing with corroborating accounts of those who have gone through a similar... ordeal. Whichever path you two choose I will respect. Just to clarify my position. The reason I wish, for the three of us to do this together, is the information you have could prove invaluable," Natalia beseeched.

Mai-Coh looked to Chian who simply nodded her head before gesturing positively toward Natalia. "We will help. It is least we can do for black wings help in saving us. I know not what information Chian, or I possess. But we will give what we can," he finished with an emphatic nod.

"I know you both have goals you are trying to achieve. Zephyria is home to a massive library. If you would like books regarding on those subjects I will work to find them for you," said Natalia.

"Will we be welcomed among the sky people," questioned Mai-Coh apprehensively.

"You need not worry about what others will think. The only ones who might hold prejudice against you are the ones who have yet to stop worshiping our former gods. They are zealots who continue to do so even though, in many cases, they were the most hurt by the gods treachery. I still do not understand why."

With their plans outlined they extricated themselves from Drogen's small cottage in the woods. None of them had realized the staleness of the air present within the cottage until walking free of its confines and into the fresh air beyond. Each of them drawing in a deep breath of fresh air.

"Follow me to the castle. Best case we will run across Fread or Krail first. Having either of them on our side before we approach my father can only work in our favor. They will listen to everything that has happened while we wait for our chance to speak."

"Does this... Fread and Krail lead the sky people," questioned Mai-Coh.

"Yes. Fread is just below my father in rank, power, and influence. And Krail is his subordinate. Fread has looked after my family and the people of Zephyria people for many years. He has always been more like family to me than others in my life, especially when compared to my stepmother and sister. *Since the death of my mother at the hands of Ether and Uther Fread has been one of the only people I fully trust, Krail being a close second,*" said Natalia.

Natalia guided them down the path Drogen had made through the underbrush of the tamarack trees guiding them until the bustle of Zephyria's market street could be heard clearly through the trees.

It is possible an appeal directly to the people of Zephyria will be necessary. If it were something smaller, like an escort mission, I could simply put in a request. I will have to consult with Fread, but if we go that route, we can speak to your people directly in the audience chamber. It is asking a lot of Zephyria, but doing nothing is not an option, ruminated Natalia.

Mai-Coh and Chian followed closely behind Natalia. Many people looked to the three with concern but upon seeing the black winged Natalia went about their business. Seeing the reactions of the zephyrian's Mai-Coh and Chian let out sighs of relief. They had been ostracized by many of the people's they after traveling across the forbidden plains. Being captured and imprisoned by the orc's made them especially skeptical of other's they had yet to know.

Natalia walked through the streets greeting anyone who stopped to talk. She asked those who stopped her about Vladimir's mood as of late, but got many ambiguous answers in return. The none to subtle evasion of her questions raising suspicion that something had drastically changed during her absence.

Upon drawing closer to the castle, the density of people waned greatly. Especially when it came to the numbers heading toward the audience chamber. The drastic decrease in citizens further amplified by the increased number of guards leading up to the audience chamber. The number of guards gathered around the castle far more than Natalia had ever seen gathered.

Is it possible they already know about the goblinkin and their plans, considered Natalia.

As the massive spires of her home came into full view, so too did the line of subjects making their way to the audience chamber to have their requests heard. The line to the audience hall itself was far shorter than she had ever seen it. Still, many of the same faces graced the line.

The more that changes the more things stay the same, she thought.

The people in line for the audience chamber were mainly farmers who needed help in harvesting their crops, where the others were convoy leaders looking for guards to journey home across contentious lands.

The group Natalia didn't like seeing, so soon after returning, were the religious zealots she had warned Mai-Coh and Chian about. Those who believed each act of the gods was nothing short of divine justice. That sentiment had also included her mother's tragic end before her very eyes. They looked at anything not given by the gods as worthless or going against the gods righteous will, even Ether and Uthers death's could not temper their religious zeal.

The line of people gradually diminished before them filtering through every couple of minutes while the larger groups such as the traders naturally took longer, as guards and travel plans needed to be taken care of, before they could continue on about their business.

The three of them found themselves filtered into the audience chamber with the group of zealots who clearly had many things to discuss with Vladimir. Every few minutes, as they collectively looked around, they added more to the massive scroll they carried.

The guards and everyone around them didn't seem to pay Natalia or the people with her any more mind than they would a farmer, something she was both glad for and perturbed by. Many acting as if they didn't recognize her. Their actions drew no ire from her, but it did make her wonder if something serious had happened to her father.

"We demand the apprehension and death of the one that usurped the position of our gods through nefarious and undignified means. Our gods and those who have looked out for us for the entirety of our existence have been usurped by a heretic. Not only have we lost our link to divinity, but one unfit to rule over the people of Zephyria has taken the throne in place the appointed of Ether and Uther. We demand Vladimir stand before us once more as the messenger of the gods delivering upon the people of Zephyria their wisdom that we may retain what it is that makes the zephyrian people who we are," demanded the leader of the Zealots.

"Drogen has not usurped power through any means other than his own and he did not wish for us to worship him as Ether and Uther *demanded* all zephyrian's to do. He is not a heretic for killing those who took the lives of so many of our people. They would have killed him and many zephyrian's had he not stopped their rampage How many of your own order were killed by the gods during their visits to Zephyria," challenged Fread.

"We demand you return power to Lord Vladimir at once. None should view you as the ruler of Zephyria you hold no authority. We demand Lord Vladimir be return to his position at once," roared the zealous leader drawing a unified cheer of support from the others of his order.

"Lord Vladimir absconded his position and appointed me to the throne of Zephyria. You have no say in this matter and coming here every day demanding to be seen within this chamber is likely to delay your audience with him indefinitely. Now if you wish to continue this farce you are welcome to do so. However, you should keep in mind that the people of Zephyria are all feeling a great sense of relief after the death of those you so strongly believe to be infallible."

"We are here because of the gods. You would dare speak heresy against them," roared the zealot leader garnering angry taunts and gestures from those of his flock against Fread. "I suppose I should not be surprised when you allow blasphemous beasts within this chamber," he raged pointing in Mai-Coh and Chian's direction.

"*Guards* remove these instigators from this chamber. They've proven themselves unfit in action and will not be heard at this time. If they want to again voice their dissatisfaction and decent then they may come back in *two days'* time. Maybe then they can garner the audience that they wish to have with the former Lord Vladimir." Fread's order garnering protests from the group in its entirety. "However, if they show up tomorrow, they are to be turned away at every instance possible. If they remain insistent to the point of walking into this chamber. They are to be thrown into the dungeon beneath the city *for a week*," emphasizing Fread his full authority on display as guards rounded up the enraged zealots.

"The gods will hear about your heresy against them and those they appointed. You will be the first to die facing their divine wrath," screamed their zealous leader.

"Leave quietly or the week in the dungeon will begin right this instant," proclaimed Fread over their obnoxious protests.

It was clear from the looks on their faces that they wished to continue more than anything However, spending a week in the dungeon wasn't an option any of them wished to face. With the threat of imprisonment looming over their heads, they relented being escorted from the audience chamber without the utterance of another word.

As the zealots were pushed out the still broken audience chamber door and down the steps into the courtyard, Fread slump down into the throne rubbing his brow as though he were trying to nurse himself from a massive headache. Seeing Fread visibly relax those around him did the same. It was then that Natalia noticed that her group, the guards, and Fread were the only other people left within the audience chamber.

"How glad I am to see you're safe and sound Princess Natalia. I know you have many questions to ask me, and likely important matters to discuss, as I do with you, but there are a few people that may need to be brought into the conversation. Did Drogen not come back with you," he questioned with an exhausted sigh.

"No the information that we bring had to be given to others as well so he sent us here to relay the information we have while he made his way to the elves, in an effort to ready them for what is coming. I must say, of all the things I expected seeing you sitting on father's throne... was not one of them," said Natalia.

"That makes two of us, and yet another matter we need to discuss," Fread said. As Natalia made to speak Fread stopped her with an outstretched hand. "Before you ask Vladimir is in good health. He's simply trying to figure out what comes next for himself."

Rising from his throne on the dais Fread made his way down to Natalia, Mai-Coh, and Chian. "Even though he knew it to be the right course of action banishing Nefar and Bernadine took a lot out of him. It's my hope, he will reclaim the throne. However, as I have talked with him in your absence I find the chances of that happening to be minuscule," he said walking up to look into Natalia's eyes.

"Was your taking over because I was not here when he abdicated the throne," questioned Natalia.

"That has a lot to do with it I'm sure, but the other reason and the reason the rest of Zephyria is aware of now, is because I am his eldest son," said Fread.

"Wait, then that would make you my brother," exclaimed a shocked Natalia.

"In a way, yes. But there is much that has been revealed to me that I never knew and that you yourself will need to hear," said Fread apologetically.

"Why would you hide something like that from me," questioned Natalia both ecstatic and saddened by the revelation.

"That at least is easy to explain. I wished to not have the stigma of royalty hanging over myself. I wished to earn my rank and the trust of the people by my own means, and not under the guise of royal privilege. I gained my position as leader of the guard with my own merits, blood, sweat, and tears. If I had my way, I would have never told another soul my lineage. Unfortunately, fate had other plans."

"But, we can discuss this further another time. There are other, more pressing matters that must be taken care of first. Like who are our new friends," questioned Fread looking up at the massive Chian before settling his eyes upon Mai-Coh.

"This is Chian of the taurean," gestured Mai-Coh. "I am Mai-Coh of the Pawnee. We come from across the plains."

"That's a first for us here in Zephyria... to my knowledge at least. You're most welcome here in Zephyria. I would love to hear tales of your homeland should the opportunity present itself."

"They were a great help to Drogen and I among the goblinkin," said Natalia.

"It seems there is more to talk about than I initially thought," said Fread with narrowed disapproving eyes upon Natalia before returning attention to Mai-Coh and Chian. "Thank you for helping Natalia and Drogen. If there's anything you need simply let me know and I will do my best to fulfill your requests."

"Thank you, Sky Leader," said Mai-Coh giving an appreciative nod which Chian replicated.

"Think nothing of it. Hmm sky leader I kind of like the sound of that." said Fread with a smile. "Now come this way. Before we discuss things any further, there are other's who arrived not long after you left Zephyria."

Fread led them out of the audience hall and down a passage located behind on of the massive tapestries hung all around the chamber. Two guards held the way open for them and it closed with the rustle of heavy fabric as they moved into the hallway beyond. This passage is a direct path to where we're going. The moment I was told of your reappearance I made sure our guests would be awaiting your arrival.

Who could be so special they have their own place within the castle, thought Natalia. *Usually, only delegates from our trade partners would receive a room within the castle itself.* Natalia shook her head pushing the thoughts of who it could be away before her mind could overtake and consume her as it had done multiple times since her torture at the hands of Bernadine and Nefar. Although she no longer felt the phantom pull of her feathers in her sleep the trauma of her torture and everything she had witnessed on their journey continued to weigh heavily upon her waking hours.

They walked past many familiar rooms, including the vault she had robbed on multiple occasions, to give relief to those effected most by Nefar and Bernadine's greed. Fread, leading the way, followed the lantern lit hallway to its very end. At the end stood a door unlike any Natalia had ever seen in Zephyria. Depicted on it was a mage holding high a staff, but what caught Natalia's eyes the most was the color of their wings. They were as black as her own.

As the door opened light flooded out into the hallway blinding everyone for a few seconds until they adjusted to the intrusion of light. Willow rushed through the door wrapping Natalia in a warm embrace. "I'm so happy to see you're in good health," said Willow dancing around excitedly while lifting Natalia as though she were weightless.

"I'm glad to see you too Willow," said Natalia giggling at Willow's happy smile and golden eyes.

"Fread's been so stressed since everyone left that he barely has time for himself anymore. I wish he wouldn't work so hard. Do you think you could talk to him about taking more time for himself. Maybe he'll listen to you more than he does me," said Willow her tongue out teasingly toward Fread as she put Natalia back on the ground.

"We can rest once everything is done Willow my love. I seem to recall that you have been quite busy yourself as of late."

"Well, I guess that means we both need a break then doesn't it?"

"So that's what you really want then isn't it," laughed Natalia. "You want time alone together." The declaration rushing blood to both of their faces.

"Well. Yes." said the embarrassed yet unwavering Willow with a mischievous smile up to her eyes.

"I look forward to our time alone together my dear. However, you and I both know there are far more pressing matters to attend to before that may happen," said Fread a look of longing clear as day upon his forlorn and weary face.

"Not long after your party left, we received a visit from a couple of beings that we could never have guessed would come to Zephyria," said Fread.

"They've been looking forward to meeting you and will have more than a few questions, I'm sure. So, be ready for that," said Willow with a smile. "Now come. Come you all, they're just inside. Oh, and who are the other two with you?"

"They are Mai-Coh and Chian. They helped Drogen and I when we were with the goblinkin in Grammora," said Natalia.

"Ooh I look forward to hearing more about that," said Willow excitedly.

"As do I," said Fread.

As The group made its way into the room Natalia felt a force unlike anything she'd previously experienced. *Not even Grock exuded this much pressure,* thought Natalia. The room seemed to have developed its own form of gravity making it hard for any of them to move, let alone breath. Natalia looked to where the pressure was coming from and saw a woman with extremely long hair looking down upon a cloaked being hunched over and studying a set of parchments with runic rubbings upon them. *How can he so easily withstand this pressure when its so intense to everyone else.*

"I do believe that's enough Lisana. You're making the young ones uncomfortable with your aura. If you keep it up, they're likely to faint before you can probe them for information on our son," admonished the studious hunched over figure. "These rubbings hold a lot of information. We'll need to give more of the translations to your librarian for research. The more we know the better we can prepare for what's coming," said Death. Never looking up from his work as he wrote upon another piece of parchment.

"We will take it to the library and have the scholars on it soon. Before that I have some people for you to meet who may be able to give us some much-needed context," said Fread ushering Natalia, Mai-Coh and Chian into the room behind the jubilant Willow.

"Who have you brought," questioned Lisana finally raising her eyes from over Death's shoulder to look their way. Her eyes moved between Mai-Coh and Chian before settling on Natalia whose abyssal black wings fluttered under her intense gaze.

Tears formed in Lisana's eyes, and she drop to her knees her eyes shifting to the reptilian slits of her true form as emotion began to overwhelm her. "Alexandria how can this be," cried out Lisana. Rising to her feet, and covering the distance between them, in order to scoop Natalia up into her arms. Wrapping her in a deep tearful embrace.

"I'm sorry, but... I am not Alexandria. My name is Natalia," she said quietly as Lisana disengaged herself retreating apologetically.

"Sorry... you look like her. It has been so very long... I'm sorry," said Lisana hanging her head low.

"An apology is not necessary. I wish I was your lost friend," said Natalia apologetically.

Death looked deep into Natalia as Lisana retreated a few steps back to his side. "Interesting. You may not be as far off as you think," said Death rising from his work in order to wrap his arms around Lisana's shoulders.

Unsure of what to say Natalia remain frozen waiting for someone to break the awkward tension burgeoning within the congestive room. "These are more of Drogen's friends. You just hugged Princess Natalia, and she brought back with her... Mai-Coh, and Chian," said Willow struggling to remember their new and strange names.

"Ah a Pawnee and a taurean. Tis nice to see your kith on this side of the plains once more," said Lisana. "Judging by your ages I would suspect you're on respective tribal quests."

"Yes, it is strange that one knows of our peoples and tribes on this side of the dessert," said Mai-Coh.

"What's strange to me is a taurean female has gone off on a quest with a Pawnee who is stuck between transitional stages," said Lisana with a smile as Mai-Coh and Chian's heartbeats rose in tempo. "Although I suspect that has something to do with why the three of you are here now."

"I think it best we get out of here and take in some fresh air," said Death. Quickly grabbing up the parchment he had been writing on.

"I agree, some fresh air would do us all some good," said Lisana. A deep sadness taking route in her eyes as she looked once more upon Natalia, and her abyssal black wings.

"I don't know if it's a good idea, but we could go to castle's courtyard to sit and talk, at least about what we went through in order to get back here. I have a rather long story to tell, as well as a book of information that I will need to translate for everyone," said Natalia.

"Does your story have to do with our son," questioned Lisana as she gestured Death's way.

"Who is your son," posited Natalia.

"Fread... Fread... Hey Fread," said Willow. Shaking Fread's arm to garner his absent attention.

Shaking his head as though he were sleeping standing up Fread looked back into Willow's eyes. "What were we just talking about," he questioned.

"You didn't tell her who they were coming down here to meet," questioned Willow.

"Well no. I thought it would be a pleasant surprise. As it was for us," said Fread. "I would have thought her name would give it away though. Did they not exchange names yet," he questioned clearly confused.

"It would seem we've been rather rude without meaning to be bowed Lisana and Death to them. I am Lisana; Reaper of Souls. And he is my companion, Death."

"You're Drogen's parents," exclaimed Natalia. Mouth agape and wings flapping at her back excitedly.

"I swear everyone just glosses over me as soon as your name is announced. Tis like I'm not even here. Although, hearing us be mentioned as Drogen's parents was a nice surprise," said Lisana taking Death by the hand.

"Fread, might you lead us to the courtyard," suggested Death.

"Can we really afford to leave here with so much going on. We only know the bare minimum of information from the etchings," questioned Fread a hint of annoyance eking into his voice.

"Children view everything as though there's no time wishing to descend headfirst into the unknown no matter the situation. Tis not until aged wisdom graces the mind that one does not simply rush in without forethought," said Death.

"I have always been the fight first ask questions later kind, but in this case, there's nothing that can be done right now. So tis best to relax and process what we can in order to figure out our next steps," said Lisana.

"We don't want or need to make any rash decisions at this time, it's better that we don't. A decision made in the heat of the moment could mean the difference between the death of a few and the deaths of thousands. I have seen the aftermath of such decisions personally Fread. Working through the information calmly and thoroughly will be far more beneficial than simply flying off the handle," said Willow critically.

At Willow's declaration Lisana's visage showed a deep underlying sadness which she pushed back down replaced rapidly with a blank stare.

I wonder what that could have been about, thought Natalia.

"I will have to keep that in mind," said Fread as he looked lovingly into Willow's golden eyes.

Willow excused herself from the room with a bow just as Drogen would have. “I will meet you all in the courtyard we’ll need food and refreshments this evening. The kitchens will need to be made aware of the numbers joining this evening for dinner.”

“Well then, we’ll go to the courtyard and await your return,” said Fread.

They made their way to the courtyard following behind Fread the entire way without a word. Natalia noticed many furtive glances from Lisana as if she were trying and failing to find the right words to say.

After winding through the castle’s many twists and turns they came to a final door which Fread pushed open allowing a cool fresh breeze to blow through and rustle the garments around each of them as they moved out into the courtyard.

The courtyard was empty of all but a handful of guards who, seeing the impressive procession coming through the door, moved swiftly to provide assistance. “Go and gather a couple more guards, I want this courtyard secured from prying eyes and eavesdropping ears. None are permitted within aside from those present, Willow, the kitchen staff, or our former Lord, Vladimir. Now go and make sure everything is secure, much is to be discussed and distractions will not be tolerated,” said Fread garnering a fist to heart salute and “YES Milord,” from the guards. As they rushed off to perform their assigned duties.

“How did one survive. It feels like an impossibility. But those wings, those gorgeous abyssal wings could not be mistaken for another. Please tell me that my eyes do not deceive me,” whispered Lisana forlornly to Death. Her eyes incapable of leaving Natalia’s wings for fear they would disappear. “She looks just like her my love. Just like Alexandria. The friend I lost when they invaded this place.”

“I know my dear. I see it as well. There is a strangeness with regard to the zephyrian’s and the angelo’s. I fear it has something to do with Natalia,” said Death. “I have asked many I have come across about the Angelo’s, but for some reason the zephyrian’s have no knowledge of them. As though they have been wiped from memory. I wonder if the loss of the angelo’s from memory extends further than the Zephyrian’s,” questioned Death.

Tears started forming in Lisana’s eyes as she looked upon the beautiful Natalia, the raven wings of the Angelo’s prominently displayed upon her back walking through the castle that had once been theirs. “If only we had not rushed to seal true magic from the world, maybe Alexandria would still be alive,” said Lisana quietly.

“It does no good to dwell on the mistakes of the past my love. All we can do is remember it in order to prevent ourselves from making the same errors in the future,” said Death.

“I will make sure not to dwell upon my mistakes of the past, when you too follow the same advice my love,” said Lisana a single tear flowing down her cheek.

“Then we will share the burden of the past together,” said Death raising his hand in order to wipe away the tear from Lisana’s cheek before pulling her in close to lay her head upon his shoulder. “I can think of only one who may have knowledge regarding her origins. The former Lord of Zephyria, Vladimir.”

Willow’s return marked the end to Lisana and Deaths conversation as Willow proclaimed “Dinner will be ready in three hours time. I told them we would be eating in the inner dinning hall.”

“Very well then,” said Death. “I believe it best to hear the story of our recent arrivals first. Before I go into what has been researched from the etchings. I may be able to infer more from the information they possess.”

Natalia recounted what had happened to her, prefacing her story with, “I only wish Drogen was here since I can only speak to my own experience.”

It was nearly two hours before Natalia was finished recounting her time among the goblinkin and the special bond she had made with Golga, Cauron, Grom, and Bogger, who wished for all the bloodshed and senseless loss of life to stop just as much as they. "With our escape I can only hope that none of the friends we made within the arena, and without were killed in backlash."

"Is there anything that Mai-Coh or Chian would like to offer in regard to their part in this story," questioned Death.

"We can recount only what happened after everyone else escaped on the scaled ones," said Mai-Coh.

"I was wondering that myself," said Natalia. "I guess it slipped my mind to ask when we returned to Moongrove."

Having been asked to recount everything that transpired after the larger groups' departure within the arena Mai-Coh and Chian shared every detail they could. Excluding Drogen's life threatening injuries as they did not ask specifically about the aftermath.

"Right then," said Willow "I suppose we should get onto the information Death and the scholars have found out from Drogen's bowl."

"I think we shall be waiting a little longer for that," said Lisana. As Krail came into the field followed closely by a couple of guards.

"I apologize for the interruption, but we've received a hawk from the Moonclave. It's addressed to Commander Fread," said Krail bringing it up to Fread's hands. Fread moved through the motion of taking the letter from Krail opening it and reading its contents. "Seraphine writes' she and the Dwarves made it to the Moonclave," said Fread.

"It is good that they made it there safe and sound. I hoped they would have sent more," said Natalia.

"Although we don't know the exact location of the Moonclave, it's likely it took quite a while for the letter to arrive. This letter seems to have been sent when they first arrived, so more are likely to come in short order," advised Krail.

"Drogen, Asche, and Keltus should be arriving there shortly," said Natalia.

"Death has more of the etchings translated, take them to the library when you have a chance," Fread advised Krail.

"I'll make sure Brena distributes them among the scholars. They'll have the equivocations for you as fast as possible," said Krail taking the parchment from Death's hand.

"It seems you've been spending quite a lot of time with Brena," teased Willow.

Krail smiled broadly at the declaration, but let no other information slip, as he left with the two other guards in tow.

"Should we discuss the information I have now," questioned Death.

"I don't think that wise we are about to be summoned to the dinning hall, if my ears do not fail me that is," said Lisana.

A zephyrian fledgling came into the clearing, clearly nervous to have so many eyes upon him. The youth took a steadying breath to calm his nerves before speaking. "I've been sent from the kitchens. Everything is ready. I can guide you to the dining hall... if you would like," said the child sheepishly. Clearly unsure of himself.

"That would be a great help. It's been a while since we last went to that particular section of the castle. You're guiding us would be greatly appreciated," said Fread drawing a smile from Willow.

Although still unsure of himself the fledgling puffed out his chest with pride at being of help to Fread and the others. Everyone rose to their feet following quickly behind their fledgling guide his wings happily fluttering with each step.

"I suppose we'll have to continue this discussion after we finish eating. Should we go to the library before continuing," questioned Fread.

"Tis as good a place as any," shrugged Death

"Can we not discuss such matters during dinner," questioned Natalia.

"No. We won't have as much control over who might be listening. There are still those that may be loyal to Nefar and Bernadine within the castle. Although I have routed most of them out, it's likely some remain. Not to mention the faction of zealots who wish for another of the gods, who did us so much harm, to once again come and take back their iron control over our people," said Fread.

"Has it truly gotten that bad," posited Natalia.

"Much has changed in Zephyria, seemingly over night, with the deaths of Ether and Uther. Some see my rise, as a form of treasonous act since Vladimir was appointed by the gods, while I was not. Krail and a few others have expressed fear that a few zealots might take it upon themselves to do something about it."

"Fear of the gods by the zephyrian's has waned and most are happier because of it. I wonder though, if their fear of the gods will grow to be a fear of Drogen and I since I am a goddess and Drogen is the reason the gods no longer torment Zephyria," said Willow.

With a new subject found, they discussed as a group, the possibility of many different scenarios with regard to Drogen and the people of Zephyria. As well as how the zealots wished for Drogen to be held accountable for his killing of Ether and Uther throughout their jaunt to the dining hall. Each voicing their own opinion on the matter, dissenting or accepting one proposition over another, and disregarding other notions entirely. All except Death, Mai-Coh, and Chian who simply chose to listen to the others and their deliberations.

The chatter died as the door to the dining hall came into view its double hung doors opened quickly by their guide to allow the group as a whole entry. Holding it as if he were a guard himself as they passed.

Lisana drew in closer to Natalia. "There's something that I would like to discuss with you and the former lord Vladimir," said Lisana pervasive sadness filling her sapphire eyes as she looked deeply into Natalia's.

"We will need to send someone for my father, it may not be till the marrow that we can all three come together and talk," said Natalia. "I have yet to see my father, I hope that he will at least be joining us for dinner."

"In the marrow then," said Lisana a slight smile curving her lips on her otherwise sullen visage.

Fread took a seat to the right of the tables head Willow taking the seat next to his, across from them sat Death and Lisana. Natalia took the spot next to Willow so that she could further observe Lisana's reactions. Mai-Coh and Chian, unsure of where to sit split themselves to either side of the table.

Noticing Fread's intentional vacation of the table heads chair Natalia found herself hoping Vladimir would indeed make an appearance. *Although he left me to be tortured at the hands of Nefar and Bernadine's men, I cannot bring myself to hate him. He is still the one who raised me. That doesn't mean I have to forgive him for what he allowed to happen to the people of Zephyria...and what was perpetrated against me,* thought Natalia.

"What is the likelihood that Lord Vladimir will be joining us for dinner," questioned Natalia motioning toward the empty chair.

"That is... unlikely," said Willow sympathetically. "He hasn't left his room, other than to go to the audience chamber every once and a while, since he banished Nefar and Bernadine from Zephyria. I feel much conflict within his heart. He truly loved them. But that love left him blind to the truth of what they were doing. He's deeply conflicted."

"That's enough Willow," said Fread. Grabbing hold of her hand and affectionately looking into her golden eyes. "We don't need rumors to go around about Lord Vladimir getting back to the zealots. One of their people could be within the kitchen staff. Waiting to deliver information to their faction in order to cause friction."

With everyone set at the table, one of the guards within the room knocked upon a door, which opened to a flurry of movement as members of the kitchen staff came striding in. Placing platters of roasted vegetables, which had been cooked along with sprigs of thyme and rosemary, wetting the palates of all present. The boards of vegetables were quickly followed up with freshly baked crusty bread. The smell of the yeast that caused it to rise adding to the aroma wafting through.

Mai-Coh and Chian looked around at the feast presented in wonder. They had not seen so much food since before coming through the forbidden plains. When they were at home with the others of their respective tribes. Yet another difference came from the serving of the dishes. Each of them filled their plates in turn passing each platter around so the next person at the table could partake.

"Is this abundance common among the sky people," posited Mai-Coh.

"No, I'm afraid that this is not common among our people. Not right now at least. One of the many tragedies that came about from the greed of the banished Queen and Princess, was the deterioration of the people's living conditions. Nefar and Bernadine saw the people as steppingstones. The truth of the matter is, we need them, more than they need us," said Fread.

"With Fread in charge things are slowly, but steadily, improving among the citizens of Zephyria. There are many who would have been considered homeless that can now support themselves. Many new shops are opening in the shopping district as well. The people who lost their livelihoods when Zephyr was overrun with goblinkin have started opening businesses and hiring apprentices in order to begin rebuilding as well," said Willow. Proudly squeezing Fread's hand affectionately under the table.

"I fear what is coming will put a large strain on our already tight budget," sighed Fread. "We were doing quite well when we could trade with the elves, dwarves, and gnomes, but with Zephyr gone, the supply chain is as well. We will need to think about alternatives moving forward."

"I know of a method... but it would only work with another Dragonkin. If only magic wasn't so restricted. If it was as it used to be, then it would be extremely simple to develop, and do so quickly... Unless..." said Lisana looking once again at Natalia. However, the look in her eyes was no longer forlorn as it had been since they met. "You said that Drogen was heading to Moonclave after sending you here," she questioned excitedly.

"Yes. Why would that matter, you said he would have to be here in order for your method to work," questioned Natalia?

"Do any of you know where this Moonclave is located." posited Lisana.

"No, nobody doe..." started Natalia. Until she realized that Lisana's eyes had moved from her, to focus entirely on Death.

"The Elves occupy the forest far southeast of here if memory serves... Oh," said Death contemplating the new information. "Should the Moonclave be what I suspect, it will prove a good guide as to which translations are most plausible. We may need to let things play out for now and see, rather than speculate unnecessarily. However, I will see what lies down this possible path."

"I take it then that we will not be discussing the rubbings until something happens to point us in the right direction," questioned Willow.

"Yes, I think that would be for the best," said Death. "Should what Lisana and I suspect come to pass, then more truths of this world and the *gods* will ultimately be revealed for what they are across the breadth of Dranier," he said. His eyes not leaving Willow's golden orbs, throughout his declaration.

Chapter Twenty-Five

"The information Natalia translated from Golga's book will prove invaluable and work to give credence to what we already know about Grock's plans for war against the races of Dranier starting with the elves, and dwarves," said Drogen to Asche and Keltus who were seated ahead of his forelegs upon his back.

This information needs to be delivered as swiftly as possible. The elves and dwarves will need time and preparation in order to repel, and defeat Grock's invasion into their lands by his hoard of minions. Still finding common ground between the two races that allows them to work together may very well be their only option. Both sides are stubborn when it comes to the other, I only hope neither side is too stubborn to understand, they need each other.

"Given our speed when do you think we'll make it to the barrier," questioned Ashe fighting to be heard against the air rushing past in Drogen's flight.

"I don't know everything looks the same from up here. I've been keeping an eye out, but I haven't seen any of the towers either," exclaimed Keltus as more treetops raced by beneath them. "It's really disorienting being up so high and traveling so fast."

They had traveled many miles after leaving Moongrove following the invisible compass Drogen possessed informing him of the right direction.

"This will be our second full day of travel. We should be seeing the towers soon," shouted Asche.

"Are you sure we're heading in the right direction," questioned Keltus.

"We have to be," said Asche. "We left in the right direction, and we haven't changed direction this whole time. We just haven't traveled far enough yet."

"I hope for all our sake's you're right. I can't wait for this ride to be over," she exclaimed with a deep frown.

Drogen paid no attention to Asche or Keltus instead keeping focus on the runic sigil at the forefront of his mind's eye. Each passing day, hour, and second brought the rune closer and the pulse more frequent. Still, the pulse remained a considerable distance ahead. Even with the distance between himself and the rune Drogen refused to rest.

I will not rest until I know the fate that has befallen my friends. Seraphine, Rumble, Tumble, and Alya please be safe. I am Dragonkin. Food is for comfort. Water is as well. And rest, rest can come when there is time to find it. Importance is the mission that must be completed for the good of all who call Dranier their home. Discomfort and sacrifice are necessary to protect what is most important, the freedom of all, thought Drogen reciting the tenets of Drakregus passed down to him by the Elders, Graven and Thane.

They traveled till dusk began to fall across the landscape in front of them blocking their eye's from seeing anything except what had already come and gone. Asche looking past Drogen's flapping leathery wing catching a glimpse of stone in the distance before exclaiming excitedly, "A tower. See I knew we were going in the right direction."

"We need to go down before we reach the barrier, it won't be good to go in like this," yelled Keltus. Garnering Drogen's attention by patting his scaled hide.

Hearing Keltus's explanation, Drogen weighed their options in his mind, choosing quickly to do what Keltus suggested. Drogen slowed his flight to find a clearing in which to land. Finding a space big enough to descend proving to be the biggest challenge as Drogen dared not release his true form with Asche and Keltus perched upon his back.

A short distance away from, what Drogen could only assume to be the barrier, a clearing just large enough for him to descend appeared allowing him to drop down inside the canopy of trees his wings wrapped tightly against his body just long enough to descend. Before crashing to the ground Drogen unfurled his wings building the pressure beneath them to cushion their landing.

Touching down lightly in the heart of the clearing. To make Asche and Keltus decent from his back easier Drogen placed his wing against his side creating a ramp for them to slide down to the ground. With his Elven companions dismounted, Drogen closed the door within his mind to regain his lither form. The red tipped black scales of his body shifting effortlessly into place.

"Let us find a tributary before we proceed. You both could use some water."

"You need water too, I know you're a dragon or whatever, but I'm sure you still need to drink at least some water to survive," said Keltus.

"I can go quite a long time without water, depending on the situation, but right now I could use some water as well, although my use case will prove to be quite different to your own," said Drogen.

"If I remember correctly there should be a stream on the other side of the barrier just before the guard tower leading into Moonclave," said Asche.

"Then we should get moving," said Drogen.

Drogen, Asche, and Keltus walked through the invisible barrier piercing the almost imperceptible membrane. The energy of the barrier brought Drogen a feeling of nostalgia, as though he were returning home. As though he were steps away from Lundwurm Tul and the embrace of his kin.

To once again hear their stories within the dining hall. As if no time has passed and the months since my extrication from Lundwurm Tul were not but a dream. I remember well my younger self wishing to leave Lundwurm Tul. To go out and explore the surrounding world as my kin had done before. To fly through the skies and fight against those who sought to destroy us. Now I find myself wishing to go back in some ways to that time. To hear their stories of accomplishment and failure, thought Drogen a solitary tear rolling down his face as he released a deep solemn sigh. *Tis unfortunate one cannot go back and experience what has already come to pass, except within the confines of memory. All I can do is look forward. I hope to once again experience the camaraderie, and must be sure to appreciate such opportunity as it arises.*

Still Drogen couldn't help but look around his heart leaping at the thought that one of his kin could be within the barrier waiting for him. *Natalia's mother spoke of Thane in the woods outside of Kethick's cave of experiments. She said the Dragonkin are still alive. I know I will see them when the time comes. I simply need to be patient.*

Shaking off the distracting thoughts Drogen moved forward one step at a time until the barrier became distant, and the sound of trickling water began tickling all six of their ears.

"We're almost to the stream... Do you find it strange we've seen no guards, or patrols. We walked past the barrier without being spotted at all, which is concerning, but coming this close without seeing *anyone*," questioned Asche clearly concerned.

"I feel the same way. Where are the wyvern riders and scouting parties. Is the council so arrogant they think nothing could happen to the Moonclave," questioned Keltus as the bank of a small tributary came into full view.

A herd of deer raised their heads from grazing and drinking from the small stream noticing their scent on the air. The deer tensed up seeing the three intruders coming out of the trees, but they didn't run. Instead, the herd released their held tension returning back to what they were doing as if the trio's intrusion was of no real concern.

Not wishing to disturb the grazing herd Ashe beckoned them further downstream, where the water began to disappear underground. Alongside the waterway lay a fallen tree covered in lichen. Calling upon the help of his silent soul Godslayer; Envoy of Death cut through the fallen tree's bark and trunk.

The tree, having been on the ground for many years, proved pithy at its core, but remained solid a short distance from its center. With the scales of his fist, Drogen formed a bowl. With the bowl formed he blew fire around its outside and inside scorching the surface.

With the vessel ready Drogen filled it in the stream breathing fire upon the procured contents. Pouring the water all over his exposed scales a thin layer of skin grew to obscure the scales of his heritage.

"Here are your clothes," said Asche. Holding out the pile of clothing she'd been given on the first night of their journey.

"Thank you," he said with a bow taking his clothes in hand and dressing quickly. The sigils' pulse a constant beckoning within his mind toward Seraphine. *I think it best to use a diplomatic approach in order to garner information in regards to everyone's whereabouts within Moonclave. Although, I doubt an open armed welcome is a plausible outcome. I will, at the very least, be able to gauge their initial reaction to my presence. I'm predicting bows, spears, and swords pointed in much the same way I was greeted upon my entering Moongrove,* thought Drogen.

"It may be for the best, that you two go on ahead. I would not wish for my presence to become a hindrance to your entering Moonclave. There will inevitably be a lot of questions asked pertaining to my appearance here," said Drogen.

"He does have a point," said Keltus. "If we are seen bringing anyone with us to Moonclave we could be brought before the council. Moonclave is supposed to be a secret only the elves know after all."

"The only thing worse would be bringing dwarves, I would think," said Asche.

"Even if the dwarves meant no harm to the elves," questioned Drogen.

"Even then the council has a way of turning everything to their advantage, and what they view as the truth, is what is considered the truth of Moonclave," said Keltus.

"Our mother never cared for the council's way of doing things, hence our leaving," said Asche.

"So, whatever has happened to Seraphine will prove to be an uphill battle. I will wait here another day, or if you wish two, in order to rout any suspicion of our coming together," said Drogen.

"One day should be more than enough," said Keltus.

"We can try and gather some information for you if you like," said Asche. "It's the least we can do for you saving us in the arena after all."

"I would hope there's a way for us to do more," said Keltus.

"We will all have a role to play in what happens next. I need to bring together the council and give them the translated copy of Grock's plans. I may need to call one or both of you as witness to corroborate the story."

"We will be there. Should you need us," said Asche as Keltus nodded her head.

"There are a few names I can bring up to give validity to my words as well. Should it be necessary for me to do so," said Drogen.

"Do you know how to get to the Moonclave from...," questioned Keltus as Drogen raised his hand.

"You need not worry yourselves," said Drogen.

Asche and Keltus having drank their fill of fresh water came over to Drogen each placing a hand on his shoulder "We'll be seeing you again soon," said Keltus.

They walked off into the woods towards Moonclave as Drogen sat upon the ground allowing the rushing waters sound to envelop him fully using the current's calming flow as a catalyst for reaching his meditative state.

As he had done many times since Ether and Uther's deaths Drogen sank within himself accessing his soul chamber and looking upon his still silent companions. The pieces of his soul whose voices he could no longer hear. Godslayer; Envoy of Death.

"I heard you crying out in my fight with Grock. Does he have something to do with my inability to hear your voices... or is there something wrong within my soul. Something I have yet to realize or understand," questioned Drogen within his own mind.

The blades remained silent not uttering a single word nor acknowledging him in any way other than coming to his call. *"I will figure this out, and we will once again harmonize and commune," Drogen promised.*

Getting nowhere within his soul chamber, he tried to release himself from his corporeal form, but found it impossible to do so. *This must be another effect of the barrier,* thought Drogen. It seems I will need to wait until I am free of its effects in order to see if Girhok and the others have moved on.

Seraphine felt and saw the pulse of the sigil upon her back stop growing in intensity and knew Drogen would be with them shortly. *He is our only hope in convincing the council that we did nothing wrong,* thought Seraphine. *If anyone can convince them of their foolishness, it will be him. Should he be unsuccessful, then we are all doomed.*

"Hey Rumble... Tumble. Have you heard anything from the other prisoner who's down here with us," questioned Seraphine.

"Aye, I thought it odd, da tree louse be sayin four when fuzzy ears not be ear," said Rumble.

"Da other one be quiet, not be sayin nothin ta us at all," said Tumble devoid of his normally cheerful and joking demeanor. "Maybe they not talkin cus day can't."

"We know there's someone else down here with us. Please, can you talk with me. Even if its just your name," said Seraphine. Pleading into the darkness. "I'm Seraphine. Do you know who I am," she questioned hoping her name might illicit some kind of response.

"If you're down here with me then the council has truly lost its way," the soothing melodic baritone of his voice relaxing Seraphine. "I am Gilvail. I came with news of the goblinkin taking elves captive. I thought taking it to the others on the council to be the best option. However, upon entering my district I was ambushed by Manzine and brought down here. And here I have sat for... I honestly don't know any more. With my absence another has likely replaced me on the council. Leaving me to rot down here," said Gilvail.

"Don't worry Gilvail when our friend arrives, I will tell him of you. I'll see what we can do to get you out of here as well," said Seraphine.

"It would take an act of the gods to garner any of our release," said Gilvail cynically.

"He be close enough," said Tumble.

"For all our sake's, I hope you're right," said Gilvail. Doubting anyone would dare go against the elven council.

Chapter Twenty-Six

Natalia awoke with a start. Her nightmares cascading images of dead bodies being loaded into carts, and the feeling of their blood flowing over her hands, crashing through her waking mind. With concern she moved around the cold dampness of sweat soaked sheets further amplifying her discomfort.

I don't know whether to be relieved or dismayed that I no longer feel the plucking of my wings in the night, she thought. A chill ran down her spine as the cool morning air touched upon her soaked night gown. Knowing further rest to be out of the question she moved to the edge of her four poster bed pulling back the curtain.

As the curtain moved away to reveal the room beyond the door of her room suddenly went wide. An unfamiliar maid rushing into the room. "Oh... You're awake. I was sent here in order to to get you up. It seems Lord Vladimir heard of your arrival and wishes to see you. At least that's what Commander Krail said." said the maid before disappearing into the closet selecting a dress and returning. "Another guest of the castle was invited as well."

"Is it Lisana," questioned Natalia.

"Oh, is that her name..." said the maid pulling Natalia to her feet and stripping her completely. "It looks like you are struggling with your dreams princess, if you like I can see an herbalist for help." Deep furrows of concern covered her smiling face hoping her suggestion to be helpful.

"Thank you for the suggestion, but past experience has made me weary of any remedy prepared by an herbalist" said Natalia with a shake of her head. "I wish I could clean myself of this sweat before going down, but such things will need to wait. I feel this conversation is of more importance than the discomfort a little sweat might produce."

"Although you don't have the time to bathe I'll make sure your bed is clean by the time you return. And this evening, I shall draw a warm bath for you to cleanse yourself Milady."

"Are you new to the castle's staff," asked Natalia curiously.

"Oh. Forgive me princess I completely forgot you weren't here when I started. My name is Ziraiy. Willow said there was an opening in the castle as many of the staff were dismissed with the former queen and princess's banishment. Many have started work as apprentices with people in the market."

"It is a pleasure to meet you Ziraiy. I am glad those who were let go have found employment elsewhere." said Natalia with a smile before Ziraiy pulled the dress down over her head.

Ziraiy moved around Natalia, Drawing the strings of her corset topped dress tight. "Lord Fread made sure they all had a place to go. I've heard he's even sent people in to check on their progress as well."

"Oh, dear princess. I dare say you need to go down to the kitchens for some food. Your dress barely fits with how thin you've become in your travels," she said walking around Natalia her eyes trained on the dress.

Natalia walked over to the mirror set into her closet door. With the previous days' events, and everything leading up to her return home it was the first opportunity she had been afforded to look at herself. The image looking back at her in the mirror seemed strange, as if it were distorted in some aspect, and displaying something counter to the truth she remembered.

"Is what I am seeing reality... or is my mind playing tricks on me... is it strange that I no longer recognize the one staring back at me in the mirror," questioned Natalia. "I will need to go and see Jesha for alterations," she said with a sigh. "For now however, this will have to do."

"If you like, I can send a few of your dresses to Jesha's shop for alterations. Then you'll only need to go for measurements and fittings," said Ziraiy.

"That would be much appreciated. If you could have her look at and repair my armors as well," said Natalia with a yawn and wipe of her eyes.

"Of course princess. I'll take them to her as well."

"Did Krail mention where I am to meet my father and Lisana this morning."

"You're to meet them in the library."

"Thank you. I will be off then. If I'm not forgetting anything in regard to dress," posited Natalia "It has been a while since I have been in audience with him."

"There's only one other thing we need to do. We need to fix your hair."

Upon mentioning her hair needing a brush out Natalia looked once more into the mirror and the tangled mess of hair creating a bird's nest like structure atop her head. "I suppose a princess should have her hair in a more refined state than a nest for birds," said Natalia with a smile.

"I'll get the knots out, but I can't promise they're not going to hurt," said Ziraiy with a wince.

Natalia took a seat in front of her personal vanity picking up the hairbrush that lay upon it for Ziraiy's waiting hand. She brushed Natalia's knotted hair diligently pulling out the many set knots garnered in her weeks away from Zephyria. Her customarily straight raven black hair fighting to retain the tangles that had long gone untamed.

"It would seem taking a brush along on adventures would do a person well," said Ziraiy her eyes sorrowful as the brush continued its relentless pull through Natalia's tangled mane eliciting ripping sounds as the hair brushed worked its way through.

"I would have to agree. My fingers proved less than adequate in detangling," said Natalia with a wince. Her eyes watered uncontrollably against the relentless assault of the brush upon her head. However, she would leave no other indication as to the depth of her discomfort. Using the pain as confirmation that she was no longer in the arena. Feeling blood flow through her fingers, as they loaded the dead into carts.

After many minutes Ziraiy lay down the brush upon the vanity. Braiding Natalia's hair so it lay between the abyssal black wings at her back. "Now you're ready to go before Lord Vladimir," said Ziraiy a smile gracing her visage as she looked back at Natalia through the vanity mirror.

"Thank you Ziraiy. I hope that today some, if not all, of the questions I have will finally be answered."

"As do I Princess. Now you better get a move on, I've delayed your departure long enough.".

Natalia nodded her head raising to her feet running over to the door of her tower room. As she approached a guard knocked. "I am coming out," said Natalia. The guard swinging the door wide upon hearing her intentions.

"I will be heading to the library, unless you have been told otherwise," she said to the guard.

The guard nodded his assent closing the door behind Natalia leaving Ziraiy, who already started working diligently upon her sweat soaked sheets.

Natalia's thoughts began to wander as she made her way down the spiral staircase that led to her tower room. Feelings of uncertainty and anxiety at what Vladimir and Lisana wished to discuss.

Does this meeting have something to do with the woman Lisana confused me with upon her first look at me. What could any of that have to do with father. What about Fread, why was he not invited to the meeting as well? So many questions, I can only hope that some will be answered, pondered Natalia with a deep sigh coming to the bottom of the long spiral staircase.

Not wishing to be seen by another soul as she mused internally, Natalia wrapped her abyssal black wings around herself sinking into the shadows. A feeling of nostalgia began creeping in around her as she moved through both guarded and unguarded doorways with nary a whisper of sound.

So many nights I did this, sneaking into the library under Brena's nose in order to read long past nightfall. She caught me so many times over the years... Until mother died. After mother's death she no longer tried to keep me away from the library. She found me many times within the stacks reading and studying everything the books had to offer. The stories and notes within the books were the only thing from which I derived comfort. The multitude of pages an escape from the harsh reality brought on by her senseless killing. At least, in the end, I was given the chance to say goodbye. Knowing what I do now. Was she saying goodbye to Fread as well without my realizing.

Natalia emerged from the shadows just before the two zephyrian guards posted outside the library door. The guards looked at her, both mouths agape in wonder how she had gotten so close without either of their noticing. "You need not worry. I would never seek to harm another of our people. However, it is best that you always remain vigilant you never know if another person skilled as I am, might come to Zephyria."

"We will keep that in mind princess," said one of the guards as the other opened the door to allow her access.

The room beyond let out a small amount of light as the door swept open. The sound of parchment scraping against book laden desks wafting out into the hallway beyond as Natalia stepped into the massive library. The guards shut the door behind her with a distinctive thud drawing the attention of the room squarely upon her entrance. While most returned to their work, their curiosity sufficiently sated with a glance, Brena upon seeing her entrance rushed her way.

"Ah princess it's so good to see you alive and well."

"Thank you, Brena. I apologize if you have been waiting long for my presence here."

"Oh, you need not worry about any of that princess. You've been on a long journey and rest is very important. Don't you let either Lord Vladimir or Lisana tell you any different," said Brena as she studiously looked over Natalia for any visible injuries.

"I will keep that in mind," said Natalia with a chuckle. "Where are my father and Lisana now," she questioned stopping Brena's frantic scouring.

Brena nodded with a final once over. "Come this way." Leading Natalia deeper into the library past the book and parchment filled desks. Going beneath the second story floor along the bookcases and shelves on the right side of the circular room led them deeper into the library. They journeyed past many light-less rooms and alcoves.

Natalia reminisced on the collection of books contained within each room, and the library as a whole, as if she had read them all the previous day. *Books on animals, beasts, beginning magic's, the works of the divine beings, the historic books, and everything else imaginable are contained within these walls. Even further in are books on a race I have always wanted to meet, the Daelon's. So much knowledge, in so many languages. It is truly grand. Only matched, I'm told, by the elven library in the Moonclave.*

Natalia cut off her thoughts as Brena stopped before a nondescript bookshelf she had frequented during many nights of uninterrupted reading. *The disappearance of Magical creatures upon the sealing of Dranier's breath*, thought Natalia spotting the book right where she had left it years prior. Natalia had worked her way through each and every book held within the library, Until she had consumed every word that had been written upon the pages and parchments.

Brena abraded her knuckles upon the wood backing of the shelf eliciting a distinctly hollow reverberation beyond. The bookshelf opened moments later to reveal a room Natalia had never seen before, lanterns lining the walls filling the room with bright light. Within the well-lit room were hundred's more books flowing to the ground from deteriorated shelves.

"So many books that I have yet to read," stared Natalia in wonder. "I thought I had read everything in the library. It would seem there are many more secrets for me to discover," her eyes lighting up at the prospect.

"It would seem you have inherited their love of knowledge as well then," said Lisana speaking in the draconic language. "But, have you been able to use the knowledge you have garnered as she did?"

"Although I have only a small understanding of this language, I can still understand the context of what you speak," said Natalia. Speaking methodically so as to get her point across even without knowing all the proper words.

Tears once again came to Lisana's eyes, but she wiped them away quickly. "Just as I thought."

"Ahem," said Lord Vladimir. Clearing his throat in order to announce his presence within the room. "It is good to see you alive and well Natalia. There is much we need to... discuss."

Natalia looked upon Vladimir taking a steadying breath before finding the courage she needed to speak. "If what you wish to speak about is mother's death, my kidnapping by Kethick, your disregard of my testimony, or my imprisonment and torture at the hands of Nefar and Bernadine's guards, then I will tell you simply. *You're* my father and I love you dearly, but I will never forgive you for standing by and allowing it all to happen," Tears welling up in her eyes as she stared Vladimir down.

Vladimir lay his head low at Natalia's declaration searching his thoughts for many moments before speaking. "I... I know there is nothing I can do to make up for what happened to you under my watch. I do not ask, nor do I deserve your forgiveness. I can only give you my word... My word that I will work the rest of my life in hopes that one day, I can be forgiven for the many mistakes I have made."

Lisana listened intently to their conversation not wishing to but in during the palpably tense moment being shared between the two royals of Zephyria.

"Maybe, one day father." said Natalia. Tears running down her face. Which she wiped away, before returning her gaze to the waiting Lisana.

Lisana bade Natalia to take a seat drawing her attention to a stack of parchments set upon the table before her. "I want to preface this by telling you the real story of Zephyria's people. This place was never home to the zephyrian people. I didn't understand why the people of Zephyria, much less their gods Ether and Uther retained no knowledge of that truth. Tis as if their memories have been... altered in some way."

"What does that have to do with me," questioned Natalia clear confusion prevalent upon her face.

"It has everything to do with you Natalia. Absolutely everything," said Lisana shaking her head in disbelief.

"These documents were found a few years after Ether and Uther placed me upon the throne. They were found in a secret room that had been unintentionally discovered during castle renovations. I brought them to Rachel so that we could go over them. I knew she would be able to translate the text and figure out their origins, even if the translations took her years. And she did, eventually. The only other person who has seen these translated documents is Fread. Although when he had chance to see them, I do not know."

Natalia looked over the pile of parchment that lay before her realizing quickly that they described another race of winged people that lived in Zephyria. A race of black winged people, a people like her. "Is this the reason Drogen referred to me as Angelo, when we first met," questioned Natalia. "And why you confused me for someone named... Alexandria?"

"Yes," confirmed Lisana. "I told Drogen only once about the fall of the Angelo's to the zephyrian's but it seems that I did not have the complete picture of what transpired here in Seraphal. Your existence proves that beyond any doubt."

"Then I am not zephyrian at all," questioned Natalia. Unable to believe the truth even as she spoke it allowed.

"No, you're not zephyrian. You are angelo," said Lisana. "Death confirmed it by looking at your soul. You're the last of your race. The last Angelo."

Natalia found herself unable to breath as the breadth of the statement washed over her completely. The truth of her black wings among the white winged zephyrian's clicking into place as her mind thundered in a torrent of questions she had never thought to ask. The room around her began to swim uncontrollably her heartbeat pounding loudly in her ears.

Just as Natalia was about to lose herself in the torrent of her own mind, Lisana keeled down turning Natalia in the chair to face her. "Breath Natalia, listen to my voice and breath," she said. Placing her hand upon Natalia's forehead, wiping away the pervasive clammy sweat that had overtaken her lithe body. Realizing Natalia could not hear her through the torrent of her mind, Lisana began to hum a lullaby she had used many times to sooth Drogen in Lundwurm Tul. A lullaby she had learned from her dearest friend Alexandria.

FLY LITTLE RAVEN TAKE TO THE SKIES,
WHEN YOU'RE OLDER I'LL TEACH YOU TO FLY,
FOR NOW FEEL THE FLOW OF MAGIC THROUGH ME,
THE FEEL OF ITS FLOW WILL TEACH YOU TO SEE.
SOAR MY ANGELO YOUR CROWN MADE OF LIGHT,
ONCE YOU'RE GROWN YOU'LL RECLAIM THE SKIES,
FOR NOW FEEL THE FLOW OF MAGIC THROUGH ME,
CLOSE YOUR TIRED EYES TILL THE MORN OF NO LIES,
AWAKEN TO THE TRUTH ONLY EYES OPEN CAN SEE.

Lisana placed her hands over Natalia's heart placing her forehead against Natalia's to form a connection through their touch. Natalia's heartbeat began to slow in her ears as Lisana continued reciting the lullaby over and over again.

The overflowing ocean of thoughts crashing within Natalia's mind slowly receded. With the regression she felt herself returning to a calmer, levelheaded state, allowing her time to recuperate. "That... song... I would swear I have heard it somewhere before," breathed Natalia. "But where."

"Your mother Alexandria was singing it to you the night we attacked Seraphal," croaked out Vladimir as though a frog set within his throat.

"You mean my mother Rachel don't you," questioned Natalia jumping up from her seat.

"No... Rachel was yours and Fread's mother, nothing will ever change that, but the one who gave birth to you was not Rachel. It was Alexandria," said Vladimir his eyes glassed over and far away.

"I thought you said nobody remembered before the zephyrian's lived on this plateau," questioned Lisana enraged at Vladimir's deception.

"It was the song; the song was the key to all these locked memories. I don't know if these memories will be locked away again. I would ask you both to sit down, while I recount the details of what happened here all those years ago. When true magic was locked away, and we waged war against the angelo's in Ether and Uther's name.

Chapter Twenty-Seven

"I was the commander of the zephyr legion. We had stationed ourselves beneath the plateau which we now call home. We were awaiting a sign or order from Ether and Uther before beginning our assault on the enemies of our divinity."

"What was that feeling just now," questioned Celestyn. "It feels as though the air has been taken from my body, and I am no longer breathing normally."

"Could this be the sign Ether and Uther mentioned," questioned Antoni. Who took furtive glances at Celestyn, as often as he could.

"Commander Vladimir, I received word that the defenses of Seraphal have fallen. We are clear to proceed with our assault. You need only give the order," said Mirko a smirk toward Antoni's infatuated looks Celestyn's way.

"Gather the garrison's. As the sun rises upon the plateau we will begin our assault. With luck we will sweep everyone before they rise from their beds." said Vladimir.

Mirko moved through the encampment raising all he came across to their feet. Bidding all of them to get ready for the battle ahead before sending them off to tell the next. As the sun rose the breadth of the zephyr war front stood before Vladimir awaiting his orders.

As his eyes traced the height of the sheer cliff left for them to climb. The sun's rays touched upon his back.

"Today we fight for the gods against their foes. We go to glory and will be immortalized for what we do this day. Ether and Uther have brought down the one thing the angelo's had over our warriors... *Magic.* It is through the gods that we have found a road to victory. Praise be to their divinity, for it is they who guide us in our conquest against the evil of the angelo's," exclaimed Vladimir. Garnering a fist to heart salute.

"Ad Deos," shouted the battalion of soldiers under his command.

"From this day there will be no more enemies to our divine beings," roared Vladimir. Eliciting another war cry "Ad Deos," Unfurling his pure white wings out from his shining full plate armor he fought against gravity to rise. With each oscillation of his wings, he gained altitude the sun shining upon his armor a shining light for the zephyr to follow.

The battalion ascended to the top of the plateau along with the rising sun landing upon the wooded outskirts undetected by the Angelo's who remained peacefully asleep in their beds. Unaware of calamities assent.

"Mirko, Antoni, and Celestyn split the battalion among you three. Antoni you'll stay here in case any try to escape. Mirko will start on the left while Celestyn will take the right. We will meet in front of the castle. It was decreed upon us that none survive to contest the power of divinity. I leave you to your duty with only one request. The heretic queen is *mine,*" he proclaimed that all could hear.

"*Ad Deos,*" responded the leaders and those of the battalion at his back.

"Ad Deos. Go and triumph over the enemies of divinity," finished Vladimir. Holding his hand high before dropping it in order of their advance.

The soldiers followed their orders unquestioningly. Splitting ranks behind their three leaders and beginning their trek through Seraphal with a fervent zeal.

Vladimir walked stoically through the heart of Seraphal cutting down any and all along his path. The sword in his hand cutting black wings and lopping heads alike. Without thought or care he walked over the fallen bodies of the heretics without so much as a pang of sympathy toward his unprepared enemy.

Screams of surprise and agony the music of a successful conquest in Ether and Uther's name. From one house a small child came running out in fear for her life choking on her own blood as she fled into the street where she fell drowning in the very blood that had given her life. The screams and howls of the dying fell to silence as the stench of flowing blood built to a crescendo of complete silence.

A wicked smile spread across Vladimir's visage as he continued his journey to the castles front steps. The light of the sun just starting its assent from the castles base. Two thirds of Vladimir's split battalion began regrouping around him as silence permeated the area. Their ranks fully consolidated as they stepped as one into the castles courtyard.

"A few of them were able to get away. However, Antoni will dispatch any who think themselves safe by running," said Mirko with a smirk.

"I almost wish the gods had let us fight these Angelo at their full power this was entirely too easy," criticized Celestyn.

"It is best we do not get ahead of ourselves. We don't know what kind of tricks they might yet employ against us once we enter the castle," said Vladimir silencing their conversation. "I have kept my eyes upon the castle this entire time no alarms have sounded within the castle."

"So, luck may still be on our side," questioned Mirko with a sigh of relief.

Vladimir nodded continuing to listen intently for anything untoward beyond the castle's door. "Go through each and every floor room by room eliminating everyone and everything you come across. Question those, who do not die too quickly, where the queen's chambers are. Once her location is know... you know what to do. While I wait for you to return, I will kill all who endeavor to escape the god's wrath."

"*Ad Deos,*" came their whispered call as Celestyn and Mirko once more split the battalion to cover more ground within the castle. As silently as possible they filtered through the castle's double doors and into the audience chamber beyond. As the last of their ranks moved into the chamber they closed and barred the doors from within.

Vladimir watched and waited for any movement. Knowing he would soon have his hands full in short order, should one of the angelo's be able to raise an alarm to alert the rest of the castle.

Alongside the wall of the castle another door opened for two angelo's desperately attempting to escape their slaughter. As they rushed through the door three of Vladimir's soldiers followed, cutting them down as they muttered and raised their hands. The shocked expression on their faces the last emotion within their minds before falling to the ground slain without mercy.

As the two fleeing angelo fell the slaughter started in full. As cries of pain resonated through the castle an alarm sounded bidding everyone escape while they still could. Many rushed for the barred double doors that looked to be their salvation only to find Vladimir circumventing their aspirations of escape.

The angelo's held their hands up. Trying in vein to call upon their magic's. Magic's that had always been apart of them, but the magic could not heed their cries for help.

Vladimir let no opening go to waste cutting down any and all who stepped through the doors. Men, women, and children alike falling with deadly efficiency to the sharpened steel of his blade. The last angelo desiring escape through the doors was hewn under a powerful downward cross cut from clavicle to hip. As he fell the clamor and commotion within the castle dwindled to tranquil silence.

Vladimir waited patiently for more who wished to escape, but no others came forth for slaughter at his hands. Many minutes passed in absolute silence before a lone soldier came out of the castle covered in blood splatter from many a great many victims.

"Mirko, have you located the queen," questioned Vladimir expectantly.

"Yes commander," he said with a fist to heart salute. "She is located in the forward most tower to your left. We are working to gain access to the room as she has barricaded herself within its confines. The only thing we have been able to make out so far, is that she's singing."

"Very good, lead the way so we might celebrate the successful conquest of these heretic's who dared go against the gods. This night we will revel in the riches wrought of our victory," proclaimed Vladimir.

Vladimir followed behind Mirko looking at the decor as they passed it by. "The first thing we shall need to do is burn all these blasphemous tapestries. Have others break the stained glass windows for they show a disingenuous history. As you work announce to all you see, from this day forth this is home to the Zephyr. We shall call our new home Zephyria, should the gods give their blessing to the proposed name that is."

"I'll see it done the moment you're within the room with the last Angelo. I'll be glad to see the end of this business," said Mirko.

"How many casualties have been reported," questioned Vladimir.

"If everything went to plan with Antoni, then we have suffered no casualties. The gods have truly blessed us in our conquest this day. Ad Deos."

"Yes. Ether and Uther are truly the greatest of the gods granting the zephyr this conquest without a drop of our blood being spilled. Ad Deos indeed Mirko."

Vladimir looked into each room as they passed taking note of any bodies within view from the hallway, but disregarding each as they had black wings instead of white.

"These black wing abominations were nothing in the face of the blessed," said Mirko. "Now this place will be ours as the gods proclaimed it to be. Are you looking forward to returning to Rachel and Freadrick?"

"You know I am Mirko, I'm sure everyone is looking forward to returning, triumphantly to their families below. It will be grand to bring them here to our new home from down in the encampment after all this time. We'll finally have a home to call our own, instead of the nomadic existence we lived in the plains. Ad Deos, for they have raised us from what we once were."

Vladimir and Mirko traversed the spiral staircase to the tower passing many other descending soldiers on their assent. The look on their faces that of jubilation for the successful subjugation of Seraphal.

Mikro was the first to walk through the already open door at the top of the stare, standing at attention against it as Vladimir stepped into the foyer beyond.

"Ad Deos, Commander Vladimir," called Celestyn.

"Ad Deos Celestyn. You are certain their queen resides beyond this door," he questioned. Pointing past the guards to the door they guarded.

"Yes Commander. We did as you ordered and verified it multiple times before our arrival, and further confirmed once we were able to gain entry. This," she pointed enthusiastically. "Is the queen's bed chamber."

"Send word to Antoni we have claimed victory. We may bring our families to our new home. Tear down, burn, and break any and all tapestries and stained glass that depicts the heretics and their ways as you go."

"I will stand guard while you're inside," stated Mirko.

"No. All of you descend the tower. I will join the rest of you soon," said Vladimir.

"Yes Commander," saluted the guards as a whole, before descending the tower.

Silence surrounded Vladimir once more as he reached for the door handle pushing the door open to reveal the dimly lit room beyond. A single curtain blocking the sun from reaching through the rooms casement window.

"Did you leave any of my people alive in your wake," questioned Alexandria. Sorrow flowing through each and every word.

"You're the last," said Vladimir uncaring for the queen, or her people's plight.

"They were defenseless without magic, and your people slaughtered them all without remorse. Why," she questioned. Clear distress expressed in her tone, but she did not rise from her seat. Overlooking a small bassinet beside the rooms four poster bed. Tears falling from her eyes and into the bassinet the entire time.

"The gods decreed your kind heretics, what other reason could I need," said Vladimir unsheathing the sword at his side. "I'll be sure to release you from your suffering quickly."

"I warn you now," she said. Holding up a blood soaked and bandaged hand to stop his assault. "If you cut me down as you plan to do, the existence of my people will disappear from the entirety of this world's minds. Only those whose magic I have used will remain unaffected by its use. The lullaby I have sung this day will be the seal to your memory, and once the seal has been removed. I hope the truth of what you have done destroys you," she proclaimed. Her eyes not moving an inch from the small bassinet.

"We shall see," said Vladimir as he pressed her head down. His sharp sword slicing cleanly through her jugular only stopping as its edge snagged against the vertebra of her spine. Blood flowed freely from her body and into the bassinet as the blood soaked cloth that had covered her hand fell away to reveal a runic sigil radiating light.

All throughout the room runic sigils lit. As the queen's body slipped out of Vladimir's surprised hands it disappeared into nothing as though she had never existed. Blinded by the light of the sigils, and the cascading magic waves emanating from them, a sense of confusion swept over Vladimir. The light within the room died down as quickly as it had begun leaving him in absolute darkness.

Unsure of what had brought him to such a location Vladimir made to leave the room through the door, which he was forced to feel for along the walls of the room. As he opened the door he heard the cry of a child, giving him pause. With the additional help provided by the lights in the foyer beyond, he walked to the side of the rooms four poster bed. Beside the bed sat a bassinet and within its confines a lone child. The tips of its black wings protruding from beneath the swaddle it was wrapped in.

"Ad Deos, exclaimed Vladimir. The gods are blessing Rachel and I with another child. Freadrick and Rachel will surely be overjoyed to add another member to our family. Now what could be your name little one," questioned Vladimir.

Looking around the room he could find no mention or information about the baby's name or origins. Even searching the bassinet proved wholly fruitless. With no other method of figuring out the information coming to mind he shrugged knowing he could always figure it out later.

Shedding the plate armor on his left arm from gauntlet to pauldron to protect his new charge from the cold metal before picking her up. Carefully Vladimir took the crying baby from the bassinet placing it comfortably in his armor-less arm.

"Let's see if a little more light helps." Walking over to the casement window Vladimir pulled away the curtains allowing the room to be filled with light from the midday sun. Upon the swaddle an embroidered name glistened in the rays of light. "Natalia."

"Well Natalia it looks like you're coming home with me," said Vladimir. Tickling baby Natalia under the chin, eliciting a soft coo through her cries. They descended the tower together, taking in many ripped tapestries and broken stained glass windows. Getting lost many times along the way in the unfamiliar environment.

As they continued on blindly he heard familiar voices coming closer "King Vladimir is that you," questioned Mirko. Celestyn at his side.

"Yes its me. Joyously it seems the gods have seen fit to bless Rachel and I with another child, along with a home to raise her in."

"Ad Deos. How fortuitous my King. Where did the gods leave the little one for you," questioned Celestyn. Moving in close to peek at the child cradled in Vladimir's arm.

"They even named her she must be special if the gods saw fit to provide her a name," said Mirko.

"Yes, and she differs from us in another way as well," proclaimed Vladimir. Gently pulling upon the swaddle releasing it from around Natalia's paltry form.

"Black wings," exclaimed Celestyn happily as she stroked Natalia's small wings eliciting another coo from the baby.

"Rachel and Fread will be overjoyed by the many blessings the gods have bestowed this day," praised Mirko.

"They truly have blessed us all this day," said Vladimir. "Has Antoni started sending our families up from the bottom of the cliff?"

"Yes he sent word our people have begun to arrive. That's why we came to find you Rachel and Freadrick are waiting for you in the receiving chamber," said Celestyn.

"It's going to take a lot of time to remember all the twists and turns of this castle," said Vladimir. "I've passed so many doors I don't know whether I'm going the right way or not."

"We'll lead the way," said Mirko. "I feel the same way as you. Luckily, our journey to find you was relatively straight forward."

Before following his two zephyr soldiers, Vladimir swaddled baby Natalia once more. They walked past many doors and corridors before finally reaching a closed door, just like many others they had passed without stopping, at the end of an extra long corridor. Mirko opened the door allowing Celestyn and Vladimir entry to the chamber beyond the three of them arriving to the applause of their entire people.

"Ad Deos," chanted the crowd as they entered.

Vladimir holding up his gauntlet covered right fist to the heavens exhorting the crowd as he pumped it in the air. The crowd parted for him, making his path to the dais located at the front of the chamber congenial.

"The gods have brought us to a place in which we can truly call home. No longer will we be subject to the whims of the plains. This place shall hence forth be known as Zephyria. The gods called this place our ancestral home and to this home we have once more returned," proclaimed Vladimir to the crowd who responded with cheers and prideful salutes.

"Not only have the gods returned us to our home for our devotion. They have also blessed Rachel and I with another child. Her name is Natalia," he declared. Holding the child up for the entire room to see, her abyssal black wings on full display.

With the declaration the room burst with excitement. Rachel ran up beside her husband followed by a prepubescent teen. With his family by his side Vladimir raised his fist once again eliciting a new chant from the crowd "King Vladimir." Only relenting when Vladimir dropped his fist to his side.

"Only if the gods will it, will I agree to rule our people," said Vladimir. "However, I do not wish to be referred to as a King. I would much rather be called Commander or Lord."

The entirety of his people communed among themselves for a few moments before a new chant followed "Lord Vladimir. Lord Vladimir. Lord Vladimir."

As the crowd chanted Fread looked over the people of Zephyria wishing to know the trust and loyalty his father had garnered through work and dedication. The young boy dropped to his knees in front of Vladimir, Rachel, and baby Natalia. "Father, once you're appointed our ruler I wish to be left out. I will work diligently to garner the trust of our people as you have done through my own merits, actions, and service. For the good of Zephyria, and its people."

Vladimir and Rachel looked upon Fread clearly saddened by his decision, but understanding completely Freads wish. "Then it will be so. You will have to achieve everything you receive with your own hands, among the Zephyr. Through your own merits you must rise," declared Vladimir.

"Thank you for granting this selfish request, Lord Vladimir."

Mirko walked up to Fread placing his hand upon the young zephyrian's shoulders. "I will take you under wing and make you a commander to rival our Lord Vladimir. The path you have chosen will not be an easy one, but it will garner for you the greatest of rewards. The acknowledgment of the gods and our people," proclaimed Mirko proudly.

"I will be in your care Commander Mirko," said Fread. "Once I have earned the right through my own merits to do so."

"Well said Fread," responded Celestyn. "Well said."

Vladimir handed baby Natalia over to the waiting hands of Rachel who gently tickled her toes. Bending down to retrieve the fallen blanket swaddling her quickly. "Oh, the gods have blessed our people with a lovely princess," proclaimed Rachel.

"Ad Deos," rang out through the chamber as Vladimir sat upon the throne of Zephyria. Rachel and Natalia at his side.

"I never asked the queen for her name. I don't know the names of any that were slain that day," said Vladimir. Tears flowing from his eyes as he looked, first to Lisana, and then upon his daughter and wept uncontrollably. "It would seem her prediction was right. The truth of what I and my people have done in Ether and Uther's name. My leading the charge in destroying an entire race of people without question... I do not deserve forgiveness. I will never deserve it for the pain I've inflicted."

"The gods mislead many, and caused mass casualties across the breadth of Dranier," said Lisana. "And there is nothing more dangerous or zealous than one who has been convert."

Natalia looked at Vladimir tears streaming down her face finally understanding and knowing the truth of her existence bringing both solace and tribulation as a torrent through her body, mind, and soul. "Then I am the last. The last Angelo," said Natalia. Shifting her puffy crying eyes to Lisana, as she could no longer stand to look upon the man sitting across the table from her.

"Yes, you're the last of the Angelo's. And your resemblance to Alexandria cannot be denied. She used the only magic left for her to use in order to save you from the fate of your people. With true magic sealed away it would have been her only option," said Lisana. "However, it was not the gods who sealed away true magic, but both the dragons and the gods together who did so."

"We reached an accord with the gods at that time to seal away magic in order to limit both sides power. We didn't understand that we were cutting our own power to near nonexistence in the process. The gods had other means of garnering strength. Their worshipers."

"Before the accord was reached, the gods went around Dranier gathering followers under their names. Raising their power to where magic was no longer necessary for victory. Their worshipers garnered for them strength and protection that we could no longer face with the sealing of true magic."

"Was the sealing of magic what led to the Angelo's downfall," questioned Natalia through hazy tear-filled eyes.

"Had magic not been sealed the angelo's would have easily repelled their threat. Even the gods feared the power of the Angelo's because they, like the dragons, could use any and all magics of Dranier."

"Did they have no other means of protecting themselves outside of magic?"

"The answer to that is... complicated. The angelo's greatest weapon was their intellect and thirst for knowledge. They gathered books from all over Dranier building this library and its many hidden rooms to study the world, magic, languages, and anything else they could possibly get their hands on. They understood all things. Only fighting when necessary to defend themselves from harm. So, combat skills were not a common practice."

"I have not gone a single day since tragedy befell my closest friend without the weight of guilt pressing down on my shoulders. When my best friend needed me most. When her people were being slaughtered. I was not here to protect her, or her people," wailed Lisana inconsolably.

The three of them sat in the room weeping until no more tears could flow. Silence permeated the room, but none spoke to break its grip upon them until Lisana cleared her throat.

"When I found out what happened here in Seraphal, I could not bring myself to come back. Death told me none survived the slaughter, and Alexandria was the last soul to arrive. We didn't know she had a daughter. If only I had known. I would have come for you before we locked ourselves away in Lundwurm Tul."

"After the zephyrian's took this place as their own under Ether and Uther's rule, all possibility of agreement between the dragons and the gods deteriorated. As I think back on that time... It was as if the gods knew nothing of the angelo. As though all memory had been lost, but we knew the truth... I knew the truth. We named the place where the first accord was struck, and true magic sealed, Seraphal as a remembrance. In much the same way as Alexandria. We wiped the memories of the elves, leaving only their Dryad mothers with complete knowledge of the truth," said Lisana.

Chapter Twenty-Eight

Drogen only took a couple of steps in the open before being spotted by a guard and subsequently surrounded by tens of others. The elves pointing drawn bows, pole-arms, and swords at his neck and face in an effort to stop his advance, which he allowed to happen.

"How did you find this place," questioned the guard with condemnation.

From the armor adorning the speaker, and accompanying side long looks and stolen glances of those barring down upon him, Drogen surmised him to be their leader.

"You were not escorted here by any of our race. *So how did you find Moonclave,*" demanded the elf. "Only an elf would know to come through the barrier."

"The barrier was easy. I simply walked through it. As for finding this place, I did have the help of an elf. Although, given time, I could have found this place without help," said Drogen with an indifferent shrug.

The guards shuddered slightly, knowing the barriers power over speech, where left debating their need steps. Understanding the barrier surrounding them to leave no doubt to the validity of Drogen's assessment, the entirety of the armed garrison differed to their commanders authority.

"Hmm," pondered the garrison leader. "You cannot speak a lie within the barrier. What's the name of the elf who would vouch for you," the commander questioned.

"I cannot tell a lie within, or without, this barrier," said Drogen his tone leaving no doubt to the validity of his statement. "I dare say there are many who would vouch for my presence here. However, I will give you the name of the one who instructed me to do so. Unfortunately, *she died* from the effects of a necrotic plague. Had she not succumb she may have vouch for me in person. Lyra the elven queen. Who might I need to speak with, to recount such a tale," questioned Drogen sadness in his eyes in remembrance.

"Lyra is dead," he questioned surprised by the information. "Then their return to us is far more tragic then previously realized," ruminated the commander. Shaking his head with a sigh.

"I am Drogen," he said bowing slightly. The elven blades came in around his neck to prevent any further action from being taken. His strange movement taken as threatening.

"I ask you now, do you intend harm upon the Moonclave or its people."

"I intend no harm upon your people or home. I will conduct myself in accordingly, unless another forces my hands to action," said Drogen.

"All of you, return to your duties. We have all heard his intentions laid out. He doesn't wish us harm," said the commander patting the air in front of him in signal to lower all of their weapons. The guards did as ordered, removing their weapons from around Drogen's neck, and slowly releasing the tension from taught bow strings. "I am Phaylor Guard Commander of Moonclave." he said. Beckoning Drogen forward.

"Tis nice to meet you, Commander Phaylor."

"I wondered why we had received no word from Sun Meadow. We've taken in a couple of people from the settlement, but they had been away for quite a time and lacked any up to date information. None of the hawks we sent out ever returned either," said Phaylor under his breath.

"Would it not be prudent to send out a party and check up on the town," questioned Drogen.

"I've said the same on many occasions, but the council... Oh forgive me, you wanted to know who to speak with about Queen Lyra. For such a pressing matter talking to the elven council should be your first priority. Luckily, they're set to reconvene for the first time in nearly a decade. They are convening in two days. So, you couldn't have come at a better time. If you like, I can have a hawk sent with your request to be heard immediately."

"Yes, that would be a great help. Am I permitted to travel within the Moonclave? Or must I remain upon the outer reaches of your domain?"

"You'll need to see what the council decides with regards to your request. But, you don't need to be here for a guard or I to deliver that information. I'll send you to an inn and from there you may go out and explore Moonclave as our honored guest. I only ask that you do not take advantage of our peoples favor and get into anything untoward," said Phaylor scrutinizing Drogen.

"I will take you up on the offer of an inn. I have not slept in quite some time. Per your other request, as I stated before, I will do nothing unless my hands are forced."

"Very well," said Phaylor with a nod. "This being your only time in Moonclave I will have a map prepared for you. However, you must surrender the map upon leaving."

"You may keep your map. I have a better understanding of Moonclave's layout then even you I would suspect," said Drogen as he looked upon the architecture of the tower and portcullis that would allow him access to Moonclave.

"Only those who built this place could understand the layout better than I," he said. Taken aback my Drogen's statement.

Though the builders of this place were not kin, the dragons were the ones to establish the outline. Either way your statement is quite accurate in its sentiments at least, thought Drogen with a smile as he stepped past Phaylor and through the portcullis beneath the tower entrance and into Moonclave. *Where oh where, have my companions been taken.*

After clearing the portcullis three directions of travel were presented to him. Two of the roads curved along the outskirts of the city from his right and left sides. Leaving only one other option a direct path through the very center of the city where another tower stood out. Taller than those he had previously seen it reached far into the sky above all the others.

Listening to the pulse of his homing sigil, Drogen walked along the central road of Moonclave. The pulse of Seraphine's sigil growing rapidly within his mind as he drew closer to the massive tower standing as the central pillar of the broader city. With a click of his fingers Drogen closed off his connection to the sigil. *So, you are there below the surface. More than likely imprisoned,* thought Drogen. *Did they imprison you all? Hmm. Is their someone with which I can confirm my suspicions?*

Looking around Drogen noted many elves coming and going from around the central tower of Moonclave, but none dared walk to close, as if they feared the pain of touching its surface. He meandered up to the tower cautiously stopping before the opaque glass doors that would allow access to its interior. Placing his hand upon the locked doors Drogen felt a surge of magic, draconic magic. *So this is where the barrier originates, if only I could see the runes. I could distinguish how to drop the barrier, and bring them all running to me,* thought Drogen.

Spreading his mind into the magic emanating from the tower Drogen's focus grew outward garnering further understanding of the barriers breadth. *Thirteen towers, one for each of the elders. The barrier forming a sphere from its center and two opposing crescent shapes on either side of the circle. Within the center lay five sections... To the north a place of spiritual and logical awakening. To the south west... Farmlands. To the east passions are crafted. Upon the west birds, and wyvern's fly. And finally south east... aqueducts feeding water to the whole of Moonclave... No not Moonclave... Seraphal.*

Drogen listened intently to the world through his connection with the thirteen towers attuning himself to anything out of place among the elves going about their daily routines. Among the citizenry other lifeforms, unlike the rest, came to his attention. Their curiously slow heartbeats surfacing to the forefront of his mind. Fascinated by the strange heartbeats, Drogen broke his connection with the towers. *I will seek out their emanations, and garner their truth.*

With his barring set Drogen made his way to the closest target of his fascination a massive willow tree located at the heart of the crafting district. Even over the distance the tree stood out of place against the breadth of trees within its immediate vicinity and beyond.

Wishing not to stick out unnecessarily among the elves, until he could garner much needed information, Drogen matched pace with those around him. The elven people of Moonclave moved slowly to their destinations. Going out of their way to avoid anyone and anything that might have decided to cross their path. Including Drogen himself.

Their lackadaisical nature and absence of urgency may prove detrimental once Grock's army arrives upon their doorstep, thought Drogen. Drogen's presence among the elves proved a blessing to his advance, for all who might have graced his path to the willow, gave him a wide berth.

With his path unimpeded, Drogen quickened his pace to the tree. His increased pace garnering many furtive glances and whispers by those he passed in haste, but nothing more. Indifferent to the lackadaisical, prattling of those he passed Drogen covered the distance to the willow quickly.

Drogen looked upon the long descending vine like branches as an imperceptible wind swept a great many along the ground at his feet. With an outreached hand Drogen brushed his fingers along a branch a smile contorting his visage as he felt the slow heartbeat emanating through its branches.

"I can feel your heartbeat," he said closing his eyes in concentration. "Your form does not conceal such a detail from me."

"Seems that even a juvenile old one is capable of seeing through our abilities," said a voice. Arising from the willow's trunk.

"You may have been better concealed among those around you, had you taken on their form instead of that of the willow," suggested Drogen.

"I suppose you're right. But, this form is so much more comfortable than the others," said the tree.

"I understand the feeling all to well," said Drogen. "Might I inquire upon some... information in regards to the friends I sent ahead."

"We are for the old ones to command."

"I know the elven princess I sent here is beneath the central pillar of Seraphal. Have they detained all the others I sent as well?"

"No, we were able to save one from the same fate. She is with Leif."

"When I traveled through Moongrove the queen's manner disappeared as though it had never been. Does her imprisonment have anything to do with that matter."

"To understand what has been done, you'll need to seek her out."

"Where is Seraphine's queen mother," questioned Drogen. Fearing something unexpected had taken place.

Another imperceptible breeze blew through the willows vines before it relayed its answer. "I will have Leif and Alya take you there," said the willow. A demur sadness prevalent in its voice. "They will be with us shortly. You may sit upon my roots until they arrive."

"Thank you," said Drogen. Walking up to, and taking a seat against the willow's trunk, awaiting Alya and Leif's arrival.

"While we wait... There is something you said to Phaylor that I would very much like to hear."

"If you wish to hear something of me I would prefer to look upon your face. My mother told me the dryads are capable of taking many forms, trees chief among them, but also the form of their children."

"Very well," acquiesced the dryad. The willow tree's long vines, roots, and trunk began contorting and shrinking to accommodate its rapidly decreasing form. The many contortions forcing Drogen to retreat a short distance from the roots on which he had only just sat. Where the once prominent willow had stood a lithe elf covered in a vine and leaf dress had taken shape. "Lyra was of my trunk. I would like to understand her fate," said The Dryad.

"Before we discuss such an unpleasant topic, I am Drogen, son of Lisana; Reaper of Souls, Godslayer; Envoy of Death, Drakregus of Lundwurm Tul."

"A name so heavy given to one so young. Only the son of Lisana could carry such a burden without being crushed," said the Dryad. "Root Mother gave me the name Harp."

"Tis a pleasure Harp. Set with me here and I will tell you what happened to Lyra in what I now know to have been Sun Meadow..."

Leif and Alya arrived at the tail end of Drogen's tale as he recited Lyra's last words. "And with her last words she was taken in the hands of a reaper to Death's waiting embrace."

With the tale's conclusion Harp's face had become covered in distraught sappy tears, the sticky liquid mingling with her vine and root dress. "Thank you old one. Thank you for delivering to me her last words. They are no small comfort in what will be the long process of grieving. Should you need anything of me, I will do all within my power to see it done. As your ancestors have always done for my ilk," said Harp.

Wiping away the sap from around her eyes upon the back of her hand Harp composed herself once more. "You know the Warren Alya. Accompanying her is Leif. She is the youngest daughter of root mother. She will guide you to Seraphine's queen mother, and wherever else you might wish to go," she ordered.

"It would be my honor," said Leif with a deep bow.

"I am Drogen and I will be in your care," he said. Bowing back before shifting his attention to Alya. "Tis good to see you again Alya. Natalia made it back to Zephyria safely, along with two new friends. There is much to go over about our time with the goblinkin, and what we came to learn. However, I believe it best to have everyone gathered before we discuss everything. The elves and dryads should be informed at the same time. If we are to relay the information efficiently."

"Okay. Okay, it's good that Natalia is home safe and sound. But what are we going to do to save Seraphine and the dwarves, who are imprisoned below the council chamber," questioned Alya.

"We don't have enough information with regards to what is happening here in Seraphal. Tis my understanding, through Commander Phaylor, the council is set to convene in two days time," said Drogen.

"The council is convening right now," said Harp. "Although they're a couple members short at present."

Drogen contemplated the new development trying to think up a strategy with the limited information available. "Harp gather all the members of the council to their chamber at the center of Seraphal while Leif, Alya, and I go and see what fate has come of Seraphine's mother."

"It shall be done old one," said Harp

"You should also know, there's another member of the council locked beneath the tower with princess Seraphine," relayed Leif.

"Then that member is already where they will be most useful," said Drogen.

"I would only ask one thing for your consideration old one. Those who have come of our trunks are young, arrogant, and ignorant of many harsh truths."

"I will treat them accordingly. You have my word, but I will not shield them from any truths that might come to light from my presence here," Drogen warned.

"I would never ask you to do so. I only ask you not judge them and their actions too harshly," said Harp.

"I will not judge harshly. I will not be their judge at all," said Drogen.

Harp bowed her head to Drogen moving back into the position her form and roots desired as she once more took her willow form. Her vines forming a canopy around the three of them.

"Now Leif do you know what has happened to Seraphine's mother," questioned Drogen.

"All I can do is take you where she was last seen. Alya could possibly guide you there herself. However, I know a few shortcuts that will get us there faster."

"Do you know what might have happened," posited Drogen to Alya.

"All I know is the council was gathered in Seraphine and Queen Silf's house here in Moonclave. They stripped Silf of her title and seat on the council. They said it was punishment for losing Moongrove to the goblinkin. Seraphine tried to reason with the council, but they refused to listen. It only got worse with the arrival of a guard bearing news we brought Rumble and Tumble to Moonclave with us. That was all the reason they needed to detain Seraphine. She told me to run when she knew they could not be reasoned with, and run I did."

"I take it the dryads are the ones who prevented the elves from finding and imprisoning you. They at least kept you well," said Drogen. Scanning Alya for any sign of injury.

"Although, I don't really like admitting it," she said with an exaggerated roll of her eyes. "The dryads kept me safely away from the elves who spared no effort to hunt me down. But I *cannot* wait to get out of this place and have a platter of meat all to myself." A sense of longing crossing her visage as she imagined it. "They aren't much for conversation either. Still, I was lucky in comparison with the others, they had no chance of getting away."

As Leif, Alya, and Drogen conversed many willows began to stir using their vines and roots to move as they released themselves from the earth. Each of their tree forms bearing in a distinct direction. Their coordinated effort's with one another, a brush of impalpable wind.

Leif guided Alya and Drogen back to the central road of Moonclave taking them along its straight path to the living district opposite the defensive district where Drogen they had previously entered. All who came across the trio's path moved away quickly.

"Are all encounters with the elven people like this," questioned Drogen as yet another elf moved far around so as to have no interaction. "Tis as if they fear any and all contact with others, even those of their own kin," he said. Noticing the same method used ahead as a male and female elf were nearing each other going in opposing directions.

"Yes. This is the way they interact with one another most of the time. Since the council told everyone of the barrier's enforcement of absolute truth upon them," said Leif.

"So the council has spread fear within Seraphal. So much trepidation the citizens they rule would rather circumvent one another than converse," postulated Drogen.

"Any deceit could cause untold harm," said Alya. "It's the same effect as Seraphine's blade truth, just... more."

Drogen nodded in acknowledgment of Alya's explanation, before turning to Leif. "Was this done to instill fear in the populous, or was it done out of ignorance?"

An invisible wind ruffled Leif's hair. "Root mother believes it to be a mixture of both."

"We are nearly to the living districts tower. Once through there's a path through the woods that will cut down on travel time, far more than if we travel along the bridges. I only hope the underbrush and shrubbery have not become so overgrown that traversal becomes more of a hassle," Leif commented.

"Should the paths here be similar to those within the rest of these woods, then your hope for hassle free traversal will likely be dashed." said Drogen.

"I hope we don't have to cut through a bunch of brush just to get to where we're going. At least using the bridges we didn't have to deal with overgrowth and underbrush. I just got my fur cleaned," pouted Alya.

Finding the right path at ground level through the forest came far quicker than either Drogen or Alya believed possible as everywhere they looked seemed completely impassible without intervention. It wasn't until Leif held her hand out through the underbrush that they found the path through.

As if it were second nature Leif led them swiftly through the forest along paths hardly distinguishable from any other section of the wood around them. The hidden paths took them rapidly through the forest, and beneath many different tree form homes. Passing beneath the canopy high structures within the living trees completely undetected by those within.

Drogen took in his surroundings, listening intently to the forest full of wildlife and the elven people around him. Simultaneously taking in Leif's every movement, as she led them along the forest floor. *I wonder if all the dryad's walk with such grace. Their every step a drifting leaf upon an unseen wind. The elves have retained some of their ancestor's elegance but have lost much in regard to natural movement.*

"We're not far now," proclaimed Leif. As a wall of overgrowth and brush going as far as the eyes could see come into view before them.

"Before we arrive, what is your take on the elves," questioned Drogen. "Harp mentioned that you're the youngest dryad. I would think yourself closer in age to the elves than the rest of your sisters, if I am not mistaken."

"Yes. I am close in age to the other elves being one of the last cuttings from root mother's limbs by the old ones. However, even compared to me, all the elves are but saplings struggling to find their way. Although They have hundreds of years ahead of them to figure out the right path, they need to grow out of their isolationism and arrogance. Otherwise, they will find themselves on the outside looking in, compared to the other races of Dranier."

"Many of them would probably see that as a welcome advancement," said Alya.

"It is unfortunate to admit, but you may be right. However, what they fail to understand is how hard it is to grow when left unexposed to the possibilities brought about by friendship and rivalry," said Leif. As wind disheveled her vine like hair.

"Arrogance can lead to many mistakes of overconfidence. A fact the eldest of my race made sure to instill upon me at every opportunity. Only through humility is arrogance tempered."

Leif touched the massive wall of undergrowth, overgrowth, and neglect dolefully. "Where we need to go is just beyond this point. Our children were tasked with both protecting and propagating the forest. Yet the forest floor is covered in underbrush. Should we have a single dry season within these woods, a single ember could turn our home to not but ash. Do they not understand that thinning the forest help's it to grow," questioned Leif. Shaking her head in dismay.

"Would you like me to cut a path," questioned Alya.

"Yes. Thank you Alya."

Alya pulled a sword free from the extra-dimensional bag Drogen lent them on their journey to Moonclave. Using the sharp blade to make short work of the first few layers of growth. Using the underbrush to express her pent up frustration and furiosity in order to penetrate deeper into the thick tangle blocking their advancement.

"How do you know I am an old one," questioned Drogen.

"We would no more forget those who brought us into this world through their magics than the elves can deny the truth of themselves. Both we dryads, and subsequently the elves, came to be through knowledge given by the old ones."

"My mother told me the story of this place, and its purpose only once, but I remember much of her tale, and the reason for the name Seraphal."

"The deceivers and their lies brought great travesty to Dranier, and all who call it their home? Had they never come then things may have turned out differently."

"I feel there is more behind your words than I understand," said Drogen.

"If you're unaware of the truth then you're truly young among the old ones. When the time comes, and you stand before your people once more, ask them for the truth of Dranier," urged Leif. "It is not something for which I may speak."

"Very well," said Drogen. "I will have to understand your meaning once I've found my own people. Finding the right questions to ask can often be far more difficult than finding the right answer. When the time comes for such things to be known, they will be." Drawing a nod from Leif.

"Just like an old one, taking everything in stride. As if knowing, and not knowing, is simply a part of the experience."

Alya and Drogen traded places as her frustration dissipated through the physical labor of cutting their path. Even with sweat dripping off her brow, Alya appeared refreshed and ready to face whatever awaited them moving forward. "I'm finally starting to feel like myself again," she said. Stretching out against a tree she had only just cleared of brush.

Three quarters of an hour passed before the brush cutting came to its end. Drogen cutting through the final layer of vines and overgrowth to reveal the clearing beyond. Alya and Leif followed closely coming through the newly formed path looking around in excitement, which was quickly followed by trepidation.

"The mansion... its... gone," struggled Alya. "There's no way it could have disappeared without a trace."

"Are you saying the place where Seraphine was taken prisoner is no longer here," questioned Drogen. Drawing a simple nod of confirmation from Alya as she looked around in complete and utter disbelief.

"Then the disappearance of the queen's Manor in Moongrove must have happened around the same time." His only confirmation a single nod from Leif.

"I think tis time we hear what has happened to Seraphine's mother, Leif." Hhis draconic rage shifting his eyes to those of his birthright staring at Leif. Tempering himself for what she was about to say.

"Yes..." said Leif. Her expression dower and strained as another imperceptible wind caressed the vine like hair of her head. "This manner and the one in Moongrove are connected through true magic. What little we can access at least. Everything would have happened simultaneously, here and there, when the ritual was performed. A ritual that is supposed to be a rite of passage for aged elves.

"What happened to her Leif. Quit dodging and tell us," pleaded Alya. Clear anxious emotion written upon her typically cheerful face.

Tears began forming in Leif's eyes as she pointed out a lone tree. A tree that had taken root at the very center of the massive clearing.

Drogen walked over to what appeared to be a very young willow, its branches and roots minuscule in comparison to the massive trees along the outskirts of the clearing. Stretching out his hand tentatively he took hold of a single branch feeling Silf's heartbeat emanating from within the small tree.

"What is it Drogen. Why is she pointing at that tree," questioned Alya.

"Because my dear Alya, this tree is Seraphine's mother," said Drogen. A seething fire of rage boiling within his mouth, as he took in the truth of the situation, and what the others of her race had seen fit to do. "Does Seraphine know," questioned Drogen holding one of her branches in his hand.

"No. The ritual was performed by four of what should be seven members of the council. Other than those who performed the ritual the dryads, and now the two of you, are the only others who are aware. No other elves are aware of what has transpired," said Leif. Tears of sap flowing freely from her eyes, and down into the root and vine dress adorning her body.

Alya too could not hold back tears dropping to her knees holding her head in her hand and wiping away drops that would not stop as she placed her forehead against the trunk of the tree that had been her best friend's mother.

"The ritual they performed... It cannot be reversed, can it? Once it is started upon an elf," questioned Drogen.

"No. We know only of a way to speed up the process. Once the ritual has been performed there is no way to reverse it. Not even the power of an old one or one of the gods could hope to stop its progress. The only thing that can be done is hastening the transformation and making the change more viable. There is a chance of death for any who have had the ritual used upon them."

"Hence your insistence that it was meant for an aged elf. One should have gone through three quarters of a millennium of life before the ritual is taken as an alternative to death."

"What can be done to speed up the process," questioned Drogen.

"The healing water of the old ones. The same waters that gave life to the dryads and the elves. It can speed up the process and might even allow for communication with the one interred within," said Leif.

"I will spread draconic water, but only when Seraphine is here to speak."

"Then you understand what must be done?"

"Yes, and it will be done," he said. Dropping Silf's thin willow branch.

"There was only one person on the council who listened to what Seraphine had to say. All the others refused to listen to anything. Twisting what she was saying in many cases as well. The addition of the dwarves was all they needed to disregard her completely. What if they refuse to listen to you," said Alya continuing to wipe away her tears.

"They have no choice in the matter," said Drogen seething with draconic rage.

Chapter Twenty-Nine

Although, the path between themselves and their destination had been cut through, Leif slowed their progress back toward the central tower of Moonclave. "You need to quell your rage. Even Root Mother is telling me so. You must beat them with logic and reason, not emotion," said Leif. Leading them at a brisk walk, but a walk none the less. It took them many hours more to reach the outskirts of Moonclave's central circle, drawing ire from Alya and Drogen alike.

I know logic is the arena through which I must fight the elven council. However, I will not suppress my emotions. My rage will simply be the catalyst from which I propel myself forward. As the elders taught me.

"The other Dryads are still trying to gather members of the council. Two, who would be on the council arrived just yesterday, but they're proving far harder to subdue than the others," said Leif. Her irritation growing with each imperceptible gust of wind as it tangled the vines of her hair.

"Did you say two arrived yesterday," questioned Drogen.

"Yes they arrived just yesterday they're the children of another queen..." a frenzied breeze whipped through Leif's hair suddenly, and she turned to face Drogen. "They're the daughters of the queen you helped lay to rest in Sun Meadow."

"Dranier truly is a small and intriguing place," said Alya.

"Tell them that tis my request they go to the council chambers," said Drogen. "See if that does not change how they're receiving you."

Another wind whipped through her vine hair a short time later as they walked along the central road of the Moonclave toward the tower still some distance away. Even at the considerable distance the dryad's in their willow forms stood out against the stone structure of the tower. Those who had returned with their charges in tow had wrapped themselves around the tower blocking off any avenue those within might have used to leave the council chambers.

"Have Asche and Keltus arrived or are we awaiting their appearance," questioned Drogen.

"It would seem there is more to your story if you know the names of the queen's two daughters," said Alya.

"As you said, Dranier is small."

"They have yet to arrive, but they're moving swiftly to the council chambers. It would seem your name carried weight with them both," said Leif.

"Have them stop before entering the council chambers. There is something I must tell them both, now that I understand their identities. Had I known who they were, I would have told them of their villages fate. And their mothers' final words, during our travels together."

"They'll be along shorty after our arrival," confirmed Leif.

"There's not much time left before what Grock has planned will come to fruition. I had hoped sending everyone ahead would have garnered some kind of assessment by the elves as to what is going on outside their boarders. Should this take too long to resolve the goblinkin will find this place far from properly defended," stated Drogen. "I must convince them, not only to release those they have imprisoned, but also that they may be fighting off a siege they are wholly unprepared for."

"Are there any other's in danger by Grock's forces," questioned Alya.

"Yes the dwarves. We can discuss everything once the elves open their ears and listened to reason." said Drogen as they crossed the final stretch of ground leading to the elven council's chamber. "We will wait for Asche and Keltus to arrive before entering the tower," he said setting down on the ground and going into a meditative state, awaiting their arrival.

Leif conversed with her sister dryad's while they waited. The impalpable winds brushing vines, roots, and limbs as they silently communicated amongst themselves.

Alya dropped to the ground taking advantage of the opportunity to transform and rest in her feline form beside the meditating Drogen. Her typical happy purr replaced by silent contemplation.

Falling within himself Drogen walked through the corridors of his mind looking once more upon the two doors within. A single locked black chain fastened tightly about the white door to a power he had yet to reach.

"*Are you the reason that they have fallen out of sink with my soul. The reason that I am unable to hear their voices within my mind. I heard Godslayer; Envoy of Death calling out to me in the fight with Grock, could it be that he is the key to releasing the final lock,"* echoed Drogen's thought's within himself.

Stepping into the void between the doors he walked once more into his soul chamber taking in the room, mentally tracing the white and black chains wrapped like constricting snakes around his soul. Walking around the room he looked upon the crystalline structures encasing the extensions of his soul. Godslayer; Envoy of Death, the dragon-scale bowl denoting a future he could not interpret, and the scale-mail armor he had painstakingly crafted to match his own scales.

"*I wish someone was here to tell me the next step of the journey I find myself on. But, I suppose the unknown is apart of living. I will figure out why you no longer speak within my mind, and I will bring my soul together once more. I only ask you have patience with my inability to recognize the proper path. We will converse once more,"* promised Drogen to Godslayer; Envoy of death, as well as himself.

"Drogen they're approaching," came Leif's call.

With the call Drogen pulled himself out of his mental depths. "Thank you Leif. Alya tis time to wake," said Drogen rousing his warren companion from her coiled soundless slumber.

Asche and Keltus broke free of the willow trees guiding them to the council chambers upon seeing Drogen stand up. "What's going on," questioned Asche.

"I thought we were gathering information to share before meeting again," protested Keltus.

"Many things have happened that are in urgent need of recounting," said Drogen before his visage became one of a dower nature. "First however, I must apologize to you both. I didn't know your relationship with another elf I became acquainted with, while saving our mutual friend Natalia from a Necromancer named Kethick."

"No. You couldn't be," said Keltus tears beginning to brim her eyes. "Are you the one who buried her in Sun Meadow?"

"Fread and I did so. After finding her aged form upon her deathbed," recited Drogen telling both Ashe and Keltus what had been done to their people in the Sun Meadow as well as

Kethick's ultimate fate. "With those final words the reaper took her to Death's waiting embrace. Had I known you to be her daughters I would have told you much sooner of the fate that befell her, and the others at Kethick's hand."

"We wondered what had befallen the village. When we returned after a long absence, having been sent to Moongrove, we noticed the forest around the village was near death. But somehow, looked to be returning to health. Wandering through what remained of Sun Meadow we discovered the skeletons of many Elves and woodland creatures driving us quickly to our mother's manor," said Keltus.

"She wasn't inside, but she never liked staying in the manor so that wasn't unusual," interjected Asche a trail of tears flowing down her face as she hugged her sister for comfort.

"We never understood her obsession with the stone building she chose to reside in, but something about it made her happy," said Keltus sobbing against Asche's shoulder.

"We found her grave, though it was not marked with her name we knew it had to be her," confirmed Asche. "We wondered who had taken the time to bury her when the others had already passed. Thank you. Thank you for telling us of our mother's final words, and final moments," said Asche. Drawing a tear-filled nod from Keltus.

"We went out in search of possible survivors, but we were ambushed by a warband of orcs. They captured us and you know the story from there," said Keltus.

"We should tell them about Harp as well, I'm sure she would appreciate knowing her grandchildren," commented Alya.

As if Harp had heard everything a fierce wind disheveled Leif's vine hair. "Should they request it, I will bring them to Harp. Harp say's she will receive them any time," relayed Leif.

"We will gladly go to meet her, but there is something we must accomplish first," said Asche wiping the tears from her sister's puffy face as well as her own. "It seems we are indebted to you for far more than your help in allowing so many to escape the arena."

"You owe me no debts," said Drogen shaking his head. "I would however ask for your help in releasing others I consider friends."

"We'll do what we can, but if there are too many dissenters on the council one voice will not be nearly enough to sway the rest," said Asche.

"Llewellyn was the only one keen on hearing our side," said Alya.

"Even if two members on the council were willing to listen, it's sure to be an uphill battle," said Leif.

"Then we must shift the council in our favor," said Drogen. "If we cannot get through to the council about releasing the others then they'll likely be less than receptive when it comes to the information Natalia translated from Golga, even with the evidence all around them."

"We wont know anything standing out here," said Keltus. Standing up straight and tall readying herself for the mission ahead.

"The Moonclave is not the only city under threat from Grock's crusade. So, the sooner a resolution is reached, the better for everyone," emphasized Drogen.

They walked up to the root and vine covered doors of Moonclave's central tower as a group. As they drew closer the tree limbs moved away allowing them passage through the tangle of willow form dryads.

A wind pushed through Leif's hair as they entered, "Root Mother and the others wish the old one luck," said Leif. The exit once again became blocked by snaking vines and roots.

"I will act as translator and the one representing the interest of the dryads. That way there's no confusion as to where we stand in these matters," said Leif. Drawing a decisive nod from Drogen as they all filtered into the room.

"How dare outsiders come into this council without being granted permission. This goes against all procedure and decorum," spouted a surly and annoyed elven man.

Not listening to the comment at all Drogen simply bowed as was a part of his decorum to the elven council. "My name is Drogen Godslayer; Envoy of Death and I have come to free my imprisoned friends. And to warn your people of what is coming from within your own woods. I warn you now to heed my words. Should you delay things more than necessary, it will be to your own detriment," said Drogen. No doubt or waver in his voice.

As Drogen straightened back up from his bow the Elders all looked at Drogen truly dumbfounded by his speech. The boisterous elf was the first to find his voice, smacking his lips together a few times to wet his tongue enough to speak. "I am the sec... The First Elder of Moonclave, King Terill. Is our being brought to the council this day your doing," he questioned. Rage filling his tone.

"From my understanding you, and a couple of others, *were already here*," said Drogen.

"Is what he says true," questioned an enraged female elf.

"So what if we were all here," questioned another. "The council does not need everyone here to make decisions."

"Terill, Elise, Elmar, Llewellyn, and Boramil, are their name's. Since they're being far from forthcoming, I figured I should get that part out of the way for them," said Leif. Pointing to each of them in turn.

"Thank you. Since their bickering has ended for the moment should we introduce ourselves as well," questioned Alya.

"Yes, please do," said Llewellyn drawing ire from Terill and Elise chiefly.

"I am Keltus and this is my sister Asche. We are the daughters of Queen Lyra."

"I thought I recognized you two, is your mother with you as well, or did she stay in Sun Meadow," questioned Llewellyn.

"Our mother died in Sun Meadow due to a plague spread by a necromancer's magic," stated Asche. "A fact you all would know if this council would have sent out a party when their messenger hawks did not return."

"I would ask you to hold your tongue, but the barriers influence is strongest here within this chamber," said Boramil dismissively.

"Does this mean one of you is here to take your mother's position upon the council," questioned Elise with a grimace. Her mouth having outrun her mind.

Asche and Keltus looked at each other unsure for a split second before Keltus stepped forward. "I am. I claim my mother's position upon this council," she said. Any doubt completely gone with her proclamation. "I will make sure that what happened to Sun Meadow and Moongrove *does not happen again*."

"Fine. Fine, you have your seat. We cannot dispute your right to the position anyway," said Elmar dismissively.

"I suppose its my turn then. I am Alya the one you have been trying oh so desperately to catch since you imprisoned my friends."

"So, you saw fit to capture yourself. Favor has truly shown upon us," said Terill. "Now we can get on with sentencing the traitor without consequence."

"And who might you be referring to as a traitor," questioned Leif.

"The former Princess of Moongrove Seraphine," said Elise.

"What treason has she possibly committed," questioned Keltus.

"She brought our oldest enemy, the dwarves, to our door," stated Elmar.

"And what reason did she have for bringing them," questioned Asche.

"You are not permitted to speak here unless called upon, but I will answer your question. It doesn't matter the reason for them being brought. The fact remains that she brought them here through the front gate of Moonclave. Committing treason against her own people," spat Boramil.

With the council going back and forth Drogen took the opportunity to look around the room at the construction of the tower itself, and most importantly the magic coursing through the runic sigils inscribed all around the structure. The draconic sigils told Drogen all he needed to know of the tower and the magic coursing through to the twelve others.

"That is enough all of you," said Drogen. Looking around the room at the group of bickering elves. He walked calmly to the dais in the middle of the room standing at the center of Moonclave, feeling the barrier and magic rush through him, body, mind, and soul.

"You have not been recognized by this council. Why should we listen to an outsider speak," roared Elmar.

"I concur," said Terill.

"You will have to force me from this dais, otherwise you will hear what I have to say," said Drogen in a calm but threatening undertone.

"Manzine remove this outsider from the dais and place him downstairs with the others. Take the warren with you as well," barked Terill.

Another elven male came sauntering into the council chamber from a door leading to the prisoners hold. "I take it you're Manzine. You may try whatever you wish to remove me from where I stand. But you will be sorely disappointed. And don't think laying a hand on Alya to be a better idea. It will end in the same result," warned Drogen.

"So you think," smiled Manzine. Splaying his fingers out toward Drogen. Vines grew seemingly out of nothing, wrapping themselves around Drogen binding him from head to toe in a matter of seconds. "Don't worry little kitten. I'll be back for you soon enough," laughed Manzine maniacally.

With a breath Drogen burned through the vines wrapping his body. Singeing the clothes and skin beneath, but he felt none of it. His draconic flames touched the dais in front of him, setting the top of it alight. However, the dais did not burn, or scorch in any way, it simply held aloft his flame.

"Nice trick. It still does not give you the right to speak in front of this council," barked Terill. Waving Manzine away with a swipe of his hand. "And there's nothing you can do to change our minds."

"Such a bold statement from one who knows so little of his origins. And the origins of the place his people call home."

"We came from the trunks of our mothers. Those I suspect surround us now. Not to mention the one you walked in with," chimed in Boramil

"If she wishes to speak then she may," said Elmar.

Leif moved to speak but Drogen stopped her with a shake of his head. "You know of your mothers, but who nurtured your mothers into the being's they are? Who laid out the plans for this place you call home? Who placed the barrier that envelops your home from which you have exerted control among your citizens without understanding the truth of what surrounds you," questioned Drogen.

"They were nurtured by Dranier itself as all of us are," interjected Llewellyn.

"That may hold some truth, but it is not the whole. It seems you will all continue to argue until you understand who stands before you. There are many ways that I could go about doing just that. However, I think the simplest method may prove to be the most effective. With a snap of my fingers... I will bring understanding to the entirety of what you call, Moonclave. No. My people had a different name for this place. A name brought about by tragedy. *Seraphal*" roared Drogen. Snapping his fingers.

Chapter Thirty

"Princess, you have a visitor, would you like me to send them in," questioned Ziraiy.

"Who is it," questioned Natalia leaning over Golga's book translating the text for Zephyria as she had for Drogen.

"Lisana princess," confirmed her handmaid.

"You may send her in," she said leaning back in the chair before her vanity as Ziraiy went back through the door. The room in which her mother had breathed her last breath, and the whole of her people had disappeared.

I wish I could have known her. She was strong enough, even without the magic they relied on, to erase a whole people from the world and save the last of her kind at the same time. No... I need to make sure these translations are right, I can't be thinking about things that don't matter... Am I lying to myself, questioned Natalia.

"Tis good to see you're awake," said Lisana looking around the room as she entered. A shiver running through her as she took everything in. "Tis strange standing in this room after so many years... How has it remained the same as it was all those years ago. As if my friend were awaiting my arrival within her chambers. She was my confidant, the one with which I expressed my woes and struggles."

"When I received word from the others that the Zephyrian's had taken control of Seraphal I was... Inconsolable my rage shook the very foundation of the city we had formed to meet the gods on even ground..."

"I apologize," said Lisana bowing her head in realization of what she had unknowingly been doing. "Natalia, I don't mean to unload such things upon you, sometimes we dragons cannot control what we say, especially when emotions are involved."

"You need not worry. I would very much like to hear more about her and my people. Now that the truth has been revealed. However, there is one question which I have been unable to comprehend. I hoped that you might shed some light on it for me. How was she able to erase all knowledge of the angelos from everyone. Everyone but the dragons, and how did doing such a thing allow me to live where I otherwise should have died," questioned Natalia tears brimming her eyes.

"Even in those days nobody truly understood the unique qualities possessed by the angelo. None except Alexandria that is. Where most races of Dranier have two, or three affinities for magic, the angelo were different. Like the dragons, they could use all magics. It was their greatest asset, their strength, and ultimately, their greatest weakness. Alexandria studied constantly different types of magic perfecting most, if not all, simply by reading. I brought her many different books in my travels, and she consumed each one as though they were the essence of her very existence."

"It sounds as if we would have gotten along quite well," said Natalia. "I spent many years sneaking in and out of the library, reading each and every book I could find within its boundaries. Had I known of the secret rooms I doubt anyone could have pulled me away," she confessed with a smile.

"I'm sure Brena was none to happy with that development," said Lisana with a smile. "Librarians usually are. I remember Alexandria getting into a lot of trouble with the librarian, for waking him up at all hours of the night while she was looking through the books for a single bit of information," she chuckled.

"Did she have the same understanding of language," questioned Natalia.

"Yes. Actually, I remember in the beginning bringing her books from different races, tribes, and dialects. It didn't matter what I brought to her, or the language it was written in. Upon reading it, or hearing a conversation, she could understand and converse in that language. As if she had known it the entirety of her life."

"I suppose I have inherited her thirst for knowledge and linguistic abilities," said Natalia speaking draconic.

"It would seem so," said Lisana matching the change of language effortlessly.

"As for your earlier question. What she was able to do was a surprise to me as well. I don't know how, or where she learned it, but she used the runic sigils of the dragons. There can be no other explanation for what she was able to do. Her spell, unlike the one we unleashed upon the elves, erased all knowledge of the angelos across Dranier. Not even the gods retained knowledge of them. Leaving only the dragons to remember their existence."

"Am I the last?" questioned Natalia. Finally looking Lisana in the eyes placing her book of translations upon the surface of her vanity.

"Yes. You're the last angelo," confirmed Lisana. Her expression sorrowful as she confirmed what Natalia had suspected.

As the mood within Natalia's room shifted a knock came upon the door moments before being swung open by Ziraiy. "There's a letter, a letter from the Moonclave just arrived Krail is gathering everyone in the Library for Lord Fread before it's read aloud."

"Thank you Ziraiy. We will go there quickly. Although the information may be out of date, it could tell us what Drogen is dealing with in Moonclave."

Natalia and Lisana wasted no time in running free of the room and down the tower stairs making it to the library in only a few minutes time. Knowing that barging into the library would draw the ire of Brena they took a moment to gather themselves before quietly, but silently opening the door. Willow, Fread, and Death were already within the room awaiting their arrival.

"Are we waiting for Mai-Coh and Chian," questioned Natalia.

"No, they have yet to decide on the course they wish to take. They're taking time to decide the best path for them," said Death.

"I'm going to show Mai-Coh the method he needs to use in order to complete his transformation. It shouldn't take long for him to understand what he needs to do. We're meeting midday today. I'm sure he wouldn't mind if you tagged along with me," said Lisana.

"I will take you up on your offer. Maybe I can convince them to stay. If only to complete the quests they set out to achieve," said Natalia. Contemplating for a moment. "I'm sure their imprisonment among the goblinkin has affected their outlook. I know it has affected me. Even though I was there for a shorter duration."

"We can read the letter now Fread... Fread hello... Fread," said Willow. Tapping Fread on the shoulder jolting him back to awareness.

"Yes... the letter," said Fread. Shaking his head looking around absently.

"You seem to be getting worse Fread. We may need employ another method to bring your soul back into resonance with your body," said Death in a low whisper. Only those closest to Fread could hear.

"We can discuss our options after getting through the matter everyone is here for," said Fread. Rising from the wooden chair he had been sitting on."This letter bears the seal of Phaylor, guard commander of Moonclave." Breaking the documents seal with a letter opener.

SERAPHINE, RUMBLE, AND TUMBLE HAVE BEEN IMPRISONED BY THE ELVEN COUNCIL. UNKNOWN WHERE THEY'RE BEING HELD, AS I HAVE BEEN RELEGATED TO SEARCHING FOR ALYA. WHO MANAGED TO ESCAPE. I HOPE THIS LETTER FINDS YOU QUICKLY, THOUGH I KNOW YOU DON'T HAVE MEANS OF HELPING IN THIS SITUATION. AT LEAST WHAT HAS TRANSPIRED HERE IS NOT CONTAINED SOLELY WITHIN MOONCLAVE.

COMMANDER PHAYLOR.

"It would seem splitting up in Moongrove was best for everyone. I know Drogen will be able to get them out, one way or another," said Natalia.

"Tis good that another of their party was able to escape as well. That means they will be less likely to push forward with what they have planned, fearing the loose end could affect the outcome," said Lisana.

"We just need to have faith that Drogen can and will affect their release," said Fread.

"Remind me once more Lisana, what were the conditions for releasing true magic back into the world," questioned Death.

"There were four conditions that needed to be met. The barrier surrounding Seraphal has to be taken down from within the central tower of the thirteen. A dragon must breathe his fire upon the central Dais, followed by the willing shedding of blood by a god or goddess. As for the last step, an accord must be reached. During our time with the gods, we could never even get past the first part. Why do you ask," questioned Lisana.

"The barrier did more than make it to where the gods could not lie, it also holds off my reapers and suppresses the soul's ability to move on through me. My reapers have been complaining about its presence since true magic was sealed by the dragons. Should the barrier fall, I will know," said Death.

"Even if the barrier falls there's no guarantee that true magic will be released. And we are far removed from Seraphal," said Lisana.

"Many will be in for more than a few surprises should true magic return to Dranier," said Death. Pausing on Willow.

"Oh, I wanted to bring this up earlier. I have a translated copy of Grock's plans from Golga's book," said Natalia.

"Good, you should probably give it to Death to go over. Maybe it will help with the translation of the etchings from Drogen's bowl," said Fread.

"Speaking of..." started Death. Grabbing a stack of parchments from a nearby table. "I have translated the first portion of the etchings. I feel as if the translations are accurate as well. I hope that the information contained within Natalia's book might corroborate the translations."

"What does the first part of the translation say," questioned Natalia. Hoping for some good news, or at least a distraction from the thoughts flooding her mind. *Between the memories of what I saw in the arena, and the information about my true origins, I need a distraction to pull myself from my own mind,* thought Natalia.

"First, Fread you said Gaia translated a portion of what was inscribed on the bowl for Drogen?"

"Yes. She translated it for Drogen while he was in Moongrove."

"If I remember what Drogen told me correctly... It was because of the information inscribed on the bowl that he found and brought Willow to us, from within the ravine that separates Moongrove from the dwarven citadel... Aragorth."

"Then she did so without understanding the context of what she was reading. The first portion of the etchings tells of battle between the youngest of the oldest. Given what has transpired here, I believe this to be referencing Drogen's battle with Ether and Uther. The first group of etchings say nothing of the ravine between the Elves and Dwarves," said Death.

"Could she have sent Drogen to free me of my seclusion? In hopes I could be saved from my, self exile," questioned Willow.

"Gaia has always had a way of bringing the children of worlds together. That they might exact necessary changes. Even if those initial meetings did not go well. They would eventually come to see eye to eye...mostly."

"So, tis possible Gaia sent Drogen to Willow in order to save her from herself," questioned Lisana.

"That is within what I would expect of Gaia. So yes," said Death. "Further into the etchings I have found reference to the fair and the stone, but they're not in conflict with each other. Instead, they are fighting the same enemy."

"Then my translated book will definitely prove useful for that part. Golga's notes say that Grock has planned to split his forces. Attacking both the elves and the dwarves at the same time. Golga even had a map showing Moonclave's location within the wood. She wrote that Grock is doing so despite his generals' advisement against it. Grock refused to listen, stating that the distance between the two was both, far enough to not arouse suspicion, and close enough to send reinforcements should one siege prove more difficult than another," said Natalia. Thumbing through her translation's. Wishing to say everything as Golga had written it.

"Unfortunately, he may not be wrong in his way of thinking," said Lisana. Shaking her head. "The elves and dwarves, even a few hundred years ago cared very little for one another. The elves hated the dwarves for cutting down trees to fuel their furnaces, while the dwarves viewed the elves as egotistical and uncompromising. Neither side was wrong. But neither side was right either. Ultimately, neither side was willing to compromise. However, neither side wanted to start a war with the other. In the end they simply decided to live as though neither existed."

"That sentiment has not changed in the slightest. Not from either side. Even though Rumble and Tumble had been exiled from their own people for fighting against the status que, established by their king regarding the elves. At least that is all they would tell me on the subject. They always fought with Seraphine and the other elves whenever they happened to be in Zephyria," said Natalia remembering many instances of such fights happening. Culminating in the trading of insults from both sides.

"See it always becomes physical with those two. They never simply talk with one another to find common ground," said Lisana. Throwing her hands up in aggravation. "I can't count how many times I had to break up a fight between that high and mighty Silf and Aragorth, just thinking about it makes my blood boil."

"I think you misunderstand," said Fread. "For as long as I was commander of the guard... I never received any reports of blows being exchanged between the dwarves and the elves who came here. Even Seraphine, hot tempered as she is, never exchanged blows with the brother dwarves. At least... to my knowledge."

"No, they never fought with anything but insults," confirmed Natalia.

Lisana thought through what she was hearing, as though such a thing were inconceivable before bursting out laughing. Drawing the ire of Brena and many others within the library for her outburst.

"What's so funny about the dwarves and the elves trading insults instead of fists," questioned Willow.

"Both elves and dwarves viewed the other as idiotic in their own ways. The elves viewed dwarves as unsophisticated. And the dwarves saw the elves as conceited. One side cannot lie, while the other side is brash and unable to hold their tongues at the best of times. So, what better way could there be for such beings to find common ground then through insults. An insult is neither a truth, nor a lie, it simply is. For both sides," said Lisana with a suppressed chuckle.

"So, what you're saying is should both sides be willing to finally work together, Grock may find his conquest far harder to obtain than he realizes," said Willow.

"This is all nothing but speculation," said Fread. Shaking his head. "They've never been able to see past each other's differences. I don't see how the threat of goblinkin attacking them would change things."

"I suppose we'll simply have to wait and see what comes to pass," said Death. "I do have another piece of information to share with Lisana. Our son's full name, as he told me through his astral form is Drogen, Son of Lisana; Reaper of Souls, Godslayer; Envoy of Death Drakregus of Lundwurm Tul."

Lisana looked into Death's eyes with shock. Both at their son's name, and that Death had not only allowed her to hear it but told her himself. "I understand now why you wanted me to hear it from his mouth. The weight of such a grand name, even among the eldest dragonkin, would be tremendous."

"I tell you this now, because one who's name carries so much weight may not have known how to bear its full weight until a chance to change it is forced upon them," said Death.

"Will you stop with the riddles and double speak already you know I can't stand when you start in like that. Say it plainly so the rest of the people here might actually understand what you're getting at will you," said Lisana haughtily.

"I'm only trying to have some fun my love. Simply put, Drogen will find himself at a crossroads and that crossroad will alter Dranier's history forever. I just hope we're all ready for the ride," said Death with a demure expression. Which he quickly schooled.

"Such a prediction coming from Death feels far too ominous," said Fread.

"What happens is not up to any of us. Drogen's fate is in his hands alone."

"Well with that trebuchet sprung how about we leave to find Mai-Coh and Chian," posited Lisana.

"Yes. Let us take our leave," said Natalia. "Unless there are other matter we need to discuss?"

"There's something that I would like to ask, but I would not wish to speak with so many around about... personal matters. Come find me after you're done with Mai-Coh and Chian. Unfortunately, I have other pressing matters to attend to with Death and Willow."

"Very well. I will come and find you once my time with the others has concluded."

Natalia and Lisana took their leave of the room working their way through the corridors that would lead them to the audience chamber.

"Drogen, son of Lisana; Reaper of Souls, Godslayer; Envoy of Death, Drakregus of Lundwurm Tul. How could a name so heavy change, and in what way," wondered Lisana.

"I do not know, but Drogen is more than capable of shouldering the responsibility of his name, and any others he might gain," proclaimed Natalia.

"I wish I could be as confident as you are. Such a name given to one so young... It must feel like the weight of the world is resting upon his shoulders."

"Drogen would never view his name as a burden. I have witnessed him speaking his full name. He says it with pride, as he declares himself fully to those who stand against him. I only wish I could do more to help, without being such a burden," said Natalia disparaging herself unintentionally.

"Is this how he views those around him," questioned Lisana with concern.

"I apologize," said Natalia. Hearing a slight edge in Lisana's voice. "I must clarify. That is how *I feel.* Standing in his presence. Drogen has never made me feel anything but welcome. He has gone out of his way to save me not once, but twice. Above all else, I want to stand by his side. Bearing the burden upon his shoulders. That his burdens do not weigh him down alone," clarified Natalia.

"Then you must declare your true intentions aloud. A goal for you to focus upon, and a mantra for which you strive. I would however caution you. Striving for another is not the right way to start down such a path. Having such a goal in mind, as a point at which to reflect is worthy of thought, but not as an end goal. Think about what would make you happy and satisfied, lying upon the fields of battle wounded and dying. And strive beyond it. That is where you will find your answer," explained Lisana.

"Then until such time as I find this... mantra, I will set a goal. To lessen the burden *I feel,* I place upon him," declared Natalia. *Although, I do not know how to accomplish such a feat.*

Lisana simply nodded in acknowledgment of Natalia's goal, as they walked through the packed audience chamber. Krail stood upon the dais as commander of Zephyria listening intently to those in attendance. When they walked free of the chamber, and into the courtyard through the splintered doors, Natalia began recapitulating Drogen's fight to Lisana. From her plucked wings, and Drogen's healing water, to the fight within the gorge below Zephyria.

"I only wish I could have been here to see it. To witness his fight against the twin gods," said Lisana sorrowfully. "I was still looking for Death. From what Death has said Drogen's killing of Ether and Uther was the catalyst he needed to release himself from the confines of his cell. For that, I am truly grateful. I hope he doesn't view me poorly for my leaving Lundwurm Tul in search of his father. I can't help but feel as though I abandoned him, for my own selfish reasons," she confessed.

"He may have, at first. I cannot say for certain. What I can tell you however, is what he told me of his time in Lundwurm Tul. Drogen didn't feel abandoned. He knew you were missing his father. Far more than you may realize. He was sad that you left, but understood why you needed to. He was happy you found the strength to follow your heart."

"Thank you, Natalia."

"Would you like to see the home he built here in Zephyria?"

"Yes. I would enjoy that very much... Is it in a secluded area? Away from prying eyes per chance?"

"Better yet, Mai-Coh and Chian both know its location. So, even if we go there now, sending a guard to locate and inform them will prove adequate enough to get them there quickly," said Natalia.

"Then let's find a guard and head over. We can look around while we await their arrival," said Lisana.

"Let us find a guard then," said Natalia with a cheerful smile.

Death, Willow, and Fread moved into the alcove, where they could see into the main library, but would not risk being overheard by eavesdropping ears. Fread sat down on a stack of books just large enough to make a comfortable chair. Using the stack behind it as a backrest. Willow choosing to stand, positioned herself between Fread and the main Library.

Before speaking they listened intently to the musings and scratching of those within the library making sure the others were too busy with their own works to be overly curious about their disappearance. With no sign of others getting close and having made certain the sections around them were clear of intruders, they began to speak openly.

"The bouts are getting worse, and far more frequent. Worse yet, I don't feel them coming," said Fread. Death setting down beside him. "It has happened twice now, that I know of, in the audience chamber. Luckily for me, Krail was there to take over before it became too apparent. However, I'm certain it didn't go unnoticed by everyone. If one of the zealots caught wind of it, they could see it as an opportunity to sow discourse."

"Is your assessment the same," questioned Death. Shifting his focus to Willow.

"Yes. Many are beginning to notice the change in his demeanor. Far more than if his symptoms had remained the same."

Hearing the library door swing open Willow and Death turned to observe the new entrant. Krail came in garnering many looks from those seated throughout the library. The rest of the library, realizing it was Krail turned back to their tasks. All except for Brena who dropped everything she was doing in order to greet him quickly.

"It would seem their relationship is developing nicely," said Willow with a sincere smile.

"I fear Fread's rapid decline may be the result of my being here. Being so near to the source of his souls end through constant contact with my presence is causing his essence to further seek release from its vessel. If not for my proximity, his deterioration may have been slower, or even have halted entirely."

"Such things don't matter now. The question is... what can be done to stop it. You said there are ways to lessen or rid him of these effects. We need to do something. He can't continue like this. I can't continue like this," said Willow. Looking despondent upon Fread, who had once more fallen into his near-death state.

"This method will ultimately need to be researched, but the binding of your souls together may lead to a reversal of most of the effects near death has caused his soul to experience. The hardest part of such a ritual would be tracking down one of your people, without true magic. Unless you know the location of a necromancer's lair," postulated Death.

"I don't know where any of those children ended up. Maybe Fread will have heard of, or know something about, a necromancer. Even if I knew the location of a Necromancer's lair, and had everything necessary to bind our souls together... Would Fread find the binding of our souls an appealing prospect. None of them know the truth, and I fear when he learns who I am... He'll no longer look at me the same way," confessed Willow. Suppressing her own emotion of fear in order to speak freely.

"If your heart is true to his soul and his to yours, then the truth will bring you closer together, not tear you apart," said Death. "Should either of you doubt the intentions of the other however, the binding could be... catastrophic."

"I don't even know where to begin."

"Tis beneficial to give one's name to start."

She looked down at the ground with Death's proclamation. "You're right. Maybe... if we journey together. Even if we don't go through with the rites. We can get everything out in the open."

"That would be for the best."

They sat in silence for a while waiting for the inevitable arrival of Krail and Brena who continued to be stopped every few feet to go over one of the translators notes on the etchings and what possible meaning they garnered from their research.

"Do you understand what *he's* been doing in your absence. Doing to those you sought to protect," questioned Death.

"I am... He has corrupted many to his way. Our brethren, and those who simply wished to be left alone. Unfortunately, without true magic, I cannot hold influence on anything more than the emotions of those around me. Two under his influence were thankfully expelled from Zephyria. If one of them were a necromancer, I was unable to tell. They, from what I witnessed, were incapable of exerting influence without access to their magics. Many, if not all don't know the truth of their missions let alone what they actually are."

"What about those located where true magic is being contained?"

"They could possibly be aware of their actions, and their missions. The question is where they were sent by Lucian. Or are they simply trying to live among the others. Had I not gone into exile, maybe I could have swayed more of them away from Lucian's influence. I fear its my fault that his influence has spread so far unchecked."

"We cannot change what has already come to pass. Only look to make better choices in the future. It would seem Krail and Brena have been able to break away from the others, and are heading our way," he warned. Taking the cue, Willow turned round in order to greet the new arrivals. "It may be wise to garner their help in this matter as well. Just remember, this is a choice that both you and Fread will need to make together, *with all faculties intact.*"

Krail and Brena stopped short of Death and Willow looking past them at the clearly incapacitated Fread. "He's getting worse isn't he," questioned Krail sorrowfully. "More people are noticing the change and have started talking. Worse still word of his condition has reached the ears of the zealots. They're calling it divine justice and proof that Fread is unfit to rule over Zephyria and its people."

"We have a solution, but we need to research it's possibility," said Willow.

"One of the problems with this method is going to be finding a Necromancer's lair," Death remarked.

"That problem isn't actually a problem. Fread has been in a Necromancer's lair. As have Natalia and Drogen. Kethick took Natalia to his lair southeast of here, if the reports are accurate. Drogen and Fread went to save Natalia, from whatever he'd planned to do with her."

"What method are you needing to research," questioned Brena.

With a pat on Fread's shoulder, he regained himself from the near-death state, startled at first by the new additions of Brena and Krail, to their party. "How long was I... when did they... We need to find a solution to this problem quickly," stated Fread. Realizing what had happened.

"We need to research soul binding, and the steps needed to enact it...and the possible effects should it fail," said Willow. A hint of sadness present in her sunflower gold eyes.

"What is a soul binding," questioned Krail.

"Tis a ritual to bind two souls together. Think of it as a marriage, *with* a few extra steps," said Death.

"And a lot more that could go wrong," interjected Brena.

"I fear a soul binding may be our only option without the release of true magic. I don't wish to rush into anything, but Fread's getting worse," said Willow gloomily.

"I will need some time to find the right book, but I know this library quite well. It shouldn't take me much time to locate the book we need," said Brena.

"I'll aid in her search as well. Maybe we can find another method, which poses less risk, in our hunt," said Krail.

"Is there anything about the ritual that is known before they go looking for, and researching, the topic," questioned Fread.

"Yes, because of Fread's near death experience the ritual needs to be in a place where the dead have risen from their graves. The most practical of these would be a necromancer's lair." said Death.

"Then I know exactly where we must go," said Fread.

"The guards should be finding and sending Mai-Coh and Chian here soon," said Natalia.

"Yes, one thing I've noticed about the zephyrian's is they're surprisingly adept at locating people," said Lisana.

"They have a good rapport with the citizens of Zephyria, so it never takes long for anyone to be located," said Natalia proudly.

"So Drogen built this house," questioned Lisana enthusiastically.

"Yes, he did, and in under a months' time."

"Being our son, I doubt he needs to sleep very often. Tis likely he built this place in a weeks' time, if not less. If he worked day and night to make the structure. Tis quite nice seeing something he built with his own hands. It makes me feel closer to him than I have felt since leaving Lundwurm Tul."

"He told me, when Fread and I came here the first time, that the table was made to remind him of the dining hall in Lundwurm Tul. Where stories were told and food was shared," smiled Natalia. Reminiscing about the night they had danced together in the castle's ballroom.

"Yes, the dining halls tables were all scorched," chortled Lisana. "Although they didn't start out that way. When we dragons get together and share stories, often times things get set ablaze. Especially when alcohols involved. I scorched more than a few of those tables myself. Recounting battles, victory, and defeat. I too miss it and think back upon it fondly."

"It would seem that you are not so different from one another as you may have thought. He gets the same look in his eyes, as you have now, whenever he speaks of his time in Lundwurm Tul."

"It would seem Mai-Coh and Chian are arriving," said Lisana her ears moving.

"Yet another commonality. He too always listens to the world around him," she said. Heading for the door.

Lisana took another couple of seconds to look at the table and the room from where she had set herself before rising and joining Natalia outside Drogen's home. Lisana closed the door tightly behind her taking a moment more to etch its design into her memory before turning to the task at hand.

With a wave of her hand Lisana beckoned Mai-Coh towards her. With Lisana taking Mai-Coh for their training, Natalia pulled Chain aside in hopes she might convince them both to stay. If only to complete the quests they set out across the forbidden plains to finish.

"You don't want to learn how to do it as well," questioned Natalia. Referring to the training Mai-Coh and Lisana were engaging in.

"No. No need with taurean," said Chian.

"Have you had any luck finding a building technique here in Zephyria that you can take back to your people?"

"No, I find no builder in sky people home. None to show how stone may shine like it does here?"

"Maybe you're looking in the wrong place. Have you asked the librarian Brena about your quest. She may have the information you are looking for?"

"No. smart sky people busy with work. Too busy for taurean. Their work more important than taurean quest."

"You are always welcome to research it yourself."

"Thought so too, but not read sky people's words," said Chian. Shaking her head. "Taurean learn with work, not with word," she said with a shrug. "Only tribe leaders learn to read. They pass down to next."

"I can help you, if you like. Working together, who knows what we might find. You with your building knowledge and me with my ability to understand other languages. We might be able to find many things that could improve the lives of your people. And maybe, my own," said Natalia.

"I would not wish to pull you away from your quests black wing."

"You would not be pulling away from anything. Everyone else has their hands full with the matters surrounding Drogen. I however, have none since translating Golga's book. And honestly... I could use a distraction from circumstances which have recently come to light."

"Only if my presence does not cause trouble."

"You are no trouble, Chian. You are a friend, and anything I can do to help, *I will*," she affirmed.

"Thank you, black wing."

"You're more than welcome my taurean friend," she said with a smile.

Looking over at Mai-Coh and Lisana they noticed discomfort along his protracted snout his teeth visibly showing in a grimace. "Why do I sit here with no result," questioned Mai-Coh. Clearly perturbed by their lack of doing anything.

"That's the problem. You are just sitting there. You need to learn to breath and fall within yourself in order to control your form. It will take some time for you to find the door within yourself," admonished Lisana.

"I do not know what you mean," said Mai-Coh bitterly.

"Then let me show you," said Lisana. Taking hold of Mai-Coh's fur covered hands and placing them upon her own. "Bend forward that our foreheads touch. Once our foreheads touch, I will be letting you within my mind. Within my mind you will come to understand what must be done. Be sure you're ready."

"I come far for healing, not give up at end of struggle," said Mai-Coh. With the decision reached he placed his forehead upon the waiting Lisana's his hands placed palm down upon her own. Within seconds of contact the rhythm of their breathing synchronized becoming as one.

"Drogen often falls into a state like that. I was not aware he could share that experience with another," said Natalia. Her mind flowing with possibilities.

"He may not know," reasoned Chian.

"I will have to ask him when next we meet, if he would be comfortable sharing such an experience with me," said Natalia. *Sharing one's body is one thing, to share one's mind seems... far more intimate. If precautions are not taken within one's own mind to lock others away from things better left alone, trouble could arise. Drogen would be the only one with which I felt comfortable performing such an act. I wonder if what we did near the river could be enhanced further through such a... connection,* thought Natalia. Blood rushing to her face.

"How long till they move," Chian questioned.

"I suppose it will take as long as it has to," she shrugged. "For now, all we can do is wait."

Chapter Thirty-One

"Have you been able to find anything Brena," questioned Krail. Sauntering into the alcove Brena had only just begun searching through.

"No. I'm afraid not. I know the book is in this alcove. I remember seeing it. Although, it has been many years. It should still be here."

"You're sure it was in this alcove and not another one," questioned Willow.

"Yes, I'm sure. I've been the librarian of Zephyria for a very long time. I know every section of this library like the back of my hand," said Brena. Clearly irritated by Willow's perceived insinuation.

"I meant no offense. I just wondered if it could be somewhere else. Maybe someone was reading the book and never put it back. Or, they may have put it in the wrong spot," posited Willow sheepishly.

"Hmm, you may be on to something there. I always had a difficult time keeping a certain princess out of the library at night. She always had a book in her hand. Often taking books to her room in order to read. I always caught her reading in the same spot at night however, the book could very well be among those she piled up around herself."

"Wouldn't books from so long ago have been returned to the shelves by now," questioned Willow.

"I would like to tell you that they were, but with the number of people that come to the library, it simply became too much for one person to handle. I have a duty to help those who come to the library, with their research as well after all," said Brena.

"It sounds like you could use some help. Even if its only to put the books back on the shelves," said Krail. "I will look into getting you help. I'm sure research would be far easier if the books were put away."

"Until that happens, we'll need to look in the other alcoves for the volume we're looking for. Unless someone can bring Natalia here on the off chance she remembers where that particular book is," sighed Brena.

"That might not be such a bad idea. Her memory is quite daunting, if anyone would remember such a detail, it would be the Princess," observed Krail.

"True, and should she return before we're done searching for the book, then we may ask her. But we should continue to look, until either eventuality comes to pass."

Willow and Krail nodded in deference to Brena on the subject as she sent them in opposite directions to look through the stacks of books left on the ground throughout the library. In hopes that splitting up would allow them to locate the right book quicker.

"Which direction is the section princess Natalia always read in at night," questioned Krail. To which Brena pointed without raising her head from her own stack of tomes.

Willow looked through many stacks of books thumbing through each stack of books and loose parchments she passed on her way back to where they had left Fread, at Deaths side. Each stack of books and parchments led to the next and the next in what felt like a never-ending hunt for information long lost, and irrecoverable.

Hours passed for the three like days, as they worked through the multiple stacks of books, and alcoves one at a time. Each book a boon to overcome as they toiled the hours away. Each of the books presented their challenges, even to Willow, as each was written in a different language or dialect than the books before them. Luckily Brena remembered the books language taking many of the books they came across out of contention. Still their progress, even with three looking, remained arduously slow.

"Found it," cried an ecstatic Krail as he came running out of a far alcove tripping over another pile of books, which skittered across the floor. Holding the book up over his head so as not to lose the precious manuscript. Catching himself with a flap of his wings to right himself before fully hitting ground.

Hearing Krail's excitement and the subsequent crash Brena and Willow rushed to him arriving only moments after Krail rectified himself from the pile of books he'd spread upon the floor. Seeing his companions rushing to him, Krail held the book out in triumph for them both to see.

"I typically don't like such outbursts in the library, it causes disruption after all. However, I will view this occasion as an exception. I thought we'd never locate that book," said Brena sighing in relief.

"So many books, how does anyone find anything in this library," said Willow. Rubbing her eyes as though they were sore from strain.

"I'll be getting you someone to help reorganize and put this library back in order, as soon as possible," said Krail. Giving the book over to Brena with a smile. "And sorry for my outburst I'll endeavor to keep such things to a minimum in the future. Although, I find doing so in your presence to be the hardest battle of all," smiled and winked Krail.

Blood flooded to Brena's face as she started swaying her hips holding the book using it, and her hands in order to cover the feelings present upon her visage. "As long as you keep it to a minimum," stammered out the flustered Brena. Before she turned around and headed back along the corridor. Where Fread and Death continued to wait.

Willow and Krail followed Brena closely. Upon returning they noticed that nothing had changed since their departure, aside from Fread.

In order to keep himself from experiencing the near-death sate, Fread exercised silently. Using his body weight and a few books to help himself remain awake and vigilant.

"Does that help," questioned Krail.

"Yes, it does. It allows him to keep time and focus on things around him. It's one of the only methods we've found that actually keeps him present. Sparring and other activities work as well, but even those have had limited success," said Willow.

"She's right. I thought my passing out when facing Lisana, could have been a one-time event. Willow and I have tried on a few occasions to spar. As long as I am able to count the strikes. Or have anything that keeps me in the moment, I am fine. But... the moment I lose that count, the moment I can no longer think in the present, I wake up not understanding what happened. Or where I am. If I continue to deteriorate... I'll be of no use to our people," said Fread.

"Krail found the book. All we need to do now is have someone translate the necessary pages. Which is something I'll be able to manage myself. Unlike Drogen's bowl, this is written in a language that I can innately understand," said Willow optimistically as she looks upon Fread.

"I've never seen this language before. Are you sure it won't be as difficult as the etchings," questioned Krail.

"Lower daelonic is actually really easy to understand. Once you get the hang of it. Death has stated on multiple occasions that the etchings are very different, when compared to other writings. Willow is a goddess, she should be able to read what's written in that book easily," explained Brena.

With a slight push of air from Fread's mouth he fell to the ground overtaken by the near-death state once more. They all turn to look at him with concern, but none with more than Willow who dropped to her knees in order to check that Fread had not injured himself in the fall.

"He is getting worse, and without true magic he will continue to do so. Within that book is the only other option for what he's experiencing," said Death. Looking at the book and then to Willow.

"Can Fread and I take this book with us," questioned Willow. Looking for permission from Brena to do what needed to be done.

"Can you take the book with you," posited Brena. "Fread is the Lord of Zephyria. You are taking him with you in order to cure his ailment, and you're asking my permission to take a book... Of course, you can take the book with you, what kind of silly question is that. We don't have time to translate another book, and if you can read it and it helps you to cure Lord Fread then take the stupid book and go," complained Brena. Throwing her hands up in the air at the absolute absurdity of the question.

"Shh," came the call over Brena's tirade. The silencing sound she employed upon others, deriving an outburst of muffled chortles from everyone within the library.

Taking in a deep breath to calm herself, Brena exhaled slowly. "Take Fread and the book and *Go* Willow," she said. Tossing the book into Willow's hands. "With everyone present, Zephyria will be able to run without either of you. For a while. We still have Lord Vladimir as well. And don't worry about informing princess Natalia. Once she, and those with her come back, I'll inform them of what's happening. *Go.* See if you can cure him, because if you cannot, I fear many hardships will result," expressed Brena. Shaking the unpleasant thoughts away from her mind.

"I will gather guards to accompany you," said Krail.

"No. This is something Fread and I must do alone. And the addition of guards will only slow us down. I fear if this goes on any longer Fread's soul may return to Death forever," professed Willow solemnly.

"Then promise me Willow, Daughter of Destruction. That you will bring him home to Zephyria no matter what," said Krail.

"I promise. I will bring him back to his people. Even if I should die in the process," she proclaimed.

"Then go as swiftly as your boots will take you."

Willow bent down at Fread's side patting him upon the shoulder causing him to jump to his feet with a start. "It is time we leave for the necromancer's lair. Our friends will make certain our lack of presence is not felt."

Once past the mental fog the near-death state caused, Fread nodded to Brena and Krail. "I leave Zephyria in your capable hands my friends. I was to meet with Natalia to discuss matters only you and I are aware of, this too I leave to you in my stead. Now let us sojourn to Kethick's lair," he said. Placing his arm around Willow's shoulders, that they could walk free of the library together.

"It shall be done Lord Fread," saluted Krail fist to heart. As they walked through the main portion of the library, disappearing from sight behind the door.

"Do you understand now what you must do," questioned Lisana. Straightening up and pulling her hands free from beneath Mai-Coh's.

"Yes." Mai-Coh shivered. "How can one door hold back so much?"

"We all place barriers within our minds, and those barriers take many different forms. Some are present because of trauma, where others are placed in order to retain. Getting past some or all of those barriers may be a part of finding the answer to your question. You may find that you are forced to relive what you've long since buried in order to stand before the door that you seek," said Lisana.

"Thank you, mother of Drogen, for guiding me," he said. Bowing his head to Lisana.

"I'm glad I was able to assist you in your journey. Tis the least I could do, for those my son has placed his faith in," said Lisana.

"Chian and I are going to look through the library when we get back. I want to help her find building methods she can take back to her people," mentioned Natalia.

"With Natalia black wings help, I will return to my people triumphant," proclaimed Chian.

"The taurean and pawnee will welcome our return," said Mai-Coh with renewed determination.

"We should be returning to the library. I hope everyone has made progress on their projects. Especially Fread, and Willow," said Lisana optimistically.

"As do I," said Natalia. *I wonder what Fread wanted to speak to me about.*

"What are you going to do now that you have the answers you seek," questioned Lisana. Catching Mai-Coh's attention.

"I wait for Chian. We did not start our journey together, but *we will* finish it together. It will prove friendship between our tribes is possible," said Mai-Coh in vehement belief.

"You will be staying a while more upon this plateau with the zephyrian's then. Many of their people do not carry weapons, thinking themselves safe from any outside harm. I also heard that you caught the attention of the more zealous zephyrian's. So, I would suggest you not take such an approach yourselves. You both have seen what can happen to those unable to defend themselves, because they were ill-prepared, or ill-equipped," said Lisan. Her eyes bearing the intensity of her heritage as she looked upon them.

"We can look for weapons that match you both within Zephyria. We have no blacksmith here in Zephyria as we trade for weapons with the elves, dwarves, and gnomes. So, a custom order may be entirely out of the question, but we will be able to find each of you something suitable to use. At least until something better comes along," said Natalia. "I have been needing to procure weapons as well."

"Tis as good an opportunity as any," said Lisana. Trying in vain to obscure her evident excitement.

"We have no money to buy weapon's we will work to procure them," said Mai-Coh

"Yes, we will," said Chian with determination.

"We should get going then. I haven't been weapon shopping in ages, I wonder what new designs have been conceived. The best weapons, aside from those we dragon's forge, come from dwarves and elves. Typically, in that order. Now a dwarven weapon with elvish enchantments, that's something rare and powerful you just don't see very often," mused Lisana.

"Speaking of weapons. When we return to the castle you should ask Willow to see the blade she carries. She told me Drogen is the one who forged it."

"I will keep that in mind," said Lisana happily.

Listening to Lisana talk about weapons brought their group to Zephyria's street of commerce where many merchants and shops were abuzz with activity. Dust and dirt flew through the air around children as they ran through the streets happily playing in mock battles using sticks as swords. Their cherubic laughter drawing a smile to Lisana's face.

"The more things change, the more they remain the same," said Lisana under her breath.

"Before we go too far. I need to see the seamstress, Jesha." *Even if Ziraiy has not had chance to bring my armors and dresses, she will need my measurements to repair and size them,* thought Natalia.

Natalia ran into Jesha's shop coming back out a few moments later with a wide smile on her face. "You would swear she is a miracle worker. She's already working on the dresses Ziraiy brought for her to take in, all she needed were my new measurements."

I will need to thank Ziraiy for her swiftness, and Jesha for the same, she thought.

"Glad to hear it. Do you know which weapon shops here have the best selection," questioned Lisana. Looking around at the many street vendors and shops.

"Yes. Come this way I will take you to Mirko's shop. He has gathered quite a selection of weapons. He is one of the people who has recently started rebuilding after zephyr was taken over by goblinkin," said Natalia.

"That name sounds familiar," said Lisana. Racking her mind to remember the context surrounding his name. "Is this the same Mirko as..."

"I suppose you would not be wrong in calling him my uncle," nodded Natalia.

As the door to Mirko's shop opened a gruff but friendly voice came from within. "Natalia, it feels like a lifetime since I last saw you."

"It has been quite some time uncle Mirko. I see you have succeeded in rebuilding your shop here in Zephyria."

"Thankfully my old shop was still available when I returned. Other than wishing I could have saved more of my inventory; things are going quite well. I've been able to gather weapons from returning guards, and caravans to fill my shop with wares. Are you looking for anything specific?"

"Yes. My friends here are looking for weapons... I don't actually know what weapons they prefer so you will need to ask them," said Natalia shrugging.

"Hmm, you come with some rather peculiar friends it would seem. Do all three of them need weapons?"

"I don't need any weapons. I have a usable sword already. Tis these three here who will be needing weapons," said Lisana. "However, I will take a look at your inventory."

"Look as you like," said Mirko. "As for you three what might you be looking for."

"My tribe use bow and arrow for hunting and war," said Mai-Coh.

"Unfortunately, I stock neither bows, nor arrows. However, I can recommend another shop. Where you can find exactly what you're looking for. If you leave from here and travel toward the castle. You'll find a shop whose carved sign is that of an elven hunter. That is where you will find your bows and arrows."

Mai-Coh nodded. "I give thanks for this information," he said. Nudging the shy Chian forward.

"M-my people are builders and warriors we only use tools made for both," said Chian timidly.

"Given the size of your muscle mass and your height I dare say you could wield a war-hammer for both. You're in luck, I happen to have a few war-hammers here in the shop. Look in the corner near the back of the shop. Its not a very popular weapon here in Zephyria, so I'll give you a good deal on it."

Chian bowed slightly in thanks before retreating with Mai-Coh to the corner of the shop Mirko had pointed them to. "Now what kind of weapon would the princess of Zephyria be looking for," questioned Mirko. Clearly intrigued.

"I am looking for easily concealed weapons that can be thrown, and something that fits my size for close quarters. Recent experiences have shown me that I need more than throwing weapons in order to survive."

"How many throwing weapons are you looking for?"

"As many as you have."

"Very well I will gather those that would be most fitting. As for a close quarters weapon... hmm a sword would probably fit you best. The question is what kind. For your stature I would suggest something like a long sword to improve your reach. However, such a thing would likely prove unwieldy and far more detrimental to you than the one you're facing. I may have something. I don't know if it is still here... Give me a moment."

"Thank you, Uncle," said Natalia. As he disappeared through a cloth door haphazardly hung to block view to the contents beyond.

Unsure as to how long Mirko would remain away, Natalia began looking through the shop's wares. Looking for anything intriguing until she stood before Chian. "Have you had any luck finding a hammer you like," She questioned.

"Yes. This hammer is fine. Good for building, and war," said Chian with a big grin. A smile that undermining her even tone. Denoting to Natalia just how enticed she was with her find.

"Has Mai-Coh gone to the shop Uncle Mirko suggested," questioned Natalia. Taking note of his disappearance.

"Once he saw Chian lost in her own world, looking through the hammers he went to the other shop. Probably in hopes of finding himself something as well," said Lisana. Looking through a collection of affixed maces, and chained morning-stars, hung along the shop walls. "I've seen quite a few weapons that may fit you, but it sounded as though your uncle had other weapons in mind."

"It sounded that way to me as well."

Mirko came out from behind the curtain holding a multitude of sheathed weapons in his arms and his pockets bulging. "I may have gone overboard, but anything you don't need or want is fine." Unfurling his arms over his shop counter, the sheathed weapons fell to its hard wood surface. With his hands free, he emptied each of his pockets of their contents. Leaving a multitude of weapons upon the counter for Natalia to rummage through. However, one of the sheathed weapons Mirko pulled back behind the counter, out of sight.

All of these daggers will fit perfectly within my armor, as soon as Jesha is able to finish the repairs. Claw weapons...these daggers can be thrown, but they are too short for close combat. Metal knuckles, they could help in a fight should one be necessary, I will grab those as well... This short sword would work fine, but it doesn't balance well in my hand. Neither does this one... She contemplated. Going over each weapon individually and sorting them into two distinct piles.

"I will purchase these weapons, those over there do not suit me. Unfortunately, I was unable to find a suitable sword within those you have shown me," said Natalia wistfully.

"I kept one weapon back. It is the one I thought might suit you best. I don't know who crafted it. Nor do I know what such a thing should be called. I actually bought it many years ago from a couple dwarves who came to Zephyr. They didn't know its origins either. All I know is, it's truly unique," said Mirko. Pulling the weapon he'd held back, out from behind the counter.

Lisana walked over to the counter intrigued by Mirko's story wishing to look upon the weapon with no known origin. With a captivated audience Mirko removed the sword from its leather scabbard placing the blade flat upon the table.

The blade measured two feet in length its circular cross guard ornately decorated with ravens in flight matching up perfectly with the scabbard depicting their touching down on the ground at the feet of a woman with books surrounding her. Parchments fell like raindrops from the ravens in flight. The hilt of the sword matched Natalia's hand perfectly. As though it had been forged for her and her alone. Strangest of all was the twisted concentric triple blade design of the sword. Its three sharpened edges narrowing at its end to a single sharp point.

"Th-this is perfect," said Natalia. Holding the sword aloft. "How can it be so light," she questioned. Placed the blade back into its scabbard. Completing the scene once more.

"Then this too is yours. Is there anything else I may be able to locate for you," questioned Mirko. Happy he was able to provide Natalia with so much.

Natalia ushered Mirko forward as she whispered conspiratorially, "I also wish to purchase Chian and Mai-Coh's weapons. I would appreciate word being sent," she said. Garnering a nod from Mirko. "I will send payment with my handmaid Ziraiy, in a couple days."

Lisana, although close to Natalia, didn't listen to what she whispered to Mirko instead she focused completely upon the weapon Natalia had just purchased, a look of Nostalgia and wonder upon her visage at seeing the weapon.

"Thank you, Uncle. I hope to be seeing you again soon," said Natalia with a mischievous smile.

"Let's head back to the castle. We've been gone most of the day, some more information should have been found by now," said Lisana.

Chian placed the hammer she found back before joining both Lisana and Natalia outside Mirko's shop. "We will work hard to pay for such fine weapons. Mai-Coh will do the same. Will come back when we have enough."

"It is good to see you have found another goal to strive for while you are here in Zephyria. I hope that I can help you in achieving those goals as well," said Natalia.

As a group they walked by many vendors, looking through their inventories, and products with intrigue. Working their way towards Mai-Coh and the castle. They had nearly reached the shop Mirko had mentioned when the gathering of a large crowd caught their collective attention.

"Tis strange... Why are there so many gathered so close together," questioned Lisana.

"Well, since we are close, let us find out what is going on," said Natalia. Equally intrigued by the larger than normal gathering.

They walked over to the gathered crowd as voices called out over those in attendance. "We find Fread unfit to rule the people of Zephyria. The gods appointed Lord Vladimir to the position of ruler. Fread has no claim to the throne on which he sits, and should be removed in place of Lord Vladimir, *our rightful* ruler," spurned the zealot leader.

"Lord Vladimir stepped down from the throne, giving his place to Lord Fread. He was chosen as the successor to the throne. I was there in the audience chamber when it happened. *Lord Fread is our ruler.*"

"What about princess Natalia. Was she not chosen by the gods as well," questioned another in the audience.

"I think you are all missing a very important point," shouted Natalia above the crowd. Causing those in front of her to move away, that they could look upon her as she spoke. "We are no longer beholden to the whims of the gods. We are free of their malice, and unjust deaths by their hand. Lord Vladimir chose Fread to rule over Zephyria, and he will be just. As he always has been with the people of Zephyria."

"If he is our ruler then why does he do nothing about the one who killed our gods. The one who has usurped their power over us."

"Drogen usurped power from no one. He freed our people from their influence and is allowing our people to choose the path that befits our people," declared Natalia. "He does not wish to be worshiped as Ether and Uther once demanded of us."

"Say what you will princess, but there will be a reckoning for what has befallen our deity, and the first to fall will be the abomination who fell the divine, followed by those he associated himself with."

"Then we will be ready. To face it as one people standing up for what we believe to be right," proclaimed Natalia to the crowd drawing cheers from all but the zealots who stared down at her from their raised perch overlooking the crowd. "You speak of the gods as though they are above reproach, but you are wrong. They have proven themselves to be unworthy of worship by their own actions against those they sought worship from. If you cannot see the truth of this now, then I do not know how you might be swayed."

Loosing much of their bluster with Natalia's speech the zealots disbanded, moving through the crowd who encircled Natalia cheerfully. "Thank you everyone for trusting in Fread, and subsequently me. Ether and Uther took far too many loved ones from us. They caused us all to live in fear for their next appearance upon the plateau we call home. We need not fear the same fate with Drogen. He does not seek worship. Nor power from the people of Zephyria. Anyone who might tell tale otherwise has never met the savior of Zephyria and its people."

"Now, we must be off to the castle. Where our people are seeking to help the one who saved us, not because we were told to, and not because we are being forced. But because it is both within our power, and ability to do what is right. We must all look to the future and the chance that we have been afforded to flourish despite deity, and divinity."

Cheers rang through the crowd as Natalia stepped back to the waiting Lisana and Chian. As soon as they were out of earshot of those she had spoken with so candidly, she visibly relaxed.

"You speak well for one so young. The books left behind by your mother have no doubt aided you this day," said Lisana approvingly.

"Knowledge is power to one able to wield it," commented Chian.

"I simply could not stand by while my own people are coerced by those who believe that all the gods and their cruelties were justified. Being of divinity does not excuse atrocities or cruelties lain upon those who provide their worship. One mother was taken before I could know her. A second was taken by the very hands of the beings the zealous view so fondly.

Simply because she claimed responsibility for a child. A child that was never even hers. Then there is the third, the one who poisoned the only father I have known. Blaming the one who saved him. The one's who took glee in having their personal guard pluck every last feather from my wings... No Ether and Uther deserve no remembrance. They deserve no worship. They deserve nothing. They have been the greatest contributors to our suffering," said Natalia. Fighting back against the tears forming in her eyes.

Taking their time in order to afford Natalia enough opportunity to dry her eyes they walked slowly. Natalia fully regaining her composure before the sign for the Elven Archer came into full view. Chian went in to retrieve Mai-Coh coming out moments later shrugging her shoulders. "Sky women say. Mai-Coh returned to castle. To tell, if anyone come."

With nothing halting their progress they made their way through the castles courtyard and up the steps leading to the audience chamber. The guards allowing them to proceed without question through the still shattered doors. A strange silence brought them all out of their own minds as they turned their eyes to the customarily boisterous and lively audience hall. The masses regularly gathered to have their voices, and requests heard had been replaced by a single contingent of guards who paid the passing group no heed, keeping diligently to their assigned duties.

"I know you're going to help Chian with her research, and that it may take some time for you to find the answers you seek within the library," commented Lisana.

"I have read every book in the library, finding the right books and parchments will prove to be the easiest part. Finding useful information not possessed by Chian's people, that will consume most of our time," Natalia proclaimed. "But I am confident we will find what she needs to return to her people victorious."

"That's good to hear. Once you have found the information Chian needs to complete her tribal quest, I wish to teach you the magics of Dranier, including draconic magic," said Lisana. Drawing an audible gasp from Natalia.

"Is such a thing possible?"

"Most of what I can teach you will be of little use without the release of true magic. However, that is not the only discipline I will guide you in. I will teach you how to use the weapon you just purchased as well."

"You know something about the three bladed sword I purchased," questioned Natalia excitedly.

"Yes. I brought its design to a divine blacksmith who fought alongside the dragons and retreated with us to Lundwurm Tul. I was not aware he had forged it. Let alone it would fall into the hands of its designer's daughter. The design for that sword was sketched by Alexandria and forged by the forge god Balthazar. Would you like to know the name she gave her design."

"Yes, I would," breathed Natalia excitedly. *What are the chances that something my mother had a hand in making would find its way to me?*

"She named it Herzblutung."

"Heart's Hemorrhage, or Heartbleeder," translated Natalia.

"Yes. Tis a weapon fit for one who must take life. But wishes not to inflict unnecessary suffering. At least, that was Alexandria's intent. Tis designed to pierce. Its grip the slightest bit oval to allow the concentric blades to twist without friction in the hand. All without sacrificing the ability to grip it tightly, should its wielder wish it not to turn as it penetrates flesh."

"I would like to see this weapon," said the intrigued Chian.

"When it arrives from Mirko. I will let you know," said Natalia happily.

"When you receive it, you must look at its pummel as well. If Balthazar followed the plans completely there will be further functionality to the blade for you to explore. As a hint I will tell you there's a reason it lacks a significant pummel."

Even with the significant height difference between Chian and the Zephyrian people she had no problem fitting through any door within the castle, a significance lost on Natalia, but not lost on Chian herself who wondered why such small beings would make passageways so large when they were entirely unnecessary. "Did the sky people build this place," questioned Chian under her breath. As they once more made their way into the library.

Brena and Mai-Coh sat conversing as they entered cutting off their discussions as they noticed the new arrivals. "You've finally returned."

"We would have been back sooner, but we unfortunately ran into some trouble with the zealots drawing a crowd around themselves. Has something happened?" posited Natalia anxiously.

"Come. We can discuss what's happened deeper in the library. That's where we all need to go anyways," said Brena. Guiding them away from the tables of working zephyrian's, and through the alcove leading to the library's depths.

Natalia stopped to glance at Chian and Mai-Coh hoping they would follow, but Mai-Coh did not rise from his seat. Instead inviting Chian to join him.

"Chain and I have not decided to join you. For now, we will not go with you," said Mai-Coh.

"Once we come out. I will begin gathering books to help in our research. We can start researching tonight if you like," said Natalia drawing a single nod from Chian. With her night ahead set, she followed the others into the alcove.

"A lot has happened. First you should know that Fread and Willow have departed with the information they needed to hopefully cure Lord Fread."

"Where has Death run off to," questioned Lisana.

"That would be the second thing that happened while you were gone. Death and Krail went into the hidden room you used yesterday nearly an hour ago," declared Brena. Seeing Natalia approach. "Are Mai-Coh and Chian not joining us?"

"They have not yet decided what path they will take in what is to come. And I will not force them to choose either way. I am going to help Chian research for her quest, that it is complete before she returns to the taurean. In the future, they may come with us, but that is only if they wish to do so. It is their choice to make," said Natalia unambiguously.

Looking around to make certain none had followed, or otherwise hidden themselves outside the secret room, Brena knocked thrice upon the concealed door. THe door swinging open for them a few moments later. Krail's face coming from inside the sparsely lit room as greeting.

With Natalia, Lisana, and Brena through the portal Krail swung it closed. Locking it that they could not be, unintentionally disturbed.

"First, I must make you aware that Willow and Fread left Zephyria a few hours ago in hopes of curing Fread's near-death state. They have to perform the ritual in a necromancer's lair," said Krail.

"Brena informed us of their departure. But a necromancer's lair... Are they going where I think they are," questioned Natalia.

"Yes, I believe so. He mentioned the banished herbalist Kethick." The name drawing a nod from Natalia in response. "I knew you had a few run ins with him, but Fread was rather tight lipped about the story, I actually had to learn most of the details from written reports, when I took over as commander. It seems Zephyria owes Drogen far more than even I understood."

"Yes. We do. Speaking of which, we had a run in with the zealots on our way back. They were speaking to a rather large crowd of people. I hope that my speech to them got through to some, but I fear they may be planning something."

"I've passed on the guard reports to Lord Vladimir. I'll make sure to add your account in as well."

"I hope Lord Fread and Willow make it back safely from where they're going," said Brena with concern.

"As do we all. Do you know what Fread wished to speak with me about," questioned Natalia.

"I do. We can discuss that matter as well. While you write your report for former Lord, Vladimir."

"With all of that out of the way. Why are the two of you in here instead of out in the library going over the etchings," questioned Lisana.

"We are here, because I needed time to absorbed and send long lost souls to their next journey," said Death. "The barrier around Seraphal has fallen, and the locks are coming undone. *Soon*... very soon. Dranier may once more breath with true magics release."

Chapter Thirty-Two

Willow looked up at the decapitated statuary formed by Ether and Uther's bodies. *I cannot help but feel responsible for your fate. Maybe, if I had been there for you, and not fallen into that sorrowful state, Lucian's influence would not have changed you so irrevocably.* Thought Willow, Sadness contorting her face. *To think he's done the same with some of the daelons. Spreading his corrupting influence through them.*

Looking at Fread, who lay motionless upon the ground, she couldn't help but sigh. "Fread," she called. Patting his arm in order to rouse him from the deathless state. "In which direction must we travel to find the necromancer's lair?"

Fread awoke, his eyes glazed over. An unsure struggle to retain himself within the present moment. "We-we must head southeast from here. Into the woods along the outer ridge of the mountains Zephyria calls its home. Once we reach the woods, I can guide us. At least... I will try."

"There are things you must know and understand by the time we reach the necromancer's lair. I fear... once you're made aware of the truth, you'll not wish to complete the ritual. But you must know the truth. Even if such an outcome does occur... Just know that no matter the outcome you, my loving and sweet zephyrian king, have proven to me that love is possible. Even for someone as detestable as me," said Willow.

"There's nothing that could be considered detestable about you. I realize we've only been together for a short time. That none of it has been easy. But every time I look into your sun petal eyes, I know I feel your love. I don't know what you have to tell me Willow, but whatever it is, it will not change my feelings for you."

"All I ask is, you listen and understand the truth of who carries you. I can only hope the love I see when you look at me, doesn't diminish for telling you."

"Where would you like to start," questioned Fread. Intrigued by her hesitance.

"An old friend told me it's customary to start with a name," started Willow. Ringing her hands in contemplation before finding the words to say. "In order to protect myself, I came up with the name Willow. My true name brought fear to those who heard it. It is a name I have not spoken for nearly a century... Since true magic was sealed by the dragons and gods."

"I know from Drogen that the weight of a name can be a burden to the one who carries it. But in the end... it's just a name," said Fread. Encouraging Willow to continue.

"My name. My true name... Is Daelon; Goddess of Passion and Emotion."

Fread looked his companion in her golden eyes. slightly taken aback by her declaration. "Wait that means you're far older than I am," said Fread with a silly grin.

"Is that really the only thing you heard Freadrick. I am Daelon. I am worshiped by those who allow their passions and emotions to reign over their lives. I am the deity of faelin, qaelin, and yaelin. Those feared most for their often treacherous and cantankerous natures. And you joke of our difference in age," she stomped in agitation. The strength of her heavy footfalls careening a cloud of dust around them.

Fread took hold of Willow's hand stopping her angry stomps with his gentile touch. "Because much like the difference in our ages. Such things do not sway the feelings I hold for you in my heart and soul."

"I have used my power to influence you, Fread. How can you trust any emotion, or passion that you have for me. You cannot trust that I am not the one influencing you," admonished Willow. Spelling out the truth of her existence implicitly. "How can you know that your feelings are genuine and your own," she screamed falling to her knees.

Fread dropped to his knees as well. Taking her head in his hand to raise her sunflower eyes to look up into his own. "Because when I am alone. When this deathless state of my soul takes hold. And upon my return to reality. *You* are the *first* and *last* thought upon my mind," declared Fread. Kissing Willow deftly upon the lips.

They kissed passionately for a short time before Fread, unwilling as he was to forfeit the sensation of his lips against hers, pulled himself away. "It will take quite some time for us to reach Kethick's lair, if we don't get moving. It took Drogen and I a few days to reach it before."

Willow steadied herself from the passionate kiss, wishing it could have lasted far longer. "That's surprising to hear given his abilities. Especially given that he lacks the need for sleep and food."

"The reason it took him so long is likely because of me. I could only fly a few miles a day before growing tired. I also needed food and water in order to maintain my stamina. He likely could have reached Natalia far sooner. Had I not joined him on the journey."

"I might not have wings, right now, but I can get us there quickly," asserted Willow.

"You have wings as well," questioned Fread.

"Yes, I do. But with magic's sealing I am unable to manifest them as I once could. And they're nowhere near as beautiful as your own."

"I'll be the judge of that," he said with a wide smile. Stealing Willow's breath away.

"Only if magic somehow gets released. The likelihood of something so momentous happening is... slim I'm afraid."

"Where Drogen is involved, momentous events are sure to follow," said Fread. Shaking his head. "I don't remember if I ever thanked him for bringing me back from Death's embrace. I'll have to do so when next I see him."

"You are suffering with this near-death state. Do you hold no resentment for him bringing you back," questioned Willow. Indignation distorting her countenance.

"I would be lying if I said I hold *no* resentment. My souls constant wish to leave my body could be considered nothing but resentment. However, he has given me a chance. Slim as it might prove to be. A chance to know and experience love with you. A love I know will prove effective in releasing me from the spiral of near death he has, unknowingly, brought upon me."

How can one such as I have found love in such a kind soul, thought Willow. Rising with Fread to their feet. *Please. Oh, please say your feelings will not change.*

"My true form is... different. Although it's been a long time since I've seen my true self, I still remember how it felt to see my reflection looking back at me. I don't want you to look at me the same way. The same way I looked upon myself," confessed Willow. "If that were to happen, I fear- I- might once again succumb to my own power. Returning to the way I was before Drogen, and you," she said raising her head.

"Unfortunately, I can only tell you the truth of my resolve. I wish there was a way in which I could prove your worries are unfounded. For now however, my word is the only assurance I am able to provide."

Willow grabbed hold of Fread lifting him, with his assistance, upon her back. Using a length of rope from her bag she tied Freads hands that even in his unconscious state he would not fall backward. Doing the same to his legs before tying all four limbs together. "With this you'll not fall from my back if you go into your near-death state," said Willow happily. "I know it is uncomfortable, but it will allow me to move swiftly, and without worry."

She realized her words had fallen on deaf ears as Fread's head fell to her shoulder, and all the tension in his muscles released.

Fread's consciousness faded in and out throughout the journey. Every time his eyes would open, he found himself further along. Often by tens of miles. Each blink of his eyes pulling him further than the last. Until, as if by some miracle, the trees of the forest, Drogen and he had entered only a few months prior, came into view.

The sun having reached its zenith some hours prior, arrived upon the midpoint of its decent. The ambiance of its rays bringing Fread back to himself, as if through his eyelids he were looking into Willow's golden eyes.

"There will be a trail to the right moving deeper into the woods. Take it and we'll be in the Elven village before much time has passed," said Fread. Utilizing the lucidity afforded him.

It took Willow only a few minutes more of travel for the trail Fread had mentioned to come into view. Trusting Fread, and his knowledge of where to go, she departed the road. Driving headlong into the thick forest without a second thought.

Willow took mental note of how diminished the forest had become. Lacking many of the typical trees and greenery she had expected to see, as they neared the village. The remaining life in the area having a sickly purple hue, clinging about the leaves and branches, as if they were suffocating under a poisonous rot.

These are the magics of a necromancer for sure. But how. How could one so powerful exist without true magic's release. I can feel the depth of corruption flowing through the forest. A corruption the forest itself is trying desperately to heal. However, no matter how hard it fights against the infection, this forest will never be the same. The necrosis the necromancer has unleashed has already done its damage, thought Willow shaking her head. "But how."

Willow continued her foray into the decay riddled forest, until buildings became visible. Knowing Fread would wish to be conscious, given their location, Willow tapped him upon the arms and legs. Rousing him before cutting the rope bindings that had secured him to her throughout the journey and discarding them.

It took some time for the shocking decay around him to register within Fread's mind. However, instinctual horripilation cascaded across his entire body telling him, in no uncertain terms, that danger was near. As his mind focused, and his body calmed down from the shock brought about by the level of decay around him, another feeling took its place. One he found both soothing and unsettling, as he continued to examine his surroundings. "This place feels different now. As though I've come home, but... not in a good way," he said with a shiver.

"This is a place where the dead have been raised and held captive from Death. Your soul was placed back within your body, although both things are different, they are similar every way that matters. They too would have sought their end through death. And like you they were incapable of going to him, barring outside influence."

"So, when Drogen killed Kethick their souls were able to find their way to Death," questioned Fread.

"Yes, once a necromancer loses their life, the magic they put out would have been canceled. But as you can see from the world around us, their influence can last far longer than they themselves do. However, there is something I don't understand. How did they use such power when true magic has been sealed away," she pondered aloud.

"We unfortunately have little information regarding Kethick after his exile from Zephyria. I believe Ether and Uther brought him here, although I have no evidence, aside from what he said before his death. Would they have been able to grant him this depth of power?"

"No Ether and Uther would hold no such power. There has to be something different here that we are otherwise unaware of. I can think of no other explanation."

"Getting to Kethick's lair could provide more answers, while we go about gathering the ingredients needed to perform the ritual."

"How do we get there," questioned Willow. Looking around for any visible clues.

"I'll lead us."

"Are you certain?" she asked with concern.

"That home like feeling. I can't explain it, but it feels as though it's calming my soul," said Fread. Perturbed by the prospect, but not willing to allow the opportunity to slip through his fingers.

"Then I will follow you," she said. Pulling out the book Brena had lent them for the journey. Shifting through the pages in order to find the spell, and the components necessary to see the ritual's completion. Although she tried to concentrate on the book, her eye's dared not leave Freads back. In case his assessment was proven wrong.

Should he fall, I'll catch him before he hits the ground. I know beyond doubt he would do the same for me. Although, for the life of me, I cannot fathom why. Could it be that he doesn't fully comprehend who... or what I am. I told him my name, yet he doesn't look at me any differently than before. If only I could show him my true self. The one locked away. If he saw me as I once was, could he possibly feel the same. No, he will look upon me in fear, or in anger, as I do when I look upon myself. I don't deserve his love. I don't deserve any kind of love, she thought. Spiraling within her mind as she walked behind her beloved zephyrian king.

The facade she endeavored to portray, of looking through the book, falling completely to the wayside as they walked past a solitary stone tower. The path behind which lead further into the wood. Fread stopped after the tower, standing before a grave with a simple tombstone. 'Lyra, Queen and Mother.'

"It would seem that someone else has been here and marked her grave. When Drogen and I came through, we didn't know her name. The one who resided in this stone house," pointed Fread. "I'm glad to see she has not been forgotten," he said. Touching the tombstone with his fingertips.

"A little further in, we'll start seeing lanterns placed in the trees for light. I doubt they've remained lit. It would make finding our way easier. Either way, they mark a distinct trail through the woods to his lair.

"Good then we'll be there soon," said Willow with a smile. "It's good to see you so alive. I feel like it's been ages since you've not fallen into that near-death state. I hope the ritual is a permanent fix."

"As do I," said Fread. Smiling back at her before leading them on through the woods once more.

The lanterns along the path that had cast the forest around them in a sickly glow were unlit, making finding the first in line far more difficult than either thought possible. Only after many minutes of fruitless searching did they spot it. The sun shining just right upon its glass to illicit a beam of visible light they could follow. Luckily each subsequent lantern along their path proved easier to spot than the first. Allowing them to gain ground quickly, as they tried to make up for lost time.

Fread stopped short at the final lantern taking a deep breath, to build up his courage. "I feel it best to warn you... Kethick had many under his influence within the cave he made his home. It's covered in mangled corpses and body parts. It's not a pleasant sight."

"Unfortunately, it's not anything I haven't seen before. There were many of his kind among those I commanded. But those beneath me only raised the dead for just causes. To hear the souls of the murdered. Or to raise an army in defense of another. They were my arbitrators of justice. It may be selfish, but I hold out hope the one you call Kethick, was not one of them."

"Who else could have been in command of Kethick," questioned Fread. Ushering Willow out from the trees, and into the clearing where the bones and decayed flesh of those under Kethick remained. Bleaching and rotting away in the sun.

"Lucian. Always Lucian. He could never leave things as they are meant to be. He enjoys corrupting any and all that he possibly can. In order to both grow and retain the power he holds over everything, and everyone. He was also the one, in the beginning, I thought my life would be the most fulfilled following. I joined him in his war against the dragons. I even submitted to his rule, when he became the supreme god of Dranier. I was a fool for doing so. The first chance he got, he rid himself of me."

"What do you mean he rid himself of you," questioned Fread. Plugging his nose in a failed attempt to block the putrid sweet smell of decaying flesh from overwhelming his senses.

"The dragons had a major role in locking true magic away. But the gods, we had a hand in it as well. We didn't know it was all a part of Lucian's scheme. The dragons thought locking away magic would limit the power of both sides. Unbeknownst to the dragons, we gods garner power through worship. Both in love, and in fear. The dragon's thought by cutting off magic they were evening the playing field. In truth they were cutting their own throats."

"What does this have to do with Lucian ridding himself of you?"

"Everything. My people are ones of true magic. We feel its flow in everything. When magic collapsed into the prison made by the combined efforts of the gods and dragons my power, and influence, among my people did as well. My namesake people, the ones I wished to protect no longer recognized me, or themselves. They simply became a part of whatever society they found themselves in. As though they'd been one of them all along. With their worship gone, so too was my usefulness to Lucian, and his designs."

"Is he the reason you locked yourself away in the gorge where Drogen found you?"

"Though it brings me great shame in saying so. Yes he is. After I ran from Lucian, he attempted to have me killed. I hid myself away in the ravine. Lucian sent many others to kill me after he located me again, but none were successful. And, they died for attempting it. Had Drogen not found me, I have no doubt I would still be there today. Keeping all emotion at bay and drowning in nothing but self-preservation and bloodlust."

"Then I must thank Drogen once more for bringing you to me. Allowing us the opportunity to grow closer."

"I will have to do the same," said Willow with a smile. Before her expression soured. "If only the surroundings were not so grotesque. This could have been a rather romantic moment."

"We should move ahead with the ritual that we can get out of here then," stated Fread.

"That sounds like a good idea," said Willow. Stepping gingerly around piles of bones so as not to disturb them.

"What does the book say we need?"

Flipping through the pages she found the passages pertaining to the ritual. "We need the alter of a necromancer, the presence of a reaper, flesh of the dying, blood of the binder, and rope to bind the hands of the dying and the binder together.

"I remember there being an alter inside the cave with a mountain of skulls piled around it. I am the dying, and you I take it will be the binder."

"Yes, and rope I hope will be relatively easy to find in our gathering from the alter. Now I wish we would have kept what I bound your hands and feet to me with. That would just leave the presence of a reaper."

"How're we supposed to know if there's a reaper here to preside over what we're attempting to do?"

"We can figure that out once we've gathered the other materials... At least I hope we can. Maybe we should have looked at the ritual before rushing out of Zephyria. At least then we could have asked Death to send a reaper here," she said. Regret contorting her face.

"Let's just get everything ready for the ritual before we worry about what is clearly out of our hands," said Fread. Drawing a nod from Willow.

It took them some time to find and gather both the rope and alter. The number of rooms along the way proving a nuisance to their progress. With Kethick's alter and a bundle of rope, found on one of the many corpses, they worked their way back to the cave entrance.

"Could he not have found a more convenient lair," said Willow. Rolling her eyes as they struggled to extricate the alter from the cave.

"I know I'll be happy to leave this place and never return," said Fread. Setting the wooden alter down at the mouth of the cavern.

"Now all we need is a reaper... Hello is there a reaper here," yelled Willow to the wind.

"Do you think that'll work," questioned Fread.

"Do you have any better ideas," she questioned. Garnering a shrug from Fread.

They continued to call for some time with no reply, nor sign that a reaper was present.

"I suppose we just have to perform the ritual and see what happens," said Willow with a shrug of her own.

"It cannot be that easy. We perform the ritual, and I get better. I've been racking my mind since we got here. Yes this ritual has a possibility of curing me, but what is it asking of you," questioned Fread. "Besides your blood and the tying of your hand and soul to mine. What is the price you're paying for doing this ritual with me?"

"There could be... Complications. Especially if the ritual doesn't succeed for some reason. The ritual could be a death sentence for you... and me. But the consequences are irrelevant. It's going to work... It has to work," said Willow. Tears beginning to flow from her eyes, springing flowers from the ground with each drop.

"We both need to know and understand the risks of what we're doing," said Fread. Comforting her by running his fingers through her hair.

"Okay... Okay I'll tell you everything that could happen. We could be destroyed completely, should our souls be incompatible with each other. Either of us could be killed should the other's heart and soul not find alignment."

"And what if the ritual succeeds, what then?"

"Then we are bound together heart and soul. Your near-death state will no longer be a factor. But you will not be living as you once were either. You would share in my lifespan. But if one of us were to die... Then both of us would die. We're giving our lives to each other, and in doing so, binding our ends as well."

Fread sat down in front of the alter, and Willow followed in kind. "Even with all of the risks you were willing to perform the ritual with me. I have already died once before. I cannot ask you to do this. It's far too great a risk. Death said even if I'm cured of the near-death state, I will have to contend with other repercussions. Many of which cannot be eased. I can't possibly ask you to make such a sacrifice for me."

"I'm doing this. Not because you asked, but because for the first time, I can envision a future I'm happy to see. And that has everything to do with you," said Willow. Grabbing hold of Freads hands. I only wish I could show you... show you what you're actually getting into. Unfortunately, I don't know how. Not without magics release."

"If you feel so strongly that you would do so despite the risks, then dissuading you clearly isn't an option," said Fread with a defeated chuckle. "Were you able to figure out how Kethick garnered so much power?"

"No. This is a place piled high with corpses, but nothing stands out that would explain the power he was able to access. Maybe Lucian devised a method of access and allowed Ether and Uther its use. Whatever method was used, I clearly have no access."

"Maybe it's not what we see, but something you have to feel," said Fread. "It's possible Kethick's method for gathering power is also keeping my soul calm."

"You may be right. Let me see if I can feel anything out of place, aside from the apparent." Willow cleared the ground around the alter to pass time as she felt the world around her. Everything about the lair and the corpses brought a deep sickening feeling to her stomach, only just holding back from retching in response. Then she felt it, a force so natural, yet foreign that she could hardly believe its presence. "There are tendrils of true magic here. But how is that possible. It was sealed in a forest southwest of here. Far removed of the mountain range the dwarves call their home.

"So, it is true magic's influence that is keeping my soul calm," questioned Fread.

"I suspect that to be the case. Although the connection is weak, there can be no doubt. True magic still lives within these woods."

"Could all the forests be connected with true magic?"

"Possibly. At least now, with the magic coming from this place, I can show you my truth," said Willow. A measure of sadness crossing her face followed quickly by resolve and determination. "Let me gather what magic seeping out of this place. Then you will see me for what I am." *And I will see the look in your eyes. The one I see whenever I looked at myself,* thought Willow. Although true magic had not flowed through her for a century its circulation came as naturally as breathing. *Its been so long, but it feels as if I am finally taking a breath after being deprived.* Raising her hand Willow summoned fire with a thought.

"Is it really that easy," questioned Fread.

"With practice, yes. I'm ready to show you who and what I am." Willow's thoughts flowed through her mind to the locked door she had been unable to access without magic flowing through her. Flinging it wide, before thoughts and doubts could hold her back from performing the action. Knowing her transformation to be imminent, Daelon closed her eyes. Capturing Freads encouraging face one last time, as a tear trailed from her eye.

Fread looked upon Daelon in awestruck silence. His mouth fully agape seeing Willow's change. Seeing the single tear falling from her tightly closed eyes, he came to understand the extent of her struggle to show him. Bringing him back to his senses. "You're the most gorgeous being I have ever lain my eyes upon," said Fread. Hoping the sincerity of his feeling upon seeing her, truly seeing her, could carve through her trepidation.

Willow opened her eyes slowly. Wanting to trust what she had heard, but not fully trusting her ears. Fread stood before her, his eyes trained upon her own, retaining their sincere glow. "Many, even among my own kind, have called me many things. Gorgeous has never been one of them. Yet you look upon me as though nothing has changed. As though I am not a monster."

Daelon's mane flowed through the air as if swimming through water, moving in invisible currents. The golden eyes of her godly being shinning brighter than they had ever shined before. The skin beneath her clothing blemish free and lustrous. Set upon her back a set of wings, but where Freads wings were feathered and white, Daelon's were made of a thin, nearly see through membrane. Having the form and function of a bat's wings.

"Because Willow..." he said. Stopping short and shaking his head. "Daelon. You're not a monster. You are the one I have fallen in love with. I do not see how anyone could look upon you, and not understand your beauty. The only explanation is they are blind. You're the truest definition of divinity I have ever seen."

"Thank you, Fread. I'm glad that I had the courage to show you who, and what I am."

"Your form and name may be different, but you are still you. We know now there's a source of magic here. Death's other solution for what to do is viable now. I can't ask you to risk yourself. Not when another, possibly safer solution, is available to us," said Fread.

"If we leave this place, you could get worse... I came here with you, knowing all the possible outcomes to the ritual. I stand before you now. Ready and willing to go through the soul binding ritual with you. Consequences or no. I feel our connection in my heart and soul, and I know you feel the same," said Daelon.

"I do, but what about the risks," questioned Fread.

"The risks be damned Fread. Everything comes with risk. It's what we do in the face of those risks that matters," she said passionately.

"Then we will perform the ritual. Without regard for risk or outcome. Because we both know, with every fiber of our being's, this is what we both want," said Fread equally empassioned.

"And with its completion our hearts and souls will forever be one," said Daelon. Taking hold of Freads hand. Guiding him to stand with her before Kethick's alter.

"With the flesh of the dying, and the blood of the binder," she read. Taking each component, as it was called for, with the sword Drogen crafted her in Moongrove. "We bind our hands before a reaper. And with this final knot, binding us together as one, so too do we bind our hearts and souls," finished Willow.

With the tying of the final knot a shift began to take place, their souls calling out to each other, while their divergent heart beats began to synchronize.

Chapter Thirty-Three

The barrier across the breadth of Moonclave fell. Its descent marked only by the sunlight glistening off its rapidly dissipating remnants. As it dispersed the entire populous of Moonclave set their eyes upon its point of origin, The council's chambers. For the first time in memory, the whole of the elven people moved with a sense of purpose.

As the citizens of Moonclave descended upon the councils tower, the willows threw wide the doors, that all present could hear the proceedings held within. With the doors open they reformed themselves over the doors that others could not gain entry, and those inside could not leave.

"Now, who among you would challenge my authority to speak and be heard," questioned Drogen. His voice resonated with the tower as he spoke. Sending his words out across the whole of Moonclave. And through him, the voices of all within.

The entirety of the council, even the newly appointed Keltus, looked at Drogen with their mouth's agape. Unable to stutter out a word or thought as they began to comprehend the situation they found themselves in.

"I will take your collective silence as acceptance," said Drogen. His eyes staring down everyone on the council before he continued. "Where should we begin?"

"How about with the people imprisoned below this councils' chambers," posited Leif. An indignant smirk contorting her visage as she looked at each member of the council.

"Yes, we should start there. Those who came ahead of me have been imprisoned long enough," said Drogen. "I must ask. Queen Llewellyn, you were one that was brought here, while the others were already confining themselves within this chamber. Are you aware of what the other members of this council have been doing short of your presence?"

"I-I don't know," said Llewellyn with a distinct frown. "We disbanded the council at the conclusion of stripping Silf of both her rank and seat on this council. Although I did not agree with the decision, I was outvoted."

"So, to your knowledge, that is the last time the council came together?"

"Yes, we had no other scheduled meetings."

"Leif, when was the last time this council came together in order to pass judgment?"

"The other members of the council were here only a few days ago, and before that. They convened in order to pass further judgment upon one judged harshly the day prior," alluded Leif.

"Is this true," barked Llewellyn. Jumping up from her seat in order to stare at Terill. Who she knew to be the likely mastermind of the conspiracy. "What judgment was passed? Why would I not be asked to be involved in the process," she raged.

"I will tell you. But only when everyone is present. Especially those who will be most affected by the answer, who need to be brought up from the prison below," said Drogen pointing to Manzine. "From the way you reacted earlier, I've ascertained you're responsible for those in the hold below. Go and get them now. Or... I will do it *myself*."

Manzine looked to Terill for support but found nothing more than a hand waving him off to complete the task. "Very well. I will gather and bring them."

Seraphine, Rumble, and Tumble came crashing through the door into the council chambers, fighting with each other to be the first one through the door. Rumble, claiming victory was the first to emerge.

"It be good seein ya again flying lizard," proclaimed Rumble. Making his way to Drogen's side.

"Good to see you too Rumble," he said with a smile.

"Where be me charge?"

"Unfortunately, we had to split up. She's back in Zephyria. We garnered a lot of information regarding... things best left for later discussion. When everyone is more, amicable."

"You told me they'd all been released from Phaylor's care. What is the meaning of this," pointed an enraged Llewellyn. Incensed by the others deceit.

"That is quite enough out of the ground hog. It has no voice here," admonished Terill. Deflecting from Llewellyn's questions.

Rumble, clearly enraged by the clear deflection, made to protest. But Tumble beat him to it. "Don't need be talkin in fronta the tree sprites. They be too young for mature talk anyway." Tumble's quip quickly enraging Terill. Drawing an almost perceptible smile to Seraphine's face.

"I will explain what happened when these proceeding are nearing their conclusion. For now, please take a seat upon the left crescent table," said Drogen. Pointing to the crescent moon shaped table opposite the council.

Alya, wishing to be by Seraphine's side through the proceedings, and knowing the next topic Drogen would be bringing to light, stuck to her like glue. Taking the seat beside her. Holding her hand in order to comfort them both.

"I will not allow you to deflect away from my question," spouted Llewellyn.

"Since it seems the others on this council are unwilling to speak, I will endeavor to explain things for them. First, you all should be made aware, they saw fit to perform worse perpetration than simply releasing the brother dwarves from Phaylor's custody into Manzine's," said Drogen.

"What did they do," questioned Llewellyn and Keltus as one.

"Seraphine, please stand, and accept my sincerest apology. I wish I could be the one to tell you what has transpired. However, tis important you hear what has been done from those who perpetrated it. Terill, would you explain to those present what fate this council thought a befitting *further* punishment to enact upon councilor and Queen, Silf."

"She was no longer a queen. Neither did she retain a seat upon this council. We need not justify our actions to you, or anyone else," bit Terill. Reacquiring his hubris. Wanting to regain control over the flow of conversation to something he, and the council, were more accustom."

"If it was within the rights for this council to pass subsequent judgement. Upon someone who had already been stripped of seat and rank, then *why are you dodging the question Terill*," examined Keltus with hooded eyes.

"We simply performed a ritual. A ritual befitting a former queen and councilor," stated Boramil arrogantly.

"Then why can none of you bring yourselves to say the purpose of the ritual aloud," questioned Llewellyn. Both of her fists striking the table with both fists. "What about you Elmar, do you have nothing to say regarding these matters?"

Manzine came back to the top of the stairs closing the door behind him. Looking at Elmar and nodding his head almost imperceptibly. Imperceptible to most, but not Drogen.

"We did everything according to council rules," declared Elmar full of bluster.

"We will not be shamed for enforcing the laws this council have made for the betterment of the forest and the elven people," proclaimed Elise.

"What part of what this council perpetrated, was for the betterment of the elven people," roared Leif. The vines and roots wrapping her body writhing like snakes around her in her rage. "And how dare any of you speak about the betterment of the forest and its people when you do nothing. Absolutely nothing to help improve either."

"The forest is alive and well. What does the forest need that we do not provide," questioned Boramil dismissively.

"You need only look upon the tree lines outside this chamber to understand how wrong you are. Do you know what happens to a forest that is not maintained. Where trees are allowed to grow so old, they simply fall over and die," questioned Leif. Looking around at each member of the council.

"It dies. It can take hundreds of years, or the spark of a fire upon dried brush, which has begun to pile up everywhere within the forest. Either way, the forest dies," said Keltus.

"Exactly. A new tree cannot grow in the shadow of those around it, for the sun cannot reach the sapling, so it cannot live. Should the trees be left to grow without thinning of their numbers, no new trees will grow, causing the forest to age and die. The trees around you are halfway through their lives, many of them far more.

"When nothing new is allowed to grow, eventually you will have no home to come back to," said Alya.

"The warren is not recognized by this council," said Elmar. Drawing out Alya's tongue in defiance of his proclamation.

"This is something that can be discussed at length some other time," said Drogen. "Answer the question. What ritual did this council see fit to perform upon one of its former sovereigns."

"We performed the ritual of transformation," disclosed Elise. Terill's hand trying in vain to cover her mouth but arriving far too late to stop her outburst.

"How could you do such a thing. That ritual is meant for those closest to their end. You all saw fit to perform such a ritual upon Silf as another form of punishment for something this council never saw fit to send any form of help for," raged Keltus incredulously.

"What is the ritual of transformation," questioned Asche.

"The second child of..."

"Enough of your posturing. Answer the question," yelled Seraphine. Rage filling her eyes as she looked at the council.

"She will be a dryad, *in due time*," declared Elmar.

"How dare you do such a thing to my mother," roared Seraphine. "She didn't deserve that. She didn't deserve any of what you did to her. Rumble grabbed hold of Seraphine before she could rise from her seat to attack the council. Tumble running to Seraphine, placing his hand upon her shoulder, his fingers tense with rage wishing nothing more than to join her and fight.

"It be all day need ta throw us back in the hole. Me brudder an me not be fallin for the same trick twice. We not not be allowen you to eadder," whispered Rumble.

"Once the ritual has been completed, it cannot be undone. The process must be completed. That is why it was meant for those at the end of their lifespans, so they could become one with their elders. That they could pass down their knowledge for future generations. To use a rite of passage as a punishment," seethed Leif. Shaking her head in condemnation of their actions.

"What is done is done, and you yourself have said it cannot be undone. None of this can cover for the treason Seraphine has perpetrated against Moonclave," deflected Elmar.

"You yourself stated none could dispute Keltus's claim for a seat on the council, what about Seraphine. She is Silf's daughter does she not have rightful claim to her mother's vacant seat," questioned Drogen.

"Her mother, and thus her, were stripped of their titles and rank. She cannot claim her mother's seat," scoffed Terill. As if the whole notion was absurd.

"Her home was destroyed by outside influence, just as Seraphine's home was, yet you did not see fit to strip Keltus, Asche, or Queen Lyra of their ranks, or seat upon this council. What makes their loss so different that they are not subject to the same treatment," questioned Drogen

"She is no longer alive to receive punishment for her lack of ability in keeping those beneath her safe," said Boramil.

"So, your reason for stripping Seraphine's mother, and thus her of any right to her mother's position among your people, is because she lived. While all those present with Queen Lyra, died. So this council would rather an entire village of its people be wiped out with little to no survivors, than have a few die in service of saving an entire village?"

"How dare you insinuate such lies within this chamber," roared Elise.

"What lies. You punished one who returned with many over one who returned with none. And you call it false. Does anyone else among you believe this to be a falsehood when the evidence is so clearly before you. Seraphine the daughter of a queen was not afforded her mother's seat, where Keltus was. If this is not true then what act has taken Seraphine's position from her," questioned Drogen.

"She brought our oldest enemy to our very door. She brought those groundhogs with her into Moonclave," said Elmar. Defending the decision.

"Hmm interesting, did this council see fit to strip her of this before or after you learned that the brother dwarves had been brought here," questioned Drogen.

"The other members decided to strip them... before word had been received," noted Llewellyn.

"So, before you knew of Rumble and Tumble were within your boarders, you saw fit to strip Silf and thus her daughter of her position. You have two daughters of queens. Each with the same supposed crime yet given two very different treatments. Why?"

The entirety of the council grew silent. None of them able to come up with defense to cover for what they'd done to one of them. Yet saw fit to forgive for another.

"I say Seraphine must be given the same treatment I received upon my arrival within these chambers," said Keltus.

"Are we simply supposed to forgive her actions in bringing an enemy to our door," raged Elmar in defiance.

"What was her reason for bringing them with her," questioned Leif. "Do any of you know?"

"They're our enemy. It doesn't matter why they were brought here," said Terill.

"What ya so afraid of tree mite. Ya afraid uh little ol me," postured Rumble.

"Don't be ridiculous why would we ever fear a ground hog," said Elise. Aghast by the insinuation.

"If you do not fear them, then why are you so threatened by their presence here among your people. Do you fear their being here will lessen your hold, and thus your power," questioned Drogen.

"We are the Elven council of the Moonclave. There is no greater position among our people," decreed Terill.

"And what exactly have you done to help your people. We have established, thus far, that you are incompetent in your care of the forest, unable to administer the laws you so hold dear evenly, and decidedly unable to defend your own people from outside threat," recited Drogen.

"You cannot say we do not defend our people," raged Terill. "We always come to the defense of our citizens."

"If you always come to the defense of your people Moongrove and Sun Meadow would still be inhabited by our people instead of an enemy and a plague crafted and sent forth by a necromancer," bit an enraged Asche. Needing to be subdued by Leif before she leapt.

Taking the opportunity Leif brought herself and Asche over to set with the others opposite the council members. Her change in position to opposing the council bringing a new level of ire to Terill, and those under his influence upon the council.

"We do not recognize the second daughter of Leif," waved off Elmar.

"Then listen to me," raged Keltus. "I know my mother sent correspondence multiple times to Moonclave, regarding the plague sweeping our lands. About the conditions of our people and pleading for help to be sent. I also know, from speaking with Phaylor, that the messages were received. Furthermore, all the hawks sent to the Sun Meadow afterward never returned. How dare any of you speak of defending our people."

"Was this information intentionally kept from me as well. Are you telling me that we could have done something to help one of the members of this council and we did nothing," screamed Llewellyn.

"We had no prior knowledge of the goblinkin threat," said Elise. Trying desperately to shift focus to something she knew they had no prior knowledge of.

"You say you had no prior knowledge, but what about the other council members who sit next to you, said Drogen scanning the room. Elmar, Terill, and Manzine, why might your heartrates be increasing so *palpably*? Unfortunately for the three of you, I was the one who saved him as well," Drogen declared. Causing their heartrates to skyrocket.

"What is he talking about," questioned Elise. Her head hung low.

"I would very much like to know as well," seethed Llewellyn.

"I think everyone present would like to understand what Drogen is talking about," commented Keltus.

"I told you to bring everyone that came ahead of me, up from the hold below. Why did you not see fit to bring Gilvail with the others Manzine. Or did you believe, as the others clearly did, that his absence would go unnoticed," inquired Drogen. The fire before him growing in intensity with his inner rage.

Manzine dared not look up through the intense flames flickering before Drogen, or past them to the other members of the council. Instead rushing through the door behind him to free the last prisoner, Gilvail. Manzine pushed Gilvail through the door and into the council chambers quickly, not wanting to solicit further rage toward himself.

"I didn't want to believe what I was hearing... you three... you three would dare usurp control from and place a member of this council in the dungeon. I could somewhat understand keeping Seraphine for bringing the dwarves. What was Gilvail's crime that he would be subject to the dungeon as well," raged Llewellyn.

"He-we-I..." stuttered Elmar. Looking at Gilvail in fear.

"You think yourself worthy of my seat upon the council Elmar? When you can't bring yourself to look me in the eyes for what you've perpetrated against me. I told you to gather the council when I returned, because of the goblinkin's incursion upon our people. But instead of doing what needed done, you conspired with other members of this council and your own personal jailer to keep the truth from reaching the ears of our people. Maybe if you would've had the gull to kill me yourself, your ploy could have succeeded."

"I...We...You..."

"Even now you're incapable of defending yourself from the truth of what you have done," barked Gilvail.

Elmar looked around trying desperately to find anything he could use to garner an upper hand with the unforeseen complication standing before him. Looking at Drogen he latched onto a final thread, one that could not be contested among the council. "The barrier is down. Lies can be spoken without its influence," said Elmar with a victorious smile.

"You dare-" started Gilvail stopping only upon hearing Drogen let out a low rumbling laugh. Shaking the council tower as he did so.

"You would dare laugh at a member of this council," said Boramil.

"No, I dare laugh at the ignorance of this council. The barrier you have placed so highly upon the shoulders of your people. The barrier you say permits only truth, has as much effect on you and your people as it does me," stated Drogen with narrowed eyes. "Meaning it has no effect at all."

"That is impossible. We know it forces those within its borders to speak only the truth," raged Terill. Jumping up from his chair.

"The truth is subjective Terill. What may be true of you may not be true of another. However, that which we know to be the truth, cannot be lied about. You may deflect away from the question at hand as Elmar has chosen to do. Or speak with two meanings both of them correct, but the underlying context. The truth, while on the surface fanciful, is still the truth. No matter what he does. No matter what he may wish he could say to the contrary he cannot. You Terill, the dryad Leif, nor I can speak falsely about what is known to be true. Now Elmar let us end this charade, that we might get on to far more pressing matters concerning the wellbeing of Seraphal."

"I agree. But first," said Gilvail. Standing in front of the cowering Elmar. Intimidating the false council member with nothing but his domineering presence. "You are in *my seat*."

Elmar rose swiftly from his chair his visage the embodiment of a scolded puppy as he skittered around the table to stand front and center before the fire lit dais.

"Now what should your punishment be for your transgressions," pondered Gilvail. Thrumming his fingers upon the table before him in contemplation.

"I wasn't the only one who conspired against you," blurted out Elmar. Trying to save himself by throwing the other conspirators in-front of him.

"I know you're not the only one who conspired against me. They'll receive their punishment soon enough," said Gilvail. "There's a mother of our kin among those present after all," he quipped motioning Leif's way. "Hmm, it occurs to me that a fitting punishment may present itself upon hearing what has transpired, since my detainment. Chief among my questions being, where is Silf."

"Leif if you would be so kind as to catch councilor Gilvail up on everything that has transpired in his absence. While he's being caught up, Manzine take Elmar down to the dungeon below. Until such time as a decision is reached in regard to his punishment," ordered Drogen.

"You cannot order one of our people to the dungeons," protested Elise.

"I'm simply following the rules known among all who live in Seraphal. Seraphine if you would, remind the council members of the law as it has been passed down to the elven people."

"It is known that should any crime be committed by one of our kin, they are to be held within the dungeon until such time as the council convenes to deliver judgment. Whether it be a few days or many years," recounted Seraphine.

"Or is this yet another rule the elven council would levy against one, but not another," questioned Drogen.

"Manzine take this traitorous usurper away from here. I'll give my punishment once I come to understand what he has seen fit to do in my stead. And don't think I've forgotten your role in all of this. I suggest you follow *his* orders," pointed Gilvail to Drogen, "Or, I may see fit to increase the severity of your punishment," he threatened.

With a break in the action going on around them, Alya wrapped Seraphine tightly in a hug before bursting into tears, the stress of the situation they found themselves in finally dissipating enough for their feelings to return. "I'm sorry. I'm so sorry. I wasn't able to save your mother from what the council did to her," wailed Alya. Drawing tears from Seraphine's eyes.

"Is there really no way to reverse the process?"

"Even Drogen is unable to reverse what they've done. Leif told him there is only one method remaining to use and that is to hasten the process. Drogen said he would do it, but not until you're present. There's a chance you can speak with your mother once more."

"They dared do what," roared Gilvail. Striking the table before him. Sending reverberations throughout the tower. "This council saw fit to not only strip our eldest queen of her position and seat but performed the ritual of transformation clandestinely. Not only did you know your actions to be wrong. You lacked the fortitude to perform the ritual openly in way of example to others who might have done the same."

Gilvail looked over the other council members his eyes falling upon Keltus causing her to shift uncomfortably under his gaze. Leif relaying to him the moments leading up to his release from the dungeon below. Asche and Keltus, I am saddened to hear what has befallen your mother and the Sun Meadow as a whole. I hope that Drogen's words acted as, at least a small comfort knowing she did not pass through Death in fear.

"I must also thank you Drogen for not only saving me from capture by the goblinkin, but for your aid in releasing me from my prison below as well. I fear however, that I may have been treated more fairly by the orcs than I've been by my own kin. There is one more task that must be taken care of first before we hear from you once more. Seraphine your mother was unfairly stripped of her title and seat by this clearly corrupt council. Whereas another," pointed Gilvail to Keltus in emphasis. "Whose mother supposedly committed the same offense retains the seat of her predecessor. I ask you Princess Seraphine will you take up your mother's mantle and set upon her vacant seat."

"She is responsible for bringing our oldest enemy into Moonclave," protested Terill.

"From what I have been informed, you sought no understanding as to why she would bring two dwarves to Moonclave. Instead, you imprisoned her and them. Deceiving another of this council into believing them released. Taking it upon yourselves to administer judgment in secret. You all lack the moral foundation necessary to place judgment upon her,' he said motioning to Seraphine. When far more heinous actions then the presence of two dwarves, have taken place."

"Of those currently on this council who among you would disregard Seraphine's appointment to her mother's position," questioned Gilvail. Elise, Boramil, and Terill rose from their seats in protest of her appointment while Llewellyn, Keltus, and Gilvail remained in their seats.

"It would seem we have a tie," said Boramil smugly. "And in matter of a tie the dissenter's position is taken."

"You're right, but there is someone here within the council chambers who speaks for the mothers of our race. They too deserve a vote in this matter. Would you not agree," said Gilvail.

"She and the Dryads listen to and are being controlled by the one standing upon the Dais. Their vote cannot be seen as unbiased," argued Terill desperately.

"Why are you three so opposed to her appointment to the council. My appointment was welcomed with open arms. What's the difference," questioned Keltus

"I agree. The crime both have committed is the same, yet one is punished, where the other is not," said Llewellyn.

"It seems to me that your protest is out of your own sense of indignant pride. You have no grounds nor evidence to support your arguments against her claiming her mother's seat," said Gilvail. Drawing the ire of the three standing council members.

"Do any of you three who stand have any tangible reason that Seraphine should not be allowed the position that Keltus was otherwise afforded," questioned Leif. Walking before each of them in turn to look each square in the eyes. Stubbornly Terill stood against the pressure imposed by Leif's finding his position untenable as Elise and Boramil lost their defiant bluster dropping once more to their seats.

"Now I will ask once more. Will you take up Silf's mantle as Queen and her seat upon this council," questioned Gilvail.

"I will accept, and I will see to it that this council works for the betterment of the forest and its inhabitants. Not to benefit the members of this council," seethed Seraphine uncontrollably.

"Come claim your position upon the council Queen Seraphine."

Taking Gilvail's cue Seraphine made her way to her mother's seat, the one Terill sat himself in as first elder in place of her mother Silf. "You are in my seat Terill. *Move*." Terill looked up at Seraphine enraged but could not protest the truth of her statement. As it had been her mother's position.

Drogen bowed to Gilvail in thanks before addressing the council once more. "None upon this council have given reason to think anything they have done up to this point has been for the benefit of either the forest or Seraphal," said Drogen. "Yet you believe yourselves right in further sentencing one of your own after an initial sentencing. Some who sit before me have clearly overstepped their bounds and in my opinion are unfit in their roles."

"None upon this council will be condemned by an outsider, no matter how powerful, or knowledgeable they think themselves to be," seethed Terill. "We are not subject to your rule, nor are we under any obligation to follow what you have to say in matters regarding *Moonclave*."

"Your race may have built this place, but we are its inhabitants," continued Boramil.

"I am not the one who will be judging the actions you have taken against one of your own. Tis the citizens of *Moonclave* who'll be your judge. I wonder what they'll have to say about these proceedings. Knowing what four members of this council, and a jailer under their employ, saw fit to do without their knowledge," posited Drogen.

"What do you mean," questioned Terill. His heart rate elevating as Drogen looked down upon him from the dais. The fire before Terill filling Drogen's eyes with light and menace.

"The magics of this tower are many. One way it can be used is to send messages between towers and surrounding areas in times of attack when information needs relayed quickly. I simply used the tower to project all that has happened within this chamber across the breadth of *Moonclave* that all within range of the thirteen towers might bear witness to what transpires," said Drogen.

"I wonder how many of our people came running when the barrier fell," questioned Keltus.

"I would suspect... most if not all wait outside these chambers," said Gilvail. "Now why don't we give our three council members a choice. Boramil, Elise, and Terill will you go willingly to the dungeon while other members of the council are selected, or will you go outside to face the people you were supposed to represent?"

Boramil, even with all of his bluster, was the first to rise walking over to the dungeon door disappearing from sight. He was quickly followed by Elise while Terill remained seated and un-moving. With a final look around the chamber he rose to his feet walked slowly to the dungeon's door and out of sight.

"You should be down there, doing your duty Manzine," said Gilvail.

"Yes King Gilvail," acquiesced Manzine.

"Wait," said Seraphine. Forcing Manzine's heart up to his throat. "Drogen what would a fitting punishment be for one who threatened to commit many atrocious acts against a prisoner in their custody. One who was only held back from committing said acts, because he was ordered to?"

"To speak of an act and to commit it are two very different things, should it be proven such an act had taken place among my kin they would be unceremoniously dispatched and greeting death. Why do you ask," questioned Drogen.

"Manzine before you go, have you ever committed acts unbecoming of a guard's duty?" questioned Seraphine.

"No, I have not," said Manzine nearly spitting his answer.

Godslayer flew out of Drogen's hand, striking between the door and frame of the dungeon door, pinning the door closed. "What are you," questioned Drogen as everyone else gasped in shock.

"None here can lie, but you, you're different, you lie, but your heartbeat tells all Manzine. Your neither an elf nor a Dryad you are something else." said Drogen. His eyes changing to vertical slits of red with swimming golden flakes.

"I could ask you the same," said Manzine. "You're strange compared to other races I met in the past... and your eyes. They flow with the gold of the gods."

"Because they are," said Drogen. "I am the son of Lisana; Reaper of Souls, and my father is none other than Death himself." With Drogen's proclamation the room fell silent. Even Leif couldn't help but hold her breath from the tension brought on by his statement.

Finally comprehending his predicament Manzine lashed out with whip like vines. Drogen stood upon the raised Dais un-moving as the vine drew a line of blood from the thin layer of skin upon his face. The end of the vine extending past and into the blazing draconic fire behind him.

With the addition of his blood a cascading font of power sprang forth from the thirteen towers of Seraphal. Their wellsprings radiating power above and below the surface. As the tendrils of magic seeped into all of Dranier everyone and everything breathed, as though it were their first.

Chapter Thirty-Four

"There you are Manzine. You're one of the Daelon's," said Drogen.

"Don't you dare speak that name. That pitiful waste of divinity could never hope to match him. She is unworthy of devotion," spat Manzine. His thin tail whipping the air at his back in annoyance.

Two horns protruded from the top of Manzine's head curving backward while leathery velum wings extended out past his arms stretching out as though stiff from lack of use.

"What do you call yourselves then, those who have forsaken Daelon," questioned Drogen.

"We are lushifare, those who know the supreme god, Lucian's love. He is the one who brings light to this world," proclaimed Manzine. "A light that has clearly been lost among the elves. So easily manipulated into getting rid of those above. I mistakenly thought pushing these idiots would prove difficult, but I was sorely mistaken. All I needed to do was slip them some information about the barrier forcing them to speak nothing but the truth. And they fell for it, without a thought to the contrary, he said shaking his head. It was entirely too easy."

"So, you're taking credit for everything that has transpired. Including the imprisonment of members of this council," questioned Llewellyn.

"Unfortunately, I cannot take credit for everything that happened. That part was their idea. If it had been mine, none of you would have been alive to tell your stories. It seems that even with my influence they could not bring themselves to take the life of one of their own. A pity to be sure," said Manzine with a snarl.

"Why have you done this," roared Gilvail.

"Because I was ordered to. The fun of doing it was purely a bonus. Spreading chaos is so much fun. Especially when those around you are so incredibly gullible. At least your women are as malleable as your men. If they had not kept me company many a night, I don't know if I could have stopped myself from raging sooner."

"That's enough out of you," said Leif. Wrapping Manzine in vines soo only his horned head was exposed.

"It seems you're forgetting something," chortled Manzine maniacally. "I can also control vines, but mine are different." Vines sprang forth from the ground at Leif's feet wrapping her tightly the surprise attack blocking her concentration. The vines around Manzine loosening just long enough for his hands to come free.

"Now that magic has been fully released, I am far more powerful than any of you. By the way my vines are coated in a special poison. Its effect is rather weak without magic. But now a single little nick will cause anyone it touches to die in excruciating agony. How about we start with you, and continue one by one around the room?"

"I will not allow you to harm anyone here Manzine," said Drogen. Walking calmly to the struggling Leif. Cracking the door within his mind his finger elongated into a claw. Which he used to cut Leif free of her bonds.

"Then it seems you'll be the first to taste my poison. I hope you can withstand its effects for at least a short time. Otherwise, this will prove to be far too boring."

"Take the council and get out of here, make sure the other dryads and elves move to a safe distance. I don't want there to be any collateral damage from his... struggle," said Drogen.

"You think I'm going to let you leave. I didn't give you permission," bellowed Manzine. Spreading his hands to form a wall of poison vines along the walls of the tower.

Drogen clicked his fingers and fire spread around the walls of the tower, destroying the vines, making them wither and die as fast as they had grown. "Go." he said. Waving his hand to make an opening in the wall of flames but keeping it burning along the floor and ceiling in order to prevent Manzine from forming his vines during the council's escape.

"I have a question for you Manzine. Were you abandoned here when the gods left? Or did Lucian send you here recently to cause trouble."

"Lucian would never abandon one of his devoted. I was placed here by Lucian hundreds of years ago. That I could gain their trust. To ruin them from within. To spread corruption and discourse to all his enemies," preached Manzine.

"When was the last time Lucian was in contact with you then," questioned Drogen. "Surely if he would not abandon you, he has reached out over the years."

"He didn't need to reach out. He placed me here knowing I would accomplish the task without fail."

"Or did he forget about you the moment he left?"

Rage filled Manzine's eyes. Magic power building up within him. Flowing down his arms in the form of vines, reaching out for Drogen's body. "I will destroy you with my poison vines. You will writhe in unspeakable agony for your false claims upon divinity."

"You can try," said Drogen. His visage aloof in its expression.

Drogen's seeming lack of concern pushed Manzine over the edge of his rage forcing Drogen out through the open doors of the council chambers and into Moonclave. Manzine broke free of the council chambers his hand forming a fist to constrict the poisonous vines. Drogen didn't struggle or fight against the vines. Allowing them to tear through his flesh and clothes, exposing large swaths of scales, concealed only by the constricting vines.

Blood poured out of the vines dripping onto the ground around Drogen's body, which Manzine's vines held aloft for everyone in Moonclave could witness Drogen's demise from all corners. "Now watch how he writhes in agony, the flesh ripped from his bones. My poison flowing freely into his blood," He cheered gleefully. Drawing gasps from elves and dryads alike.

Manzine let loose the constricting vines from Drogen, allowing his body to fall to the ground in victory. "The creature before you will not last much longer. I suggest you say your goodbyes now. The rest of you are next. Manzine of the lushifare who serve's the supreme god will be sending you to Death soon."

"Hey Drogen it seems this one really likes to hear himself talk, are you just going to lay there and do nothing, or are you waiting for something? I still need to go and see what the others on the council did to my mother. I would appreciate you not wasting time unnecessarily," ranted Seraphine angrily.

Drogen rose to his feet, quickly bowing to Seraphine. "I apologize, I was hoping to garner what information I could from him as to why Lucian is targeting my family. He imprisoned my father and sent Ether and Uther after me as well." he explained.

"How dare you acts as though you're alright. My poison acts quickly, I'm sure that it's seeping through to your heart as we speak," barked Manzine indignantly.

"Just finish it," said Asche "They need to see the extent of what the other members of the council did in order to pass judgment."

"As you wish," said Drogen. The flesh covering his scales peeling off as he walked away revealing the sun dampening black, red tipped scales beneath.

"That is impossible. How are you walking around? What is that hidden armor," questioned Manzine. Walked backward losing every ounce of hubris he had as he cowered in fear.

"The fact you don't know from my scales what I am, is all the proof I need to know you were left here," said Drogen.

"The dryads, unlike the others who call Moonclave their home, were left with the memories of my people. You however, being here with them, were not. Which means that Lucian left you here years ago, and likely, never thought about you again," said Drogen.

"My... my poison... How?"

"I am a dragon your poison means nothing to me," said Drogen. Envoy of Death appeared in his hand, descending into Manzine's heart.

"None can stand before his divine light," gasped out Manzine. Struggling to speak his final words. "It is like standing before the sun."

"Then I will blacken his cursed sun," said Drogen. Pulling Envoy of death from Manzine's heart cavity.

"Why must the gods manipulate their peoples into such actions. Actions that lead to unnecessary bloodshed. Grock is using his own people in much the same capacity. Tis a shame. Tis a monumental shame that so much blood should be spilled," said Drogen. As much to himself as to those gathered around him. "Worship without thought, or question. Divinity that cares for their followers as little as they do their enemy. All fodder for their cause. Lets go," he finished dropping Envoy of Death from his hand. The blade disappearing before it ever touched the ground.

"Yes, let's be off. Do we need anything to give my mother a chance to speak," questioned Seraphine.

"Yes, those who have gone through the ritual will need the water of an old one," said Leif. "It is only with their healing waters that they might regain their voice and speak. Although, it is not a guarantee."

"We still have water in the bag Drogen gave us," said Alya. Holding up Drogen's extra-dimensional bag.

"I hope it's enough," said Asche. Looking skeptically at the minuscule bag in Alya's hand.

"What about the mole men," questioned Seraphine teasingly.

"Ye best be off ta ya tree huggin. Me Brudder an me not be needin that show I be wanten ta ear what that pain in da rump got erself inta, when ya return," said Rumble. Garnering an enthusiastic nod from his brother.

With a nod of his own Drogen started toward the clearing where Silf lay waiting. Those around him speaking between each other, but if he heard anything he didn't show it.

Many of the elven people around the council wished to follow along in order to pay their respects, but Gilvail assured them they would have time to do so after Seraphine was afforded her chance.

Following Drogen through Moonclave and the tower leading into the Living district. The remaining five of the elven council, Asche, Alya, and Leif made there way through the path Alya and Drogen had cut through the underbrush. The journey that had taken many hours, due to cutting there own path, taking a little over half the time.

Seraphine lost her footing upon entering the clearing, Keltus and Llewellyn taking up the task of righting and helping her move closer. Her fellow council members sat her down before the tree encasing her mother, as tears flowed down her cheeks. She touched the juvenile branches of the sapling willow tree tenderly wishing to feel her mother's presence once more through the contact.

"Please mother speak to me, allow Drogen's water to be enough that I can hear your voice one last time," she pleaded through tear filled sobs.

Alya opened Drogen's bag calling audibly for the waterskin, they had used during their journey to the Moonclave. Pulling it free she handed it to Drogen who took it deftly. "Should such a thing happen. I may not be here to give aid," he said sending fire into the waterskin.

"The ritual shall be sealed away that none can use it until such time as an elder wished to go through the ritual. It cannot and will not be used as a means of punishment ever again," said Gilvail.

"Do the other members of the council agree," questioned Leif.

"Yes," said all of the council members in unison. All except for Seraphine whose voice and eyes remained trained upon her mother.

"In order to ensure that this never happens again we will leave knowledge of the ritual with our forest mothers, and not within elven hands, or those upon the council," said Keltus.

Once more an invisible wind swept through Leif's hair. "Root mother agrees with young council member Keltus. Drogen spread the water of the old ones that Seraphine might hear her mother's voice."

Drogen nodded pouring the golden draconic water out over the small willow tree. They waited many minutes as the water absorbed around it growing flowers around the tree trunks base as leaves and flowers began to bloom upon Silf's small limbs. As the flower's bloomed they radiated light as though fire burned along their entire length.

"Mother, please speak to me. If only to let me know that you're all right. That you're not in pain," said Seraphine. Brushing away her tears as she looked upon her blooming mother's branches.

"No pain," came Silf's voice from the willow. "Please my sweet child, don't shed tears for me. I will be fine here where our house once stood. It is time you start your journey into the future. I know it doesn't seem like it now, but you are strong. Far stronger than I have ever been. The elven people are sure to have a bright future with you, and those around you, to lead them into a new age. I only ask that you do not make the same mistakes I did, and don't let the prejudices of the past hamper the elves' path forward."

"I will take your words to heart mother, as will the other members of the council. I love you. I only wish I had been able to do something to prevent this from happening."

"This was all out of your control Seraphine. It may take you some time to come to terms with what has happened, but please, move past it, and look to the future," said Silf. The last syllables of her articulation's fading to an inaudible whisper.

Seraphine choked back on her sobbing gasps to stop herself from crying any more. A try at feigning strength against the sadness that proved futile as Alya's arms wrapped her into a tight embrace. With the feeling of comfort coming from her closest friend the levee she endeavored to raise fell completely. All her pent-up emotions and frustrations, from being imprisoned and talking with her mother; for what could be the last time, coming out in a flood.

She wept for many minutes with Alya comforting her the whole time, while Drogen placed a comforting hand upon her shoulder. Seraphine cried until all of her tears were expended before she found strength enough to stand. Alya released her but, remained close in case she once more collapsed.

"I will make you proud mother. I will lead our people into a new, more prosperous era. One that will see our people rise to be the best they can. To care for the forest and all who call it their home. And to not let the past dictate the future any longer," proclaimed Seraphine with an unsteady bow to the willow. "I will return when I have fulfilled my promise to you, and when I need advice. Although you may not be able to hear or speak with me, your presence will surely give me the answers I need."

With her declarations done Seraphine turned away to the other members of the elven council with prominent puffy cheeks and eyes. "I wish to convene a meeting of the council tomorrow. Drogen came here with information. Information I have no doubt will prove to be important for our people to know."

"You need time to grieve," protested Alya.

"There will be time to grieve later. Right now, is a time for action," said Seraphine. Straightening her spine before walking back out along the path to Moonclave proper.

Seeing Seraphine's resolve the rest of the council followed suit with Asche following closely behind them.

"Are you not coming," questioned Alya.

"No. Not yet," said Drogen. "Go with them Leif. I will be along shortly."

Leif nodded to Drogen taking Alya under the arm so they could walk together out of the Living district leaving Drogen alone with the willow bound Silf.

Drogen waited many minutes making sure that nobody was watching or looked to return. Satisfied all were gone he began to speak. "Was all of this truly necessary Silf. Whatever could be the point of making your daughter experience such despair. Or would it be more appropriate to call you Root Mother?"

"When did you figure it out," came Silf's voice.

"I suspected when I met Harp that something was amiss. She, like you, wore a dress made of her own leaves, however if you are asking when I knew for certain. It was the moment I touched upon your branches. Your heartbeat is not something you can hide from me."

"The old ones were always able to distinguish the truth, from what others try to show," said Silf.

"So, why all the theatrics. I understand that what the council saw fit to administer as punishment was unacceptable. Hence my going along with what you wanted done. However, you didn't need to remain as you are. You could have revealed the truth at any time. So why?"

"I have guided the Elves from the very beginning. I only recently came to realize that many of the choices I made were not right for them. Or I had made the right decision but implemented it in the wrong way."

"To what are you referring," questioned Drogen.

"I thought expanding out of Seraphal to be the best option. I was right to bring them out of the barrier but flawed in my execution. Because of this, not one, but two settlements were lost. Had the barrier been taken down and the elves forced to come into contact with others, as opposed to remaining stagnant, then things with the council may have turned out differently."

"Then it would seem the dragons are to blame for a lot of the trouble caused by the barrier as well."

"I cannot blame the old ones for something I could have taken down myself," said Silf. "Even though I wished for them to see the world. I also wished to protect them. In so doing I sealed my own fate. They need to look past my mistakes and into the future."

"Do you not fear this to be a mistake as well?"

"I fear nothing less, and it was hard, so very hard for me to see Seraphine in such despair. But Seraphine will be the one to lead the elves into a new age. She has found friendship, and camaraderie with many, outside our people. Those connections will provide a path forward for the elves. A path I proved incapable of leading them toward."

"I know that Seraphine will prove to be a great leader of the elves. I know the friendships she forms with other races, moving forward, will garner a far greater life for Seraphal and all that call it their home. That is all I have ever wanted for my children," said Silf.

"I should be off to follow the others before they become suspicious of my long absence. May the next journey of your life bear fruit for the children of these woods to grow and become better than their predecessors," said Drogen. Bowing to Silf.

"Thank you old one. Finally, I may rest a short while," said Silf with an audible yawn. "Please look after our people as your mother once did. And, when you see her again, please tell her I'm sorry. Sorry for not listening to her sooner. If I had, maybe things would have turned out differently."

"I will tell her, when I am afforded the chance to do so. I do have a question to pose to you. Before I go to the others. In your time among my kin were there any who could not hear their weapons among those who forged their own. I can no longer hear Godslayer; Envoy of Death within my mind."

Silf's branches lay still for a short time as she contemplated Drogen's question. "No. All who forged weapons could converse with them. I have no recollection of any incapable of doing so. It may not be Lisana's side that renders you incapable of conversing at this moment, but Deaths." suggested Silf.

"I have come to suspect the same," he said with a sigh. *If only I could figure out the final lock. Then they could resonate once more with my soul. And then, I will hear their voices once more. It was only in my fight with Grock that I was able to hear them. Maybe he is the key.*

Drogen turned away from Silf's Root mother form and began the long walk back through the cut in underbrush and overgrowth path. *For now, tis best the others get some rest. It has been a long and tiring day for everyone after all. If the information given, translated by Natalia, from Golga's book is accurate then the elves have only a short time left to prepare before Grock's armies arrival.*

Thinking through the trial and tribulation of the day's events even Drogen felt mentally exhausted. Which he would take care of through meditation. With his thoughts going over the day he made it onto the central road of Moonclave, subconsciously searching for his friend's heartbeats. It took him little time at all to find Alya and Seraphine, who had decided it best to wait for him along the road. Just inside the crafting district.

"Before you ask everyone else went about doing other things," said Alya.

"Queens Keltus and Asche both went with Leif to see... Harp. I don't remember anyone by that name, but I cannot say I remember ever meeting a Leif either," Seraphine shrugged. Clearly trying to fight against her sadness with humor.

"Gilvail left to see just how much of a mess Elmar made of the Aviary District and to talk with Phaylor about Rumble and Tumble staying here in Moonclave," continued Alya.

"So, the brother dwarves will be welcomed here," questioned Drogen absently.

"Yes. They will be the first. To see if we can get along, in some capacity," said Seraphine. "Although I doubt that will ever happen," she finished with a roll of her eyes.

“Shes just saying that while rolling her eyes because they’ve grown on her like a dwarven beard,” said Alya. Nudging Seraphine’s side with her elbow playfully.

“Ah, whatever. I’m sure they’ll find some way to make it difficult,” she said with an exaggerated pout.

“I’m glad to see being locked up hasn’t affected your sense of humor,” said Alya.

“Is someone bringing the dwarves here, or have they been given other arrangements,” posited Drogen.

“Oh, I forgot Llewellyn is actually going to get them personally. We have rooms set up here in the Crafter’s District,” said Seraphine.

“Are we staying with Phatropa again,” questioned Alya.

“Yep, and I asked them to prepare lots of food and drink for tonight as well. We’ll eat and drink to our release, to victory, and to those who are unable to join us in celebration,” said Seraphine. Continuing to think about her mother.

“Then we should get there fast, if the dwarves get there first, I doubt there will be any drink left for the rest of us,” said Alya. Pulling them both away by interlacing her arms with theirs. Heading quickly for food, drink, and rest they all sorely needed.

Chapter Thirty-Five

"Did you feel that rush earlier... It is hard to describe the feeling it gave me. Like drawing breath for the very first time," said Natalia looking to Lisana for answers.

"That my dear angelo, was the release of true magic back into the world. It would seem that teaching you magic will be far more useful than I previously thought," quipped Lisana happily.

"It felt as though it reached into the depths of my very being."

"That is exactly what happened. In many ways your body and soul *are* breathing for the first time. You've grown up in a world devoid of true magic growing up in one as well. So, this is truly the first time anyone has drawn upon the breath of Dranier, for a very long time. True magic is akin to the world reaching out for contact that feeling of breathing you described is your body, mind, and soul reaching back."

"Does this mean I am capable of using magic right now," questioned Natalia.

"You were always capable of using magic, the types of magic were severely limited, but Alexandria proved its use to be possible even with true magic being sealed away. True magic simply makes it easier. Runes, and sigils are no longer the only method that can be used. With true magic, all you need to do is visualize what you want and make it so. That is both the beauty and the danger of true magic."

"I remember reading a book of magic in the library many years ago. It had been hidden behind other books on the second floor of the main library. If I remember right the book stated that danger followed those of magic who thought themselves able to control its every aspect."

"There were many who tried to take in, and control true magic before its sealing. They wanted nothing more than to control all of its effects and outcomes as they pleased. They died not understanding the requirements necessary to hold such power. Those foolish enough to seek control over true magic for themselves are inevitably, the first to fall."

"Are there other danger's in using true magic?"

"There is danger in everything Natalia. Magic just like a sword is something to be respected. A sword can cut an enemy just as quickly as it can cut its wielder. Tis how we use our tools and weapons that determines how the danger actualizes itself. So yes, you can use magic. As anyone can but, do not ever believe yourself its master," warned Lisana.

"Thank you Lisana. I will be mindful of your warning's," said Natalia. Bowing to her.

"Now if we're done with the questions we should get on with our spar," smiled Lisana expectantly.

Natalia gripped Herzblutung with her left hand pointing its twisted concentric blades straight toward Lisana's heart. Using her wings, she pushed herself foreword quickly covering the distance between them. Feigning a forward thrust as she came in close Natalia used her right wing to launch herself in a circuit around Lisana. Herzblutung traveling across Lisana's hanging parry deflecting the slashing strike harmlessly away as she stepped out of Natalia's reach.

"Tis good to see you have some experience with a sword. I dare say you have had instruction before."

"Fread taught me how to use a sword. However, I didn't understand the significance of holding a sword until leaving Zephyria. Out there I witnessed the harsh truth of carrying a weapon, and the consequences should one fail to wield it properly. The consequences I witnessed ... I still wish I did not see," said Natalia. Remembering the dismembered bodies in carts that had been taken to the arena's kitchen.

"What do you want to achieve from further practice of swordsmanship," questioned Lisana.

"What do you mean," questioned Natalia. Confused by the question.

"I do realize that my asking this may seem strange. I am the one who spoke of training you to use Herzblutung after all. But that was before seeing you fight. Learning to use a sword is practical and will serve you well in the future without doubt. Right now, even without my training, you might be better served garnering experience. Many could live a long and happy life with the skills you already possess. So, I ask, is there a reason for which you might wish to improve beyond what you are currently capable of?"

Natalia slid Herzblutung away before sitting on the ground in the same way Drogen often did when contemplating his thoughts. *Is there a reason for me to continue practicing with the sword? What goal do I want to achieve. If I am capable as I am, then it may be more practical to put my efforts into learning magic. Why would I need to learn more about using a sword? I am proficient as I am... Because I want to,"* thought Natalia surprising herself with her own answer.

"At first, I wanted to learn and train with a sword in order to help my friends, especially Drogen in whatever comes next. He taught me for a short time before I intentionally got myself caught and brought to Grammora. Before that, I learned to be a thief, to help the people struggling in Zephyria because of Nefar and Bernadine's greed. I have done most things out of necessity, or because I thought it would help others in some way. I even thought about throwing myself completely into magic studies, because that may be the next practical thing that I can do to help everyone. But for this," said Natalia. Pulling Herzblutung from its scabbard. "That would be a lie."

"Then what is your truth," questioned Lisana with a smile. As though she knew full well her answer.

"I want to continue improving with the sword because it is hard. Unlike reading, languages, and comprehension, which comes naturally to me. This is something that I must work to improve upon myself. I can read all I want about fighting, stances, and attack patterns, but putting all I learn into action. That is the difference. That difference is what makes me want to continue learning and improving in any way I can," professed Natalia.

"So, you do this for yourself, and not for others? I've heard far less reasonable explanations for improving oneself," she said with a nod. "I will continue to instruct you and teach you in every way possible. Knowing what one wants and having the ability to recognize it are often the hardest to spot within oneself. Tis a sign of maturity far beyond your age, and a key to finding your mantra."

"I will be in your care moving forward for both the sword and in the use of magic," said Natalia. Rising to her feet and into another bow, which Lisana returned in kind.

"Do you remember what I told you yesterday, before we entered the library?"

"Yes, you said we should look at the pummel of the sword, and there is a reason for it not being... pronounced."

Natalia held out the pummel end of Herzblutung for Lisana to see. "All I see is a hole in which something may be placed. What it could be for... I do not know, nor understand. I would assume it to have some function that I have yet to ascertain."

"You're quite right. Tis to insert the haft of a spear."

"So, this is actually the tip of a spear and not a sword," questioned Natalia.

"Tis both and designed with both purposes in mind. That's how Alexandria designed it. Tis unfortunate she was unable to see the birth of her creation, but none so tragic as being unable to witness her daughter wielding it. I know, without doubt, she would be very proud."

"I wish I could have known her. But learning about her through her closest friend will have to tide my heart," said Natalia. A distinct sadness wafting over her.

"Before you travel far down the path on which your mind takes you. When are you continuing your search in the library with the taurean Chian," questioned Lisana. Trying to help keep Natalia's mood from sinking too deep.

"We are meeting in the library this afternoon. I found quite a few instructional manuals, but they contain information already known to Chian. Although she is unable to read her understanding of building and its intricacies are spectacular. It is like she can see everything in her mind from a simple picture, and a small description."

"I met many of the taurean in the past, they are phenomenal builders. They and the gnomes had a big hand in building the structures necessary to contain true magic. The taurean love building. This entire city we sit in now was built by them as well, with the help of a few dwarves of course. Mythral is much too difficult to work by anything other than a dwarven forge, an elemental, or a dragon's breath."

"Chian said the taurean are incapable of making the structures around here," said Natalia. Puzzled by Lisana's exposition.

"Tis strange to hear. They were the greatest builders of Dranier. Designing and building some of the greatest structures across its surface. Tis unbelievable to think they've lost their great knowledge," shrugged Lisana.

"Chian said they do not learn to read or write until they are older and among the elders of their tribe. The young, in turn, learn from those elders how to build."

"I thought it strange she was looking for techniques here when they built this place. There is another room in the library, Chian may need to see," said Lisana. "Wherever the taurean's built they left their knowledge that any who wished to build for themselves could have the knowledge to do so. Their loss of knowledge may be an effect of true magic being sealed, but I doubt that is the case."

"Where in the library do we need to look in order to find where the taurean left the information," questioned Natalia.

"You have to go to the deepest portions of the library. Going far beyond the special chamber that houses many of the magic books is a seemingly empty wall. Of course, there will likely be books stacked to the ceiling in front of it. Unlike the rest of the library there will be no shelves. Either by climbing up the stacks of book themselves... or flying as it were. Either way you will need to get to the second story where you will find a seam between the two floors. You will find a hidden stone door leading to the stores of information."

"This is so exciting. I almost want to go find Chian now," said Natalia excitedly before sighing aloud. "Unfortunately, I don't have time to do that right now. I have to go and see Krail to find out what Fread wished to speak to me about. I hope they return swiftly, there's no telling when those zealots might start something."

"Has there been any word on them, or their return," Lisana questioned.

"No, it's only been a day. It will take them a while to get back. If they have even reached the woods yet."

"I wonder if they'll choose to go through with the ritual now that true magic's release will provide them another option."

"Either way it is their choice to make. Well, I better get moving. I would not want Krail to send guards after me for being late," said Natalia with a mischievous smile.

"I hope Drogen has his eyes set on you. You would surely keep him on his toes."

"He has more than that," said Natalia aloud. Slapping her hand over her mouth and running away in embarrassment.

"Tis good to hear," yelled Lisana. Responding to her hasty retreat, with a mischievous smile of her own. "Very good to hear."

Stifling the embarrassment of her unintended confession, Natalia made her way to the castle's courtyard. Having chosen the location of their bout to be beneath the window of her tower bedroom, the journey took no time at all. Standing out in front of the courtyard were many waiting to be heard in the audience chamber. Some of those in attendance showing themselves to be worse for wear, including the seamstress and her daughter, Jesha and Shiesa.

"Oh, princess Natalia," said Jesha. Clearly relieved to see a friend among those gathered.

"It is unusual to see you coming in for an audience," noted Natalia.

"I..." to which Shiesa took hold of her mother's hand. "Forgive me dear. We, need to... um... reveal something. No... we need to... this is going to be so hard to explain," wavered the distraught seamstress.

"I am your friend Jesha nothing you reveal is going to change that," said Natalia. "For either of you. If it will make things easier for you, come with me and we can talk privately about what this is all about," she said. Worried for her friend.

"If you will allow me to be so bold princess."

"It is not a matter of being bold Jesha. It is a matter of being comfortable. Come. Follow me, and I will do what I can to help you."

"As long as you don't have more pressing matters," said Jesha.

"Both of you just follow me," she said. Grabbing Jesha and Shiesa by their hands and pulling them into the audience chamber with her. Natalia noticed Krail's eyes upon her, and with a shift of her head, bade him to follow.

Moving through a door along the right-hand side of the audience chamber, Natalia led Jesha and Shiesa into a short hallway. She swiftly opened the first door they came to, revealing a small sparsely decorated conference room with a small square table and four chairs.

"If you don't mind, I signaled for the head of the royal guard, Krail to follow us as well. If need be, I can have him wait outside. But, if what you need to talk about required you to come for an audience, I thought having his attendance may be prudent," said Natalia. Explaining herself further upon seeing a look of fear appear on Jesha's face.

"Do you... trust Krail," questioned Jesha.

"Yes. I would trust him with my life, as all who live here in Zephyria should," proclaimed Natalia as Krail walked through the door.

"We don't have much time. Those zealots are getting closer to the front of the line. Something about how they are acting today has me... concerned," said Krail. Looking over his shoulder before closing the door behind him.

"I... I will make... We will make it quick then," said Jesha. Stumbling over her words, as she felt rushed.

"Krail do not rush them. It is clear that whatever they are going through is going to be difficult for them to speak of," admonished Natalia.

Realizing his error Krail took a calming breath. "I apologize if I have made you feel rushed. Please take as much time as you need to get out what you need to say."

"Thank you," said Jesha. "Oh, where should I start...," posited Jesha.

"I hep mama," said Shiesa with a pouting expression. "Man come for cloth. see Shiesa. Mean man yell at mama cause of Shiesa, but Shiesa not bad. Why mad at Shiesa," questioned the little girl. Looking up at her mother with a smile, proud of her explanation.

"Thank you Shiesa," smiled Natalia encouragingly.

"Yes, thank you my darling girl for your help," said Jesha with a smile that fell short of her eyes.

"So, what happened with the man that brought you here in such a state," questioned Natalia.

"Everything was going as usual until... magic came back," she said quietly. "Shiesa is too young to understand. She doesn't yet know how to control... Her change. When the man saw her, he threatened us. I didn't know where else to go," she said stifling a cry. "I came here hoping to find a friend for support. That's when... I saw you princess."

"What do you mean by change," questioned Krail.

"I am... We are not... oh why does this have to be so hard. I'm trusting you two with this. So please know that what you see. It-it's still me. Jesha."

Natalia and Krail bade Jesha to show them looking slack-jawed as, who they had thought to be a Zephyrian, changed before their eyes. "You are of Daelon," questioned Natalia thinking through the books she had studied in the past. "A... Tiefling, and that would make Shiesa one as well," she deduced excitedly."

Shiesa came over to Krail holding her hand out and pulling upon his gloved one. "Pwease no be mad at mama. Shiesa and mama fwend to Kwaiw an Pwincis."

Krail looked down at the young girl holding his hand and couldn't help but smile as she asked so sincerely for friendship. "Th-thank you for your friendship little one. We're all friends here. You don't need to worry."

"Yes. Neither of you need to worry. You will be safe here in Zephyria. I give you my word," proclaimed Natalia.

"Do you know who it was who saw Shiesa," questioned Krail.

"No, it was the first time I had ever seen him. However, I did recognize his voice from a few shopping trips. He was one of the people speaking to the crowds that formed between all the shops and stalls," said Jesha shaking her head. "Other than that, I have no idea."

"That is not good," said Natalia. "He must be one of the zealot speakers. I fear your concern to be more than warranted."

"Natalia, take the two of them to your chambers. Things could get messy, if the Zealots try and use their being here against Lord Fread. Urh, Fread and Willow just had to be gone at this time as well," cursed Krail under his breath. That Shiesa did not hear his outburst. "Luckily Vladimir is upon the dais today, since Fread and Willow aren't here. Lord Vladimir is actually what Fread wished to talk about, but we don't have time for that right now."

With no time to waste, Jesha pulled Shiesa up into her arms. Krail pushing the three of them through the door and into the hallway beyond. Running past in order to survey the audience chamber ahead carefully. Making sure the zealots had not made it up to speak.

Taking the opportunity, the crowd within the audience chamber permitted Natalia began to move in a manner that would allow their circumvention of the zealots. Guards, under Krail's direction, began trailing behind them. Keeping their distance in order to not draw attention, but also close enough to respond quickly should the situation call for intervention.

"Stop right there," bellowed the leader of the zealots' order, drawing the attention of everyone in the room squarely upon him, and those he had spotted wading through the crowd.

Of course, it could not be that easy, thought Natalia letting out a sigh in resignation.

"You would dare to disrupt these proceedings before your time," bawled Vladimir. Enraged by the insolent outburst.

"I apologize Lord Vladimir," said the man. Kneeling down in exaggerated fidelity before Vladimir's raised dais.

"You had better have a reasonable explanation for your outburst Antoni. I have come to understand you are giving your *true Lord*, Fread a hard time. I would very much like an explanation for this as well," said Vladimir. A menacing edge in his voice.

"You were chosen by our true divinity, and he was not. You are the ruler of Zephyria not him," said Antoni. As though his logic regarding the matter were absolute and unquestionable.

"I passed my title on to Fread. In so doing abdicated the throne of Zephyria. The gods Ether and Uther no longer hold sway over Zephyria, its people, or me. They are dead and gone Antoni, and they will never return. It was well within *my power,* to do what has already been done."

"Then your position should have been given to Queen Nefar, princess Bernadine, or princess Natalia instead of the bastard child of a former Queen."

Rage filled Vladimir's eyes at the clear provocation. "Ether and Uther took my first wife from me and saw fit to bring to the throne a woman and her daughter who tried not only to kill me, but also Natalia. You look so favorably upon the gods, but if you knew the truth as I do you would weep where you stand Antoni. All of Zephyria would weep," warned Vladimir. Falling back onto the throne.

"I need no other knowledge when there are beasts living among the people of Zephyria. Beasts that would be seen as abominations to Ether and Uther," proclaimed Antoni.

"For whom are you referring Antoni. Yourself, me or are you talking of Celestyn."

"Celestyn was given a hero's death by the divine. She was a saint in their eyes. I speak of the four beasts who walk among us, two of which hide themselves in plain sight," bellowed Antoni. Pointing to Jesha, the shaking and scared Shiesa in her arms. "These two who pretend to be zephyrians are anything but. They're blasphemous beings who must be dealt with swiftly."

"They are not. They are simply trying to live their lives as everyone in Zephyria is." protested Natalia.

"Show them. Show the others of Zephyria what you really are," raged Antoni. Running forward, trying to rip Shiesa out of Jesha's arms."

"Don't you dare touch my daughter," raged Jesha. Magic flowing through her causing her body to change to her true self. A Tiefling for all of Zephyria to see."

"See. I told you these beings before you go against everything we hold dear as zephyrians. They are an abomination."

"No Antoni. We are the abominations. This woman is simply trying to protect her child. Which is what Rachel my wife was doing when she was taken, and I did nothing. When my wife was replaced upon the throne of Zephyria and her daughter given the status of princess, I did nothing. When the daughter I raised from a squab returned from the dungeon stripped of each feather upon her back. I did nothing. Still all of that pales in comparison to what we did following blindly behind those deity we thought were here for us. I will stand by no longer as tragedies and travesties are committed in the name of a deity that cared nothing for us. You are to release her, and her daughter Antoni, they are under the protection of the royal guard of Zephyria."

"How can you go against those who gave us everything we have, those who formed the land on which we stand for our people. Those who gave us everything we ever needed," admonished Antoni. Against Vladimir's rebuke.

Tears began forming in Vladimir's eyes as he looked upon Antoni, and everyone else within the room. "Because old friend if nothing is done, the past will inevitably repeat itself. I see you doing it now, because the past has been lost within our memories. Your actions prove that some among us have the capacity to repeat mistakes we made in the name of divinity. Commander Krail, find and bring Lisana here quickly."

"Yes, Vladimir it will be done." said Krail. Fist thumping against his heart in salute and acceptance of the task.

Krail grabbed a few guards sending them off in multiple directions to search of Lisana. They were gone for many minutes before Death walked into the audience chamber holding aloft Reaper of Souls caressing its haft as he whispered to the blade.

"She will be here shortly," said Death. Placing the scythe within his left arm and resting his back against the audience chamber's wall.

The guards Krail sent off to find Lisana came back a short time later having been unsuccessful in finding their target within the castle itself. As the last guard returned so too did Lisana walk into the audience chamber.

"What's all of this about," questioned Lisana. "Whatever it is it better be worth interrupting my meditation. Oh, a Tiefling... And her daughter. I suppose the little one couldn't stop the transformation when magic was released," she said lackadaisically. "Are they the reason I was summoned?" she posited with a shake of her head.

"These beings go against the divine. They need to be destroyed," screamed Antoni. "And what is this one supposed to do that will prove Ether an Uther's teaching's wrong. We should be grateful for them, and everything they've done for Zephyria and its people," he proclaimed stubbornly.

"I fear that should the truth of our deeds continue to be forgotten, some among the people of Zephyria will take it upon themselves to commit further travesties. I cannot allow it to happen again. *I will not* let it happen again," said Vladimir. Standing in resolve. "Please sing her song that all of Zephyria will understand what *we* have done," he concluded. Tears flowing from his eyes as he looked not to Antoni, not to a guard, Death; or Lisana but to the one who stood as the last of her race. The daughter he'd raised with his first wife Rachel as a blessing of the gods. He looked upon Natalia dropping to his knees upon the dais of Zephyria weeping aloud.

So, without protest, and without malice, she sang Alexandria's song. With the aid of true magic, casting her voice to the whole of the plateau. She repeated the verses over and over again. The memories of the past flooding back into each of their minds. As their flow waned, and Lisana stopped singing, the whole of Zephyria fell to their knees. Weeping for what they had done in the name of divinity.

Part 3

War Upon the Horizon

"Golga. Up Time," announced Hargo. Waking his sleeping General.

"Roccan and Cauron here?"

"Yes. Wait for Golga."

"Where?"

"Outside, tell when ready."

"Just send them in Hargo."

"Yes general," he said. Nodding in acknowledgment.

Roccan and Cauron came into Golga's small abode as she rose from her furs, greeting her fellow generals with a wide mouthed yawn.

The descent of their forces set to ensue within the hour. Cauron and Roccan leading the force to Golga before splitting and sending a contingent force to attack the elves, while the rest of the force attacked the heavily defensible dwarven citadel.

"When is dwarf siege ready to start," She questioned with a stretch.

"First force in position. Give order now, take three cycles," confirmed Roccan

"Bridge over ravine completed in three cycles," questioned Golga. Garnering a nod from the others. "Both good and bad news. Hope others find use, for more than Grock's war."

"Is this why you had them build close to orc taken elf land," questioned Cauron.

"Speaking of, when will they be ready to attack elf home," questioned Golga. Intentionally dodging the question.

"Thirty cycles," announced Roccan.

"Warband sent to fight elf home too small. I thought Grock would see through. Grock have too much faith infiltrator make conquest easy. Hope they find them quick. We do not want elf to fall. Do not want any to fall. Grock think too high of self. Elf will resist. Elf will help dwarf. Elf and dwarf will help kin stop Grock," said Golga.

"Good. Grock does not care. Split force leaves conquest open, and uncertain," said Roccan with a nod.

"Grock does not care for kin. Only result. Only Conquest," said Cauron with disgust.

"Have we found ally in vaudune, hob, raske, or gob," questioned Golga. Hoping they would follow her lead when it came time to make their stand. Though, she remained doubtful of the possibility. Even after seeing Grock's own inefficacy in the arena against Drogen. Allowing those who would have died in the arena to remain alive and showing them all that Grock was in fact not infallible, or unbeatable. For the first time they'd been given hope. Hope they could find a way out from under the tyrannical god and his machinations for conquest at the expense of all their lives.

Hargo shook his head, hanging it low. "Want proof. Not stand against Grock with no proof. Proof not dead. Proof Grock be hurt. All fear Grock. Only some fear Dragon."

"He must prove better than Grock, or others do not follow," said Cauron.

"It too much risk. Have no proof," surmised Golga with a sad nod and sigh.

"Grock hurt others will follow. Grock killed more follow. Grock win... *Dranier fall,*" said Cauron. Shaking his head.

"We have no power to stand against Grock. Only god or dragon hope to kill Grock. We must do what help to save most. Elf know attack comes, it is time to gather, defend, and fight back. Must win, despite odds" said Golga cementing her own resolve.

"Will they understand what Golga give," Cauron questioned.

"Natalia understands. Make others understand too," said Golga.

"Yes, Natalia understands. Not mean elf or dwarf will choose to. May not trust what given by Golga."

"It no longer in our hands. No more to do but wait," commented Hargo.

"No. There still more we can do. More help to give. Call Grom and Bogger I have job for them," ordered Golga.

"Yes general. I find Grom and Bogger," said Hargo moving hastily away from her war tent.

"Sending them out a good value of remaining time? They are not able to travel alone. They could die before reaching anyone. Never make it to the right person to deliver message," commented Cauron.

"They will understand risk. All Dranier is at risk. Failure not an option. Failure means all fall to Grock. No time for failure. We must fight. We must win," insisted Golga.

Chapter Thirty-Six

Although they had tried to return the same day, they had left Zephyria. They were both exhausted, and far too drained after the binding ritual to return more than a few miles. However, even in their exhausted state they could not keep their hands, and bodies away from each other. Their early night turning into revelry of body, mind, and soul as they succumb to their passions without restraint.

We have fallen into the passions of our bodies before, but this time... this time it was different. Almost spiritual in depth. Is this an effect of the soul bond, wondered Fread.

Feeling movement beside him, Fread shifted his attention. A bright smile lighting his face as Willow's sunflower orbs looked into him, through tired, yet enthusiastic eyes.

"I wish we could remain like this for eternity. Locked in each other's embrace," commented Willow, wiping the sleep from her eyes so she could look at Fread without the lingering haze of sleep.

"Last night was... Intense" remarked Fread. Looking into her soul, as she stared back into his.

"Yes, it was. I suppose that will be a benefit of the soul bond," said Willow with a wistful giggle.

"A welcome benefit, we will need to get beyond the forest to see if my near-death state has been cured. I hope, for both our sake's, that I am," mumbled Fread.

"I was able to access true magic outside the necromancer's lair, something I thought impossible, with true magic being sealed. I hold no doubts that we've been successful in curing you."

"Was that feeling I experienced after the binding my body bringing in magic as well?"

"Yes. I believe it was. I was born into a world of magic and remembered the feeling. You may have been too young at the binding to have noticed the difference when magic was sealed away," contemplated Willow.

"You may be right... how then did I take in true magic, without knowledge of how to do so," questioned Fread.

Propping herself up on her elbow Willow contemplated silently for a moment. "Maybe you learned how to do so through the binding," she said with a shrug. "I'm sure we will figure more out once we get out of the forest."

"Speaking of, we should probably get moving. I know we got here quickly, with you carrying me. However. I would rather return using my own feet and wings. It will take us more time to return doing so, but I don't think we will be missed even if we take a little more time to return, I trust those I left in charge of Zephyria will be more than capable of handling anything that comes up. And do so swiftly. Still, getting out of this forest quickly is a pleasant prospect. I would rather not remain any longer than needed," said Fread looking around at the destruction and corruption Kethick's necromantic magic continued to reap, even after his demise.

"I could not agree more," professed Willow. "This unease I feel, since the soul binding, is it coming from you then?"

"I'm afraid so. It seems there are many things we'll need to get accustomed to after the ritual," he sighed. Fread led them away from Kethick's lair. Using the lanterns, which had mysteriously reignited, out of the woods and into the abandoned elven settlement. "We left in such a hurry that I have no armor, nor weapon with which to fight, should the need arise."

"Do you think we can find something usable here?"

"We should at least try."

Looking through and around the houses garnered Fread a helm, a broken long sword, and a waterskin. We should leave the waterskin here. We don't know what methods Kethick used in his experiments. The water could be one of the sources he used to further this travesty.

"Just like one he's corrupted to his influence. I used their abilities to help other, and to punish wrongdoers. Only Lucian would think to use their gifts to commit such cruelties," commented Willow. Shaking her head in anger. "If only I had fought against him from the beginning. Thought to take my family away before his corruption could spread. I just wish I could go back. That I could have done things differently."

"Willow... Willow... Daelon," shouted Fread. I can feel your regrets for the past. Look at me," he said. Pulling her eyes up to his own. "We cannot reverse what has already been done. All we can do is look to the future. We cannot allow the regrets of the past to cloud our outlook. It's what we do from this point forward, for your people, and mine that we must focus on. Not the failings of the past. We will get through everything together. One step at a time."

Taking hold of Willow's hand Fread lead them back along the trail that would bring them to the main road. The road that would take them straight back to Zephyria. As they moved away the trees, bushes, and brush became thicker, as if every step they took was slowly healing the forest around them. The purple hue of necrosis which permeated the trees, behind them gradually dissipating in conjunction with the thickness and health of the forest.

Fread and Willow let out a sigh of relief upon reaching the forests edge. Taking a deep breath of the fresh air, expelling the gloomy necrosis from their lungs.

"This feeling... How strange. Did magic reach this far before, or has something happened," questioned Willow. Feeling true magic seeping into everything around them. "Magic has returned to Dranier. There can be no other explanation."

"I told you, when it comes to Drogen you should always expect the impossible to come to fruition," said Fread with a smile.

"I hope you know I can feel that *I told you so*, smugness," said Willow. Poking her tongue out at him.

"I feel so energized. As though I could run all the way to Zephyria without rest," commented Fread. Trying to divert attention from the shared feeling.

"Nice diversion Lord Fread," commented Willow with a chuckle. "I'm feeling the same way. Have you noticed any symptoms from the near-death state since leaving the settlement."

"No. Not that I noticed most instances before. I've not lost any time. The true test will be if I can stand before Death without my soul trying to escape."

They traveled swiftly along the road leading back to Zephyria. Moving far faster along the route than Fread thought himself capable of. His stamina, and resilience to fatigue far greater than he had ever experienced. "Is this also a part of our new bond," he questioned. Easily keeping pace with Willow.

"It must be. How else could we have traveled so far without rest, food, or water?"

"Another change to keep in mind I suppose," said Fread with a smile.

They had traveled a quarter of the distance back to Zephyria when an arrow from a crossbow came flying in where they had just been. They made to run away from their attackers quickly, but something made Fread stop. A voice in his head that he had never heard before.

Message. Golga. No Kill.

"Did you hear that too," questioned Fread.

"Yes, I did. I didn't know there was telepathy among the goblinkin," said Willow in a whisper.

"Can you tell which one its coming from?"

"No. but I think it will be the one who isn't aggressive toward us," she assumed with a shrug.

Out of the woods came a small band of goblinkin. Swords and crossbows drawn down upon them leaving them no avenue of escape before being encircled. At the back of their ranks stood another of their kind, clearly their leader, as he stayed back barking out orders.

Hoping to distinguish who they were to save Fread simply thought *Drop your weapon.* Among those present none disarmed themselves. *Well, it was worth a try.*

Before any of the orcs could get in close enough to stab them Willow transformed showing her true self to the goblinkin before wading in for an attack.

As an orc came in for a strike against Fread its blade fell to the ground. As if Fread had swiftly disarmed them before their exchange could happen. Fread pulled his blade to the side grazing the flat of the blade along the orcs tunic and with a turn threw him to the ground where he lay immobile.

Daelon, noticing Fread's feint, took the opportunity to bring out her sword. Something about the blade catching her eye as she held it out. Along the flat of the blade, where nothing had previously been, was a single word. "Solace," said Daelon, and her sword responded.

Yes, my liegess. Do you wish to provide these beings solace, or agony as they die, questioned the blade within her mind.

I would rather not have them suffer. There's far too much suffering in this world," thought Daelon. Looking upon the blade.

So, you have truly found me then, this is not a fluke, whispered the blade.

Daelon struck down the first orc in her path the orc falling to the ground, without so much as a sound, as if it had simply fallen asleep on its feet.

And what of my liege, questioned the blade within both their mind, even though the blade was not within Fread's grasp.

"Does this mean we can hear each other through you as well," posited Fread. Unnerved by the prospect.

Yes. while I am in use, we may all converse without restraint. So, what of you my liege. Would you wish them solace or agony, questioned the blade as Daelon cut through more orcs who fell just as silently to the ground as the first.

I would not wish a torturous death upon any, who do not deserve such retribution.

How pragmatic of you. Then all who feel the cut of my blade shall experience solace, or the travesties they committed in life. Their memories shall determine which. May they find solace in their deaths that they could not garner in life, said Solace within their minds.

You called her liegess and me liege. Does this mean you are a part of us, questioned Fread.

Yes, my liege. I am a part of your souls now, as you are a part of me. I am the connecting factor between you both, now and forever.

Does this have something to do with Drogen. He is the one who forged you, questioned Willow.

A blade forged by his hand, and bathed in his fire, is not to be trifle with.

Will I still suffer side effects being near Death. Like the near-death state, I suffered previously.

No. We are free from such... effect. We are of one being now, and forever. We are soul bound. That is what it means to be as we are.

With a final swing of Solace, the last orc fell to the ground, but unlike the rest it writhed in some unseen agony before going completely limp. *That one caused much suffering the souls of his victims will find solace in its return in kind.*

"I hope you're the one who spoke to us," said Fread. Holding his hand out to the only goblinkin remaining alive.

Daelon looked upon Solace, not knowing what to think, so in lieu of thought she wiped Solace of blood returning him to the sheath at her side. With Solace slid home she looked upon Fread and an orc whose face was scrunched in confusion. "Oh, he cannot understand us," said Daelon. Shifting back into, what she felt to be, a nicer form. "Luckily I can speak their tongue."

"Are you the one who spoke to our minds," questioned Willow.

"Yes, I still not good. Not understand how. New with breath. Bogger give message for winged menace."

"Bogger... Why does that name sound familiar," questioned Willow.

"You're the orc Natalia said captured her, but kept her safe," commented Fread excitedly. "Wait, how did I understand what he said," he questioned in confusion.

"Maybe it's another effect of the soul binding ritual," suggested Willow.

"We need to figure out everything we share now. If we don't know everything it could pose a danger to the two... three of us going forward," commented Fread. Looking down at the sheathed Solace.

"We don't have time for that right now. If you're here I suspect we've run out of time," said Willow.

"Golga send Grom and Bogger tell time start war," said Bogger.

"How much time do we have before the elves and dwarves are attacked," questioned Fread.

"Bogger go fast take worg. Grom do same but travel down long. Take Bogger three cycle get here, two more wait..." he said calculating on his fingers. "Gogla tell Bogger 30 cycles. You know math more than Bogger tell Bogger how long," he questioned hopefully.

"If it took you five days to arrive and find us then we have 25, as you call them, cycles before, the first attack," commented Willow.

"We need to get back to Zephyria quickly. We need to gather forces and join our allies against Grock's onslaught," said Fread.

"Thank you, Bogger, for giving us this information...You said Grom was going somewhere else. Do you happen to know where," questioned Willow.

"No Grom separate from Bogger, Not know where Grom go. Only know go down not up." he said. Shaking his head.

"We should send word to Moonclave and Aragorth of the impending attack so they know when it will happen, and how much time they have left to prepare," said Fread.

"Hopefully Drogen fixed the situation Phaylor mentioned in Moonclave."

Fread nodded his hope for the same. "We can hope. The first step will be making sure Grock's plans don't go unnoticed by those he is targeting."

"Good. Can give message for Bogger to pain in backside."

"I suppose you're referring to Natalia," said Willow. With a giggle she tried and failed to conceal. "Quit trouble Bogger. She big trouble for Bogger. Tell her quit trouble Bogger. Bother Grom for change," said Bogger. Crossing his arms with an under bitten exhale.

"We'll be sure to tell her Bogger," said Fread. Unsure of how to take the strange orc.

"Bogger not orc. Bogger vaudune. Vaudune help," he said. Touching his forehead.

"Let's get going," said Willow. "We have less than a month to prepare. Those most at risk will have far less than that. If word doesn't arrive quickly."

"I hope we can see each other again, on better term's," said Fread with a wave.

"Bogger hope not. Fly people pain in Bogger butt," he said. Grumbling as he walked back into the forest. Throwing his hands up as he disappeared.

Chapter Thirty-Seven

Drogen moved freely outside his body taking in the Moonclave before turning his attention to his true objective. Projecting himself out across the forest past Moongrove and into Grammora. Setting himself down within the arena where he hoped Girhok would no longer be.

Where many had gone with the reapers, appeased with Grock's loss of captives, and subsequent loss of control, Girhok and many others still remained. The reapers walking between them for when they finally chose to leave the mortal plain.

"Why do so many of you remain Girhok," questioned Drogen. Coming up beside the dead orc swordsman's spirit.

"We remain, because Grock may still have victory. Only when Grock suffer defeat will leave to death satisfied. Small win not win overall." said Girhok. Shaking his incorporeal head.

"It seems that many have gone to death satisfied with Grock's loss, but I understand. You gave your life for Grock and his cause. You, and those who remain will not be ready to rest until Grock's plans for Dranier have shattered to pieces. Only then will your souls be satisfied."

"Yes. Defeat only way."

"Then defeat it will be. Although, how I might accomplish such a feat is beyond even my understanding. Grock has power beyond my own. Power that nearly killed me in our previous fight. Had I not been able to escape quickly... Grock would have claimed victory," said Drogen with a sigh. "As I am now, I am not his match. Even with true magic my chances of victory are... minuscule."

"Then we watch as world falls to Grock," lamented Girhok.

"I will do everything I can to prevent that from happening. Even if I might die in the process," said Drogen. "I do not fear greeting my father in this form as my body falls in battle. What I truly fear is greeting him without having done all that I can to save the ones who have placed their faith in me."

"Then you different then Grock. Grock kill own to save self. You die save other. Not same. You better, Girhok would been better with you."

"Drogen, hey Drogen. We should get going," called Alya.

"Unfortunately, it seems I must call this discussion short. I am presenting the information about Grock's attack against the elves and dwarves today. This is at least a start for undermining Grock's plans. Once Grock has fallen, I will come see you again," said Drogen with a bow.

"You said you die by Grock," remarked Girhok.

"Then I will die in battle with sword in hand to defeat Grock, even if it's with my final breath," asserted Drogen. Pulling himself back swiftly to his body in Moonclave. Drogen awoke from his meditative position on the inns floor his eyes focusing upon Seraphine and Alya setting on the small bed they had shared through the night.

"Where do you go when you do that," questioned Seraphine.

"Well, this time I went to the ruins of Zephyr, or as the goblinkin call it now, Grammora."

"Why would you want to go back there," questioned Alya incredulously.

"I defeated one among the goblinkin who truly respected the sword and its teachings. Unfortunately, he was felled by my blades. After his death, his spirit chose to stay where he had fallen. Grock promised that in death they would in turn be apart of him. Thus his devotion to Grock resulted in nothing, but his demise. Only Death may bring within, the souls of the departed."

"What does he want then," questioned Seraphine,

"He, and many others who died in Grock's service wish to see him defeated and his machinations for Dranier destroyed."

"Well then, we need to do everything we can to make that happen," commented Alya.

"That is where the information I have comes in," said Drogen

"Let's go down and eat breakfast, afterward we will head for the council. Do we have a timeline for when the attack's will begin," questioned Seraphine opening their rooms door.

Following Seraphine and Alya, they went down for breakfast. Seeing the always energetic and happy Phatropa bringing a bright smile to all of their faces. "She's more elf than any others I have seen," commented Alya. Caught up in Phatropa's always graceful movements around the room.

"Because, her grace of movement is closer to your ancestors than that of the other elves, I have met thus far," denoted Drogen.

"You can almost imagine the tempo of her song with each step she takes," nodded Seraphine.

"What can I get you all to eat," questioned Phatropa as she walked up to their table. "And congratulations on taking your mothers seat on the council Queen Seraphine."

"Thank you Phatropa. We'll have whatever's quick and simple. We have a lot of work to do and very little time to do it."

"I take it the council is having another meeting today then. I will have Aurix make your breakfast quickly. We wouldn't want to have one of the council late on her first day. That simply will not do." With her assertions Phatropa headed to the back of the inn where, they assumed, Aurix worked on preparing meals. "Your meal will be out shortly," came Phatropa's call.

"The book you have does it need to be translated," questioned Seraphine.

"No. Natalia translated it on their journey back to Moongrove after their escape."

"Have you had chance to read it at all," questioned Alya.

"I have, but only by the light of a fire on my journey here with Asche and Keltus, otherwise no. Things have progressed nonstop since coming here. I've not been afforded the time."

"You came here with the other new queen Keltus, and her sister Asche... Were they among those you helped escape in Grammora," questioned Alya.

"Yes they were. I believe it prudent to have everyone listen to our tale. It will show the people of Moonclave the threat they are facing from people that have experienced life among the force coming against them."

"Then that's what we will do. Once Moonclave understands what is coming we will need to start preparing."

"Yes, you will. With the release of true magic, they will be more of a threat but, so too will the citizens of Moonclave."

"Do you think we will be able to learn how to use magic, in what may prove to be a very short amount of time," questioned Seraphine.

"There are those among your kin that will remember how to use magic, they will be the best to teach the rest to use it. We simply need to find those most capable in its use."

"Here you go dears. We have some porridge, fruit, and milk for you. Is there anything else you would like. Oh, silly me here's some honey as well."

"Do you have any meat," questioned Alya.

"Oh dear, No I'm sorry we elves don't eat meat. We do have eggs if you would like. Non-fertile of course... Oh what about mushrooms," suggested Phatropa.

Weighing the options Phatropa presented Alya sighed out sadly. "Give me eggs and mushrooms then."

"I know it's probably not the same, but it will fill your stomach nicely," said Phatropa. Always presenting with her joyous smile. Taking Alya's request Phatropa disappeared once more to the back of the inn emerging moments later with a large, stemmed mushroom; with the flutes removed, two eggs and a pot of steaming water.

Bringing the ingredients to the table Phatropa cracked the eggs swirling them inside the pot of water for a few minutes before adding the fluted and cut mushrooms into the pot to steep. "Let everything set in here for a short time take them out and throw them into your porridge dear. And after you're done, if you like, drink the mushroom tea as well."

"Thank you Phatropa. I don't think I've ever seen something like this before," commented Alya.

"Well, if you like it, you can have it each morning if you like," said Phatropa. "I must be off more patrons are coming down. I hope your meeting goes well Queen Seraphine, and you all have a blessed day."

Rumble and Tumble came downstairs from their room stomping loudly upon the stairs with each step they took.

"For being so small you make a mighty racket," commented Seraphine. With everyone in the inn below staring at them.

"Aye me brudder an me be used ta stone, not flimsy wood," said Rumble.

"Di'nt want ta sleep in de bed, too easy to break." said Tumble with a devilish smile. "Specially wit two."

"So just like Drogen you slept on the floor," questioned Alya.

"Aye, though that be to soft to. I be missin the stone ah home fur sure."

"You mean Aragoth," questioned Alya.

"No fuzzy ears. Aragoth no longer home to me brudder or I. It not been home for long time. I be meanin home wit me charge. De princess Natalia," said Rumble forlornly.

"We be needin ta give er a good wallop fur what she did, goin off wit out us," spoke Tumble. Cracking his knuckles before letting them fall to his side. "We be missin da little troublemaker. Always keep us on our toes that one."

"We all feel the same way. I'm gonna be giving her an ear full the next time we see each other. You have my word on that," said Seraphine in a huff.

"At least she's safe," said Alya.

"Knowin that one. She wone be fur long," countered Rumble. With a nod from Tumble.

"Never outa trouble fur long."

"After we're done eating, we'll be heading to the council's tower. Drogen, Keltus, and Asche are going to be telling us all about their time among the goblinkin. Will you two be joining us as well," questioned Seraphine.

"Though I hate bein wit you tree flies fur too long, dis has to do wit me charge. Me brudder an me will be attenden," asserted Rumble.

"Tree flies and vole's, lets see where it goes," rhymed Tumble with a grin.

"I don't know. I've seen a vole or two in my day, they're cute, can't say the same for you two," said Alya with a grin of her own.

"Let me put me beard up, and you be seein a resemblance," countered Tumble. Pulling his long beard up over his face.

With Tumble's display they couldn't help but laugh, any tension they had felt for the tasks ahead melting away.

"Okay. Okay I see it," said Alya. Fighting back tears as she laughed.

"Done you be furgetin it fuzzy ears."

Everyone finished their breakfast quickly, or as quickly as they could with Alya and Tumbles continued antics drawing attention away from everyone's meals. Upon finishing they felt full of energy, and prepared to face the day ahead.

They walked as one out of the crafter's district taking the main road, the straightest path to the central tower. Many other elves, and willow trees remained outside the council's chambers. Many having been there since the barriers fall. Still those stationed outside the tower said nothing to the groups passing only watching diligently.

"Why do so many sit outside the tower," questioned Alya.

"I don't know. I thought they would have gone back to whatever they were doing by now. To think there are so many who remain after everything Moonclave learned yesterday."

"The reason they remain as they do is likely that they wish to know what comes next," said Drogen.

"I hope they are ready to hear the truth in that regard as well," commented Leif. The doors closing tightly behind them.

"As do I," commented Seraphine. Looking around the room to the other waiting council members. "I apologize it would seem you have been waiting on our arrive. Our meal ran a little long with all the... distractions."

"Ya be callen me a distraction den," alleged Rumble.

"Done be full a yur self brudder. She be talken bout the vole," remarked Tumble with a hearty belly laugh.

"Yes, it was a rather large and boisterous vole that stole everyone's concentration at breakfast," said Alya. Stifling a laugh.

"Well, your vole problems aside, we should get on with this meeting. There's much I need to do. Elmar did a rather fine job of mucking everything up in the aviary. We barely have any wyvern's left for patrol duty because of his mismanagement," complained Gilvail.

"I hope the other districts are not in the same trouble as yours is. It could prove to be quite detrimental if it is," said Keltus. Shaking her head. "Lucky for us the aqueducts are self-sufficient. There were many blockages due to lack of maintenance. Asche and I spent much of the night clearing them. There are many more we need to take care of."

"We will need to find and appoint for the remaining three positions on the council, and do so quickly," commented Gilvail.

"You may be right, but there are other matters that need to be discussed right this moment so the whole of Moonclave has time to prepare. Selections can happen another time," said Seraphine.

"What about the former councilor's," questioned Llewellyn.

"Let them sit and stew awhile. It is the least they deserve for what they have done," said Gilvail with a dismissive wave of his hand.

Seraphine once more took her seat at the center most chair, of the seven present, to the right of the central Dias. "Let us table these discussions for later, and get onto what we're all actually here for," she said with a dismissive wave of her own. "Drogen if you would kindly take to the Dias and relay what you would to the Moonclave that everyone within its borders will know and understand what is coming."

Drogen moved to the Dias as Seraphine bade him do. Taking position before the fire that remained lit atop its surface. "Where would you like me to begin," questioned Drogen."

"Ye best start from when ye left after da blockhead princess oh ours," asserted Rumble.

"What does he mean by block headed princess," questioned Gilvail.

"Oh... I guess that detail was never stated to the other members of the council, since they took it upon themselves to lock everyone up without question," said Seraphine. "These two dwarves are the personal guard to Princess Natalia of Zephyria."

"Those dimwitted ignoramuses would lock up the personal guard of a foreign princess," shouted Gilvail. Rising to his feet and walking quickly toward the door that would take him to the prisoners hold.

"Calm down, we simply have to find a fitting punishment for their crimes. The information we are getting now is far more important than their punishment... Although I rather like the though of doing so myself," said Seraphine.

"Please go on Drogen... You are projecting everything out into Moonclave again aren't you," questioned Llewellyn.

"Yes, everything that transpires here is and will be shared to the rest of Moonclave through the towers," Drogen affirmed. "Then I will begin. After leaving Moongrove I travel..."

"Mai-Coh, Chian, and I escaped just before Grock's, and the other giants hammers fell upon us. The final activation of the rune bringing the three of us to the room I was permitted to use in Moongrove. A few more days passed before the other's, who had escaped another way, arrived as well. They had made a detour to drop a few others off in another location. When they arrived Natalia had a translated copy of Golga's book in her possession, which is what I hold in my hand now," said Drogen. Holding the book up that everyone in the council chamber could look upon it.

"Queen Keltus, Princess Asche, what other information can you add to Drogen's story," questioned Gilvail.

Asche walked between the crescent table and the dais to stand before Drogen and the council.

"Keltus and I were caught by a contingent of orcs after traveling through Sun Meadow, where we found our mothers unmarked grave. We only learned yesterday that Drogen and a Zephyrian by the name of Fread had been the ones to do it. To which we are eternally grateful," she said. A hand over her heart and her head hung low in respect to Drogen. "In our grief at finding our mothers grave and our village dead we were lost in grief. Grief the orcs took full advantage of. We were not prepared for a surprise attack. So we were captured and imprisoned. We were taken to the place the goblinkin had dubbed Grammora. The rest Drogen has told you."

"Do you agree with their assessment of the... bugbears," questioned Llewellyn.

"I have to. They did much for those in their care while in the arena. I know it might be a long shot as they are goblinkin and we have had problems in the past with such races here in the forest, but their actions have spoken volumes to everyone who was held captive under Grock's rule."

"Drogen has stated himself they are his generals. Can the information any of them has provided actually be trusted, and not a diversion from their true objectives," questioned Gilvail.

"We cannot know for certain whether the information is accurate until everything comes to fruition. However, you have witnessed for yourself how close the goblinkin have come to your territory. We have all witnessed what they are doing, in one way or another. To do nothing is tantamount to giving them everything they want."

"Even if we think the plans laid out in the book to be false. Drogen is correct. We cannot allow the goblinkin to attack without recourse here in Moonclave. Not as they have done with Moongrove. We must defend our people and our city or face the consequences of our inaction."

"We all know the goblinkin are a threat to our wellbeing and to the Moonclave as a whole. Furthermore, if the information is accurate, as I believe it to be, the dwarves will be under threat as well," said Keltus.

"If we prepare, and the goblinkin forces attack us then we can fight off their invasion," said Keltus.

"If the information is less than accurate, we can fight the goblinkin facing the dwarven citadel, and the dwarven king will be *massively* within our debt," said Gilvail. Weighing it all in his mind. "This may all around be a win win for us either way."

"Do we know when the invasion is supposed to take place," questioned Llewellyn.

"No. unfortunately they have no set time for their attack. We could be facing them in a couple of weeks or tomorrow. That is why I wished to give this information quickly, that you had all the time possible to prepare."

"Can commander Phaylor hear us at the defensive district," questioned Seraphine.

"Yes, he simply needs to touch upon the tower, and we'll hear his voice as well," said Drogen. Sending his feeling out to the tower as Phaylor placed his hand upon it. "He can now reply through me."

"Phaylor, we need you to send scouts to check the area for any sign of goblinkin activity. We don't want to be caught unaware of an impending threat. Take the remaining wyverns within the aviary," relayed Gilvail.

"Yes, councilor Gilvail. It will be done without delay," said Phaylor. Pulling his hand from the tower.

"We will know soon enough how accurate the information contained in that book is," said Keltus. "Although, I truly wish for it to be inaccurate, everything I have seen leading up till now tells me otherwise. Still, I am holding onto hope that it is not."

"As are well all dear," said Llewellyn shaking her head sadly. "As are we all."

"Say this information is accurate. What needs to happen before those who wish to end this before it has begun will change sides?" questioned Keltus.

"The requirement is likely for Grock to lose," asserted Asche.

"I suppose that's where Drogen will come in."

Drogen stepped down from the dais. Without a word in support or in contradiction of their assessment. "I will leave the book Natalia translated with this council as they prepare for Grock's offensive actions. If I would be permitted, I wish to tell Natalia's guard more regarding our time among the goblinkin."

"You need no permission to come or go from us," asserted Keltus. With all the others of the council responding in kind.

"It will take some time for Phaylor's scouts to return. Is there anything else we should discuss," questioned Llewellyn.

"A people without clear, and defined leadership are likely to fall," commented Drogen. Walking free of the council tower with Rumble and Tumble in tow.

"He's right. If we don't select leaders for the remaining three districts an invasion could come from any one of them without our realization," said Keltus.

"True, if we are to be successful and save Moonclave from this outside threat we must fill each position swiftly. We can allow no holes within the council, or the Moonclave," said Seraphine.

Chapter Thirty-Eight

The dead eyes of bodies loaded into carts stared through her as she loaded them all one by one into a cart to be taken away. Each set of eyes piercing her heart. She continued to pile the bodies higher and higher using her wings to carry parts up the teetering tower of corpses.

As she lay the final corpse atop the pile they slipped along their base falling down on top of her as she careened to the ground. Struggling against the weight of the bodies atop her Natalia's eyes became uncovered, her head moving out from beneath the rest of the corpses. As her eyes adjusted she found herself within the kitchen's of Zephyria. A place she had spent many hours in her youth. However, unlike the kitchen she remembered, this kitchen was covered in blood and run by a fist of orcs. Each of them taking from the pile to their station until she was next on the stack. Though she tried to fight it, to move her body, she couldn't no matter how hard she tried. The orc pulled her limp corpse up on the table bringing its massive cleaver down.

Natalia awoke screaming from the depths of her soul. Ziraiy and two guards rushing in as she battled against the blankets laying atop her sticky sweating body.

"Princess Natalia. You're alright. It was a nightmare. You're safe in your room," said Ziraiy. Soothingly throwing the curtain back around her four-poster bed. Wrapping her in a hug, hoping to calm the flailing princess.

"Z-Ziraiy. Is that really you... Please say it is," wailed Natalia. Tears streaming down her face as she shuddered uncontrollably.

"If you guards would please leave," said Ziraiy. Holding Natalia. "She doesn't need an audience for what she's experiencing."

The guards looked at each other in concern before nodding and leaving the room securing the door behind their retreat.

"It's okay princess, let it all out. You're holding onto a lot, aren't you. If you like, I will sit and listen any time you need to talk. I don't know if it will help, but I am here for you," said Ziraiy. Running her fingers soothingly through Natalia's hair.

Natalia cried uncontrollably into Ziraiy's shoulder. Her abyssal black wings shaking under the weight of her emotions. Try as she might she couldn't get the images of the corpses out of her mind. Their lifeless stares a haunting reminder of their loss and demise within the arena.

As her tears dried up her eyes and cheeks became puffy and sore. "I'm so tired Ziraiy. I don't know what to do. The nightmares are so intense... I see no way out of their embrace. Oh' Ziraiy is there anything I can do," sobbed Natalia. Even though no more tears would flow from her eyes.

"I will contact my herbalist friend as soon as I see that you are alright. He will know what to do to help you. I know you have had a history with herbalists. Just know that I trust him to do what is right. He wishes nothing more than to help people with his craft," said Ziraiy. A deep sadness in her eyes seeing Natalia so disturbed.

"Then it seems I must put my faith in you as well. That you would not lead me wrong," said Natalia. "I'm sorry. I don't know if I can do that. You've only been my attendant for a short time. I'm sorry I just. How can I know for certain that you, or they are not targeting me? As Kethick once did."

"You needn't be sorry princess. I know trusting someone so new is difficult. Especially with the many scars of your past. I too have found such things difficult in the past. I will tell you a secret, maybe then you will come to trust me... If not I can have the draconic woman Lisana come and oversee things, if you like. The truth is I have found working for you to be a new adventure in my life. An adventure that I truly appreciate being afforded the opportunity to have. However, I am not a Zephyrian, I feared that if anyone else found out I might be harmed in some way. It has happened to me many time in the past. Even among those who I have trusted. It has been difficult to find anyone I felt I could trust enough to show my self to. However, you saw another who was unlike you and chose friendship," said Ziraiy. Looking into Natalia's eyes with tears of her own. "So, whether it be another mistake or not I will show you the truth, in hopes that it may allow you to find some form of trust with me."

Ziraiy looked over to the door where the guards would appear should Natalia so much as speak in a raised voice before sighing heavily. "It has been so long since last I did this," she said. Releasing magic through her body, pushing down the being she was pretending to be in order to show herself for her true form. "I know that I am grotesque to look upon. I much prefer the pure white wings of those who call this place their home. As well as the beautiful wings that adorn your back."

Where once sat the unassuming middle-aged Zephyrian Ziraiy sat something else entirely. I am what is known as a faelin the first of Daelon.

"Are you like Jesha and Shiesa, they were called tieflings," questioned Natalia. Far more curious than scared.

"We are similar yes. They are second of Daelon or qaelin. We are similar to cousins if that helps," said Ziraiy with a smile.

"Thank you for showing me. Are there more of your kin among us," questioned Natalia.

"There may be. We were unable to remember ourselves without true magic. It's possible that there are others. I must however warn you. There are those who do not follow Daelon as well. They're the ones to be weary of. They are lushifare and follow, who they call the supreme god, Lucian. They're prone to rage should anyone speak ill of him. Tis a good test to see that you're speaking to daelon and not lushifare. I ask that you keep such in mind, said Ziraiy. Now that you know, should anything go wrong with my friends' potion, you may do with it as you need." she said. Wapping Natalia in a tight embrace.

"Thank you for trusting in me with who you are. Ziraiy. And thank you for your comforting hug. Maybe... Maybe talking about what I experienced, will help me in some way," said Natalia. Looking up at Ziraiy. "Were you within the audience chamber when I was brought up from the dungeon?"

"Yes princess all of Zephyria gathered in the chamber. I saw what happened, and I witnessed the one called Drogen restoring your beautiful wings. Your friend was mighty angry for you."

"Yes he was, then you will understand that the experience was traumatic, in multiple ways. Then maybe you'll understand why I did what I chose to do. Drogen brought us all to Moongro..."

"I-I see. That is quite troubling. I wont tell him all that you told me, but with this he may be able to give you a more refined and tailored potion," said Ziraiy.

"I hope your friend is able to help."

"As do I."

With her story told. Natalia rose from her vanity chair, where Ziraiy had been brushing her hair.

"I must really get going. I was supposed to meet Chian some time ago in the library. Hopefully she has not already left. Thank you again Ziraiy for listening. Somehow, I do feel slightly better."

"I'll go and see what he thinks. I hope he can help, at least to temper your nightmares that you may sleep."

Natalia walked over to the door of her room Ziraiy changing back to her unassuming zephyrian form as the door opened. "I hope so as well," she said. Walking through the portal and into the foyer beyond. "I would appreciate if what you witnessed this morning did not become rumor among our people."

"Yes Princess," called both guards.

With her damage control out of the way she made her way swiftly to the library hoping that Chian had remained, to at least look through the books she had stacked up. *Although she cannot read, many of the books have detailed drawings,* Thought Natalia. *Please still be there. I really want to find that room Lisana mentioned with you and distract myself for just a little longer.*

She ran full speed through the doorways closing them swiftly behind her as she neared the library, she noticed a gathering in the hall outside the library. *What has drawn so many people here?*

"Excuse me. I need to get through I am supposed to have been meeting someone here," said Natalia. Drawing eyes to her and a parting of the group. Allowing her access to the library beyond. "Chian," she called. Receiving no response. Only after taking in the light of the room beyond did she manage to understand why so many were out in the hallway.

Within the room Chian stood toe to toe with a massive wolf whose back lay just under her breast line. Its body a thick mixture of fur and muscle. The wolf looked around the room as though it were seeing its surroundings for the first time before letting out a howl that reverberated through the castle. Books fell from the shelves to the floor jostled free by the sound.

Still Chian didn't back away. She stood before the wolf her hand outstretched and slightly hesitant, but continued her trajectory to place her massive hand upon the wolf's nose. "Mai-Coh, You scare sky people. You scare me. Ask you change back," she said slowly. The giant wolf looked around the room sniffing the air as he did so before hanging his head low, and closing his eyes.

The wolf slowly began shrinking in size the bones within its body cracking, breaking and reforming quickly to accommodate the new shape until a fully muscled, almost elven man stood before them panting and sweating uncontrollably before passing out on the floor in front of them all. "I did not mean to bring fear," said the man. Moments before passing out entirely.

"Is that really Mai-Coh questioned Natalia as she rushed into the room to Chian's side."

"Yes is Mai-Coh. He change to great wolf of Pawnee clan. Thought only elders capable," said Chian. "Big wolf."

"Yeah, very big wolf. Is this part of what Lisana taught him," questioned Natalia.

"Think so," said Chian with a nod.

"Sorry I arrived so late. I had a difficult night," said Natalia looking down at Mai-Coh's quick breathing body. "Is he gonna be alright."

"Yes, his clan do this. It all part of him. Did not know it hurt so much."

"Drogen's first time transforming was similar to this as well. Only after performing the action many times does the pain begin to wane. If I remember correctly the elders of his race forced the transformation over a hundred times. It was to dull the pain and make the transformation instantaneous."

"Mai-Coh must rest."

"I will have someone go find Lisana. She will understand what comes next better than anyone else I would suspect," commented Natalia. "Guards, find Lisana quickly and bring her here. Tell her everything you witnessed should she ask the purpose."

"Yes, Princess Natalia," voiced the guards. Fist to heart in salute.

"Chian if you would bring him and follow me. We will take Mai-Coh somewhere private in the mean time. I'm sure the library staff would like to return to their work as quickly as possible," said Natalia taking charge of the situation quickly. "Where is Brena," she questioned members of the library staff.

"She's with the etching expert. They are compiling everything. We finished translating the final set of etchings last night. We were just starting to celebrate when... Well, you saw what happened. Well then you should continue with your celebration. You have all achieved a great feat and deserve to celebrate such a grand accomplishment," asserted Natalia. "Do not let this unexpected event to prevent you from enjoying yourselves. If anything you should view what you witnessed as further achievement. You see Mai-Coh has overcome many obstacles and hardships in order to do what you witnessed. An achievement he garnered here in Zephyria. Celebrate yourselves, and the achievement you just bore witness too."

Cheers rang out all around her as she concluded her speech bringing everyone back to a more festive and congratulatory mood. With the party back underway Natalia bade Chian to follow her into the dark alcove on the right side of the library. Natalia looked around making sure no one had followed them before opening the door to the hidden room full of magical texts.

"Mai-Coh can rest here while the guards go in search of Lisana. Hopefully, it won't take too long to find her."

"Thank you, Natalia black wing," whispered Mai-Coh under his breath. As Chian lay him down upon the table.

"You're welcome, Mai-Coh. Lisana should be here soon. If you will be alright, there is something I wish to take Chian with me for."

Chian made to protest but Mai-Coh shook his head tiredly. "I will be fine. I just need to rest. The change took far more out of me then I thought it would."

"Are you sure Mai-Coh. I stay if want," said Chian.

"Yes, my blue furred friend. I will be fine. I will rest until Mother of Drogen's arrival."

"Where go," questioned Chian. Exiting the hidden room. Chian looked back at the door, deep concern on her face, hoping Mai-Coh would truly be alright.

"Lisana told me something very interesting this morning about who built this place. I was told from a young age that the gods had built Zephyria for us. Knowing what everyone in Zephyria knows now. Many probably think the angelo's built it. However, that is also not the case."

"A dragon building this place make sense. Want tall ceiling when in large shape," commented Chian.

"Lisana said we will find a hidden door between two floors on a wall where no bookshelf was built," said Natalia.

"Like that one," questioned Chian. Pointing to a wall stacked floor to ceiling with books.

"How can you tell there isn't a book shelf behind all those books," questioned Natalia.

"No wood fallen. Books stacked high but none fall down."

"Here I was thinking I would point it out first from memory," said Natalia. Flying up into the air Natalia began grabbing stacks of books bringing them down to Chian so they could be stacked once more out of the way. As the stacks of books began to decrease from around the second floor Natalia began running her fingers along what she believed to be the seam connecting both floors together.

"Move left three rows twelve up in column," said Chian. Looking up at the wall.

"How can you tell," questioned Natalia incredulously.

"Brick is different," said Chian. Without further explanation.

Natalia simply went along with Chian's assertion feeling up the wall with her finger tips. Just as Chian had said the brick was different than the others around it. It was rougher in texture compared to its neighbors. Unsure how else to proceed Natalia pushed on the brick and it depressed slightly under her hand, but she could push it no further.

Seeing Natalia's struggle Chian climbed the stacks of books coming to rest beside her. With her more powerful hands Chian pressed the brick in easily and with it opened the hidden door into the musty room beyond. The bricks were set in relief of a specific shape. Her shape drawing a look of wonder to her eyes. She moved through the opening in the wall her shape and size fitting perfectly within the expertly crafted stone relief.

"Let me see if I can do this... Lisana is starting to teach me how to use magic at night. Hopefully I can give us some light so we can look around," said Natalia. Drawing only a nod from Chian as she continued staring at the detailed work that went into making the door.

Natalia concentrated on what Lisana had told her. *Think of what you want, and simply picture yourself having it,* thought Natalia. In her hand a small ball of light formed casting a luminous glow over the room before them.

As their eyes adjusted to the light more of the room beyond came into focus. Books lined shelves around the room with a single table and chair placed in the direct center of the room. Chain moved over to the table looking at the carvings in its surface. "These are the marks of the many clans of the taurean. My people built this place," said Chian. In both confusion and wonder.

"Yes Chian, from what Lisana has told me they built much of this world. Including the place where true magic was once sealed, The Moonclave," confirmed Natalia.

"Taking a book off the wall Chian opened it flipping through the many pages before placing it back on the shelf. This is the knowledge of my people, and how they built this place." said Chian. "If this is true, why is it written with word and sketch. Not just sketch."

"I do not know."

Looking at the multitude of books around the room, and the writing on each of the covers, Chain looked back to Natalia. "If offer still there. Can you teach me to read the writing of my people," she questioned.

"Gladly," said Natalia with a smile. "And if you like, when things settle down. We may be able to go to the Moonclave as well."

Chian nodded happily in response, looking around the room at all the information her people had left with both hope and pride.

Chapter Thirty-Nine

"Where is he," questioned Lisana as she opened the door to the library. Instead of the usual silence she was greeted with enthusiastic cheers to success and the success of others going forward. Although a welcome surprise it left Lisana wanting, for an answer to her question.

Looking around for the librarian Brena she found her and Krail enjoying the festivities alongside everyone else. She waded through the boisterous crowd and up to their table before being noticed by either of them. "Where's Mai-Coh," questioned Lisana.

"Sorry we didn't see you come in. He was taken further into the library to rest. At least that's what onlookers have said Chian and Natalia did," said Brena.

"They more than likely moved him exactly where you are thinking," said Krail.

"Where is Death? He went to investigate when we returned from working through the last etching translations," said Brena.

"Good. Then I'll leave you to your celebration," said Lisana.

She walked swiftly to the hidden room, not bothering to look if any were watching because her ears were enough. Lisana threw wide the door and upon the table lay Mai-Coh quietly sleeping. "Good, at least he didn't die from the transformation," said Lisana.

"Was that an option," questioned Death. His voice coming from the chair closest to the door.

"You know very well that anything can happen. The pain of transformation, especially the initial is terrible. Just as is practiced by my kin, he will need to transform until the pain is no more. Tis arduous, and could kill him still. Luckily for him he will have access to dragon water. Getting through so many transformations without it, would prove far deadlier to one who doesn't know when to quit."

"Then what Drogen is able to do with his dragon water must be truly magnificent," said Death.

"Yes, I wish to know the full extent myself. Krail said that Drogen reattached his wing after it had been completely cut off. Not even the elders water is so powerful. Is it our mixing that has brought such healing ability about," questioned Lisana.

"We cannot know for sure. He is something knew. Something that neither Gaia or I have ever seen before, and he is still growing, and coming into his power. He needs only open the door," said Death.

"Brena said that the translations are done. What have you found out?"

"I think going over the translation would be best done with everyone present."

"Okay, then we wait for Fread and Willow's arrival as well," said Lisana. Drawing a nod from Death before returning his focus to Mai-Coh.

"I'll wake him after he rests a while more. The first transformation is always the hardest to get through. I still remember the sound of my bones breaking, scales sliding and the feeling of being ripped apart even now. It will inevitably be the same for him."

"What race does he belong to anyways. I remember the pawnee being able to transform, as he does, but from what the guards told me he was massive," said Lisana.

"Yes the pawnee are far smaller than I believe him to be, although I have yet to see his transformation his soul cannot lie to me. He is not of the pawnee. Only one race I know of is so massive, and they are of Daelon. He is vendijo. Why he is with the pawnee I could not say. I doubt even he knows," said Death.

"It would seem that much has changed since true magic's binding on the other side of the desert. Speaking of, I wonder how the others are doing. If they've had time to build up our forces," contemplated Lisana.

"We will not know until going there. Once Drogen knows tis likely he will wish to come with us. Do you know if he was told the truth of Dranier?"

"No... I don't believe he has been enlightened. Especially since his time in Lundwurm Tul was cut short."

"Are we going to leave that conversation to the elders, or should we be the ones to tell him the truth," questioned Death with a sigh.

"You could not have known my love. You have lived so many lives, there are bound to be certain things that go unseen," said Lisana. Trying to comfort him.

"It doesn't make our mistake any easier to fathom or fight against. We thought ourselves more knowledgeable, and that ignorance has caused immeasurable pain and suffering," said Death.

"I know we have a lot..." started Lisana. The door to the hidden room flying open.

"We need to gather everyone now," said Fread. Walking into the room with Willow fast at his heals.

"What's going on," questioned Lisana.

"We received word from one of the goblinkin that Natalia befriended in Grammora. We have less than a month before the goblinkin begin their siege," said Willow.

"Lisana if you would go and gather Natalia and Chian, I believe you know where they are," said Death. Receiving a nod as she walked out the door.

"Now just to make sure that my eyes do not deceive me. This one," said Death. Pointing to Mai-Coh, "is one of yours. Correct."

Willow stepped forward to take in Mai-Coh, her eyes scanning him with true magic, receiving a response back as it flowed through him. "Yes he is, but how. How did I not see it before. Many of their clan find the transformation hard, but he said he was of the Pawnee. Does he not realize his true origins," questioned Willow.

"It would appear so," said Death. Looking between Willow and Fread. "I see the ritual was successful. Fread's soul is content once more within its vessel."

"So it seems. Although there has been... an unforeseen complication," said Willow. Pulling the blade from the sheath at her side. "Solice," read Death aloud. "Let me speculate a moment, this blade was forged by a dragon, and you used it to perform the ritual."

"Yes, how did you know that," questioned Fread.

"Because the same thing happened to Lisana and I," said Death. Pulling reaper of souls from within his cloak. Although, her blade was already quite aptly named. As if it were fate itself pushing us together. Any downsides you might have had from the ritual will have been negated with a dragon made blade as well. You should count yourselves lucky."

"Yet another thing we'll need to thank Drogen for when we see him again," said Willow.

Death began laughing taking in the true absurdity of those standing before him. "Drogen comes for your soul, after forging a blade for you," pointed Death from Fread to Willow. "Then you two go and perform the soul binding ritual. If I didn't know any better, I would think he's moving fate itself with his actions alone."

"Is that really Mai-Coh," questioned Fread. "He looks so different."

"In many ways he is. This is the first time he has gone through the transformation. I think it would do Mai-Coh good to hear about his true people from the one who raised them Daelon," said Death. "You can go over your knowledge while Lisana helps him to master his transformation."

"Oh, so he's the friend you mentioned then," said Fread. His smile causing blood to fill Willows cheeks.

"Tis good to have friends especially friends who will tell you the truth no matter how hard it might be to hear," said Death.

Lisana walked into the room with Natalia and Chian, who were both carrying a stack of books. "They were exactly where I suspected they'd be." After the three of them had entered Brena and Krail followed as well. "I figured I would gather these two as well, since I was out," said Lisana.

"Well everyone is here, where should we start," questioned Natalia.

"I suppose we should start with getting Mai-Coh up," said Willow.

"I agree he and Chian have not decided whether to join us, with what is coming, or not to. I wouldn't want to pressure either of them," said Natalia.

"Thank you Natalia black wing,," said Chian with a nod.

"Mai-Coh," called Lisana to the sleeping form laying out on the table. She touched his arm bringing him groggily out of his deep sleep. "If you and Chian do not wish to join us in our discussions regarding Drogen, and the goblinkin, then you'll need to rest else wear. When we're done here, I'll find and aid in healing your wounds."

Mai-Coh looked around the room, and the audience that had filtered in without his notice, as he slept. "Chian, do we stay, or go?"

"We stay Mai-Coh, much to learn from sky people, sky people and black wing friends. We stay. Help how we can," said Chian.

"I knew you would come to same conclusion. We stay and join sky people. Help friends," nodded Mai-Coh letting out a groan. "Need help to sit in chair."

Everyone moved to help Mai-Coh quickly, but Willow and Death were the first to help him off the table and into a seat. "I also need to speak with you. There are things I would like to clarify and have clarified, if possible," said Willow with a sad smile. Seeing Mai-Coh wincing in pain.

"I will help any way I can."

"Mai-Coh will need to get some rest even after I help him heal. We should get on with this meeting quickly," said Lisana.

"I agree," said Death.

"Then I would like to relay what we just learned on our journey back from the necromancers lair," asserted Fread.

"I take it that the ritual was a success then," questioned Brena.

"Yes, it was, with some unforeseen complications, but none of them... bad," stated Willow. Completely unsure as to how to categorize the effects of the ritual. Passing the book, they'd borrowed, back to Brena.

"We can discuss the details later. What happened afterwards is far more important," said Fread. Tapping his foot. "We were attacked by orcs, we were able to dispatch them, but one of them spoke into our mind. He's one of the goblinkin that Natalia mentioned before, Bogger. He came with information about when the first siege will happen. They are set to begin their assault in twenty-five days."

"Where they fight first," questioned Mai-Coh.

"We don't know. He was only sent with the number of days. We don't know where they plan to strike first," said Fread.

"The information Golga gave me said that Grock has planned to attack with a split force. One toward Moonclave, and the other to Aragorth," said Natalia. "Wait what about Grom they are typically together?"

"He didn't know where Grom was being sent. Only that he was sent to the south," said Willow.

"We should send word to both Aragorth and Moonclave telling them they need to prepare for siege," said Krail.

"We need to amass forces as well, to aid our allies against Grock's threat," said Fread.

"Going to help your allies is a great thought, but you also need to be weary, and guard Zephyria as well. The Daelon's are passionate, and more often then not wish to live their passions out as much as possible. However, those who follow Lucian are different, they want to spread chaos wherever they go," said Lisana.

"We must learn from the mistakes of the past, and from those who made those mistakes," said Krail. Thinking through the options they had moving forward. Knowing they would need to amass a force to help their allies.

"I suggest we call for volunteers to fight against the goblinkin alongside our allies," said Natalia.

"I cannot help but think the force would be rather lacking if it were comprised of only voluntary forces," said Fread.

"We need to retain a force here capable of meeting any outside threat swiftly," said Krail.

"Then split the difference and have volunteers from within the ranks of your guard, and the citizens of Zephyria. You should talk with Vladimir. He will likely know how to break the forces apart most effectively. He was always a great strategist," said Lisana. Sadness haunting her face.

"I have to agree, Vladimir will know how best to proceed. Krail and I will approach him on the subject," said Fread. "And while we're at it send word to Moonclave and Aragorth."

"Then it would seem to be my turn," said Death. Standing up from his seat at the head of the table. "Brena and the others inside the library have proven most helpful in translating the etchings from Drogen's bowl. What everyone must understand is Drogen is in danger," said Death.

"What do you mean *danger*," questioned Lisana and Natalia quickly.

"Exactly as I have said. If things go as the etchings state, Drogen will be hard pressed in his battle with Grock."

"He triumphed in the arena facing Grock after we fled. Mai-Coh and Chian are proof of that," protested Natalia. "Tell them, tell them how Drogen beat Grock and saved everyone from the arena," she said. Pleading with Mai-Coh and Chian.

"We triumphed, but... Drogen, our dream walker, nearly did not survive," said Mai-Coh. "Drogen click fingers as giant and Grock hammer fall. When open eyes see Drogen, his body look fine. But beneath hurt bad have a hard time breathing before dragon water."

"Why did he not tell us when we arrived," questioned Natalia. Tears streaming down her face realizing how close she had come to losing him without even knowing it.

"Did not wish friends to worry," said Mai-Coh.

"Drogen shoulder whole world to keep friends safe," said Chian.

"We need to do something," said Lisana. "We have been separated for so long and you're telling me now that he is going to die. I will not allow it to happen, even if I have to kill Grock myself."

"There is only one way for him to survive. He needs to access the other power he was born with. The power of a god," said Death.

"Then we need to go to him quickly," said Natalia.

"Yes we do," seconded Lisana.

"None of you will be of help to him as you currently are. As it stands, any of you could prove reason for a forfeit of his life." Those around him made to protest but fell silent as he released his aura throughout the room. "Before any of you protest let me explain," Death said. Pointing to everyone in turn as he went around the room.

"First, we have our angelo princess who has received barely one night of magic study, and a few traded blows with Lisana. Next is the goddess who keeps her true identity hidden even among friends because she fears they will not accept her once they know the truth. We have the new ruler of Zephyria, who has only just recovered from his near death state and has yet to explore the full extent of the new connection that he has formed. A taurean who knows nothing of her peoples work, or how to build as her ancestors once did, and finally a vendijo who has only just gone through his transformation. None among you are ready for battle, none of you are ready to face the threat of war upon yourselves, let alone in protection of an ally," he said. Bringing the truth to light for everyone."

"He's right. We cannot go into these matters throwing caution to the wind," said Krail. "No matter how difficult it is to acknowledge our faults."

"How are we supposed to progress so far in such a short amount of time," questioned Natalia.

"I have a method for you," said Lisana. "The others will not be able to use it, but it will allow your studies to proceed at a quicker pace than the others."

"Then I will be in your care for this as well," said Natalia.

"As for Chian, you will need to put all your time and effort, into studying your people's writings and methods."

"I want nothing more, but Natalia black wing just began teaching me to read."

"I will help you with that as well, though my method may not be very pleasant at first, it will prove effective in its quickness," said Lisana. "As for you Mai-Coh I will be helping you with your transformations. We will be using my dragon water, but be prepared this will not be a pleasant experience."

"Fread, Solace, and Daelon will need to train together, and experience every aspect of their bond in order to see the extent of their connection. From the look I feel from your three souls you will be at it for a while," said Death.

"Daelon," questioned everyone as they looked to Willow.

"You need not hide yourself here Daelon others of your kin have already begun to show themselves in Zephyria. You need not worry any more. Especially since you've married the king of Zephyria body, mind, and soul."

"Ziraiy showed herself," questioned Willow.

"You mean Natalia's handmaid," questioned Fread.

"Something happened yesterday that you are unaware of," said Krail

"Tell them both what happened while Daelon shows her true form. Then we must all start on the tasks ahead of us," said Death. Daelon revealing to them all her true self, garnering gasps of awe from the others in the hidden room.

Chapter Forty

"Where should we begin with these discussions," questioned Seraphine.

"We can always let the prisoners sit in their cells for a few more days," said Gilvail. "Their punishments remain to be figure out, and its not like they need food down there either."

"Then we should appoint council members. We do have three positions to fill," commented Llewellyn.

"Those who saw the council as a means to garner power have run Moonclave for far too long. Their methods were disheartening for many in Moonclave, and outside it as well. We need people on the council who are known and trusted by our people. Does anyone have a suggestion as to nominations," questioned Keltus.

"I would nominate Phaylor for councilor of the defense district. He is loved by the Moonclave and has served as battalion commander for nearly a hundred years under Boramil. He voiced his concerns about the council and their plots to me many years ago. I wish I had taken it to heart at the time," said Gilvail.

"I agree. Phaylor is a great choice to take over for Boramil," supported Seraphine.

With a nod he continued. "That will take care of the defense district. That leaves the craft, and knowledge districts left to fill."

"Who in the crafting district is both trusted and loved in Moonclave," questioned Seraphine in a whisper to Llewellyn.

"What about Phatropa," suggested Alya. Taking a seat at the vacant crescent table on the right side of the dais.

"Phatropa... the maid at the inn run by Aurix," questioned Gilvail incredulously.

"Do you have any better suggestions," questioned Llewellyn. "I dare say she would fit the roll quite nicely."

"What about Transil. He did return with you from Moongrove during the retreat right," implored Gilvail hopefully.

"He would be a good candidate as well," admitted Seraphine.

"Either way, they need to willingly accept the position," conceded Gilvail. "Transil has always gone his own way. I doubt he would be willing to give up his freedom for the council. Still he might surprise us."

"That leaves the district of Knowledge," said Llewellyn.

"I don't really know anyone within the district myself," said Seraphine.

"Elise is the only one I had chance to meet over the years," said Gilvail. "Most in the knowledge district have remained within its walls for centuries, Unless something has changed during my travels and imprisonment."

"No, Gilvail is quite right. I met a few in the past, but I cannot say I ever heard their names," confirmed Llewellyn.

"I think Drogen would agree, meeting with those who spend all their time researching the knowledge of the past would be best. We don't want to make any unnecessarily rash decisions" said Seraphine.

"They could have someone in mind to represent them as well," pointed out Alya.

"The warren has a point," said Gilvail. Rubbing his brow in a concerted effort to dissipate his growing exhaustion. "Left without other options, we might nominate Leif for the position."

"She cannot accept the roll," said Seraphine. Shaking her head. "The Root Mother has forbidden any of the dryads from serving on the council. Leif warned me of it this morning. As if she knew it was going to come up."

"So the mothers of our race are completely out of the question then. With that being the case, who should we send to the district of knowledge to find our new council member," questioned Gilvail.

"I will go. If I am to take on my mother's role, I need to know every person within Moonclave," said Seraphine. Determined to live up to and surpass her mother's legacy.

"It may be prudent to have more than one member of the council in attendance," contemplated Llewellyn aloud. "I will accompany her as well."

"Thank you Llewellyn. I look forward to it."

"We should at least ask Phaylor, Transil, and Phatropa to appear," said Keltus. "They will need to decide whether to take the positions or not. We shouldn't wait around with them in the background without knowing yay or nay either. If none of them are willing to take on the duties then we'll be right back where we started when time is likely of the essence. Should they not wish to take the position we need to find others quickly."

"That is exactly what we'll do then. Lucky for us, we have someone here who will be more than capable of completing this task," said Gilvail with a smile.

Seraphine looked around not understanding until her eyes stopped on Alya. "You're right we do have someone who can do it, and quickly too."

"Fine. Fine. I'll do it, but only if you ask nicely," said Alya. Scrunching her face in mock resistance.

"Alya my friend, would you kindly deliver summons to Phatropa and Transil. Commander Phaylor will need to wait to receive his summons until the scouts return unfortunately."

"Okay, it may take some time to locate Transil. Unless one of you knows his location. You may be waiting quite a while for them to arrive here. Even with my speed."

"She has a point," said Llewellyn.

"Could we use the tower in the same way Drogen did to communicate, or at least find them," questioned Keltus.

"Better yet, why don't we have the dear come and demonstrate how to use it for us," posited Llewellyn.

"I don't know if the dwarves will like that. He only just left with them after all," said Alya.

"I'm sure they'll make an exception for their fuzzy eared friend," said Seraphine with a maniacal laugh.

"And here I was thinking being put into a cell had calmed you down. I guess It only helped to make you more cynical," said Alya. Her tongue out mockingly. "I'll see what I can do."

Alya disappeared outside the council chamber for only a short time before returning scratching her head slightly confused. "He said to think of who you want to contact and let your consciousness flow out to find them."

"Well... That sounds... complicated and vague," said Seraphine. Scratching her own head.

"I guess we just need to do it and see what happens," said Keltus with a shrug.

"Any takers," questioned Gilvail apprehensively.

"Oh, for the sake of Moonclave I'll do it," said Llewellyn. Clearly done with everyone else's unease. She rose from her seat with vigor, walking swiftly to the dais, but stopping just before reaching the step up. Looking into the fire light set upon its surface. Swallowing the lump in her throat, she climbed the dais closing her eyes that she could drift away. "It's so easy... Yet so complicated," She stuttered. Feeling the whole of Moonclave around her.

"Transil may be too difficult for your first search. You should focus of Phatropa. We all know where she will be," said Gilvail.

"Yes, focus your search first by the district, then to the place within the district, then to everyone within the building, and finally Phatropa herself among them," suggested Seraphine. Thinking it the most logical approach.

"If you think yourself an expert at this, you should have done this yourself," bickered Llewellyn. "Sorry dear. I didn't mean to snap its just the level of information going through my mind is hard to sort through with so much going on."

"Are you really connected to Moonclave through all thirteen towers then," questioned Keltus. "I know Drogen said it but, I still find such a thing impossible to believe."

"All on the council must experience this. It's truly inspiring, and humbling, all at once. We must also require it of any king or queen moving forward," said Llewellyn.

"Once we've all experienced the connection we'll put it to a vote. Should we all feel the same it will indeed need to be so," said Gilvail.

"I don't know how much more of this I can handle honestly. It is quite overwhelming," said Llewellyn. Shortly before cutting off the connection and stepping down from the dais. Shaking her head of the growing fog. "He stood there the entire trial. How did it not overwhelm his scenes. Could we be missing knowledge on how to focus the information?"

"I shudder to think of how overwhelming it would prove to be, casting the voices of the council out across the whole of Moonclave, as Drogen did," speculated Seraphine. Causing Llewellyn to shudder as she walked back to her council seat.

Each of the gathered council took turns standing and attempting to focus through the dais. And each of them disengaged their connection from the platform, wholly unsuccessful.

"He did it so effortlessly," complained Gilvail. Massaging his forehead in an attempt to dissipate the stress placed upon his mind. "I agree with Llewellyn every member of the council must experience the connection."

"We should vote it now then," surmised Seraphine.

With a raised hand in vote the decision passed unanimously. "Maybe waiting till Phaylor returns before bringing together the other, perspective king and queen councilors, would allow us to be more efficient with our time," backpedaled Keltus. Not wishing to try her hand at the dais too soon.

"We do need to find a suitable person to fill the knowledge district's empty seat. Doing so may take quite some time," affirmed Seraphine.

"Well then. Let us go to the knowledge district and find a worthy candidate. Do you think Drogen will come with us as well," questioned Llewellyn.

"I'm sure he'll go. If he's ask to. However, having a good reason for his presence wouldn't hurt. Just in case he has other plans," commented Alya.

"We should go and fetch him then dears. Mind leading the way dear," Llewellyn asked Alya. All of them rising their feet.

"I don't know how long his conversation with the dwarves might take," said Alya with a nod. "But, I will lead us to them."

"We can always just drag him along with us to the knowledge district, without any explanation. I'll just hook my arm in his, and he'll come along, I hope," said Seraphine. A slight hint of embarrassment rising blood to her face.

"That is another method you might employ. One only a close friend, or more, might get away with," said Llewellyn with a knowing smile.

Chapter Forty-One

Drogen told the dwarven brothers of his and Natalia's time among the goblinkin. Explaining, as best he could, the friends they had garnered during their imprisonment. The dwarven brothers remained steadfast and engaged through every little detail. Asking questions about Natalia's state of being, after each and every ordeal.

"Tha bleedin idiot goin off wit no way out. She be more den enough trouble fur me brudder and me. She be in need of a good wallopin fur sure," cursed Rumble stomping his feet in his angry rant.

"I believe the Hobgoblin... Or was he an Orc," questioned Drogen. A hand running through his red tipped black hair. "Either way Bogger seems to think much the same," he remembered with a smile.

"Wallop the birdy, a lessen of two, one fur the past. An one fur da future me brudder will do," rhymed Tumble with a consternated brow.

"Tis good to hear you speak normally again Tumble," said Drogen. His ears picking up on the disbanding of the council, and their trajectory toward him. "It would seem there is something the council is needing us for. Since Alya is leading... Seraphine and Llewellyn directly to us."

"At least ya add time ta tell us bout our dunder-eaded princess. At least she be fine in Zephyria wit da flyin folk," said Rumble. His anger cooling slightly.

"Are the two of you planning on staying here, or going to Aragorth."

"We not be goin ta Aragorth. Not unless word fail ta reach em," said Rumble. Shaking his head. "Go de rest of me life witout seein dem boulder eads again, an it be too soon still."

It would seem there's more to these two being in Zephyria than I initially realized, thought Drogen. "What are you planning to do then? Head back to Zephyria?"

"Aye, we be in charge ah carin fur da pinhead after all. But we not be goin till the battlin be done. Da princess be mad we leaven er friends ta go da er."

"Cut the orcs watch em fall, kick da eads ya gotta ball," chanted Tumble. Dancing enthusiastically.

"You two better not be talking about playing ball with our heads," said Seraphine. As she, Alya, and Llewellyn moved into earshot.

"Bagh. Da ears ah tree bugs make fur terrible sport," admonished Rumble. "Day not roll right of da foot. Orc eads be round. Make fur good rollen."

"Well isn't that a... charming image," winced Llewellyn.

"That was definitely my fault. I know better than to ask," said Seraphine. Shaking her head.

"We didn't mean to interrupt your talk, but... Seraphine has something she wants to ask you," said Alya. Pushing her forward.

"Really," Seraphine admonished. Before relenting to the push. "Would you come with us to the knowledge district? We need to find a candidate to replace Elise. And, if at all possible, a suitable punishment for what she's done."

"Very well. There's something I wished to look into as well. I presumed the information would be where knowledge is kept," said Drogen.

"Oh, if I may ask? What are you looking for dear? Your search may provide us the perfect method of finding our perspective king or queen," said Llewellyn with an encouraging smile.

"Two things, One will help the elves prepare more effectively for battle in a short amount of time. And the other, pertains to an issue of a, personal nature," said Drogen cryptically.

"Then we should head for the Knowledge district quickly. If you are able to provide Moonclave a method of preparing more efficiently for battle, then we have no time to waste. We know the attack is coming. I only wish we knew the timeline we are working with," said Llewellyn.

"Will you three be coming as well," questioned Seraphine.

"Me brudder an me got no need fur books. Would like ta be shown to a blacksmith if anything. We can help forge weapons fur battle," said Rumble.

"I have other matters to attend to as well. Keltus has asked for help cleaning the aqueducts. I don't know what the job entails, but I told her I'd be happy to help," said Alya. A slight look of regret on her face.

"Do you know if Bailfar has begun working again, since our return from Moongrove," questioned Seraphine.

"Yes, he reopened his shop in the crafters district. From what I've been told he doesn't leave his shop very often. I asked him why on one such outing, he said he was practicing a new technique someone had shown him in Moongrove."

"I'm sure he would be more than accommodating to the mountain moles here," said Seraphine. "He's often said he'd like to see how they work their forges."

"Ah a termite wit a taste fur steel. Dat be somethin worth seein," said Rumble. Dragging his brother off with a wide grin plastered across his face.

"Are you sure you won't need help finding it," shouted Alya after them. Garnering a simple, tap upon Rumbles nose as they headed off. "Well, since they're going to follow their nose to find Bailfar, I may as well get on with Keltus and Asche's request," she said. Changing into her more agile tiger form. Shaking off her clothing, she stuffed them into the extra-dimensional bag before running off to the south.

"I hope she knows I'm gonna want that bag back," said Drogen. Watching Alya run off.

"You might have to fight her for it... Or give her meat," said Seraphine with a chuckle.

"What do you think her reaction will be when she finds out there's meat inside the bag," questioned Drogen with a slight laugh.

As soon as the realization of Drogen's statement processed, Seraphine burst into a fit of uncontrollable laughter. "She's not gonna be very happy learning that later," she said. Wiping joyful tears from her eyes.

"We should be off as well," said Llewellyn. Chuckling herself.

The three of them looked toward the knowledge district, and the massive building working as a portcullis to the distant tower along the outer reach of Moonclave. They began their trek along the left most road outside the council chambers. The most direct path to their destination. The road before them was clear, as most others who called Moonclave home walked past the massive building as though it were not even there.

"Any idea what we're in for," questioned Drogen.

"No. The only one either of us know, with any familiarity, is Elise," said Llewellyn. "Otherwise no other elves have made contact with them. Not for, by my estimation, over a century."

"The only one I know who ever went into the building was my mother, though I doubt she found the time to do so recently, given... well. The last time would have been... half a century ago when we came back to Moonclave for necessities we lacked in Moongrove."

"I've wondered myself how they can live in the library, and never come out for food or drink," said Llewellyn.

"Hopefully we can answer that, and many other questions we have, within its confines," said Drogen. Reaching for the entrance he pushed the massive wood and mythral bound door wide. Allowing Seraphine and Llewellyn first access to the foyer beyond.

As their eyes adjusted to the dingy darkness of the massive collection of shelved books many things began to stand out to them. Firstly, The books, which should have been on shelves, were spread out over every flat surface. Coating the floor as if they were tiles to be walked upon. Secondly, the distinct lack of activity, which resulted in stark and resounding silence. Thirdly, a distinct lack of anyone or anything notably differentiable within the massive collection.

"This place is an absolute mess," said Seraphine whispering. As if cutting through the silence would provoke an unseen attack.

"It could take years to put all of these tomes, and documents back together. It's as if it has been ransacked and deserted," commented Llewellyn. The disbelief in her voice matching her expression.

"You can come out now. Hiding from me will never work," said Drogen calmly into the soundless void.

"I... I apologize. I thought you were Elise," came a small, but masculine voice after a sharp inhale of surprise. "Not that I would disparage a member of the council," said the elf realizing that his words could be taken as speaking out against his Queen. "I didn't know there were others coming today. If I would have known, I would have tidied up. Or at least... tried to," he stuttered. Looking around at the monumental mess of books littering every possible flat surface.

"You don't need to worry about Elise for a while. This is Llewellyn and I am Seraphine. We are members of the council and this is Drogen. Our mothers would refer to him as an old one, if that gives you any context."

"Oh. Members of the council and an old... One... *Members of the council and an old one,*" shouted the elf. Shaking in disbelief. "If you're here does this mean I'm being punished as Elise told me. Please, I don't know what I did to receive punishment. But I can help you locate information. I hope my usefulness will help lower the punishment I receive," said the elf timidly.

"And I thought you had long exposition," said Seraphine. Elbowing Drogen playfully.

"You're not in any kind of trouble dear. You need not worry yourself. We've come for information. No punishment necessary, even if it cannot be found," said Llewellyn sympathetically. "What is your name dear?"

"My name... Oh forgive me I have been so rude," bowed the timid elf. "I-I am Tsuga."

Drogen bowed in kind to Tsuga in greeting, rising back quickly while Tsuga remained in position as if awaiting punishment for being rude. "You may rise Tsuga. You need not fear us. Are there any others here in the knowledge district? Besides you and Elise of course."

"Why yes. Yes, there are many others here in the library... Its finding them that is the challenge."

"How many others," questioned Seraphine.

"Fifty last time I checked. Queen Elise has everyone gather every year or so to take a tally for the council."

"Did she ever tell the council such information," Seraphine questioned Llewellyn.

"No, she never shared that information openly within the council chambers. She may have said something to the others, but never to me," confirmed Llewellyn in a whisper.

"I would like you to gather everyone within the library. There are matter's of the council that need to be discussed and having everyone present will make it simpler," said Seraphine.

"I... I can't do that. H- However I would not want to be punished by my Queen if I gather everyone without her permission," said Tsuga.

"Elise is no longer Queen of this district. She no longer holds the authority to punish anyone," said Seraphine.

"Queen Elise is... No longer... queen..." Tsuga collapsed his legs losing all tension as his knees buckled and hit the books on the ground in front of him. "Then I no longer have to fear her punishments?"

"No. you no longer have to fear Elise," said Llewellyn in a soothing voice. "So please once you're ready and able. Go and gather everyone else within the library."

"We would be most grateful," said Seraphine.

"I will go now... it may take some time to find everyone, but I will do it as quickly as I can."

"Thank you Tsuga. We await your return... Is there anywhere for us to sit, that isn't covered in books by chance," posited Llewellyn. Looking around for any visible opening.

"I'm afraid not. No place in the library is free of books. Its been many years since anyone has bothered to return a book to the shelves I'm afraid. The whole library is in this state, making finding information rather... difficult. Luckily, finding everyone else will be much easier."

Tsuga disappeared into an unlit alcove behind a wall of books. The wall teetering as he squeezed through and behind it. The council should have interceded here sooner," said Seraphine. Feeling sorry for the clearly traumatized elf.

All of the knowledge contained in this great library, discarded to the floor and stacked instead of being returned to the shelves," complained Llewellyn with a shake of her head.

"Yes, tis a shame indeed, luckily returning them to their rightful place will be a simple matter," said Drogen with a click and wave of his hand.

The books moved as if they knew exactly where they were supposed to be. Each of the tomes stacking and returning while he simultaneously mended the fallen shelves around the entire room. The last to return to their cubicle shelves were the numerous rolls of parchments, stacked and stored within the many tables dotting the room. Books that did not belong within the front foyer, or the shelves that lined that walls stacked themselves upon the unearthed desks to be re-shelved in the correct area later.

"Now we have a place to sit and wait for his return with the others," said Drogen. Taking in the massive room appreciatively. "Tis quite grand when tis clean."

"How is such a thing possible," questioned Llewellyn and Seraphine. Both their mouths agape.

"With magic's release, such things are quite simple. The books remember where they once set within the confines of this library. They just needed a helping hand to return. As for the rest, magic requires but two things, knowledge and concentration. With those two things out of the way, one must simply want something done, and allow the world around them to make it happen. You'll understand how it works soon enough.

"Is that what you wanted to find here," questioned Seraphine.

“No, not initially, but it may be prudent to have a magic tome found as well. The book I wished to find for the elves is regarding something called the seraph’s trance. With it, preparations for Grock’s attack can be made faster, and more efficient,” said Drogen.

“Is it similar to your meditation,” questioned Seraphine.

“Tis incredibly similar. However, how similar is what will determine whether or not I can teach you myself. It may be something you must garner the experience for yourselves. I hope, for the sake of both Moonclave and Aragorth, that the former is a possibility.”

Chapter Forty-Two

"Word has been sent to Moonclave and Aragorth regarding the timing of the attack. However, it will take some time for our warnings to arrive. I estimate two days for Aragorth, and seven or more for Moonclave," said Krail.

"Did you also warn of Drogen's injuries in the arena. I doubt he's been asked about them. It's likely that nobody there knows of his injuries," questioned Fread.

"Yes, I made sure to include another message for Seraphine detailing what Mai-Coh and Chian shared with us."

"Good, hopefully Seraphine can stop him from leaving before everyone is ready and able to help in the fight. How are the others doing in their training? Have there been any notable updates. I cannot help but hope for their quick progress."

"Of note is Lisana did... something that has allowed Chian to understand her people's language quickly, as well as a few others. Princess Natalia has received some ability that makes sleep less necessary. From the reports I've received, she's currently secluded in the library practicing what Lisana taught her, and reading every new book she can get her hands on."

"What of Mai-Coh, and Willow," questioned Fread.

"Mai-Coh is going through quite the hardship at present. If his screams of agony are any indication. Willow and Lisana are overseeing him. Making sure he doesn't overdo it. I hope, for everyone's sake, they can get through with it quickly. We have received reports of frightened children on market street. Even Drogen's house in the woods doesn't seem to be far enough away to deaden the sound. Unfortunately."

"Speaking of children, how are Jesha, and Shiesa doing. Have they been able to return to their lives without issue?"

"Yes actually, that is a bit of good news. They've gone back to work, and from what I've heard Shiesa and the fledglings are playing together without issue. They are doing well, and nobody's caused issue with their presence, or appearance."

"I hope it remains that way." Fread looked down at the stack of papers littering his desk releasing a deep sad sigh as he came to the question that had been plaguing his mind since learning the full truth of Zephyria. "And what of our people... Now that everyone knows the truth."

"Many are having a hard time coming to terms with the truth of the past. Coming to terms with what living here now represents. I have heard many discussing a return to our nomadic ways. Viewing whatever is out there upon the dunes as more favorable than remaining here. Others believe that staying is the right thing to do, and want to build a monument to the Angelo's as a reminder of the past. In hopes that the knowledge will prevent another tragedy from being committed in the future."

"What of the troupe of zealots," questioned Fread.

"Some have left the order, while others decided to remain. Those who remain however, no longer view Ether and Uther favorably. They have instead begun worshiping Drogen."

"I doubt he'll like that. But he'll not be able to control such things, even if he wanted to."

"I dare say there are many among the citizens of Zephyria started doing so in secret, quite some time ago."

"When do I need to go to the audience chamber to listen to requests?"

"It is about that time. We should probably head that way."

"I hate having to request volunteers from our people so soon after Zephyr being seized, Ether and Uther's demise, and the knowledge of the past being brought back into the light. So much has happened in such a short time. I don't know how such a request will be received, especially given the context of helping save those who are unwillingly fighting for Grock."

"We've committed, and gone through many hardships, that's for certain. However, our people are strong and will survive against all the adversity. Because we have to. This volunteer force to help our allies may surprise us all. We were placed in the same position, and if not for Drogen we would likely remain so. Our people need something to give them renewed purpose, and helping those experiencing the same hardships we once had, could ignite that purpose."

"I hope you're right Krail. Has Lord Vladimir given an answer about sitting down to discuss strategy and splitting the guard in order to aid our allies?"

"No... He's been rather silent on the matter. I get a feeling he's waiting for something, or someone to guide him along the right path. I think he wanted to keep the knowledge of what our people had done to himself. In hopes that our people would not have to feel the pain and regret," said Krail.

"Antoni, the Zealots leader, forced his hand. He's likely still grappling with everything," said Fread. Hanging his head solemnly. "Either way our people need a goal. Something to achieve and strive toward," he said. Standing up behind the stacks of paper littering his desk. "Have some of the guard's work through these documents. Have anything pressing brought to me directly. Otherwise, they can delegate the tasks amongst themselves."

"Yes Lord Fread," said Krail. With a fist over heart salute.

"And thank you for providing worthy distraction from my thoughts. Although, the amount of paperwork you were able to come up with is quite alarming. I appreciate your efforts my friend," he said with a smile and high reaching stretch. "Well let's head off. Can't keep our people waiting."

Fread and Krail walked through the door of his tower office on the right side of the audience chamber. Choosing that particular tower offered him, as Lord of Zephyria, a prime location. Allowing for quick access to the audience chamber as well as the castles kitchens. Seeing out over the walls of the castle was another benefit to the office, as he could look down and see Zephyria, and its people from within the room.

They traveled quickly down the spiral staircase which opened into a spacious hallway. To the left as they exited lay small rooms for guests of the kingdom, and to the right, doors leading to the kitchens. Further down the hallway lay an open archway leading to the furthest reaches of the castle, circumventing the audience chamber completely.

Moving through the archway lead Fread and Krail to the center most entrance of the audience chamber. Where he could access the Dias and sit upon the throne of Zephyria, without trying to walk through those gathered within the chamber itself. Krail opened and held the door for Fread allowing him to walk.

Krail, flying down from the Dias, took his place at the head of the guards. "Allow those outside to enter for their audience with Lord Fread of Zephyria," he called. Saluting with fist to heart. Receiving one in kind from those standing in front of the still broken door.

All who could fit inside the chamber did so, filtering in until the chamber both upstairs and down, were packed with people. Many standing shoulder to shoulder. "It would seem that all of Zephyria has come to hear what I have to say this day. This is the first time I have called all of our people to audience. Seeing all of you gathered here gives me great hope, and pride in our people."

"Many things have happened in a very short time. We lost Zephyr; our trade city to invasion, the gods; many of us have always worshiped were cut down, and the tragedies of the past, have come to light. I know, with everything that has happened, we are all searching for something, anything we can do. Or believe in, once more. We need a purpose. A goal for our people to strive toward."

"I know there are many who believe we should return to how things once were. When we wandered the dunes of the forbidden plains as a tribe. Others have suggested returning to Zephyr in hopes of reclaiming the city, and rebuilding it to its former glory. Still more have suggested remaining and memorializing the Angelo, in some way, that we do not forget. Nor allow the mistakes of the past to be forgotten, or repeated in the future."

"If you would allow one, still young to endeavor a suggestion as to what we might do? I would have you hear me. We are no longer the same people we were in the past. Returning to nomadic life, although an option, was never of benefit to our people. The sins of the past, are just that, in the past. Abandoning this place serves no purpose, and it does not bring the fallen back. That being said, building a memorial for the past is something that we *must do*. We need to understand and know the history of what we did, in order to make sure that other generations of our people do not facilitate the same mistakes as their forefathers."

"We cannot make right what has already been done, but we can see that the future of Dranier is not marked by similar tragedy. This should be the goal of our people. To help others facilitate common ground and understanding, between all peoples of Dranier."

"To that end. We have received word that our allies to the south are in trouble. The same forces that took Zephyr from our people threaten's to do the same to both the elves and the dwarves. Grock's forces are set to strike within the month against them both."

"However, there is more to this endeavor than may first meet the eye. There are many among the goblinkin that commit these acts unwillingly. We, as a people, have committed atrocities in the name of the gods. As the goblinkin endeavor to do now. It is my sincerest wish, and hope, that we can work together in order to prevent what took place here from happening again."

"Now, I turn it to you, my people. All of us have felt the sting of the past within our hearts and souls. Will we take up arms that our sins do not become the sins of others. That we strive to bring peace, when others want not but war. I force none of you to join in this fight. I do not demand your service. I ask for willing volunteers amongst our people. Volunteers who will be led into battle by m..."

"Me." Came a deep voice from behind them. His blood red armor set creaking slightly as he walked to the front of the dais. "I will lead our people once more to battle, not to conquer in the name of the gods. To help prevent another race from committing the same travesty as I did all those years ago. I know this cannot lessen the burdens of the past, but to prevent those burdens from being placed upon another's shoulders, is the right thing to do. Who among you will join me. That we may prevent another from following down the same path," inquired Vladimir.

The audience chamber was silent as the people of Zephyria contemplated the correct course of action. Their minds whirling in sadness and doubt. The losses they had suffered and the past that might have repeated itself, without their knowledge of the past, only days prior.

"I will join you." Came a voice that none expected. Wading up to the front, Antoni dropped down to his knee before the dais. "First, I must apologize for my actions against you Lord Fread. I believed with my entire being that Ether and Uther were infallible and had a reason for everything they did. I followed blindly their every whim and wish. I dove into pray of them even after they took Celestyn from me. I do not wish for others to be so blind that they do not see the truth as I do now. In keeping with this self-made pact, I will be the first to volunteer."

With Antoni's declaration a hundred others raised their hands. Fread looked around at the volunteers with tears in his eyes. "I would not ask you to do this alone my people. I will also be asking for volunteers from among the royal guard of Zephyria." With his declaration spoken every guard within the audience chamber stepped forward. Saluting fist to chest as one.

Chapter Forty-Three

"I figured this would take some time, but a week, it takes over a week to find everyone. How big is this place that it takes over a week," cursed Seraphine. Throwing her hands up in protest as she leaned her head back in the crook of her chair. "Someone's got to go out and get food again soon."

"You told Alya to bring us food, when she gets a chance, yesterday. Don't you think she'll bring something soon dear," questioned Llewellyn.

"Yeah, we can hope. Otherwise, someone's gonna have to go gather food again. I might as well go do it myself. I feel like I need some fresh air anyways. I really hope this doesn't take much longer. We have a lot to do in order to prepare for Grock's peons."

"I know we do. Phaylor sent scouts further into the forest hoping to learn how close they are to us. They haven't had much luck unfortunately."

"I hope everyone realizes the threat the goblinkin pose. I know those who went through loosing Moongrove with us do. But the others, I fear, are going to be harder to convince since they haven't experienced the same loss."

"There's likely going to be speculation as to the scale of attack we'll face. Until it's seen firsthand," nodded Llewellyn. "This is the first time the Moonclave has ever been under threat. All our battles with the dwarves have been conducted along the ravine that separates our forest from their mountain home, or an exchange of formal complaints."

"This is the first true threat to our home that most here will have ever faced. That we know of at least. Our dryad mothers may know about some other battle, or Root Mother may. However, I doubt we'll be getting anything useful, not for the threat we face. Drogen's been searching since that poor dear Tsuga went deeper into the library. Has he mentioned what he's looking for?"

"No, he's been silent. Simply looking through the many tomes and returning them to the shelves," said Llewellyn. Shaking her head. "If we knew the layout of the library maybe we could be of help to him. But I dare say, you and I are quite out of our depths when it comes to this place. As you said dear. We don't know how big this place is that it takes over a week to find everyone living in it."

Seraphine scanned the room taking in the light hanging over Drogen's back casting a shadow to the ground around him but also illuminating the books lain out before his eyes. Each of the books on the ground were written in different languages most of them indecipherable to her. All she could make out were the figures within the texts showing a warrior's movements.

Drogen lifted his head from the books turning his eyes toward the door Tsuga had run through the week prior. "It would seem Tsuga has finally returned."

As if on cue the door flew open and out Tsuga tumbled followed by a cacophony of others who simply walked over, or around their timid counterparts splayed form, until he was able to right himself.

"I... I'm sorry it took so long to find everyone. It feels like every section of this library has another section attached to it. Which has only gotten worse since a few days ago. Oh... wait how long was I gone for," questioned Tsuga. Looking around at the cleaned room that had been a complete wreck when he left. "Have I been lost for a month *again*?"

"Lost. For a month... Again," exclaimed Seraphine incredulously.

"How is there so much here that you could be lost for a month," questioned Llewellyn. People continuing to flow through the door and into the anteroom of the library.

"Wait if you get lost in the library for a month how do you find food," questioned Seraphine.

"Food? Is this your first time here or something," questioned one of the elves. Emerging through the door. Breaking away from the others, the female elf moved to stand beside Tsuga. "All are sustained within the library. We need neither food nor water to survive within its walls. Our only need here is the pursuit of knowledge."

"How strange," stated Llewellyn. Unsure of how to process that particular bit of information.

"Yes. Its one of the many strange things about the library. Wait... Where's Elise she usually oversees these things, or has something happened," she posited. Looking at Tsuga.

"We'll go over all the details when everyone's present. I assure you. But first, what's your name," questioned Seraphine.

"Oh, I forget people don't know me outside the knowledge district. I'm Amanita. I'm the one who has authority when Elise is away."

"Well then, it would seem you're the one we are needing to speak with," said Llewellyn.

"Elise has been imprisoned below the council chambers of her own accord. Along with three other members of the council," said Seraphine. Trying to gauge Amanita through her reaction.

"Let me guess, following Terill's advice finally got the better of them all," posited Amanita with a sigh. "I told her doing what he wanted would backfire. If only she'd listened to me. But what do I know. I'm simply too young to understand the way things are done." Clearly reciting words, she had heard from Elise many times.

"Then she knew what she was doing was wrong," questioned Llewellyn.

"Love can leave you blind to the obvious," commented Amanita. Shaking her head.

The stream of people coming through the door began to stem its flow as the chamber itself filled to near capacity with elves. The mix of people in various states of tiredness from fully awake to nearly falling over in exhaustion.

Drogen remained seated looking through the books he had found, as though no others had arrived. Content to continue working uninterrupted. As the final elf moved through the door and into the room, he rose from his seat, walking over to the table where Seraphine, Llewellyn, Tsuga, and Amanita waited.

"Is this everyone whose presence is known within the library," questioned Drogen.

"Yes, this is everyone." said Tsuga.

"How is it that so many live in the library, and the council was never made aware of your numbers," questioned Llewellyn.

"I didn't know our numbers were not being reported. If that's the case, then what was Elise doing having us all come together all these years," contemplated Amanita.

"That is something a new member of the council will be capable of finding out. Have any ideas who might be willing, and able, to fit the roll," questioned Seraphine inquisitively. Pushing herself between Amanita and Tsuga in order to give each a supportive nudge.

"We need to ask those who call the knowledge district their home who they want to see serve them on the council," said Llewellyn.

"Right. Right, I know. But they can put their names into the list if they want to. Can they not. Time isn't on our side after all."

Llewellyn nodded her head but stopped short. "You may be right, but we need to find someone the knowledge district trusts. Not those we've only just become antiquated with dear."

"Yeah, you have a point," said Seraphine. Looking at Drogen who was standing by, patiently waiting. "Do you have anything to add?"

"No, not as of yet. Although, if we want everyone to hear what's going on, I believe it best to start speaking quickly. Many of the elves look to be exhausted, and ready to collapse at any moment."

Looking around at the menagerie filling the room she couldn't help but agree with Drogen's assessment. "Let's get on with our business then." Taking herself out from between Amanita and Tsuga Seraphine moved in to address the gathered crowd.

"I am the newly appointed Queen of the Living District, Seraphine. Due to the actions taken by former members of the council, my mother Silf is no longer able to fill the role she once held. Thus, I have taken her place. With me, I have Queen Llewellyn, who oversees the farming district. We've come before you today looking for someone who will lead the Knowledge district. Elise, by her own actions, has deemed herself unfit for her seat," proclaimed Seraphine.

Expecting protest, or at least some discord regarding the removal of Elise as their Queen, Seraphine paused. Surprising, to both Seraphine and Llewellyn, no protest of any kind came from the declaration throwing them both off, as Seraphine tried to continue.

"W-We gathered you all... Here to find a new Queen for... to take Elise's place on the council," said Seraphine. Struggling to find the right words to say to the strangely silent crowd. "You really aren't going to protest her removal?"

"Why would they," said Amanita. Who walked up from behind them. "Elise was the only one aloud to leave this place. She kept us all here doing research. Many of the people here haven't been outside of the library since before Silf and Lyra left to form their own villages."

"After they left, we were all put to work finding information for Elise, and the council, non-stop. Some of us have never gone outside the libraries walls," confessed Tsuga.

"What was she making everyone research," questioned Llewellyn.

"Lately it was something to do with a being coming to Moonclave. Something we've never seen before. It was deemed so important that we needed to find all the information pertaining to Old Ones. Elise wanted every reference, and material gathered for her to look through. Everyone scattered to find every bit of information we could. Elise said it was priority one. Without it they could not ensure the safety of the Moonclave," said Amanita.

"I suppose that would have been my doing," said Seraphine with a sigh. "I told them the person coming to represent me was powerful enough to raze Moonclave to the ground, and he had killed both Ether and Uther the gods of Zephyria."

"How can such a being exist. The stories I've read say that they're far too powerful for anyone to stand against," said Tsuga with a shiver. "I hope they're not like the gods, if they are, everyone and everything could be in serious trouble."

"You have nothing to fear regarding, as the Dryads call us, the old ones. Only the gods themselves need fear us. Unless one was unwise enough to stand in the way," commented Drogen.

"Well... with the barrier... I suppose you can't lie about such things," trembled Tsuga.

"The barrier's gone, but he cannot lie regardless of the barrier being up or not. None of us can, it would seem," said Llewellyn.

"But everything we found regarding the barrier says it was put in place that deceivers could not walk with lies, or deceit, as their objective's would be lain bare through absolute truth," said Amanita. Reciting the passages from memory.

"Yes, and the deceivers have not set foot within Moonclave since," said Drogen.

"Wait, so the barrier isn't to force truth, but to keep those who would wish to deceive from walking though," questioned Llewellyn.

"Yes. Those who were in the barrier when it was raised could only speak truth, while those outside the barrier who wished to deceive could not cross its invisible threshold. Any who tried would lose the memory of where they had found the barrier. Keeping its location secret from any who would wish to deceive.," explained Drogen.

"Then we didn't understand anything. We lacked necessary context," reasoned Tsuga.

"I think we're losing the room. I see people falling asleep," cautioned Llewellyn.

"Right," said Seraphine. Turning to address the room once more. "Among those who call the knowledge district their home, who would the people of this district wish to lead them. Representing them as king or queen upon the council of Moonclave." The room went silent, until everyone simply pointed Amanita's way.

"Awe, really you guys. I appreciate you all wanting me, or are you actually pointing at Tsuga," questioned Amanita. Stepping away, some of the fingers followed her. While others remained steadfast upon Tsuga. "I thought so, it seems we have a split room."

"Then how about a competition. I came here to help them prepare for the battle they will soon face, and for information for a more personal issue as well. Why don't we see which of you is more capable of finding the information, and from there a decision may be reached," proposed Drogen.

"Ooh that sounds like fun actually. What do you say Tsuga. It will be like the games we used to play," posited Amanita teasingly.

"Th-that does sound like fun," he said with a smile. "What are the rules then?"

"Do we really need rules?"

"No... I guess we don't. Elise always put restrictions. I suppose I got used to there always being stipulations."

"True... But I don't think we need restrictions this time. What information are we searching for," she questioned excitedly.

"Before I tell you, I must make you aware, *time is of the essence*. We don't know when the first volley against Moonclave will be launched by the goblinkin, under Grock's command," cautioned Drogen. "Dissemination of this information could save Moonclave and its citizens from ruin."

"Then we'll also split the room. That way we can cover more ground than if we tried to find the information alone," said Tsuga.

"I'll give you both the same information to look for. Twill be up to the both of you to decide how to search within the library. If the other members of the council have no objections of course," Drogen quarried.

"I find nothing objectionable," stated Llewellyn.

"Neither do I. This will inevitably allow us to both find the information we need and provide the council with a member from the knowledge district. I will reiterate, as Drogen stated, time is not a luxury that is on our side."

"This information can help our people and home prepare for the fight ahead. So please, for our people and Moonclave, bring what he asks back quickly," stressed Llewellyn. Bowing her head to Tsuga and Amanita.

"The information you will be looking for is on the seraph's trance, weapons of the old ones, earthen magics, and mushin."

"We will do our best," said Amanita.

"Tis all we can ask," said Drogen.

"Everyone split between the two of us. Those following me we will use the other door," said Tsuga. Moving to take his spot at the head of the group.

"We will go through the usual door then," spoke Amanita. "And let the search begin."

Amanita led her people back from whence they came. Tsuga on the other hand, lead his group along the library's wall of books, stopping along the wall of bookshelves. Pushing against one of the bookcases. The bookcase itself swung wide open and through the hidden door the rest of the elves disappeared.

"Please take less time," pleaded Seraphine. To the empty room.

Chapter Forty-Four

"They've brought books back every few hours since they left. Aren't they close to finished? I'm so tired of waiting," complained Seraphine. Sitting down next to Drogen. Her legs folded beneath her in a meditative position.

Many books had been piled onto the desk in front of Drogen. Working his way through each tome quickly, he formed two stacks. One imperative stack, for Moonclave's success. The other, books best left for future, or advanced study, as it would do little to aid in the approaching assault.

As the hours and books continued to collect, days passed. On the second night one of the elves from Tsuga's group brought, from the library's depths, the necessary literature for achieving the seraph's trance. Although split between tome's and rolls of parchment the various mental exercises combined to describe how elves in the past had achieved the trance state for themselves.

Taking the opportunity afforded them, between deliveries of manuscripts, Drogen taught Seraphine and Llewellyn, as the combined knowledge advised. 'The trance state of Seraphal,' as it was called within the teaching's would allow the people of Moonclave to function and work with only four hours of down time within the semiconscious, but immobile state. They would no longer need sleep, and would therefore be, more effective in defending and preparing Moonclave for siege.

Looking over the magic tomes brought in by Amanita's team Drogen heard movement and a low voice behind him. "You're supposed to be practicing, not talking Seraphine," admonished Drogen as he continued.

"Do I really have to sit perfectly still to do this, its such a bother, and so boring," complained Seraphine. Finding the whole experience both daunting and tedious.

"Yes. And accomplishing this, will boost both efficiency, and viability for teaching the rest of Moonclave the seraph's trance. Tis necessary, if Moonclave is to have enough time for preparation. It will also allow for you all to learn how to use true magic, sense it too has been released."

"Furthermore, most of the goblinkin, now that magic flows through all once more, will not expect magic attacks. There will undoubtedly be many changes with regard to the goblinkin as well. For example, trolls, with magic's renewed flow, will no longer be able to walk beneath the sun. However, magic's influence will have made their regenerative ability nay impossible to deal with by normal means."

"Isn't there a way for us to learn all of this faster?"

"Yes. Tis all apart of why the both of you must learn and understand the trance state. There will be a much higher rate of success if the information is disseminated from multiple perspectives."

"I know you can use this state, but what makes it difficult for you to teach us how to use it," questioned Seraphine.

"My method of trance, as with all dragonkin differs greatly from that of any other, my trance state especially. In one way the elves, and therefore the dryads, differ is they must remain perfectly still in order to achieve the trance. I however, do not. Tis this that allows me to move in ethereal independence while my body moves and fights."

"So, elves need to learn from other elves," said Seraphine. Letting out a long sigh in resignation.

"Some of the elves already know but have lost the knowledge. Likely as a result of the memory spell my kin invoked before retreating to Lundwurm Tul. Still, those who have experienced the state will teach those who have yet to. Take Llewellyn for example, she was able to go into the trance, with very little instruction."

"Then why can't she teach everyone else, including me how to do it," questioned Seraphine hopefully.

"Because, she does not know how it was originally achieved, only that she can achieve it as the patterns necessary have already formed in her mind. A clear path forward, for those lacking in these patterns is essential for those who have never achieved it. Each person's method will likely differ in multiple ways. Having multiple points of reference will prove more effective."

"Fine, fine, I'll do it. I don't really understand any of it though," said Seraphine in a huff. Finally settling down into a comfortable meditative position.

Drogen sighed, understanding her frustration. Peeling his eyes away from the tome 'wind slash and all its uses' he looked at Seraphine. "If you continue to have trouble, speak with Llewellyn. Bouncing questions off each other may improve both of your understanding. Giving each of you better insight. And thus, better insight for the whole of Moonclave."

Llewellyn sat immobile along the library wall where she'd been for only a couple of hours. Seraphine looked at her shallow breathing form trying to decipher what allowed her counterpart to so effortlessly do nothing. Especially when her mind would not allow her the same experience.

How can she sit without doing anything? Is her mind blank, or is it the opposite? Would it be bad to wake her from the trance? Should I wait until she's ready to awaken herself... Time feels as though its... pushing in around me. How am I supposed to save everyone? I can't keep everyone safe. I couldn't even save my own mother. How can I be a queen? I am not worthy. I can't fill my mother's seat. I am unworthy. I am nothing. I am worth...

"Seraphine," called Drogen wrapping his arms around her back as anxiety ran rampant through her body and mind casting her flesh into a cold sweat. Her heart beat thundering in her ears as she subconsciously moved to spread herself out across the floor. Though her mind continued to real, feeling Drogen's embrace, her heart beat began to decrease.

"Breath Seraphine. Take a deep breath in through your nose, and at the end of your breath, pull in once more. Then out through your mouth."

After a few minutes of her focus Drogen began to speak, but in a subdued and soft cadence. Lulling her to rest. "Focus your ears, and mind upon my voice. Allow the sensations. The fears. The anxieties. All of them *fall* away. As the world itself *slips* and *falls* away," he said. Caressing her hair to impart comfort.

Drogen kept his arms wrapped around Seraphine until her breathing returned to normal. Turning her around in his arms Drogen sat down taking Seraphine with him to the ground laying her head upon his lap.

Seraphine slept upon his lap for some time before she returned to the waking world her heart and mind once more under her control. Although even after her rest she felt both physically and mentally drained.

"If you like. There is another method. I have never attempted such a connection before. However, I do believe it to be possible. In the past, the elves learned the seraph's trance, not from the dragons, but from the angelo's. There method of giving information differed greatly from most others. They could spread knowledge through physical connection."

"Then how can you do it," questioned Seraphine.

"I believe this ability was originally of my kin, and shared with the angelo. We both shared a *deep* connection with magic itself. My method and ability's within the trance state will not work for you. However, you may find some information within that will be of aid."

"No, I'll wait for Llewellyn you said it yourself; we elves have to figure this out on our own. I can figure this out, I'm just being impatient is all."

"What just happened and how you came out of it, remember it. I would suffer great pain to learn your heart had given out, whilst I could not aid in calming your mind dear Seraphine. I would also hope the breathing technique might encourage your trance state."

"Okay, I'll sit here next to Llewellyn as well, maybe some of her ability will come to me through proximity," said Seraphine. Sharing a hopeful yet muted smile.

Another couple of hours passed without a word spoken. Instead of falling into the trance state, she fell asleep. The stress of her anxiety's rise and fall continuing to plague her even after much time had passed.

Llewellyn rose from the ground looking sadly to Seraphine, who she knew, continued to struggle. "The poor dear has had so much placed upon her shoulders. Do you know if she has grieved her mother, or started to come to terms with everything else that's happened?"

"No. I don't believe she's afforded herself the chance. I hoped you might be able to help her. Keeping all of those emotions in could prove debilitating when the time comes for action. The trance state will prove a great help to her in that regard as well. Still, she may need someone to temper her mind and heart against the raging rivers of thought set to overwhelm. Until she is capable of doing so herself, of course," said Drogen. Returning to the books on the table in front of him.

"While she rests is there anything I can help you research dear?"

"Yes, this stack of books pertains to using true magic we are going to need multiple people who can understand its workings as well. I hope that at least one of the people within these walls has studied magic and how to use it," he said. Pointing to a large stack of tomes and parchments. "The elves of the past were most adept with earth, water, and wind type magics. Research and understanding of these will go far to improve the livability of the elves and dryads against this and possible future invasions."

"Then you wish for me to learn magic from having absolutely no knowledge on the subject much like you're doing with Seraphine and the trance state," realized Llewellyn.

"Multiple perspectives and methods lead to better and more complete understanding," he said with a nod.

"When do you expect the others to return so we can determine their understanding?"

"I expect they will be back soon. They've gathered a lot of information already. More than I thought they would find at least. Even if this library is larger than it looks. Tis still finite in size."

"What information are we waiting to receive."

"Information on the old ones, and their weapons. I don't know if this library, or any library for that matter, would have that information. I wish I could speak with one of my kin. Maybe they could shed some light on recent experiences."

"I hope they can find something that helps you. You've been here for a very short time, but have changed the elves and Moonclave for the better."

"Whether my intervention here is good or not has yet to be determined. That distinction can only be known in the future, and we cannot know what the future might hold for any of us," said Drogen.

"What about the other subject you were looking into. Is that something we'll be learning as well," questioned Llewellyn. Taking a seat next to Drogen, that she could thumb through the tomes of magic he wished for her to read.

"Some among the elves and dryads may go down such a path. However, most will not be able to experience mushin for a very long time, if ever. No, I am researching mushin that I may better understand what I am capable of doing when pure instinct is allowed to take over without thoughts weight upon action."

They worked in silence for a time. The sound of Seraphine's restful breathing the only indication of life outside the continuous flipping of paper. Llewellyn flipped through the pages earnestly taking in every word and practicing as she went along. The concepts and abilities within the book coming almost as naturally to her as breathing.

"I cannot explain the feeling of using magic, even though this is my first time doing it... It feels as though it is not."

"That is because magic, like breathing, has always been apart of you. Although that part had been stripped to its minimum. Magic has always been, and forever will be apart of us all. True magic, is at its root, the fulfillment of will. Should you want it you need only allow yourself to obtain it, though you must possess the concentration and knowledge to do so. This is both the benefit, and the detriment of magic."

"You said that we elves are most attuned to earth and water magics. What are the dragons attuned to?"

"My kin are attuned to all magics of Dranier, as though they are simply an extension of our hands. The same as the weapons made of our scales."

"Then you would be able to save us from any calamity the goblinkin might bring without all of the studying."

"Perhaps. I could do just that. Save the elves and the forest from calamity at Grock's hands."

"If that's a possibility then what are we doing wasting time here instead of preparing with the others," questioned Llewellyn. Placing the book of magic down on the table in order to look at Drogen.

"I may be enough to stop Grock's conquest against the Moonclave. However, what happens when the next attacker comes knocking upon your door, and I'm not here. The knowledge locked in this library is only as good as those who are willing to learn and understand it. The knowledge that you are taking in now will help the elves and the forest survive against not just this attack, but every attack that may come in the future. With or without my or anothers intervention."

"So, you are giving us knowledge for today and tomorrow," reasoned Llewellyn.

"The best survivors are not the ones who look to the present or next day, but those who look far into the future at a goal they strive to make reality."

"How can one so young be so wise."

"Maybe it has something to do with being raised by those who've lived for untold centuries. It could be that my soul differs in some way from others. I do not know," said Drogen. Shaking his head. "However, what I do know for certain is, decisions made in haste or reaction are doomed from the start."

Llewellyn nodded her head in acknowledgment of Drogen's words picking the book of magics back up and returning to her diligent study of the text. "Some of this information is going to take far longer than a few hours or days for anyone to figure out. What does it mean that water is three parts formed into one for example..."

"Once you understand the truth of everything with regard to the bonds shared between them and what makes them one you will understand the depths of what true magic is capable of. Understanding the parts that make up the whole, will garner deeper, more precise control over that which magic manipulates and bend."

"Are you saying that someone could take materials they know the composition of and form them into whatever shape they wished with magics help. But they would need to understand their composition completely to do so."

"Yes, and if one knows the base of the things around them, then they can extract, or manipulate them at will. True magic is something that one may use without thought, but the more thought and concentration brought to the mind while manipulating those pieces will garner for the manipulator a better, and more refined result."

"C-can you show me an example of what you mean."

With a click of his hand a ball of fire formed in his palm. "For fire you need three things, air, fuel, and ignition. Flowing more air through will boost the flame, where too much will smother it completely. Now what do you think the fuel for this fire is, as it sits in my hand," questioned Drogen.

"I-I don't know."

"For this water is the fuel, or more precisely a piece of the base elements of water is the fuel. The problem is that should too much of the element be broken apart at once catastrophe would ensue. This is the inherent danger present to magic, and a risk that you and all who use magic must understand. Without knowledge and concentration working in concert, life is forfeit." said Drogen. Smothering by adding more air to the flame snuffing it out completely.

"We will need to make clear the importance knowledge will have for those who wish to learn and use magic. I doubt anyone realizes the inherent danger."

"There's danger present in all things. A sword is a danger to its enemies and its wielder, magic is no different. Respect must be given to both, or ruin is sure to follow. Tis important for you both to remember," commented Drogen. Knowing Seraphine had finally awoken from her slumber, during his explanation.

"Nothing really gets past you does it," questioned Llewellyn. Walking quickly to Seraphine's side. Lending a hand in getting her back to her feet.

"Not if I can help it," said Drogen with a smile. "Hmm, it seems your rest ended at the perfect time. The others have finally returned."

Both the hidden and the regular door flew open as though they'd been waiting for Drogen's announcement before descending once more into the main library. Tsuga and Amanita leading the charge.

"You're finally back," rose Seraphine excitedly. Jumping up from where she'd been sleeping and falling slightly into Llewellyn's arms. "Any luck finding other books?"

"Unfortunately, no. We couldn't locate any books regarding the old ones and their weapons within the library. It was difficult finding anything on the old ones in the first place," said Amanita.

"Elise would have been very disappointed and would have no doubt punished..." started Tsuga. As Drogen held up his hand bidding him to stop.

"I thought finding such information here would be a long shot, but I still hoped there would be some insight as to what I'm experiencing. Knowledge of such things will simply have to come with time," said Drogen with a shrug.

"The rest of the information that you were able to find will prove beneficial to the whole of Moonclave and for that the council thanks every one of you," said Llewellyn.

"To that end there's something everyone here needs to know. We do not have long before Moonclave will be under siege by the god Grock's forces."

"H-How long do we have," questioned Tsuga fearfully.

"We don't know, yet. Word has yet to arrive from commander Phaylor who has dispatched scouts. I am certain we will hear word from them soon. Still, we need to prepare against the attack as best we can in the time we have remaining," announced Llewellyn.

"That also involves helping everyone within the Moonclave prepare as well. The books that you retrieved from the library will help the council do just that. How many of you can use the Seraph's trance," questioned Seraphine.

Three-quarters of the over fifty present, raised their hands. "Well, it was much faster to work and more efficient to do so. Elise could send any of us off into the depth at any point in time," explained Tsuga.

"We can also use the state for better comprehension and retention of information," stated Amanita.

"Good, your knowledge on the subject will be a welcome boon for those without understanding or experience," said Drogen. Nodding to Seraphine. "And how many of you have, at least a rudimentary understanding of magic?"

Far fewer raised their hands, but Tsuga and Amanita were quick to do so. Doing so enthusiastically.

"Splendid," commented Llewellyn. "I'm starting to understand magic, but most of the concepts simply go over my head if I'm being honest. Even with a display of how magic works, from Drogen, I have a hard time grasping it."

"Then we have many differing perspectives for both the trance state and use of true magic, which is exactly what we need." said Drogen. "I suppose the only remaining question left becomes who will be the one to lead the knowledge district as king or queen upon the council."

"Right..." mused Seraphine aloud. "Which of you brought back the most books then," she questioned. Looking at the stacks of books on the desk where Drogen remained seated.

"They both returned with the same number of tomes and parchments, by my calculation. The contents of which will prove beneficial both now, and into the distant future for the elves, dryads, and Moonclave as a whole."

"Hmm... That doesn't really help us in deciding which one of you is most fit to lead in the council does it," said Llewellyn.

"Are there any other criteria that might help," questioned Seraphine.

"Actually," said Tsuga. Stepping up. "I don't think I have what it takes to sit on the council... I don't... I mean."

"That is precisely why you must take the seat Tsuga," said Amanita.

"No that's why you have to take the seat," burst Tsuga. "I'm not cut out to lead, but you are. I am much better here in the library finding information, you know that."

"On that...I cannot disagree, then why don't we do it together," questioned Amanita.

"Is that even possible?"

"Well, yes if you had been joined by a member of the council, it would be possible," said Llewellyn.

"It seems that we're in luck then," commented Amanita. "Tsuga and I were bound before a member of the council many years ago. Our binding was overseen by two members of the council. The ritual was performed in front of our forest mothers. Does that work?"

"Wait you two are bound," questioned Seraphine. Skeptically looking at both Amanita and Tsuga before turning to Llewellyn. "Well then... I have no objections. What about you?"

"No-No objections dear."

"With that decided we should bring everyone to the council chamber and announce the appointment. We also need to figure out how to most effectively teach everyone what they need to learn without any further delay," said Seraphine.

"Actually, that part will prove to be quite easy, this city was built in such a way that disseminating information may be the easiest part of this whole ordeal," said Drogen.

"I take it you have a plan then dear," questioned Llewellyn.

"I do. The people of Moonclave need only place their hands upon the towers used to form their home. Those who touch the tower will have access to the information of all who have the necessary knowledge through me," said Drogen.

"Since we have everything figured out, we need to go to the council and consult with the others. Tsuga and Amanita will come with us for introduction, and to take their seats beside us. Hopefully everyone we selected before coming will quickly gather as well," said Seraphine.

"We'll figure that all out once we go and see," said Amanita joyously.

"I hope we'll be of help to Moonclave...I hope I can be helpful in some way. To everyone," said Tsuga under his breath.

"Hold your head up high Tsuga. You've already contributed greatly to the knowledge district, so much so that half of those within its walls chose to follow you, and not just me. The same will be true outside the library. Just you wait and see," said Amanita. Embracing Tsuga and kissing him on the lips. "One of these days you'll see in yourself what I've always seen in you. I just know it."

"Let's go everyone," called Tsuga. Blood rushing to his face, as he fought against the passion bubbling up inside for his Amanita. "You always know exactly what to say in order to get my blood boiling," whispered Tsuga into her ear. A statement lost on everyone except Drogen. Who couldn't help but smile at the timid elf's sultry declaration.

Chapter Forty-Five

The entirety of the knowledge district left the confines of library, following their appointed councilors in lockstep, to the central tower of Moonclave. Other elves and even dryads turned to witness the group's passing. Upon reaching the outer portion of the tower, Tsuga and Amanita split the districts ranks around the building. Allowing their once secluded people a chance to mingle with others of their race.

Drogen opened the council chambers door allowing everyone to pass before moving in himself. Looking around the room, he noticed quickly the absence of the councils other members. "Before the other members of the council are called. I believe it prudent to have those from the knowledge district an opportunity to learn of their predecessors exploits."

"That would be a great help. We don't know much about the rest of Moonclave, or what Elise and the others were trying to accomplish," commented Amanita.

"Well then let us go over all the sorted details. There is much about our current situation... And much I would rather not speak of at the moment," said Seraphine. Her eyes downcast toward the polished crescent table.

"Actually. That will not be necessary. Not here at least. Those outside need only place their hands upon the tower and I'll relay it all directly. I should however warn this will be the first time I've done such an exercise. I intend for this to be a test for relaying information across the breadth of Moonclave."

"Wait. You plan to teach everyone in Moonclave the Seraph trance and magic all at once," she questioned. Her mouth, as well as Llewellyn's, fully agape having experienced the monumental strain of the dais.

"Precisely. Doing so will allow for a more timely accomplishment of the trance and magic without having to garner the knowledge for yourselves. With this Moonclave will have the knowledge to defend itself from outside forces. I will be the intermediary for the transfer this time. However, those on the council will need to familiarize themselves with the full extent of what these chambers are capable of."

"The power the dais possesses is... immense, I don't know that any one member of the council will be capable," said Llewellyn. Growing concerned.

"Then, do not leave it as a single king or queen's burden. You will find its power far easier to manage by combining your efforts," said Drogen.

"Then having everyone experience the dais will prove not just a benefit, but may also prove invaluable in the future," said Seraphine.

"If you believe it wise dear, may we feel your method of using the dais? Is such a request even possible," questioned Llewellyn.

"Tis possible, and you may," he said with a nod. Walking over to the dais Drogen stepped up once more before its fire lit surface. Holding his hand out to the group he beckoned them forward.

Llewellyn and Seraphine grabbed hold of Drogen's hand and arm without hesitation. Amanita and Tsuga, although reluctant at first, did the same taking hold of his other hand and forearm. Closing his eyes in concentration, Drogen and the others, felt everything through the thirteen towers of Moonclave. He allowed them to adjust for a few moments as the overwhelming sensation coursed through their bodies before proceeding.

Drogen's voice spoke both outside and inside their minds as he projected it outward. His voice radiating from each of the towers. *"Those who wish to know what transpired within these council chambers, place your hands upon the walls of each tower. Through this connection you will know everything the council saw itself fit to do, through the eyes of those who bore witness."*

Each hand placed upon the towers throughout Moonclave became another pull from the dais upon Drogen and those with their hands upon him. The sensation, foreign yet not entirely unpleasant, brought their minds and memories together. Drogen let the knowledge and memory of what happened, starting with his entrance to the council chambers, flow into and throughout the minds of their connected conscious.

Others, through the connection, broadcast both their feelings and knowledge of the events as they unfolded within their minds. As Manzine began his attack within the memory Drogen spoke into Seraphine's mind alone. *"Do you wish to show them your reunion?"*

"No, but they do need to see what the council did. Everything else I wish to keep to myself," said Seraphine. As though she were having a normal conversation with Drogen. Except within her mind.

Acquiescing to her request Drogen showed everyone the result of the council's actions, against Silf. With the memories conclusion everything faded away. The combined conscious returning to individual personalities with Drogen's slow meticulous dispersion of power back into the dais itself.

Everyone who'd been holding Drogen released themselves, completely exhausted by the experience, and mental focus. "I... We," said Seraphine. Looked at everyone else with heavily lidded eyes. "Will need to rest for a while before doing anything like that again."

"Agreed," proclaimed the others. Grabbing hold of each other so they didn't collapse from the effort walking would undoubtedly be.

"While you rest, I will call the other members of the council for you. Are there any others you wish to invite," questioned Drogen.

"How are you not exhausted like the rest of us," questioned Tsuga with heavy eyes and labored breath.

"This place was built with my kin in mind. Tis not surprising that others would find such things more difficult than I," said Drogen.

"We'll leave calling the rest of the council to you then dear," said Llewellyn. As they all fell into their seats.

"Call for Phaylor, Phatropa, and Transil as well. They're the others we discussed," said Seraphine.

"I will do just that; are there any others you wish to come as well? Asche, Alya, Rumble, or Tumble," suggested Drogen.

"That may be prudent as well," contemplated Seraphine. Scratching her head as she thought.

"If they wish to join, they can. However, this has more to do with placing people on the council than passing on information at this time. So they may come at their own pace," suggested Llewellyn.

"As you wish." Drogen allowed himself to be swept away by the radiating power of the dais. He focused his mind on those heartbeats he knew. Harp, Silf, and Leif were the first to come to mind, but he dismissed the sensation of their heartbeat without a second thought. Thinking back to his time in Moongrove Drogen recalled each heartbeat, narrowing it down as he went. Within a matter of a few moments, he'd located Transil, Shylva, and Bailfar, and dozens of others he had been fortunate enough to meet in Moongrove.

"Transil, the council requests your presence," announced Drogen into Transil's mind.

Transil's heart rate jumped at the mental intrusion. Forcing him to take a calming breath before replying. "What does the council want with me?"

"They elect you to the council for the crafter's district," stated Drogen.

"No thank you, I love my freedom. The council will be nothing but a lead weight around my neck. Ask someone, anyone else to take on the roll. It will not be me," stated Transil. Leaving no room for doubt.

"Very well. I will relay your declaration to the council," stated Drogen. Allowing for a few extra moments, in case the musically inclined elf changed his mind. Before ultimately cutting off the connection.

He moved quickly through each person the council wished to contact leaving Phaylor for last. Stretching out beyond the main portion of Moonclave to the guard district he pushed his consciousness as far out as possible. Still, he could not feel Phaylor's heartbeat among those stationed near or around the crescent moon shaped area the towers allowed his consciousness to cover.

"Phaylor is outside of the towers reach. I can contact those within range for an update."

"Please do dear."

Drogen broadcast to those within range of the three defense towers. "Second in command of the defensive district. Place your hand upon the tower that the council may converse with you."

While they waited for Phaylor's second to follow the direction, Gilvail, Keltus, and Phatropa arrived together. As everyone took their seats a hand was placed upon the tower, connecting through Drogen. to council.

"This is the second in command," said an elf. Clearly unsettled by the new sensation.

"Have you received word from the scouts or Phaylor," questioned Llewellyn.

"Yes, we received word from the forward scouts a few days ago. They're set to return today, with a prisoner in tow. The letter I received was brief, but commander Phaylor mentioned one of the goblinkin they found surrendered without a fight. Unfortunately, that is all the information we have at the moment."

"They surrendered without a fight? Why would they do that," questioned Keltus aloud.

"When your commander returns have him bring the prisoner here personally," ordered Seraphine.

"It will be done my queen. Is there anything else the council needs," posited the elf.

"Yes dear. All of your people need to have clear access to the towers. We'll be using them to give information needed to fend off whatever awaits us. Touching the towers will be essential in our preparations moving forward," stated Llewellyn.

"I was afraid you would say that. Luckily commander Phaylor ordered the towers cleared upon hearing the council during the trial. We stand ready."

"Are you in need of any supplies," questioned Keltus.

"Not at this time."

"Then we leave the defense district in your capable hands," stated Gilvail.

Drogen cut the connection as Phaylor's second removed his hand from the tower. Bringing himself back to the council chambers and the new arrivals.

"When Phaylor returns we'll offer him the position. Until then, we have others who have a decision to make for themselves," said Gilvail. Looking around at the new faces within the chamber. "I take it Transil will not be joining us then?"

"He was emphatically opposed to his appointment. Stating the council would be a lead weight around his neck," affirmed Drogen.

"Unfortunately, he's always been like that," said Gilvail with a sigh. "Doesn't want a single thing to tie him down so he can go anywhere and do anything he wants whenever he wants. I thought a seat on the council might do him some good. But alas, I cannot force him to take the seat."

"We have one I nominated for the council here. Perhaps she will be willing to take on the roll Transil is not," commented Seraphine.

"I hope so," stated Llewellyn.

"Everyone please take a seat. That we may discuss appointments," said Keltus. Taking her seat at the right crescent table. "If the three of you would kindly stand before the dais that we may speak to the reason you're here."

Amanita, Phatropa, and Tsuga stepped in front of the crescent table where the four council members sat standing before the fire lit dais and Drogen. Phatropa, unsure of herself, looked around nervously, but retained her signature smile throughout.

"Amanita and Tsuga, will you take seats upon the council, For the knowledge district," questioned Seraphine.

"Only those who are bound may serve upon the council together," stated Gilvail in objection.

"We were bound before both Queen Silf and Queen Lyra. We stood in the forest beneath our mothers vines as the ritual suggest be done," stated Amanita.

"It happened just prior to Queen Silf and Lyra leaving to form Moongrove and Sun Meadow," affirmed Tsuga.

"Then I withdraw my objection," said Gilvail with a nod.

"D-D-Don't you need more proof," questioned Tsuga.

"You know what happened within this chamber. The truth of us and our mothers, do you not."

"Why... Yes... Oh. You're quite right. We are unable to lie. Sorry it seems I forgot," said Tsuga. Shirking back at his unintended mistake.

"No need to worry dear. Tis good that you forgot such detail. It proves without doubt, you hold no room for dishonesty or deception. Just what this council needs moving forward," said Llewellyn.

"I agree," said Gilvail with a nod. "Now, let us move onto the elven maiden who Seraphine and Llewellyn would have lead the crafters district," he said. Moving his attention, and the attention of the others to the increasingly nervous Phatropa. "You're Aurix's daughter are you not?"

"Why yes King Gilvail," she stated with a smile. "Did he instruct and train you?"

Phatropa tensed up noticeably as her mind wandered for a moment taking a deep steadying breath. "Yes, he did," said Phatropa. A smile on her face that none upon the council had ever seen. A smile that made the rest of them slightly nervous.

"That smile is all I needed to see. I suppose you're his child after all," said Gilvail. Showing a wicked grin of his own.

"Yes, yes I am," she stated proudly.

Slightly disturbed by the strange sight unfolding in front of her, and everyone else in the chamber, Seraphine had to clear her throat before feeling comfortable enough to speak. "Hmm, then I take it there will be no further... disagreement?"

The silence present after the question spoke clearly to everyone in the room. "Good then we need only ask the question. Will the three of you take your place upon the council of Moonclave and becoming the Kings and Queens overseeing your districts within," questioned Llewellyn.

"We do," spoke Amanita and Tsuga confidently.

Once more all eyes turned to Phatropa. "I have one question. Can I still work in my father's inn? When the councils duties do not interfere of course."

"Why yes dear. You may do as you please, but the council's duties and our duty to Moonclave must take priority over all else. We must lead our people by example of course," proclaimed Llewellyn.

Phatropa contemplated for a few moments clearly weighing everything out in her mind before saying yes or no. "I'm sure my father will understand, and be able to find someone to work in my place. When my duties overlap. Yes. I will do everything I can to help Moonclave, and those within the crafter's district."

"All in favor of the three who stand here raise your hands," said Llewellyn. And all upon the council did so.

"With the members of the council in unanimous support. And with the questioned in favor of their own appointment, it will be so. Take your seats upon the council of Moonclave," stated Seraphine. With her declaration the three newest members of the council took their seats.

"I wish I would have received my seat at the same time as these three. They didn't even make a big deal of my joining at all," complained Keltus. "Oh well, there are far more pressing matters to attend to," she continued with a sigh.

"Don't worry too much about that Keltus. Once we have time, after we defend Moonclave, a formal party will be held for the newest members of Moonclave's council. This is little more than a formality," consoled Gilvail.

"That is something we should all look forward to dear," said Llewellyn. Showing a sympathetic smile.

"Yay, I love parties," stated Tsuga. Garnering laughter from everyone else. Except for Drogen whose expression turned quite dower. An expression he hid behind the flaming dais.

"Now the only one left to appoint is Phaylor, upon his return. What was his seconds name, he'll most likely be the one filling Phaylor's soon to be vacant position," questioned Gilvail.

The room grew silent as none of them had even thought to ask the elf's name.

"His name is Quercus," came Phaylor's voice into the council chamber through the dais.

"Thank you for the information Commander. I take it Quercus told you of the council's request then," questioned Gilvail.

"Yes. I had planned to bring the prisoner to the council as quickly as possible. However, something he stated should be known before I make the journey. The orc has stated he left his leader a fortnight ago, or as he put it, fourteen cycles. However, that is not the important part.

The one who sent him to be captured made him remember a saying. First boom twenty-eight. Which he keep reciting in *very* rough elvish."

"If what he says is correct, we have at most two weeks left before the goblinkin attack either Moonclave or Aragorth," said Gilvail. The blood drained from his face.

"Th-that's barely any time at all," stammered Keltus in shock. "I hope for all our sake, that your method works. If not, we stand little chance against invasion. Even with all the warriors we have, we will no doubt be outnumbered and overrun by goblinkin." looking up through the flaming dais to the one being she knew could pull off the impossible.

Chapter Forty-Six

"I can start the dissemination process at any time. However, everyone within Moongrove needs to have uninterrupted physical contact with the towers. Should they release themselves from the tower they will lose out on the proceeding information."

"The problem then becomes time and stamina," concluded Llewellyn.

"What are you talking about," questioned Gilvail and Keltus together. Having arrived at the tail end of their discussion.

"Drogen, with the knowledge districts help, found information necessary for our continued survival. He can give that information to everyone at once through the towers. Ensuring we are prepared for invasion."

"I don't know how something like that's even possible," remarked Amanita. Still unsure of the whole process. Even after experiencing a part of the dais's power herself.

"So are we just waiting for Phaylor to arrive with his prisoner," questioned Keltus.

"We're waiting for Asche, Alya, Rumble, and Tumble to arrive as well," announced Seraphine.

"Why did you call for them," questioned Gilvail.

"Alya and Asche have been helping to clear the aqueducts outside of Moonclave. The water ways are important for insuring we do not run out of resources should the siege last for any length of time. The council needs to know how the clearing is going, and if more help is needed," said Keltus.

"As for the dwarves, that is another matter entirely. We've sent word to Aragorth many times over the weeks. We have not received word back. Unless Phaylor received a hawk during his scouting mission, we have no way of knowing what the status of the dwarves," explained Llewellyn.

"Are you hoping this, Rumble and Tumble, will go to Aragorth? Is this only to make sure they've received word of the coming attack," questioned Amanita speculatively.

"Yes, but that is far from the only reason we have to worry."

"We know Grock has split his force from the book Drogen brought... The dwarves are likely the only thing standing between Moonclave and the bulk of Grock's forces," surmised Keltus. Grasping the actual importance of the citadels fate.

"While we wait for Phaylor to arrive the newest members of the council must experience the Dias by themselves. It is important you all understand its power and depth, without Drogen's help and guidance," stated Llewellyn.

"It didn't seem that difficult. Sure, it was mentally exhausting, but I don't see how it differs from using magic in any way," said Amanita. Rising confidently from her chair and wandering to the dais.

Drogen dropped down from his perch taking only a single step to the side in order to allow Amanita passage before him. Grabbing hold of the dais she pulled her eyes to the floating draconic flame.

"Close your eyes Amanita. Allow yourself to feel Moonclave as you've never experienced it before," stated Drogen. As Amanita closed her eyes her mind became one with the thirteen towers.

"She is a confident one for sure, but I dare say this will prove a humbling experience, as it was for the rest of us," said Llewellyn. Looking to Amanita with concern.

"Is it truly that difficult," questioned Tsuga. Rubbing his hands together anxiously.

"We'll find out for ourselves soon enough," stated Phatropa. Placing her hand supportively on the shoulder of her timid counterpart. "While Amanita is having her experience, I did have a question. What is this... trance state you're referring to?"

"In short, tis a mental exercise created in the original city of Seraphal by a race known as the Angelo's. With it the elves will no longer need to sleep. Instead, with meditative practice, you simply need to remain stationary a few hours a day," edified Drogen. More to the entire council than just Phatropa.

"Oh... Since I already have this ability, can I help those who have yet to do it," she questioned. Clear excitement in her voice at the prospect.

"Wait. How do you know how to do it when you didn't know its name? We're the same age, and everyone else lost the knowledge when the old ones left. At least that's Drogen's theory. I can't sit still long enough. That or I fall asleep," complained Seraphine.

"Actually, I figured it out on my own. I actually taught my father to do it. He was far faster at figuring it out than I was. Your theory may explain why," contemplated Phatropa. Nodding her head.

"Your knowledge will prove to be invaluable. I doubted there would be anyone who retained the experience. Having achieved it on your own from start to finish will no doubt allow most, if not all, of the elves to learn the seraph's trance," complimented Drogen with a nod of his own. "Your method's will impart the missing elements for Seraphine as well. The more who know and have experienced the use of both the trance, and magic, the better off Moonclave will be."

"Amanita, can you tell how far out Phaylor is from arriving," questioned Keltus.

As if the question had pushed her over the edge Amanita cut her connection with the dais stepping down quickly shaking her her head. "My head feels like its on fire," she stated. Rubbing her eyes. "And I'm exhausted beyond belief. I couldn't get any deeper than a single district, and that in itself took all my concentration to achieve."

"Tsuga or Phatropa who will take to the dais next," questioned Gilvail.

"I will, stated Phatropa rising from her seat. Everyone else has experienced this in some capacity whether it was through Drogen or by themselves except me," said Phatropa. Defending her position on the matter.

"You don't need to defend your position to me," said the apprehensive and fidgety Tsuga. "I am more than happy to go up after everyone else is done, or not at all."

Phatropa nodded her head to the rest of the council as she walked over to the dais, taking her place upon it. Focusing her eyes upon the flame before her, she exhaled a long deep breath. The power of the dais a coursing torrent through her body and mind.

"Once you and Phaylor experience the tower's power, and the magic that it holds, we'll need to work in pairs or larger," said Llewellyn.

"Why would we need to do that," questioned Tsuga and Keltus. Drawing everyone, who remained focused on Phatropa, to the conversation.

"Drogen said we may have an easier time focusing if we do so together," stated Llewellyn.

"We should leave this for another time. We need to focus on getting the information we have to our people. Using the dais, as of now, is beyond our abilities," said Gilvail.

"Phatropa if you would tell us how far Phaylor is from this council's chambers," questioned Seraphine.

Phatropa struggled against the mental focus and strain trying desperately to fight her way to the information she was being asked to retrieve, resulting in a loss of control both mentally and physically as she crumbled.

Drogen reached out grabbing Phatropa hearing the change in her heartbeat as her mind blacked out from the mental strain.

"I think it best not to push yourselves when working individually. It may cause those around you further issue if they cannot contact their council member. Having any leader incapacitated, during a siege, could prove detrimental," cautioned Drogen. Shaking his head.

"Is she going to be alright," exclaimed Keltus and Amanita. Quickly coming to Phatropa's aid.

"Phatropa will be fine, she only needs rest. She'll regain consciousness soon, and with the trance she'll recover quickly."

"Can you tell us how far away Phaylor is, before Tsuga takes to the Dais" questioned Amanita. Not wanting her other half to push himself unnecessarily.

Drogen placed his hand on the dais feeling its connection flow through him and in a matter of moments found Phaylor and the prisoner in his charge. *So, she sent Grom to relay the information,* thought Drogen.

"Phaylor will arrive within the hour. Tsuga should be done with his time upon the Dais just prior to his arrival."

"He got that without even standing on the dais. What makes him so different compared to everyone else. I don't see any physical differences," questioned Tsuga.

"The surface of a person is only a small part of what makes a person dear," cautioned Llewellyn.

"He's a Dragon, that's reason enough for his abilities to outshine our own," said Keltus.

"I assure you he's lacking in other aspects, like not understanding currency at all," said Seraphine. Winking to Drogen, placing Phatropa in her seat with Amanita and Keltus's assistance.

"What use is currency when the materials necessary are so easily found or made," commented Drogen with a shrug.

"I'd hate to know what an old one considers to be hard. Especially if locating precious metals is considered simple," remarked Gilvail.

"As would I," nodded Amanita. "Alright Tsuga your turn. And make it quick. It sounds like once this Phaylor person gets here, things will become extra interesting. Far more interesting than the library has ever been," she said giddily.

Tsuga stepped up to the Dais cautiously. Remembering the feeling of its power flowing through him previously. With an audible gulp he took his place.

Asche, who held aloft the door for Alya, Rumble, and Tumble made their way into the chamber. The dwarves being their typically boisterous selves, sauntering in with glee filled expressions on their ash laden faces.

"It be good ta swing a ammer again after so long. Thought me muscles be gone from da lack," stated Rumble. Visibly flexing his arms.

"Swing da hammer watch em fall, beat the steel into a ball, smooth the balls ta throw no catch. Toss da ball watchem retch," sang and danced Tsuga excitedly.

"You know how they are. Get them singing and you just can't help but play along," said Alya. Smiling and giggling as Tumble took her hand and began dancing in a circle with her to his own made-up beat. Tumble's antics even bringing a slight grin to Gilvail's face. Though he hid it quickly.

"Now, what be so important tha me brudder and me are needen ta ear sky lizard," questioned Rumble.

"Sky lizard is that what the dwarves call the old ones, or Dragon's" questioned Amanita. "That reminds me. I really want to see what an old one actually looks like," she stated. Looking to Drogen with an expectant gleam in her eyes.

"Amanita, maybe Drogen doesn't want everyone in Moonclave to see his true form," admonished Gilvail. His eyes betraying the truth of his curiosity despite the implication of his statement.

"Well, why not. Many other members of this council have seen his other form. Do not act as though you are above the same curiosity," countered Amanita. "How many people here have seen an old one's true form... That we remember, or know of?"

"Many in Moongrove witnessed him change... Also, everyone who just came in has seen it as well," stated Seraphine. A mirthful grin and giggle in satisfaction. Having been among the first to witness his true form.

"My sister and I actually rode on his back to get here," stated Keltus. Joining in the jovial exchange at Drogen's expense.

Ache, remembering the feeling of their swift flight over the forest, nearly retched as if she were once more experiencing the sensation.

"Now that is a story I would very much like to hear. Especially with his arrival happening a full day after your own," said Phaylor. Pulling upon Grom's bindings. Leading the orc into the council chamber.

Tsuga, hearing Phaylor's commanding voice, broke his connection. Taking a moment to regain his bearings, he stumbled upon weary legs back to his council seat to rest beside the waiting Amanita.

"Tis good to see you again Phaylor," spoke Drogen.

"Your definition of causing problems and mine seem to be very different," admonished Phaylor. Pointing his finger in jesting accusation toward Drogen

"I told you. I wouldn't do anything. Unless first something was done to me. I only obeyed the rules we both set forth upon our meeting," said Drogen with a cheshire grin.

Phaylor couldn't help but chuckle at the absurdity of it all. Shaking his head the entire time. "So you did."

Turning his attention to the captured orc Drogen bowed. "Tis good to see you as well Grom. Did Golga send you here with information not present within her book," questioned Drogen. Drawing sidelong glances from those around him.

"When you learn speak gob," questioned Grom with a tilt of his head. "Only winged friend speak gob," he said. Scratching his head before shrugging it off as nothing to dwell on.

"I didn't realize I could honestly," said Drogen confused. *When did this start. I couldn't understand the goblinkin the entirety of my time among them,* he thought, going back over his memories. Confounded, by the new development.

"Good be easy for Grom then. Tall armor tell time Grom hear. Grom know more. Tall armor does not understand Grom," he said. Pointing his thumb toward Phaylor.

"What other information do you have," questioned Keltus.

Phatropa who had remained motionless within her chair suddenly came back to her scenes with a jolt, her body moving automatically into a defensive stance. As though she expected an attack at any moment. She looked through the room for any threats stopping on Rumble, Tumble, Alya, Phaylor and the bound Grom before settling herself back into her chair.

"You came to just in time dear. This orc, whose name is... Grom, is relaying further information," said Llewellyn with a welcoming smile.

"Many more have arrived since I stood on the dais. Uhh, I have a splitting headache. I *do not* recommend going until you can't take it anymore," said Phatropa. Shaking her head in an attempt to remove the mental cobwebs.

"Okay... Drogen please ask Grom what other information he has," said Keltus. Bringing everyone back to the task at hand.

"What other information did you bring us. Aside from when the attack is going to happen," questioned Drogen.

"Grock build bridge. Wood to mountain. Almost done, with breath help." stated Grom

"Which mountain did they build a bridge to," questioned Seraphine. While Grom scanned the tower room. His eyes landing on Rumble and Tumble who he pointed to excitedly.

"Built bridge tree to dwarf. But higher up," continued Grom. Rubbing his chin as if he were trying to think of the right words.

Working through Grom's scattered words, Seraphine jumped from her seat hitting the table with her balled fists. That's why they took Moongrove. They didn't want anyone to see what they were up to. They didn't want interference with their construction effort."

"That's a troubling development. They're using the ravine and forest as cover while they build their bridge. Their bridge, even if its higher up... The ravine even if its closer to Sun Meadow, it will allow Grock swift action against whoever becomes the bigger threat," said Gilvail.

"It also makes its use by anyone else impossible, as its location would be right in the middle of his goblinkin army," added Phaylor.

"There be any word from Aragorth," questioned Rumble. His face filling with dread as though he already knew the answer.

"No, we haven't received anything from the citadel. We've sent multiple hawks these past weeks. Nothing's returned," consoled Phaylor.

"There be three things I be seein fur the cause. Me kin not want ta respond. Da letters not be reachin um. Or, and I be hoping it not be the cause, they already be under siege," said Rumble. Hitting fist to heart, in what Drogen could only presume to be, an attempt to stop his heart from racing.

"Based on the timeframe Grom has given, if it's accurate. The third option is the least likely," said Keltus.

"I hope, for all our sake's, he is right. If the attack against the dwarves has moved up. How much time can we possibly have left for preparation," Postulated Seraphine. Realization sank into each of them with Seraphine's words. The weight of their time restraint coming wholly into focus.

"We can't know the timetable hasn't advanced. The attack on Moonclave may not be weeks, but days, or hours away," spoke Llewellyn. The gravity of their situation finally setting in.

"All we know is what we've seen so far. The scouts have only been able to push a short distance into the forest. Everything outside of Moonclave is so overgrown that getting through it takes far too much time. Lucky for us, the overgrowth will hamper the goblinkin's attacks as well," commented Phaylor.

"That still leaves us with little working information. Even with the information we have, we know nothing," expressed Gilvail.

"We have no idea where the attack is coming from. No idea what Grock has seen fit to send against us. Nor do we know when we might be inundated with goblinkin," spoke Keltus through gritted teeth.

"All the information in the world is useless without knowing exactly what we're dealing with," said Alya. Taking a seat opposite the council with Asche, Rumble, Tumble, and Phaylor.

"I fear me kin not be sendin word back, bout nothin," said Rumble. Shaking his head. "Dem blasted ingrates need a good hit bout the head fur dare stupidity," he raged. Smacking his fist against the table. "Dem damndable, thick skulled, no good, bearded boulders."

"I take it from your rage, you believe they're simply ignoring our attempts to communicate," questioned Llewellyn. Slightly relieved. hoping it to actually be the case.

"Dat be da mountian way. Receive a letter. Never say," rhymed Tumble with a sneer. "The question be. Will our kin welcome, me brudder an me," he finished. A forlorn look set upon his face.

"We be needin ta saveum from demselves. Real question be, will dem goats listen ta da likes uh us. They never done so before. Either way, we be needin yur help sky lizard. Me brudder an me not be makin da citadel in time ta be makin a difference. Not witout movin quick as possible," said Rumble. Looking up to Drogen before dropping his head in concentration.

"We know from the information Golga provided, Grock is splitting their force. He's attacking both the dwarves and the elves, within the same interval," said Keltus aloud. Trying to work the problem.

"We don't know what forces are being sent against us. If we knew what the force is primarily comprised of... then we can prepare more effectively to counter it with Drogen's help before he needs to leave with the rock eaters," strategized Phaylor. Nudge Rumble playfully.

"Then why not ask Grom if he knows which of his kin were sent against us," said Amanita. Looking to Tsuga.

"O-on your way here," began Tsuga. With Amanita's encouragement, in goblin-tongue. "What other goblinkin did you meet?

"Grom see no kin," he said. Shaking his head before holding his hand way above himself and standing on his tippy toes. "All big, no small like Grom."

"That cannot mean... What I think it means," questioned Tsuga. Blood rushing to his feet.

"I'm afraid its exactly what it sounds like. Grock isn't sending orcs or goblins to fight us. He's sending ogres, trolls, and the like," said Gilvail. Deflating in his chair along with everyone else.

"We don't have time for this. We need to get everyone ready for the attack. It doesn't matter what Grock is sending. What matters is our survival," said Asche. Trying to rally the council with her encouragement.

"Drogen can you get all of the information we have out to the people quickly," questioned Alya. Wishing to aid in Asche's energizing efforts.

"I can and I will. Even if I must do it in one fell swoop. Everything they need will be disseminated across Moonclave."

"Once the initial lessons have been learned, we must all work together. Only with our combined effort will Moonclave be ready to whether the coming storm," stated Llewellyn. Rising from her chair.

"Llewellyn is right, we have to show everyone in Moonclave that hope remains. We need to lead by example. Showing both strength and unity against this looming threat. With our unity Moonclave itself will be strengthened," proclaimed Gilvail.

"To that end we must finish what we started this day. That includes electing our final member to this council. Through our unity we'll show everyone who calls Moonclave home. We face this threat together as one," stated Seraphine.

"Phaylor of the defensive district. We called you here to this chamber to ask you a very important question. The answer of which will greatly affect you, and our people's future," announced Llewellyn.

"I will do everything within my power to help and protect the people of Moonclave. As I have always done," said Phaylor. Dropping to one knee where he stood.

"Splendid. We of the elven council ask you Commander Phaylor. Will you claim for yourself the last seat of this council. Rising from your current position to that of king, and council for the defensive district of Moonclave," questioned Gilvail.

Phaylor rose from the ground his face both humbled and radiant. Looking at the other members of the council he slammed his fist against his armor in salute. "I will claim this seat that I may continue to protect our people and our home," proclaimed King Phaylor with pride.

"Go to the dais and feel its power flowing through you. Through it you will know all that we must protect. Once you're done, take your place here beside us. And let us begin, in earnest, our preparations for war," declared Seraphine.

Chapter Forty-Seven

"Leave the minimal number of personal behind to defend Zephyria from possible outside invasion. If an unfriendly race, such as those who call themselves lushifare, learn that Zephyria has been left unguarded… It could prove devastating. Lucian is not one to leave a vulnerability unexploited," cautioned Willow.

"What could these lushifare do in the time Vladimir and the other volunteers are away," questioned Fread. Trying to understand both the necessary, and the less than, when deciding on who Vladimir could take. And who was essential to guard Zephyria.

"Look what everyone who wants to fight has accomplished in the weeks since Natalia's return. Especially Natalia. Although, she may be the exception to the rule."

"I would both hope and expect so. She's become quite… intimidating. At least that's what the guards who've witnessed her transformation these last couple of weeks have said. I wish I had time to look in on her progress. Sadly, there's been far too much going on for that. Figuring out the proper numbers to send and leave has had to take priority."

"There's still time," started Willow.

"No. We're out of time. That's the problem. Those heading to the battlefield bellow need to be on their way as quickly as possible if we have any hope of meeting the goblinkin before they're able to fully mount their offensive. I would rather our men fight in order to preserve our allies, than have to mount a rescue for those that remain alive. The numbers we send could mean the difference between saving hundreds and saving a mere few. Hence the predicament we find ourselves in," said the confounded Fread. Rubbing his fingers along his brow in frustration.

"Yes. But sending ten more against a horde of thousands would be akin to bring kindling to a raging fire. No matter how we look at what Grock is doing, he has the advantage of numbers, however that advantage is also disadvantageous. The dwarves have their citadel, and the elves their forest. The hordes of goblinkin are fighting within their enemies strength. Yet he has also seen fit to carry out two sieges at once, splitting his force further. There has to be a way we can effectively maneuver against those loyal to Grock," reasoned Willow.

"So, what you're getting at is… What if sending them to the front line isn't our best course of action? What would benefit our allies while simultaneously lessening Grock's appeal to his worshipers. The book Natalia translated for us said they wished to consolidate their force against Grock, but need Grock himself to push them away in some way."

"Exactly, what can a small force, leaving enough soldiers to defend Zephyria and its people?"

"A small force. Led by Vladimir to attack… There supply routes! Yes. With an army so large and far from Grammora and any other goblinkin settlement that we're aware of, they will need supplies. Commandeering even one supply caravan will put doubt on Grock's conquest and may just bring others to side against Grock," speculated Fread excitedly.

"It could also drive them closer to Grock. Such a ploy could bring animosity to Golga and those looking to turn against Grock more than it drives them into her arms," warned Willow.

"No matter what course we take it will ultimately be up to the goblinkin themselves to choose. This could be exactly the right course for us to take, but we will not know for certain until it is too late to change course." acknowledged Fread. Releasing a deeply held anxious breath.

"Go, find Krail. Have him gather these volunteers," he said. Handing Willow a list of three dozen handwritten names. on a rolled parchment. "Have them ready themselves for battle under Vladimir's command."

"What are you going to do now," questioned Willow. Rolling the parchment and tying it with ribbon.

"Lord Vladimir called me to his chamber. It seems there's something important he wants to discuss, before leaving for the battlefield."

"Have we received word from Moonclave or Aragorth," questioned Willow hopefully.

"Yes, we received word from Commander Phaylor. Seraphine has taken her mother's seat on Moonclave's council. I'll need to remember to call her Queen Seraphine, instead of princess. I'm not sure if Natalia has been told yet. If not, I would very much like to be the one to inform her. Aragorth however, they have been completely silent. Looking through the work orders I would estimate our last contact with them was nearly three months ago."

"I hope their lack of communication is less ominous than it sounds. I'll let Krail know you want to tell Natalia about Seraphine's new position while I deliver your list. If I know him, as I believe I now do, he'll be in the library with Brena," she said with a smile.

"It is their free day. So, I wouldn't doubt it. If need be, ask one of the guards on the list to go around and gather the others. I had better go and meet my... father... That is still awkward to say. It being a secret for so long. This will also allow me to inform him of the plan we just formed."

"Where do you want everyone to meet?"

"Have everyone meet in the audience chamber. They will be seen walking through the streets of Zephyria, that our people can witness those who would risk themselves for both our allies and what is right," said Fread.

"You should save the flashy speeches for the audience chamber," said Willow. Showing a dubious smile.

Grinning Fread re-stacked some of the paperwork on his desk before getting up and walking out of his tower office. *Who would have thought something so mundane as paperwork would be so pleasant an experience after so many near death experiences. I wonder what else I might have missed, during those times,* thought Fread.

Descending the spiral stare of his tower office Fread worked his way, skirting around the audience chamber, to a little used door along the right wall. The door leading him into the depths of the castle and up to where his father had lived since their conquering of Zephyria. *I hope what he wishes to discuss doesn't make things any harder than they already are.*

Climbing the stair to Vladimir's chamber Fread placed his hand upon the door to his father's room. With a deep steadying breath, he knocked hard upon the hardwood door. Announcing his presence beyond before pushing against the jam.

"Come in Fread," came Vladimir's muffled voice as the door swung open.

Vladimir stood at the center of the room with two maids. Each of the maids gathering and attaching the crimson armor over his thick padded gambeson. The blood red armor Vladimir had commissioned, from the elves, and worn since his ascension to the throne of Zephyria. “It would seem people calling me the Crimson King was far more apt than I, or they understood. Under my leadership the zephyr committed genocide against the angelo. I wonder now... Was this armor a subconscious reminder of what I did in their name,” reflected Vladimir. The maids busily working around him.

Knowing the question to be rhetorical Fread simply continued to watch the maids as they worked diligently placing each individual piece around his body. “Unfortunately, we cannot change what happened. We can only pass down the truth of what we did to our future generations. They must learn from the past to safeguard the future from the mistakes of their predecessors.”

“In keeping with safeguarding the future. I take it, from your presence here, you have formulated a plan of attack for those I will lead?”

“Yes I have. I’m sending you with three dozen from the garrison and every volunteer you see fit for service. However, with what I believe to be the best route for helping our allies this may be more than necessary.”

“Those numbers seem lacking, for the front lines. That means your plan is not on the front, but elsewhere. What would such a small force be capable of accomplishing that may be hindered by having too large a number,” questioned an intrigued Vladimir.

“Disruption. While the goblinkin under Grock are focused on the war efforts with their split force, they need supplies for both fronts. Supplies they need in order to maintain the front lines. Furthermore, this will leave Zephyria defended from any possible outside threat and allow your force to move with speed and precision against supply targets,” said Fread.

“Hmm, that is a good plan... However, if the forces are split in twine as we are led to believe then we may be forced to choose which caravans to attack along the roads. It may be more advantages to send two forces of men to be most effective,” contemplated Vladimir. Stroking his chin in contemplation. “Either way, it would be best to start with a small force. Calling for reinforcements when necessary.”

“I will have a secondary force set and ready. Following your departure.”

Having finished securing the armor around Vladimir’s legs and chest the maids set to work about his shoulders and arms. “Now onto the other reason I asked for your presence. I know this may be asking far too much, but it has weighed heavily upon my mind. If at all possible, do not allow Natalia to leave Zephyria while this war is being waged.”

“She’s been training with Lisana every day in order to fight. I doubt she’ll take such an order well.”

“I know Fread. I have no right nor say in this matter. Not after everything I have done. However, she’s the last of her race. The last angelo of Seraphal. Should she lose her life then...”

“I understand... But I cannot ask her to stay. Natalia has found friendship and camaraderie with every race in this fight. She knows, better than any of us, the cruelty of the gods. Asking her to sit on the sidelines... she will not. The thing you are not taking into account is no matter what has happened. And despite everything that has come to light. She is still your daughter. Maybe not in the same way that I am your son, but you raised her. I know for certain. If duties did not hold me here... I would be fighting beside her, every step of the way,” asserted Fread.

“It would seem I am outnumbered in this then,” he said. Grinning in resignation. “If we are incapable of keeping her out of the war, then maybe we should ask a favor of those more capable of watching over her.”

"I see we were both thinking along the same lines. I already asked and they agreed without any dissent or fuss. I suspect they'll be paying a visit to the front line. This does involve their son after all."

With his armors tightened and held firm around his body Vladimir began inspecting himself in his full-length mirror searching for anything out of place. One of the maids holding out his helmet for inspection, while the other fastened his sword belt about the waist. Taking hold of the helmet with both hands Vladimir placed it fully upon his head the leather inner lining, formed from years of use, contoured perfectly to his head.

"Thank you both for your assistance in fitting my armors. You may return to your tasks," said Vladimir.

"Your men are gathering in the audience chamber as we speak. Those you wished included are among them."

"Then it is time we descend to the audience chamber below," said Vladimir. Taking off his helm to hold it comfortably within the crook of his arm.

Vladimir led the way down the staircase and through the hidden door behind the dais. Within the chamber all who would accompany him to the battlefield were gathered their numbers far beyond what Fread had called for.

Seeing the numbers present within the chamber Fread understood. He himself wished to join in the fray. That they could exact some form of righting to the wrongs committed in the past. As well as those committed against them when Zephyr was overrun. Looking out over the group standing before him, he understood nothing he said would convince those present to stay behind.

"It would seem that for all my planning and assessment, I had forgotten the very reason I wished to become commander of Zephyria. The trust and commitment of our people. I looked to dissuade a large force from being deployed. I wished to keep a large enough force here in Zephyria to prevent something that may very well never come. However, looking out over those who stand before me... I cannot bring myself to do so. So, tell me, my people, for what have you gathered here."

Silence fell over the chamber as the whole struggled to form into words the underlying feeling and strength driving them in mass to stand before their king. "We gather to right the wrongs caused by the zealous in the name of divinity. We gather to protect and teach both friend and foe that there is another way. That there is always another way," spoke Antoni. Walking to the front. "To be arbiters of peace to friend and foe alike."

"Then it is time. Time we show the world our resolve. Show Dranier that we are not bound to our mistakes. That we can overcome past failings in order to prevent others from going down the same path in the future. Remain steadfast in our belief that peace is an option. Even if neither side can see the path forward. For peace to be an option we must exude uncompromising strength. Zephyria from this day forward fights for peace through strength and steadfast conviction." His words bolstering and invigorating both himself, and those gathered.

"Lord Fread, Lord Fread, Lord Fread," chanted the assembled soldiers. Thunderously hitting their gauntlet covered fists against polished armored chests.

"I turn you over to your commander and the one who will lead you in this war," announced Fread. Garnering thunderous applause. "These men and women of Zephyria are yours to command, Lord General Vladimir."

Vladimir stood tall upon the dais raising the helm in his arm up onto his head and placing it down. "We go into this war looking to keep bloodshed to the minimum. Our first mission will be the disruption of supply routes. Afterwards, we fly as one to the fields of battle. We must do all we can to end this conflict. Whether through talk or action, we cannot know for certain. However, we cannot allow our mistakes to become those of another when we are capable of preventing such travesties from happening again."

With Vladimir's declaration the audience chamber erupted once more into salutes and cheers. Cheers which had to recede before he could continue speaking. "Now follow me through the streets of Zephyria that our people may see our new resolve and resolution. We fight for *order*. And we fight for *peace*. For all who call Dranier their home."

The room split in twine allowing passage for Vladimir as he walked purposefully to the door Drogen had destroyed using Ether and Uther's bodies as battering rams. Stepping through the door Vladimir said only a single word and the battalion fell lockstep in behind him. "March."

"I see it was a good idea to train and retrain everyone while we had the opportunity to do so," said Krail. Coming up behind Fread through the hidden door.

"With so many going Zephyria is going to be less than safe. Should some unseen threat happen to be looking our way."

"Yes, but we have something they will likely underestimate, should they think invasion is an option."

"What might that be?"

"We have you and Willow. Who have the love and devotion of our people. If such a thing were to occur. I know we can whether the storm."

"I will ensure yours and Zephyria's hope, is not misplaced," said Fread. Watching as the last armored zephyrian walk into the midday sun. Their armor reflecting back toward the dais until disappearing completely from sight.

"It is quite a lofty goal. Some might say unobtainable," said Krail.

"Achieving the impossible is simply a step upon the appropriate road."

"That sounds like something Drogen would say in this situation."

"Even without his presence here, he has guided my thoughts and actions through his own."

"Then it would seem the king of Zephyria has found faith where many others have as well."

Chapter Forty-Eight

"Did you see Lord Vladimir and the others heading out to join the fight princess," questioned Ziraiy. Setting out Natalia's clothes for her to dress.

"I know. I saw them leave while I was in the shopping district yesterday. I wanted to go and join the fight. But, maybe their leaving first will work out in my favor."

"Does this mean you're planning to do something the former lord, and present lord might not be particularly fond to find out?"

"It is like you have known me my entire life," said Natalia with a rye smile.

"Oh dear you're going to be rather troublesome aren't you. Well probably best I don't know. That way when they forcibly question me in the dungeon I don't have anything for them," said Ziraiy with a dimpled grin.

"The armors Jesha repaired, are they in the closet?"

"Yes, along with the hammer and bow, as you requested princess."

"Thank you Ziraiy. I have one other request, then I want you to take the rest of the day off. Go to the kitchens and gather some ratio... some food for the next few days. I plan to lock myself in this room in order to... study independently for a while."

"I'll gather some food for you, so that you may... study without unnecessary disturbance." said her personal maid. With a wink.

"Then it looks like all I need to do is inform every one of my impending seclusion," she said. Smiling to Ziraiy as she moved out the door of Natalia's room.

Natalia, looking at herself in the mirror, grinned. Hopping up from her chair and dressing quickly she moved to her casement window throwing it wide, that the morning air could filter in around her filling her lungs and whipping playfully through her hair.

I can almost feel it in the breeze. This is the perfect day to start an adventure. I'll have to thank Krail for removing the baring from my window... when I return home of course. Well then. No time like the present, she thought jumping from the tower window and flapping her wings as she controlled the air currents around her with magic. The magic allowing her to fly more easily, and further, than she'd ever been capable of in the past.

Covering the ground between her tower and the audience chamber, Natalia flew over a couple of remaining guards and maids. The castle ground attendants stopping to wave excitedly. Seeing their princess maneuvering overhead.

Setting herself down lightly upon the lowest step of the audience chamber, Natalia walked calmly to the door Chian continued to study diligently. "I didn't think I'd find you here. I was going to head for the library to look for you and Mai-Coh. I have a few things I'd like to discuss with you both today... when you both have time," said Natalia. Trying not to sound too suspicious as maids and guards shuffled past.

"Mai-Coh will find later. I look. Fix broken door. Put books and knowledge to work. Mai-Coh talk with King of sky people," said Chian. Not taking her eyes from the pieces of door that remained. Reaching out she touched the hinged section. Whispering under her breath, the castle began to shake, as if a tremor was surging through the structure.

"Many problems. Not all can be seen. Can fix, but need more than sky people have," said Chian.

"What do you need that is not available in Zephyria?"

Chain didn't say a word. Simply pointing to the rarest material of any within the castle. Metal only found in one place. The dwarven citadel of Aragorth.

"We should talk with Fread. There may be some stored in the castle."

"Then to Mai-Coh and leader of the sky people we go," said Chian. Looking to Natalia with a nod. Finally prized her eyes away from the double doors, and structure in front of her.

"Do you know where they are?"

"Where all are most days."

"Then we should head to the library," commented Natalia. Grabbing hold of Chain's massive hand. "Later today I would very much like to meet both you and Mai-Coh at Drogen's house in the woods. There are things I wish to... discuss. And time may be of the essence, if we are to be successful," she whispered cryptically. As the young Zephyrian, who previously guided them to the dining hall, worked his way up beside them.

"Princess... I was tasked with gathering... food for your... time with books," said the boy. Thinking about the words before correcting himself. "Your time in st-u-dy," he finished with a smile.

"Yes, I requested for Ziraiy to have a few days' worth of food delivered to my room. That way I can study in peace for a few days. Did she ask you to help her?"

"No, I ask to help. Zir-aiy not know what Prin-cess like," he said. Sounding out the larger words.

"Oh, I understand. Thank you for helping Ziraiy, for me. I know gather things that *you know,* will last for let's say... three days. We can't have food going to waste after all. Also, you should pick some of the things you like and send them up as well. That way I have a good variety," said Natalia. Encouraging the fledgling who nodded happily.

The young kitchen boy ran through the audience chamber excitedly for accomplishing the task he'd made for himself. The beaming smile on his face bringing a smile to everyone he passed along the way.

"Young treated well with sky people. Not always true of other tribes."

"Yes. They are. If only to shelter them for a short time from the harsh realities present in life. Realities known to us all in time," commented Natalia.

Having walked to the library so often their journey felt, to them, as though it took no time at all. Both nearly walking past the room entirely, only stopping when the guards questioned their passing.

"Thank you for turning us around. It would appear we were lost in thought," said Natalia apologetically. With a smile and nod the guards opened the library door allowing them to pass.

After the translation work had been completed work within the library had fallen off. Returning to its typical state with one notable exception. The stacks of books and manuscripts that had been littering table tops and the ground, across the breadth of the library, were steadily receding as shelves within received much needed repairs.

Working on organizing the many stacks Brena looked up for a second taking note of Natalia and Chian's entrance as her newly appointed assistant brought forward an impressive stack of flattened parchments to sort and organize. "It feels as though we'll never be done re-shelving everything. Still, having help is making the process much faster, and entirely more fun. This stack needs shelved in alcove five."

"Ooh, this will be my first time in that one," said the adolescent zephyrian excitedly. "What information is stored there," he questioned. Lifting books from the table and looking to Brena excitedly.

"Actually, why don't you ask the princess, I'm sure she knows even better than I do what's within that particular section of the library."

"Really! Hello Princess Natalia," said the boy. Holding his head low and shifting his feet nervously, as he'd not noticed their presence.

"No need for you to be nervous. Lift your head, and let me think a moment... Ah within it are books regarding the many races that call Dranier their home. Many of them are very out of date. Especially those regarding the goblinkin, but they still retain a lot of very useful information," smiled Natalia to the energetic assistant. "How are you liking your work here in the library?"

"I like it a lot Princess, there's so much to learn. I could read a book in here every day and never reach the end," he said. His eyes shining at the prospect.

"Then it seems you have truly found your place."

All smiles, the boy excused himself. Skipping his way through the main alcove, and through the portal, to the other sections of the library beyond.

"What name does this young one have," questioned Chian.

"His name is Fabian. Krail told me he was teaching himself to read out in town. He's one of the young ones who came from Zephyr after the goblinkin invaded. Poor dear lost his father in the siege. Told me he was a guard on the wall."

"It looks to me that Krail has found the perfect fit. Speaking of Krail is he here with Mai-Coh and Fread as well?"

"No, he's off doing things along market street. Making certain everything's going well since so many left with Lord Vladimir. He's taken it upon himself to speak with everyone's family who joined in the war effort."

"What of Lisana and Death?"

"I'm afraid I haven't seen either of them since yesterday," said Brena. Shaking her head.

Mai-Coh and Fread emerged from the doorway where Fabian had gone. "I asked a favor of them. They're likely working on fulfilling my request," said Fread.

"What could you have asked death and a dragon to do, that they would agree too," questioned Willow. Walking up behind Fread and Mai-Coh.

"I suspect it won't be long now before everyone knows, but I think I'll keep it to myself. For now at least," said Fread with a mischievous grin.

"Well, I actually have something I need Mai-Coh and Chian for. There's something in my room for both of them. I'd like them to come with me. If they have the time. Oh. On a side note, I will be staying in my room to study for the next few days. I would prefer to be left undisturbed, if possible," said Natalia.

"Is that what the tomes you requested are for," questioned Brena with a frown. "I thought you already read everything in the library. Even the new books Lisana uncovered?"

"Zephyria needs to have a better understanding of those who follow both Daelon and Lucian. We need a way, other than insulting their deity, to differentiate between them. In order to keep everyone here in Zephyria aware and safe. Should Lucian's people try to infiltrate Zephyria. I am merely being cautious."

"Having more information regarding any potential threat will help. I'll have the kitchens send food to your room," said Fread.

"No need. I have Ziraiy working with the kitchens to gather everything I need for my time in isolation. I had hoped to tell Death and Lisana about what I'm doing."

"I'm seeing them later today. I'll let them know once they return," said Fread.

"Thank you. With this information I will make sure everyone in Zephyria is able to distinguish friend from foe. Truthfully, I hope the information proves to be unnecessary, but it is better we are prepared in case it is not," said Natalia.

"Willow and I are heading to the tower to go through some more paperwork that seems unending. If anyone sees Krail send him to the tower as well."

"Well then, let us head up to my room. I have a surprise waiting for you both," said Natalia. Giddily pulling them out the door toward her room. Followed out by Fread and Willow who split left.

"You have something for us, Natalia black wing?" questioned Mai-Coh.

"Yes, I do, they arrived a few days ago actually. But everyone was busy leading up to the departure. This just happened to be the perfect opportunity."

"We did not know exchanging of items to be a custom of the sky people," said Chian inquisitively.

"Well... this is more a present than an exchange of gift... You don't need to feel obligated in any way to repay, or give in return," said Natalia Who continued to drag them through the hallways. "There is something else I would like to discuss as well... When there is no chance we will be overheard."

With a nod they silently agreed to Natalia's wish saying nothing until they were all behind the closed and barred door in Natalia's room. Waved her hand before the door a sheen of magic flowed across its surface. "This will stop anyone from listening in."

Natalia moved into her closet, throwing the doors wide before stepping in. "It took a while for Jesha to repair my armor. The leather she had procured previously having been used up she had to wait for another trader with the leather we needed. Thankfully the gnomes brought some to trade, or else my armor might have never been repaired." Handing the armor to Chian through the door, Natalia grabbed the weapons she'd procured. Worked her way back into the room after a slight struggle.

"These are for you two," said Natalia dragging the heavy hammer for Chain across the floor to place its handle into the palm of her hand. In her other hand she held out the unstrung bow for Mai-Coh. "These weapons, I hope, will help you on your next journey. Whether it be on this side of the forbidden plains or on your journey home."

"These are the weapons Chian and I saw last time we walked through the market of the sky people," said Mai-Coh in astonishment. "Th- thank you Black wing,"

"Thank you, black wing," said Chian with a bow. "But why does black wing bring out armor," she questioned. Rising back to her full height.

"That has to do with the spell I put on the door. I already have all the information needed to distinguish between Lucian's people and Daelon's. I made sure to mark all the books so the important parts are distinguishable for the others. I also wrote out the most important things to remember."

"What does this have to do with the door," questioned Mai-Coh.

"I don't want anyone to interfere with what I have planned. I am leaving Zephyria for the Moonclave. I cannot stand back and wait while my friends are in danger of loosing their lives. So I am leaving tonight. However, I also wanted to invite you both to join me. Chain you mentioned wanting to see the elven library. Especially since your people constructed it. The problem is going with war so close at hand will prove to be an entirely different experience than going during a time of peace."

"I would see the library built by my people," said Chian. Looking to Mai-Coh who shrugged in response. Differing to her judgment. "The library could be threatened or destroyed by invasion. The knowledge left by my ancestors lost forever. The reason my people no longer have the knowledge of the past, could be lost forever. No. I cannot allow my people to remain as they are. I must return to my tribe the knowledge. It is what I am here to do," she proclaimed.

"We join you black wing," said Mai-Coh with resolve.

"We leave tonight. Once I have everything prepared for the trip, I will meet you at Drogen's cabin. With any luck we will have three days head start before anyone notices our disappearance," said Natalia. Calculating everything she needed to accomplish, before departing Zephyria.

"Tonight, at Drogen's cabin," said Mai-Coh. Taking hold of Chian's arm, before bowing to Natalia. "I give thanks to you black wing, for the gifts you have given," stated Mai-Coh. Leading Chian out of Natalia's bedroom door.

Chapter Forty-Nine

Drogen focused his mind on the information he was receiving through the physical connection he shared with Phatropa, as her hand rested upon his shoulder. The knowledge within her mind regarding the trance state and its manifestation flowing through the towers and out to the elves through their own connection's across Moonclave.

As the font of information moved from a wave to a trickle Phatropa dropped her hand cutting off the connection entirely, a deep weariness setting in and contorting her features. "I'll need time to recover after enduring such mental strain, so who's next," she questioned. Taking a cross legged seat upon the floor to begin her trance.

"I believe it best I go next. I would think my ability to easily reach the trance without effort will be helpful to those who have experience without knowledge. After wards should be Seraphine. Who has yet to achieve the state. If she can achieve the state while connected to Drogen our knowledge and understanding are sure to be far greater. And come with far greater success," reasoned Llewellyn.

Placing her hand on Drogen's shoulder Llewellyn fell into the connection through him imparting her own experiences. Transmitting the relevant experiences through the connection Drogen felt many more drop their hands from the base of the tower. *I hope the number of attachments dropping in such a way is a good sign. Only time will tell how effective this method of learning has actually been,* thought Drogen.

As Llewellyn's experience with the trance state came to a close Drogen beckoned Seraphine to the dais. She had purposefully been left out of the connection in order to experience the trance state through the dais. In hopes that her lack of experience could help others overcome their own difficulties in achieving the state.

Before Seraphine's hand reached out to receive the connection Drogen felt the numbers still holding the towers diminished to less than a hundred. Llewellyn dropped her hand as Seraphine placed hers upon Drogen's shoulder. Her lack of experience became overshadowed by the knowledge of those who had garnered their own experience with the seraph trance allowing her to achieve the state, while Drogen transmitted her experience out through the towers.

With Seraphine's achievement of the trance those remaining followed. The numbers falling until only one remained, and then none. As the last hand fell from the tower Drogen cut off the connection placing his hand upon Seraphine's own holding her in place as he turned. Catching her before she could fall to the ground.

"With this everyone in Moonclave is able to use the seraph's trance. All that remains for them to learn are the fundamentals of magic," said Drogen.

"H-How long will it take before everyone is ready," questioned Tsuga.

"For those who've experienced the state, but simply lacked the knowledge they once possessed, it should take no more than four hours' time. The same amount of time as it takes Phatropa. For those uninitiated, it could take as long as six. The time needed will decrease with time, knowledge, and experience. However, tis my hope that using the towers might reduce that time. Still, it will depend on the elves on an individual level," stated Drogen.

"Would it be wise to have those who awaken from the trance state learn magics fundamentals as soon as their able then. It would split the number of people receiving the information. It would also be less stress on everyone mentally," posited Amanita.

"I would suggest doing so. This will allow you to begin dividing everyone along different scheduled breaks for their trance state. Even without the need for sleep times of immobile rest are necessary. This needs to be a consideration for both preparation and battle," advised Drogen.

"Let us work out and establish a rotation time based on the districts. This will make certain that we are never left defenseless, as they are incapable of moving," said Phaylor.

"The same will be necessary for the defensive forces on a smaller scale," consulted Gilvail.

"Yes. I will need to establish a system for the defensive district that we are not left without proper guard at any time."

"When Llewellyn wakes, we'll start teaching true magic. Until then we have messages from the scouts to look through. Including a hawk that arrived from Zephyria for Seraphine," said Gilvail. "I must thank you once more Phaylor. Despite Elmar's mismanagement you were able to keep the aviary running."

"It was, and still is our only reliable form of communication beyond the towers. If the hawks had stopped then we would have truly been isolated. I only wish I could have saved more of the wyverns. Had I realized sooner how bad everything had become, I could have retained more wyvern for the riders."

"Has word returned from the dwarven citadel," questioned Drogen.

"No, we continue to send word to the dwarves, but receive nothing in return. We simply don't have enough people in the defensive district to send a party out to the citadel. We need as many people here as possible to defend Moonclave from assault."

"Then my taking them to the citadel looks to be our best course of action," stated Drogen.

"I would like to argue against your leaving, but if the dwarven citadel falls... We stand no chance," said Amanita.

"So, saving the dwarves, and their citadel is necessary if we want to survive," questioned Tsuga.

"That looks to be the case," said Gilvail with a frown. "Don't anyone of you tell those ground hogs. They won't be able to hold their heads up if you do."

"I will inform the dwarves of our immanent departure. The hours between now and our leaving will allow them to finish what they're doing as well," said Drogen.

"What have they been doing," Tsuga questioned.

"They've been helping Bailfar in his forge since regaining their freedom, as far as I know," said Gilvail.

"Tis no doubt. Tis the case even now," said Drogen with a slight nod.

Sending his consciousness out to where he knew the dwarves to be Drogen called for the brothers bidding them to the central tower upon completion of their tasks. Drogen could tell by the dwarves' heartbeats that they were doubling their efforts in order to finish their work quickly. Taking their renewed vigor as acknowledgment of is request, Drogen pulled himself back into the audience chamber.

From their quickening heartbeats, those who retain knowledge of the seraph trance will be up and moving soon. Phatropa, and those from the district of knowledge, who found their own path to the trance, will be first it would seem.

Phatropa rose from her seated position with a long stretch of her tight muscles. "I feel much better now. Does this mean it's time to learn magic," she questioned enthusiastically.

"Let a few more rise from their trances while we all get into position," said Amanita rising from her chair with Tsuga. "Whenever you're ready Drogen."

"Come to the dais. I will call all who've awakened to touch once more upon the tower. That they may learn to use true magic through your teachings," said Drogen. Broadcasting what needed done throughout Moonclave.

Hands reached out and touched the towers immediately. Many others following suit while those within the audience chamber moved in behind him. Amanita and Tsuga opened their mind, letting flow everything they had learned in their years of study within the library.

The information released through Drogen crashed through the conduit of his mind in a nearly overwhelming torrent of information. Information quickly and precisely condensed within him and shared through the tower's connection, in a single precise stream of consciousness.

As the information within Armina and Tsuga's minds fell to the wayside, they dropped their hands. Exhausted by the strain placed upon their body and mind. With the transfer of knowledge complete Gilvail, Phaylor, Phatropa, Tsuga, and Amanita steadied themselves. Using each other, in order to return to their waiting council seats.

"I feel like my mind is gone... empty," stated Tsuga. Struggling to find the right word.

"Should we expect this every time," questioned Amanita with a yawn.

"Tis strange you two feel that way," commented Phatropa.

"The experience was vastly different for me as well," said Gilvail.

"That likely has more to do with Drogen than it does with the dais this time," reasoned Phaylor.

"I would not doubt such a conclusion to be the case," remarked Keltus. Who had only just begun to stir from the trance. "Well then I suppose it's my turn to learn magic."

"Ca-can you give us a minute... I don't think either of us have the strength right now," commented Tsuga. Drawing an exhausted nod from Amanita in response.

"You two need not worry. Your bodies and minds need only rest within the trance. I can disseminate everything to the rest of the elves. I simply need to remain upon the dais in order to retain the information in its entirety."

"Then we leave it to you," said Amanita.

"I only wish we had a way to repay you," said Tsuga. He and Amanita positioning themselves for the meditative trance.

"As do I," echoed those able to within the chamber.

"This is all knowledge the elves would possess had your memories not been erased by my kin. I am simply returning what you lost." Sinking into the connection Drogen felt many across Moonclave rising. "It would seem the second group is waking. Once Llewellyn rises, I will spread the knowledge again."

A few minutes more passed before Llewellyn's heartbeat returned to normal. "Oh dear, I hope this next part doesn't prove to be as tiring as the first," she said shaking her head.

"It wasn't so bad for us, but Amanita and Tsuga need time to recover," responded Phatropa.

"So, it would seem," said Llewellyn taking note of the meditative positions of them both.

"Those who have recently risen place your hands upon the tower that you may learn," spoke Drogen taking hold of Llewellyn and Keltus's hand, once more transmitting the combined knowledge of Amanita and Tsuga.

"Oh, that was a much nicer experience than any of the previous," said Llewellyn. As Drogen released them both.

"Those who remain have only just achieved the trance state. It may take some time for them to return to the physical world, from their minds," said Drogen.

"Then wait we must. Are the burrow slugs on their way here yet," questioned Gilvail.

"Aye we be ear," came Rumbles gruff voice. The door facing the Crafter's district swinging open wide. "Ya bark louse be needin ta learn some manners. Yah insult ta the face, not ta the side. Thought ya be knowin better," admonished Rumble with a grin.

"It would seem my time in the dungeon has ruined my sense of decorum," said Gilvail. "To think I'd be reprimanded so by a rock eater."

"Smack a stone eat the ore still be more than bug in fleour," sang Tumble.

"Quite well done with that one," commented Phaylor.

"Your voice leaves much to be desired. But for some reason, its also... soothing," said Seraphine. Regained herself fully.

"Told ya we be growin on ya," said Rumble with cheeky grin.

"I'm really glad Alya wasn't here to hear that," said Seraphine with a sigh. "I'd never hear the end of it."

"Oh yah not be needen ta worry bout fuzzy ears. I sure she be findin out," said Rumble.

"Is it too late to put him in the dungeon... Just for a little while," suggested Seraphine with a giggle. "Anyways why are the two here already? What else have I missed?"

"The most pressing would be Drogen has nearly finished teaching everyone in Moongrove the basics of magic," said Llewellyn.

"The only ones left to learn are those who have only just experienced the trance. Which means it's your turn to learn," informed Keltus.

"Really, but I've only just gotten up," sighed Seraphine. Resigning herself to the inevitable tiredness.

"No need to worry. We initially thought the same way. However, only Tsuga and Amanita needed to rest afterwords. They're the ones who had to supply the information after all," said Llewellyn.

"Then I would prefer to get it all over with as quickly as possible. Are we waiting for many more," questioned Seraphine.

"I can still hear the heartbeats of a few who remain within the seraph's trance. Their numbers continue to dwindle with each passing moment. Still, waiting a short while more, would be advisable," said Drogen.

"Then we can discuss the actions needed with the dwarves," said Gilvail.

"What ya be meanin wit action," questioned Rumble. A slight step back as he reached for a weapon that wasn't there.

"You could have said it in a less threatening way Gilvail," bit Llewellyn. "We still have not received any response so your plan of heading to the citadel is the only option left."

"Zephyria has sent word many times over, and they're a far greater distance then the citadel. I wish we could leave things as they are, but if either of us fall, the other is not far behind," said Phaylor. Stressing the importance with his tone.

"Aye, I think I be preferin the threat, it be easier ta deal with," said Rumble. Looking to his brother.

"Du brudder dwarves be goin ome, dare beards regrown, be in exile no more."

"I take it you're leaving the moment you're done giving everyone the knowledge we need," questioned Seraphine.

"Yes. That is the plan," said Drogen.

"I had hoped we would receive something from the citadel. I had hoped that you would not need to go. I don't like sending any of you to Aragorth. A part of me wants to tell you all to stay here. I want, above everything else, to act selfishly. To keep all of my friends here and safe. But I have to think of what's best, not only for the elves, but for Dranier as a whole. Leaving Grock to conquer without resistance puts, not only Moonclave and Aragorth in jeopardy, but all of Dranier. He will not stop at just us. He will go to Zephyria, Anu-grah, and Tegrus," said Seraphine reaching out to place her hand into Drogen's establishing a connection that none of the others could hear. *"But you will not be leaving without knowing everything that I feel and wish for the future."*

Drogen felt the rush of emotions, thoughts, and fantasies cascading through Seraphine's mind into his own in a wave that threatened to wash him away. "Those who remain without the knowledge of true magic reach out and touch the tower before you," spoke Drogen. Splitting the connections Drogen pushed out the knowledge to the remaining elves. With the knowledge transmitted fully he cut himself away from the tower's connection. Until all that remained within the connection was him and Seraphine.

"When you return, and we are alone... or not," said Seraphine within his mind. Sending forth imaginings of fantasies involving herself and Natalia. *"Then I wish to be with you."*

"Then there is much to look forward to," said Drogen. Sending through the connection his feelings for her, and the thoughts she'd shared. *"I endeavor to return once everything has come to its conclusion. One way, or another."*

"That is all I can ask," said Seraphine. Their mental connection falling away completely. They walked free of the dais their hands intertwined. "I wish I was going with the three of you, but I am needed here. Please, make sure you take care of each other."

"Aye, ya leave da flyin lizard ta me brudder an me. Ya need not be worryin Queeny," said Rumble.

"I'm glad to hear it. Everyone come and witness Drogen's truth. May we burn it into our memories that no manipulation of memory can relieve us of his majesty. Without his effort, Moonclave would not have the chance of surviving. that it now has," proclaimed Seraphine.

Amanita and Tsuga stirred from their trances upon the proclamation coming to their feet quickly. The council and the dwarves, as a whole, filing out behind Drogen.

Outside the tower many elves were beginning to practice and understand magic. Everyone within sight stopping their practice to witness the council and who they followed.

All upon the council bowed their heads to Drogen an action he returned in kind. He turned and looked Seraphine in the eyes closing them as he bowed his head to her.

"The Council thanks you for everything you've done to help us prepare for the war that knocks upon the gates of Moonclave," said Gilvail.

"We thank you for everything you've done for us and the Moonclave," said Keltus. Remaining bowed.

"As does Root Mother, for all of her children, give thanks," came Leif's voice. Walking out from among the previously practicing elves.

"Then I leave Moonclave and its people in all of your capable hands," said Drogen. Releasing Seraphine's hands, which fell to her side. "I would ask you all to stand back."

Keltus, having seen his true form before, stepped back many paces. Seeing Keltus's actions the others around Drogen followed suit, creating a large circle.

Drogen stripped himself of his clothing and with a claw cut around his entire form. The skin falling away, revealing the scales beneath the thin layers of epidermis. And with their reveal the sun itself looked to dim further than its decent among the treetops would demonstrably allow. Drogen opened the door within his mind, and in the blink of an eye manifested his true existence.

Those unaware, or simply frightened by the display fell over themselves in fear, stopping only when they noticed those around him did not. Drogen's long neck turned down to look upon the council, the dwarves, and Leif. "Rumble and Tumble let us be off to Aragorth. If luck is on our side, we may yet save them from themselves," said Drogen. His booming deep voice reverberating in resonance with Moonclave itself.

Rumble and Tumble looked to Drogen's tail and with a shrug to each other made for it climbing up his scaled back stopping once they reached a comfortable position in which they could grab and hold one of the spikes along his spine.

"You better hold on tight," yelled Keltus to the dwarves.

Drogen pressed into his haunches, launching himself into the air. With a thought, air began to flow around him and as he unfurled his wings the magic air pressure filled them. With each beat he gained greater altitude until he could easily fly above the treetops toward Aragorth.

As the council returned to their chamber Seraphine took note of the letter that had been placed before her seat. The letter they had received from Zephyria.

"Has anyone read what Fread sent from Zephyria yet," questioned Seraphine.

"No, we didn't read it. We never even thought about it. Everything else took precedence. That and it may prove prudent that everyone knows what their letter says," said Gilvail.

Seraphine cut the seal free from the rolled letter unrolling it on the table for everyone to see. "They may be sending forces of their own to help fight Grock's minions. That is a bit of good news for sure."

"It would seem that a lot has happened in Zephyria as well, this mentions Lord Fread and Commander Krail," pointed out Phaylor.

"Oh dear," commented Llewellyn. "There's another message here... From a different hand entirely."

"I recognize that handwriting. That's from Princess Natalia. What does it say," questioned Seraphine.

"It would seem we should have opened this the moment we received it," said Amanita.

"It says that Drogen was mortally wounded in his fight against Grock. If Mai-Coh and Chian had not rendered aid he would have died from the injuries," read Keltus.

"Seraphine grabbed the letter swiftly from Keltus's hand reading over Natalia's writing multiple times, hoping that it would change, but no matter how many times she read its contents it would not. Tears welled up in her eyes. Realizing the truth behind Drogen's statement to her. *'I endeavor to return once everything has come to its conclusion. One way or another.'* "You better return to us Drogen. If only for me to kill you myself for not telling me the risk you face," raged Seraphine to the council chambers.

"There's nothing we could have done to stop him dear. Even if we wanted to. His existence is far beyond any of us, I'm afraid," consoled Llewellyn.

"I...it would seem that all we can do now is... pray," suggested Tsuga.

"The old ones are the closest to divinity. I wonder if they too may grow in power, as the gods do, with our worship," contemplated Amanita.

"Well, it couldn't hurt," said Gilvail with a shrug.

"I doubt he'd view it the same way," said Seraphine. A smile gracing her face through the tears. "I think he would be quite perturbed actually. Which makes me want to do exactly that even more." Wiping her eyes, she folded Natalia's letter placing it within her dress, over her heart. The letter a constant reminder, to pray with her heart and soul, for his safe return.

Chapter Fifty

As the door closed behind them Natalia undressed completely to adorn her body in her thin but comfortable gambeson, the under armor adding slightly more bulk, but far greater resistance. With her gambeson secured she slipped her newly mended, and refit studded leather armor securing it tightly.

Walking in the leathers caused many creaks and sounds, as the new pieces of armor had yet to ware in. With a wave of her hand over herself she cast a spell, silencing everything around her. Testing her spells effectiveness, Natalia began contorting her body and stomping her feet. Listening for any utterance. Pleased with the spell's effectiveness, Natalia grinned. *All that remains is Ziraiy's arrival. Enough time to write a letter for Fread and Willow, I hope.*

Natalia started and stopped many times trying hard to come up with the words to say. Wanting to succinctly convey the reasons, and feelings driving her decision. *I should leave something for Brena and Krail as well... But, where do I even start.*

In hopes of moving past her sudden mental block, she leafed through the tomes and parchments Brena had gathered from the library. Making certain she had not missed any key passages, though she knew them to be correctly marked with nary a glance.

I never would have thought, this..., thought Natalia holding the blank parchment up in front of her eyes. *Would be the hardest part, about leaving Zephyria.*

First, I must apologize for deceiving you all... With the first words written the others slowly began to flow out onto the parchment, and upon her sentiments conclusion she scribed her name. Her signature beginning and ending in large flourishes. Denoting to any who saw it that despite the trepidation, she wholly believed it to be, the right course of action.

Looking over her writing one last time Natalia rolled up the parchment. Her eyes scanning every line as it disappeared. With a click of her fingers a small flame sprang to life at the tip of her finger. Using the flame, she melted a piece of sealing wax, sealing the document with the press of a stamp. As she removed the seal the intricate portrayal of a raven in flight greeted her eyes, similar to that depicted on her tri-blade sword.

"I'll take this stamp with me as well. Should the opportunity present itself I'll be able to send letters to Zephyria," commented Natalia to the empty room.

Looking around the room a shadowy figure caught her eyes. Springing up at the sight, Natalia pulled and threw one of her many hidden daggers. Pullling Herzblutung from its sheath before touching back to the ground. Ready to defend herself. The shadowy figure threw its hands up, the thrown dagger caught in one hand as she stepped out into the dim light.

As Ziraiy moved out into the light Natalia visibly relaxed, placing her sword back on her hip with a sigh of relief though her heart had yet to calm from the surprise. Looking at her personal maid she noticed Ziraiy was speaking, but none of the sound reached her ears. *The spell!* Exclaimed Natalia though it too could not be heard.

Waving her hand counter to her cast she lifted the silence spell. “I take it this means you’re do-,” questioned Ziraiy. Tossing the dagger by the tip and catching it by the hilt while looking at her charge with concern. “Did you not hear me come in?”

“No. I did not, but that is entirely my fault. I thought I had cast the silence spell on my armors. Evidently, I cast it over myself instead. There is still much I must learn with regard to magic. This just proves it all the more. However, first I must apologize to you. I have acted in an imprudent manner toward you,” said Natalia. Bowing her head ruefully.

“No. you have nothing to apologize for. That is the proper response to an intruder in one’s room. I would have been quite worried had you not acted in such a way princess. Especially when startled by something, or someone that does not belong. No harm has been done. So please, raise your head,” she bade with a motherly smile. Moving forward, Ziraiy held the daggers hilt out for Natalia to grab and put away. Which she did quickly.

“Were you and the kitchen’s fledgling able to gather the necessary supplies?”

“Yes, Apicius was a great help with navigating the kitchens.”

“Please tell him that I appreciate all his help. And thank you Ziraiy, for all your help since my return to Zephyria. I do not know when I might be back from my journey, but I hope... when I do return. You will have continued to work in the castle and may once more choose to fulfill this role for me,” she said. A smile and a tear upon her visage.

“You need not worry yourself for me princess. When you return, I will be right here at your side,” said Ziraiy. A tear forming at the bottom of her eye as well.

With their goodbyes done, Natalia flung wide her casement window, spread her abyssal black wings, and flew from her tower window into the night. Where none could bear witness to her silent escape. Over the market district, to the waiting Mai-Coh and Chian.

She touched down silently at the trailhead leading to Drogen’s small cabin amongst the tamarack trees. Looking around, for any that might have somehow followed her flight, before advancing into the tree line.

Walking cautiously free of the trees into the clearing where Drogen’s house set Natalia saw a bright moving light emanating from within the structure. *Good they were able to make it. I hope they have not been waiting long,* thought Natalia.

Excited for the journey ahead she threw the door wide, “Are you both ready,” she questioned. Her jaw hitting the floor in shock as Mai-Coh and Chian were not the only ones waiting within Drogen’s small house. *F-Fread, W-Willow, Krail, Brena, Death, Lisana, Mai-Coh, Chian... I have made a serious miscalculation.*

“I-I-I,” stuttered Natalia uncontrollably.

“It would seem she’s rather surprised,” said Willow.

“I would have to agree,” teased Krail with a giant smile.

“Lucky, she hasn’t gone into shock,” admonished Brena “I told you we should have waited outside.”

“If you would princess there are things we need to discuss before leaving Zephyria,” said Lisana. To change the subject.

With her plan’s shattered, Natalia’s mind began desperately trying to catch up to the scene unfolding in front of her. Taking Lisana’s advice she sat down in one of Drogen’s handmade chairs. Looking around the room, she couldn’t help but feel as though she were about to be scolded. “I-I apologize... for...”

"That is quite enough of that young angelo. You're not in any sort of trouble. Just relax, and listen," attested Death. Assuaging her concern.

"Our father asked that I keep you here in Zephyria, which we both agreed, would never happen. We three are much alike in that regard. If I didn't have the safety of everyone in Zephyria to worry about, I would have volunteered to fight against Grock's force," said Fread. Looking into Natalia's eyes.

"If you knew then... why didn't you say anything," questioned Natalia.

"For one, I hoped you would come to me. But honestly, knowing all that has transpired between you, Vladimir, and Zephyria itself, I knew that possibility to be... small. I was actually surprised you didn't run after the garrison when they left."

"I wanted to do that myself. But *somebody* had to stop me," said Lisana. A soft elbow nudging Death's arm.

"As did many," said Krail.

"That aside. I knew it wouldn't be long before you would leave. Who would be going with you, was the only thing I was unsure of. I knew you would likely ask Mai-Coh and Chian to go, if you decided on heading to Moonclave, and you did."

"But, how did you know," she questioned.

"Do you honestly believe I didn't know what you've always been up to. Although you didn't know I was your stepbrother, I took it upon myself to protect you. No matter what you were up to during your nightly escapades through the castle."

"I-I... They."

With a wave of his hand, he stopped her. "I didn't mean to go off on so many tangents. Back to why I am here, and what I've been meaning to say. Please, come home safe from your journey, my beloved sister. And know should this next leg of your journey last weeks, months, years, or decades. You will always have a home to come back to."

"It would seem that Lord Vladimir... our father, made the correct choice leaving Zephyria in your hands... brother. The crown suits you well. I will return when the opportunity presents itself. You have my word. Thank you for always looking out for my best interest," said Natalia. Tears in her eyes to match Fread's. Any many others throughout the room.

"Speaking of looking out for your best interest, I have asked Death and Lisana to go with you. In hopes you will all meet with Drogen upon your arrival. I may have actually forced her hand in the matter, although... Now that I think about it, the convincing seemed to be the easy part," contemplated Fread with a smile.

"There's still a lot I need to teach her in both magic and the use of Herzblutung," said Lisana with a shrug. "And the library in Moongrove has an even bigger selection of magic tomes."

"I look forward to continuing my studies," affirmed Natalia with a chuckle.

Willow moved around the table wrapping her arms round Natalia lifting her up from the chair to her feet. "I know we've not known each other for long, but I can't help but feel a deep kinship with you. Please have a safe, and fruitful journey," said Willow.

"Thank you, Willow," said Natalia. Dropping into a whisper. "Please make sure you take good care of Ziraiy, Jesha, Shiesa, and everyone else in my stead."

Willow pulled back slightly at the list of names, receiving a smile and knowing wink in response to the clear question present upon her face. "I will," she said with a smile. Giving Natalia a slight bow..

"It's gonna be rather quiet around here again, without you trying to sneak books away to your bedchambers in the middle of the night," commented Brena with a smile.

"Speaking of, those books you sent up have been marked with parchment, telling of effective methods to discern those of Daelon from those of Lucian. With the books, there is a parchment with the seal of a raven in flight upon it. I have written within it the names of each book, and the number of markers contained in each. In case any become lost," announced Natalia. "There are also messages for each of you," she stated. Blood rushing to her face in embarrassment.

"Good can't wait to read it," said Krail with a toothy grin. "I'll also make sure that things don't completely fall apart. While those two lock themselves away."

"I don't know. It seems to me you're the one everyone should be looking after," said Natalia. Laughing mirthfully.

"You've definitely got me their princess," said Krail. Wrapping his arms around Brena's body from behind. To hold her lovingly in his arms.

"It would seem, tis time to leave," said Lisana.

"Yes, it would," said Natalia. Walking to and opening the door.

"Sorry princess but I haven't actually made it that far yet. If you would kindly close the door." Closing the door Natalia looked at Lisana inquisitively. "You didn't think we were walking to the Moonclave did you. Magic has been released, not that such a trifling thing would have prevented me from doing this in the first place."

"Do what," questioned Fread.

With a wave of her hand upon the door of Drogen's cottage runic sigils appeared, appearing to draw themselves out of thin air. "Of course, it would have taken far longer to mark the runes without magic. Now open the door," said Lisana. Grinning from ear to ear. "If we walked, or even flew, to Moonclave now, we'd miss all the excitement."

Natalia opened the door once more, but instead of the tamarack forest night that she expected to greet her, she was staring at the inside of a massive circular tower. "Unfortunately, this will only work, this one time. Maybe if he'd have made his door out of a stronger material it could have worked again. Well let's get moving. We'll probably have a lot of explaining to do to the elven council using this method, but tis the fastest way there," commented Lisana with a triumphant chuckle.

Lisana pushed everyone through the door, as their stunned expressions proved them to be incapable of moving themselves, without assistance. Only Death walked through the door under his own power. Followed closely by Lisana. "When we go to see the dwarves, I'll have to get them to make some Mythral doorways. At least then we won't have to deal with the portals deteriorating on us," commented Lisana. Closing the door behind her.

As the wooden door shut silence returned to Drogen's cottage. None of those who remained wanting to move. In case what they had just witnessed was actually a dream.

Fread stood up slowly, moving cautiously toward the door, unsure whether to touch it or not. Slowly he inched his hand out, his fingertips just touching the wood. With his slight touch the wooden door turned to vapor, as though it had never been. Staring blankly into the darkness Fread let out his held breath. Recognizing the familiar outline of the tamarack trees.

Chapter Fifty-One

Drogen felt the brother dwarves shifting around on his back fighting admirably against the force of the wind as it battered against them threatening to blow them off the moment they lost grip upon his spiked spinal ridge. Keeping a watchful ear on the dwarves, in case either of them began to fall, two other familiar heartbeats came within range of his draconic ears.

Alya and Asche were running quickly through the forest, their heartbeats denoting desperation. Looking through the trees for a clearing to set down, he found one with ample room, along the same path on which Alya and Asche continued to travel. Barely missing the tree tops with his wing tips he set down lightly upon the ground.

Rumble and Tumble, glad for the break released their cramped hands from around Drogen's spike ridge sliding down his back and tail to the ground as though it were a slide. With the brothers back on solid ground Drogen closed the door in his mind.

"Alya and Asche are heading this way. From the sound of their heartbeat's something unforeseen has transpired."

"We be needn a better way a riddin. While ya wait on da elf an fuzzy ears me brudder an me be findin a better way," said Rumble.

"Ride da lizard thru da sky, keep yah hand or loose yur hide," sang Tumble.

Drogen nodded his head to the brother's before they moved a short distance away talking back and forth amongst themselves as they worked the problem.

Alya and Ashe burst through the copes of trees with abandon nearly running right past Drogen, Rumble, and Tumble entirely. "Alya Asche," spoke Drogen. Calling attention to himself as his scales made it nearly impossible to distinguish himself from the night around them.

With the advent of the unexpected, yet familiar voice, they both skidded to a stop to look around. Finally seeing Rumble and Tumble, they both breathed a sigh of relief.

"I thought I heard Drogen," commented Asche.

"You did," said Drogen from behind them. Causing them both to jump in fright.

"My scales make it hard to distinguish myself from the world around us. That is why you're having a hard time seeing me."

"There you are," said Alya and Asche at once. Their eyes well suited for distinguishing object in the darkness of night. "It's good you're here. We have a big problem heading our way, and it's not coming through the front gate."

"I wondered why neither of you were learning among the towers. So Grock's forces are not coming through the forest, but from the side?"

"Alya and I have been working our way through the aqueducts cleaning them out. We were doing the final few down toward the ravine," said Alya.

"But, we never made it to the ravine. When nightfall came multiple fires started both alongside and inside the ravine. Far too many looked like massive bon fires rather than campfires," recounted Asche with a shiver.

"Could ya see da citadel at all," questioned Rumble. The brothers coming back to join the conversation.

"It was already getting dark when the ravine came into view. Even if it were not, we could not have seen Aragorth through the trees or the mountains alongside the ravine," said Alya demurely.

"I'm taking them to Aragorth. Word hasn't been returned, and if either side falls, the likelihood of the other following is a risk we cannot afford to take. I'll see what I can do along the way to lessen their numbers. Go quickly and inform the council. Tell them to focus their efforts along the sides of Moonclave instead of from the defensive district, where they believed the attack would originate. They may be looking to bombard Moonclave from multiple sides," considered Drogen.

"If only we retained more wyvern's. Maybe we could have been more proactive in our scouting," cursed Asche.

"Ingenuity in times of trouble will help far more than languishing for what is not present," cautioned Drogen.

"I'll have to keep that in mind," said Asche. Bowing her head slightly.

"Go, and make sure that scouts are sent out above the knowledge district first. If they are attacking from multiple directions then they will likely want to attack from opposing sides to devastate everything between their forces. If no elf can do it, talk with your mothers, they too have stake in Moonclave's survival," said Drogen.

Alya and Asche began their run through the wood once more disappearing into the trees quickly. Their heartbeats receding from Drogen's ears moments later.

I should have asked for my extra-dimensional bag back, thought Drogen as he turned to Rumble and Tumble. "Have you thought of a solution?"

"Aye, we be needin some leather, or saddle bits. Ye know where we be findin da like," questioned Rumble with a smile.

"Well I can always fly back to where Alya is. I wanted to get my bag back anyways, and there's plenty of leather in it," said Drogen. Noticing a crestfallen look fall over Rumble's face. "Although, I did tell Alya and Asche I would cut down on the number of enemies before they can begin their siege. What do you think Tumble. Should we go back after Alya. Or, find leather among the goblinkin on our way to Aragorth."

"Take da Orc an Worg ta ground, Take a saddle an sinch er down. No more hold, or loosen hide, only wind an uh pleasant ride," sang Tumble. Wringing his hands in anticipation.

"How many saddles do we need," questioned Drogen. Taking on his true form.

"We be needin a few," said Rumble. Taking the forward most spot between the spikes, at the base of Drogen's neck, with Tumble directly behind. "Done ya be goin too fast now, me brudder an me not be wantin ta fall from such height."

Using magic to aid in his accent they began their journey once more toward Aragorth. At a slightly slower pace, affording the dwarves an easier time.

The first indication of their proximity to those Asche and Alya had seen came in the smell and sting of wafting smoke as it passed into their eyes and noses. The smell of smoke quickly followed by the scent of the rancid fat's many of the orcs chose to coat their armor in.

"That be the smell ah orc if I ever smeld it," shouted Rumble. His voice fighting the buffeting winds.

The smell of the goblinkin below growing until the air itself felt unclean. Causing Rumble and Tumble to plug their nostrils in hopes of combating the overwhelming stench.

"That not be orc stink. That be da stink ah troll," Rumble corrected. Holding his nose tightly closed.

Drogen continued on hearing the heartbeats within and without the ravine taking in their numbers as they gained ground. A short distance away from the advanced troupes Drogen set down once more, cautiously masking his descent within the trees.

"From the heartbeats I can hear, there are no orcs among them," said Drogen. Shaking his head. "Nor are there goblin, hob goblin, or any other that I might have considered on the smaller side of Grock's forces."

"Then that other orc be right. Grock didn't send da small ones. Only the biggins. Dem tree sprites be in fur a hard fight. I be afraid ta see what Aragorth be facen. No small ens here means day all at da citadel," said Rumble.

"No orc or gob about da field. Not a chance Grock'll yield," rhymed Tumble.

"I doubt his yielding is among the cards Grock will play," said Drogen.

"Wha be da best course," questioned Rumble. Stroking his long beard in contemplation. "Owe many be there?"

"They are well over six hundred strong. From their heartbeats most are trolls and ogres. Within the gorge however, there are a great many giants as well."

"Whatever we be deciden ta do. Best be deciden it quick."

"Between the giants, ogres, and trolls I believe the trolls will prove the hardest for the elves to deal with. They have use of magic, but fire magic is not among their typical talents, talented as they are. My mother often told me that the elves, although gifted with the use of water, earth, and air magics, struggle with fire. Tis as if they fear it down to their souls, is how she once described it to me."

"Den we be goin after da trolls," reasoned Rumble.

"I believe that to be the best coarse of action. I can take them down quickly, nullifying their regenerative ability. If we had more time I could accomplish more. However, I fear that leaving the dwarven citadel alone much longer, especially given the distance Grock's forces have traveled, puts both the elves and the dwarves in far too much danger."

"Aye," confirmed Rumble.

"It would seem your wish for a more comfortable ride will need to wait a while longer. Although, so long as you don't find yourselves moving opposite my scales you both should come out... relatively unscathed," stated Drogen. Smoke plumes flowing from his toothy grin.

"I thought of tiein meself to a spike. Now I be thinkin uh full saddle. Sinch an all, be a better idea," commented Rumble. Smiling with a mirthful laugh.

"Saddle da dragon, ridem high, da sinch let loose an da dwarf'll fly," sang Tumble. Accentuating his song with a descending whistle. Ending with a clap of his hands.

"On that note," said Drogen. Walking a short distance from the dwarves to retake his form.

Once more the dwarves placed themselves between the spikes at his neck holding on with all their might as they ascended. Flying low and slow over the encampment Drogen noted every location he could containing trolls. Knowing full well, he only had a single shot of being rid of the forces, without endangering Rumble and Tumble in the process.

Taking his time he made a couple of passes gliding out over the encampment and back into the trees that his wings did not give away his location, or intentions. With a final pass he returned to the woods at their forward encampment.

Coming in low, in order to ensure the complete annihilation of their ranks, Drogen took in a deep breath. An inferno sprang from his mouth, bathing everything in light and flame as alarms sounded throughout the encampment. The conflagration engulfed everything in its path, nullifying the trolls regenerative ability entirely. Although they tried to mount some kind of defense against his onslaught their rise came entirely too late. Resulting in far greater losses.

Although his attack lasted only a brief few moments, it devastated the entirety of the troll forces. Their ashes spreading out upon the breeze formed by his passing wings set adrift along with the ash of their camp fires. With his attack concluded, and every troll incinerated far beyond their regenerative abilities, they flew quickly toward Aragorth. The distinct sound of distant engagement resonating in his ears.

With his superior vision, the outline of a massive boulder careening up from within the ravine caught Drogen's eyes in the dark night. The boulder disappearing from sight as many more followed out of the ravine, along the same trajectory. The massive stone boulders falling heavily into the side of the dwarven citadel. Their cumbrous strikes a climax of plangency.

Chapter Fifty-Two

"I really want to learn how to use this magic," commented Natalia. Scanning the wonderful craftsmanship upon the enchanted mythral archway. Prying her eyes away from the curious magic in order to assess any possible threats within the cylindrical room.

"If only we could have worked together a short time longer. Maybe then we could have convinced the dwarves, elves, gnomes, and all the others to make more enchanted archways. If we had, getting from one place to another would be so much simpler. Not to mention the time and money savings with trade," commented Lisana. Looking upon rune etched portal.

"It would make matters of travel and trade much more convenient," said Natalia. Turning her studious mind once more to the archway. Her mind working meticulously to take in every bit of information it might offer. "These are draconic runes. Are they the same as those Drogen used in his runic sigils, for what he called a home rune?"

"They may look similar, but are quite different. The ones we carve in wood or stone are shortened and made to fit upon the material used. Those placed upon the archway are the full draconic sigils. Those that require extreme precision, knowledge, and craftsmanship working together seamlessly."

"Great precision is indeed necessary when dealing with the manipulation of the space and time between two places. Other forms of magic are far more forgiving with minor mistakes. Still, more knowledge leads to greater understanding, and greater power," stated Death. Training his eyes upon Natalia expectantly.

"I recall hearing those words before, along with a warning. To not think one'-self better than magic. Nor to think one's-self able to control it," stated Natalia.

"Just making certain you remember. And have taken the lesson to heart," commented Death with a slight nod.

"She knows and understands, I'm the one whose teaching her magic after all," said Lisana with a huff.

"How will the tree spirits welcome us. When we walk free of this place," questioned Mai-Coh. Finally bringing himself into the conversation, after losing himself in the new sights, smells, and sounds.

"Well... I didn't really think that far ahead. Even with their memories wiped concerning the dragons... The dryads can still vouch for me. If tis necessary," said Lisana. Shrugging dismissively. "Nothing to worry about."

"We know two tree spirits from Grammora. Helped them to escape with the dream walker Drogen and Natalia black wing," commented Chian.

"That would leave Death... See all your worry is for nothing. We all have someone here who can vouch for us... and Death... Well let's get going. We don't know when, or if the battle has started yet. I cannot wait to meet Drogen after so long," said Lisana enthusiastically.

"And this is exactly why he asked," said Death. Shaking his head.

Holding her hand out and twisting her wrist a set of stone stairs formed from the towers floor creating a descending staircase to the floor below. The stones grinding loudly against each other as they descended. Moved to the top of the stair, Lisana enthusiastically bid the others to follow.

A great commotion and alarm sounded as they descended to the audience chamber below. The elves within the chamber forming a defensive line, as they prepared to fight the new, and unforeseen intruders within their midst.

Chian, curious as always about anything architectural studied everything she could. Taking in both the structure and the magics allowing for their operation. Turning back to look at the staircase she traced the runes she could see in the air before her. Committing them to memory. Her eyes noticing the precise workmanship present upon each of the stone blocks. Allowing it to slide effortlessly into and out of place. "Wondrous." The only word she could use to describe everything.

Thinking through the knowledge left by her ancestors in Zephyria, she knew the tower and staircase to be similar to those described within the hidden tomes. However, the information had been left incomplete. Seeing the theories, turned to practice, Chian knew their coming to Moonclave would indeed be worth whatever trouble they might find themselves in. Distracted, as she continued to be, by the architecture, Chian barely noticed the swords and other sharp implements, pointed her way.

"Natalia," screamed Seraphine. In excitement, rage, and joy all at once seeing her friend. While also remembering the circumstances leading up to their separation. Even with the mixed emotions Seraphine threw her arms around Natalia. Lifting her up in the air. "Don't you ever do that to me ever again."

"I apologize. I did not anticipate the consequences my actions would hold for me, nor those I hold in my heart. I thought I could do it alone, that it would somehow help me deal with, and rise above what Nefar and Bernadine did to me," confessed Natalia.

"You better promise me you'll never do something like that again. Or I'm not letting you go," threatened Seraphine. Putting a little extra pressure into her hug to drive home how seriously she was taking her declaration.

"I promise. If I am thinking about doing anything reckless. I will invite you along," declared Natalia. Knowing this to be the real source of Seraphine's anger towards her actions.

"You better," stated Seraphine. Dropping Natalia to the ground. "With that out of the way. Welcome to Moonclave Princess Natalia of Zephyria. I have a lot of questions about everything that's happened. However, two more pressing questions come to mind. First who're the people you brought with you," she questioned with a smile. Which quickly turned anxious. "And two, *where* and *how* did you all manage to get into *Moonclave* without *anyone* noticing?"

"The second part will be easier for me to explain young one. I am Lisana Reaper of souls, and I brought everyone here through the mythral archway on the second floor," she stated. As though doing so were a natural occurrence.

"Wait, I know these three," said Keltus walking into the chamber after hearing the raised alarm. Mai-Coh, Chian, and Natalia helped Asche and I escape from Grammora. Thank you three again for everything you did to help us escape and return to Moonclave alive," she proclaimed. Bowing her head.

"We did little compared to the dream walker," said Mai-Coh. Drawing a nod from Natalia, while Chian continued to be otherwise enthralled.

"Dream walker," questioned Seraphine. "Wait... you mean Drogen. Does that mean we all have that in common as well," she posited aloud. "Hold on, did you just say Lisana Reaper of Souls?"

"Yes, and this is Death," stated Lisana with a wide grin.

"I-its nice to meet you b-both... I-I-I'm Seraphine. I'm uh prin... Queen of the living district, and a... uh close friend of D-Drogen. Although, I would... very much like it to be more than that," she stammered. Visibly nervous as she shifted her weight back and forth from foot to foot.

"It would appear there is another one," said Death. Grinning as he looked from Natalia to Seraphine.

"It appears so. Looks like you have some competition Natalia," said Lisana teasingly.

"I would hope more for a partnership than a competitor," commented Seraphine. Before turning around in hopes that the blood rushing to her face would be concealed. Only then remembering exactly where she was, and who stood around her. With the realization blood filled her face all the more. Resulting in an awkward gate, as she walked stiff legged back to her seat.

Hoping to distract from her embarrassment Seraphine began introducing the other members of the council. Phaylor; of the defensive district, Gilvail; of the aviaries, Keltus; of the aqueducts, Amanita and Tsuga of the knowledge district, Phatropa; of the crafters district, Llewellyn; of the farmlands, and I am Seraphine; of the living district.

"I don't know whether to take the physical embodiment of Death being here as a good sign or a bad omen," contemplated Phaylor. Shifting nervously in his seat.

"You needn't worry yourselves. I'm not here for any of you. I have another purpose that I must fulfill, when the time comes," said Death cryptically. "I have also been charged with the protection of the last Angelo by Lord Fread of Zephyria. Otherwise, I'll not be interfering in such *mortal* matters."

"That means we don't need to worry about trying to fight death then," said Gilvail. Sighing in relief.

"I-I understand the other people's presence now, but w-who is Lisana," questioned Tsuga.

"Well Death and Lisana here are Drogen's parents," stated Seraphine. As many others around the council felt their blood rush to their feet in surprise.

"Speaking of our son. Where is he," she questioned. Listening intently for his heartbeat.

"Unfortunately, he's already left. We didn't read the letter in time to stop him from flying away I'm afraid," said Llewellyn solemnly.

"He left with Rumble and Tumble to Aragorth. We never received word from the citadel and their fall would ensure our own," said Amanita.

"Then we should head to the dwarven citadel," said Lisana. Moving toward the closest door.

"No, we must wait for the right time," said Death.sSaking his head. "When the time comes. We'll all go together. Until then, it would be best for everyone to stay. The elves and dryads will likely need help against the goblinkin. Especially if trolls have been sent."

"You may be right. With magic sealed they were able to walk in the day and their ability to regenerate could be dealt with using simpler methods, like lopping off their heads or piercing their hearts. With true magics release they'll be far harder to deal with. Especially without the cauterizing effects of fire magic. I hate when you use logic against me," commented Lisana.

"No, you don't," said Death with a grin. Receiving a wave of Lisana's hand and roll of her eyes in response.

"How can we help you prepare," questioned Lisana.

"What we're struggling with right now is the use of magic. Drogen transferred the knowledge into each of us through the dais, but even with all the knowledge we're struggling to use and understand it," grumbled Keltus. Trying and failing to produce anything more than a drop of water in her palm.

"Having knowledge, and implementing it are two different matters entirely. Knowledge is taught, but wisdom only comes through experience, trial, and tribulation," stated Death.

"I thought you said you wouldn't be interfering in such *mortal* matters," teased Lisana.

"Giving the knowledge of aged wisdom could hardly be considered interference," countered Death.

"Do you know how much time you have? Before their forces arrive," questioned Lisana.

"We don't. I've sent out many scouting parties along the most likely routes of egress, but none of the search parties have come back with more than a few long burnt-out fires, along common trails. We've found nothing that concretely states where they plan to attack from, or that they're attacking Moonclave at all," said Phaylor. Clearly frustrated.

"If only we would have retained that orc in the dungeon or something. We may have been able to garner more information. Information he possibly didn't even know he had," started Gilvail.

"Grom risked his own life to bring us the time of their attack, and what the forces are comprised of. I would not allow such kindness to result in punishment," admonished Seraphine. As though she had argued the same point multiple times before.

"We need as many allies as we can get. Those within our enemies ranks especially," said Keltus.

"Or they will turn into our greatest regret. However, we cannot know the truth until everything falls as it may," stated Phatropa.

"It would seem we have visitors, and they're definitely in a hurry," said Lisana. As the doors of the council chamber flew wide.

"Avren," questioned Death. Surprised as Alya and Asche came rushing in.

Alya, still trying to catch her breath looked at Death curiously, shaking her head in response. "I am Alya. Avren is my mother's name."

"We don't have time for this," stressed Asche. "Their attacking from the ravine!"

The council as a whole stood up from their seats. Cutting all other conversation short.

"How many are there," questioned Phaylor.

"We don't know. It was far too dark to see. Luckily Drogen heard us running and stopped. We saw him attack, but we have no idea how effective he might have been at reducing their numbers," stressed Alya.

"We never expected them to attack from the ravine," complained Gilvail demurely.

"If they were coming through the ravine, then why were so many fires made along the forest paths," posited Amanita.

"They were distractions from the main force," concluded Phaylor. His hand striking the council table in frustration.

"It pulled our focus and allowed the main forces movements to go unnoticed. With us focused on the forest the goblinkin could move upon us at their leisure," concurred Gilvail.

"Using the ravine, instead of the forest, will have cut down on their movement time and energy considerably. We would have been caught completely unaware had the two of you not gone to the ravine," concluded Keltus. Praising her sister and Alya's tenacious clearing of the aqueducts.

"Even with giants the underbrush and overgrowth would have hindered them greatly. We should have thought it a possibility from the beginning," said Seraphine. Admonishing herself for not seeing it before.

"It would appear, what we believed would hinder their efforts. As it hindered our own, did nothing but put us at further disadvantage," stated Llewellyn.

"Drogen told us to send scouts to the forest outside the knowledge district. He believes they may be attempting a pincer, attacking from both sides," spoke Alya.

"Phaylor how many do we have who can search the forest north of the knowledge district," questioned Seraphine.

"I'll need to speak with Quercus to be certain, but I believe we only have one scouting party at the moment. It would be much simpler to find out had Drogen remained to help from the dais," stated Amanita sadly.

"We don't have time to practice using it either," complained Phaylor gruffly.

"We don't have time for any of that. We need to find where our enemy is located, or we doom ourselves to fall. It has come time for us to act. We can no longer just sit here commanding others to search. If we don't have enough people, then we must ask our mothers for assistance, and go to where it is most needed ourselves."

"Keltus go and speak with our mothers. Tell them what we suspect and bid them to search the forests around Moonclave for any sign of incursion. Who of those present is most familiar with the forest north of the knowledge district?"

"I am. I do know the area well. It's where many of the herbs and spices my father uses at the inn are most easily gathered. I will go there straight away," volunteered Phatropa.

"Did no one think to ask for our mothers assistance before," questioned Amanita skeptically.

"Often one is blinded by their own focus. Focus upon a single spot in lieu of the entire work leaves all other perspective to be lost," stated Death.

"That was another of Drogen's suggestions, but it seems you beat us to it," remarked Alya.

"H-how long do we have before they're in range," questioned Tsuga sheepishly.

"Although the distance is difficult to judge in the darkness... I would think we have less than a day before they're in range. Maybe even less if, as I suspect, there are giants within the ravine itself," advised Asche.

"If as you suspect, there are giants in the ravine. Are they not already within range to attack us," questioned Llewellyn.

"Amanita and Tsuga go with Phatropa to search the outskirts around the knowledge district. Gilvail and Phaylor take to the aviary and defensive district. Send hawks with scouts around to each tower. That way messages can be sent and received quickly should anything be found. If there are other positions the goblinkin hold we must know about them now," instructed Seraphine.

"Phatropa's party, before you go to search the forest, I have another important task for you. Go to the crafters and gather every available weapon. I don't care if they are dull from use, or as sharp as razors, we need every weapon ready for service. Take as many, as you find along the way with you. Have them gather weapons from their homes as well, those that have them," ordered Seraphine.

"What of the rest of us dear," questioned Llewellyn.

"We know that a force is coming from the ravine, we need eyes in that area. Gather as many as you can, among those who have grasped magic, and set them to work on raising our defenses in the area. Asche, Keltus, and Alya go with and assist her as well. You have a greater knowledge of the area, then anyone else. You'll be our first line of defense and our warning for the first volley. Alya, when you are no longer needed in the west head east to the knowledge district. Your superior sense of smell will no doubt inform us long before their forces arrive. *GO NOW,"* commanded Seraphine. Her tone one of unquestionable authority.

"Yes, my queen." Rang their voices within the chamber as they disbanded, going about their tasks with haste. Seraphine looked taken aback by the others of the council calling her their queen, as they too held the heavy title.

Phatropa, seeing the confusion in Seraphin's expression spoke lightly, before hastily departing after the others. "We may all be kings and queens of our districts, but you, even if you have not realized it. Are clearly, queen of us all," she attested.

"It would appear that you are indeed your mother's child," stated Lisana with a knowing nod and smile.

"I'll take that as a compliment. Although I can't help but fear what it means for my future. Lisana, mother of Drogen, if I may ask your help. May you aid me in addressing my people through the dais," she asked. Bowing respectfully to Lisana.

"It would be my pleasure Queen Seraphine," said Lisana. Bowing in kind.

Lisana stepped upon the dais holding her hand out for Seraphine to grasp and with her embrace they became one with the thirteen towers of Moonclave. Casting their consciousness across its ether, that all within could listen and hear their queen speak.

"I call upon all who have made Moonclave their home. The elves, our mothers, and any other's that might view this place favorably. Even if you, for certain reasons, have hidden yourselves away amongst us. We are on the precipice of invasion. From the deity, Grock's forces. His army knocks upon our door, but we cannot give up or give in. This is our home, the only one, many of us have ever known. I will not see it taken over. We have lost far too much already."

"I say *no more. No more* will we allow the goblinkin to overtake and claim our homes for their own. *No more* will we run from the battlefield, they wish to create. I ask all Moonclave to stand, take up magic and arms, to defend our homes and lives from this incursion at the hands of a power mad god. We will not become a stepping stone along Grock's tyrannical path. We will deny him his conquest. Eliminating any who wish to travel the same destructive road."

Her thoughts complete they cut their connection from the dais. With the loss of her minds focused concentration on her objective Seraphine struggled to keep her feet. Lisana taking her by the arm, steadied her while Natalia ran over to assist. Sitting Seraphine down comfortably in her chair.

"The dais is quite taxing on the mind," commented Lisana. Shaking her head. "Even I am not wholly unaffected by the power that flows through it."

"What about Drogen? He had no issue relaying information through the connection, or spreading the knowledge of magic to everyone in Moonclave. How can he do it so easily, if you struggle to use it as well," questioned Seraphine. Taken aback by Lisana's declaration.

"I do not believe Drogen would be unaffected by its power. Tis a font of magic for the whole of Dranier. It would be impossible for any other than Death or life themselves to do so much and remain as they were without rest between such mental strain," spoke Lisana in consternation.

"Then when Drogen left... he was," said Seraphine. Tears forming in her eyes. "We asked far too much of him. We continued to do so without realizing he too was being strained by its use. He left to the dwarven citadel after standing, and relaying information, from the dais for the entire day without rest. If he faces Grock as he is, Drogen will. We will have caused. I-I will have caused," she wept.

Before Seraphine could fall completely into despair. Natalia wrapped her arms around her. "I'm certain he would not view it in such a light. In the short time we have known him he has acted selflessly. He probably thought to spare you this knowledge, as he did regarding his encounter with Grock in Grammora."

"Maybe, he found a method of lessening or counteracting the mental strain," considered Death aloud. Drawing hopeful looks from everyone as they all wished for Drogen's safe return.

"Then we can *beat* him ourselves. For leaving us to worry for him," blubbered Seraphine. Continuing to fight back her tears. "There's no time for tears. No time for grief. No matter what happens grieving my mother and regrets must wait," spurred Seraphine. Fighting and grasping her resolve.

"Tis the best and worst aspect of regret. No matter how one looks at the actions they take in the moment. Regret is always a later issue," commented Death. A deep burdensome sadness taking hold of his visage.

"We have to believe in him. That no matter what he will return to us," proclaimed Natalia. Dropping her voice to whisper directly into Seraphine's ear. "Especially since *I am winning*."

"You little minx," remarked Seraphine in surprise. "I guess that means I was right about that armor changing your personality. You're right he must return to us safe and sound. I cannot allow you to remain in the lead after all."

Taking some time to regain their composure, Seraphine and Natalia began recounting to each other about their time apart in finite detail. Hours passed as they passed stories back and forth, all the while a deep pit of worry forming in both of their stomachs. As they began to reach the end of their recanting, a lone hawk flew in through the window touching down upon the table before Seraphine. With a deft hand she took the letter from around its stick like leg. Unfurling the unsealed parchment she saw only two words written, but those two words made her blood run cold. "Trolls, West," she read aloud. The thick sappy blood of a dryad sticking to the letter like glue.

Chapter Fifty-Three

Drogen flew full speed to Aragorth, Rumble and Tumble struggling the entire way to maintain their seat's, between his spinal spikes. Still, they did not, and would not, call for him to slow his pace. The sound of massive boulders crashing against the dwarven citadel was all they needed to hear. To understand the dire situation their homeland faced from the goblinkin assault.

Using the cover provided by the night, Drogen dropped into the ravine his breath of violet fire leading his headlong charge. The fires burning everything in their path, boiling water and blood alike as they licked the flesh of their unsuspecting targets. One giant fell to the might of his flame exploding outward as its blood converted to vapor combusting instantly under the pressure. The same fate shared by the trees and waterway beneath the giant's feet.

Covered in bone, sinew, and the rising steam, all within the ravine retreated fearfully. With their retreat underway, Drogen rose from the depths of the ravine breathing bright blue flame out before the citadel. The flames pushing back against the horde occupying the area.

I cannot continue to breath such flames, else Rumble and Tumble will endure the same fate as the giant below, thought Drogen.

As Drogen touched down beside the ravine Rumble and Tumble quickly dismounted. Sliding down his back to the ground. Feeling the weight of their bodies fall free of his own, he closed the door within his mind.

Knowing the brother dwarves to be unarmed, their weapons having never been returned, he cut a wide path through the goblinkin line. Each action taken with his blades made in order to protect the unarmed dwarves and aid their advance toward Aragorth's drawbridge entrance.

Seeing the corpse-grinding fate presented by Godslayer; Envoy of Death the most intelligent among the invading force chose to retreat. The trolls however did not. Instead beginning to swarm, as flies upon refuse, surrounding and cutting off the path Drogen had just formed with sheer numbers alone.

Drogen worked tirelessly cutting limb and torso away from one troll only to have three propagate in its place. Each cut limb causing its previous owner to writhe in pain from the regeneration, while the limb itself regrew into another of their race, adding to their ranks as Drogen, Rumble, and Tumble continued their painstaking pace toward the citadel.

Surveying the land through the mass of troll flesh surrounding them, Drogen tried to make out any other recognizable landmarks from his previous sightings of the citadel. As he cut through two trolls, he saw the remnants of guard towers he'd spotted before. Where once they had stood proud of the citadel overlooking the landscape, they now lay low fallen to be trampled underfoot of, trolls, ogres, and orcs alike.

With the defensive towers toppled the dwarves are left with only one point of defense and egress. Aragorth itself, thought Drogen continuing his survey of the battlefield as he lopped limbs and heads alike.

"Will they let you in," he questioned. Moving diligently onward while expanding the ranks of trolls to a near flood.

"Aye, we be dwarves. They not be letten one alone," confirmed Rumble confidently.

"Not even a couple uh outcast, as me brudder an me," sang Tumble. Dodging back from the raking hand of a troll that got a little too close for his liking.

"Will yah stop makin more uh the damned things," complained Rumble. "Yah better ave a plan or an explanation soon, or we be fillin a belly stead uh slicen um."

Pushed through the final swath of trolls blocking the draw bridge Drogen exclaimed, "Get down." Fire boiling in his mouth.

Quick understanding drove Rumble and Tumble to the ground mere seconds before molten flames burst from Drogen's mouth. Engulfing the massive number of trolls and turning them into molten piles of flesh. The massive number of trolls he'd created, forming a thick wall of smoke and fire between them and the other goblinkin who had been forced to retreat, due to the rapidly growing, and regenerating, numbers of trolls Drogen formed with his deadly blades.

"Their corpses will burn for a while blocking the citadel from further assault from the front. The ravine side is another matter entirely. I doubt their assault to be halted much longer," stated Drogen. Scanning the flaming wall of troll flesh for any possible point of incursion.

"Aye, this be more than enough cover. Me only wish to ave taken a few heads meself in da process. I be goin back ta the tree mites fur me axe, an me brudders hammer," lamented Rumble.

"You'll have your chance before long. Now how do the two of you get into Aragorth," questioned Drogen. "The troll's bodies will continue to burn, but as soon as morning comes, they'll turn to stone. Snuffing the fires."

"It be easy nough. Less there not be one in da citadel," said Rumble. Looking up the mountainside for any visible movement. With a sigh, Rumble took up a fist full of stones. "It be the hard way then." Chucking the stones against the surface of the draw bridge with great precision, Rumble's stones brought forth a plangency of chime. Each note vibrating pleasantly through the ground at their feet, resonating with the solitary-mountain-citadel.

"Me brudder an me be goin home," remarked Tumble solemnly. His typically mirthful rhymes replaced by a hard-edged tone as Rumble continued throwing stones against the portal of the home that had long before forsaken them.

As the crystalline sounds faded away, Rumble returned to their side, shrugging and shaking his head. "They not be hear. They be gone to the city. Aragorth be closed to all who not be knowen the chimes. Closed as the day we be sent away." Turning around to look at the draw bridge once more Rumble shook his head. "I not be suffren da fools much longer. Too blind ta see. Too deaf to hear," he uttered under his breath.

Drogen's eyes moved to the burning troll corpses and the outline of thousands waiting to to cross the line. "You both have come to realize the symbiotic nature necessary for yours and the elves survival. They must survive even if it is despite themselves. Surely, there's at least one among the dwarves who realizes this truth as well."

"Aye, an ye be lookin at um," said Rumble with a bemused grin. "An ya see what that belief done ta me an me brudder."

"Brudder dwarves, wit their brudder's no more. Beards cut from knee ta snore," rhymed Tumble in obvious dejection.

"So that's what brought you both to Zephyria?"

"In a round bout way. Went ta Zephyr first. That be where we met Fread. He be a parta the guard then, not commander. He be the one ta appoint our position in da castle. To look after da princess," reminisced Rumble.

"Well, if they won't allow you entry, I'll just have to make an entrance for you," said Drogen. Looking at the solitary mountain standing before them, noting once more its unnatural distance from the mountain range at both its back and front.

"Ya can try, but it be far more than it be appearen. None be gettin in without a lot ah doin," said Rumble. Turning his back fully to the citadel as they had done nearly a century before. Making to step toward the burning troll corpses, moments before the sound of metal scrapping against metal began filling the air behind him.

The drawbridge, slowly at first, began its long decent to the ground. Rumble and Tumble, although still apprehensive in their expressions, were excited within their heartbeats, at witnessing the drawbridge's fall.

"I'll leave the necessities of diplomacy to the two of you," said Drogen. The drawbridge touched ground sending out a shock of sand and dirt from around its base.

"An what ya be doin in da meantime," questioned Rumble.

"I'll be holding back the horde. There's no telling when Grock might arrive. And although you say there's more to this place than meets the eye, I doubt Grock will find much trouble in destroying whatever defenses this citadel boasts," stated Drogen.

"Either way, ya best not be dyin on us. We be wanten ta go back ta the winged one, she not be receptive wit out ya," grumbled Rumble. Stepping onto the bridge determined to see this part of their journey done.

Tumble walking beside Rumble, across the rapidly ascending bridge, looked back at Drogen for some sign of acquiesce toward Rumble's comment. An acquiesce, protest, or acknowledgment that never came.

Hearing Rumble and Tumble's heartbeats fade away, Drogen let out a breath of relief. Taking a short moment to compose himself, before the shift in tides with the rising sun, he sat down before Aragorth. Calling upon Godslayer; Envoy of Death, Drogen sank into himself once more, hoping his holding the blades both physically and mentally might elicit a response.

"I only wish you could speak to me as you once did. I don't know what I must do to hear your voices again. I fear I may die without so much as a whisper from either of you. I know you can hear me. I feel it to the depths of my soul. Even if you will not speak to me, I must ask for your assistance in what comes next," spoke Drogen. Running his fingers along their etched runic names.

What is it that I lack. Am I ignorant of the truth. Or am I to blame for this...apprehension. I know that my father has made up half of who I am, but what does that truly mean. What does it mean to be the son of Death, Lisana. What does it mean to be a part of their converging bloodlines? What does it mean for the future of Dranier, and all of its inhabitants? What does it mean to be... me, contemplated Drogen.

As the sun rose upon the horizon, the little light produced by the immolated bodies of the troll line began to diminish. Black clouds blocked the suns initial vestiges, allowing Drogen a few more precious moments of reprieve.

"When troll done rosten start the fighten. Beat short rounds and dragon to dirt," announced an orc. Many cheers followed by the sounding of war-horns throughout the encampment at his back.

Opening his eyes to look at the line of eager goblinkin through the flames he cocked his head in intrigue. *How can I understand them now. I could not do so before. Even after living amongst them in Grammora. I relied solely upon Natalia's expertise. Is this a change caused by my first encounter with Grock,* considered Drogen. Calling forth his draconic bowl. *I hope they were able to glean something. Even though these markings continue to elude me. Tis no small comfort to have it within my grasp again.*

Looking over, the strangely alien etchings in hopes of garnering some unknown detail. He couldn't help but find disappointed. *You're supposed to represent my life, and thus its end. Should I be grateful I have yet to understand what these markings mean. Or is my lack of understanding fates way of ensuring my hands do not move against what is... Predestined? Is my understanding connected to what I lack? What I lack in removing the final lock from the white door?"*

Practicality tells me I will likely die upon this battlefield. Their numbers driving me ever closer to my father's side. NO, I cannot think in such a manner. I must prevail. I must not perish here upon this battlefield. I will not allow those for whom I care to fall. Thus, I cannot fall. I will protect all who would stand against conquest and tyranny. And with my strength free them of its oppression," proclaimed Drogen. Drawing strength from his own conviction against the shadow of doubt weighing heavy upon his heart.

A distant lighting strike bathed the world in light as the rays of the sun careened over the coming storm. Turning the burn scarred flesh of the trolls to solid stone. The goblinkin's War-horns sounded alongside the distant mountain, where their line had been forced to retreat, in order to mitigate the heat of their burning compatriots' corpses.

The footfalls of the goblinkin, thunderous in their own right, began their advance, but Drogen paid the looming threat no further head. Fear, anxiety, and stress fell away as he sunk deep within himself. Standing before the two large doors housing his inherited power. To the left a black door, embellished with a red dragon. To the right, a white door decorated ornately in gold filigree. Only one lock and chain remaining across its breadth. The single chain blocking access to the power that lay just beyond.

Reaching out Drogen grabbed hold of the lock, squeezing with all his might in an attempt to break its hold. The harder he squeezed the lock the more visions came to his mind. The death of Balthazar. Ether and Uther's cruelty to the zephyrian people. And Grock's uncaring nature toward anything but himself.

Pulling his hand away, he flung himself back into his corporeal form. *To be Drakregus, one must be able to let go of thought. To let go of feeling. To let go of everything that makes them a part of the world. To be Drakregus, is to be war itself. To feel only the motion of battle. To move despite thought, interruption or interference. That is the state of the Drakregus. The achievement of Mushin.*

Understanding what he must do Drogen let the world fall away, the incalculable number of goblinkin quickly advancing past the stone line of fallen trolls becoming nothing, the worries, fear, anxiety, and doubts all falling away. As if he were cleansing himself within a stream, and the dirt was washing away. With his cleansing he took a deep breath letting it out slowly the world melted out of focus. At once he felt nothing, sensed nothing, was nothing.

The first to arrive before him where goblins, their numbers a torrent of heartbeats filling Drogen's ears, the prospect overwhelming in its breadth and depth, but Drogen found no fear. The trolls and orc followed closely behind, some on foot, others riding on back of dire worgs, but Drogen had no thoughts. The last in line where the ogres, their massive frames dwarfing Drogen by nearly double, in his sealed state, but he made no move from where he sat.

As a goblins gnarled dagger came down to impale Drogen through the heart his hand moved on its own, knocking the dagger free from the goblins hand. The dull blade rendered most effective in his hands, sailed through the corroded arteries of half a dozen more. His left hand crushing the goblins skull in hand before throwing it into the coming horde, like a battering ram, killing or wounding five more.

Without thought or feeling Godslayer; Envoy of Death appeared in his hand. The blades rolling around his body, an asp ready to strike. With his double seax blade he stepped forward. Each step blood flowed, heads rolled, and limbs fell with deft precision. His deadly blade dance punctuated by eruptions of all consuming fire.

Chapter Fifty-Four

"How goes the preparations in the aqueducts? Have we managed to add sufficient wards and barriers to the area.," questioned Seraphine.

"Ashe, Alya, and Llewellyn are working with many from the knowledge district. We have also had many come forward that are...not of us. They say they are of... Daelon. Either way they are proving to be quite adapt at other forms of magic. Unfortunately, none of them are well versed in fire magics."

"When this is all over, we'll need to thank them for their assistance," insisted Seraphine.

"Yes, we will. There have been a few incidents regarding them. However, they are quite different then we are. And with Manzine's... appearance many are being pushed away, or disregarded entirely. Luckily our mothers, seeing this trend have come to aid them, showing them kindness and bringing our kin closer to these followers of Daelon." said Keltus with a hopeful smile.

"They've seen fit to protect our home from Grock's forces. They are as much a part of our home as we are. This is not the time for in fighting, I will have to thank our mothers for stepping in as well. And the barrier's"

"Oh right, Barrier's and traps have been prepared in the forest to the south. Any of them who think coming through the forest to be a good idea, will be severely disappointed or very dead. That brings us to the biggest problem we will have to the west, The giants. No matter what we may be able to accomplish against the ogres and worgs, we have no good method of defending or defeating giants," affirmed Keltus with a shake of her head.

"Then it may only be a matter of time before all the defensive measures might be rendered useless to the west. What of the trolls to the east? Has a method of dealing with their regenerative ability been made," questioned Seraphine.

"Bailfar is working with Aurix and Lisana on a solution for the trolls as we speak. Lisana's knowledge of herbs and acids is proving invaluable if Bailfar's musings are any indication. They're hoping to have the right concoction made and ready to test shortly. On that note the weapons Bailfar and the dwarves crafted have been distributed between both points as well."

"They had to have worked the entire time we were in the knowledge district to have produced so many weapons," contemplated Seraphine aloud. *Yet another name to add to the thank you list.* "What of our guests from Zephyria. Have they been able to find what they're looking for in the library?"

"Unfortunately, they have been unsuccessful. I have been meaning to ask, but shouldn't we be asking for their assistance. We have formed an alliance with Zephyria after all," questioned Keltus.

"I believe asking for their help, at this time, would be a mistake on our part. They may be willing to help us to fend off an enemy that is far beyond our capabilities. However, if we ask for help with something, they see as minor, it could destroy our chances of receiving aid when we need it most," reasoned Seraphine. "Asking Natalia, who I have no doubt would agree, would have the same result. Death himself has said he will not act unless it is to save Natalia. Putting her in harms way could be seen as an intentional effort to bring Death into our affairs. I for one don't want to see what happens to someone who, even if accidentally, causes an affront to Death himself."

With the thought coming to fruition in her mind, a shiver ran down Keltus's spine. "So, we need to deal with as much as absolutely possible before asking for their aid. When next would you like a full reporting?"

"The time it's taking for them to start their assault is worrying. Let's make the next report for tomorrow, sooner if there's any movement," said Seraphine.

Seraphine watched as her fellow queen councilor hastily exited the chambers. Only after silence once more permeated the room, did she allow herself to relax in her seat. "I wonder if our mothers would be willing to intervene further. Beyond their rolls as lookouts," questioned Seraphine. Speaking to the empty room.

"Yes, we are," came Leif's voice. As she sauntered into the council chambers. "Although I don't much like your tone in calling us lookouts."

"I apologize, the stress of leading everything going on here in Moonclave must be affecting me far more than I realized. It feels as though I'm holding the fate of our people squarely upon my shoulders. So please forgive me both now, and for what I might say in the future," said the clearly stressed Seraphine.

As Leif made to speak her piece, an impalpable breeze brushed the vines on her head, stopping her in her tracks. "Root Mother wishes for me to convey a message to you. A true leader does not lock themselves away. They must show strength to both their people and their enemy through their actions. Surrounded by those they would command. You must remember Seraphine you do not carry the weight of Moonclave alone. We must shoulder this burden together."

"Thank you, Leif. And thank you, Root Mother. I seem to have lost myself within the walls of this chamber," said Seraphine. Looking around but stopping momentarily to take in the brightly burning fire upon the central dais. "Do you know where Natalia and those she came with are?"

"Yes, they made their way into the library at sunrise," said Leif.

"Good. At least within the library they'll be safe." *Where should I begin,* contemplated Seraphine. "Let's head to the farm and aqueduct districts. They're likely to be attacked first, even with our heightened defenses, we'll be in trouble if giants are amongst their ranks."

As she stepped toward the chamber door Seraphine felt frigid claws reaching up from the pit of her stomach. With a concerted effort, she pushed against the feelings before they could take hold and overwhelm. Waging a battle of her own within the depths of her mind. Closing her eyes she took in a steadying breath, calming herself before stepping through the chamber door, and into the larger world beyond its comforting confines.

Leif walked silently beside Seraphine as they traveled west. All who passed her stopping and asking for advice, or if she happened to need anything from them. A sight that would have been viewed as unimaginable only weeks prior.

Any who chose to speak with her, she would hear, give suggestion, or course. Seeing them off with the grace and dignity of her station. "They see me as something... more, yet I cannot look at myself as they do. It may be shameful to admit but, I'm far out of my depths with all of this," confessed Seraphine. Shaking her head.

"It's as if I'm a rouge actor, among the people, and most especially the council. How am I supposed to be an effective leader? I fear they'll come to see me as the fraudulent Queen that I see myself as. Do they not view me as a usurper, especially when there are far more qualified candidates. All of them far more credibility than the recently imprisoned daughter of the former queen."

"The mind can often play tricks upon us. Casting doubt against belief, against the roll we play, and upon what we see staring back at us, in a pool of clear water. No matter what others may say to the contrary, the mind can and will twist the truth of what others, and we actually see."

"And what is the truth," questioned Seraphine in a low whisper. Her mind continuing to cast thoughts of doubt and inadequacy.

"None are ready to lead when responsibility is placed upon their shoulders. We all must learn what shouldering such responsibility entails. But one must also be willing to take necessary risks. To make mistakes. All in order to learn for themselves what it takes, and what things are beyond one's ability to control," spoke Leif. Intangible winds dancing through her vines.

One day these shoes of my mothers. I hope they come to fit me as well as they once did her, thought Seraphine as a single tear rolled down her face.

As they neared the aqueducts and farmland's the smell of fresh running water and growing crops filled the air, bringing them both a much-needed respite, from the uncomfortable feelings presented by Seraphine's demure mental state.

"We should head through the central tower both here and to the east. Going through the Library is a chore, but with a guide through its depths the journey is much faster than going through the other towers," advised Leif.

"We'll ask Amanita and Tsuga, or if they're already out, it may be wise to grab the previous queen of the knowledge district. From what I understand she's been rather chatty, and is driving her co-conspirators mad," bid Seraphine with a slightly wicked smile. "Can't say I feel for any of them. If they had their way, I could have been executed, or received any number of other punishments, for simply being my mother's daughter."

As they drew down upon the tower splitting the aqueduct and farmland districts, the concussive crashing of stone felling trees, and impacting the ground, rocked them both from their internal contemplation.

An imperceptible wind whipped against Leif's hair and with it she moved quickly to the tower Seraphine only steps behind. Each door within the tower was thrown wide as they ran toward the crashing sounds just beyond. Flinging the last door so hard that it nearly broke along its hinged side, Leif propelled herself up into the trees with rapidly growing roots and vines.

Seraphine, still a novice with magic, couldn't hope to keep up with Leif's pace. Making the door many minutes behind her dryad companion rendering her incapable of finding the path through which she traveled.

Outside the tower Seraphine spotted the cause for the sound that had brought them running. A boulder, half as tall as the tower at her back, had fell and rolled over everything in its path. The boulder stopping only a hundred yards from the tower itself. Scanning the boulder and the wood surrounding it for any sign of blood, she could not help but breathe a sigh of relief, finding none.

I have no idea where she went, and I hardly think I could catch up to her. I guess this means I should find Llewellyn and make sure there aren't any injured. This boulder came uncomfortably close, I hope none of the others have made it this far.

Moving swiftly to the western rally point Seraphine only let herself feel relief when she found everyone gathered, with no injuries in sight. "Are there any injured, or in need of help," posited Seraphine. Cautious in her optimism.

"No, everyone is fine dear. Just a little shaken up I'm afraid. That boulder came far too close for comfort," elaborated Llewellyn.

"Unfortunately, this proves our fear. Grock did indeed send giants against us. We cannot hope to face off against giants, not if they are allowed to get much closer. Sure, we could manage to do some damage, from whichever tower they come to, but can we hope to fell it before catastrophe," posited Seraphine.

"They're clearly within range to attack with boulders. This time we got lucky. They're tying to figure out Moonclave's exact location. A few scouts, who returned just before that boulder fell, saw the giants' throwing stones and trees in multiple directions," informed Asche. Walking free of their erected war tent.

"Then there's much we can do to prevent the giants from ever finding Moonclave, and we must," said Seraphine low. Before clearing her voice to garner the attention of everyone in the encampment. "Moonclave faces an uphill battle. They wish to squeeze us from both sides to ensure our defeat. Even with the odds stacked against us we must look for victories. The more little victories we claim, the better our chances of coming through this scarred, but otherwise unscathed."

"With giants at their disposal, they believe themselves to be victorious already. But I refuse to stand idly by while we are threatened from a distance, picked off like ants. Those of you who wish to take part in claiming for themselves one small victory... Follow me, that we may ensure our survival," posited Seraphine.

Few among the gathered raised their hands in acceptance of the new task, but Seraphine paid them no heed walking through their middle toward the giant threat. "Two of you go and inform Phaylor or Quercus of our mission. Have them send any they can spare to aid our efforts."

Placing her hand on the hilt of her companion sword Truth Seraphine let out a high-pitched whistle calling all at her back, who dared, to follow. *I know what must be done to protect Moonclave and everyone who calls it home. Although this means the possibility of sacrificing myself for my people. I will ensure through my own strength that none who meet their end, go in vain.*

Swiftly she ascended from the ground to the treetops flinging herself along, like she'd done as a child, using limbs and natural vines to aid in her haste. All the while, scanning the forest, in hopes of glancing Leif amongst the foliage.

Having not lived among the old growth for many years, Seraphine's initial progress slow and cautious, as her mind fought against her muscle memory. *Why do I fear what used to bring me such joy. My muscles, though clearly fatigued, are screaming for my mind to allow what they already know to happen. I must trust myself. Trust my body. Push away my doubts and simply be one with the forest, as I have always been.*

With renewed confidence in her strength and ability Seraphine's movements became more natural, as though she were every bit apart of the forest as the forest was a part of her. Speeding past nesting animals and grazing fawns, who had, yet to be scared off, she could feel and hear them all.

The halfway point between Moonclave and the still distant ravine, denoted by the natural thinning of the trees, caused her to shift direction, knowing her trajectory would bring her out closer to the gorges end, than where the giants would be.

Leaping and bounding through the trees as though it were second nature, the sound of boulders cracking, and splintering trees in the distance drew her in. A boulder nearly ten times her size descended from the sky above her, its only warning the earsplitting shattering of the treetops, forcing her to the ground and away. As she tucked and rolled along the forest floor the boulder crushed the tree she'd been standing on, sending splinters of wooden shrapnel into everything within its path.

Luckily this tree blocked most of that, thought Seraphine touching the tree's bark in thanks for it shielding her. *I really need to figure out this whole magic thing. The knowledge is here. I just need some time to figure it out, but I have no time for that right now. The scouts were right. They're throw's do seem to be random. Which means they haven't located Moonclave,"* she thought with a mental fist pump. Not wishing to look too excited.

Hearing no other boulders descending she returned to the treetops, knowing that the traps lain out in the area, from the progress reports, would be deadly to anyone unfortunate enough to encounter them. Redoubling her efforts she continued at her breakneck pace, only slowing when the massive hairy feet of a giant came into view, from below the canopy.

Circling behind the giant, Seraphine climbed as high as she could into the trees crown. Doubling over on a branch just beneath the thick foliage she slid the leaves away, peaking out in hopes of seeing how many giants Grock had sent. Meticulously she scanned the area, spotting three heads above the canopy for her efforts.

Hastily she descended the tree to the forest floor. "Three giants. Hopefully Grock thought that number enough to deal with us," she said aloud. Knowing in her heart that her people had followed. Even with the odds so stacked against them.

"The giants are starting to throw trees like javelins as well," said Asche. "I narrowly escaped one of those javelins right before that boulder came down."

"I hope for all our sake, the trees are traveling far over Moonclave. I would hate to learn just how far they can throw a tree. Especially when they can, so effortlessly, throw those massive boulders," remarked Llewellyn.

"Did anyone see Leif along the way," questioned Seraphine.

"I'm afraid not my queen. Even with our quick pace she had many minutes on us, and is much faster than we can match. She's out here somewhere, but until she makes herself known, I doubt any of us could spot her" remarked Asche.

"I only hope she's safe. How many have come with us?"

"Twenty in total. Some stayed behind, but only because they needed to. Didn't want an unforeseen enemy attacking Moonclave before our victorious return after all."

"We need to take out the giants and do it as quickly as possible."

"Taking all three down in one fell swoop would be the best method, but with only twenty... I don't think it's possible."

"Actually... It may be. The twenty who came are adept with magic. With their help, it may be possible to take all three of them down at once. However, we should ask the dears if they believe it possible to do so. Just in case I'm wrong in my assessment of their abilities," warned Llewellyn.

Gathering around their queens the group of magic users looked, all together, uncertain. Having only been able to use magic for a short amount of time driving many of them to shake their heads, dismissing the idea entirely.

"Anything you can think of that could provide us with an advantage. Using magic or otherwise" questioned Asche.

"We're simply looking for suggestions. Please all of you speak your minds. We cannot know it cannot be done, if we fear to even try," said Llewellyn. Attempting to drum up participation amongst those gathered.

"We could attack them from the treetops, they wouldn't expect that," suggested one. With that one suggestion, came a flood of commentary. Both for and against it.

"Clam yourselves," cautioned Seraphine. "We don't want to be wiped out before we can strike because we are too loud," she said. Shutting everyone up as they shrank away from the sound of a tree trunk striking and shattering another tree far too close for comfort.

"Sorry," said the group in a whisper.

"Okay, I heard use vines to trip them to the ground. And go for their throats, if we're going to attack from the treetops. Are there any other suggestions," questioned Seraphine.

With no other's forthcoming Seraphine began formulating a plan. "Actually, it may be best to incorporate all three suggestions. YES. This could work," she said excitedly. Drawing shushing sounds from those around her. "Sorry," she apologized in a whisper.

Regaining her composure Seraphine began laying out their plan of attack. "Those who're capable of producing thick vines will be in charge of felling the giants."

"You'll need to work in pairs. Otherwise producing enough vines to fell a giant, will be far too strenuous," commented Asche. Having worked closely with the magic users building traps.

"To ensure their safety, and concealment from the giants, a distraction will be necessary. Without a worthy distraction the giants could avoid the vines entirely," stated Llewellyn. Catching on to Seraphine's plan.

"Exactly. To make certain those below go unnoticed we'll need to distract the giants from the treetops, leading them into our trap. If they're focused on the treetops, they'll not have time to worry about what might be happening at their feet. That just leaves the most dangerous portion of this whole plan. Attacking and killing the three giants before they can regain their feet. We only have one chance to get this right, and no matter which portion of the plan we are carrying out, the chances of being injured or killed are astronomical," conferred Seraphine to her small force.

"We're dealing with giants after all," stated Llewellyn.

"Whatever risk we face is far outweighed by those we'll be saving," declared Asche. Bumping fist to heart giving weight to her sentiments, and conviction.

"The six most adapt at forming vines will split yourselves between the three of us. Six more for the treetops. The rest of us will fill in where we're needed and attack the giants when they're down. Any who find themselves free at any point are to remain in position as sentries. Our task is already complicated. We don't need interruptions or unforeseen enemies stopping us at a critical moment," ordered Seraphine.

With their orders given each team split, moving after a single target. Taking her team to the giant furthest away Seraphine, sent the vine weavers ahead, bidding them to work quickly.

Their targeted giant, being the closest to Moonclave, brought tension to Seraphine's throat. *We need to take care of this giant quickly. If even one of them is able to find Moonclave, then it will prove easier for the others to as well. Luckily the forest itself conceals much of Moonclave from sight, even from giants, but if those camouflaging trees were to fall it would inevitably be a beacon for others to follow.*

Silently they moved into position ready to commence their attack. Wishing to give the root weavers ample time, she staid their attacks. Choosing to watch and wait for an opportunity to present itself, as they needed every advantage possible.

With a heavy hand the giant uprooted an elder oak tree from the ground raising it over his head and the canopy of trees to throw the javelin. Seeing the giant's intentions. Seraphine raised and dropped her hand commanding them to commence their attack. Arrows, branches, and stones rained down upon the giant's head and arms from the trees around it. Each of the implements aided by, another of their groups, wind magic.

Distracted by the new sensation the giant lost grip upon the massive tree in its grasp. The heavy trunk slamming into the side of its head and cutting at its ear. With the tree's fall the giant raged striking out at all the other trees around it with heavy front kicks leveling its targeted trees and felling one or more behind them.

Retreating from the raging giant the elves continued their assault from a safer distance. The magic user propelling them further in order to make up for the new disparity. Concerned with the strain being placed on the magic user, Seraphine looked to where she knew him to be.

The male elf's body, seeming to blur under the strain of his concentration, became foreign to her, but not so foreign to their surroundings. Antlers grew from the tops of his head, forming into points around his crown. Oaken bark covered his body as oak and holly leaves, acorns and berries covered a majority of his body.

The look in his eyes reminded Seraphine of a wild animals, but even seeing those wild eyes and his change of appearance, she couldn't help but feel safe within his presence.

"What are you," questioned Seraphine before she could catch herself. Knowing it not to be the time for such conversation.

"Yaelin. Third of Daelon. Kurnun," remarked the antlered man. Struggling to hold his concentration.

The giant swung its arm around trying to fight off the stinging pelts of its constantly moving, and unseen enemy. Further enraged by its lack of understanding, the giant began to charge haphazardly. Choosing a direction of charge by where the stinging strikes engaged its body.

The heavy footfalls of the stomping giant alerting the waiting ground team to its lumbering approach. Chasing headlong after the stinging sensation the giant didn't see the thick vines lain out along its path, until it began its uncontrolled descent to the ground. Its lumbering body crashing into and crushing trees, acting as a cushion to its fall.

Even with the giant brought prone, those within the trees continued to bombard it. Throwing anything they could readily get their hands on. The magic user of their contingent, who had once more dawned his elven form, supplying necessary force to their efforts.

Even with magics aid their actions did nothing to subdue the giant, however, before it could bend its knee and rise, the vine weavers stepped forward. Creating large thick vines around the giant's arms and feet in order to keep their adversary prone. With no other option available they anchored their vines to roots and trees around them. Making absolutely certain that the giant could not rise.

Dropping out of the tree with Truth drawn Seraphine walked up to the giant's mouth. With a shallow cut, just enough to draw blood, "How many of you are there," she questioned the giant. Unsure if it could possibly understand.

"Two hand," spoke the giant. Trying to fight its bonds.

With the giant's declaration Seraphine paled, but the magic user stepped forward in order to ask another question.

"Not how many with Grock. How many here," questioned the Kurnun. Pointing to the forest.

"Half hand," commented the giant. The third of Daelon translating.

"Then we don't have more than the three to worry about," breathed Seraphine in relief.

"Let's be done with this. I hope the other groups were successful in dealing with their giants, but if they were not, they will need help," stated Seraphine.

Holding out his hand to Seraphine, the Kurnun bid her take it his eyes already closed in concentration. Following his lead Seraphine took his hand and felt magic's flow circling through her body, and with it came understanding, Drogen's dissemination of knowledge, had lacked.

Bidding those around her to do the same, they combined their efforts, for the first time. Thick thorny brambles began to grow around and beneath the giants' body tearing and cutting through its body as the vines upon its back held it in place.

Though the giant struggled, it did so for only a short time, as the brambles pierced through its heart and head. The thorns and stems drinking in the fallen giants' blood producing bright red fruits and flowers as they consumed the giants' entire body.

Only upon confirming for themselves, after making triply sure the giant was in fact deceased, did they begin to realize their accomplishment. Though for most it remained beyond their mind's comprehension. Further compounded by their heightened battle state's waning.

Although she wished to relax and celebrate their monumental victory, Seraphine rose to her exhausted feet. "Unfortunately, we can't rest just yet. We must make sure the others have been successful," avowed Seraphine.

Although exhausted from their success, they backtracked to where the other two parties would have encountered their foes. Only slowing their pace as the second squad, led by Asche, joined them on their way to Llewellyn's party, having enjoyed similar success.

Thrilled by her compatriot's success, Seraphine held high hopes, that Llewellyn had found success as well.

Chapter Fifty-Five

Running through the trees to where the giant had previously trekked, they found the broken bodies of both elves and ogres. All of whom had been crushed within the imprints left by the giants feet upon the ground, while others found themselves impaled upon tree limbs.

"Two of you take the bodies of our fallen people and return to Moonclave. Everyone else follow me," ordered Seraphine. Quickly picking up on the giant's path easily.

Instead of the giants pushing of the trees, or uprooting them to throw, they were instead trampled and crushed under its feet and body. *So they were able to fell the giant, but it regained its feet before they could kill it,* determined Seraphine.

Running along the giant's path, at full speed, they felt the giants reverberating footfalls long before spotting their target. The vibrations from the giants movements caused many of their muscles to spasm from their fatigue. Even Seraphine found herself struggling to continue as the vibrations became more and more intense through the ground. In hopes of mitigating some of the effects they once more took to the tree tops.

Even with the trees absorbing the shock, I have to force my legs and arms to keep moving forward. I know it must be the same for the others complained Seraphine internally though she portrayed strength, to any onlookers, at all times.

As soon as the giant's feet came into view Seraphine slowed the others allowing some to rest, while sending Asche and a few others out as scouts, in hopes of locating Llewellyn, and those under her command. *Please say we're not too late.*

"This giant has traveled a great distance. Lucky for us it turned away from Moonclave, but that doesn't render it any less of a threat. Those who absolutely need rest, remain here as look outs. I don't want any surprises coming up from behind us. Any who feel they can still fight follow me. We need to take care of this giant, and any other ogres hidden in the area. We'll deploy a similar strategy as before. But this time we do not have surprise on our side. We will need to move in tandem. vine weavers, work quickly to wrap the giants legs. Everyone else attack from the treetops as before," she ordered. Sending them off.

We need to take care of this before more, or worse giants, decide to show up. I will need to provide a secondary distraction, just to make certain they're distracted, thought Seraphine running full speed toward the giants feet.

Seeing the vines extending along the ground she launched herself over them coming out in a roll to her full height. The giant, distracted by the renewed attack happening at its face and neck began to swing its arms around defensively. With the distraction above Seraphine pulled Truth from its sheath, running the sharp blade across the giants exposed toes in a flying leap.

As the giant recoiled from the pain in its foot, its big toe grazed Seraphine's leg throwing her body into an uncontrolled cartwheel. Unable to control her speed, or landing, she slammed hard into the trunk of an ancient oak tree, knowledge of which struck her body as acorns fell around her, dislodged by the impact.

The vine weavers continued their work on the elongating slithering vines. Unaware in their concentration, of Seraphine's injuries. Looking her body over for wounds, her breath caught. *How could I be so foolish. What was I trying to do, get myself killed for nothing,* thought Seraphine admonishing herself, as she rolled her back up the tree for a better view of everything unfolding around her.

Even with her self admonishments, her method proved successful, throwing the giant into a rage filled stomping and flailing tirade. Further punctuated by magic aided stones and arrows cutting long gashes along its face and arms. The giants blood flowing and soaking into the ground as it hopped on one foot.

Those she placed as lookouts suddenly dropped from their trees as ogres burst into the open, heading straight for the enraged giant. The elves, using their knowledge of the forest to their advantage struck the ogres down as they passed, completely unaware to their presence until they lay bleeding out on the forest floor.

Their efforts greatly successful in thinning the ogres numbers, left but four of what had been a contingent of fifteen. Those four rushed to their giant charge, trying in vein to stop its hopping. Providing the vine weavers ample opportunity to raise their vines to the back of the giants hopping knee.

With a push the giant fell backward, still clutching its cut and bleeding foot. Wasting no time, the vine weavers extended and tied tens of other prepared vines together across the giants legs, torso, and arms. Immobilizing it completely.

The four ogres moving to cut away the vines, found themselves each facing a fist of elves for their trouble. With the ogres aware of their presence their battle became much harder. Even with five elves fighting the thick-skinned ogre would take them many minutes of continuous fighting. Fighting they were far too exhausted for.

Using the last vestiges of their stamina, and concentration, the root weavers came together. Holding hands in order to disperse the strain of their spell, as they were collectively exhausted. For their combined effort what started out as a sapling beneath the giants skull, quickly developed. The tree rooting and growing thicker and taller through the prone giants upper body killing the giant instantly. The nutrients from its massive form, and spilled blood, providing sustenance to its rapid growth. Faltering from the strain and effort of killing three giants, the vine weavers collapsed.

Although covered by the tree and giants corpse from view by the other elves Seraphine witnessed the last on the weavers line fall. "Gather the weavers, and return to Moonclave quickly," shouted Seraphine over the fighting.

The elves, fighting hard against the ogres, relented. Retreating to the vine weavers. Throwing their unconscious compatriots over their shoulders, they hastily dispersed into the woods, fanning out to ensure they could not be easily followed.

The ogres moved around the tree made of the giants corpse angrily. Their fists striking the tree as they walked around its trunk and rooted corpse.

Trying to move away, Seraphine pulled herself around the ancient oak. As she tried to rise from the tree she couldn't help but cough. Covering her mouth, in hopes of stiffing the sound, she felt wetness upon her hand. Pulling it away in order to look, she noted it to be blood. Hearing footsteps at her back she couldn't help but lament her actions further.

I cannot call this a good death, but at least I will go to Death knowing Moonclave and my people are safe, she thought as another cough of fine red blood escaped her mouth. *If only I could have made those thoughts and wants come true before my end. Everything I wanted to say and do with both you and Natalia,* she pondered licking her lips. *Oh the fun we could have had together.*

Closing her eyes, for what she knew to be the last time, Seraphine waited for the death blow she knew to be coming, as the ogres footsteps drew closer.

"Grom defend elf friend, wait for other friend find," spoke Grom directly into her mind.

"Ogre leave. Grom kill. Grom find first. Go back," he ordered the ogres "You disappoint Grock. No giants left. Leave all ogre to Grock rage if not go," he threatened. Making the ogres turn and run quickly.

As the ogres crashed through the forest, in order to distance themselves, Grom wrapped Seraphine's arm round his shoulders. Hefting her up, as best he could, in order to bear the brunt of her weight.

Seraphine used her feet as best she could. Struggling with each step against her injuries, and lack of stamina. "Thank you Grom. For saving me. I just hope it's not in vain," she stated. Her voice exhausted and shaky. "What of the others, did the others make it back alive."

"Grom tell them run. They listen to Grom. Because Grom know other elf, and other elf listen. They go, try find more, come back. Not see ogre coming. Not know others come till too late. When return giant dead, ogres come for elf friend. Why others leave elf friend?"

"They didn't know I was injured. I ordered them to take others back to Moonclave. They did exactly what I wanted them to. They retreated so they could continue to fight those Grock has sent against us."

"Grom want friend to live. Grom want all friends live. Even if Grom not live to see friends. Grom understand elf friend reason. Grom think same, not same as other, but same as dragon."

"It seems you have far more in common with us then you do with Grock, and those who blindly follow him," said Seraphine offhandedly.

"Because more same with Drogen then with Grock," said Grom with a smile. "Grock kill many with anger. With rage. Drogen kill to protect. Not same," he said. Shaking his head. "Not same."

"No definitely not the same. I think I'm getting worse. I need time to rest, and use the state Drogen taught me to regain my strength. Can we stop for a short time?"

"No. Not stop. Take elf friend home. Take friend to help hurt. Grom not stop till friend safe. Not far now. Grom send mind to elf. Get elf friend fast help."

"Thank you Grom. You're a good friend," said Seraphine. Displaying a cherubic smile, despite the pain of her injuries. With Grom's assertion Seraphine breathed a sigh of relief. Her remaining stamina falling to naught. With the last of her mental ability Seraphine collapsing in on herself. Falling deep into the seraph's trance. Knowing, for certain, she would be safe in Grom's hands.

Chapter Fifty-Six

The sound of horns in the distance roused Seraphine from her meditation, turned sleep. Taking some time to recognize her location, as the many shelves of books, tables, and chairs came into focus around her.

"You're finally awake, you had everyone worried I'll have you know, especially Llewellyn. She's been by your side every second, since the vaudune Grom brought you to her," chastised Lisana.

Looking across the table she'd been placed against, she noticed Llewellyn with her head on the table, sleeping. As if seeing Seraphine get up through her eyelids Llewellyn launched from her seat embracing Seraphine embracing her tightly. "Ouch," exclaimed Seraphine. Causing Llewellyn to back off. Though she gripped Seraphine's arm in order to comfort Seraphine, and herself.

"You should have asked for help, ogres and trolls may be easily felled, with the right knowledge. Giants are a different matter entirely; I must commend your ingenuity in dealing with their threat. Though I must say again, you should have asked for help."

"I sent word to Quercus to send others down to assist us," said Seraphine.

"Yes, you did dear. Quercus sent everyone he could spare. We were gathering in order to attack the giant and ogres. We didn't know the giant had been felled. Not until Grom popped into our minds. The others of your party joined us moments later, they thought you were right behind them."

"True magic hasn't been released for very long, yet so many are increasing both proficiency and knowledge. I hoped it would be so, especially in the aftermath I witnessed, upon seeing it sealed," commented Llewellyn in melancholy.

"I thought we'd lost you dear. If not for Grom, we would have," stated Llewellyn.

"How...How long have I been unconscious?" questioned Seraphine.

"Three days, your body needed to heal. Speaking of which you should continue resting. The rest of Moonclave is fending off the trolls in the north. The acid I helped Bailfar and Aurix make is effective at stopping their regeneration. Furthermore, without the giants throwing trees and stones, their siege ability has diminished greatly," said Llewellyn. Reading through some of the books left out by Drogen.

"What about Leif? Did she return," questioned Seraphine.

"Oh, she returned all right, she was in nearly as bad of shape as you. If I hadn't been here to help in the healing process, tis likely neither of you would have recovered from your wounds."

"Leif and many of our mothers, took out ogres, while we took care of the giants. They pushed and threw them back into the ravine. The only ones that escaped were those with the giants themselves."

"It would seem the dryads' pension for theatrics and overexertion has been passed to their children. I'd say this should teach you a lesson, but past experience tells me such a notion will only land on long deaf ears," remarked Lisana. Crossing her arms and looking expectantly to Seraphine.

"I apologize, both for inconveniencing you, and for not asking for help," she said. Bowing respectfully and humbly to Lisana.

"You are far from an inconvenience. I simply don't want you to lose your life in some desperate attempt to garner my or deaths approval. You already have it," said Lisana. Rising with a massive grin.

Seraphine, making to protest, was cut off before she could effectively organize a rebuttal. "I should be the one apologizing. Death is reluctant to leave Seraphal. Unwilling to find and help Drogen. Tis all getting on my nerves. I know he's hiding something about Drogen, probably because he's afraid of what I might do when I find out."

"Could it be a good secret, like a surprise," posited Llewellyn hopefully.

"The secrets Death keeps, more often than not, are ruinous," said Lisana. Worry clear as day in her voice as she looked past Seraphine and Llewellyn. Searching her memories.

"Drogen will find a way to return. He's far stronger than any of us. Aside from you, and Death of course."

"In the past I had a hard time matching him. The bond has closed the gap between us. But defeating an opponent, doesn't always mean besting them in battle. There are many methods of winning against an adversary. Some do not require bloodshed," remarked Lisana.

"Drogen told me much the same in the past," commented Natalia. Appearing from the shadows before an adjacent bookcase. Leading her to stand between Llewellyn and Seraphine.

Having neither heard, nor seen her approach, both elves jumped from their seats in surprise making Seraphine cringe against the strain. "Ouch."

"Sorry, I forget others cannot see or hear me from the shadows," said Natalia apologetically.

"Don't feel bad, I can't distinguish her from the shadows either. If not for her heartbeat, I doubt even I would know when she comes and goes. Yet another gift you inherited from Alexandria," stated Llewellyn.

As if not hearing Lisana's comment, or simply choosing to ignore it, Natalia began scrutinizing Seraphine from head to toe. "At least you have awakened. You are looking much better as well. Although still not fully healed, if that wince of pain was of any indication. Here I thought you were looking forward to Drogen's return. If only to get on the same level with him that I have achieved," she commented offhandedly.

"I am," assured Seraphine. Puffing out her chest but faltering back as pain shot through her body.

"Kind of hard to do that if you're dead dummy," exclaimed Natalia. Admonishing her friend with a finger.

"I'm sorry. I swear it won't happen again.," said Seraphine. Bowing her head. Elicited another. "Ouch. Wait a minute. You did the same thing I did. At least I didn't go off with a couple of gob... Okay Grom saved me but... Oh forget it," huffed Seraphine.

Natalia wrapped her wings and arms around Seraphine in a light, but affectionate embrace. "I am glad to have you here. Alive and well. Soon Drogen will be with us to celebrate our combined victory over Grock, and the war he tried to wage against us."

"Certain things must progress forward, many of which none present would or will like to know. However, just because a state is reached outside of the norm does not mean the end. Often an end leads to the chance of new, or true beginning. One only need be given the chance.

The choice to proceed with the natural order, or to break what is considered natural with one's own existence," commented Death. Striding into the room from the deeper library. "Either way, the truest test of resolve is what will determine Dranier's future."

"I swear, you love speaking in riddles and half measures. Is this a new personality trait Lucian implanted in that thick skull of yours, after imprisoning you," questioned Lisana rolling her eyes disapprovingly.

"I had to find ways to entertain myself being chained to a wall for so long. The lushifare and trolls could hardly manage after all," said Death. A grin on his face that didn't reach his weary eyes.

"No," remarked Natalia looking Death's way. You cannot mean he will die. That he will not survive his fight with Grock," she raged. Stepping to Death himself without fear. "You knew this whole time that Drogen would die if he faced Grock and you said nothing."

"I told you; none present would like to hear the truth," said Death. Lisana's draconic claw wrapping threateningly around his neck.

"You had us wait here, knowing our son will die. How dare you delay us from going to him the moment we arrived," exclaimed Lisana. Rage and fire filling her mouth as she looked into Death's eyes.

"He will not end through me. Not if I can do anything to prevent it from happening. But tis not my choice to make. Tis his own choices that will decide. Tis only his end if he chooses it to be. However, should he choose to live despite me, he'll no longer be able to die. Not now. Not ever. He'll be as Gaia, and I are. Knowing no age. knowing no rest. Destined to watch as everything and everyone he has ever known, loved, cherished, or despised, falls within me. This world will be but his first as a complete being," remarked Death. Sorrowfully looking into Lisana sapphire eyes.

"Then his choices are to walk with you in his fall, or to see all he knows crumble and fall as he lives eternally," realized Natalia. Dropping to her knees. Realization of what such a choice would mean.

"It seems like an impossible choice for anyone to make. I love him, I want to be with him and Natalia both. Selfishly I want him to come back no matter what. But given the choice..." spoke Seraphine. Tears welling up in her eyes as she and Natalia embraced.

"Why, why didn't you tell us all of this before now," raged Lisana. Tears rolling down her face anticipating his answer through their shared connection.

Together they spoke, and the truth of Death lay bare for them all to see. "Because, I could not bear to see the death of my only son," they said in unison. Both dropping to their knees to embrace, tears falling in streams from their faces.

The depths of despair Drogen's mother and father felt in their realization matched only by Natalia, Seraphine, and Llewellyn. Their tears spilling freely as they wept.

"W-We must go. Even if it means we see him fall, and never rise, we must go to him. I have to see him. Even if it proves to be the last time," sobbed Lisana.

"I have feared this day, from the moment I translated the etchings," said Death. Shaking his head. "This weight has come closer to destroying me, than Lucian, or anyone else has," acknowledged Death. "I don't know that I have the strength."

"You do have the strength. Because you have me. We do this together," stated Lisana emphatically.

"As will I," exclaimed Seraphine, Natalia, and Llewellyn.

"When the time comes, you will know. It will be your faith in him that will show him the right path. Even so, he may choose to walk with me instead. The choice is squarely set upon his shoulders, and his shoulders alone," forewarned Death.

"We must end things here quickly. I cannot leave Moonclave while it's still under siege," proclaimed Seraphine.

"Don't worry yourself about Moonclave dear. We've got everything with the goblinkin under control. Quercus and Phaylor are sweeping the forest to the south, taking care of any stray ogres."

"What about the trolls to the north?"

"From what I heard the acid has proved greatly effective at stopping their regeneration. The bigger issue has become finding something that can actually hold up to its effects. The more pressing matter will soon become what to do with the boulders they're leaving behind. The acid effect remains even after they turn in the sun as well."

"Maybe they can be used in the future to defend Moonclave then," posited Seraphine.

"That may prove more dangerous than necessary," said Llewellyn. Shaking her head disapprovingly.

"You may be right," said Seraphine. Hugging Llewellyn tightly "Ouch."

"I hate to see you leave. Especially while still being injured. But it seems to me you'll be in good hands. Go and be with the ones you love dear. We'll be fine until you return to us Queen Seraphine."

"Thank you, Llewellyn. I'll make it back as quickly as I can. And if I have any say at all, with everyone celebrating behind me," she declared. "No matter *what* it takes to make it so. Also, do you know where Asche and Alya are? I doubt they'd forgive us, if they weren't invited along. Especially given what we know now."

"They should be with Phatropa working on ridding the forest of trolls and those few remaining ogres."

"Good, I wanted to see those fighting to the north before moving out anyways. While we're heading out, will you gather some provisions for our trip to the dwarven citadel. I hope we can reach it in a couple of days' time, but I don't know if that's even possible."

"Unfortunately, the dwarves don't possess a transfer gate. Thus, we cannot deploy that method," commented Death.

"I am more than capable of getting everyone there within the day. Although, taking so many, I'll need to rest at least once on the journey," stated Lisana.

"Do we know anything about Drogen, or the dwarves, condition at the moment," questioned Natalia.

"If the number of souls that have been streaming in are of any indication the goblinkin are experiencing a slaughter they could not have seen coming," stated Death.

"Then Grock has yet to arrive," said Seraphine. Hopefully, pulling herself up from her chair. Using the top of the table to leverage herself in order to minimize the pain.

"I really wish you had more time to heal dear. But I know, even if I asked for you to stay and rest, it would inevitably fall upon obstinate ears. As it would, if it were me in your place. The least I can do is gather a couple days' worth of supplies," affirmed Llewellyn.

"Thank you, Llewellyn," said Seraphine with a bow. Which she straightened from quickly.

"Let us go and find Asche and Alya. Are Mai-Coh and Chian still helping in the west as well," questioned Natalia. Drawing an unsure shrug from the others.

"When they're not in the library looking for that room nobody can find," spoke Amanita. Coming through the hidden bookcase door with Tsuga at her side.

"D-Don't worry about them. We'll inform them where you've gone, when they return this evening," assured Tsuga.

"Thank you for your assistance. Tell Chian, when we return, I will continue helping her search the library for her people's hidden store," declared Natalia.

"They'll be informed," said Amanita.

"How did you hear all of that anyways," questioned Seraphine.

"The library has many magics within its wall. One of them is to increase how far one can hear with the use of wind magic. I actually think it's similar to how our mothers communicate using the wind. So, are you all ready to go?"

With everything necessary taken care of they moved through the library as one. Following closely behind Amanita and Tsuga, using the non-hidden door behind their receiving desk. They moved quickly past many alcoves, and many teetering towers of books. Each turn within its ever-lengthening hallways making Seraphine constantly wonder how, and where they were navigating the maze of parchments, tomes, and alcoves.

As she turned with the others for the final time, she found everyone in front of an under-whelming nondescript door. Looking behind, where they had only just been, she found herself staring at a blank stone wall. A wall she noted as having a single stone out of place amongst all the others. As though it were of a different material entirely. Brushing the idiosyncrasy off as her own mind playing tricks, since the books that had been present when they turned the corner, disappeared as well.

Chapter Fifty-Seven

"Let's find them quickly, we need to be off as quickly as possible if we ever hope to get to Drogen before something happens to him. We may still be able to do something, anything to prevent what is written in the etchings from coming to fruition," said Natalia. Realizing they may still be able to do something if they can get there fast enough.

"I'm afraid that is not possible Natalia. None. Not Death, Gaia, nor I can prevent what is written upon one of our bowls. Many have tried, but what is written upon the scale bowl of the dragonkin will always come to be. Maybe not in the way one believes it will. Hence the reason it took Death, and everyone in the library so long to translate the etchings effectively," said Lisana forlornly.

Seraphine, upon hearing Natalia's thoughts on saving Drogen, felt hopeful, but upon hearing Lisana's explanation felt herself fall deeper into disappear, wishing for the pain she felt throughout her body could lessen the pain she felt growing in her heart. "Now, I fully understand why you didn't want to go," commented Seraphine. Shaking her head after meeting Deaths lachrymose eyes.

"The easiest to reach will most likely be Alya. She can hear further than the elves will be capable of. As long as she's in her other form at least," said Seraphine.

"Oh really. And from what clan does she come from," questioned Lisana.

"Alya is one of the Warren."

"Ah, the tiger people. I actually formed a pact with their species in the past," said Death. Stepping forward. With a nearly imperceptible whistle released from his lips a white tiger came tearing through the wood toward him at a ferocious pace. "Calm yourself, I would not have called you too me in such a way, if it were not important," he remarked. Dropping to his knees before Alya.

Alya, breathing heavy from her exertion, turned back into her usual self. Her expression one of absolute rage. "Who do you think you are. Calling me like a common house pet to your side. How can someone be so rude," said Alya. Poking Death with her finger before looking around at those gathered around her. "We'll just have to discuss your rudeness later. I heard you were recovering in the library, why are you out here," she questioned. Looking squarely at Seraphine.

"I didn't want us to leave without you knowing. We're heading to Aragorth. To where Drogen is. Death didn't tell us everything from the etchings. We need to get there quickly. Hopefully before Grock arrives," said Natalia. Stepping forward.

"I'm needed here. We've almost gotten rid of the trolls, but they've begun to multiply. We only have a short amount of time before the sun goes down as well. At least I can sniff them out among the rocks, even before nightfall. Go I will inform everyone on this side to what you're doing. I would give you his bag to take to him, but its being used for all those fire ball things Bailfar and Aurix are making. Oh and Asche, if shes the other one you wanted to talk is actually working in the south today with Mai-Coh and Chian. They found a group and needed some assistance in clearing them out, especially since nearly the entire defensive district is here looking for the frozen trolls," said Alya quickly. Clearly trying to be done with the conversation in order to return to her task.

"Thank you Alya. I hope we'll be seeing each other very soon," said Seraphine.

"As do I, but next time, have someone else call. Especially if this one cannot stop himself from being rude," said Alya. Pokeing Death with her finger once more before turning back to her tiger form and running off into the woods.

"Do you think Alya realized who she was poking like that," questioned Natalia. Whispering into Seraphine's ear.

"I don't think so, I doubt she would have done so had she actually realized."

"What did you say to her that got her so worked up," questioned Lisana.

"What are you supposed to say when you're calling in a giant cat. Here... kitty kitty," said Death with a slight grin.

"No wonder she was so mad. Don't tell me you used to do that to Avren as well," questioned Lisana shaking her head and looking at Death with disapproving eyes. Yes, her mother used to do the same thing, even knowing full well who I am. She is truly a great friend. I hope to see her again one day soon," remarked Death both Natalia and Seraphine's mouths agape knowing Alya's quest to find her mother.

"Well then with all that out of the way, we should be going," said Lisana. Looking at them both with a chuckle at their expressions.

"Here take this before you go," came Llewellyn's voice as she threw wide the towers door. "The library is quite strange, I had sworn I lost my way within the books, but somehow I got here just in time, how is that even possible," she questioned. Looking at the door she had just opened.

"Sometimes the library lines up perfectly," said Amanita.

"And sometimes it doesn't," cautioned Tsuga.

"I think I'll wait for the two of you to guide me back in," said Llewellyn. Pushing a bag full of supplies into Natalia's hand. "Thank you again for what you gave me while I was waiting for this one. I know we don't need to eat in the library, but it did provide me some comfort I must admit."

"You're quite welcome, thank you. I hope we wont need them but it will be better if we have them just in case."

Lisana stripped herself stuffing all of her clothing into her own extra-dimensional bag. Throwing it to Death to carry as she regained her blood red draconic form. Elongated black pupils, surrounded by a sea of sapphire blue, looked back on them. Unfurling one of her wings to form a ramp to her back. She let Natalia, Seraphine, and Death climb upon her back. They set down between the comb like spikes at her back holding tightly to them as she crouched and launched herself into the sky a couple of Dryads pulling back on the trees in order to allow her to rise unimpeded.

"Without the others we wont need a break," said Lisana. Her deep draconic voice rumbling through everyone sitting upon her back. "Natalia, that air spell I taught you. Now would be a great time to use it," she remarked. Spreading and beating her wings in a headlong rush to Aragorth.

Chapter Fifty-Eight

How many more must die to my blades, before they no longer test the line, thought Drogen as yet another horde of goblins, aided by their orc counterparts tried and failed to push in around him.

Splitting the plain between the dwarven citadel and the goblinkin incursion with Godslayer; Envoy of Death, garnered him something he needed above everything else, time. *Rumble and Tumble will have made the citadel. I can only hope they'll be effective in gathering their kin to mount a counter offensive against those loyal to Grock.*

Using mushin within his meditative state, ensured Drogen remained ready and able to fight at a moment notice. Though even his muscles felt strained, their nay constant use over the week fatiguing his movements greatly. *If I'm to fight Grock I must find time to rest and recover. Mushin guided meditation can only get me so far. I've ambidextrously fended off the goblinkin's advancement upon the citadel. However, even I have my limits, and they're quickly approaching.*

The first day I annihilated their ranks. Pushing them back along the plains. Forcing them to where the mountains turn high next to the deep and treacherous ravine. I hoped cutting a line across the plain before them would deter them. Yet, every day and night more cross the boundary, and every day and night more fall to Godslayer; Envoy of Death.

I wish you could speak to me, Godslayer; Envoy of Death, then it wouldn't feel as though I wage this battle alone, thought Drogen spinning the combined might of his blades effortlessly round his body, hand, and neck removing life and limb from any who dared cross the line.

"As long as I stand before you. None shall advance upon the dwarven citadel," exclaimed Drogen. Using the goblin-tongue. Although he still couldn't understand how, or why he could.

"Grock come. Orc rid of pest. No dragon. Only bug. Crushed under boot," exclaimed an orc. One whose only contribution to the others, as Drogen observed, was running those beneath him over the line. Never daring cross it himself.

"I thought orcs cherished strength above all else. Yet you, an orc, show no strength. Sending others across a line you fear tread yourself," admonished Drogen. "Although, I understand where you picked up such tendencies, Grock's ways are ingrained within you after all."

"You die by Grock. He kill you. One who not know place in Grock world," raged the orc. Slamming his pristine war-hammer onto the line, he remained unwilling to cross.

"And where is the mighty Grock now? He sent his armies to war, yet he does not show himself before those who would sacrifice for him. Why is he not among those he sent out in his name. Not at the head of his armies, fight for what he believes so strongly in. When you die for his cause, will he know your face. Will he appreciate the sacrifice you make in *his* name," questioned Drogen.

"No peace, orc want war," exclaimed the orc. Thumping fist to chest starting a chant among the goblinkin. Many of whom doing so with great reluctance. Chief among those being Golga, who looked upon the zealous display with disgust, which she quickly hid behind neutrality.

"The time has not come for your true feelings to be known. You'll know when the time comes," thought Drogen. Feeling the probing of his thoughts from Bogger within the goblinkin ranks. *"Has there been any word from Grom, with regard to the elves?"*

"No, nothing of Grom. Nothing of elf," spoke Bogger within his mind. His voice raising in surprise. *"Behind."*

Drogen side stepped as a giants hammer came down from on high. The stone where his feet had been forming to the mallets maul. *"Thanks for the warning,"* said Drogen a slight grin forming at the edge of his lips. *"Let me pass one unto you. Trust only what you witness for yourselves."*

Taking the initiative while the giant began lifting its hammer Drogen ran in splitting Godslayer; Envoy of Death in two. Trotting for the giants exposed legs at full speed with Godslayer; Envoy of Death leading his charge.

The giant kicked out with its foot as he came in close, the giant becoming off-balanced with the sudden shift. Drogen rolled beneath the giants massive raised foot. Taking the opportunity his roll afforded, he cut from the front of its arch through its callous covered heel. The painful slice forcing a yowl from the giants lips, as it dropped the haft of its maul.

Blood gushed from the wound as Drogen ran free, behind the giant, bringing him in line with its rapidly descending foot. Another rage, and pain filled howl spewed forth as it stomped into the ground reflexively, as if to squash an ant.

Looking for an opportunity to strike again, turned into a sidelong dodge The maul of a second hammer plunging from above. Its mass blotting out the mid-day sun.

Dashing toward the second giant, inside the hammers range, he heard the grotesque crushing of flesh against stone. The giants missed strike falling long. First crushing the first giants femur to its foot before grinding it to paste against the stone.

The pain of its leg being crushed, enrage the first giant to strike his second. The second, trying and failing to fall away from the incoming swing, caught the hammer across the side of its face, eliciting a series of cracking sounds as its jaw, and neck twisted. Its visage and vertebra shattered from the decisive blow.

The second giant fell stiffly. The flailing of its arms, ringing a bell like note as its body impacted the dwarven citadel. The war-hammer fell from its raised hand, crashing down behind Drogen, as he stepped forward, the impact indenting and reverberating through the ground.

Hearing the heartbeats of four other giants descending upon him, Drogen took on his true form. With a breath of white-hot flames, Drogen backed himself up against the dwarven tower. Using the sturdy structure to protect himself from being flanked.

Bludgeons fell like rain upon him and the citadel, followed quickly by massive unnaturally dense, earthen boulders. Still, he persisted fire turning the boulders into a molten lava bath upon his blood red tipped abyssal black scales.

I hope what Rumble and Tumble said about this citadel is accurate. Else it will fall under their onslaught long before I do. But what could be keeping them. Through it all they've remained unnaturally silent. How much longer must I persist without rest.

Two massive hammers cut a harrowing path through the goblinkin encampment. Felling tent and kin alike. As their wielders reached the plain, giant hands and feet crushing the unfortunate souls in their path. The armors of the dead adding texture for the giants, to gain purchase, despite the slick blood. Regaining the bludgeons, with a shake to dislodge blood and bodies alike they spotted their brethren fighting near the citadel. Disregarding the objection of those around their bloody path, the giants trotted full speed toward the distant tower.

Kull, who'd taunted Drogen, roused those around him. Sending everyone he could convince across the line and into the fray, following in the giants wake. With great satisfaction he relished seeing the dragon struggle. A struggle that would intensify with the addition of those he continued to send over the drawn line.

Still, many needed no such convincing. Chief among them the zealous champion Gulvon, who declared his advance with the blowing of a war horn. "For Grock." Those few remaining holdouts rallied behind their champion with pride. With compatriots at his back and side Gulvon ran across the line, the tip of his bastard sword leading the charge.

Gulvon's conscripts attacking the dwarven citadels drawbridge with everything they could. Using swords, knives, pole arms and any other object they could find in order to strike upon Aragorth's entrance. However, nothing they brought to bear against the structure left so much as a scratch upon its surface.

Hargo looked upon those crossing the line with trepidation and sympathy for what he knew would come. "We stay back. They run to death. Doubt ten giants last against him."

"I agree. Have raske come to our side," questioned Golga expectantly. Bathing herself within the confines of her war-tent.

"Would like say yes," he said. Shaking his head. "Say they need more. Proof when Grock come, Drogen not run. Drogen fight. Drogen Win."

"Even with his stamina. He's fought without rest this quarter cycle. I fear he grows weary. These giants were hand-picked by Grock to stay in reserve. Now I understand why," commented Golga. Stepping free of her bath to dry.

"Roccan and Cauron return," spoke Bogger within their minds. *"Grock not happy with progress."*

"When Grock fights for his own cause. *Then* he can complain about progress," raged Golga under her breath.

"Grock send all kin to slaughter long before coming himself. Wish had gotten away with Orna. Not forced to fight. Not forced to die," said Hargo with a mournful resigned sigh.

"We will not die. Nor will we sacrifice ourselves for something we do not believe in. Must have faith that dragon can destroy Grock. Drogen will free our kin, and Dranier of Grock," proclaimed Golga hopefully.

"Hope Golga right. Until certain, raske not move against, or for Grock."

"At least they plan on staying neutral. Have they taken the hidden marks?"

Yes. All marks in place. All await time, even raske, confirmed Bogger walking into Golga's tent. "Even with protest upon their lips, they mark willingly," he explained. Touching his fingers to the side of his head.

"Received word from Grom?"

"Yes war-chief, Grom say elf friends hurt, but not destroyed. Only trolls left to meet death."

"Grock will be livid hearing such unwelcome news," said Golga with a wide tusk filled grin. "Glad elves fight and win."

"Still, not enough for Grock to fight," stated Hargo demurely.

Golga and Bogger shook their heads. "Grock will not fight. Grock will continue doing nothing. Grock will watch all kin die. Do nothing to risk harming himself," commented Golga in revulsion.

"We are nothing to Grock. Only pawn in game of conquest. Nothing more," confirmed Bogger. *Bogger hear Grock thoughts. Grock think nothing of kin. Think nothing of sacrifice. Only think of other god night and day. Lucian and no other."*

"What make Dragon different," questioned Hargo. Remembering the people Drogen had saved from the arena's fate, in defiance of Grock.

"Dragon wants peace. Only kill who step over line. Dragon keeps word to friend and foe. Even when does not speak. Wants to save, not sacrifice."

The giant, with the pulverized leg, picked up by the new giants, came sailing toward Drogen's draconic form. Seeing the flailing giant coming, its heartbeat quickened, he breathed a stream of white fire. As the charred corpse hit the citadel it blew apart covering the battlefield in ashen bone, from the rapid boiling of what had once been the giants blood.

Turning his flame to the two giants, while fending off the attacks of the two remaining before him, proved fruitless as their hammers blocked his fire from reaching their bodies. The compressed stone dissipating the heat.

Drogen dropped himself low as the third giants hammer narrowly missed its mark, striking hard against the dwarven citadel. The hammer strike breaking off a massive chunk of the citadels rocky wall. Beneath the fallen stone shone a bright unmarred iridescence.

The giant's hands and arms vibrated uncontrollably through the hammers haft. The oscillations forcing the giant to recoil as the sensation traveled through its body. Drogen closed the door within his mind quickly as the hammer descended upon him. The shifting allowing him to effectively dodge the falling bludgeon moments before plummeting upon his head.

Seeing Drogen's hasty dodge from beneath the falling hammer, the other three giants closed the gap. Their hammers creating a canopy against the sun's rays, as they expeditiously plunged to the ground. With a thought Drogen brought forth Godslayer; Envoy of Death, their ethereal forms turned corporeal in his hands, as the giant's massive cudgels struck.

The heavy strikes of the giants made his arms go numb under the immeasurable weight and pressure. With his arms shaking from the strain his knees began to buckle. Pushing back against their combined strength and dropping Godslayer; Envoy of Death allowing him to kick off into a sidelong roll toward the ravine's edge.

The giants ran swiftly after his hasty retreat. Their hammers primed and ready to strike.

Reaching the sheer edge of the bluff Drogen felt for the soul chains wrapping each around his feet. *Though my hands feel numb they did not falter or break under their combined pressure. I am Drakregus. I will not be so easily dealt with by the likes of you,* thought Drogen. Pulling back on his blades with a twist of his legs as he returned to his feet.

Godslayer; Envoy of Death hurtled in from behind his unsuspecting prey. With their hammers raised high above their heads, they had no hopes of countering his deadly soul bound blades. They bit deeply into the calf and leg of two, of three giants. Arrogantly believing themselves safe, moving directly against him.

With the unforeseen wounds the giant's mallets were flung sidelong, narrowly missing Drogen harmlessly careened into the ravine. The hammer of the third, and quickly advanced fourth however, did not miss its mark. The hammer of each giant crashing in from both sides of his prone body.

Tis time to find the truth I know I must find, he thought. With a click of his fingers the hammers fell upon him, but he felt nothing of their strikes as he sank within himself. Deeper than he had ever tread within his mind closing the door to the outside world completely as the giant's hammer's rose to reveal his motionless body below.

Chapter Fifty-Nine

Grock walked between the rows of tents and goblinkin gingerly, his gate one of a gloating nature as he tread lightly to Drogen's body. With a wide cheshire grin he waved his hand over his enemies form. From the ground beneath Drogen came earthen stone, which formed around his body, in order to hold his corpse high.

"I wonder how it feels, knowing that you have died for nothing. You've lost and now Lucian's plans are one step closer to completion," Grock whispered into the air with a gleeful chuckle. "The dragon is dead. It will rise no more against my conquest. This is the fate of any who stand against me. This one has proven itself weak, and what do we do with weak," he questioned. Roaring in satisfaction.

"Destroy all weakness; Slaughter to Prevail," chanted the goblinkin back to their deity. A fervor renewed by his presence and victory over their collective adversary. All at once the dead, those who fought against the dragon were forgotten. As if their sacrifice for Grock was simply a means to the dragon's end. That they too were weak, and thus, culled for that weakness.

Hargo shook his head sadly. "There be none to win against Grock now. We lose all the moment Dragon lost life. All will die for glory of Grock," he said. Detesting the thought.

Golga looked through the fold in her tent watching and hoping for any sign that her faith in Drogen had not been misplaced. That there was still a chance for him to succeed. No matter how thin such a thread might be. Standing up, after the shock subsided she walked in the growing frenzy, Hargo at her side, moving to stand before the hanging corpse of her hope set up on display.

Victoriously Grock sauntered over to the closed portal into the dwarven land. Having returned to the nominal height of those around him Grock moved to his giants. Arms raised in congratulations, before reaching out and grabbing one by the hand. Savagely Grock bit a chunk from the giants outstretched hand and as he swallowed, grew to its size.

The giant let out a yelp in pain, as its deity grew before him, holding the giant's hand that it could not retreat. "You narrowly allowed it to escape my wrath for that you have proven yourself weak." Grock's war-hammer, which he grabbed from his side, grew in size to match his newly gained stature.

The giant, try at it might to break Grock's grasp found its struggle to be futile as the spiked end of the war-hammer bore through its skull and brain rendering it lifeless. As the giant crumpled Grock discarded it forcefully over the ravine's edge. "Let this be a lessen. Weakness of any kind will not be tolerated."

Those giants that fell by Drogen's blades quickly followed clearing the battlefield of their hefty corpses, and allowing Grock access to Aragorth's secure drawbridge entrance.

The beak of Grock's hammer rang out across the battlefield as it pushed between the drawbridge and the citadel. Grock yanked hard against the structure his strength overwhelming the counterweights upon its other side as the rattle of massive chains emanating, from within the structure, in its descent.

A war howl of victory from Grock, the blowing of horns, and pounding of drums signaled the start of their victory march into the dwarven citadel. Trolls, ogres, orcs, goblins, worg's, and the like moved onto the drawbridge thumping their chests in time with their footfalls. As the sun above their heads turned to shadow.

Another dragon descended from above their heads its fire breath rending all upon the drawbridge in flames. Their shrieks of unimaginable pain sending the others skittering away in fear. Grock moved to strike the dragon down with his war-hammer, but found landing a blow difficult as the dragon expertly skirted his every strike.

Within the dragon's fire a shadow descended into the citadel. Propelled, and guarded from the flames by some unseen force before disappearing from view. Another shadow descended to the ground from the blood red dragon's back. Its body covered in Abyssal black robes and a scythe.

Though the figure stood no taller then Grock's ankle the intimidation exuded by the cloaked figure drove even more of the goblinkin away, many diving into the ravine in lew of facing the new threat themselves.

The cloaked one closes the bridge. Dwarves given more time, spoke Bogger excitedly into Golga and Hargo's minds.

Grock, moving to prevent the door from being raised, found himself bathed in Dragon's fire. A fire that would have cut through everything in its path had it not been for the golden barrier surrounding the entirety of his being. With the distraction and threat of immolating flame the cloaked figure, with strength far greater than his size might denote, shut the door hard against the citadel.

With the door shut, the dragon swept down from the sky cutting off its attack against Grock in favor of blowing a precise jet of flame around the drawbridge's perimeter, welding their point of egress shut.

Grock moved in to break the weld before it could harden and set, but found himself once more shrouded in bright blinding flames as the cloaked figure waded in for a strike at Grocks legs. The scythe bit into Grock's shield deeply pushing him back and away as the weld cooled and set.

The blood red Dragon descended quickly the cloaked figure jumping up on its back in a practiced motion. Tackling Grock's shielded body the dragon toppled their deity. As Grock fell the three reaming giants, who had gathered behind him, joined his descent. Stumbling against the unforeseen strike two of the three to the ground. The third jumped backward its foot slipping in the blood of its skull crushed brother sending it careening into the ravine.

The giants hand reached out for Grock's hand and was unceremoniously repelled. Repelled by the golden barrier A golden light that faded away completely from its eyes as it sank into the ravine. Its last thoughts the glow of gold, and pain, as its body crumbled on the jagged rocky outcropping and corpses below.

Never look through eyes of dying again. Too much, complained Bogger nearly retching from the experience. *Maybe Bogger show to Grock, when time come. Show despair Grock give kin.*

Golga and Hargo paid Bogger, nor the others around them any heed. Walking through the chaos, through the zealous, and the fearful to stand before Drogen's hanging earthbound body.

And for the first time in her life Golga closed her eyes and prayed. Preyed to the only being that had ever treated them as more than fodder for slaughter.

The Dragon and rider look this way as well. Sadness and rage from both, said Bogger.

The dragon, having toppled Grock and the giants unfurled its wings taking to the sky after testing the golden barrier, to no avail with its clawed feet. Chaos continued to course through the goblinkin as a burst of fire engulfed those who had not thought it best to flee. Flames licked at Golga and Hargo's backs, but they refused to move from in front of Drogen's body. Though the heat of the flames could be felt the fire, though it consumed all around them, never touched their bodies.

Opening her eyes upon Drogen's face she felt her heart sink into the depths of despair. Feeling completely lost and uncertain about their future as the one she placed her greatest hopes upon had fallen, and with him her hope for a better existence for the goblinkin.

Before the giants attacked. Drogen said something strange to me, commented Bogger as the blood red dragon flew over Grock's army diving into the ravine cupping one wing to its side as it descended to follow the ravine before swiftly rising and disappearing into the forest on the opposite side.

"What did he say Bogger," questioned Hargo. That he could remove Golga from her internal contemplations and worries.

"Trust only what you confirm for yourselves," said Bogger. Followed by a joyous laugh into both their minds from their vaudune companion.

Chapter Sixty

The bright white glow from the drawbridge at their back cast heat and light into the citadel until it cooled and solidified behind them. The cooling giving Natalia and Seraphine hope Grock would be further delayed in his bid for conquest. However, even with the citadel's drawbridge sealed, every sound at their back gave fear and breathless pause for many moments.

Natalia, using her newfound knowledge of magic, cast out a ball of light. Sending it as high as the ceiling above would allow. Long dark shadows persisted in the pervasive darkness, as massive pillars and statues came into focus, within the unfamiliar surroundings.

Curious by nature, Natalia wandered over to the statues looking for any indication as to who they might be. "Aragorth Patriarch of Dwarven kind," she read aloud. Easily translating the dwarven marks. Seeing another statue, a little further in, Natalia moved swiftly to it. "This one has no name beneath it... It is completely blank. The statue looks to be male, and he's holding a hammer. Oh, the hammer has writing on it. Un-ster-blich I think is what it says. It is really hard to make out without actually going up there."

"I think their proportions are off," said Seraphine. Taking in the statue's massive stature while also, begrudgingly, acknowledging the precision of the stonework. "I haven't heard a dwarf talk about or mention anyone other than Aragorth. Of course, I haven't had the displeasure of meeting too many of the ground trolls either," she said with a shrug.

"Rumble and Tumble never mentioned anyone else either. Of course, I could hardly get them to speak about Aragorth at all. Let alone what brought them to Zephyria in the first place."

"What I find most troubling right now is the sound of the goblinkin trying to break down their front door. Why are there no dwarves here to greet the invading force. Rumble and Tumble had to have made it inside. Drogen would have..."

A rain of stones turned to a thunderous clatter against the stone facade of the Dwarven citadel, turning into a ball, protecting their fronts. Each strike receiving a bells toll in response, creating a cacophony of clashing chimes.

"A-are we just going to pretend we didn't see him hanging there," questioned Seraphine. Scrunching up her face in order to stay strong against the rise of emotion she felt percolating up from the pit of her stomach.

Natalia remained with her head low, using the chimes overhead in order to focus away the pain she felt inside. "Death said he would talk to Drogen. We may not know how, but I have to believe, we all have to believe in him and Drogen. Especially Drogen. If we stop... If I stop..."

Seraphine ran to Natalia wrapping her in a tight hug. Feeling the warm embrace and cherishing the sensation, she wrapped her wings round them both in order to retain the feeling if only for a bit longer. "I feel the same way. I only wanted to know it feels the same for you. That I'm not alone, with these thoughts and feelings."

"No. You are far from alone. I feel the weight in my heart will never allow peace in my mind. However, we have no time to dwell. Not now. I cannot fathom what good we may prove to be for the dwarves, but we must do everything we can to help them fight Grock."

"I'm sure we'll be useful in some way. And if we're not, we stay out of their way."

"I hope they have something for us to do. I don't care if it's clearing out storerooms. As long as it provides distraction from all these thoughts and dread swirling through my mind. The world threatens to encircle and consume me whole."

"I know Drogen would have something to say about such thoughts, but... I have nothing," confessed Seraphine. Drawing a tear-filled chuckle from Natalia, despite the desperation in her heart.

Natalia's laughter proved infectious as Seraphine followed suit regaling her with an impression of Drogen, in order to prolong their fits of laughter. They cleared their eyes from their tear-filled laughter a few chuckles remaining in their fit. Their inexplicable outburst bringing them a more hopeful outlook.

"We should be going to find the dwarves then. The goblinkin could eventually get in here, although it will likely take them a great deal of effort with whatever Lisana did to secure the door," remarked Natalia.

"Yeah, we'd better get going then... I wonder what the dwarves are going to do when they see me. I'm an elf after all."

"You are not just any elf Seraphine. You are an elven queen. You are also in the company of a zephyrian princess."

"That didn't seem to matter to my own people, when I returned home. We can only hope that Rumble and Tumble's reception here was more kind than it was in Moonclave," said Seraphine ruefully.

Using her finger in order to control the light Natalia sent it out along the outer reaches of the citadel's antechamber. Along the upper walls of the shinning metallic inner structure stood platforms with massive ballista. Their massive rawhide drawstrings in definite working order.

"This whole citadel is a defensive tower," remarked Seraphine in awe. "If they've got so many defenses, why aren't they defending themselves."

"Let's get going. With any luck we can find the dwarves, and a way to finish this war quickly."

"Moonclave should be routing the last of the trolls. They'll be free from the goblinkin soon. After that, I don't know what they'll do afterwards. One thing's for certain, if the dwarves fall our routing of their forces will have been for nothing. We can't allow that to happen."

"I hope Lord Vladimir, and all those he took with him, are doing well. They left Zephyria in hopes of cutting off Grock's supply routes. If they have been successful, the goblinkin will start having to fend for themselves in order to gather necessary supplies. Which will certainly bring tension between the goblinkin and Grock. Especially if he says something that puts them off of following him entirely. Grock's loss will hopefully be our gain in the fight against him," said Natalia hopefully.

"I hope you're right. Still, we can't expect quick results. It will take some time for them to realize their supplies aren't coming, and possibly far more time before it is so bad that Grock needs to step in," warned Natalia. Guided them both onward and down.

What started out as a large chamber quickly decreased in size and breadth, before thinning out into a long corridor. Many different junctions, doors, and bends crossed and weaved in interconnected tunnels. Leaving Natalia and Seraphine in a state of confusion.

"Did you learn any magic that can help us find our way in this maze of tunnels," questioned Seraphine.

"Actually... No, I read everything on magic within the library. Lisana has also been teaching me. Unfortunately, that was not a part of the teachings. Maybe, if I had more time in Moonclave's library, I could have learned something useful for finding the correct path."

They worked their way along the many different hand carved pathways through ground and stone alike. Most paths, resulting in dead ends. With nothing to visibly distinguish the correct path they continued to wander aimlessly. Making each move along the correct path a painstaking process of elimination.

"This is taking forever. It doesn't help that everything looks the same either. If not for the lack of chiming around us, I'd be doubting we've made any progress at all," said Seraphine.

"I need a break; my concentration is waning. My light is continuing to dim, Without rest we will be moving blindly through the tunnels. Far more than we already are," said Natalia. Sitting down in the middle of yet another alcove filled with multiple pathways and tunnels leading off in numerous directions.

"These tunnels must be a defensive measure, to obstruct invaders. I wish Moonclave had such measures. The forest being overgrown likely helped prevent a more direct attack against Moonclave, but it also prevented us from effectively locating threats. There's much that'll need to change in order for us to keep our autonomy," considered Seraphine.

Natalia cut her use of magic in order to give her mind and concentration a rest plunging them both into absolute darkness. Worked through a glowing spark of remembrance, the pervasive darkness drew Natalia back into the dungeon below Zephyria. Back where the guards, who were following Nefar and Bernadine's callous orders, pulled out each individual feather from her abyssal black wings. Before the memories could overwhelm her, she trained her mind on other, more pleasant memories, but they too turned against her. Turning to the many bodies she loaded into the arena's carts, which unbeknownst to the rest, were dismembered in the kitchens.

Trying to focus on anything else Natalia held tightly to Seraphine's words. "Lisana told me. Magic is more powerful when multiple beings use it together. If we find the right knowledge, the council may be capable of creating a method of defense. Not unlike these tunnels, for Moonclave. When we get out of here, I will help you. I am helping Chian find her peoples writings as well. Certainly, within that vast library, we can find something effective."

"I look forward to it. But first, we need to find our way out of these tunnels. How are the dwarves able to distinguish between the right and wrong path. I don't see any difference between them, especially without light to guide us."

"I would suspect it is much the same way your kin do not find themselves lost in a forest. It is a part of who you are," reckoned Natalia.

"I've never even thought about that. Even as a child, going into the woods, I always knew which way I needed to go to find home. Maybe we're not as different from each other as the past would have us believe," thought Seraphine aloud. "If you tell those two, I ever said such a thing, I'll find some way to deny it."

"How are you going to deny anything, when you have no choice but to tell the truth?"

"I don't know... I'll have to think of something," she grinned. "Of course, I won't need to, if one of my sweet loves doesn't say anything," she said with flirtatious eyes Natalia could feel, even in the dark.

"Okay. Okay. I won't say anything. I cannot see what you are doing in this darkness, but I swear I can see it plain as day in my mind."

"Have you rested for long enough," questioned Seraphine hopefully.

"Yeah, I believe I have let's get going. We don't know if or when Grock will regain entry."

"Hopefully they cut down on the number of these random tunnels the further in we go."

With a sigh Natalia lifted her hand producing a ball of iridescent light. They walked down many different tunnels each more twisted and winding than their predecessors, but far fewer of them leading to dead ends. With less time being spent backtracking they began to advance more quickly.

"How much further can they be. It feels as though we've been traveling for hours already."

"I hope we will get wherever we are going soon as well, but I know about as much as you do when it comes to this place. Not a lot of information has been shared about Aragorth. Even though we are trade partners, I do not believe any other Zephyrian has been granted access."

"I doubt any, but the dwarves, have been permitted for a very long time. Well... except that other statue we saw beside Aragorth's. Come to think of it. I don't think I've met another dwarf. None but Rumble and Tumble... I wonder why," pondered Seraphine. Going through her mind for a possible answer. Wait we did see a great many when I met Drogen and Willow in the ravine. They didn't look interested in talking at the time."

"The further we travel the more questions arise," remarked Natalia.

As they'd hoped would be the case, fewer of the tunnels led off into deviating directions. However, where the number of tunnels had decreased in number they had also decreased in size. Most leaving Natalia and Seraphine either hunched over, or on their knees in order to move through the tighter areas.

As the tunnels grew tighter Seraphine's heartbeat began to increase beyond her control. Its influence upon her mind a hammering beat threatening to consume her entire being. Try as she might to calm the swell, she could find no solace within herself, as its influence drowned out all other thought. "Natalia," she cried out. Closing her eyes tightly as she reached out for help against the swell.

Natalia stopped in her tracks and turned around. Recognizing from within herself, the look of distress upon Seraphine's face. With her concentration squarely on aiding her friend Natalia's magic light was extinguished casting them both back into complete darkness. She pulled Seraphine into her embrace fully, holding her as she calmly spoke into Seraphine's ear. "Listen to my voice. Breath in through your nose and out through your mouth. I know it's hard, but you are not alone. I am here by your side. It will pass, but you must breathe."

Natalia rubbed Seraphine's body tenderly giving her another stimulation to focus on. One that was not the racing of her own mind and heartbeat. As time progressed around them Seraphine slowly began to regain herself. Her breath and heart slowly returning to their normal state while her body sweat uncontrollably, causing a deep chill to set in for them both. But Natalia refused to let go, until she knew for certain that Seraphine had recovered.

"How long has this been happening," questioned Natalia with concern.

"I-I don't know. It feels as though it just suddenly started happening and now... Now I have no control over it at all," she lamented. A chilling shiver shooting through her body.

"I know the feeling. Although, I may know when mine started. I believe it started with my time in Zephyria's dungeon," said Natalia. Losing her hold on Seraphine slightly. "You were there when they brought me up from the dungeon. My wings plucked, but I wanted to keep the other part a secret. Maybe that was the wrong way of going about it. I have been having night terrors since then," acknowledged Natalia.

"Even when we were traveling together. How did you keep it a secret?"

"Drogen helped me, but even he cannot cure the mind. No matter how powerful he may be. If I am being honest, the night terrors are what made me think of going with Grom and Bogger to Grammora in the first place. I wanted something, anything to take my mind off of what they had done."

"You were their victim," said Seraphine.

"I told Drogen the same thing. Do you want to know what he told me?"

"Yes."

"He told me no," she recalled with a chuckle. "He told me to never be the victim. To be a survivor, an avenger, anything else. But never a victim. He told me the moment I view myself as the victim, is the moment I relinquish control over what they did. Even now, I doubt I understand the depth of what he meant with so few words. At its base, I had two options. I could fall into despair, *or* I could fight. I chose to fight. I chose to conquer and better myself *despite* what they perpetrated against me," imparted Natalia.

"Then I too will push against this uneasiness. I will fight and *I* will win," said Seraphine. Clinching her fist in resolve.

"Then this too, we do together," said Natalia. Grabbing hold of Seraphine's hand with her own in a firm grip, which she reciprocated in kind.

Seraphine stood up slowly, hunched over from the low ceiling, helping Natalia to her feet as well. They stepped forward in unison. Their simple unassuming movement belie the tacit formation of a life's long pact.

Chapter Sixty-One

A great flood surged through Drogen's mind enveloping his entire being its currents swept him away within his own mind. Outward sensations that had previously precluded themselves from within the confines of his mental state became all too forward and consuming as he fought back against the abyss threatening to consume him.

Each thought forced Drogen against the crashing waves each derision of cognition a bridge to the unwelcome sensations he desperately coveted an escape from. Until his mind no longer retained the strength necessary to struggle against the torrent. The ebb and flow of his shattered self. carrying him deeper than he had ever been, within the confines of his mind.

Just as the pain his body continued to experience threatened to consume him entirely in strife, the currents, and his suffering lulling to a placid dull ache. Relegated to the outer reaches of his sub-conscious where the sensations could no longer reach him.

Drogen floated lazily upon the placid pool of his sub-conscious unsure of what might come next. *"How do I return to my center. To my soul chamber,"* spoke his mind to the void. Eliciting an echo in response as his thought traveled. *"What has brought me here. As opposed to any other place within me. Could I have sustained more injuries at the hands of Grock's giants than I thought?"*

"We brought you here. You already know why. Though you have yet to admit it to ourselves," spoke Drogen's own voice back in response. Yet the voice had not come from his consciousness upon the pool, but below.

Though he struggled to do so, Drogen turned himself round till his face lay within the waters. Reaching out with both hands he felt for what he instinctively knew to be there Godslayer; Envoy of Death.

"Although I lack understanding of where this flood originates. Your presence here shows that they too are a part of me. Apart of us," stated Drogen

"Yes, all are a part of the whole," Echoed his own voice back.

"Tis good to hear you once more Godslayer; Envoy of Death. Is this a result of being so near the end. Or could this be fate's way of giving us the illusion of choice, in aspects beyond our understanding or control," pondered Drogen as he reached out. Finding no hilts on which to hold.

"Fate. Destiny. What sway do such falicidic aspects hold upon us?"

"Fate cannot bind us. We are greater than such concepts as... destiny."

"Yet what Gaia told us stands as testament to wisdom we most certainly lack," reminded Drogen.

With his reach for the blades producing no results, Drogen instead called for them, as he always had. Knowing for certain, no matter the circumstance, they would always come to his call. *"Godslayer; Envoy of Death,"* he called into the waters. With his call he felt their weight fill his outstretched hands.

As his grip tightened upon the hilts of his seax blades the world around him inverted throwing the calm waters into tumultuous waves once more. However, instead of fighting the feeling he allowed it to take him fully. His sub-conscious mind finding harmony within the crashing cacophony.

As the waters around him began to calm, Drogen found himself upon his feet his trusted blades in each hand. Looking down upon the water he saw his own reflection. However instead of his red tipped black scales he saw a figure in white and gold robes staring back at him. The sapphire eyes of his mother's piercing gaze looking back and though him.

Turning his back to the image Drogen pulled Godslayer; Envoy of Death up to his eyes a deep sadness causing the waters around him to shift restlessly. *"If this has nothing to do with fate, or destiny, then why. Why, could you not speak to me before this moment,"* questioned Drogen.

"We spoke. We always speak. But you did not listen."

"Could not listen."

"Why could I not listen. The last time I heard your voices was in my fight with Grock."

"You know why."

"We all know why."

"Then tell me," spoke Drogen in frustration. The pool at his feet beginning to churn.

"It takes more than half to make one whole. We know the truth, that which you have been unwilling to admit to anyone. Even yourself. We can no longer hide in fear of what might be."

"Fear is what continues to bind us. What prevents us from becoming whole."

"Will opening the door irreparably change us."

"Will it make us something we are not. Will it corrupt us to their way."

"To our enemies' way," as if to accentuate their point the waters bellow his feet once more showed his reflection adorned with white and gold robes a sinister malicious smile upon his reflection as he stands upon a pyramid of corpses.

"To the way of destruction and pain for all of Dranier. To spread terror to those we see as beneath us as they do." In the reflection he stood above the world. His white and gold robes moving in the breeze, as carnage and flames ravaged the world below him.

"No. Not all of them wish for conquest or pain," Drogen reminded himself. *"Willow is of them, and she is our friend."*

"Then why must we fight the others. What makes the others our foes when Willow is not?"

"Is it simply because we are Drakregus?"

"What is a war dragons' purpose if not to seek war?"

"Could our true purpose as Drakregus be to bring peace," pondered Drogen.

With his thoughts whirling in contemplation Drogen combined Godslayer; Envoy of Death into one using his thoughts as a catalyst for their movement within his expertly trained hands. The waters at his feet ebbing and flowed with their movement as he scrutinized each aspect along the strange path his thoughts had taken.

With a final twisting flourish of Godslayer; Envoy of Death the waters returned calmed to a reflective surface once more. Looking down at the blades who were, and always had been an extension of himself he understood what needed to be done. *I can no longer allow the fear of losing myself to the power beyond the door prevent me from opening it. I will retain who I am. I must retain who I am."* With his thoughts the reflection upon the water's surface began to shift and change. Light, like stars in the night sky began to shine through the abyss reflecting upon the water's surface.

"If only there was a way, I could confirm this to be the correct course. Even if my body, mind, and heart tell me tis so. Hesitation continues to plague me."

"Another is here. One who knows. But we must ask the right question."

"Without the right question, an answer means nothing."

"The door is open, and he has walked in," spoke his swords.

Drogen nodded his head before looking up from Godslayer; Envoy of Death allowing them to fall from his hand and dissipate into the ether of his mind. And with their dissipation so too went the waters.

With a calming breath as he closed his eyes, Drogen stepped forward. With another step he returned to the center of his being. Opening his eyes the many pedestals on which the most important aspects of his being had been placed, came into focus. The black and white chains rising out of each to connect back to the fires of his existence.

Godslayer; Envoy of Death, the dragon-scale bowl; formed from the extra scale that had grown over his heart, the scale male armor; he had made to perfectly emulate the scales of his own body, and finally the two doors; those doors which held that which he had inherited from both Lisana, and his father Death.

Looking around his soul chamber a cloaked figure appeared. His head hung solemnly as he stood in silent reflection.

"If this was to be my end, I suspected a reaper would be here. But to have my father himself come. I must say, I am honored. Even beyond being your son," spoke Drogen his eyes trained upon his chained soul."

"I would not have come myself, but Lisana insisted that I must. Seeing my own son... Life-less," spoke Death. Shaking the thought from his own mind. "However, unlike all the others, you have another option. You can return to life, but in so doing... you'll never know an end. You will be the truest of gods. Living alongside Gaia and I forever."

"It would seem fate has such in store for me," said Drogen. Tracing the many chains with his eyes. "I have but one question for you who sired me. A single question that may rid me of these thoughts that have plagued my subconscious mind for far to long."

"Such importance placed upon a single question can only mean one thing. You've already decided what course to take. What possible influence could one answer make," reasoned Death.

"The answer is simply the proof I need. To know that what I choose is indeed true to who, and what I am. That it will always be true, to who and what I am." Pausing in contemplation of the right question to ask "Even faced with the inevitable regrets of the past and those the future indubitably holds. Do you Death, enjoy living?"

For the first time since entering his soul chamber Drogen looked to the cloaked figure standing next to the door. There upon Deaths visage grew a wide joyous smile. And with a single nod Death spoke. "Yes."

With a smile of his own Drogen walked over to the abyssal black chain that had remained steadfast across the white and gold filigree door and clenched his fist around the lock.

"Do not make this decision without thought to what it truly means. Should you continue, there will be no going back. You will live forever, time flowing around you without stop nor rest. Tis not an easy existence. We three alone will know no end," warned Death again.

With a final squeeze of his powerful hand Drogen turned the lock to dust, the particles scattering through his fingers and falling to the ground at his feet. With the lock crushed the chain fell away, joining the others along its jam. Placing his hand upon the door, Drogen felt the power reaching out from behind it, with both reverence and apprehension.

"I find this gives me another regret. That your mother those who have found great love in you, and I had to witness your demise and the grotesque display Grock saw fit to make of your body," Death lamented aloud. "If only I had been... stronger. We may have been able to arrive in time to change the outcome in some way," he said. Shaking his head in dismay.

Pulling his hand back from the door Drogen turned round to look upon the father he had yet to know or understand. "It would seem there's been a misunderstanding," Drogen whispered calmly. "I had thought, should any be capable of seeing beyond the facade that lay before them, it would be Death. I suppose I should take my ability to deceive you as worthy indication that Grock, and the others, have been fooled as well," he said. Snapping his fingers.

A distinct rhythm filled the soul chamber around them, and with its reveal Drogen walked back to the ornate gold and white door housing the other half of his soul and power. "I look forward to seeing everyone again very soon." he said. Pushing wide the door within his mind. And with the doors opening, Death's astral body was forcibly driven out.

Chapter Sixty-Two

They continued to walk their way deeper into the carved stone-ways each one bringing them closer to the depth dwelling dwarves. Though the number of misleading tunnels had diminished greatly, they still found themselves backtracking along occasional dead-end routes. Each new tunnel leading to bouts of uncertainty and hope that their journey would soon end.

"I hope we didn't get turned around on one of our many backtracks. I'd hate to wind up back where we started. Are you getting hungry too," questioned Seraphine.

"Yes, I am. Unfortunately, we did not plan well for this trip. Hopefully we can procure food from the dwarves, when we finally reach them," said Natalia hopefully.

"Hopefully they've got more than meat to eat," said Seraphine. Sighing as her belly grumbled.

"And if they do not?"

"Either way we need to eat, in order to maintain our strength," she said with a shrug.

Natalia held out her hand stopping herself and Seraphine to listen intently. "Do you hear that. It sounds like... metal scrapping metal maybe they're working on something."

"I like that we can hear something after so long. I don't know if I like that the first thing we hear, is the grating of metal against metal."

"I wish our ears were more attuned to the tunnels. Even with the sound guiding us, with the sound bouncing around as it is we are still likely to pick an errant path," said Natalia. Her practicality pervading the excitement in her voice.

"Let's see if I can," said Seraphine. Cupping her hand around her pointed ears in order to funnel the sound more effectively in. Closing her eyes, she listened intently to the sound as it filled the few off shooting tunnels around them. "That's not the sound work, that's the sound of battle," she cautioned.

"That means the dwarves would be fending off attacks from above and bellow, had Lisana not sealed the drawbridge as she had. Do they not have enough sentries to guard and defend the tower?"

"They probably don't know messages have been sent from Moonclave and Zephyria. Especially if the messages are brought from the citadel above. Rumble and Tumble are likely the only sources of news they've received."

"We need to do whatever we can to help them drive the invaders back. If Grock's minions above find a way to open the draw bridge everything we have done to this point will have been for nothing," exclaimed Natalia over the near deafening sounds of combat permeating the tunnels as they continued to move in closer.

Seraphine nodded her head in agreement, as they both started running toward the sound of battle. Without pretense or hesitation, they galloped out of the tunnel emerging onto a wide stone bridge.

Lamps lined the sides of the bridge at equal distances casting only the barest of light onto the bridge and into the void along its short-walled sides.

Natalia, still concentrating on the magical ball of light, lifted her hand sending it to the apex of the cavern.

At the head of the bridge a garrison of dwarves fought against their would-be invaders. A menagerie of goblins, orcs, worgs, barghest, and worghest stampeding haphazardly against the defensive wall formed by the dwarven shield guard. Their approach contained, from overwhelming the dwarves, by the stone gateway at the bridges head.

The dwarves stepped forward in unison their heavy, and spiked, half bell shields crushing those sluggish in movement between spike and wall. Each step forward pushing the gob-linkin back, giving their enemy no room for advancement upon the line. Those not pinned by shield or pushed back through the large archway, they fought desperately to flow through, found themselves falling into the black void beside the stone bridge. Their cries ending with a sickening splatter, as they quickly discovered the basal of the spanning structure they wished to tread.

Natalia and Seraphine, thinking better than to rush in behind the occupied dwarves called out in order to garner their attention. "What can we do to help," they posited. In dwarven and common tongues. Their calls from behind the dwarven line being met with the loosing of crossbow strings aimed directly at their advance. Upon seeing Natalia and Seraphine, the dwarves who'd fired in hast, looked on in horror as the blood drained from their faces.

Hearing the catches being released from their strings Seraphine raised her arm up in a futile attempt at blocking the certainly deadly arrows, vines forming in haste around their bodies in hopes of halting the arrows.

Raised her hand up before her, Natalia added to Seraphine's defensive spell forming a barrier as well. With her concentration fully placed on the barrier, the light she'd been maintaining snuffed itself out, casting the battlefield in near darkness.

The number of arrows heading toward them became impossible to determine given the minuscule light provided by the bridge's sconces and lanterns, which spanned far too large a distance between each to be effective for either of them.

Natalia narrowed her focus as the arrows began striking the rapidly grown vines. Pushing herself into Seraphine allowing her to condense the air shield in hopes that any strike from the front and overhead would stop before reaching their targets.

Those arrows, that had fortunately been cast wide, dug into Seraphine's vines, many only a few inches away from drawing blood from each of them. However, the greatest concentration of arrows had found their mark with deadly precision. The heavy bolts of the dwarven crossbows struck roughly against her concentrated magic barrier. The magnitude of the attack threatening to break her concentration completely. Concentration she desperately needed to maintain.

As the thwack of the final arrow fell upon her their raised barrier. Natalia and Seraphine lowered their arms, letting out a steadying breath against the tension. Both of them feeling bruises form along her forearms from the air shields unforeseen dissipation recoil. Drawing groans of pain from both of them.

Seraphine, spreading her hands apart moved the vines from in front of them allowing them both a way to pass.

"We be ear ta help ya bleedn clods," raged Natalia. In perfect dwarven. "I be comen out dare meself an wacken the lota ya if ya think a pointin dem blasted bolts me way again," she chided belligerently.

Seraphine, checking herself for wounds, looked under her raised arm in shock and bewilderment. Having never heard the always prim and proper Natalia, speak in such a crass manner. "Didn't think I'd ever hear you speak like that to anyone. I must say, I'm quite proud," said Seraphine wiping at a fake tear in appreciation, while cautiously lowering her arms.

"Gotta get through dem thick skulled dung heaps sum ow," yelled Natalia to the dwarves. "Wit one a yah I be needen ta talk ta. We be ear ta help if ya be letten us talk afore firein again," she scolded impudently. "Wha da matter. Ya not recognize ya own speak,"

"We be need'n no help from a bat nor long ear tree mouse," piped up one of the dwarves. Clearly the one leading the defensive force, as at his command the bell shield wall moved forward pushing back against the goblinkin. Blocking off any further means of egress to the bridge, aside from climbing the spiked bell shields themselves.

"Ya be as stubborn an ard headed as me damn guard. Be tinken yur selves' better den all da udders. Not be foolen any but ya selves," raged Natalia. "Move out me way. I show ya wha me be able ta do an help ya even if ya to orc headed ta know ya be needn it."

Clearly still enraged by the greeting they received; Natalia pushed herself through the back of their ranks, using magic to move dwarves aside, in order to walk unimpeded to the bell shield line. Taking Herzblutung, the tri-bladed concentric dagger, from the sheath at her side she grabbed a fallen javelin from the ground. Removing the shaft in order to place her own weapon upon it.

The hefty dwarven bell shields blocked her from advancing past and into the invasion force itself. Looking at the bells construction she recognized quickly that it would be impossible for her, or ten of her, to lift a single one of them out of the way. Possibly even with magics aid.

At the center of the shield lay her only point from which to display her ability and use to their war effort. A single reinforced horizontal slot, just big enough to fit the head of a sidelong halberd through, acted as both a window to the other side and a place through which weapons could be thrust or fired.

Channeling wind magic through the wooden shaft, which drew bright blue lines along the wood grain, of her spear she concentrated its flow into the concentric grooves between the three blades. With a single thrust of the weapon through the slot the gathered magic flowing out like a shot spiraling and condensing upon a single devastating point. Erupting forth, its pinpoint size mien its devastating power.

All those along the path of her magic fell to the ground. Their hearts pierced through in an instant. Those who had been fortunate enough to not have their hearts pierced by Natalia's magic found themselves unable to hold their weapons having completely lost use of any extremity that had been unfortunate enough to be along its precise path.

With so many injured or fallen from Natalia's single thrust the invaders worked themselves into a frenzy, falling over themselves as they ran away in absolute terror. With a sigh, and deep sadness, Natalia watched as they trampled over their fallen comrades, without thought of anything more than their own survival.

I hope this display has more of you flee. I did not wish to see so many dead. I know this too will haunt my nights. But maybe, it will allow for more to choose living to see another day instead. Am I wrong for wanting them to see another day? I too had to live under the thumb of gods who sought their own self interest above the people who worshiped them as divine. I can only hope they too will see a day when they are free of Grock's machinations. Or am I just fooling myself since I see so much of myself and my peoples struggles in them, considered Natalia.

Pulling back on the shaft of her spear she grabbed hold of the Tri-blades handle twisting it free of the quickly deteriorating shaft. As the wood came loose it fell to the ground where it splintered into millions of fine strands, its remaining strength expended with the channeling of magic.

Taking the opportunity Natalia provided, the dwarves moved the bell shields forward through the path of destruction she had rout. Still met with resistance even after the display of overwhelming power, the dwarves forward press had become much easier to take and maintain then their previous efforts afforded.

"Be supposen ya got some use," scoffed the dwarf under his breath. Even though the expression on his round face told a contrary tale. Black wings be tellen me. Ya da princess ah dem pigeons. Why a long ear one be ear wit ya," questioned the dwarf dismissively.

"I am Princess Natalia, and this long ear, is Queen Seraphine of Moonclave." Upon her announcement of their titles the blusterous dwarf began to shift on his feet nervously and move the tongue in his mouth as though all the moisture within it had dried up completely. "I-I ask ya not be too ard on me men. Only followen me order. We be bein invaded ya see," whispered the dwarf apologetically.

Seraphine rubbed her chin in feigned contemplation making the uncomfortable dwarf sweat a little more before answering. "No need to worry, your men were only following orders. However, you might advise them to look and listen before firing in the future. In order to avoid making a possibly catastrophic error," suggested Seraphine with a smile.

"Aye, as me name be Onyx Dwarvenguard. I be seein it done."

"We come with news from Moonclave and Zephyria. We have all been facing Grock's forces in different ways, sending word here many times, with no response. I also believe my personal guard came to deliver information on the war front as well. Did Rumble and Tumble come through here," questioned Natalia hopefully.

"No, not seen dem two since dare exile. It seems dare beards finally come back. Musta gone direct to Aragorth. Dis be a defense post, it not lead ta the city only the mines. I be supposen da two a ya been lost in da tunnels fur a while," questioned Onyx.

"Don't really know how long it's been. We had to backtrack quite a bit before finding the right path many times before reaching you here." said Seraphine with a sigh. "We had to stop and sleep twice, along with taking many breaks."

"Aye, dem tunnels be a good defense fur invaders. Not fun fur da unfamiliar," chuckled the dwarf mirthfully. "Shale, lead dem ta Aragorth, they be needn ta deliver message to da King."

"As ya command." Came a feminine voice from beneath a dwarves metal helm. "This way, word uh da outside be ard to come by. Da king wanna be earen it quick."

"Before that, would you mind if I sealed off this passage for you," questioned Seraphine.

"Nah we gots a way uh sealen um out. Done ya be worryin. Just ya go ta me king," assured Onyx.

Shale walked by Seraphine and Natalia leading them back into the tunnel system they had only just escaped. Looking at each other they both nodded silently hoped the journey within the tunnels would be far shorter than the previous. With a sigh and a shared look, they followed the plodding dwarf Shale.

Natalia held out her hand concentrating another ball of light inside it. Using its luminescence to look over the rising bruises along her forearms, from barring the weight of the dwarven bolts against her barrier.

Seraphine looked at the bruises along Natalia's forearm with great concern having not been able to see them on the dimly lit bridge. "Your bruises look worse than mine. Are they from blocking all those bolts with your barrier, or mine," questioned Seraphine. Concerned her inadequate knowledge had led to their injuries.

"It is from my barrier. Unfortunately, I was unable to protect us both completely from the bolts. Your barrier blocked the bolts and the power behind them. I didn't account for the power of their bolts. I will need to ask Lisana what I missed, in making the barrier. Maybe I needed an anchor of some kind to prevent the recoil," contemplated Natalia. "There is much to learn in the ways of magic. I would wager most questions I will not know to ask. Until I have experienced using magic in combat like today," she smiled excitedly.

"Every time I see that smile of yours, I know trouble's sure to follow. Long gone is the timid princess of Zephyria, I'm so proud," said Seraphine. Playfully shoving against Natalia's shoulder.

Shale led them through the tunnels without speaking a word, although Natalia and Seraphine could tell the female dwarf was listening intently to their playful conversation.

They traveled back along the route that had brought them to the bridge, the sounds of fighting completely removed from the tunnels casting everything in uncomfortable silence. Silence they refused to allow to consume them, as it had previously. Holding each other's hands for comfort.

After traveling for many minutes, a loud ominous rumble, along with the sound of crashing stone, filled the tunnel around them. The sounds clearly emanating from the direction of the bridge, but if it was alarming to Shale, she made no indication.

"Are we missing something, that clearly came from the bridge did it not," questioned Natalia.

"Aye, it come from da bridge. Day be blocken da tunnels afore more dem bugs show up," said Shale. As though it were only natural to do so.

"Doesn't that make using the mines impossible until the debris is clear. My method would have at least aloud you to continue using the mines."

"Better da mines be closed den full ah gobs. Be useless till gob be gone anyways. Not be da only one it done to ether. An not be da last. Best usen a method we be known work."

"There are other places the goblinkin have come through? How long have you been dealing with the invasion," questioned Natalia.

"Nary a mont. If me time be right," contemplated Shale. "Ard ta know fur sure. Been in da tunnels most uh it."

"We thought it was odd not seeing any dwarves inside the citadel above where the goblinkin have gathered," said Seraphine.

Shale stopped in her tracks before turning to look Seraphine in the eyes. "Wha ya mean none in da citadel," she seethed with a tight fist.

"It looked completely abandoned when we walked through it."

"All the weapons looked to be in operating order, but nobody was there to either greet, or try to dissuade our entry," remarked Natalia.

"It be worse den I be thinkin. Need ta see me king quick," she said. Turning and running as quickly as her shorter legs would allow her to travel.

Shale's quickened pace turned the already complicated to remember turns through the menagerie of tunnels into a chaotic mess that neither Natalia, nor Seraphine, could make rhyme or reason of. However, Shale confidently took each turn, as though she were moving on instinct rather than memory.

Even with their increased pace and a guide they traveled for many more hours than either Natalia or Seraphine had hoped, leading to very dry mouths, to accompany their already hungry bellies. "Be nearen Aragorth. Get ya food an water dare," stated Shale. Hearing their bellies rumble uncontrollably.

"Thank you," said Natalia apologetically. Holding her stomach in an attempt to quiet the borborygmus of its emptiness

Even with Shale's assurance of their closeness it took more time than either Natalia or Seraphine liked before they could hear the sounds of civilization filtering in around them.

A few turns in the tunnels and another change in direction brought them to a bright, nearly blinding light. At the end of the long tunnel the sound of crashing water drew them in. The sound making all three of them lick their lips in anticipation. As they neared its source the light grew brighter only allowing sight of what lay beyond its luminous glow when they moved past.

Chapter Sixty-Three

Waterfalls cascaded down from the upper most layer of rings that formed the outer most domain of the city Aragorth. The waters descending and disappearing far below. Through the great falls yet another marvel caught their eyes as the flow of molten lava, its bright yellow glow, stood in stark contrast through the clear flowing waters. The flowing magma providing light within the dwarven city.

"Come an drink," said Shale. Cupping her hands beneath the water and bringing it to her mouth. "Be finen food, after drinken yur fill."

Taking Shale's lead, Natalia and Seraphine cupped their hands and drank hungrily. Until their stomachs began to ache in protest.

"Uh now my stomach hurts. Now where do we find food," questioned Seraphine hopefully.

"Aye food be near ear. Need walk a wee bit further," stated Shale. Pointing along the circular wall.

"Good. By the time we get to where the food is our stomachs will have stopped hurting," said Natalia. Feeling the water slosh around in her otherwise empty stomach.

"Dis way den," said Shale. Bidding them to follow swiftly. "Sooner ya both be fed da sooner ya be able ta see me king."

The trio moved rapidly along the upper lairs wide pathway, Their view obscured by the waterfalls, or magma flow, rendering their view of the inner most cavern nothing more than a constantly shifting waterborne image.

Although they were not dwarven, and moving at an unusual clip, their quick pace set by their guide Shale, roused no more than a passing glance. Their accompanying expression ranging from shock and joy, to outright anger, with few exceptions. Still the citizenry of other dwarves did nothing to block or hinder the trio's swift pace, bringing them quickly around to where the upper ring descended to the next layer.

A few dwarves, lined up before the precipice of the decent, disappeared in rapid succession. As they edged closer Natalia and Seraphine, they couldn't help but swallowed involuntarily, caught off guard by what lay ahead.

Two set of stairs descended along the caverns side. Another, parallel stare descending from the waterfall's edge as well. Between the two stares lay a grouping of three long smooth channel. Those coming up from below hiked up the stairs, using either set to do so. Their numbers leaving only one method available to reach the adjoining layer below.

"Best ya let some time go between ya two, or ya be a tangle uh limbs at da bottom. Speaken uh limbs. Hold yurs tight ta yur sides, or atop ya. Done wanna be loosen an arm or leg on da way down," said Shale. Failing to hide her grin as she sat down atop the carved crevice. Holding her arms atop her body she lay back allowing for her rapid descent to the bottom of the stair. The floor below leveling out to slow and ultimately stop her gained momentum.

Seraphine looked at the channel and then the stairs trying to muster her courage. With a gulp in resignation, and not wanting to hold up the growing line of dwarves behind them, she sat down at the top of the crevice. "Drogen, give me strength." Before laying back and letting herself fall. Fear and exhilaration assailed her senses throughout the descent. But as the floor evened out, and her momentum slowed, she couldn't help but smile. A smile shared by the wing cloaked Natalia as she joined them.

"I be sorry. I didn't think bout dem wings ah yurs. It look like ya figured it out all da same. Da two ah ya be lookin like one ah da yongens," commented Shale with a wide knowing grin. "Still ya avent seen the best part. Dem waterfalls be gettin in da way ah da best view ah Aragorth." Helping both Natalia and Seraphine to their feet Shale purposefully faced them toward the wall. "Dis be me favorite part wit da youngens from above."

Seraphine and Natalia stepped out of the channel toward their guide before turning around to see what Shale could possibly be talking about, and the sight before them had both their mouths fall agape.

At the center of the vast cavern stood a massive castle faceted with every variety of precious stone, metal, and jewel imaginable. The flows of water and lava descending down on either side of the structure and into the dark void below. Each aspect of Dwarven craftsmanship on full display. From massive suits of armor; holding ornate swords and pole arms, to the expertly cut and faceted jewels around each stone doorway; inlaid with platinum, gold, silver, and other precious metals. Including the most coveted of all, mythral.

At Natalia's side, her dagger began to hum, as if it were resonating with the sight of the castle. Looking down at Herzblutung she felt as though she heard a voice, but dismissed it as a trick of her overwhelmed mind from the site lain out before her.

"We'll move out once ya ave yur wits back about ya," said Shale mirthfully. "Dat lookel never get old."

Slowly Seraphine and Natalia overcame their confounded feelings, though they couldn't help but continue to marvel at the castle, still two layers removed.

"The closer we come to that castle the more lost we will likely become in its marvelous intricacies," said Natalia in awe.

"Ya best not be doubten it, but the first sight ah da castle be da most special uh all," Shale reminisced. Shaking her head against a flood of memories. "We be nearen da food vendors. Lotsa food ta eat dare. Ya both can pick an choose, as we go."

Running through the gathered crowds on the second round became more difficult as many, instead of allowing them to pass, stood in stubborn opposition. Forcing them to detour around those gathered groups. Still, the inconvenience was overshadowed by the smells wafting through the air of roasted meats and vegetables. The smell of food causing their mouths to water uncontrollably, and simply not see the rude acts being perpetrated against them.

With the smell of food guiding them, they unconsciously increased their pace, stopping only when they found the first in the massive line of food vendors stations against the rings outer wall. Their location set along the wall in order to allow those uninterested passage without inconvenience to themselves, the vendors, or those waiting.

"Be needn three," said Shale. Leading them through the line at the first stall.

"Two silver," said the gruff dwarf. Looking at Shale's entourage with a huff.

"Wha ya playin at. Tree dis mornin wah only one," complained Shale. Raising her fist in threat.

"Aye, bu dat be dis mornin. It not be mornin any more," said the dwarf "Best I be able ta do now be a sliver an a big copper. Since ya be such a loyal customer an all."

Shale simply rolled her eyes at the supposed discount pulling out the money and handing it over. Taking the money, but checking it over first, the gruff dwarf pocketed the money then handed over three metal skewers of roasted meat.

"Do you sell any roasted vegetable," questioned Seraphine. Her mouth-watering just looking at the dripping skewers.

"Bah what good be a veg when ya got meat," said the Dwarf. Crossing his arms in annoyance.

"Ugh just give me the skewer," said Seraphine. Taking it hungrily from Shale. Before taking a bite, she thanked the creature for its sacrifice, though she didn't know what it had been when it lived. Upon finishing her thanks, she quickly devoured every last meaty morsel.

Following suite both Natalia and Shale did the same eating every last bit the skewers provided.

"Dare be many a vendor afore da castle. I be maken sure da both ah ya be full to the brim, by da time we get there," assured Shale.

"Let's get moving then," said Seraphine. Her stomach pains receding, as the food hit bottom.

Although they didn't stop at every vendor along their path, they did stop multiple times to buy food as they went. Each vendor charging the three a different rate each time. Even if they served the same foods as another. The varying prices only increasing the closer they came to the final outer ring of Aragorth.

By the time of their last decent, using the carved stone channels, all previous hesitation and fear they had felt had dissipated, rapidly replaced by the thrill and wish to experience more of the exhilaration provided by the slide.

Descending to the final layer brought them directly in line with the dwarven castle of Aragorth. The path to the castle a single avenue carved out of stone blocks. To either side of the massive central road set a multitude of stone structures. Making up the whole of dwarven civilization within the carved out mountain they called home.

Leading them along the main avenue Shale set their pace toward the distant castle calling to them sternly whenever they stopped to gawk at some aspect of the bustling city alive around them, for far too long.

Dwarves of all shapes, and beard lengths, walked through the city going about their daily business. Some of which, stopped in their dealings to stare at the strange sight of an elf and zephyrian walking in the streets. Many sharing murmurs and whispers as most had never seen anything other than dwarves their entire lives. As they hurried along to the castle, an entourage formed. Pacing them on their journey.

Nearing the castle's entrance, dwarven sentries; wielding javelin's and pole arms, stood guard along the path. Noticing the unusual entrants they began to move, looking to detain Natalia and Seraphine. However, upon seeing Shale of the Dwarvenguard, they quickly returned to their post.

Looking up at the castle standing before them Seraphine and Natalia couldn't help but marvel, once more, at its absolute majesty. The details they'd been able to glean over the great distance of the second, third, and fourth lairs, paling in comparison to the observable details up close.

Every portion of the castle had been ornately decorated. Each space large enough to hold one of the massive cut and refined gemstones, or stone within a facet upon its face, had been tastefully filled. To give further luster and elegance to the structure itself. Massive defensive towers, reaching up to the third layer closest to the flowing lava, further illuminating and illustrating the greatness of those craftsmen who raised the structure into the statement it had become.

Shale allowed them time to take in the many sites and intricacies of Aragorth's castle. How could they not as, each doorway, stone, jewel, filigree, and facet had been meticulously and expertly crafted. Each set into the structure without so much as a single mistake visible to the naked eye.

As if being released from an invisible hold Natalia and Seraphine shook themselves bringing their eyes to the ground, so as not to be trapped in the castles majestic allure anew.

"I would love for Chian to see this. She would be most impressed by such fine craftsmanship," spoke Natalia.

"When this war with Grock ends, we can bring her, and Drogen down here with us," said Seraphine. Hoping beyond anything else, that it could and would happen.

"Dis way," said Shale. Motioning to the guards, standing outside the great arching double doorway, to open the castles doors.

The castle arching doors, being so large that a giant standing on the tips of its toes and extending its arm to reach above its head, would be hard pressed to touch the top of the door. Let alone the arched frame it occlude securely within. The guards, knocking on the door in a rhythmic pattern, initiated a series of heavy clicks, bangs, rattles, and groans from the other side before growing silent once more. With a single finger to the unhinged side of the french hung doors, they glided open, as if entirely weightless.

"If only to see that, Chian must be brought here," whispered Natalia into Seraphine's ear. Receiving a slow, but earnest, nod in response.

Massive pillars lined either side of the foyer. The columns reaching high above adding to the feeling of great opulence, and grandeur. So as not to loose either Natalia or Seraphine Shale grabbed their hands, practically dragging them along, to where they would meet King Aragorth. Passing many doors along the way. Each of them distinct in their materials and make until, at the end of the long entrance hall, they came to a door made of the dwarves most prized and loved of metals, mythral. Large torches stood in sconces along each of the doors french hinged sides. The light causing a cascade of light to fall upon the door itself producing an aurora across its face, beget only by expertly polished mythral.

Once more the guards stationed outside the door tapped upon it rhythmically, but this time, produced a clear and precise chime of bells. Upon the ringing of a final solemn note the doors opened. As if doing so of their own accord.

A voice rose within Natalia's mind as the final note diminished to silence. Try as she might to find its source, she could find no indication. *Is this another aspect of my experiences at the hands of Nefar and Bernadine's guard, or something else. Or is this from my time with the goblinkin,* Natalia questioned within herself. Shaking off the uncomfortable thoughts, she quickly fell in line behind Shale and Seraphine.

Flanking along both sides of the central walkway, as they entered the massive chamber, stood an entire battalion of dwarven soldiers. Each carrying long polearms. At the head of the room, and line of Dwarves, set Aragorth's throne. However, unlike the rest of the castle around them, it had no ornamentation, filigree, precious stone, or jewel. Instead, it had been carved from a single block of limestone.

Shale knelt down before the stone throne. As decorum stated for Seraphine, she remained standing before the throne, of her equal in status. Natalia however, unsure of her own standing, moved to kneel beside Shale. Seraphine's hand came down, preventing Natalia from completing the action. Looking at Shale for protest against Seraphine's prevention, she found none.

The guards behind them struck the ground at their feet with the butts of their pole-arms in tandem, their hard hits reverberating through the floor and into each of them, as they awaited Aragorth's arrival.

Chapter Sixty-Four

The white light consumed Drogen as yet another force far beyond his control pulled him through the white and gold filigree door. Except Drogen did not struggle against its pull as he had the raging waters that had swept him away. Choosing instead to clear his mind completely and allow what lay beyond the door to exert its influence. *"Tis all a part of the whole after all,"* contemplated Drogen.

"Dis be it. Our time ah bein ear an not a part uh da ole be done."

"Or will there be yet another end for us. One yet unseen. What makes this one different then all the others who've come before." questioned another voice.

"Wha ya be meanen bout diffren. Dis one be ah us true and true. Ya be daft not ta be seen it. He be da son ah Death an is mudder be a dragon. Dem two be at war wit one anudder fur a centry afore finen each udder true."

"How could Arawn father a child. Danu herself is incapable of doing so. Through anything more than her power to bring life. Though Gaia was greatly capable of deceiving those she took as her lovers. Still Azrael could never hope to do so, when Tellus has never been able to."

"Aye. I be admitten it be strange fur sure. Still, he be ear. An he be da one ooh open da door."

"Since you know this one personally, you take care of this portion of his journey. The others will be quite interested to learn of this development. Until they too become one with the whole," said the second voice. The final tendrils of its speech falling to a whisper as it seemingly traveled further away.

Drogen, who had been listening intently to the strangely familiar voices back and forth, came to a sudden realization as the second voice he could not mistake for any other. "*Balthazar*," he questioned. "How is it possible that you're here."

"Aye I be ear. An I not be alone ear eader. I be one uh da gods. Da god ah war, metal, an a good drink," stated Balthazar. Smiling as he walked into view, through the white wispy fog surrounding Drogen. "As fur owe I be ear. Ya saw me ammer, but once in yur life. Ya remember wha runes be upon its face. Da name uh me closest companion?"

Drogen thought back to the first and only time he had seen the blacksmiths true weapon. Playing through the events, they began unfolding around him. The fog showcasing memories of the past. However, they were not memories from his own point of view, but those from Balthazar's. *"Many runes were transcribed along each face of your hammer, but one stood out against the bevy of others. Unsterblich, your hammers name was Unsterblich."*

"Aye, I be Balthazar de Immortal. Owever, immortality be attain in many ways. Not always be ow one tink. Not mean ya be livin in da sence of uh mortal. Me immortality be linked wit you Drogen, wit War. I be yur guide ta what be comin next. Till we all be one wit da ole," said Balthazar. As though it had become his mantra.

"What comes next."

"It be good ya earen yur swords again. Day be needn ya to ear um speak. An ya need be listnen ta dem when day do. Day be aparta ya. Ta da depths uh yur being," explained Balthazar.

"They spoke truths I've been struggling to reconcile. Tis one of the reasons I could not hear their call, but I feel there is more than my fear holding back their voices."

Aye, thar be anudder reason fur it. Now dat ya open da door. Fur da next part ya be needn ta call dem blades ah yurs. We be needn ta walk through da door an inta yur soul chamber as well," instructed Balthazar.

"Come Godslayer; Envoy of Death." called Drogen. The blades appearing within his grasp, as they always did. However, as Balthazar had alluded to, their voices did not reach his mind. *"I will not allow their voices to return to silence. What must I do in order to restore them, now that I have opened the door."*

Without answering Drogen's question Balthazar beckoned him through the white door and into his soul chamber. As they walked through, the door swung closed, with exception of a near imperceptible gap where power continued to emanate. Stopping just before Drogen's chain bound soul, Balthazar raised his hand, and silently pointed.

"My soul is the answer to the question," pondered Drogen. Assessing the chains coiling like serpents around the fires of his existence. Looking down upon Godslayer; Envoy of Death and the single chain that flowed from each handle he finally understood. *"They can no longer resonate because they are only half of what they should be. They are haves that must be made whole. As I have become, by breaking the lock, and throwing wide the door."*

"Ye be as in-tune wit yeself as ya always been. Me dear friend. Now ya be understanden what ya mus do," commended Balthazar with a large toothy smile.

"How does one reforge a blade within their own soul. They are both a part of me. Thus they are, even within the realm of my mind, capable of being changed. Same as I have, and will continue to, once I better understand what lay beyond the white door. This space is within my influence as well, because it too is a part of my whole," contemplated Drogen. Settling his eyes upon the single remaining pedestal standing proud of his chained soul he continued. *"This is my soul, and within this chamber, things are as I wish them to be."* And so the pedestal changed into an anvil, as though it had been so all along.

"That just leaves a hammer. Since I have fire covered."

"That's where you're wrong Drogen." Interjected the second voice from beyond the slightly ajar white door. "Your draconic flames were enough for them before, but now, they will prove to be... inadequate. No matter how hot you are capable of making them. A far hotter, primordial flame, will need to be used in order to reforge your blades."

"I be da one teachen em. Ya bes be waitn yur turn Tyr," Balthazar admonished.

"Fine, I'll just go speak with the others then while you continue your part. I'm sure those pacifists will have something intriguing to say. Or maybe Musashi," said Tyr dismissively. His voice faded away once more.

"Ya be aven yur ands full wit dat one fur sure," said Balthazar. Shaking his head. "Aye but he be right. Yur breath not be hot nough ta do what need be done. Dem swords need reflect ya as a whole. Usin yur fire gain bring no change, no resonance. As fur da hammer, ye be known da name ya need be callin. Ya need only call an she be ear."

"*Unsterblich,* thought Drogen. Balthazar's hammer appearing atop the anvil. *With you I will fully forge out the truth of my existence. Godslayer; Envoy of Death, tis time to forge you anew, so that I may hear your voices into eternity."*

"Once ya do wha come next. Dare be no goin back. No return ta owe tings were. Ye be one uh three. I ask ya be sure dis be da right path. Dis be near ya las chance ta change yur mind," cautioned Balthazar.

"Whether this has transpired through destiny, fate, or by simply following the path that I have sought out for myself. I do not know. What I do know, and understand, is I am the only one who has been born capable of becoming a true god alongside Death and Life. There must be a reason, or purpose, behind it that I do not see. Beyond helping those I care for," reasoned Drogen.

"An what if dare not be?"

"Then I must discover reason myself. I will have an eternity to figure it out," said Drogen with a sincere smile. *"I have also come to realize something very important that my counterparts have yet to grasp about themselves. Life herself gives rise to those without meaning, soul, or ambition. Death enjoys living despite all the hardships and regrets that come with living.*

"What does that make you Drogen, Son of Lisana; Reaper of souls, Godslayer; Envoy of Death, Drakregus of Lundwurm Tul." questioned Balthazar.

I do not know, for now I must embrace both sides of my soul I am Gottdrak. Both dragon and god of Dranier. Tis my hope that upon reforging Godslayer; Envoy of Death I will come to understand my truth, and the aspect I represent between life and death.

"Ya already be known what aspect ya be representen. As all who be callen da hall beyond that door home ave afore ya. We be one an all da former lives ah War," spoke Balthazar. Shaking his head.

Drogen nodded with Balthazar's claim but said nothing as he stepped closer to his bound soul. Reaching out he touched one of each color of chain running his fingers along their links before closing his eyes. *"The chains will fall from my soul once I accept both halves of the whole."* spoke Drogen. Removing his hand from the chains.

"And how ya go bout doin that," questioned Balthazar.

Drogen called forth the two doors to stand opposite each side of his bound soul. The chains shortened along their hinged sides until taut and immobile, completely binding the serpentine chains. With a click from his fingers from both hands, both doors flung wide and with their opening came a surge of power and strength. Power and strength that scorched and melted the chains to nothingness. Releasing the shackles binding his primordial fires.

Chapter Sixty-Five

The royal guard of Aragorth remained kneeling over many minutes, as a band of clergy helped Aragorth, to his limestone throne. Only when their great ruler sat, and raised his lethargic hand, did they rise. Smashing the butt of their pole-arms against the ground to signal the completion of their rulers command.

The dwarven monarch's old wizened distant eyes looked out from the throne. Their great depth pervading the innumerable lines of age upon his grand visage. Upon his gray-haired head, set the crown of his station fitted with every manor of jewel, filigree, and mythrals distinct iridescent sheen.

"Who are you to stand before King Aragorth," questioned not the king. But one of the clergy beside him. "Why have you seen fit to bring them before his majesty Shale Dwarvenguard."

"They come wit news from da citadel above," said Shale. Raising to look into the clergies' eyes.

"Your king ordered Aragorth's every entrance sealed, ta combat the goblinkin incursion," spoke the clergy in common tongue, but with far more eloquence than either Natalia or Seraphine had thus far heard from a dwarf. "None are permitted entrance. Especially not into our *great* city," spoke the priest menacingly. Casting her eyes down upon the trio.

"Day found me regiment. We be fighten um off, on da east mine bridge. Witout da elp uh da black wing an long ear, da push would been many hours still, an more uh me brudders dead. Er magic push da stinken ones back, so da udders could collapse da tunnels. Me Dwarvenguard now hold da bridge cusa dare elp, High Priest Kyan," explained Shale.

"As for who we are and why we stand," interjected Seraphine. "I am Queen Seraphine of Moonclave and this is Princess Natalia of Zephyria."

"Ah a Queen and a Princess, that still does not explain why you do not kneel before his majesty," admonished the priestess. "I suppose, I must forgive your lack of decorum. You are the first to stand before the Throne of Aragorth in over a generation. The short memories of long eared tree mites will not be held against you."

A clear ire rose in Seraphine's face, at the priestesses supposition of proper decorum, and unwarranted admonishments. "What gives you the right to stand and speak to a Queen and Princess from another people in such a way."

"I was appointed by Aragorth himself to this position. I have his permission to conduct the court in any way *I* see fit. Should he feel that anything I say or do is beyond my roll, he will undoubtedly let all in the chamber know," said Kyan smugly.

"I know many rulers, one stands beside me, and another is my... Father The crimson king Lord Vladimir of Zephyria. My friend here may certainly speak for herself on such an issue.

But I for one am certain that none of them would allow a groundhog's *ordure* to speak, in *their* stead," emphasized Natalia.

"I agree, they would hardly permit another, below their station, to stand in front of them as they sit upon their throne," spoke Seraphine. Seething in rage.

"We did not come here to speak with the clergy. We are here to speak with Aragorth himself," said Natalia.

"You have no say in who you are permitted to speak with. Neither of you do."

"You'll not allow us to speak with Aragorth. Your king who is seated behind you," questioned Seraphine suspiciously. Turning to look at Natalia Seraphine noted the same incredulous expression. *Something about this doesn't feel right,* thought them both.

"If we are not permitted to speak with Aragorth then... Point us in the direction of my twin guards, Rumble and Tumble. That we may be on our way. Back to our own lands."

"They came some time ago. Speaking ridiculous lies, no doubt placed into their heads by the likes of the elves and zephyrian's, during their exile from Aragorth," spoke Kyan dismissively. "You will find them where they belong. In the stockades being pelted with food and whatever other grotesque things the citizens of our fine city have to offer such repugnant's"

"However, we cannot allow either of you to walk through our streets armed as you are. Once you have the other two within your company, *Shale* will return you through whatever hole you came from."

"So she can witness Grock's army beating upon your front door," stated Seraphine. Her statement's causing the dwarven guard within the chamber to shift from foot to foot. A clear indication to Seraphine that they remained blissfully unaware of the true threat they face.

"You speak lies, bark louse. Your wish to rile up the people of Aragorth will prove futile. We would already know of any threat before it ever reached us, through communication with the citadel above."

"The abandoned citadel that's currently being pelted with boulders and anything else Grock's forces might want to throw at it, you pig headed molekin," insulted Seraphine with a cheeky grin. "Or is there another way we could have come through. And before you even try, I'm an Elf, unlike you. *I cannot lie.*"

"Say I believe your worm riddled brain, and there's an army at our front door. How then were you able to enter. If the citadel is abandoned you would have been forced to face an entire army in order to even a tempt to drop the drawbridge," postulated Kyan sarcastically. Drawing laugh's from the gathered priests at her back. With a dismissive wave of her hand, "Gather their weapons and take them away."

"What about all the messages that were sent to Aragorth. Surely not all of them were intercepted by the Grock minions," posited Natalia. Reluctantly removing Herzblutung's weapon belt from her side."

"Cobal, have we received any outside correspondence."

"No me Priestess," yelped Cobal. Far louder than necessary. The dwarven acolyte nervously shifting his weight.

Seeing the nervousness of the dwarven clergyman, Seraphine quickly devised a plan in order to get to the bottom of what was really happening. "I would ask that one of your priests hold our weapons, and take us to Rumble and Tumble."

Looking Seraphine over curiously as she touched her swords hilt three times, Natalia began to grasp her plan. "Shale has been wonderful, but as you alluded to earlier, she is needed elsewhere."

"Yes. Yes. Shale will be of far greater use helping to block off more of the tunnels from the goblins that have found their way into the tunnels. Disciple Zirco retrieve their weapons. They may take those despicable outcasts with them. They remain without deed, and name. Those third born are of no use to Aragorth."

"Actually... I was hoping Cobal would be kind enough to show us around," said Natalia. Shifting from side to side, looking down and away as she spoke.

"Oh really," said High Priest Kyan as she looked over to the nervously shifting dwarf. "Alright then, I suppose I can allow it."

Zirco having retrieved Seraphine and Natalia's weapons, brought them up the steps before the other clergy. Handing them over to Cobal with an impish grin.

Cobal began to descend the steps, but the outstretched hand of their ruler stopped him dead in his tracks. Aragorth reached out toward the dwarf with wrinkled fingers before curling them, in a gesture, for the weapons to be brought to him. Looking to High Priest Kyan for direction, the already nervous dwarf, shook as though he were breaking a fever.

The High Priest looked back at the outstretched had of Aragorth with fear in his eyes. As if the movement itself was impossible for him to even imagine. Still, Aragorth's old wrinkled-hand held steady as the stone throne on which he sat. Although clearly disturbed by the king's sudden movement, Kyan turned away from the display, tossing her hand in deference.

Cobal, perspiring profusely, inched forward. Kneeling before his sovereign, Cobal held out Seraphine's sword for the elder dwarf.

Aragorth ambled to the front of his throne, placing his hand upon the swords hilt. With the touch his far away eyes noticeably brightened. In a swift practiced motion Aragorth drew the sword free of its sheath. Cutting a line across Cobal's outstretched hand.

Thought Cobal winced noticeably from the cut, he dared not make a sound, or move away from his kneeling position before the throne. In the same movement Aragorth returned it fully, its seating producing a dull thud.

Placing Seraphine's sword upon the ground at Aragorth's feet, Cobal brought up Natalia's sheathed sword, that it could be studied by his monarch's wise eyes.

Aragorth wrapped his hand around the circular shaft of the concentric blade pulling it free from its sheath. Bringing the blade up before his eyes bringing a change to the monarch. A change, from the visage of High Priest Kyan, that was unexpected and objectionable. As the grizzled elder dwarf looked down upon the kneeling dwarf and spoke. "Wha ya lot be given me," spit Aragorth in near convulsive rage.

Kyan moved swiftly between Aragorth and her disciple. "W-w-w-we can go over your concern. I-I-I-In private chambers my King. We've gone over all of this before. D-D-D-Don't you remember. I-I-I know aging is hard on the body and mind, but this is not the right."

"I not be talken ta you ya dung eap in cleric cloth," seethed Aragorth. Pushing Kyan aside.

Kyan moved away slowly, to dissuade Aragorth from possibly striking out with the dagger. Even with distance between them, he didn't lower the blade, nor the threat that it posed.

"Now wha ya dereliks be given me." His knuckles cracking under the strain of his hand's unyielding grasp around the hilt of Herzblutung.

"I-I-I apologize for our sovereigns' outburst. His advancing age..."

"If ya done be shutten ya yap an letten dis one speak... I be runnin ya through wit me master's final work," raged Aragorth. Pointing the tri-blade sword toward her heart with menace filled eyes.

"I done kno..." started Cobal. But before the last syllable could escape his lips his body contorted in pain.

"In all me years dare be two things constant. Da young tink demselves better den da old. An no matter ow anoyen a tree louse be, day not tell ya a lie," spoke Aragorth. Kneeling down to look in Cobal's eyes. "An now, neader can you, naw witout pain runnin true yur ole body."

Tears welled up in Cobal's eyes as he looked into the knowing sorrow of Aragorth's own. Struggling against the pain, Cobal looked toward Kyan. Who looked down upon the clergyman menacingly in response, shaking her head coldly despite seeing the coursing pain running through another member of her order.

"Da pain not end till da truth be spoken. Now ya best be out wit it Cobal. Or ya be in fur more pain den ya can andle," he said deliberately. Taking hold of Seraphine's sword Truth in his other hand, Aragorth rose back to his feet, reclaiming his throne.

Aragorth brought Natalia's Herzblutung up to his eyes taking in each detail as he waited for the effects of Truth's magic to overwhelm the cleric's senses. "Ow did ya come by me master's last work," he questioned. Cobal beginning to convulse in pain. His winces and breaths coming out with agonizing strain.

"I purchased it from my Uncle's weapon shop in Zephyria. He does not remember who gave it to him, or when he received it. Only that it came to him while he was running his shop in our market city of Zephyr... Long before Grock's force overtook the city," said Natalia.

"Den I mus be sure ta thank dis uncle," said Aragorth. Continuing to admire the blade. "Me master never tol me ooh it be fur. Only it be fur anudder. It nah be fur Dwarven ands." Growing silent, as though in reminiscence it took many moments for Aragorth to begin speaking again. "A bit ah da soul. Da soul ah its maker be locked wit in dare creation. If nah fur dis blade... I never uh come to me senses. An if not fur dis one," he said holding up Seraphine's sword, Truth. "I not be knowen da truth ah ooh be tryin ta do me in. Me guard detain da High Priest an er order," he commanded. Raising Herzblutung high above his head before hitting the hilt upon the arm of his throne. Breaking it off from the blow.

"We-We've given you nothing," exclaimed Kyan in defiance.

"I be earen da truth fur meself," impressed Aragorth. Pulling Truth from its scabbard.

Natalia, Seraphine, and Shale gathered together, backing away as the city's clergy were forcibly knelt before their king. Aragorth's royal guard holding weapons at their backs. To each of the detained, a single cut was placed upon their arm, slicing through their robes to draw blood upon Truth.

"Now we be findin out da truth. Wha ya be given me," he questioned. Raising his hand before any of them could speak. "An afore any ah ya be thinkin a speaken a lie, I be suggestin ya look at da result uh such *action*," pointed Aragorth toward Cobal. Who continued to writhe in agony upon the floor. Letting out tortured screams, with every caught breath.

With the threat clear to them all, and an example present before them, the line of clergy disseminated into a cacophony of raised voices. With only one among their order remaining silent, Their High Priest Kyan.

Cobal, hearing the others speak, chose to save himself from the pain. Speaking the truth, the pain stopped. Even with its regression, he lay exhausted on the ground covered, in a pool of his own sweat and bile. Having thrown up from the excruciating pain.

"You say nutting ta defend yeself genst me accusation," questioned Aragorth to the silent High Priest. As the others returned to silence.

"I not be needn ta explain me self fur doin what be right," spoke Kyan. No pain flowing through her body."

"An wha bout what ya doin be right," questioned Aragorth.

"Cus ye not be me King. Me king be da one oh send me ear ta take down all ye false dwarves. Da Verger be da true dwarves not ye ooh abandoned um," spoke High Priest Kyan. Her facade slipping entirely in her rage.

In response, Aragorth ran his finger down Truth's edge drawing his own blood upon the sword. Ripping a piece of cloth from the arm of Kyan's tunic he wipe the blade of blood before returning it to its sheath.

With a heavy sigh he sat Seraphine's sword down across the top of his throne, past the broken arm, Herzblutung remaining in is grasp. A deep sadness permeated the air around him as he returned and sat before High Priest Kyan. Allowing a few moments of silence to pass, before addressing her accusations.

"Dat be a name... I not be earen fur a long time. I not be sure ah ooh be tellin ya of dem we lost, but it not be me dat did em in," he said solemnly. Shaking his head as his eyes traveled back through time. "Day be da reason fur me masters leaven. Day be da reason we not within dem sacred halls ah old. Day be da reason I abandon *dat name.*"

"Ya abandon me kin. Ya abandon dem all. Now day be nutten but ghosts," proclaimed Kyan.

"He split me an me brudder apart, wit his corruption. Dem udder ones did nothin ta elp. Me master warn um of da truth. Day refused ta listen. An it nearly led us all to our end. Da fay came ta elp, but day could do nutten ta save em. Day sealed dare own fate trusten in him, above me master. An wha did da elves receive in return? Me blame fur dare inability. Fur me inability ta save um. Da refusal uh dare matriarch fur access to da forest an its resources, only pushen me resolve ta ave nothin ta do wit da fair folk. When day did nutting but try an elp," recalled Aragorth. Turning his solemn eyes toward Seraphine, before refocusing his attention upon the kneeling clergy. "Now yunguns, wha did day promise ya. Wha day give ya fur surrendren to da gobbos? An ow were ya supposen ta accomplish da task?"

"We ta clear da way, fur the gobs above. Bring em all ome ta fight dem comin from bellow," said another of the clergy.

"Aye, an let me guess wha day promise ya. Day say da gobbs come an tear up da place. Day kill me, an in da suffren after, one uh ya rise to da occasion. Put yeself on da throne an mantle ah king ta rebuild da Verger, wit dem left alive," questioned Aragorth shaking his head.

"Ow-Owd you know wha me true king tell me," questioned Kyan. Shaking her head in disbelief.

A single tear formed in the old monarch's eyes as he looked down upon his misguided cleric. "Cus it be da same deal me brudder took from da deceiver. Da one ooh killed me people, an filled me old ome wit da ghosts ah da dead. Dare bodies unable ta rest fur eternity fur what he day did ta dem," explained Aragorth. Taking hold of Kyan's shoulder, and placing his forehead upon hers.

Though the cleric tried to fight against the monarch's grasp she couldn't get away. They staid locked together for a short time before he released her from his grasp. "Why ya not tell any uh us, if dis all be true. Why ya keep it all ta yurself" she questioned in disbelief.

"I taught that keepin me people away from da udders, an da sins uh da past dat I could save um meself. Afore day could make da same mistake me brudder made. Even in me age, I make da mistake ah taken everytin on meself. If not fur deas two inviten demselves ear, I would ave add to watch it apen again. I mus give all da knowledge uh da past to me people. Not old it all meself."

Aragorth pointed out three guards. "Go to me room in da castle. Along da outer wall uh me room, pull da sconce an enter da room. Dare you find me papers. It be all da knowen I gadder from Bathara." Walking back and forth before his throne, he continued to grip Herzblutung's hilt. As though it were his one and only life line.

"Day be gone fur a little while, so I will ask da lotta ya. What ye been given me ta keep me locked in me own ed."

"We been givin ya waking shade me king. It be a gift uh da udder king," said Zirco.

"Den it be wearen off, given uh bit uh time," said Aragorth with a relieved sigh. "Ya lot didn't ave da guts ta kill me yeselves it would seem. Or was dis a part uh da deceiver's plan as well. Ah way uh gainen support fur yeselves, wit me death?"

"It be part uh da plan me king," confirmed Cobal in remorse.

As they waited for the royal guards return the chamber turned silent. Taking the opportunity the silence provided, Natalia and Seraphine stepped up beside the kneeling clerics in order to speak with Aragorth.

"We came to speak with you King Aragorth. I know you are currently dealing with... heavy matters. But what we have to tell you is quite pressing for your people as well. It has cost the lives of many people. One whom I love to the depths of my very being," spoke Natalia.

"Dare be an army beaten gainst me fron door," said Aragorth "I be well aware. Dis be needen uh fix first. Den I be focusen on da true threat to me people."

"I hope whatever Lisana did to the door holds long enough for you to move your army through the tunnels," said Seraphine.

"I be knowen everyting ya be knowen. Got more den enough time afore day be breken dat seal. Dat dracon friend uh yurs sealed da doorway wit er fire after all. Er breath fuse da door an make dare entry nay impossible."

"How can you know any of that," questioned Natalia.

"Ye be daft. I already tell ya dis dagger contain a piece uh its maker. We leaven a piece in all we be createn. Dis be me master's work. True him, I be known all ye know. All I need do, is listen an ear," said Aragorth in explanation.

"It's hard, finding out those you've lived and grown with, could hold such incredibly deceitful and deadly machinations. Many who once set upon Moonclave's council have been imprisoned for such. Figuring out the correct punishment for what they did, is something I find myself struggling with," confessed Seraphine.

"My stepmother and sister were banished for what they did to both the citizens of Zephyria... And to me," said Natalia frankly. "Not that I am trying to advise you on how to deal with such actions," she expounded quickly. Seeing the growing ire upon Aragorth's deeply furrowed visage.

"De young always look ta solve all de problems uh da past. Da problem be dat the past be impossible ta solve. Try as we might, all one be able ta do is look to da past, ta not make da same mistakes in da future. Me problem be, I old all me knowen uh da past in me ead. Not in de ands uh dose maken choices in da future," acknowledged Aragorth.

The royal guard, that had been sent to gather materials from the secret room in Aragorth's quarters returned. Their arms overflowing with parchments, crystal bowls, and a vile filled with gold flecked fluid. The liquid within moving rapidly within the confines of the thick glass jar, as though it were sentient and searching for any means of escape.

"I been researchen all deese years a way ah tellen when one ah da deceiver's minions add come ah callen. In opes uh keepen me people safe uh his ways. An wit it, I be able ta tell ooh ah ya took part in da ritual. Though, I suppose, I could ask ya since Truth been used. Dis be me final question ta da lot uh ya. An da one dat decide year fate. Did ya go true da ritual, wit da deceiver?" questioned Aragorth. Looking at them all intently.

"What is that strange liquid," questioned Natalia.

"It be all that left uh me brudder, after da deceiver got done wit em. He forced me, ta kill me own brudder. Spillen me own flesh an blood, I be seein da deceivers influence over em. It come out ta grab old uh me as well. Lucky dare be a bottle near me feet ta old it."

"Why was there a bottle at your feet," questioned Seraphine offhandedly.

"Ya be knowen full well why dare be a bottle at me feet," barked Aragorth back with rage. His rage subsiding slightly, as he looked between the bottle of flowing liquid and those who lay beyond it. "I'd oped da day would never come dat I need do dis ta me people again."

Pointing to one of the guards carrying a fine wooden box Aragorth moved Truth to the side of his throne in order to sit comfortably. Placing the box upon his lap he pulled out crystalline bowls, each one larger than the last.

Started with the smallest, Aragorth pricked his finger with Herzblutung using his own blood, in order to produce the chime. Each increase in size simultaneously decreasing the produced tone, he continued through until only a single bowl remained.

The largest of the bowls stood as the outlier, where the others had been completely clear. The final bowl shined in an iridescent rainbow reflecting the chambers light., he opened a piece of rolled leather, pulling out a metal syringe.

Using the syringe, Aragorth punctured the corked glass bottle, pulling a small amount of the flowing liquid in. Emptying the contents of the syringe into the mythral bowl. He pricked himself again, as his finger had stopped bleeding, and placed his finger on the ridge of the bowl.

"Any uh dem ooh reacts ta da sound, are ta be cast free uh dare misery," ordered Aragorth to his guard. In acceptance, the guard struck their arms against the stone floor at their feet.

Running his finger along the bowl's brim elicited a droning chorus of sound, which filled the room completely. At first there were no reactions to the sound, but as his finger circled for a fifth time many of the clergy began to emanate unnatural light through their vain's. With the golden light to guide their weapons, all who shone fell by the royal guards swift and decisive action.

With their deaths, Aragorth gave the closest guard to him the syringe, as he continued rubbing the rim of the bowl. As if pacified by the bowls song, the golden blood moved toward the sound. The liquid subsequently procured by the guard, and injected into the glass bottle, to merge with the rest.

"It do de lot uh ya good ta remember dis moment. Fur dose ooh take the blood uh du deceiver be bound ta his will. It be true blood dat de deceiver brought ruin to me brudder an me old home. Take me research ta da clerics hall an ave all de knowen I been olden be given ta me people. It be good ya didn't take part in da ritual Kyan, Cobal, Breccia, Sill, and Mash. Unfortunate, da rest uh yur order not have yur foresight on da matter," sighed Aragorth sadly.

"I-I-I sorry fur me ignorance me King. It be my lack uh fait in you an da past that bring many in me order ta forsake. Please me King, punish me in place uh de udders."

"Aye, it be yur job as high priest ta keep da faith of all who call Aragorth dare ome, but de blame not be all on ye. It be on me as King. Still, you all be punished fur wha ya may uh done, by earen an readen bout all dat appened wit da deceiver in da past. Guard's take dem to the clerics quarters an don't allow um ta leave till it all be known and written fur da masses ta know. An take da pour dead witya when ya go."

"Now, back ta udder pressin matters. Thar be an army knocken on me door, an not a dwarf in sight ah stoppen it. Shale round up all da teams blocken tunnels. Send um ta da citadel above. We be needen ta make room fur our counterattack, now dat the bad ens be dealt wit afore day given away our advantage. An gadder dem two Kyan put in da stockades fur no good reason.

Day come ome from exile. Day been punished more den enough. An day be in need uh apology," said Aragorth under his breath.

"Can we get our weapons back then? We're on the same side after all," reasoned Seraphine.

"Aye ye can ave yur weapons back, but I be needen dis one a we bit longer," he said holding up Herzblutung.

"That is quite alright with me King Aragorth. I only have one request, that I may inquire about your services for the blade sometime in the future. When there are fewer pressing matters to attend to," stated Natalia.

Aragorth looked at Natalia and the blade with a raised eyebrow in interest, before simply nodding in agreement. Rising from his throne Aragorth looked over his guard. "Ave all ead da call, we rise to war," he bellowed. Receiving a cacophony of sound as the guard's arms struck repeatedly against the stone floor at their feet.

Chapter Sixty-Six

Although efficient in their preparation's, Aragorth's military might took many days to converge and rise through the rings and carved caverns leading to the surface and the waiting goblinkin. Leading his people at the head Aragorth marched them unerringly toward the wide open, upper citadel.

Following closely, the cart pulling vendors, brought their wares excitedly. Knowing any coin, the soldiers couldn't pay themselves, would be furnished by Aragorth, for their aid in the war effort. Food vendors, blacksmith, and armorers being chief among them, carrying smaller implements, forges, and the like.

In total the journey took every part of two days to accomplish, as most portions of the carved tunnel could only accommodate moving in a single file line. The vendors, having to cut their way through many of the smaller sections to accommodate their burdensome carts, took another.

Shale, having been sent to gather forces from the tunnel teams, succeeded in bringing five fists. Deploying each to a battlement within the citadel, Namely the ballista stations. Each of them connected by ascending rope catwalks reaching far into the hollow mountain's upper reaches.

The low vibrating twang of the heavy ballista reverberated through the citadel when each release. The dwarves, worked in teams of five, loading the heavy bolts, cranking back upon the hide rope; using the leverage of a block and pulley system, while two adjusted the positioning along the weapons two axis. The last dwarf of each group using hand signals, for precise aiming, firing the siege weapon upon strategic targets.

"Any uh ya dat can be spared, See to da bridge. We be long pass time uh bringin da fight ta da lot outside," ordered Aragorth.

"What can we do to help," questioned Natalia. Seraphine nodding enthusiastically in support.

"We not be needn elp right now, although... Go an elp gadder arms fur da front. Most uh me men be gatheren bell shields. Bring all dem arms ta side uh da bridge. Be needn many as possible fur when da bridge come down."

"Any specific kinds of weapons you want closest to the bridge," questioned Seraphine.

"Aye all de pole arms go to da front everytin else ave back aways. An any ya be findin along da way dat be looken fur sometin ta do, gadder um to yur cause as well," announced Aragorth loudly. So all nearby could hear the order.

"We will see it done," said Seraphine and Natalia together.

As they moved through the bustling ranks of armed and armored dwarves, they continually recruited those who looked lost, or simply unsure of their roles to play. Their main recruits being those too young, by dwarven standards, to have experienced wartime preparations. Those recruited, though outwardly gruff being ordered around by someone other than their own, were inwardly relieved to be of assistance to their far more in-tune brethren. Though they would hardly admit so in front of either Seraphine or Natalia, the jubilant smiles on their faces as they carried weapons to the front, betrayed the truth hidden under their gruff exteriors.

After many hours of gathering weapons and placing them along the outer wall for easy access, they had amassed an impressive collection of arms. All of them ready and waiting for those who might need them. However, the number gathered, paled in comparison to the division of military might, gathered within the mountain citadel.

"It be good ta see so many younguns among da ranks," said Aragorth. Examining those around him intently. "Loss many, along wit me brudder. So many I be doubten me people come back, but we be a ardy bunch. Seein so many uh dem ear be given me ope. Ope fur da future uh me people."

"We gathered every weapon we could find and laid them out for easy access as you requested. I only wish we could have found more," said Natalia.

"Dem blacksmiths be worken ard ta make an repair weapons already. All dem been gatheren wit ya, be placed by a smithy. Dat make tings move swiftly fur repairs and restocken da front. Now come wit me. Dare be sometin needn done afore da bridge be free. An da battle begin. Lucky dat your draken friend sealed da bridge, fur me people sake. Doe it be a pain in da rump ta clear away," he commented. Shaking his head while leading them away from the front, where spiked bell shields had formed a defensive line.

Aragorth brought them both to the center of Aragorth to look upon the two statues within the chamber. Looking up on the statue of himself Aragorth shook his head, as though seeing himself in stone were not, in his opinion, proper. Standing before the only other statue within the chamber he looked up with reverence in his eyes, before kneeling and bowing his head.

Seeing Aragorth's actions, Natalia and Seraphine followed suite. Although they didn't know the significance of the one they showed reverence to, it felt like the right thing to do. For many minutes they knelt before the statue, until Aragorth himself rose.

"We wondered, when we came through here who this statue represents," said Seraphine inquisitively.

"It be me master. Da god ooh elped me people an loved us all as is own. He be da one me clergy supposed ta teach da udders of. An he be da one ooh uncovered me brudder an da deceiver's corruptin ways, witin me people's heart. If only he be ear wit us. He leave me people ta elp dose ooh could stop da deceiver. Da only ones ooh could do so, from what he be sayin when he leave. I ope he be right. Dat one uh dem be able ta beat da deceiver, an any under is influence."

"What is this gods name," questioned Natalia. "All we've been able to see is the name engraved on the weapon he carries 'Unsterblich,'" she read aloud. Though she remembered it still within the steel trap of her mind.

"Aye, dat be apart uh is name. He take dat name from dat weapon uh is. Cus uh da truth of Dranier's past. Truth dat da deceiver be wanten ta ide. Wha dat truth be, e never told, ah blast dat blade ah yurs," said Aragorth. Finally realizing he was still under Truths influence. "Is name be Balthazar Unsterblich; da patron god uh da dwarves, me master, god uh da forge, an war. Now cut me wit dat blade, an take dis over sharen away will ya," barked Aragorth brusquely.

With a bemused giggle at the old dwarf's declaration Seraphine pulled truth from its scabbard allowing Aragorth to cut himself upon its sharpened edge and end any further influence the blade might have upon him.

"If Truth still held influence over you... What about the clergy you cut with it, would they not also remain under its influence," questioned Natalia.

"Aye, an it be uh good punishment fur da lot uh dem. Till ya come back true uh course," said Aragorth with a sly grin. A grin quickly cut off as a cheer rang out from the drawbridge. "It be time ta mount da counterattack," he announced. Excitedly moving to the front line, through his gathered kin.

"Dis day we fight fur our ome's an loved ones. Dat day not ave ta experience wha we warriors' must ta save our kin from death. We be fighten a might far larger den our own, and far ugglier to," Aragorth chimed. In order to add a little levity to their harrowing situation. "Day believe day already won dis war. It be our job ta teach em better den ta believe anytin uh da sort. Now gadder yeselves an prepare. If day want war den we bring dem what day be asken fur," proclaimed the king. Holding high Herzblutung. "Drop da bridge. SHIELDERS ADVANCE!"

The drawbridge fell swiftly, the sickening sound of blood splatter and cracking bones accompanying its quick descent to the terrain bellow. Taking the opportunity, the bridges descent facilitated, the bell shield dwarves advanced through the massive opening creating a shield wall atop the bridge. With each advance of the dwarven wall more shielder's pushed in at their brothers backs. Bolstering and widening the line, while simultaneously driving back the sieging force, before they could implement counteractions.

Goblins, barghest, and worgs, who had been forced to the front as meat shields for the orcs and ogres, fell swiftly before the dwarven shields, pole arms, and spikes present. Many being ground into bloody paste, as the dwarves continued their relentless advance.

Using the tower itself to prevent the possibility of being flanked from behind, the dwarves continued to push through the mythral gateway, strengthening their line with every step. As the remaining shielder's took their place, dwarven archers began raining arrows down upon the goblinkin. Their crossbow bolts finding their marks, without much need to aim, thanks to the sheer number of enemies.

"Bring out da bolter," ordered Aragorth. Looking out over the shield wall from within the citadel.

From a far corner of the hollow mountain a team of ten dwarves, both pushed and pulled with rope, upon a uniquely built ballista. Where the ballista above were made to move and acquire targets, this one had been constructed to fire bolts straight into the ground. Though the device had been placed upon wheels, the dwarves struggled to move the bolter, even with the heightened innate strength present within their species.

As the bolter made its way through the gate, behind the line of dwarven shielders and archers, Aragorth, Seraphine, and Natalia followed.

"What is that thing supposed to do," questioned Seraphine speculatively.

"Ya be seein ear afore long," said Aragorth dismissively. "Switch out," he ordered. And with his utterance all on the front line transferred their burdens to those fresh and ready behind them.

"Drogen would be quite enthralled with your people's prowess, seeing how coordinated your warriors are," commented Natalia. Scanning the battlefield over top of the dwarven shields. Looking for the distant stone construct, on which she knew Drogen's body to be. However, the quickly setting sun upon the distant horizon made discernment of anything from their vantage near impossible. Dusk set in upon them. The rise of the waning gibbous moon showering the battlefield in its light, as it ascended from below the tree's, a fair distance removed of their backs.

"I not be known ooh ya be talken of. But de dagger be callen out to ya, at da speaken uh da name. Doe I not be known wha such a ting be meanen, I know it be time ta give ya back me master's work," said Aragorth. Holding out the sheathed dagger, hilt first, to Natalia.

Natalia could tell from his expression giving the blade back made him uneasy. Realizing his hesitation was likely due to his mental state, under the influence of what the clergy had referred to as waking shade. "Should I witness any change in you, I will place the dagger back into your hand, you need not worry," reassured Natalia.

"I tank ya fur dat. I not be knowen ow long day been drugen me. Dare may be some effects I not be seein in time ta stop," commented Aragorth. Nodding as the dagger's sheath left his hand.

Following the bolter, and those maneuvering it to the right side of the dwarven line, Aragorth silently motioned for the line to split along the side of the citadel, allowing a means for the massive device to move through.

"Gone be ard moven true ear me king," spoke one of the dwarves. Shaking their helmed head.

"What be blocken da way Crush?"

"From de smell I be tinken fried troll."

"Aye, I be smellen da stink from ear. Wha ya suggest we do ta get da bolter true," questioned Aragorth.

"It be best ta lift de thing over da stone's. It not be far ta where da bolter be useful. But de weight be ard ta manage," said Crush. Contemplating the problem.

"Actually, we might be of help in this matter," said Natalia. Wrapping her arm around Seraphine's waist with a smile, drawing everyone's eyes in curiosity. "I believe I can lessen the weight, making it a lighter burden. Seraphine here can help to pull the wagon with her vines as well."

Crush, Aragorth, and the others looked them both over skeptically, so much so that they began to doubt their own ability. Until Seraphine stepped, and gave her a supportive push, forward. "We've got this. We'll show them a little of what we can do. Then we can join in the fighting. I for one want to get to Drogen's side as quickly as possible, and if this helps do that I'm all in."

With a nod, Natalia stepped forward. Pulling Herzblutung from the sheath at her side, she began concentrating magic into the spaces between the blades. Stopped after only a short time. "The magic is dissipating far too quickly using this method. The blade alone cannot retain the magic. It could dissipate too quickly and prove far too dangerous. With a spear shaft I'll be able to channel more power into the blade and maintain it longer. However, the channeling will make the shaft unusable."

"Aye, an I be suspectin dis ta be da matter ya wished ta speak ta me bout in da future," said Aragorth with a knowing nod. "Well one uh ya bring a weapon shaft fur da winged one," he commanded. A couple of soldiers running off, scrambling in search.

Moments later they returned holding three wooden shafts between the two of them. "Good tinkin, may be needin more den one. Some dem hafts be long in age. Cobbal bring dat one uh yours. Angelit, you be assisten da princess wit wha she be needen."

"Yes me king," said Cobbal and Angelit together.

With the wooden shaft connected to the concentric spear Herzblutung Natalia stepped forward humming to herself as she thought through the problem before her. *Using wind magic as I do with my wings will help reduce the weight making it easier for the dwarves to lift, but I need a more efficient method,* contemplated Natalia. Moving swiftly through the books categorized within her mind she quickly found the answer she sought.

Concentrating and channeling power through the wooden haft of her spear, magic formed within the spaces between Herzblutung's blades. Allowed her magic to flow out, attach, and spread throughout the bolters surface. Filling the space within its confines. *A base of two fills the void, reducing the weight of what lay inside,* she thought. Aiding her concentration by focusing on what she wished to accomplish.

With a nod, in confirmation it was time to act, Aragorth bid the ten dwarves to lift the bolter. A feat that would have taken another ten to be reasonably accomplished. Still skeptical, the dwarves prepared themselves for the back breaking weight. Testing the heft gingerly at first. Only when they each held it high over their heads did they understand just how much weight had been reduced. With a collective glee-filled smirk on their faces, they strode across the fried troll boulders, sitting the bolter down once they had cleared them entirely.

"Ya sure ya not be needn a job ear in da citadel. We be moven all kind a heavy tings an yur magic would make da job a ole lot easier," questioned Angelit. Walking beside Natalia and Seraphine with the extra wooden spear shafts.

"I would love to stay and learn more about the citadel, and possibly access your library, but I have other matters that I must attend to. Perhaps I could teach you how to use magic," posited Natalia. "Although I am still learning many of the intricacies myself. Teaching and learning in the same instance often leads to far greater understanding."

"Hmm, I ave ta tink bout dat. Bein a soldier be well an good, but it never been to me liken. May be I not looken fur me purpose in da rite place," contemplated Angelit aloud.

The rapid onset of the dwarves from the citadel had successfully forced the goblinkin into a short retreat. One that Aragorth wished to take full advantage of. "Gather de bolter shot," ordered the monarch. Sending a call though the shield line.

"Five uh ya protect da bolter wit me da elf an winged one," ordered Aragorth. "We be needen ta work fast. Ta use dis advantage. Now line er up an fire."

The dwarves worked quickly firing sharpened wooden poles into the ground, forming palisades in a line from the citadel to the ravine's edge. Growing vines around the palisades, Seraphine reinforced, and bound them together. Seeing the palisades being formed from behind the citadel goblins, orcs, and hobgoblin's, that had been cut off from their brethren behind the dwarven lines, came out in droves. Trying to prevent the full formation of the defensive measures.

Seraphine heard the approaching warband before the others. Cautioning them all in a few gestures to garner their attention. Looking to Natalia she gestured to the sky, and that was all Natalia needed to see, in order to understand what Seraphine wanted.

With a thought a ball of light appeared at the tip of her spear, having done the spell so many times, it came to her as naturally as breathing. Sending the spell high into the sky above them it illuminated the gathered force blinding them, as she shined it deliberately their way. Upon the spell completion, the shaft of her spear disintegrated. With practiced ease Natalia caught Herzblutung as it fell, motioning for Angelit to hand over another of the hafts.

With her spear reformed Natalia, Seraphine, and the dutiful Angelit stepped forward, with the fist of dwarves and their king, to defend the others as they continued building their fortifications.

"I been raren fur a fight, fur a long time," said Aragorth. A grin showing more than a few missing teeth. "It be good ta ave a weapon in me and an gobs ta kill."

With four fists of goblinkin, a mixture of goblins, orcs, and a single ogre making up their ranks. “I call dibs on the big one,” said Seraphine and Aragorth in unison.

“How about we go by number felled,” questioned Natalia.

“It be a bet den. An no inflaten yur counts. I be wachen ya both ta be sure,” said Aragorth mirthfully.

With a thrust of Herzblutung a current of water erupted out from the spear tip cutting through the hearts of two goblins who had made the unfortunate choice of running in front of one another. “That’s two for me,” said Natalia. Though she didn’t sport enjoyment within her voice for the killing, as she knew others would.

When the defenders met the goblinkin a wheel of carnage ensued. The dwarves worked seamlessly with their ruler encircling two fists rending their blood upon the ground at their feet in short order. Those wielding halberds, coming in with long range attacks, while their King and two others worked on those within the pole-arms range with flail, hammer, and axe.

With their two fists down, and their number counted, Aragorth looked up to where Seraphine and Natalia worked to bring down the others. “I be afraid fur anyone ooh cross dem two,” commented Aragorth. Witnessing the carnage wrought against the goblinkin by the combined efforts of Natalia’s spear, Seraphine sword, and Angelit’s one handed ax.

“Aye,” concurred Crush. Looking on in awe.

“We can’t be letten dem tree show us up. We still be in da fight till da last uh um fall,” he said. Raising his axe high in the air. Pushing it forward, he led their charge against the dwindling number of goblinkin.

They met the remaining force head on. Two moving ahead in order to slow the ogre’s progress toward the others. With a sidelong strike of his flail, the final orc fell to the ground dead at Aragorth’s feet. “Dat be six fur me,” he announced. Puffing out his chest.

“Oh come on I only got five,” said Seraphine with a frown. “What about you?”

“I lost count,” lied Natalia. Causing Truth to act in response, and Seraphine to shake her head.

“How about we just do it together. We can use this as an... opportunity. A way of bringing our three people’s closer together.”

“I be in support uh dat idea,” commented Aragorth. “Make me wish id took de advice uh dem twins even more,” he whispered with a sigh.

With their bet concluded, without a clear winner, they attacked the ogre as a team. Working within their own strength’s allowing them to blend their combative abilities together taking down the hard skinned ogre with efficient ease.

Having successfully dealt with the prominent threat, behind the citadel itself, the palisades went up quickly. The two team’s of dwarves finishing their hard work as the moon following its long trajectory, disappeared along the horizon, giving rise to the morning sun.

Tired but satisfied with their quick, but robust work they took a much needed breathe. “We leave da bolter ear till after da war be won,” questioned Crush hopefully.

“Aye we leave it ear. Its job be done, an it be unwieldy. Got alf a mind ta push er over da edge an tell Ignes it fell, cus uh da weight,” commented Aragorth. Looking it up and down. “Be needen a lighter one in da future.”

With the palisade built and reinforced, from the leading edge of the upper citadel to the ravine, the sieging force could no longer access the space. Allowing the front line of dwarves to expand across the plain without worry of being flanked from behind, by Grock’s larger force.

Even with the added defenses, the battle to maintain their place in front of the citadel, and garner more was hard fought. Even with the benefit of the dwarven shield wall, superior tactics, and knowledge. It took the dwarven line many days to advance to the mountainous region. In an effort to completely cut off Grock's forces ability to flank the dwarven line.

Every few hours the dwarven line would switch, for those who were ready to hold and push the line. Those exhausted from the great effort, resting their weary muscles and feet a short distance removed of the citadel. After three days of slow progress the entire force cheered for achieving the mountain and cutting off any further possibility of an assault from the rear of their line.

With their rear secured, more bolter teams were deployed from the citadel, each team coming together. After another three days of hard work, the laborious task of the defensive palisades behind the dwarven line were complete each of them reinforced through Seraphine's tireless efforts.

The shield wall of dwarves continued to push forward. Each small step forward leading to many injuries and deaths, mainly for the goblinkin, even the shield wall failing to prevent the dwarves from losing many of their own. Most deaths, on the dwarven side, being from lucky shots. Bolts and broken weapons, flying through the reinforced opening in the shield, or the many boulders thrown over their defensive line by ogres and giants. Giants who disappeared almost as quickly as they appeared, within the ranks of their foes, much to the ire of the dwarves. Believing the giants were being concealed after each thrown stone, though they couldn't understand how.

Chapter Sixty-Seven

Within both encampments, dwarven and goblinkin, the fighting had ultimately come to a standstill. Though most of the deaths were on the siege's side, thousands more remained to fill and take place of the fallen. Although the dwarves had succeeded in pushing the goblinkin back to the mountain's their ability to progress entirely halted, due to the sheer mass of Grock's, perceived force. Days with continual regression and stalemate at the front line, bringing the bugbear generals ever closer to experiencing Grock's rage.

"Not long now before Grock start killing us instead. You sure Drogen not dead. All is not lost to Grock," questioned Roccan.

"I see it with my own eyes. Bogger and Hargo see it too. Drogen not dead. Only need time to recover. Have faith Drogen save kin from Grock, said Golga."

"Have marks been spread and covered," questioned Cauron.

"Yes last have taken mark. Covered and await time. Even ones not sure, hold hope," spoke Bogger into their minds.

"Good even hold outs come around. Grock done nothing while supply go missing. Leave army hungry."

"*Quiet Grock comes,*" spoke Bogger. Moments before Hargo came in announcing the same.

Hargo, held open the war tent's flap, to accommodate Grock's massive bulk. Though his size had diminished greatly in the interim, since consuming the giant's flesh, he still retained some of its features. Though in a diminished state. Leaving him with the height of an ogre rather than that of its giant cousin.

"Why are they continuing to be pushed back," he seethed. Having to duck himself into the tent. "I told you to send everything against them. Don't think yourselves above replacement. There are trolls, ogres, giants, worgs, barghest, orcs, and any number of other of your kin here. And instead of advancing my conquest, you sit here."

"There are no troll. Most burned before war started. Last burned by blood dragon, but you should remember th," spoke Cauron.

"The giants and ogres," said Golga. Holding her hand up to stop Cauron before the aging bugbear could succeed in getting himself killed. "We sent all against dwarves. None return, all dead. Most after cast one stone. No other want to go. Think ogre and giant cursed."

"Bigger problem lack of food," said Roccan. Continuing to shift the conversation. Hoping to spread Grock's ire, instead of giving him focus upon a single target.

"Tribes flee in night, because no food. Choose hunt in wood, rather than starve," Hargo informed.

"There's plenty of food. All they need to do is gather the corpses. They can cook their unworthy hides, at least that way they can provide use. Since their lives were completely worthless. There had better be progress soon, or even your status as Lucian's pets, will not save you from being fed to *my* army for dinner," proclaimed Grock coldly.

Grock stomped away from Golga's war tent like an impetuous child. His footfalls moving far and away from the front line. Where those who worshiped him as their deity, continued to die in droves.

"Grock not been informed of elf victory," inquired Cauron with a raised brow.

"No. Tell Grock elf attack go well. Think all come back. Join this attack," said Golga. Gnashing her teeth in contempt of Grock, before letting out a sigh.

"Need to force Grock focus away. Give Drogen time to recover."

"Golga still believe Drogen will win against Grock? When Drogen fall by giant before Grock fight," questioned Cauron. Growing increasingly unsure.

"Faith Cauron. If Drogen loose. All lost, for gob and Dranier. Grock win all die."

"All ahead either way. Grock loose better for all. Grock win... too dead to worry," spoke Bogger cynically.

"Drogen must win, for sake of all. Look to Drogen for help. Time come to help Drogen. Show faith Drogen will win. Without faith loose everything," said Golga.

"Attack, attack from hole." Came shouts of surprise from outside the war tent.

"Hargo go look," ordered Golga. Rising to her feet in concern.

"Wing ones come, white feather, not black," informed Hargo. Moving back into the tent.

"Tell wing ones Drogen plan. Send those of Grock across line," said Golga both aloud and in her mind. That Bogger could relay the message, while her seconds in command fulfilled it.

The head of the flying forces stood upon the wind, an imposing figure in blood red full plate mail. His white wings working effortlessly, even with the armors weight, as he led those behind him into the fray.

The goblinkin, being caught completely off guard by the Zephyrian forces sudden appearance, worked themselves into a frenzy. Retreating quickly away from the ravine's edge.

Upon seeing her father, Vladimir the Crimson King flying in the skies above the gathered goblinkin, Natalia couldn't help but let out a joyous cheer. Igniting the determination of the dwarves around her.

"Allies have arrived to aid us in our struggle to break their siege. Let us show the new arrivals our determination and strength. SHIELDER'S MARCH," ordered Aragorth.

Each step of the shield wall reverberated through the ground beneath their feet, as if their footfalls were those of a fist of giants.

"Arrows from the forest," came a call from the front line. Bolts raining from the sky, pushing the goblinkin away from the raised stone. The stone continued to hold Drogen's body, just before the line he had cut across the plain. From mountainside to ravine. His black scales with red tips dimming the sunlight, subconsciously drawing their eyes to his hanging form.

"Hold," came Aragorth's call. Seeing the line Drogen had drawn with his sword.

"Only those under Grock pass the line. Until he rises," spoke Bogger the Vaudune into everyone's mind. The image of Drogen's hanging form holding their hope. As well as hope for the dwarves, zephyrians and elves; on the other side of the ravine. Approaching the line.

"I not be one fur taken da words put into me ead... Wha da two uh you be tinken," questioned Aragorth skeptically. Deferring to Seraphine and Natalia's greater knowledge on the goblinkin.

"Grom was the one who told us about the threat facing Moonclave. He also saved me from dying in the forest, when I was surrounded by ogres. I don't know anything about this one though," confessed Seraphine.

"That's Bogger. He is a friend and Grom's... Partner in crime. I suppose that would be a good analog. We can trust what he says. He is likely being commanded by Golga, Roccan, and or Cauron, to tell us as well. Without their help in Grammora, I would not be here right now. The only other one who did more to protect me was Drogen," said Natalia. Looking up to where Drogen hung upon the rock for all to see.

"Dis be da one day expecten ta rise," questioned Aragorth.

"It be him on da rock dare," came Rumble's voice. Causing Natalia to whip around. A tear forming in her eye, hearing her loyal guard after so long.

"Doe da one above look dead as stone, wit one look ya see da rise an fall. Uh chest as air fill lung in frona all," rhymed Tumble walking up beside his brother.

"Dare be much I be needn ta say ta da too uh you, but dare be too much goin ta do it ear," said Aragorth to the twins. Sadness prevalent upon his face. Though he tried to hide it in changing the subject. "It be strange, sometin bout wha ya be sayen bring an old rhyme ta mind. One me brudder would sing," said Aragorth. Closing his eyes as he recalled the words his brother had sung to him many times as children running through the verger homeland of Bathara.

As the light of the sun reached its highest in the sky Aragorth began to recite from long dormant memory the words of his brother's song.

He comes with mountain son
Namesake nipping at his heels,
Correction, Protection, opposing direction,
Understanding,
The pounding drumbeats have wrought.
He meets them halfway,
Tips of blade drawing iron line in the sand,
The bodies a pile,
Sinew and Bile
No strike can abate a body filleted,
wading the bloody shore,
None can save the Lord of War.
Bludgeons of might,
Ring through the night,
There he lie upon stone of floor,
Pronounce him dead,
He'll rise no more,
nevermore the Lord of War.
A Finally mistaken, fatal, awaken
Their lives forsaken,
Forfeit for what they have done,

Come forth Eclipsing one,
Blacken the cursed sun,
meet them in battle,
Desolate the chattel,
We're about to be overrun.
Here comes thee Eclipsing one,
Here comes their final sun,
set upon its zenith,
The war has only begun.
No Way he died,
Breathe, Heartbeat, Alive
No place to survive,
stars upon his hide,
pressing their lives to the scales of Demise
Each time he falls he'll rise once more,
give heed the final score,
see him cry the Lord of War,
All find peace forevermore,
Hand, fire, sword
None may stand before,
THE LORD OF WAR

As his brother's song receded back into the depths of his memory Aragorth glanced up to the hanging form bound to stone, red and black eyes flecked with flowing gold, peered back.

His draconic eyes looked down upon Natalia and Seraphine and he couldn't help but feel relieved at both the sight and sound. Especially since the heartbeats of Rumble and Tumble stood close to their side. With a pull of his hand, against the binding stone, the ringlets round his wrist gave way. Pain spread through his entire body as he lurched forward, hanging from by his other wrist, limply from the stone. *It would seem I've healed marginally well. But I have not healed completely. I'll need dragon's water to fully recover.*

"Yes, and then we can end this," spoke his reforged swords within his mind.

"Golga will be glad to know her faith in you was not misplaced," said Bogger within Drogen's mind. Confused by the advent of other voice within Drogen's mind.

"I feel the power locked beyond the door flowing through me. However, I still have limited knowledge of what that means. Even after spending some time with those who've been locked beyond it. Still, I will do my best to make certain your faith in me is not misplaced," thought Drogen.

"Gob get more from faith in you, than ever given by Grock," said Bogger. Mentally bowing in deference.

A swift pull of his other hand brought Drogen into a free-fall toward the ground, where Seraphine and Natalia awaited him with raised arms.

Using wind magic Natalia slowed Drogen's decent until his arms lay comfortably across their shoulders. "Thank you both."

I need far more practice with magic. I should have formed the barrier as a dome instead of a convex shield. The recoil was far more severe than I accounted for," thought Drogen. His lungs burning from internal bruising and cracked ribs.

"We thought you were dead," said Natalia and Seraphine. Tears in their eyes hearing his voice again. When they thought the possibility nay impossible despite Death hopeful assertions to the contrary.

"Only when the heart stops beating can one truly be considered dead, although I must admit, I came far too close for comfort this time," he confessed.

I wish we knew where Death and Lisana went after we arrived. They'll be overjoyed to know you didn't die.

"My father already knows I didn't succumb to my injuries. He came to me personally after all. For now, I need to recover from the wounds that have yet to heal, and for that I ne..."

"Water, bring us some water," shouted Seraphine. Her voice reaching into the crowd of dwarves and flying zephyrians that had congregated around them.

Moments later Aragorth himself stepped forward raising a bucket filled to the brim with water up to Drogen. "I be figuren dis one be up on de rock fur many a day. He be needn more den a bowl ta quench dat thirst," assured Aragorth.

"Thank you Verger Granod Sedem," said Drogen with lethargic eyes. Taking the bucket of water from Aragorth's hand he shot draconic fire upon its surface, turning the liquid inside into golden healing water. Bringing the water to his mouth, Drogen drank deeply feeling the healing liquid move through his body. Healing his internal injuries completely. With the waters working quickly within his body he poured the remaining contents over himself regrowing the skin over his scales. "You wouldn't happen to have my extra-dimensional bag with you," questioned Drogen. Looking into Natalia and Seraphine's eyes.

"Afraid not," said Seraphine. Eyeing him up and down suggestively.

"Its not the time for that," said Natalia with a mirthful grin. "You'll get your chance later. We have more pressing matter to attend to."

"Ya your right," said Seraphine. Shaking off the pleasant thoughts going through her head.

Coming back to reality, from their imaginings, they noticed a distinct change in the dwarven line. As their demure stature had fallen further. Following their kings lead they kneeled to Drogen.

Seeing the old king kneeling down, Drogen knelt himself holding his hand out to the king, bidding his rise. "I don't know why you kneel before me. I'm no more, or less than any one of you. Please rise, that we may speak as equals in this fight against Grock's conquest."

"What can we do but push back against his forces," questioned Seraphine.

"One uh dem mind speaked into our eads. Only dose followen Grock be crossen da line ya drew cross da ground," informed Aragorth.

"Then that makes things much simpler. He has lost the favor of those who would worship him, and with it, he'll have lost everything."

"What do we need to do, in order to end this," questioned Natalia.

"For those defending their homes and lives from invasion, all that needs to be done is to defend the line. As for me, I must come to understand myself. Or I risk falling once more to Grock, even with his loss of favor."

"Ow ya go bout doin dat," questioned Aragorth with a frown.

With a shrug and a slight smile Drogen replied, "Trial by fire has always been my favored method of learning. I think I'll start out with a walk across the line. That I may speak with our allies on the other side."

"What can you accomplish by being so incredibly reckless," questioned Seraphine. Shaking her head. "We already thought we lost you once. I don't ever want to feel that ever again.

"I want to protect as many of the friends we made as possible. I cannot do that if I fear Grock, or what he might do to them, if they are unable to push your line back from this stalemate," said Drogen.

"The possibility of saving all of our friends is little to none," countered Natalia.

"Maybe, but more will survive with my intervention than if Grock is left to his tyranny unchecked," replied Drogen.

"Then we are going with you," said both Natalia and Seraphine in unison.

"And before you try and protest, you are not going to change either of our minds," said Natalia. Grabbing hold of Drogen's arm in unwavering determination. Seraphine following suite with equal determination moments later.

"It would appear I have no say in this," said Drogen with a sigh.

"Yeah, and you better get used to it," said Seraphine hotly.

"I shall try," said Drogen with a small grin. "Then let us meet with our compatriots on the other side of the line." Walking through the dwarven ranks on his way to the front.

Seraphine, Natalia, and Aragorth following, the fully nude Drogen, closely as a line formed to the central shield of the dwarven line.

"Why did you feel the need to kneel before Drogen. Seeing you and your people do so came as quite a shock when you had yet to meet him," questioned Natalia. Raking her mind for a possible answer, from the eclectic knowledge she had access to within her mind.

"Only one be left... Or I be supposen he not be," began Aragorth sadly. "He call me by me true name. Not one given to meself by virtue uh bein King ear in Aragorth. An only one be callen me dat wit narry a glance in me direction. Dat be me master, Doe I not be knowen owe it be so. I know he be, in some way, me master. Though he not be looken da same as he did afore. I be owen all me self an me people's prosperity ta em. Far more den any else be knowen."

"Are you coming with us as well," questioned Seraphine.

"Aye, ye both be leaders uh de udder forces. It not be wise ta ave me out uh da talken. It be me people's lives on da line as well. I be wanten ta meet dem ones who ye be talken bout too. I be seein fur meself da character uh dose who go gainst Grock. Even doe doing so be deadly. Day be sounden akin ta me struggle, wit da deceiver."

"They differ from the other goblinkin that you have likely met in the past, they are known as bugbears, and their names are Golga, Roccan, and Cauron," Natalia informed them.

"An ooh be da leader uh dem tree," questioned Aragorth.

"They are all three generals. But Golga, from the notes in her book, is just under Grock when it comes to commanding the gathered forces."

The dwarven shield wall stretched from the ravine to the mountain side twenty short paces removed of the line Drogen had drawn upon the plain. On the other side of the wall the sounds of battle could still be heard, but any enemies that crossed the line were dealt with by the combined efforts of Zephyria's flying force, and the expertly placed arrows of Moonclave's archers and mages.

Before they reached the front, a hole formed in the shield wall, allowing Drogen and the royal entourage, to pass. As soon as they had distanced themselves just far enough from the shield wall that they would be unaffected by the movement the dwarven defensive wall reformed behind them.

As though he were on a simple jaunt through a field of flowers, Drogen sauntered through the combating forces. Unworried for the many sharp implements that could come upon him as he strode through. Seraphine, Natalia, and Aragorth in stride beside and behind him.

Looking across the battlefield, Drogen noted the multitude of dead and trampled bodies strewn across its breadth. None of those fallen given more than a cursory glance before being trodden under foot by those who would later join them. Mixing torn bodies, spilled blood and crushed bones into the conglomeration of rend flesh, excrement, and bile permeating the air throughout the battlefield.

As though through his presence alone, the battle would come to a close, everyone stopped what they were doing. If only to watch the eclectic company pass them by. "It be strange seein da people ear stoppen ta watch us pass," said Aragorth. Looking behind them to see that none of those behind had continued their struggles against the other.

"I think anyone would, if not in wonder, in fear," said Seraphine.

"Why would they be stopping in fear," questioned Natalia.

Looking to Drogen as he strode through the enemy ranks without care Aragorth nodded his head in understanding. "Aye. What be more ta fear one ooh wear plate ta fight in da front, or one who walk true dare enemy witout fear, naked as de day day be born."

"Would they not think the one walking through was crazy for doing something so... disadvantageous." questioned Natalia.

"Aye day might, if day not be knowen. But, would ya be willen ta risk yeself ta prove what ya be tinken be true. I be doubten most would," spoke Aragorth.

"Its also likely that many who are fighting saw Drogen go down themselves, and now he is walking through their ranks without so much as a weapon upon him," commented Seraphine.

"Bogger, lead me to the tent that houses the generals, there is much to discuss," thought Drogen. Feeling the sensation of Boogers intrusion.

"As you command, our sanctif Drogen"

"What is the meaning behind your words," questioned Drogen. Followed Bogger unmolested through the goblinkin army.

"See Drogen as beacon of hope. Hope against oppression of one who call self-divine for all gobs. Unlike other kin, not view Grock in same light. Drogen treat gob not as enemy, not as fodder. See as equal. Make Drogen sanctif. Divine for warrior who seek peace through strength, not conquest."

"I ask not a soul to worship me as deity."

"Make Drogen worthy. Why bug, hob, raske, gob, orc, vaudune, and more gather for Drogen. Why many forgo fight when Drogen walk past battlefield. All see time to choose," insisted Bogger.

Bogger's words struck a chord deep within Drogen's soul telling him without a doubt the vaudune was right. *I'll be a deciding factor for this war's outcome, and likely, many more in the future. But what does it all mean? Why has everything changed so much? Why do I feel as though I'm far from realizing the true complexities of my roll. Tis times like these I wish I could speak with the Elders. They raised me to be Drakregus, but in my youthful ignorance, I never questioned what that truly means,* he thought to himself.

They stepped into Golga's war tent after walking through the encroaching forces for nearly an hour. The sun remaining in the early vestiges of its rise above them.

"Go inside the generals await you. I will keep watch. Grock will no doubt be informed of your arrival by one of the zealous. More than likely that coward of an orc," he shared in ire. The image of the orc sending others over the line but not going himself showing in Drogen's mind.

Hargo moved the tents flap out of the way, allowing Drogen and his entourage to pass. As they entered the war tent the eyes of Golga, Roccan, and Cauron shot in surprise before shifting into a deep sigh of relief.

Chapter Sixty-Eight

"We have little time," said Golga.

"Grock come soon need plan," advised Roccan. Looking at Drogen hopefully.

"Unfortunately, I have no plan. I only just regained my body after all," said Drogen. Shaking his head.

"Not good. Said dragon would have plan," said Cauron in concern.

"When the time comes. I will know what to do. Just leave Grock to me. You should focus on those that remain loyal to Grock's conquest," assured Drogen.

"What makes you think, that whatever comes to you, will have any merit in your fight against Grock," questioned Natalia.

"Tis what I instinctively feel," he said with a shrug. "Tis as if it calls to me, through the door. However, it remains just beyond reach. I know when the time comes, I will know what to do."

"We must have faith," said the Vaudune Grom within everyone's mind.

"Good to hear you again Grom. Thank you, for saving me in the forest," said Seraphine.

"Grock approach. DUCK," Yelled Bogger into their minds. Moments before a massive war-hammer crashed through the tent, and wooden structure beneath it. Flinging it across the encampment, and over the ravine's edge.

"Hello Grock," spoke Drogen. Using a language none of the others around him could recognize. None but Grock.

"You are one of us. Why do you stand in opposition of our conquest."

"Why do you allow those who give you strength to die while you toil away at the back of the line."

"They are but fodder. As all below us are," said Grock. Puffing out his chest.

"No, they are all that stands between strength and ruin. It would serve you well to remember that. We stand at the precipice of a choice. One that decides the fate of Dranier. Would you have your army fight against the combined forces of all you wished to destroy. Or, will you concede? The choice is yours."

Grock looked down on Drogen mirthfully before bursting into a belly laugh that chilled everyone else to their core. "You are unworthy of the threats you speak. I will not concede, and none who work against me will survive their betrayal."

"I will not allow any of those who would stand against you to die without a fight. The real question is who has betrayed who," he posited. Making a show of looking to Grock's own generals. "It would seem to me, you have lost sight, of what your people once looked to you for. You have betrayed their faith, in both action and inaction."

"They do not owe me faith. They owe me fealty," raged Grock.

"They owe you nothing. You owe them for absolutely everything that you are," countered Drogen. Rising to his feet and stepping into Grock's range. "They are the strength of the gods. Without their reverie and faith, you are nothing."

Grock's war-hammer came round for Drogen's skull but, was met with one of Drogen's reforged Oslo blades, its name shinning with brilliant golden light. "I am more than I was Grock. I doubt you can say the same," he said. Biting menace in his voice. "Furthermore, you are being quite rude. I came to speak with the ones leading this force. From what I have witnessed, you are *far* removed of the position."

With a downward stroke of his oslo, Grock's war-hammer sank to the ground. Now what path is it that your generals wish to take, in this conquest of yours.

"Bugbear does not want to fight with others. Want make friend. Bring all together. Not sacrifice other gob for nothing," iterated Golga. Shaking her head. "Bring all kin together. Rise above how kin are seen. Show all that gob are more than others know."

"You are nothing without me. Without his divinity," growled Grock. Stepping toward Golga.

"Gob think same no more. Dragon prove Grock is wrong," spoke Roccan pridefully. Moving to intercept Grock himself. But finding his way blocked.

Drogen walked before Grock, oslo in a cross guard. His stance able to become a thrust with a single step. "A Dragon stands before you. Ready for battle. Yet you would go after those you view as weaker than yourself. What does an act of aggression toward your definition of a lesser say about the god Grock. Would you view your own actions as a show of great strength, or great weakness," ridiculed Drogen. Hoping to transfer Grock's focus back upon himself.

Succumbing to his rage, from Drogen's pointed insult filled insinuation's, Grock focused squarely on the glib Drogen. Taking hold of his war-hammer with both hands for a heavy sidelong swing.

Within his mind, and aloud, Drogen called out for Grom, Bogger, and the generals behind him. *"Tis time. This will not end until one of us can no longer rise."*

Drogen knew that the message had been received as those around him scattered without another word. All of them knowledge, that anyone caught between the two would be slaughtered when the austere nature of their battle began its crescendo, to its inevitable climax.

The rumble of heavy footfalls began to approach. The distant footsteps causing tremors through the ground as they drew closer. As if on some unheard cue, battle erupted within the goblinkin ranks. A single sign distinguishing those who fought for Grock and his conquest, and those who fought for its conclusion. Those fighting against their own deity bore the mark of a dragon upon their armor. A mark that had been previously hidden beneath a false layer of armor, over the hearts. Choosing the path Drogen's actions had shown possible.

"We bes be getten outa ear afore dis ole place erupts," yelled Aragorth. Projecting over the sounds of battle filtering through the tents around them.

"Hold short time," said Golga. A small band of orcs, raske, and vaudune forming ranks around them. Each bearing the mark of a dragon, in the armor over their hearts.

"Even with their armors marked, distinguishing friend from foe is going to be quite difficult. Until the smaller skirmishes reach a conclusion," yelled Natalia. More sounds of battle cropping up around them.

"More for Drogen then Grock. Grock fight over line. No care for line meaning. Only conquest," stated Roccan.

"Only those fear death more than Grock remain. Still see Grock as divine, not Drogen," said Cauron.

"Grom is helping my people take out any of Grock's minions left on the battlefield," advised Seraphine.

"Dat Bogger be doin da same fur me kin as well. All uh dem be pinchen da front wit da Zephyr."

"Then all we have left to do is wait for the fighting to conclu...," began Natalia. A tremor narrowly knocked them all to the ground. Though still a great distance away. The colossal creature's head threatened to block the suns rays entirely. Casting a long shadow over the mountaintops high above.

"By da gods," exclaimed Aragorth in surprise.

As they collectively looked to the sky above, their hearts sank to the souls of their feet. Staring back at them, though it remained hundreds of yards removed, from between two peaks were the eyes of a giant. But not those that had been throwing stones against the citadel, or tearing a pathway through the forest. No what stared back at them was a titan primal force capable of wiping them out with a single swipe of its hand.

From the ravine behind them a deep roar sounded, and with its reverberations came a blood red Dragon, colossal in its own right, but still far removed of the titan size. Upon the dragon's back rode Death grasping, the scythe's haft, Reaper of souls.

"Death said he wouldn't intervene," exclaimed Seraphine. Shock in her bulging eyes, as she tried to take in the awe-inspiring image unfolding in front of them all. *At least if I die here and now this will be the final image that I see,* she thought. Her mind overtaken by the display.

"They either knew I was here and are keeping their word to Fread, or that thing is something beyond our ability to handle. Either way, I must go and help them in any way I can. Even if I am only capable of acting as a distraction, while they deal with the threat," said Natalia. Gripping Herzblutung.

"Hate ta be sayen it, buh I be open it be da first one, an not be da second," said Aragorth with a shudder.

"I could not agree more," said a voice behind them. Vladimir and the Zephyrian army, balancing themselves upon the sky above. "I had hoped it was a part of the force moving against Grock."

"That not part of kin," said Golga. Using the more common tongue of Dranier, looked around, as the sounds of battle had stopped.

"Long time since see titan. Hope not to see again," said Cauron. Following Golga's example. His face sagging as if suddenly overcome with age.

"Titan reason bugbear with Grock. titan come bugbear home. Take to one call self su...preme. Supreme gift bugbear to Grock for war," proclaimed Roccan.

"Same story father tell when titan come back. Should listen more to father. Father tell Golga run, not follow father. Too young see error. Now father gone and Golga not remember home."

"It be da deciever's influence. It be da same way wit me brudder. He took ta da deceiver, an it cost me em, me master, an undread's uh me kin," lamented Aragorth.

"I hate to ask, knowing how few weapons the dwarves had in the first place. But I need more shafts for my spear, if I am to be at all effective at attacking, or distracting this titan for Lisana and Death," said Natalia.

"I ope he not be ear fur me yet. I be too spry ta die. Take all uh dem ya need. An be sure ta put in a good word fur me wit em, jus in case," said Aragorth. Wringing his hands.

"You got it," said Natalia. A slight grin toward the dwarven king.

"Ya got a good daughter dare Vladimir da Crimson King uh Zephyria."

Although he smiled at the comment a clear sadness overcame Vladimir, as he looked upon her face. Still unsure if he could even be considered a father. When his past actions had proven his inadequacies, in the roll. Least of which being his inaction in saving her from torment, at his wife and stepdaughters hands.

"Aye he does. An he best not be furgetin it," said Natalia in dwarven to the king. *I want nothing more than to hate you for everything that you have done. For your inaction against Ether and Uther when they took the life of the only mother I ever knew. Your believing Nefar and Bernadine over me, and so many other things. You are the only father I have ever known, try as I might to hate you, to loathe your very existence with every fiber of my being. I still love you as my father,* she thought. Returning her eyes to the titan.

Rising slightly into the sky Natalia watched as Death and Lisana stopped the titan's forward momentum. Death striking with Reaper of souls against the titan's skin while Lisana breathed a cone of fire upon anything and everything she could manage to hit. Though she concentrated most of attacks upon its face.

"I bess be careful round dis one. Make me apology ta dem twins erd by er," he said. Whispering to Seraphine as Natalia flew around the encampment gathering wooden shafts from the ground, Rumble, Tumble, and other dwarves. Those who had made their way into the encampment, searching for Aragorth.

"If I was your advisor. I'd be suggesting the same," said Seraphine with a knowing smile.

After gathering a few more shafts, Rumble and Tumble ran up to Natalia their expressions a mix of anxiety and fear. "Ya be a pain in me brudder an me arses ya dunderhead princess," said Rumble. Stomping his feet hard against the ground as they handed her the ones they gathered.

"I know I am Rumble," said Natalia. Throwing a hug around the gruff Dwarfs neck. Pulling Tumble into her embrace as well.

Rumble tried to continue seething in anger, but it subsided quickly. From both his body and visage as he felt the warmth of her sisterly embrace. With another huff Rumble and Tumble returned the gesture in kind. Only dropping their hold when Natalia herself began pulling away.

"Now don be tinken dis get ya out uh trouble wit me brudder an me," said Rumble with a loud harrumph. Protesting as he tried furtively to retain the last vestiges of his anger.

"Princess be fine, always be kind. Make enemy inta friend all da time. Buh what we to do wit a giant outgrew it own size," questioned Tumble. His typical energetic rhythmic fashion returning.

"For that, you need to ask Seraphine and Aragorth. I will be leading the forces of Zephyria against that thing. We all need to work together, or defeating this titan before it can reach the mountain. It could wipe us all out with just the falling debris."

"Dragon and robed one not enough to take titan down," questioned Golga. Looking up at Lisana and Death working in tandem to fight back against the titan, but even the hot flames emanating from Lisana's mouth did little more than scorch the hair where it touched. Death fared no better, the scythe cutting in against the titan leaving little more than a papercut.

"We must rise and fight, or everything that may come from our combined efforts will be for naught," said Natalia. Gliding to the front of Zephyria's flying force. With nearly a dozen wooden shafts secured, and divided between the Zephyrian force, the collective force of Zephyria rose into the sky. Their augmented flying speed monumental. With the aid of Natalia's magic, the wooden shaft of Herzblutung glowing brightly with the power coursing through it.

"We all be aven much ta discuss, an atone fur, but it not be da time. Now be da time fur action," announced Aragorth. Looking to the gathered forces around him. We must all work together if we ave any chance uh dealen wit dis threat. Gob, Elf, Zephyrian, Dwarven, an anyone else I not be knowen bout ear."

"We need a chain of command. I say Aragorth should be at the top, he is the oldest of us all, and he understand's the defenses and terrain around the citadel far better than any one of us could," suggested Seraphine.

"Aye, bu did ya ave ta mention me age," Aragorth grumbled. Shaking his fist in mock anger. "Fine I be willin, everyone need be followen me orders den. Gol...ga, ye be da leader uh da gob's we be needen elp in da citadel. Dare be more bolt throwers den got shooters." The old king extending an olive branch.

"Lead da way old one," said Golga. Her toothy smile garnering a disapproving finger from Aragorth in response.

"Elves... Ow ya people be uh use across da ravine," questioned Aragorth. Looking across at the distant elves.

"Actually..." said Seraphine. Clearly hearing something in her own head that the others could not. "Grom says the ravine is covered. Whatever that means," she said with a shrug.

"Well, if ya got it figured out send da biggest an da smartest ones ya got over ta da citadel. We be needen ta break a few uh dem bolt throwers ta aimum at da titan. May be needen machine elp to if ya got any fur dat. Dat be remind me, DWARVES GRAB DA BOLTERS, we be needen dem too. NOW MOVE," exclaimed the Monarch. Jumping for emphases.

The battlefield whipped into a frenzy as the enemies turned allies tried to fall into some sort of rhythm, though tensions were high in the beginning, the established chain of command aloud everything to quickly fall in line.

Those at the back of the dwarven line passed Aragorth's orders to the ballista squads for them to retake, aim, and fire upon the titan. Many of whom having taken to doing so before ever receiving the order. Each team worked tirelessly to load bolts and fire rapidly while keeping care not to aim near the flying fire breathing dragon, or its scythe wielding rider.

Seraphine ran to where her people would be coming across the ravine, wanting to see the method they would be deploying in order to cover the distance. As she stepped up to the ravine long willowy vines started growing and thickening into heavy twisted ropes forming a natural bride large enough for ten to walk across, shoulder to shoulder.

The earthen magics of her kin flowed until the bridge became robust enough to support everything and everyone that might need to cross it, both presently and far into the future. Phaylor stood at the head of his elven troupes. Ordering them forward as soon as the bridge was fully formed. At his side stood the Vaudune Grom.

"It would seem there is much we need to thank you for in the future Grom," said Seraphine. Phaylor stepping off of the bridge to stand before her.

"Queen Seraphine where are we needed," questioned Phaylor. Deferring to her, in order to follow what he knew to be the proper chain of command.

"We need the strongest and most technically inclined to go help the dwarves with their weapons. Many of them are locked into a specific position and need to be retrained upon the titan. We also need a way of reaching that thing without putting ourselves, or those currently fighting it in danger with our presence."

"Actually, I think we can help with that," said Leif. Followed by many other dryads and those she could recognized from the Knowledge district.

"Then I defer this to you." said Seraphine. Ecstatic seeing Chian, Mai-Coh, Alya, and to her great surprise, a gnome.

"I don't believe we've met before," said Seraphine to the new arrival.

"I am Deus of Anu-Grah my band of misfits teamed up with Vladimir to disrupt the supplies for the gobbos. Although now it would seem everyone is working together... Was anything we did even worth it," questioned Deus under his breath.

"I suspect that your disruptions to the supply network likely helped many on the fence about Grock and his plans be pushed over the edge actually," said Seraphine.

"Many flee because no food. Full tribe gone in night. Grock do nothing. Turn many to Drogen side. All who remain, who hard to convince, turn when Grock make last mistake. Tell those want food. Go to battlefield. Eat dead," said Bogger into their gathered minds. Showing them all Grock's declaration, while speaking it in his own words.

"Well then where might you need a few machine enthusiasts," said Deus. Trying to shake the strange feeling of Bogger's mental speech from his head.

"The dwarves need help with their ballista and many other things inside the citadel," she pointed.

"Then that is where we will go," said Deus. "Come on Carme let's see what we can do to help the bearded folk and Anu." Pointing into the sky, following Lisana's outline with his finger.

"I hope Golga, and whoever took over for me, made it out of the arena okay. I was really worried when she sent me away without taking them," said Carme. Who was looking around while following Deus. An entourage of their people, at her back.

"Chian, you're probably most needed at the citadel as well."

Chian nodded chasing after, and passing the gnomes, as she ran for the citadel. The hammer, Natalia had gifted her, placed in a loop upon a woven vine belt.

Despite the growing onslaught of weaponry trained upon it, the titan continued to draw ever closer to the mountains. Their high peaks their only defense between them and annihilation.

Chapter Sixty-Nine

Each step leads to a cut, each strike against skin, each move uninhibited by thought. There is only action nothing more, nothing less. Thought Drogen. Wading into Grock's range with an upward strike of his double oslo aiming for Grock's inner thigh as he duck, rise, and step past Grock's swing.

Though trained and battle-worn from countless battles, Grock's movements did not flow into each other. Each of them a hulking swing or overhead strike with vast amounts of power, but no finesse, or restraint given to his movement. A necessity for any who wished to protect themselves from mortal wounds.

Most strikes resulting in Grock's hammer smashing into the ground or errant swings through the air. But the golden barrier surrounding Grock's form would not budge under Drogen's deathly accurate strikes. *It will not yield. If I cannot cut through the barrier, then this becomes a battle of attrition. One that I cannot hope to win. We must cut the barrier.*

"We will, when you're ready to look upon us for help."

"Fear continues to hold us back."

"We are reforged. Yet we are too blind to see what it means."

"Then we fight till the truth is revealed," said Drogen. Looking at the blurry golden runes upon his oslo blades. Yet to reveal the names they could speak, but he still could not hear.

Grock, unimpressed by Drogen's continued inability to cut his barrier, turned away from Drogen to look upon the titan with glee.

"The supreme sent his greatest threat to aid in our conquest. None of them will survive the titan. I doubt death, or that red lizard could hope to stand against it either. Not after what Lucian has done. You should sit back and watch, as what remains of Dranier falls to his reign."

"That is where you're wrong Grock. They will not fall. They will not give up, and because of that neither will I. One should never turn their back on their enemy, until they lay dead upon the ground," proclaimed Drogen. Throwing himself headlong into Grock's exposed back. His double oslo cutting a line from hip to shoulder, against his golden barrier. However, unlike his previous attempts, that recoiled from the strike, the blade bit in. Cutting shallowly into the flesh at Grock's back. And for only the third time in his life, Grock experienced fear.

Growing angry at the barrage hefted against its advance the titan started swinging its arms wildly. Bating many of the bolts out of the sky before they could get close enough to touch its skin.

Extending his arm, the titan swung around wildly. Attempting to swat Lisana and Death out of the sky. The zephyrian's began, flittering about its massive body, poking and prodding any opening they could find like a swarm of wasps.

Lisana and Death continued focusing on the titan's face and neck. Death cut with his scythe along the titan's exposed eyes, attempting to blind it, unsuccessfully. "Even its eyes," cursed Death.

"How have you become so weak," questioned Lisana. Producing another breath of fire, focused upon the spot where the scythe had slashed.

"I cannot fathom, but I think I have an idea as to who's to blame. When I find Lucian, I'll rip his throat out with my own hands for this," he raged.

"Tis not good, if things persist as they are we'll have no way to stop it from wiping everyone out."

"Fire isn't working we need to change tactics. I may have enough power to hold it, but beyond that, I have nothing," confessed Death.

Lisana curled her wings in around her dropping like a boulder as the titan struck out against her flight. Unfurling her wings, with a deep breath, she let loose a cone of acidic breath, oil of vitriol. Which she helped the elves develop, to combat the trolls regenerative ability. However, even the extremely caustic acid could not penetrate the titan's skin. Before it could be used against the Zephyrian's or those down the mountain Lisana let loose a flood of water from her mouth.

While making the acid inert the titan's hand moved to swat her from the sky once more, forcing her into a downward dive, toward its feet. The missed strike hitting the peak of the mountain behind them.

The mountain top flew through the air and into the forest beyond the ravine where the newly constructed bridges had been erected. Boulders and stones falling across the defenders ranks. Crashing heavily from the dwarven citadel to the very end of the goblinkin's war-tents, and everything in between.

Those along the peaks destructive path ran toward the mountain, in hopes of escaping the calamity. Others, knowing themselves incapable of covering the distance ducked, hoping any stray rocks would fly overhead, and out of harm's way. Many were unfortunate taking pieces of the rapidly descending mountain top's stray boulders as they careened past.

Vines descended rapidly from the mountain top attaching to the ravine's edge creating a makeshift canopy over them. Sending a majority of the boulders into the ravine. Where the canopy prevented the larger boulders from descending upon them, it couldn't prevent the smaller ones from falling through.

Cries of anguish and pain rang out, as Alya regained her feet. Seraphine, who had been right in front of her moments prior, had been replaced by a large boulder. She fought desperately to lift the boulder away. Only stopping when she heard a moan from the other side. Hopping the boulder in a single bound Alya sniffed the air finding Seraphine's scent quickly along with that of Mai-Coh and what she suspected to be a hobgoblin, she had yet to interact with.

Standing over Seraphine's body was a massive wolf. Causing the hair on the back of Alya's neck to stand entirely on end. *"It's okay. The Wolf is Mai-Coh,"* said Grom in her mind. Lifting up against the heavy stone Mai-Coh moved his head in a beckoning way, clear pain present in his eyes as he looked to Alya for help.

Seeing Mai-Coh's struggle Alya quickly shred her clothing turning quickly into her white tiger form. Ducking under Mai-Coh's foreleg She grabbed Seraphine by the arm with her mouth, pulling her out quickly.

With Seraphine free of the fallen debris Mai-Coh quickly changed, running free of the debris, though it pained him greatly to do so. In order to escape the boulder before it could finish crushing him under its massive weight.

"Is our tree spirit friend alright," questioned Mai-Coh with great concern.

Changing back quickly as Mai-Coh did Alya lay her head upon Seraphine's chest. "Her heart's still beating. Maybe she just hit her head? I don't see blood anywhere which should be a good sign. It looks like she just got knocked out."

Mai-Coh let out a sigh of relief. "Should take her to tree spirits, they will know what to do," he said. Walking up to them.

Rising to her feet Alya placed her hand on Mai-Coh's arm for support, lifting Seraphine with her rise. The touch making him flinch and her to pull away quickly. "I'm so sorry, I forgot you were hurt, are you okay."

"Is not pain that makes me jump. I am not used to feeling touch upon skin. I spend whole life covered in fur. Feeling touch to skin is still... strange," observed Mai-Coh. Taking hold of Seraphine's left arm.

"You're hurt. You don't need to strain yourself further, holding her with me," said Alya. Concerned as Mai-Coh threw Seraphine's left arm over his shoulder.

"I feel broken ribs, but they heal soon. No worry needed."

Leif came running to them moments later with a group of elves, Grom and Hargo at her side. "Thanks for bringing them, Grom," said Alya in relief. Drawing a smiling nod from him.

"I was sending my sisters up the mountain when I heard Grom's call. We didn't have enough time to make a barrier that would block everything. I wish we could have; many have died because we could not. Grom told us Seraphine was hurt. I narrowly escaped death myself had the raske Hargo not been there to shield me," said Leif.

"Hargo have hard skin. Not much hurt raske. Magic make skin stronger too," explained Hargo. Struggling as he was, to speak in their tongue.

"It would appear there are many different types of goblinkin. Many more than we thought there to be. I look forward to learning more about you, the vaudune, and all the others," said Seraphine. Her eyes swimming.

"Are you alright," questioned Leif in concern.

"Don't worry about me." said Seraphine. Lifting her head awkwardly, to look at Leif. "Once I'm done with the trance, I'll join in the festivities. Until then, we need to do everything we can to take down that titan."

"Yes Queen Seraphine," acknowledged Leif. Running back to where the others were beginning to rise, with the use of vines, ascending quickly to the newly formed plateau. "You two go and help however you can. Just leave me here for now. I'll be fine."

"Grom and Hargo can you take her into the citadel?"

"We take to beardies," said Grom. Nodding his head enthusiastically.

"Should get Bogger on way. Bogger help take forest friend to beardy friend. Hargo Keep safe."

"Okay, I leave her to you then," said Alya. Taking off with Mai-Coh, in the direction Leif had gone, rising to the mountaintops using their more agile beast forms.

With help provided by the mechanically inclined gnomes the dwarven citadels defensive weaponry had all been brought round, in order to fire on the titan. The problem then became lack of bolts for the massive war machines. Munitions they desperately needed if they stood any chance of defeating the gaining titan.

Lisana and Death fought tooth, scale, and nail to bring it down. But even with their power and strength, could do little against the primordial titan as it continued pushing against their greatest efforts. "Why can I not take care of this weak being myself," seethed Death in frustration. "Something is truly wrong; this is a consequence of losing access to the souls of other planes. I know it."

"We don't have time for this. Its already taken a mountain top we cannot allow it to do more damage, and while you may be free to die and return whenever, not everyone else has that luxury. I highly doubt they would wish to experience that unpleasantness anyways," scolded Lisana. Shooting a torrent of wind into the titan's face. Attempting to push the giant off balance.

"How is this thing here to begin with. There were none of this kind on Dranier before my imprisonment," posited Death. Reaper of Souls cutting a large swath across the titan's hip as Lisana dove under its swatting hand yet again.

"There can be only one explanation and we both know the answer," cried Lisana. Using her hottest fire as metal tipped bolts found their marks around the titan's frame. But even the heavy bolts could do nothing to slow its progress.

"This thing has to have a weakness, we just need to find it, and do so quickly," said Death. Cutting in yet another completely ineffective slice. "Now I wish I had kept some of the power from consuming Ether and Uther."

"Natalia, use whatever magics you found and fire on the titan, we need to know what magic is most effective against it, or we're all doomed," ordered Lisana. Taking in a deep breath and releasing a cone of ice from her mouth engulfing the primordial in swathes of blue ice. Hoping the vast fluctuation of temperature would damage the titan's nay impenetrable skin.

"Everyone protect Natalia while she concentrates on the magics," ordered Vladimir. Having come to understand magic long before, but only regaining the knowledge with his memories of the past.

"You need not protect me. However, I do need those with spear shafts to remain close. I will likely be going through many in a short time," said Natalia. Affixing yet another haft to Herzblutung. Power pulsed through the spear flowing between the concentric blades to the tip of the spear. With a thrust of her weapon, a shot rang out, as the air around her spear had been pierced.

Her wind magic, as it had done to the goblinkin within the tunnels below Aragorth, formed a small puncture upon the titan's chest. However, unlike the goblinkin below, the magic did not pierce. Instead, finding the route of least resistance, ripping upward across its chest. Creating a nearly imperceptible gash.

"Maybe if I use wind magic to pull," posited Natalia.

"Don't even think about it. This thing doesn't have lungs in the natural sense. It survives on essences far beyond anything you are capable of controlling, or understanding," warned Death. Passing her on a subsequent run.

Taking the advice to heart, Natalia began to work through her magical repertoire. Learned through Lisana's teachings, and her own study. Having been burnt through with magic her spear's shaft turned to dust, forcing Natalia to grab Herzblutung upon the hilt in order to replace its haft. Torin, the zephyrian placed at her side, handed her another spear shaft without so much as a word.

Ice, fire, acid, water, air, earth, all have been proven useless against its tuff skin. Things that would kill any one of us without question have proven worthless against it. What magics do I have left at my disposal.

The dryad's and elves work their magics to subdue the titan under a blanket of vines, and roots. Their tireless efforts amounting to little more than a slowing effect upon it. The numerous bolts from the massive ballista within the citadel simply bounce off its skin. Acid that eats through everything it touches glides to the ground like oil. Fire does little more than burn the hair from its massive body, no matter how hot it becomes.

Sink it into the ground, but then it could simply burst through the mountains with its strength alone. Drop a mountain on top of it, but I do not know the composition, and the likely hood of such a thing working when the bolts have not... improbable. It does not breath air, thus taking it out or replacing it with something else, will not work. Looking around and through her mind all possibilities she could think of lead to further stalemate.

"Lightnin magic." called out a voice she didn't recognize. Breaking the hopelessness of her inner contemplation's.

Looking around for the one who spoke, to thank them for the suggestion, she was surprised to find Mai-Coh, Alya, Leif, and a number of elves atop the plateau at her back. The elves reinforcing the dryads as they worked diligently to stop the giants' movements. While Mai-Coh and Alya, retaining their bestial forms, surveyed the scene unfolding before them.

Holding her spear high in the air Natalia closed her eyes envisioning the sights, smells, and feelings that accompany a thunderstorm. Combining them all with the knowledge she gained from years spent reading about natural phenomenon, and their cause. She called electricity to her touch, and through her, it flowed into Herzblutung. The smell of ozone and the tingle of static causing her hair and feathers to flair through her entire body.

Death feeling a crackle upon the air, new it was time to act. Jumping from Lisana's back Death drove foot first to the ground his cloak billowing, but never rising, around him. His stature growing to that of his adversary, alongside Reaper of Souls until Death matched the titan. Pushing in upon the titan with his quickly waning power Death stepped behind the titan, placing the sharpened edge of his scythe against its neck, in order to bend it backward with all his strength. Leaving the titans chest open to the sky while its extremities were quickly bound by the elves and dryads.

Lisana dove upon the titan covering its body with a cone of water.

Insulate the air, slice through the pressure between the positive and negative. And with a path through, pierce, concentrated Natalia. Opening her eyes she felt unfamiliar, yet congenial, power releasing in waves around her. With a step upon the air, she stood before the titans nearly prone chest. Its eyes looking back at her with pity, as she thrust Herzblutung down upon its heart.

A blinding flash of thunderous light burst from Herzblutung cracking the sky above. The massive bolt flowing through her spear from the sky and into Reaper of Souls, and death stood upon a platform of air a foot off the ground. Leaving only one path for the lighting to reach its destination. Through the titan itself. Herzblutung acting as a conduit, piercing the titans heart.

As the blinding light of the massive strike cleared, and everyone felt safe enough to open their eyes. Those that could see the fallen titan were drawn to the massive wound upon its chest.

The titan's body had been covered in black fractals, each of them growing in size, density, and complexity, the closer they came to its perforated heart.

Deaths arms felt numb from the strike. As he stepped out from beneath the titan's body his own body began to shrink, along with Reaper of Souls. Seeing Lisana descend to him Death ran to her side. With his arms barely functioning the scythe lay precariously over his shoulder.

As Lisana touched down he could sense the rising ire within her. Climbing her tail, he sat upon the ridges of her spine and awaited her assent.

Natalia's wings flapped lethargically her body flying higher, as her mind began to go black. Her mental stamina completely spent. As the world fell away, so too did Herzblutung, fall from her grasp. Its haft blowing away in the wind. Herzblutung and Natalia began to descend in a free fall toward the ground.

Seeing her corkscrew descent, Lisana and Vladimir plummeted toward her, trying to match her velocity so as not to hurt her, in their haste. Being much faster, Lisana reached Natalia first. Death, reaching out with near catatonic arms, pulling her to safety.

Noticing the glint of Herzblutung in the sunlight, Lisana caught the blade, in her fore-claw, by its hilt. With Natalia secured Lisana unfurled her wings, using the drag they created to slow their speed before ascending to the plateau, Vladimir, having dove, doing the same a short time later.

Lisana and Vladimir touched down, upon the plateau to triumphant cheers, rising up from Dranier's combined force. Their merriment and mirth permeating the mountains themselves.

"It would seem we arrived just in time to render aid," said Leif joyfully. "I'm also glad I sent a few of my sisters to Aragorth's citadel. They were able to help form more bolts for those ballista."

Death brought Natalia down from Lisana's back allowing Lisana to take her slimmer form. The blood red scales folded inward around her body as she stood up on her hind legs. With her secondary form achieved she began searching through the bag she had attached to her leg. From the bag she pulled out clothing, with which she quickly adorned herself.

"I for one am just glad it's over," said Vladimir. Studiously looking over Natalia's limp form with great fatherly concern. Though he thought himself unworthy of the title.

"Before you start worrying yourself into his arms," pointed Lisana to Death. "Natalia simply used too much of her concentration. She only needs some time to recover, from what she just did. Just how she managed to pull thunder out of thin air is another question entirely. I doubt even her mother would have devised a spell so reckless to herself," said Lisana. Shaking her head in both anger and admiration. Though which would be the most prominent when Natalia awoke, time could only tell.

"You're just mad because you didn't think of it first," said Death. Narrowly dropping Natalia. Causing Vladimir to come running to his aid. Taking Natalia under the arm, he called Antoni over to help. Garnering Torin's help as well.

"Such power is truly terrifying," said Antoni. Clear apprehension in his voice as he followed orders.

"I didn't know something to channel magic through, could be so effective. Do you think she could teach me to wield magic too," questioned Torin in wonder.

With a sigh Lisana pulled Herzblutung out from under her arm. "Yes, magic grows stronger with a conduit, but tis a massive downside, going through hafts so often. However, even a conduit cannot help those who have no affinity for the weapon they wield."

"So, had her entire race been lost, as our former deity Ether and Uther wished it to be. We would have been lost here as well. The power she holds was feared by Ether and Uther, why else would they wish them completely wiped out. I cannot help but think of the many ways things may have been different had we come to the Angelo looking for peace, instead of war," lamented Vladimir.

Lisana and Death stepped up to Vladimir and Antoni as they began beating their wings, in order to bring themselves down from the top of the newly formed plateau. "We cannot change the mistakes of the past. Only live to see that those mistakes are not repeated in the future. The first step is passing our stories, no matter how tragic, or damning, down through the ages," said Death. A look of internal strife present upon his customarily stoic face.

"Now where is my son, while all of this is happening," questioned Lisana. As if in response, the ground began to shake beneath their feet.

Chapter Seventy

Drogen felt the impact of Grock's hammer through the ground in a side step just beside its flat maul. Kicking out, with his left foot toward Grock's leading leg, forcing Grock backward in order to escape the blow.

Using the new positioning afforded by his missing kick, Drogen slipped his double oslo blade, catching it just before the start of the second blade, thrusting at Grock's exposed neck. The tip of his blade puncturing the golden barrier, but still not reaching Grock's flesh, before his retreat.

Continuing his forward momentum Drogen used the forward weight of his slipping thrust, allowing it to descend in a clockwise spin sending it across his back, into his left hand, turning its gathered momentum into an upward strike. The oslo cutting through Grock's divine cloak from groin to chin. The golden barrier, just strong enough to slow his blade, allowing Grock time to disengage the attack.

So far Ethereal has shown only half its name, the other's name is Envoy, yet I know for certain it is no longer Death. Though such a name certainly remains... fitting for one sired by Death himself.

"We must push ourselves further. To claim what we already know to be true. This is but the first step on our journey as one," spoke his swords.

"Though you speak with the tongue of divinity, you still lack the one thing that makes us truly divine. You lack the protection of a divine cloak. Though you can cut it you remain nothing before me," said Grock. Swinging his war-hammer up toward Drogen's face, from the ground.

Drogen crouched as the hammer rose the air pressure of the sing rustling his hair as it moved harmlessly past. Splitting his blades, he rose between Grock's engaged arms. Thrusting with Envoy, using his powerful legs to rise. In realization of his mistake, Grock moved his upper body backward, Drogen's blade cutting from the tip of his chin to glabella. Forcing Grock to drop his war-hammer, in the process.

"You say I lack the robes of divinity, yet you've not realized how thin your own has become. Have your actions, against those who would follow in your wake, proven more devastating then you initially thought. Could this be the reason you sequestered yourself at the rear of your forces. Allowing them to die, while you cower in fear," prodded Drogen.

A massive bolt of lightning cut through the sky above rending them both blind, but Drogen knew well how to fight and win, even when his eyes could not see. Working himself up to the stunned Grock, Drogen struck out against his blinded foe, each of his slashes reaching their mark with absolute precision, using Grock's heartbeat as reference.

But his strikes did not reach their marks as a wall of stone had grown between himself and Grock rendering his strikes moot and useless though he could still follow Grock's heartbeat.

As his vision returned, the foreboding shadow that had been present, no longer loomed over them or the battlefield further removed of their own.

Grock's thick earthen walls fell as he sliced through them, his ears focused on Grock's heartbeat. As cheers rose from the combined army behind him. "It would seem your bid for conquest has been thwarted. Everyone has found reason to work together, toward a common goal. This will likely lead to talks of peace, across Dranier."

"It would seem his supremacy's reinforcements didn't live up to their reputation," said Grock. Spitting on the ground in anger. His voice and heartbeat moving as though he were ridding the earth, a surfer upon the waves. Turning the ground itself into a water like state, causing Drogen to sink.

"It's time I show you just how inadequate you are, before a true *god like me*," proclaimed Grock. A sinister mirth upon his bisected visage. Using the earth as a ferry toward the base of the plateau, covering most of the ground, before Drogen could pull himself free.

Calling forth and unfurling his wings Drogen chased after Grock expeditiously, recognizing the expression plastered across Grock's face as anything but altruistic, toward himself and those he cared for.

As Grock reached out to the stone mountain he swung the war-hammer sidelong into the mountain side creating a massive cavern as the stone turned to dust under Grock's, magic powered swing.

Drogen crashed into Grock's back his swords slicing in with a double thrust, but deflected outwards, as they cut against Grock's divine robes. Try as he might Drogen could, once more, do nothing to cut the barrier.

"Gulvon pray for Grock. Kill Dragon. Dragon nothing before divine Grock," praised the cowardly orc. Groveling on the ground at Grock's feet with a short sword on the ground instead of in his hand.

"You're all useless. I'll finish him off myself," raged Grock. Smashing Gulvon into the ground with a stomp. Twisting his foot in emphasis upon Gulvon's blood spurting corpse. With Gulvon dead under foot, Grock churned through the hard rock mountain. Turning it all to sand. Treating a tunnel, from one side of the mountain to the other.

Fighting through the dunning sands, Drogen chased Grock through the tunnel. Constantly two steps behind, rendering him incapable of landing a decisive blow. *If that coward had not intervened this would have already ended. How you became a champion in the arena I may never know. Even your end was that of cowardice, crawling on your knees,* thought Drogen.

Grock burst through the other side of the mountain throwing sand, rock, and rubble into the air outside. With magical force Drogen pushed through the sand, sending it cascading out over Grock and everything beyond in order to effectively clear the path.

Grock sprinted from the tunnels exit, and beyond, with Drogen hot on his heels.

Coming back out into the high noon sun Drogen was forced to squint his eyes. Registering both the terrain, and possible hazards beyond within a matter of seconds, as he chased Grock down, his wings beating with abandon.

"Because of the supreme my victory is assured. You'll all be crushed under foot like the scum you are," snarled Grock. His vigor renewed. Slamming his war-hammer into the titan's lightning blackened chest cavity. The sound of breaking bone filling the canyon in his strike. Echoing a foreboding tone

Diving in at Grock's exposed side, Drogen's blades, buried themselves in Grock's side and chest, as he hooked around Grock's body over the fallen war-hammer. Continuing with his forward momentum Drogen pulled upon Grock's body trying and failing to pull him loose from his war-hammer.

Though weak the barrier shirked Drogen's swords out of Grock's body, forcing Drogen into a full twist to dissipate his own momentum. Readying himself for Grock's inevitable attack Drogen reformed his double sword extending its reach with a slip, pointing Ethereal at Grock's neck.

With a snarl, Grock ducked the blow pushing his hand down into the titan's body and coming back with a large chunk of its massive heart.

Stepping into his failed strike Drogen pulled his double oslo downward, with all his strength. As the sword came down, Drogen heard Grock's heartbeat clearly in his mind, each millisecond of his swing, it grew in intensity. Before he could comprehend what had transpired, a wall of stone slammed against him, throwing and skittering him over, the ground below the dead titan. Splitting Ethereal from Envoy Drogen sank them into the sandy ground slowing and stopping the uncontrolled movement.

As his movement ceased, Drogen cast wide the door in his mind releasing his true power, and with it released a massive cone of infrared flame from his mouth. Bathing the sandy field, the titan, and Grock in one breath.

I can only hope that my depletion of his shield integrity might allow my flames to reach him, as they did Ether and Uther, thought Drogen. His heart sinking as Grock's continued to become larger and stronger.

When he finally ran out of breath, after many long minutes, the titan's body came into view. Its remains, unscathed by the flame, even in death. The sand around the titan's body, turned to molten glass, flowed in around the corpse adhering as it cooled.

Grock rose to his feet next to the titan's massive head. Rising to the height of the very being he had consumed.

Grock smiled down at Drogen with malicious intent. But instead of stomping at him, he began chanting. Moving his hands in practiced motions. Unsure of what Grock had planned Drogen beat his wings deploying wind magic beneath them in order to aid in his rapid ascent. Only realizing the folly of his actions when a massive shadow blocked out the rays of the sun from above.

The sand wave crashed against him, sending Drogen plummeting into the earth below. Struggling against the cacophony of heavy waves he fell deeper and deeper into the sand. Unable to move against the crushing weight. In a last desperate attempt at saving himself from succumbing to the immense pressure, Drogen breathed infrared fire, turning the sand to molten glass, and shutting the door within his mind.

Using air to cool the molten glass, he formed a thick bubble around himself creating a chamber and stopping his descent. The solidified glass protecting him from the sand, his prison of immurement.

As the shifting sands ceased their movement, they solidified, exerting exorbitant pressure upon his glass prison. Causing cracks to form, but it remained intact.

"This is it Drogen, your final chance to be released from the burdens of your namesake. Do you choose to leave passing through death, or will you choose to live without end. The middle ground between life and death," questioned Tyr. His voice traveling out from beyond the white door, within Drogen's mind.

"I have been asked and have answered the same way each time. What makes you think this time would be any different," questioned Drogen defiantly.

"We ask because we must make absolutely certain this is the path forward for us all. Yes, you say you are committed to be everlasting. However, deep within us all is still apart of us that is unsure. A part that looks to all that has happened, and wonders if life is truly worth living. Especially when one must endure through greatness. And greatness of loss, none more so than those who are eternal."

"Ya be doubten yur name. Be doubten da name ya kin give ya as uh atchling too. Ya can ave no doubt, dis be da correct path fur ya Drogen. Not cus yur da, ya ma, nor dem udders be needen ya. Not fur Dranier, or any udder reason. It mus come from da soul itself."

"I reforged my blades, is this not acceptance enough," questioned Drogen. Although he already knew the answer.

"No, not when ya not be able ta see an ear dare name.

"Your Name," interjected Tyr.

"I have accepted that I am both god and dragon, but not the truth behind my name," reflected Drogen shaking his head in understanding. *"Is this the correct path for me. To live forever watching everyone I know and love, pass through death when their bodies can no longer retain their being. To experience the heights of existence, and the lows of existing,"* he contemplated silently. *"I must choose this path. And the consequences that arise from the choice. I will be the one to stand, for those who cannot stand for themselves. The one to bring together both allies and enemies, in order to facilitate a better existence for all."*

"And should a force greater than your own stand against you," questioned Tyr.

"If peace is not an option... Then WAR it will be," proclaimed Drogen. His body enveloped in robes of black, trimmed in blood red. Just like the scales his manifested divinity, covered. With a snap of his right hand the walls of his tomb condensed further forming solid granite around him.

"This is a small portion of what it means to be a true god. To unlock more of what lay beyond the door. War must look to others," spoke Tyr. As he and Balthazar faded away.

With a click of his left hand a ball of azure fire formed, casting light within the chamber. The ball floating before him as he called for his swords, within his mind. "*Godslayer; Envoy of Death,"*

"We will always come. Though you now speak the wrong names. We are you, and you are us. We need no names, to recognize the call," spoke the blades.

Holding the swords up to the blue flame, the etched golden runes shined brilliantly upon the reforged double oslo swords. *"Ethereal's Peace; Envoy of War,"* they said as one. As one they had finally become.

Chapter Seventy-One

Splitting Ethereal's Peace; Envoy of War, Drogen drove them up into the granite before him. With a twist he cut through the granite layer allowing it and glass to slide and shatter upon the floor at his feet. Revealing less compacted earth above.

With a point of focus made, he pulled all air from the chamber into his lungs, letting it out in one devastating magic enhanced breath. Blowing earth and fire miles above, what could have easily become, his tomb. The light of the mid-day sun shining down upon him, as he launch himself out of the sand glass tunnel.

Having thought Drogen defeated, Grock advanced upon the plateau. The dryads and elves, under Leif's guidance, wrapping Grock's lower body in previously grown roots. While others grew more, throwing the thick and heavy vegetation around Grock's upper body.

While those of Moonclave weighed Grock down, magic users, and the citadel launched their own assault against his advance. Lightning and water magics, accompanied and chained with metal tipped bolts, flew in against Grock.

Having launched himself, like a cannon ball high into the sky, Drogen looked down upon Grock. Flinging the door to his draconic heritage wide, he grew spontaneously. With a deep breath, a torrent of flame slammed mercilessly into Grock's exposed back.

"Why won't you just die and leave me to my work," raged Grock. Spinning around to look upon Drogen. His divine cloak shirking off magic, fire, vine, and bolt alike.

"You don't have the strength to finish what you've started," said Drogen brazenly.

Using earthen magic Grock lifted his hand bringing towers of solid stone out from beneath the sand. Forming massive pillars beneath Drogen's flying draconic form. Closing his fist the earthen towers launched from the ground, as if released from a trebuchet.

Curling his wings in, Drogen dropped from the sky. A rain of earth following his decent. Turning over midair, he shot the falling debris with white hot flame. Turning the bludgeons stone to molten rock. Which glided harmlessly off, his scaled hide.

Closing the door in his mind as the ground neared, he righted himself using his retained wings, absorbing the impact with his legs.

Raising his hand Grock pulled more stone from beneath the sands, forming them into towers. Which he collapsed with the closing of his fist, atop Drogen's head.

Calling and dropping Ethereal's Peace; Envoy of War, chains formed upon their split hilts. Each chain running through his grasp, alternating color, matching those that had once bound his soul.

Wind magics flowed through his soul chains, and into each oslo. Forming a barrier of air as the magics pooled along their fullers to flow, like a pen to their points. Swinging the blades round himself in a continuous pattern of circuitous movements, forming a dense protective barrier. Halting the falling columns, before they could reach their intended target.

Drogen formed a door with his blades from within the dome of debris. With a wind enforced front kick, launched it across the field between himself and Grock. Continuing his magical manipulations around his feet, Drogen propelled himself headlong toward Grock's turned back. Ethereal's Peace; Envoy of War, trailing behind him by their soul chains.

Grock, having returned to his advance on the mountain plateau, found himself struggling against the dryad and elven vines, as they had continued to lengthen, thicken, and multiply. Try as he might, to reach their defensive position upon the plateau, he could not overcome the weight. His powerful arms continuously collapsing from the strain.

Progressively more bolts rained down upon Grock, from the dwarven citadel. The Moonclave reinforcements readily supplying bolts for the dwarven ballista. Each round of shots coming in a continuous explosive wave, using the gnomes penchant for alchemist compounds to their advantage. Following the plangency of a hollow chime. With the resonance of a slightly deeper tone from below, the elves and dryads that had been consistently growing vines, switched out. For those who had been afforded some time to recuperate their stamina and concentration.

Taking the opportunity provided by their switch out, Grock managed to raise his hand in line with the plateau. As his hand descended, a bolt of lightning ruptured upon it. Blasting it up and away. Followed in quick succession by dwarven bolters, hoisted and fired by two teams of Zephyrians with wind magics aid, provided by a team of dryads.

"Another one, and one accustomed to the barrier no less," seethed Grock. Pulling his hand close amid the surprise and pain. Electricity pulsing, from his fingertips up to his shoulder blade. While the bolter shots did little more than bruise his skin.

Drogen's rush at Grock's back culminated in a twisting whirlwind of blade strikes. Ethereal's Peace; Envoy of War slicing repeatedly into Grock's back breaking through the barrier. Although his blades sliced through the barrier, the density of Grock's graphene skin remained nay impossible to slice, pierce, or puncture. *I must draw his attention away from the plateau and those beyond, if they are to survive.*"

"What's the matter Grock. Does your fear of defeat render you incapable of facing me, or must you be told what to do by Lucian, before you may act," probed Drogen. Hoping that mentioning, the one Grock himself called supreme, would sway his rationality. As mentioning Daelon had to Manzine.

"No matter what you do. Little dragon. Little god. Whatever you might be. You cannot hope to defeat me. You are too weak. You have no divine cloak. No followers of your own. But you can. You can have power. Power beyond your wildest dreams. All you need to do is prostrate yourself before the Supreme's merciful radiance. Through him all become powerful, for all upon Dranier were birthed of his glorious light."

"Then hear me. For my answer to you will be the same as it was to the lushifare Manzine. I will blacken his cursed sun," said Drogen. Emphasizing every word of his threat.

"You are nothing before me. You are nothing before him. I will cut you down now. Before the disappointment of your lineage can come to despoil the ground on which he walks," sermonized Grock. Turning to Drogen with ardent eyes.

Beneath Grock's vine covered hands rest his war-hammer. Its maul and shaft growing from beneath the thick vines to match Grock's titanous form. Gaining strength through his conviction, Grock raised the maul of his hammer high over his head and back. The tangle of vines become weightless in his fervor.

Seizing upon the provided opportunity, those upon the plateau and within the citadel, redoubled their efforts. The ringing of the drawbridges many distinct chimes lending sound to their coordinated efforts, against Grock's back.

As Grock's bludgeon fell toward Drogen he cast Envoy of War to the sky, piercing the maul. As the sword gained purchase, Drogen pulled with all his mite upon the chain. Wrenching the hammers trajectory wide.

"He is wrong. There are those who would follow me. Not because I wish them too, but because it is what they wish to do. Even though I insisted they do not. I feared what might become of them, and me, upon opening the door to my inherited power. Yet, there is no change in perception. No change in what is right, or what must be done to ensure peace for those willing to fight for it. Whenever I close my eyes, I hear their voices calling to me. Those I have met and have yet to meet. All of their voices. I hear them, though I am certainly unworthy of it. I will not allow their voices to go unanswered," thought Drogen reaching out for the white door and throwing it wide. The voices of his friends, followers, and the like flowing out to envelop him.

"Th- this is impossible," stammered Grock as he looked into Drogen's titan sized eyes.

Combining Ethereal's Peace; Envoy of War together he took advantage of Grock's surprise. Sliding the double oslo around Grock's back, cutting into the mountain's, he pulled upon the blade. Forcing Grock forward and away, from those he wished to protect. The razor-sharp edge, of his double oslo, slicing into Grock's back and hip.

Recovered from his shock, Grock turned a circuit, using the weight of his war-hammer in aid of the rotation. With his regained balance he kicked out toward Drogen's side.

With a hasty retreat, Drogen stepped back. Grock's kick impacting Ethereal's Peace; Envoy of War making it turn a circuit within Drogen's expert hand, bisecting Grock's face, frontal bone through mandible. Grock's saliva and golden blood flowing freely out of his bifurcated mouth.

Lurching forward with rage filled speed Grock swung his hammer upon Drogen haphazardly.

If I dodge the blow those on the plateau and beyond could be killed, he thought bracing himself for the inevitable impact. As the war-hammer struck his stomach, the air forcibly purged from his lungs.

Launched backward he sank Ethereal's Peace; Envoy of War into the ground absorbing some of the momentum to protect everyone at his back. Even with his weapon acting as an anchor he felt the mountain roughly impact his back.

I hope they were able to brace for the impact. Quickly righting himself, he noticed several heartbeats rising with him.

"We will aid you. As best we can," spoke Leif directly into his ear.

"I appreciate the help. Are you certain you wish to risk yourselves in this manner. There may be little aid you can provide, against one who would call himself divine," he said. Preparing himself for Grock's coming onslaught.

"You're fight for us all. The least we can do is lend a helping hand," assured Alya. Purring and nuzzling into him.

"Our other friends will aid you dream walker Drogen. They will recover soon. When they are ready, Chian will ring the bridge," explained Mai-Coh.

"This is the tone you must listen for," said Bogger into Drogen's head. A chime ringing out from the citadel.

Going on the offensive, that Grock could not force him back into the mountain again, Drogen waded in against him. Side stepping Grock's hammer strike to deploy a counter thrust with Envoy of War, but the strike was only a feint, disguising his real attack.

As Grock parried the sword with the shaft of his hammer, Drogen kneed him in the solar plexus. Before extending his leg. Forcing Grock to double over and move back in one swift movement. Though Grock's divine cloak dissipated much of the force.

"I have a plan. See what you can do to aid in its execution. However, if you must choose between continuing to live, or perishing in this battle. You must all choose to live," remarked Drogen.

"Already working on it," assured Grom mentally. Grock's war-hammer coming up from the sand. Creating a deep furrow in its travel and revealing green roots spreading out beneath.

The vines upon the ground behind Drogen began to writhe and grow, like serpents stretching out around Drogen. Reaching out for Grock's legs and feet, in an attempt to tether Grock to the ground.

Feeling the growing vines Grock retreated, tripping over the titan's corpse in his haste, but managing to keep himself upright.

Not willing to let the opening go to waste, Drogen moved against Grock, bringing his blades to bare, before Grock had a chance to recover. With a slip thrust, to extend his reach, Drogen pushed Ethereal's Peace; Envoy of War toward Grock's chest. Forcing him to fall backward, or risk impalement. In his fall Grock reached for Drogen's legs. Attempting to grapple him to the ground. Finding nothing but air for his trouble.

Sidestepping Grock in order to gain a more favorable strike Drogen cut downward with his double sword sinking Ethereal's Peace into the ground, just beyond the dead titan's head. Grock pushing himself in a sidelong roll. away from Drogen's strike, and up to his feet.

In Grock's rise a look of deep concentration pulled upon his face. Opening his hands, the earth below Drogen's feet began to move violently. Once more threatening to engulf him, but as quickly as the sand had begun to churn, so too did it stop. As a massive wolf and white tiger began biting and tearing at Grock's flesh with their rending teeth. Ruining the concentration and focus necessary for Grock's use of magic.

Drogen came on in a flurry of blows, his double oslo in constant movement with each step. Forcing Grock on the defensive, and allowing Drogen to slice into Grock's flesh, from multiple angles. Drogen's speed far greater than Grock, and his heavy war-hammer, could hope to parry. For even when Grock managed to parry a strike, another followed, faster than the last.

However, even delivering consecutive blows to Grock's body, they barely managed to cut deep enough to draw blood. Let alone a mortal wound. As Drogen struggled to inflict a decisive blow the dwarves, zephyrians, elves, bugbears, vaudune, goblinkin, and the like began marching out to meet them.

"Need something more. We cannot win a battle of attrition," spoke Ethereal's Peace; Envoy of War within his mind.

"Yes, but what can we do. The door to divinity has been opened, yet we continue to struggle," sneered Drogen. Catching a glancing blow to the side, with Grock's hammer. Forcing air from his lungs once more.

"Then open the other door," suggested the blades.

"What might come about, having both doors within open at the same time. I did so when reforging you, but what could the ramifications be for doing so now," considered Drogen thoughtfully. Stepping into Grock's range splitting the blades for a close thrust. Trailing Envoy of War up for a slice upon Grock's exposed stomach, as he pushed forward.

"Only one way to know for certain."

Try as he might to calculate the risk of having both doors open at once, Drogen knew beyond doubt, his subconscious was right.

With a thought Drogen closed the door to his divine power shrinking back to his smaller frame. Grock's war-hammer missing completely, as his body rapidly descended. From where his head had been, miles up in the sky. Within his soul chamber Drogen called forth both doors, and with a deep steadying breath against his growing doubt, compelled them open.

A tsunami of power flowed through him as both aspects of his inherited power coalesced into one. And with their synchronicity came comprehension.

Drogen's body grew in showcase of his heritage. His spinal ridge pushing out from the tip of his rapidly growing tail to the base of his elongating head. His size matching that of Grock and the titan that lay upon the ground. Though he had lived less than a quarter of a century, by his count.

Grock looked on in fear as the light of the world dimmed in Drogen's presence. Even the sun, shining brightly above the battleground, waned to a shadow of its typical glory. Upon the abyssal black of his draconic scales, some of the blood red tips came through. But most had changed entirely. Taking on a non-casting brilliant shifting golden light. A reflection upon his back, of the stars in the sky, behind the shrouded sun.

Flying into the sky above Grock Drogen held aloft the split Ethereal's Peace; Envoy of war. Each blade resting within his draconic hands, as the battlefield below grew silent. But for a single bell like chime. *"Begin,"* he thought. To those listening in upon his mind.

"Grock you started this war, and used all who worshiped you as fodder. Sitting back and watching them all march to their demise. All for conquest in your name. A leader of any merit would stand upon the front lines of his ambition. Placing themselves alongside those they command. You have proven yourself unworthy of their devotion. Unworthy of those who would sacrifice themselves for the cause you have championed."

"Those who stand before me, Drogen, Son of Lisana; Reaper of Souls, Ethereal's Peace; Envoy of War, Gottdrakregus of Lundwurm Tul, whether you be friend or foe. I have but one question for you," he announced. Raising Ethereal's Peace; Envoy of War high above his head. *"WAR OR PEACE!"*

In answer to his question the eclectic military might of Dranier dropped to their knees. Their weapons out across outstretched hands in reverence. Signifying their wish for Peace.

Looking out upon the battlefield, at everyone bellow, Drogen noted upon Grock's face a concerted effort to remain standing. Dropping down to one knee Grock fought against Drogen's influence, succeeding, but only with monumental effort. When he finally did return to his feet his exhaustion was evident.

"Then peace shall reign," roared Drogen. Swooping down toward Grock. Ultraviolet flames leaping from his mouth and into Grock's eyes.

Drogen's flames licked at Grock's exposed skin. Obscuring his vision completely as he raised his hand and war-hammer, attempting to shield himself from immolation. Each passing moment within the flaming cone abating his divine cloak. As if he were losing, what remained, of the faithful he relied upon.

Flames leading the charge, Drogen attacked with racking, clawed fore-legs. His claws fragmenting the paper-thin barrier with little effort.

Somehow remaining upright, Grock pushed Drogen away with one hand allowing him to swing his war-hammer toward Drogen's side. But as the maul impacted, he felt the exerted energy dissipate against the abyssal barrier, of Drogen's divine cloak.

Pressing his forelegs against Grock's war-hammer and hands Drogen's talons and claws locking them both together. With Grock's hands occupied in their battle of strength, Drogen snaked his head up high. Drawing in a deep breath he released a dense stream of white-hot flame directly upon Grock's bifurcated visage.

Although paper thin, Grock's divine barrier protected him from Drogen's molten fire. The thin shield persisting, despite Drogen's best efforts.

With a great amount of effort and strength, Grock pushed Drogen backward, his draconic talons cutting long furrows into the ground.

An arrogant smile appeared upon Grock's face as he continued pushing through the weight and fire Drogen pressed against him. "You are still too weak," proclaimed Grock triumphantly. Despite his mangled mandible.

But in his arrogance, he did not see the true intention behind Drogen's continued use of draconic fire. Only when the binding chains of Drogen's blades began to exert there constricting force, did he come to realize his mistake.

Though Grock had been the one pushing Drogen around the battlefield. Drogen had been guiding their movements. The furrows created by his claws cutting a circular hole at the center of their battleground.

The chains of Drogen's blades leading to the mountain Plateau and out into the forbidden plains.

Natalia and Seraphine, standing on the plateau, held hands with elves and dryads. At their center growing an oak tree. The roots, with help from Ethereal's Peace, splitting the mountain in twine. Its chain wrapped around the trees mighty trunk while its blade lay within the mountain itself. Its twin upon the plain. Envoy of War, and three sets of eyes within its branches.

Plying as much pressure as possible around Grock, Drogen constricted the chains at every presented opportunity. Gaining the most ground, when Grock tried to breath.

In a desperate attempt to escape, Grock attacked with all his might, using his free hands and war-hammer to deliver blows. Though he fought hard. He could not escape Drogen's grasp and moments later lost feeling in both arms. Dropping the war-hammer to the ground at their feet.

"What do you choose Grock, War or Peace. I noticed your struggle against me. Were you fighting against a part of yourself that knows this conquest of yours has reached its end. Or perhaps, tis a part of you that never wished for this conquest in the first place," posited Drogen.

"WAR. War is all there is. Peace is only possible through his light. You will be taken in his wake as all of Dranier will. You will fail, and you will fall, for he is truly divine," spoke Grock with a zealous fervor. Though he struggled to breath throughout.

"Are you one of Daelon's that was corrupted by Lucian? As the one in Moonclave was" questioned Drogen.

"She is unworthy of his eminence," croaked Grock. Golden blood flowing freely from his ruined mouth Drogen's constricting pressure unrelenting in its proliferation.

"So not of the lushifare then," said Drogen. Remembering Manzine's behavior upon being considered one of Daelon's people. "Then you must be one of the divine. As Ether and Uther were." Continuing to evaluate what he knew, and didn't know, about the deity of Dranier.

"Drogen placed Ethereal's Peace against Grock's neck the double-edged blade pressing against what Grock could still control of his thin divine barrier. Before you walk through Death. To what lay beyond. We will converse once more. There are many you must answer to. Before I will allow you to go to him," commented Drogen.

"You only prolong your path toward the inevitable," gasped Grock. "You will be taken by his div..." Started Grock as Ethereal's Peace sliced the barrier drawing another line of golden blood, from Grock's neck. For many agonizing moments, for Grock, they remained in that position. Drogen's oslo inching through the barrier, and his neck, until he succumb.

In Grock's final moments a look of clarity filled his eyes, as though he were waking up from within his own mind. "Thank you, brother," mouthed Grock. Ethereal's Peace cleaving his head free of his shoulders.

With Grock's death Drogen's soul chains dissipated. As Grock's body fell his golden blood flowed and pooled upon the sand, quickly being absorbed. However, something strange within the rapid flow caught Drogen's astute eye. For a portion did not absorb into the sand. Instead, the sentient golden liquid lunged for him.

Acting quickly against the unusual threat, Drogen took in a short breath, letting out a cone of immolating fire. Destroying the vicious liquid before it had a chance to harm him, or anyone else.

Closing both doors within his mind Drogen's body returned to its usual shape and size though the scales upon his body remained forever changed in their appearance. They remained abyssal in color, tips of red still present throughout, but he continued to shine with golden light. The stars shifting as he did, under the constellations above.

Suddenly a chill struck him, and he knew a reaper had come to collect Grock. "Reaper, there is much this one must answer for. One in particular that he must be brought in front of. Keep this ones soul where it lay for now. When I return, we will go to Asmora. In order to release the souls of those who needlessly died in Grock's bid for conquest," spoke Drogen. To what others would suspect to be empty space.

"As you command *War*," spoke a cold voice next to his ear.

As he began to walk away an unsettling feeling of alarm began to rise within him. Stopping him dead in his tracks. "What is your name reaper?"

"I am Zurek."

"Strange. Counting you, I have met two reapers. Yet you feel. Odd as though you are a part of Daelon's people," probed Drogen. Separating himself from his corporeal form just in time to see the reaper Zurek snarl in disgust.

"So, there are some among you that have fallen to Lucian as well," he said. Calling forth Ethereal's Peace; Envoy of War. "Yet another aspect that must be overcome," commented Drogen. Cutting the reaper in two with a circuit of his double sword.

"Such weapons have no effect on me," Zurek shrieked in defiance. Not understanding the truth until his body was pulled into Drogen's double oslo blade. "You are participating in this war. You do not follow Death. Thus, you fall under *my* domain."

As the reaper's body absorbed into Envoy of War a bright red ichor began to pool upon the ground, extinguishing the sentient gold that flowed in with it. Moments later manifesting into a large hound. The dog sitting obediently in front of War. Knowing it would never betray him. "Guard this one Zurek. Make sure none with that strange affliction dare come near this... or the titan's soul," ordered Drogen. Eliciting a single bark of confirmation from his loyal companion.

Chapter Seventy-Two

Those who had journeyed around the defensive palisades of the dwarves, grouped together as one entity. While Alya, Leif, and Mai-Coh trotted over from behind.

Unsure of his next actions, and feeling exhausted, from the strain placed upon his body by the long drawn-out battle, Drogen sat on the ground. Waiting for those who wished to see him.

The sound of large wings filled the air behind him, drawing his ears to the heartbeat at the center of the wing-beats. At first, he thought the heartbeat to be one of the heavily burdened Zephyrian's. But the truth, he could barely believe his ears for what they registered. Rising up onto his feet he stood, waiting for the dragon's descent to the ground. Holding himself in a bowed position, awaiting her arrival.

As the dragon touched ground a cloaked figure jumped from her back a scythe resting comfortably against his shoulder. With her rider dismounted, Lisana closed the door in her mind. and ran full speed toward the bowing Drogen.

As Lisana stepped into Drogen's view he shifted his vision up to meet her gaze. Their eyes meeting as his mother pushed him up straight. Wrapping him in a tight loving embrace. An embrace neither of them had felt, for many years. "I'm sorry I left you. That I left when you had yet to finish training in Lundwurm Tul. There's nothing I can do or say that can make up or explain away my own selfishness," languished Lisana. Tears flowing down her scaled eyes.

"I only felt such a way at the moment of reading your letter. Even then I understood. I could see over all the years, the yearning holding fast to your heart. It was time for you to go out into the world and look for him. I still needed to learn how to take care of myself. I cannot and would never hold your leaving against you. It was the correct moment for the both of us, though we may only be realizing it now."

"Tis true what those who call you friend have told me," she said. Pushing Drogen slightly away in order to look into his eyes once more. "I commend you for choosing your friends so very well."

Behind Lisana came the sound of someone clearing their throat, drawing them both to its origin. Death waited silently behind her, and she reached out grabbing his hand to pull him in close. "Drogen, this is your father. Death himself," said Lisana with a mirth-filled smile.

"Tis good to be in your presence... outside of the astral," commented Drogen awkwardly. Looking into the eyes of the father he had yet to know.

"I agree," said Death. Just as awkwardly. Unsure of what to do next, they both bowed to each other, further intensifying their shared awkwardness.

"I really hope the others get here quickly. At least then we won't have to feel how awkward this situation is," said Lisana. Bringing them both together in a hug. "I know it's strange right now, but we'll figure this all out with a little bit of time."

"Yes, we will," said Death looking at Lisana appreciatively before turning to look at the ground near Drogen's feet "Why is there an ethereal hound guarding Grock's soul," he posited. Curiously cocking his head in consternation.

"His name is Zurek. He guards against any who have been taken in by the one who once bound him in service via blood," explained Drogen. Leaving Death himself speechless by the revelation.

"How could he," questioned Lisana. A shadow of power beginning to spread from Death.

"He is the reason I no longer feel connection to the other planes, planets, and souls. He is the reason I am weakened," proclaimed Death. Rage filling his eyes. "Lucian will pay for all he has done," he seethed. Tightly gripping Reaper of Souls long haft.

"That we may discuss later. For now, I think it best to enjoy this victory with all the others. They too are caught up in Lucian's machinations. Taking in the victories is just as important as acknowledging our faults, or what needs are to arise in the future," said Lisana. Nodding for emphases. "And they all deserve to celebrate this victory, without the weight of what comes next upon their minds."

Aragorth, Vladimir, Golga, and Deus were the first to arrive, at the head of the combined forces of Dranier. Mai-Coh, Leif and Alya arriving from the distant tree a few moments later. The dryads, elves, Natalia, Seraphine, and Chian arriving shortly after, upon descending the vine and oaken plateau, and following the battalions' path respectively.

"Day be fine. titan ert da tree bug wit its throwen uh da mountain, but she be recoveren well nough in dat trance ting she be talken bout wit da udders."

"Natalia is recovering as well, she was the one who felled the titan with lightning magic, the crazy girl," said Lisana. Shaking her head in feigned fury, as her expression denoted pride.

"I very much wish to go to them, but seeing the number's here, something tells me that may be something I must wait on," said Drogen. Looking over the collected company.

"Aragorth, Vladimir, Golga, Deus, Leif and all those behind and beside them bowed themselves before Drogen, Lisana, and Death. We thank you, divine old ones. For both your aid, and the love you have shown us all in your actions," said Leif.

"You have shown us all that there is a better way. That those past mistakes, although painful, can be turned into a force for good. Even when we cannot see such an outcome ourselves," said Vladimir.

"Drogen see all as equal. None above. None below. Wish not see dead ones. Matter not if gob, hob, hest, dwarf, elf, or bear. Drogen not like Grock," professed Golga. Thumping her chest proudly.

"I not be knowen ya fur long, but ya ave a peace uh me master witin ya. An I be see'in it all da more, wit ow ya bring all uh us ear together. Fightin against da tyranny of anudder," said Aragorth.

"Ya fought in the arena. And saved many for doing so. Even when you were presented the chance to escape with some of the others," said Deus. As Goya the gnome champion came up beside him and Carme.

Goya bowed once more as he stood directly in front of Drogen. "Thank you for showing us all there is another way. That we do not have to stand by and watch powerlessly while our people suffer at the hands of tyrants," said Goya.

Looking at Lisana and Death for words of advice or wisdom, Drogen saw them both looking away, as if in embarrassment for themselves and him. Seeing no help forthcoming Drogen let out a silent breath taking a moment to collect his thoughts.

With a bow of his own to the people of Dranier Drogen bid them to rise alongside himself. "I did nothing but show you all that within each of you is one capable of standing up and fighting against the injustices and tyrants that may plague you, and your people. Furthermore, I will tell you all, as I have stated to the people of Zephyria. I do not wish to be worshiped," he stated emphatically.

"Just know, I will always lend a hand to those who would wish for peace in times of strife. That I may take upon myself the burden's lain too strenuously upon their shoulders. Tis not my place to tell any of your kith or kin what is the correct path for any of you moving forward. You must all come to such knowledge for yourselves," he said. Making certain that they knew he would never lord himself over them or, touch their sovereignty.

"Thank you all, for your assistance in dealing with Grock, and the titan. Now if I may. Tis a long walk back even in the company of those I hold dear," he said. The sea of warriors divided up the middle allowing him; accompanied by Natalia and Seraphine, Lisana, and Death a pathway to walk through their middle.

As he walked through, they once more bowed to him, coming back to their full heights as he passed. Upon reaching the rear of the collected company, the eclectic battalion turned and followed Drogen back to the dwarven citadel, where the injured, and dead had been gathered from the battlefield. Chian, Mai-Coh, Alya, and Leif running to join them at the head.

"I doubt I could have subdued Grock without all of your assistance. Growing those tree's where you did is what made it possible. The two of you biting and ripping at his skin, even though it was for a short time fully distracted him from everything else that was happening. And you Chian, without your notes in broadcast we would have had a much harder time coordinating, even with Grom and Bogger's telepathic abilities. Any sort of distraction could have proven deadly," appreciated Drogen.

"Thank you both as well," said Drogen inside his mind. Drawing answers from not only Grom and Bogger, but Ethereal's Peace; Envoy of War as well. Making Drogen crack a smile. With his appreciations out of the way, they moved quickly to the citadel, where Drogen called for water. That he could heal the wounded of their injuries.

Aragorth, having seen Drogen's ability fist hand took note of the injured ordered barrels of water brought forward, as opposed to buckets. Into each Drogen breathed his fire, filling mugs, bowls, cups, and other implements full of the healing liquid to administer it quickly to all the injured, bringing about their complete rejuvenation.

"I half thought Krail had been talking up some other water, as what healed his amputated wing. But even those without their limbs are regaining them. Your healing water is beyond any I have ever seen," mentioned Lisana. Looking through the conglomeration of healed injuries.

"Can your draconic waters not heal as mine do?" questioned Drogen. Having been unaware that his healing ability was anything of note.

"No Drogen. Restoring limbs to those who lost them, even when the limb is retrieved, has always been thought impossible. Much like the competent handling of two swords, which you have also proven."

"Could this healing ability be an aspect of my father's genetic influence combining with that of your?"

"Tis a question we may never know the answer to. Maybe if Gaia were here with us, we could come to some determination. However, that would be... Unlikely to occur without much searching and effort," explained Death.

Looking through those being healed and those who remained injured, having not received the healing elixir yet, Drogen listened for the heartbeats of Natalia and Seraphine. Through the many hundreds gathered he located them off in a far corner administering the dragon's water while Rumble and Tumble fussed over them both like a couple of worried mothers.

Unfurling the wings at his back Drogen flew directly to them, his wing beats creating a drum like resonance within the citadel itself as the wind pressure struck against the opalescent mythral structure.

Touching down beside the twins Drogen knelt down in observation of Natalia and Seraphine for any physical injuries that he could possibly alleviate with the healing elixir, they were administering to others, despite having injuries themselves.

Although Seraphine had been in worse shape before her time in the trance, her injuries had greatly recovered.

Natalia's mental condition, after using the trance, had recovered from her use of lightning magic. Only for her to exhaust herself once more aiding the elves, dryads, and Seraphine grow the mighty oak upon the plateau. Upon completing their distributions, they meditated within the seraph's trance once more.

A welcome uneventful hour passed before they both began to stir. Upon opening their eyes, they found themselves surrounded by the various leaders of each group.

"Tis good to hear, and feel, both of your heartbeats within my mind. I apologize to you all. I know my fall worried you," commented Drogen.

"When we saw you attached to the stone, we thought all was lost," said Natalia. Moving in close to Drogen, along with Seraphine.

"All did when see Drogen fall," said Golga. "Could not believe. Went to body, but not see dead. See hope, Bogger confirm hope nod dead."

"What did you see that gave you hope," questioned Seraphine. Laying in Drogen's lap and holding Natalia's hand to her heart.

"See chest rise and fall. Still breathe. Still hope," declared Golga.

"Bogger hear thoughts, not that Bogger understand, but hear Drogen voice," commented the vaudune.

"It is strange hearing him so positive," said Natalia.

"No worry, black wing still pain in Bogger butt."

"Ya be a right pain in me brudder an me rump too," commented Rumble with folded arms.

"I don't know that referring to a princess in such a manor is a good idea. Especially with so many rulers around," commented Alya in a conspiratorial whisper.

"Princess, queen, god, king, dragon, gob, cat, cow, dog, mouse, or flea ya all be a pain in du rump ta me," rhymed Tumble gleefully. Giving them all, much needed, levity.

"I'm just glad we have reached a conclusion with Grock," said Natalia. Sighing in relief.

"In the physical sense," said Drogen. Cheers and toasts springing up behind them. Everyone who faced the titan and Grock drinking merrily together. All of their differences put aside in the joys of victory.

The dwarven food vendors began passing out food and beer from kegs and stalls that never seemed to run empty. Many of them becoming lost in the merriment and festivities themselves. The blacksmiths and armorers chief among them, as they no longer needed to man their stalls.

Aragorth walked free of the rambunctious crowd, narrowly being sucked in by one of the many groups of drunken dancers, clear nervousness present upon his ancient face as he moved in behind Rumble and Tumble. "Dare be sometin I be needen ta say... Now dat du two uh dem be awake. Rumble and Tumble come an stand ear afore me," he said. Motioning them forward.

Unsure of Aragorth's intentions, they looked at each-other apprehensively. Their minds going back to the stockades, having only been released a week prior. Having no avenue of escape, or wish to run from what might be coming, the brothers sighed and shrugged in unison, before acquiescing to Aragorth's request.

It wasn't until they looked back upon him that they noticed his head bowed to them. "Wha ya be doin," questioned Rumble.

"I be apologizen, in da only way I be knowen how. In me anger I cast ya out uh da citadel. Ya be wanten ta work wit da udder's uh Dranier. But me pride, an wha appen wit me brudder... Make me tink ya wrong. When it be me dat be wrong. Add we work wit da udders afore all dis..."

"An fur da effort uh growen ya beard ta come back, ya be stocked. Made ta suffer da udders tinken ya did sometin wrong. Dare be nutten I be able ta do... ta give back da time ya missed wit ya friends an loves. All I be able ta do now is bow me ead, an beg ya forgiveness. Doe I not be deservin of it," lamented Aragorth. Not lifting his head at all, as he pontificated to Rumble and Tumble.

"Bugh, for da sake uh da Dragon's lift ya ead," complained Rumble dryly. "Ad ya done dis a few years inta me brudder and me exile id uh given ya a good wallop. Made it wurt da trouble. Tings bein as day are doe," he said. His voice losing some of its gruffness. Add me brudder an me not been exiled, we never woulda met deese pains in da rump," said Rumble. Finishing with an exasperated harrumph for good measure.

"What about you Tumble," encouraged Natalia.

"Me brudder an me be feelin da same. Bugh da biggest regret, we be sent witout name," rhymed Tumble sadly.

"Aye ya two been young. Too young ta fine ya last name," said Aragorth. Shaking his head sadly. It not be too late doe. Ya elped bring all uh us togedder. Ya bring me master, back ta me. If it be pleasen da both uh ya. I be given ya a name right ear an now," announced Aragorth looking around as he did so. His eyes settling on Drogen, before returning to the twin's. "Rumble an Tumble I give ya da name... brudders Drakoon."

Rumble and Tumble dropped to their knees in acceptance of their name, pride upon their faces. "Da two uh ya be da ones worken wit da udder's uh Dranier. Elpen bring da people uh da mountain out inta da world. Out wit all da udders. Sometin da two uh ya shoulda been doin fur a long time. Dis be da mission uh da Drakoon."

Cheers erupted within the citadel giving everyone another reason to celebrate and party, a party the vendors seemed all too prepared for, as they opened yet another batch of kegs. With food and libations flowing aplenty, everyone became swept up in the party atmosphere. All of them getting along, as though they had always been the best of friends.

Although they all knew there would be growing pains and struggles as they started looking forward to a time of peace between them all. They pushed such thought from their minds to live within the feeling of shared achievement and victory.

Epilogue

Lucian lay out upon his throne of light, looking down upon the two failures that had come crawling back to him, disgusted by their very presence. "Not only did you fail to bring down the monarch, that others aided in facilitating, you were exiled in the wake of Ether and Uthers deaths. And you have the gull to stand before me," said Lucian. His rage filled power pressing them to the ground, from their feet, in anguished fealty.

"Ether and Uther should have killed the beast the moment they found it. Their deaths could have been avoided had they obeyed... my... orders. I should have done to them what I did to the others. At least then I wouldn't have to deal with the aftermath of their incompetence."

"Nefarine, and whatever your name is. You both disappoint me, but your supreme is just. I will give you *one...last...chance*. However, should you fail, your lives are forfeit. There is nowhere you can run. Nowhere you can hide, that my light cannot and will not reach to snuff your lives out. You are Lushifare, you best not forget what that means," proclaimed Lucian. His presence pushing them flat upon the ground. "Now get out of my sight," he seethed. Releasing his exertion slightly. Allowing them to crawl slowly away from his high dais.

"Nuntius, what information have you garnered from the returned," questioned Lucian impatiently.

"My supreme. I-It would appear. Well... It would seem."

"Get on with it Nuntius, or do you wish to die again."

"N-n-no my supreme," squirmed Nuntius fearfully. Wanting nothing more than to run. "Grock has fallen in battle, as has the titan."

"When will they be returned here?"

"Th-they're not coming back my supreme."

"Did you not send Zurek. To ensure they would be returned to me in their fall?"

"Y-yes supreme, b-b-but you see, Zurek is among those who will not return."

"What did you say," said Lucian. Moving to the edge of his seat.

"Z-z-z-zurek is no longer within the connection. Another was sent, but cannot get close, for a hound."

"They are the carriers of the dead, how can a dog block them from returning to me *what... is...mine*," sneered Lucian.

"I-it's not a normal dog. I-It's different. Something the dead bringers c-c-cannot deal with," started Nuntius. Shirking away as the pressure of Lucian's presence began to overwhelm her.

"Useless. All of you useless. Fine, they were of no real consequence anyways I can always bring another titan to heel, with everything I possess. All three of them gone. All without contributing anything to their supreme. The others better start pulling their weight, or I'll be forced to make an example of them myself."

Breathing out a sigh of relief, that she had gone through the exchange unscathed, Nuntius poured over her notes. Stumbling across a lost note she had only recently found. “T-t-t-there is something else my supreme. Though I don’t see the significance, I thought it best you be told. It was a part of Grock’s last report,” said Nuntius. Fidgeting nervously with her notes.

“What use is information from the dead, when they are not here to deliver it themselves? Oh, quit your fidgeting, and spit it out already,” he said with ire.

“G-g-g-grock report the castle fell, and h-h-he escaped... I found it strange that he let us know he escaped. Then I thought, maybe someone escaped the prison. But that’s never happened before. And how does a castl,” spoke Nuntius excitedly. Her head flying from her body. Allowing her to look back at herself, until everything turned black.

“Now this is far outside my expectations. The chains were supposed to hold him for eternity. Yet he freed himself in a mere twenty years’ time. With magics release Daelon, and hers, will have their faculties returned. It would appear facing you is coming faster than I anticipated. However, it is not I that will fall. I’ll be the last one standing. All of my preparations have led up to this. Not even Death himself can hurt me now.”

“Nefarine, bring yourself and your worthless daughter back in here. I have your mission,” said Lucian in disgust.

“Yes, my Supreme,” said Nefarine and Bernadine. Their wings and tails scrapping against the floor as they crawled across its reflective surface once more.

“Investigate and report back to me, the reason my favorite toys will not be returning. You may even have the opportunity for revenge,” tantalized Lucian.

“As you command my supreme,” said Nefarine passionately.

“And reassemble this one before you go,” he said. Allowing them to bring their heads up from the ground enough to see Nuntius’s decapitated body beside the dais. “I’m sure the reapers have stashed her soul away. Now get out of my sight.”

The pressure ceased from around Nefarine and Bernadine’s bodies allowing them to stand up for the first time since their arrival, nearly a month prior. Taking Nuntius’s body through an adjoining door, Bernadine threw her half of the corpse to the floor.

“Does this mean we have to go all the way back just to find out something he can send things we can’t see ourselves to figure out,” questioned Bernadine angrily.

“Do not disparage the one chance we have at returning to power. The supreme is giving us an opportunity to show him that we are worthy of his love,” said Nefar zealously. Dragging the body away. “Now help me down the stairs dear. We can’t be disappointing the supreme. Not with our return to royalty so close at hand.”

Lord of War

(Part 3)

Beware.
In the fin not fall,
Another hears the mantle's call,
The halls within demand once more.
War Torn,
A parter beyond the veil,
Wade-for blood and gore,
To even the score only one may prevail,
Defeated locked beyond the white door,
Forevermore within the halls of war.
Watch his rise,
In the others fall,
Leave none forsworn,
Our lord of War.
Prophecy of the Dwarven King
Verger Granod Igneous,
King of Bathara

About the Author

B.W. Goodwin graduated with honors from the International Culinary Schools at the Art Institute of Phoenix with an associate's degree in culinary arts and a bachelor's degree in culinary management. He was born and raised in Arizona and lives on his family's property in the small town of Tonto Basin. He is passionate about role-playing games, anime, manga, and fantasy in both literary and visual mediums.

Made in the USA
Middletown, DE
10 September 2024

60088534R00295